America's enemies, be warned: there is no weapon more dangerous than a wounded and cornered Mitch Rapp. . . .

The powerful #1 bestseller of a young Mitch Rapp on his explosive first mission

KILL SHOT

"Nail-biting."

—*Goodreads*

"Vince Flynn has never been better."

—*The Providence Journal*

"Flynn is a master—maybe *the* master—of thrillers in which the pages seem to turn themselves."

—*Bookreporter*

AMERICAN ASSASSIN

"There is a reason Flynn is #1 on the bestseller lists."

—*New York Post*

"Captivating."

—Glenn Beck

"Terrific."

—*Toronto Sun*

And don't miss these "complex, chilling, and satisfying" (*The Cleveland Plain Dealer*) Mitch Rapp thrillers!

EXTREME MEASURES
PROTECT AND DEFEND   ACT OF TREASON
CONSENT TO KILL   MEMORIAL DAY
EXECUTIVE POWER   SEPARATION OF POWER
THE THIRD OPTION   TRANSFER OF POWER

Novels by Vince Flynn

And with Kyle Mills

VINCE FLYNN

AMERICAN ASSASSIN

Pocket Books

New York   London   Toronto   Sydney   New Delhi

Pocket Books
An Imprint of Simon & Schuster, Inc.
1230 Avenue of the Americas
New York, NY 10020

This book is a work of fiction. Names, characters, places, and
incidents either are products of the author's imagination or
are used fictitiously. Any resemblance to actual events or
locales or persons, living or dead, is entirely coincidental.

Copyright © 2010 by Vince Flynn

All rights reserved, including the right to reproduce this book
or portions thereof in any form whatsoever. For information
address Atria Books Subsidiary Rights Department,
1230 Avenue of the Americas, New York, NY 10020.

This Pocket Books paperback edition September 2017

POCKET and colophon are registered trademarks of
Simon & Schuster, Inc.

For information about special discounts for bulk
purchases, please contact Simon & Schuster Special Sales at
1-866-506-1949 or business@simonandschuster.com.

The Simon & Schuster Speakers Bureau can bring authors
to your live event. For more information or to book an event
contact the Simon & Schuster Speakers Bureau at
1-866-248-3049 or visit our website at www.simonspeakers.com.

Manufactured in the United States of America

10 9 8 7 6 5 4 3 2 1

ISBN 978-1-5011-8080-4
ISBN 978-1-4391-0051-6 (ebook)

To the victims of the
Pan Am Lockerbie terrorist attack
and their families

ACKNOWLEDGMENTS

WRITING is by necessity a solitary process. Fortunately, my wife, a beautiful, stoic Scandinavian from Northern Minnesota, understands this. Lysa, you are an amazing partner. Every year you bear the brunt of these deadlines. Even when I am physically around, I am mentally elsewhere . . . trying to figure out the twists and turns of the story. I can never say thank you enough.

Publishing, on the other hand, has very little to do with solitude. It is a dynamic, exciting industry where things can go wrong, or right, at countless junctures. I am extremely lucky to be surrounded by some of the best people in the business. From Sloan Harris and Kristyn Keene at ICM, to Emily Bestler, Sarah Branham, Kate Cetrulo, Jeanne Lee, Al Madocs, David Brown, and Judith Curr at Atria, to Louise Burke and Anthony Ziccardi at Pocket Books, to Michael Selleck and Carolyn Reidy at Simon & Schuster, and the entire sales force . . . you are all top-notch. For twelve straight publications, most of it during the most tumultuous times the industry has ever seen, you have managed to make each launch better than the previous.

To Lorenzo DiBonaventura and Nick Wechsler for continuing to push the boulder up the hill—I do not know how you do it. To my friend Rob Richer, who helped give me the flavor of Beirut in the early nineties, to Ed Schoppman for facilitating the hardware, to Dr. Jodi Bakkegard for straightening me out, and to all those who choose to remain in the shadows, thank you. To those whom I may have forgotten—my sincere apologies.

And last, to you, the reader. I have wanted to tell this story for fifteen years. How did Mitch Rapp become Mitch Rapp? Crafting this novel has been one of the greatest thrills of my writing career. Thank you for your support and enjoy the read.

AMERICAN
ASSASSIN

PRELUDE

BEIRUT, LEBANON

M ITCH Rapp stared at his reflection in the dusty, cracked mirror and questioned his sanity. There was no shaking, or sweaty palms. He wasn't nervous. It was just a cold, calculated assessment of his abilities and his odds for success. He went over the plan once more from start to finish, and again concluded it was likely that he would be severely beaten, tortured, and possibly killed, but even in the face of such prospects, he couldn't bring himself to walk away, which brought him right smack dab back to that part about his mental health. What kind of man willingly chose to do such a thing? Rapp thought about it for a long moment and then decided someone else would have to answer that question.

While everyone else seemed content to sit on their hands, it was not in Rapp's nature to do so. Two of his colleagues had been grabbed from the streets of Beirut by a nasty little outfit called Islamic Jihad. They were a tentacle of Hezbollah that specialized in kidnapping, torture, and suicide bombings. The jihadis had, without question, already begun the interrogation of their new prisoners. They would expose the men to unthinkable pain, and they would begin to peel back each layer of the onion until they got what they wanted.

That was the savage truth, and if his colleagues could delude themselves into thinking otherwise, it just meant they had consciously or unconsciously gravitated toward convenient conclusions. After a day of watching the very people who said they would handle the situation do nothing, Rapp decided to look for a solution on his own. The bureaucrats and foreign service types back in Washington might be content with letting things take their natural course, but Rapp was not. He'd been through too much to allow his cover to be blown, and beyond that there was that nagging little thing about honor and the warrior's code. He'd been through the wringer with these guys. One he respected, admired, and liked. The other he respected, admired, and hated. The pull for him to do something, anything to save them was strong. The gang back in Washington might be able to simply write off losing the faceless operatives as a cost of war, but to the guys who were in trenches it was a little more personal. Warriors don't like leaving their own to die at the hands of the enemy, because secretly, they all know they might be in the same position one day, and they sure as hell hope their country will do everything in their power to get them back.

Rapp eyed his fractured reflection; his thick, uncombed head of black hair and beard, his bronzed olive skin and his eyes, so dark that they were almost black. He could walk among the enemy without attracting so much as a suspicious glance, but that would all change if he didn't do something. He thought of his training and everything he'd sacrificed. The entire operation would be exposed, and that meant his career in the field would be over. He'd be stuffed behind some desk back in Washington where he'd rot for the next twenty-five years. He'd wake up each morning and go to bed each night with the nagging thought that he should have done something—anything. And ultimately he would emasculate himself by questioning the size of his balls for as long as he lived. Rapp shuddered at the thought. He might be a little crazy, but he'd read enough Greek tragedies to understand that a life filled with that kind of recrimination would eventually lead him to the psych ward. *No*, he thought, *I'd rather go down swinging.*

He nodded to himself and took a deep breath before walking over to the window. Rapp gently pulled back the tattered curtain and looked down at the street. The two foot soldiers from Islamic Jihad were still positioned across the street keeping an eye on things. Rapp had dropped a few hints around the neighborhood about what he was up to, and they had shown up barely an hour after he had pressed his seventh hundred-dollar bill into the willing hand of a local merchant. Rapp had considered killing one lackey and interrogating the other, but knew word would spread so fast that his colleagues would be either moved or killed before he could act on whatever intel he could gather. Rapp shook his head. This was it. There was only one avenue open to him, and there was no sense in delaying what had to be done.

He quickly scrawled a note and left it on the small desk in the corner. He gathered his sunglasses, the map, and a large wad of cash and headed for the door. The elevator was broken so he walked the four flights to the lobby. The new man behind the front desk looked nervous as all hell, which Rapp took as a sign that someone had talked to him. He continued out the front door into the blazing daylight and held his map above his head to block the sun while he looked up and down the street. Looking out from behind the sunglasses, he pretended not to notice the duo from Islamic Jihad. With his face buried in the map, he turned to the right and started heading east.

Within half a block, Rapp's nervous system began sending his brain alarms, each more frantic than the previous one. It took every ounce of control to override his training and millions of years of basic survival instincts that were embedded like code into the human brain. Up ahead, the familiar black car was parked across the street. Rapp ignored the man behind the wheel and turned down a narrow side street. Just thirty paces ahead a rough-looking man was stationed in front of a shop. His left leg was straight and firmly planted on the pavement and the other bent up behind him and placed against the side of the building. His big frame was resting against the building while he took a long drag off his cigarette. There was something vaguely familiar about him, right down to the dusty black pants and the white dress shirt with the sweat-stained armpits.

The street was otherwise empty. The survivors of the bloody civil war could smell trouble, and they had wisely decided to stay indoors until the morning's sideshow was concluded. The footfalls from behind were echoing like heavy shoes on the stone floor of an empty cathedral. Rapp could hear the pace of his pursuers quicken. A car engine revved, no doubt the black BMW he'd already spotted. With every step Rapp could feel them closing in from behind. His brain ran through scenarios with increasing rapidity, looking for any way out of the impending disaster.

They were close now. Rapp could feel them. The big fellow up ahead threw his cigarette to the ground and pushed himself away from the building with a little more spring than Rapp would have guessed him capable of. He filed that away. The man smiled at him and produced a leather truncheon from his pocket. Rapp dropped the map in feigned surprise and turned to flee. The two men were exactly where he expected them to be, guns drawn, one pointed at Rapp's head, the other at his chest.

The sedan skidded to a stop just to his right, the trunk and front passenger door swinging open. Rapp knew what was next. He closed his eyes and clenched his jaw as the truncheon cracked him across the back of the head. Rapp stumbled forward and willingly fell into the arms of the two men with pistols. He let his legs go limp, and the men struggled with his weight. He felt the arms of the big man wrap around his chest and yank him upright. His 9mm Beretta was pulled from the back of his waistband and he was dragged the short distance to the car's trunk. Rapp landed headfirst with a thud. The rest of his body was folded in on top of him, and then the trunk was slammed shut.

The engine roared and the rear tires bit through a layer of sand and dirt until they found asphalt. Rapp was thrown back as the vehicle shot away. He slowly cracked open his eyes, and as expected, he found himself enveloped in darkness. His head was throbbing a bit from the blow, but not too badly. There was no fear on his face or doubt in his mind, though. Just a smile on his lips as he thought of his plan. The seeds of disinformation that he had spread over the past day had drawn them in just as he'd hoped. His captors had no idea of the true intent of the man they now had in their possession, and more important, no idea of the violence and mayhem he was about to visit upon them.

PART I

CHAPTER 1

SOUTHERN VIRGINIA
(ONE YEAR EARLIER)

MITCH Rapp removed the blindfold from his face and raised his seat back. The brown Ford Taurus sedan rocked its way down a rutted gravel road, twin plumes of dust corkscrewing into the hot August air. The blindfold was a precaution in case he failed, which Rapp had no intention of doing. He stared out the window at the thick wall of pines that bracketed the lane. Even with the bright sun he could see no more than thirty feet into the dark maze of trees and underbrush. As a child he'd always found the woods to be an inviting place, but on this particular afternoon it had a decidedly more ominous feel.

A foreboding premonition hijacked his thoughts and sent his mind careening into a place that he did not want to go. At least not this afternoon. Still, a frown creased his brow as Rapp wondered how many men had died in this particular forest, and he wasn't thinking of the men who had fought in the Civil War all those years earlier. No, he thought, trying to be completely honest with himself. Death was too open-ended a word for it. It left the possibility that some accident had befallen the person, and that was a convenient way to skirt the seriousness of what he was getting himself into. *Executed* was a far more accurate word. The men he was thinking of had been marched into these very woods, shot in the back of the head, and dumped into freshly dug holes never to be heard from again. That was the world that Rapp was about to enter, and he was utterly and completely at peace with his decision.

Still, a sliver of doubt sliced through the curtains of his mind and caused a flash of hesitation. Rapp wrestled with it for a moment, and then stuffed it back into the deepest recesses of his brain. Now was not the time for second thoughts. He'd been over this, around it, and under it. He'd studied it from every conceivable angle since the day the mysterious woman had walked into his life. In a strange way, he knew where it was all headed from almost the first moment she'd looked at him with those discerning, penetrating eyes.

He had been waiting for someone to show up, though Rapp had never told her that. Or that the only way he could cope with the pain of losing the love of his life was to plot his revenge. That every single night before he went to sleep he thought of the network of faceless men who had plotted to bring down Pan Am Flight 103, that he saw himself on this very journey, headed to a remote place not dissimilar from the woods he now found himself in. It was all logical to him. Enemies needed to be killed, and Rapp was more than willing to become the person who would do that killing. He knew what was about to happen. He was to be trained, honed and forged into an ultimate precision weapon, and then he would begin to hunt them down. Every last one of the faceless men who had conspired to kill all those innocent civilians on that cold December night.

The car began to slow and Rapp looked up to see a rusted cattle gate with a heavy chain and padlock. His dark brow furrowed with suspicion.

The woman driving the vehicle glanced sideways at him and said, "You were expecting something a little more high-tech perhaps."

Rapp nodded silently.

Irene Kennedy put the car in park and said, "Appearances can be very deceiving." She opened her door and stepped from the vehicle. As she walked to the gate she listened. A moment later she heard the click of the passenger door, and she smiled. Without an ounce of training he had made the right decision. From their very first meeting it was apparent he was different. She had audited every detail of his life and watched him from afar for several months. Kennedy was exceedingly good at her job. She was methodical, organized, and patient. She also had a photographic memory.

Kennedy had grown up in the business. Her father had worked for the State Department, and the vast majority of her education had taken place overseas in countries where an American was not always welcome. Vigilance was a part of her daily routine from the age of five. While other parents worried about their kids' wandering out into the street and getting hit by a car, Kennedy's parents worried about her finding a bomb under their car. It was drilled into her to always be aware of her surroundings.

When Kennedy finally introduced herself to Rapp, he studied her for a long second and then asked why she had been following him. At the time Rapp was only twenty-two, with no formal training. If Kennedy had a weakness it was with improvisation. She liked things plotted out well in advance, and being so thorough, she had gone in assuming the novice would have no idea that she had been running surveillance on him. She had recruited dozens of people and this was a first. Kennedy was caught off guard to the point of stammering for an answer. The recruit was supposed to be the one struggling to understand what was going on. Rapp's recognizing her was not part of the script.

Later, in her motel room outside Syracuse, she retraced her every move over the past eight months and tried to figure out where she had slipped. After three hours and seventeen pages of notes, she still couldn't pinpoint her mistake. With frustration, and grudging admiration, she had concluded that Rapp had extremely acute situational awareness. She moved his file to the top of her stack and made a bold decision. Rather than use the normal people, she contacted a firm run by some retired spooks. They were old friends of her father's, who specialized in handling jobs without creating a paper trail. She asked them to take an objective look at Rapp, just in case she had missed something. Two weeks later they came back with a summary that sent chills up Kennedy's spine.

Kennedy took that report straight to her boss, Thomas Stansfield. Midway through reading the file he suspected what she was up to. When he finished, he slowly closed the two-inch-thick biography of the young Mitch Rapp and made her plead her case. She was concise and to the point, but still Stansfield pointed out the potential pitfalls and obvious dangers of leapfrogging the initial phase of training. She countered perfectly. The game was changing. He had said it himself many times. They could not sit back and play defense, and in this ever more interconnected world they needed a weapon more surgical than any guided bomb or cruise missile. Having spent many years in the field himself, Stansfield also knew this person would have to be uniquely autonomous. Someone who conveniently had no official record.

Kennedy ticked off eight additional reasons why she felt this young man was the perfect candidate. Her logic was sound, but beyond that there was the simple fact that they had to begin somewhere. By Stansfield's reckoning this was an endeavor they should have started a good five years earlier, so it was with a heavy sigh and a leap of faith that he decided to proceed. He told Kennedy to forgo the normal training and take him to the only man they knew who was crazy enough to try to mold a green recruit into what they needed. If Rapp could survive six months of schooling at the hands of Stan Hurley, he might indeed be the weapon they were looking for. Before she left, Stansfield told her to eliminate any connection: Every last file, surveillance photo, and recording that could ever tie them to Rapp was to be destroyed.

Kennedy pulled the car through the gate and asked Rapp to close and lock it behind them. Rapp did as he was asked and then got back in the car. One hundred yards later Kennedy slowed the vehicle to a crawl and maneuvered diagonally in an effort to avoid a large pothole.

"Why no security on the perimeter?" Rapp asked.

"The high-tech systems . . . more often than not . . . they draw too much unwanted attention. They also give a lot of false alarms, which in turn requires a lot of manpower. That's not what this place is about."

"What about dogs?" Rapp asked.

She liked the way he was thinking. As if on cue, two hounds came galloping around the bend. The dogs charged straight at the vehicle. Kennedy stopped and waited for them to get out of her way. A moment later, after baring their teeth, they turned and bolted back in the direction they'd just come from.

Kennedy took her foot off the brake and proceeded up the lane. "This man," Kennedy said. "The one who will be training you."

"The crazy little guy who is going to try to kill me," Rapp said without smiling.

"I didn't say he was going to try to kill you . . . I said he is going to try to make you think he's trying to kill you."

"Very comforting," Rapp said sarcastically. "Why do you keep bringing him up?"

"I want you to be prepared."

Rapp thought about that for a moment and said, "I am, or at least as prepared as you can be for something like this."

She considered that for a moment. "The physical part is assumed. We know you're in good shape, and that's important, but I want you to know that you will be pushed in ways you never imagined. It's a game. One that's designed to make you quit. Your greatest asset will be mental discipline, not physical strength."

Rapp disagreed with her but kept his mouth shut and his face a mask of neutrality. To be the best required equal doses of both. He knew the game. He'd been through plenty of grueling football and lacrosse practices in the humid August heat of Virginia, and back then it was only a simple desire to play that kept him going. Now his motivation to succeed was much deeper. Far more personal.

"Just try to remember . . . none of it is personal," Kennedy said.

Rapp smiled inwardly. That's where you're wrong, he thought. It's all personal. When he responded, however, he was compliant. "I know," Rapp said in an easy tone. "What about these other guys?" If there was one thing that made him a little nervous it was this. The other recruits had been down here for two days. Rapp didn't like getting a late start. They would have already begun the bonding process and were likely to resent his showing up late. He didn't understand the delay, but she wasn't exactly forthright with information.

"There are six of them." Kennedy scrolled through the photos in her mind's eye. She had read their jackets. They all had military experience and shared, at least on paper, many of Rapp's qualities. They were all dark-featured, athletic, capable of violence, or at least not afraid of it, and they had all to one degree or another passed the extensive psychological exams. They had all showed a facility for foreign languages. In terms of a sense of right and wrong, they all hovered near that critical six o'clock position on the mental health pie chart. That thin line that separated law enforcement officers from career criminals.

Around the next bend the landscape opened up before them. A freshly mowed lawn roughly the size of a football field ran along both sides of the lane all the way to a white barn and two-story house with a wraparound porch. This was not what Rapp had expected. The place looked like a rural postcard complete with a set of rocking chairs on the big white porch.

A man appeared from inside the house. He was holding a cup of coffee in one hand and a cigarette in the other. Rapp watched him move across the porch. The man swiveled his head to the left and then right in a casual manner. Most people would have missed it, but Rapp's senses had been opened to the reality that the world was divided between those who were part of the herd and those who liked to hunt. The man was checking his flanks. He stopped at the top of the porch steps and looked down at them from behind a pair of aviator sunglasses. Rapp smiled ever so slightly at the realization that this was the man who was going to try to break him. It was a challenge he had been looking forward to for some time.

CHAPTER 2

RAPP looked through the bug-splattered windshield at the ballbuster he'd been warned about. Even from across the yard he could see the displeased look on the guy's face. He had medium-length brown hair swept to the right and a full Tom Selleck mustache. He was in a pair of faded olive shorts that were a little on the small side and a white V-neck T-shirt. As the car came to a stop Rapp noted the faded black combat boots and white tube socks that were pulled all the way up to his knees. His skin was a leathery, dark brown and all of it, even his cheeks, seemed tightly wound with muscles and tendons. Rapp wondered about the eyes that were conveniently concealed behind a pair of sunglasses. He thought about his plan, and he figured he'd find out soon enough.

"How old is he?" Rapp asked.

"Not sure," Kennedy said as she put the car

in park. "He's older than he looks, though, but I wouldn't bring it up. He doesn't like talking about his age." She unbuckled her seat belt. "Wait here for a moment."

Kennedy exited the vehicle and walked casually across the gravel driveway. She was wearing black dress slacks and a white blouse. Due to the heat and the fact that they were more than a hundred miles from headquarters, she'd left her suit jacket in the backseat. A 9mm Beretta pistol was on her right hip, more to avoid a tongue-lashing from the man she was about to face than from any real fear that she'd have to use it. She looked up at the man on the porch and brushed a loose strand of her auburn hair behind her ear. Stopping at the base of the porch steps she said, "Uncle Stan, you don't look too excited to see me."

Stan Hurley glanced down at Kennedy and felt a twinge of guilt. This little beauty could jerk his emotions around in ways very few could. He'd known Irene longer than she'd known herself. He'd watched her grow up, bought her Christmas presents from strange exotic places, and spent more holidays with the Kennedys than without them. And then a little less than a decade ago, all the joy had drained from their lives when a delivery van packed with over two thousand pounds of explosives pulled up to the U.S. embassy in Beirut. Sixty-three people perished, including Kennedy's father. Hurley had been away screwing one of his sources and had narrowly dodged the bullet. The CIA had lost eight valuable people that April day and they had been playing catch-up ever since.

Hurley was well aware that he had almost no control over his temper, so it was his habit to keep things brief when he was upset and talking with someone he liked. He said simply, "Afternoon, Irene."

Kennedy had been expecting and dreading this moment for some months. Normally Hurley would have greeted her with a warm hug and asked her how her mother was, but not this afternoon. She'd done an end around on him, and Stan Hurley did not like people going over his head for approval on something this serious. The chill in his mood was obvious, but still she pressed on, asking, "How are you feeling?"

Hurley ignored her question and pointedly asked, "Who's in the car?"

"New recruit. Thomas told me he filled you in." Kennedy was referring to their boss.

Hurley's eyes were shielded by the polarized lenses of his aviators. His head slowly swiveled away from the car toward Kennedy. "Yes, he told me what you were up to," he said with obvious disapproval.

Kennedy defensively folded her arms across her chest and said, "You don't endorse my decision."

"Absolutely not."

"Why?"

"I don't run a damn Boy Scout camp."

"Never said you did, Stan," Kennedy said in a biting tone.

"Then why the hell are you wasting my time sending me some titty-boy college puke who doesn't know the difference between a gun and a rifle?"

The normally stoic Kennedy allowed a bit of irritation to show. She was well aware of the special hold she had over Hurley, and a look of disapproval on her part was far more potent than a direct attack.

Hurley looked down at her and could see she was unhappy with him. He didn't like that one bit. It was the same with his own daughters. If one of his boys had so much as looked at him sideways he would have knocked him on his ass, but the girls had the ability to get past all his defenses. Get inside him and create doubt. Still, on this issue, he knew he was right, so he held his ground. "Don't make this personal, Irene. I've been at this a long time, and I know what I'm doing. I don't need you going over my head and then coming down here and dumpin' some untested rookie in my lap."

Kennedy stood sphinxlike, refusing to yield her position.

Hurley took a drag from his cigarette and said, "I think you should save us all the headache and get back in your car and take him back to wherever you found him."

Kennedy was surprised by the genuine resentment she felt. She'd been working on this for more than a year. Her analysis and her instincts told her Rapp was just the man they were looking for, yet here she was being dismissed like some complete neophyte who had no understanding of what they were trying to accomplish. Kennedy slowly climbed the porch steps and squared off with Hurley.

The veteran backed up a bit, obviously uncomfortable with someone whom he wouldn't dare lay a hand on entering his personal space. "I got a lot of work to take care of this afternoon, Irene, so the sooner you get back in the car, the better off we'll all be."

Kennedy squared her shoulders and in a tight voice asked, "Uncle Stan, have I ever disrespected you?"

"That's not what this is—"

"It's exactly what it's about. What have I done to you that has caused you to hold me in such low regard?" She inched closer.

Hurley's feet began to shuffle. His face twisted into a scowl. "You know I think the world of you."

"Then why do you treat me as if I'm still a teenager?"

"I don't think you're incompetent."

"You just think I should stick to analysis and leave the recruiting and training to you."

He cleared his throat and said, "I think that's a fair statement."

Kennedy put her hands on her hips and stuck out her chin. "Do me a favor and take off your sunglasses."

The request caught Hurley off guard. "Why?"

"Because I know your Achilles' heel, and I want to see your womanizing eyes when I tell you what someone should have told you a long time ago."

Hurley cracked a smile in an attempt to brush her off, but she told him again to take his glasses off. Hurley reluctantly did so.

"I respect you," Kennedy said, "in fact I might trust you more with my life than anyone in this world. You are unquestionably the best man to whip these operatives into shape . . . but there's one problem."

"What's that?"

"You're myopic."

"Really?"

"Yep. I'm not sure you really understand the type of person we're looking for."

Hurley scoffed as if the idea was preposterous.

"That's right, and you're too stubborn to see it."

"I suppose you think the Special Operations Group just showed up one day. Who do you think trained all those guys? Who do you think selected them? Who do you think turned them into the efficient, badass killing machines that they are?"

"You did, and you know that's not what I'm talking about. I'm talking about our third objective."

Hurley frowned. She knew right where to hit him. He quietly wondered if Stansfield had put her up to this and said, "You think this shit's easy? You want to take over running this little operation?"

Kennedy shook her head and smiled in amazement. "You know, for a tough guy, you're awfully thin-skinned. You sound like one of those damn desk jockeys back at Langley who run their section as if they were some Third World dictator."

She might as well have hit him in the gut with a two-by-four. Hurley stood there speechless.

"You've created a cult of personality," Kennedy continued. "Every single recruit is you twenty to thirty years ago."

"And what's wrong with that?"

"Nothing, if you're talking about our first two objectives." Kennedy held up one finger. "Training operatives with the skills to get down and dirty if they have to and," she held up a second finger, "creating a highly mobile tactical assault team, but when it comes to the third," she shook her head, "we're still at the starting gate."

Hurley didn't like hearing this, but he was not some unaware idiot. He knew what he'd been tasked to do, and he was acutely aware that he had so far failed to make any progress on the most delicate of the three programs. Still, it wasn't in him to cede the point so easily. "I can teach anyone how to kill. That's easy. You point the weapon, you pull the trigger, and assuming you can aim . . . bam, a piece of lead enters the target's body, hits a vital organ, and it's done. If you've got big enough balls I can teach you to slide a knife through a guy's armpit and pop his heart like a balloon. Fuck . . . I can show you a thousand ways to punch someone's ticket. I can teach you battlefield techniques until I'm blue in the face . . ."

"But?" Kennedy asked, prodding him in the direction she knew he was headed.

"Turning a man into what we're looking for," Hurley stopped and shook his head, "it just ain't that easy."

Kennedy sighed. This was the opening she was looking for. Touching Hurley's arm she said, "I'm not saying it is, which is why you have to start trusting the rest of us to do our jobs. I have brought you a gift, Stan. You don't realize it right now because you think a guy has to go through boot camp before he's ready to have a run at your selection process, and normally I would agree with you, but this is different. You're just going to have to let go of some of your control issues for a bit. What I have in that car is exactly what you've been looking for, Stan. No bad habits that'll take you months to undo. None of that stiff military discipline that makes all these guys stand out like a sore thumb when we dump them into an urban setting."

Hurley glanced at the car.

"He's off the charts on all of our tests," Kennedy added. "And he's yours for the shaping."

With a deep frown Hurley studied what little he could see of this raw lump of coal that Kennedy was about to dump in his lap.

"That is," Kennedy said, "if you can swallow your pride and admit that the little girl you used to bounce on your knee is all grown up and just might be better at spotting talent than you."

Checkmate, Hurley thought to himself. I'm stuck with this puke. At least for a few days until I can figure out how to make him quit. "Fine," he said with a defeated tone. "But no special favors. He pulls his weight just like everyone else or he's gone."

"I don't expect any favors, but," Kennedy said, pointing a finger at his face, "I am going to be very upset if I find out you singled him out and gave him some of your famous extra love and attention."

Hurley digested her words and then gave her a curt nod. "Fine . . . I'll do it your way, but trust me, if I so much as get a whiff of weakness—"

"I know . . . I know," she said, robbing him of the final word. "You'll make him wish he'd never met you." Kennedy had pushed it as far as she was willing for the moment. Rapp would simply have to show the crotchety old bastard what she already knew. "I have to head over to the Farm to take care of something. I'll be back for dinner." She turned to head back to the car and over her shoulder she yelled, "And he'd better look no worse for the wear than the other six, or you're going to have one very unhappy niece on your hands."

CHAPTER 3

RAPP watched Kennedy drive away, his heavy, oversized lacrosse duffel bag hanging at his side. The scene was a bit surreal. It brought back memories of being dropped off at summer camp when he was nine and watching his mom drive off. Just like today, he had gone of his own free will, but this time there were no tears in his eyes. Back then he'd been a boy afraid of the unknown. Today he was a twenty-three-year-old man ready to take on the world.

As the car drove down the lane, Rapp could feel the weight of his decision. A door was closing. He had picked one path over another and this one was undoubtedly the one less traveled. It was overgrown and more treacherous than his imagination could do justice to, but then again his youthful self felt invincible and was filled with schemes to cheat death. He would undoubtedly be pushed to quit, but he was confident that would not happen. He'd never quit anything in his life, and he'd never wanted anything anywhere near as bad as he wanted this. Rapp knew the score. He knew how his chain would be yanked and jerked every which way and he would be forced to endure all of it. The prize at the end was what it was all about, though, and he was willing to endure all of it for his chance.

Rapp could feel the man's eyes on him. He let his heavy bag fall to the ground and watched him come closer. The man with the 'stache and the sunglasses blocked his view of the long driveway. Rapp instantly smelled the acid mix of coffee and cigarettes on his breath. He wanted to take a step back, but didn't want to appear to be backing down, so he stayed put and breathed through his mouth.

"Take a good look at that car," Hurley said sourly.

Rapp tilted his head to the side and watched the sedan disappear around the corner.

"She ain't coming back," Hurley added in a taunting voice.

Rapp nodded in agreement.

"Eyes front and center," Hurley snapped.

Rapp stared at his own reflection in the polarized lenses and remained silent.

"I don't know what kind of fucking bullshit you pulled on her. I don't know how you managed to con her into thinking you had what it takes to make it through my selection process, but I can promise you that every day you're here, you will curse her a thousand times for walking into your life. But you better do it silently, because if I hear you utter one single unkind word about her, I will make you feel pain you never thought possible. Do you understand me?"

"Yes."

"Yes!" Hurley barked. "Do I look like one of your faggot college professors?"

"No," Rapp said without twitching.

"No," Hurley howled with a veiny throat. "You call me sir when you talk to me, or I'll stick my boot so far up your ass you'll be chewing leather."

A fleck of spit hit Rapp in the face, but he ignored it. He'd figured something like this would happen. He'd already taken a look around and hadn't seen any others, so this was probably his best chance. "Sir, permission to speak?"

"I should have figured," Hurley said with a sigh. He placed his hands on his hips and said, "All right, Ivy League. I'll give you this one chance to say your piece. I can only pray you're going to tell me this was a bad idea and you'd like to go home. And I've got no problem with that," he added quickly. "Hell, I'll drive you myself."

Rapp grinned and shook his head.

"Shiiiiit!" Hurley drew out the word as he shook his head in disgust. "You actually think you can do this?"

"I do, sir."

"So you're really going to waste my time."

"It appears so, sir. Although, if I may . . . I suggest we speed things up a bit."

"Speed things up?" Hurley asked.

"Yes, sir. My guess is once you step in the ring with a man you can probably figure out inside about twenty seconds if a guy has enough talent to make it through your selection process."

Hurley nodded. "That's right."

"I don't want to waste your time, so I say we find out if I have the goods."

Hurley smiled for the first time. "You want to take a run at me?"

"Yes, sir . . . so we can speed things up."

Hurley laughed. "You think you can take me?"

"From what I've heard . . . not a chance in hell."

"Then why are you in such a hurry to get your ass kicked?"

"I figure you'll do it sooner or later. I'd rather do it sooner."

"And why's that?"

"So we can get on with the important stuff."

"And what would that be?"

"Like you teaching me how to kill terrorists."

This was a first. Hurley took a step back and studied the new recruit. He was six-one and looked to be in perfect shape, but at twenty-three that was expected. He had thick, jet-black hair and dark bronzed skin. He had the right look. Hurley sensed the first glimmer of what Kennedy had alluded to. More amused than worried, Hurley nodded his consent and said, "All right. We'll have a go at it. You see that barn over there?"

Rapp nodded.

"There's an open cot in there. It's yours for as long as you can last. Throw your crap in the footlocker and put on a pair of shorts and a T-shirt. If you're not ready and standing in the middle of the mat in two minutes I'm sending you home."

Rapp took it as an order. He grabbed his bag and took off at a trot for the barn. Hurley watched him duck inside, noted the time on his digital watch, and walked back to the porch, where he set down his coffee mug on the edge of the glossy white floorboards. Without so much as glancing over his shoulder he unzipped his pants and began to urinate on the bushes.

CHAPTER 4

RAPP found the cot next to three bunk beds. It was standard military surplus. Not great, but a hell of a lot better than the floor. After stripping to his underwear, he opened his bag and pulled out a pair of shorts and a plain white T-shirt. Kennedy had told him to pack only generic clothing. She didn't want him wearing anything that could give one of the other men an idea where he came from. They were all under strict orders to not discuss each other's past. Rapp folded up his clothes, placed them in the footlocker, closed it, and set the bag on top. He would have unpacked the bag, but he heard his instructor approaching. Rapp took up his position in the middle of the well-worn wrestling mat and waited eagerly for his shot.

Hurley stopped near the entrance to the barn, took a long drag off his cigarette, and began to loosen up with a few side stretches and shoulder rolls. He was not expecting much of a fight, so after a quick calf stretch he took one last puff off his cigarette, stubbed it out against the sole of his boot, and entered the barn. The new recruit was standing in the middle of the mat wearing shorts and a T-shirt. Hurley gave him the once-over. He was fit, just like all the others, but there was a certain casual, relaxed posture that he found off-putting.

"Shoulders back! Eyes front and center!" Hurley shook his head and mumbled some incoherent words to himself. "I don't have time to babysit." He bent over and took off his boots and socks and set them neatly at a ninety-degree angle at the edge of the mat, socks folded on top. He took off his sunglasses and set them on top of the socks. Stepping onto the mat, he asked, "Rules?"

Rapp didn't flinch. "That's up to you, sir."

Hurley bent back, continuing his stretching, and said, "Since no one's here to monitor this little ass kickin' I suggest we keep it civilized. Stay away from the balls and the eyes, and no throat strikes."

"Choke holds?"

"Absolutely," Hurley grinned. "If you want it to end, all you have to do is tap out."

Rapp shook his head.

"Fair enough." Hurley caught his first glimmer of something he didn't like. There was no sign of tension on the kid's face. He looked as relaxed as a schmuck who was about to play a round of golf. Two possibilities presented themselves and Hurley liked neither. The first was that the recruit might not be the little mama's boy that he thought, and the second was that he might be too stupid to know he wasn't cut out for this line of work. Either way, he might have to waste more than one day of his valuable time trying to drum him out. Hurley was shaking his head and muttering to himself when he realized there was a third possibility—that the kid actually might have the goods.

The potential hazard made Hurley pause. He glanced at the young college kid and realized he knew surprisingly little about the man standing in the middle of the mat. The jacket he'd received from Stansfield was so sanitized that the pertinent details would have fit onto one page. Beyond the general physical description and test scores, every other piece of information had been redacted. The man was a blank slate. Hurley had no sense of his physical abilities and general bearing. He didn't even know if he was left- or right-handed. A frown creased Hurley's well-lined brow as he ran through some more scenarios.

Normally, when Hurley stepped onto the mat with a recruit, he already had the advantage of having read an extensive personnel file, as well as having watched him for several days. You could tell a lot about a man by observing him for a few days. He silently called himself a dumb-ass for not thinking of this sooner. There was no calling it off at this point. His bare feet were on the mat. If he called it off, it would be a sign of weakness.

Hurley set his apprehension aside and reminded himself that he'd bested every man he'd run through here. He moved forward with his normal swagger and a lopsided grin on his face. He stopped ten feet away and said, "Ready when you are."

Rapp nodded, dropped into a crouch, and made a slow move to his left.

Hurley began sliding to his right, looking for an angle of attack. He glimpsed his opening when his opponent made an aggressive head fake that was an obvious tell of what would follow. In that moment, Hurley decided to dispatch the kid quickly. He wasn't going to waste time with defensive blocks and holds. He was going to make this kid feel some real pain. Maybe bust a couple of his ribs. That way, even if he proved to be a stubborn fool, there'd be no hope of his keeping up with the others.

Hurley anticipated the punch, ducked into a crouch, and came in to deliver a blow to the kid's midsection. Right about the time he pivoted off his back foot and let loose his strike he realized something wasn't right. The kid was a lot faster than he had anticipated. The little shit had doubled back on his own weak fake and was now a good two feet to the right of where Hurley had thought he would be. It looked like he had been suckered. Hurley knew he was horribly out of position, and exposed, but he wasn't the least bit alarmed. He pulled back his punch and prepared to go back in again on a different angle of attack. He was in the process of delivering his second blow when he realized again that something was wrong. Hurley sensed more than saw the big left hook bearing down on his face. In the final split second before impact he braced himself by pulling in his chin and dropping his hips.

The crushing blow landed just above Hurley's right eye.

Punches are funny things in that each one is different. You've got uppercuts, hooks, jabs, round-houses, haymakers, and rabbit punches, to name a few. If you've sparred enough, you've felt all of them, and you learn to recognize each one by feel almost the instant it lands. A little scorecard in your head quickly analyzes the blow, and there's a brief con-versation that takes place between the part of the brain that analyzes the thousands of instantaneous signals that come flying in and the part of the brain whose job it is to make sure the brain stays online. Hurley had been doing this for years, and as a man whose job it was to judge talent and teach, he had grown very accustomed to giving instant feedback to the man whose ass he was kicking. On this occa-sion, however, he was too busy trying to stay on his feet, so he kept his mouth shut.

The punch hit him so squarely that Hurley ac-tually went down to one knee for a split second. The turtle move had saved him from getting KOed. If his head had been exposed any further the force of the blow would have snapped his jaw around so quickly his equilibrium would have gone offline, and he'd be down for a nice long nap. The ringside announcer in Hurley's brain made him aware of two things in extremely quick succession. The first was that he hadn't been hit this hard in a long time, the second was that he'd better launch a counterat-tack, and do it quickly, or he was going to get his ass kicked.

Hurley pivoted from his back to his front foot and launched a flurry of combinations designed more to get this kid to back up than actually hit him. The first two were blocked and the next five found nothing more than air. Hurley realized the kid must have been a boxer and that meant he'd have to get him down on the mat and twist him into submission. No more punches. Before Hurley had a chance to regroup, he felt the leg sweep catch him perfectly in the ankle of his right foot, which happened to be bearing about 90 percent of his weight. What happened next was simple physics. The sweep took him out so cleanly that there was no hope of catching himself with his back leg, so Hurley went with it. He landed on his ass, tucked and rolled back and sprang onto his feet. The fact that the kid had just swept him was not lost on Hurley. Boxers did not know how to use leg sweeps. There was a split-second pause while Hurley looked across the mat at the new recruit and wondered if he'd been lied to about his lack of military training. The respite did not last long.

Once again Hurley found himself on the receiving end of a combination of well-placed punches. He had to get this kid down on the mat, or he really was going to get his ass kicked. He backed up quickly as if retreating for his life. The kid followed him, and when he launched his next attack Hurley dropped down and slid in. He grabbed the lead leg and stuck his shoulder into the kid's groin, while pulling and lifting at the same time. The kid tried to drop his hips but Hurley had too good a hold. Hurley was about to topple him when a double-fisted hammer strike landed between his shoulder blades. The blow was so solid Hurley nearly let go, but something told him if he did, he would lose, so he hung on for dear life and finally toppled the kid.

Hurley was on top of him. He found a wrist and jammed his thumb into the pressure point while maneuvering the rest of his body into position for an arm bar. He rolled off and delivered a scissor kick to the throat of his opponent that under the rules was not exactly fair, but neither was their business. The kick barely missed, but Hurley had his opponent's wrist in both hands now and was ready to lean back and cantilever the kid's damn arm until he hyperextended the elbow. Before he could lock in the move, though, the kid did something that Hurley did not think possible.

Rapp had somehow reversed into the hold and was now on top of Hurley, who still had a good grip on his wrist. Hurley's head, however, was now firmly locked between Rapp's knees. Rapp hooked his ankles together and began to close his knees like a vise crushing a coconut.

Hurley jabbed his thumb as deeply into the wrist of his opponent as he could, but it didn't get him to back off a bit. He could feel the early stages of a blackout coming on and scrambled for a way out. He released his left hand from the wrist hold and grabbed a handful of the kid's thick black hair. Instead of letting go, though, the kid squeezed his knees even harder. White lights were dancing at the periphery of his vision. Hurley couldn't believe he just had his ass handed to him by some college puke.

Still, he did not stop looking for a way out, and with the darkness closing in, he found his answer sitting only a few inches in front of his face. He vaguely remembered a brief discussion about rules before they had started but that wasn't important right now. Making sure he didn't lose was what was important. In a last-ditch effort to avoid calamity, Hurley released his opponent's wrist and lashed out with his now free hand. He found the kid's gonads and with every last ounce of strength he clamped down and began to squeeze.

CHAPTER 5

KENNEDY returned to the lake house just after six in the evening. She was tired, hungry, and not in the mood for another confrontation with Hurley, but there were certain developments that needed to be discussed. One of the unforeseen and increasingly difficult aspects of her job was the inability to communicate freely with her colleagues. Foreign intelligence agencies that operated in Washington were always a threat, but no longer her biggest concern. Now she had to worry about her own government and a new generation of journalists who wanted to break the next Watergate, Pentagon Papers, or Iran Contra scandal. Combined, they had ended hundreds of careers and done untold damage to national security. It was the new sport in Washington to pound on the very agencies tasked with keeping America safe. Surprisingly, Kennedy was fairly ambivalent about it. As her mentor Thomas Stansfield had told her many times, "Great spies don't complain about the rules, they find ways around them."

She parked the car in front of the house and climbed the porch steps, dreading the thought of going another round with Hurley. Kennedy opened the screen door and entered. The rooms to her left and right were empty, so she went down the center hall to the kitchen. Her feet stopped where the hardwood floor transitioned to linoleum. Sitting at the kitchen table was a bruised and battered Stan Hurley. He had a drink filled with ice and Maker's Mark pressed against a fat lip and a bag of ice held against his swollen right eye. Leaning against the counter directly across from him was Troy Tschida, a thirty-two-year-old former Green Beret and Hurley's right-hand man. Tschida tried but failed to suppress his amusement over his boss's battered physical appearance.

"You think this is funny?" Hurley snarled.

"Absolutely not," Tschida said with dramatic, false sincerity.

"You prick. Wait till I stick your ass in the ring with him. You won't be laughing after he lands a couple punches."

"What happened?" Kennedy asked, genuinely not sure what they were talking about.

Hurley hadn't seen her enter, because the bag of ice was covering his right eye, and he didn't hear her because his ears were still ringing. He turned his head and removed the bag of ice to reveal an eye that was so swollen it was almost entirely closed. The skin above the eye was a shiny bulbous red.

"What happened," Hurley said in a voice rising with anger, "was that fucking Trojan horse you dumped in front of my house this afternoon."

It clicked and Kennedy thought of Rapp. "You're saying my recruit did this to you?"

"Don't fucking play games with me. I am in no mood." Hurley slammed his glass down on the table and grabbed the bottle of bourbon. He filled it to the brim.

"I have no idea what you're talking about," Kennedy said sincerely.

Hurley took a big gulp and said, "My ass. He's your recruit. You give me some cut-and-paste fuckin' jacket on the guy that reads like a ransom note. I know nothing about him. He's here less than a minute and he up and suggests we find out if he has the right stuff." Hurley stopped to take another drink and then in a falsetto voice designed to mimic Rapp said, "Let's speed things up, and find out if I have what it takes to do this."

"My recruit did that to you?" asked Kennedy, still not entirely sure what the man was talking about.

Hurley slammed his glass down again. This time brown liquid sloshed over the lip of the glass. "Yes, God dammit! And don't stand there and act like this is a surprise to you." He pointed an accusatory finger at her. "You planned it. You set me up."

"I have no idea what you're talking about." Kennedy shook her head and asked, "Are you trying to say my recruit bested you?"

"Damn close." Hurley turned his attention to his drink and mumbled to himself.

"Your boy had him beat," Tschida interjected with a smile, "but Stan here broke the rules and put the kid's balls in a vise."

"You think this shit is funny?" Hurley barked.

Tschida smiled and nodded.

Hurley looked like he was going to launch his glass across the room at him, and then at the last minute decided to use the bag of ice.

Tschida stuck out his right hand and caught the bag with ease. "Don't be a baby. After all the asses you've kicked around here, it's about time you got a little taste."

"My problem," Hurley shot back, "is getting ambushed by this young woman here. Someone I helped raise, by the way." Hurley turned his one good eye back on Kennedy. "No military experience, my ass. Where did you find this kid?"

Kennedy was still in a bit of shock. She herself had seen Hurley tie NFL-sized linebackers into pretzels. Nowhere in her research had she found anything that would lead her to believe Rapp was capable of going toe to toe with Stan Hurley. "Stan, you need to trust me. I had no idea he could best you."

"He didn't best me! He almost did."

"Yeah, but you cheated," Tschida said, taking perverse pleasure in the torment he was causing Hurley. "So, technically, he beat you."

It took every last bit of restraint to not throw his glass at the gloating Tschida. Hurley turned his attention back to Kennedy and asked, "What are you up to? Why in hell would you try to sucker me like this?"

"Just calm down for a minute, Stan. I am telling you right now, we found nothing in our research that said he was capable of this." Kennedy gestured at Hurley's battered face. "It was my sincere hope that someday he would be able to do this . . . but not this soon."

"Then your research sucks. You don't learn how to fight like this in your basement. Someone has to teach you."

Kennedy admitted, "He's been going to a martial arts studio for the past year."

"That would have been nice to know," Hurley fired back.

"Stan, you have been bitching up a storm that this guy is a waste of time because he hasn't had Special Forces training. You think a year of training in a strip mall is equal to what the army puts guys through?"

"That depends on the instructor."

"And the student," Tschida added.

Kennedy folded her arms and thought long and hard before she spoke. "There is one other possibility."

"What's that?"

"I know you don't like to talk about your age, but is it possible that you've lost a step."

Tschida started laughing so hard his big barrel chest was rising and falling with each chuckle.

Hurley was seething. "I'm going to put your

ass in the ring with him, first thing in the morning. We'll see how funny you think this is then."

Tschida stopped laughing.

Kennedy pulled up a chair and sat at the table across from Hurley. "Please tell me what happened."

"You're not jerking my chain?"

Kennedy shook her head.

"You weren't trying to pull a fast one on me? Set me up?"

She shook her head again and said, "No. In fact I was worried that he would be on the receiving end of a beating. Not the other way around."

Even through his anger- and bourbon-induced haze, Hurley was starting to grasp that Kennedy was telling the truth. "Where did you find this guy?"

Kennedy gave him a look that he instantly understood.

"Shithead," Hurley said to Tschida, "go check on those clowns, and if they're screwing around bust 'em out and make 'em snap off a hundred up-downs."

"Got it." Tschida moved out, all business.

As soon as the screen door slammed, Hurley looked at Kennedy and said, "Who is he?"

She couldn't keep him in the dark forever, but she would have preferred to wait a few more days. Setting her apprehension aside she said, "His name is Mitch Rapp."

CHAPTER 6

RAPP lay on his cot, his head propped up on a lumpy pillow and a bag of frozen peas on his groin. Dinner had been served buffet style on a folding table at the far end of the barn. His appetite wasn't really there, but he forced himself to eat. There were seven of them plus two instructors, and among them, they polished off a giant pot of spaghetti, a plate full of rolls, and all the salad and corn on the cob they could stomach. The men were tired, hot, and ragged, but they stuffed their faces all the same and washed it down with pitchers of ice water and cold milk. Rapp had spent the last five years eating at a training table and knew how it worked. Tough drills in heat like this didn't exactly spur the desire to eat. It had the opposite effect, but you had to ignore it and shovel down the food. The physiology was pretty straightforward. They would be burning five-thousand-plus calories a day, and that meant either they had to eat a ton of food or they would begin to lose weight. With his frame and current weight, Rapp could lose ten pounds, but anything beyond that and he would open himself up to injury and illness.

Rapp tossed the copy of *Time* magazine on the floor and adjusted the bag of frozen peas. One of the instructors had pulled him aside as he was clearing his plate and told him he wanted him to get on his back and start icing. He then gave him strict orders to report any blood in his urine. Rapp simply nodded and took the bag of peas. After his sparring match and before dinner he'd had a few hours to reflect on what had happened while one of the instructors led him through a tough circuit of calisthenics and then a ten-mile run through the woods. Rapp made it seem like he was struggling, but he wasn't. Especially with the running. He could last all day if he had to, but he didn't want to show these guys too much too soon. Besides, give a teacher the choice between a straight-A student who has all the answers and an earnest one who gets better over time, and they'll pick the earnest one every time.

Rapp was still trying to absorb what lesson there was to learn from his earlier throwdown with the man whose name he still did not know. He was not happy that the man had changed his own rules in the middle of a fight, but there wasn't a lot he could do about it now. He had to focus on how it would affect things going forward. It was important to know how far he could push it, and if these instructors weren't going to abide by the rules, they could hardly expect him to do so.

Rapp's first chance to meet the other men was after his run. They were at the pull-up bars behind the barn doing four sets of twenty-five. In addition to the mean old bastard running the place, there were three more instructors. Just as his recruiter had told him, no one was to use his real name or discuss any personal information. The first two instructors were easy to keep straight. The short skinny one was called Sergeant Smith and the tall skinny one was called Sergeant Jones. They would start their days with Smith and end with Jones.

Rapp had to do two sets of twenty-five with a thirty-second rest between so he could catch up with the other recruits. After each man had polished off a full one hundred pull-ups Sergeant Smith went nuts. He lined them up and paced back and forth dumping disdain on them.

"One of you faggots doesn't think he needs to do a full pull-up," the instructor started. "Thinks he can go halfway down and not quite all the way up. Well, I don't like anything done half-assed so you ladies get to start over."

Then the invective really started to fly as he called into question their manhood, honor, intelligence, and lineage. Rapp noted that he treated them as a group rather than singling out the supposed offender, who he wasn't so sure even existed. He'd watched the other men, and none of them seemed to be slacking off. The sergeant was simply moving the goal line in hopes that one of them would grow sick of the games and quit. As he looked around, though, he didn't see that happening. The other six were hard individuals.

"Four more sets on the quick. Let's go!" the sergeant barked. "And do 'em right this time, or I'll send you ladies on a nice long run and you can forget about dinner."

There were two bars, so the men lined up and started over. Rapp was waiting for his turn when one of the other recruits poked him hard in the kidney. Rapp turned around and took inventory of the man who had jabbed him and was now cussing him out in a voice only the two of them could hear. The man looked like one of those professional rugby players from Europe. He had a heavy brow made heavier by a single black eyebrow that traveled laterally from one temple to the other. His eyes were coal-black and wide-set, but his most prominent features were a hook nose that looked to have been broken at least twice and a dimple in the middle of his pronounced chin. Rapp thought of two things almost instantly. The first was that it would be a waste of effort to try to knock him out with a punch to the head. The guy's neck was as thick as the average man's thigh. The second was that he didn't fit in. At least as far as Rapp understood the intent of what they were up to. The man's features were so distinctive as to make him almost impossible to forget. He looked more like an enforcer than a stealth operative.

"Do 'em right this time, shithead," the big man said testily.

Rapp was sweaty, dirty, hot as hell, and not used

to taking crap from anyone. He had done his pull-ups correctly. If anyone could be accused of not doing them all the way it would be the very man who was in his face. Rapp was tempted to set the tone and knock the guy on his ass, but he figured there would be plenty of time for that later. He turned back around without responding and stepped to the line.

"That's right," the big man said, "be a smart boy and keep your mouth shut. Just fucking do 'em right this time."

The rest of the afternoon proceeded without incident and they were allowed to jump into the lake to cool down before dinner. Rapp steered clear of Victor but kept an eye on him. He had learned that was the big man's name. Or at least the name he'd been given. Since they were forbidden to use their real names, the instructors gave each of them a fake first name. Rapp's was Irving, which they had already shortened to Irv. The other five guys were Fred, Roy, Glenn, Bill and Dick.

They all seemed decent enough and pretty much kept their heads down and their eyes alert. There were a lot of knowing glances and silent communication. Since they were forbidden to talk about their past, there was no mention of military service or the units they had served in. This created an interesting situation for Rapp. The instructors more than likely knew he'd never served in the military, but the other recruits had no idea.

It created a weird dynamic when you dumped a group of guys in a situation where they were forbidden to talk about their pasts. It pretty much killed small talk, so little was said during dinner. Rapp retired to his cot so he could ice his groin and was staring up at the slow, churning revolutions of the ceiling fan that hung from the rafters directly above him. He was thinking about the match, going through it move by move wondering what he could have done differently, when Victor appeared next to his cot.

"What's your name?" he asked in a hushed voice.

Rapp glanced over to the door where one of the instructors was giving orders to one of the other guys.

"Irv."

"No, dumb-ass." He shook his head. "I mean your real name."

Rapp was starting to think he didn't like Victor. He'd been warned by his recruiter repeatedly that talking about your personal life was grounds for immediate dismissal from the program. Just ten minutes earlier, while they were eating, the instructors had reminded them of this again. Rapp impassively looked up and said, "Didn't you hear what the instructors told us?"

A lopsided grin fell across the other man's face. "That's just a bunch of BS. It's a game. They're just trying to fuck with us." He glanced over his shoulder to make sure no one was close enough to hear and said, "Come on . . . where you from?"

"What's your angle?"

"Huh?"

"What are you up to?"

"Just trying to get to know the guys . . . that's all."

"Try not to take this the wrong way, but it's none of your business who I am or where I'm from."

"Is that so?" His face flushed a bit and his jaw tightened. "I'll tell you something. I don't need you telling me what is and isn't my business."

Rapp didn't like his predicament. He was on his back and vulnerable, but he didn't want Victor to think he was easily intimidated. "It's not me telling you," he said in a casual voice, "it's them." Rapp looked over at the instructor by the door.

The instructor finished whatever he was saying and left. It was just the seven recruits now.

Victor started laughing. "There goes your mother. Looks like your ass is mine."

Rapp decided lying down was no longer the best position to be in. He quickly swung his legs off the cot and stood. In a conversational tone that was loud enough for the others to hear, he said, "What's your problem, Victor?"

"You're my problem."

"I gathered that," Rapp said from the other side of the cot, "but could you be a little more specific. Maybe it's something I could fix."

"I doubt it," the bigger man said with disdain. "You look soft to me. Like you don't belong here."

"Well . . . why don't we find out." Rapp gestured to the wrestling mat.

Victor laughed as if the idea was preposterous. "You don't stand a chance."

Rapp nodded as if to say maybe, maybe not, and walked over to the edge of the mat. "I'm sorry about your mother, Victor."

"What did you just say?" Victor asked.

"I said," Rapp half yelled, "I'm sorry about your mom."

"You'd better watch yourself!" Victor's eyes had taken on a wild glare.

"Or what?" Rapp asked.

The other five guys all dropped what they were doing to see what was going on.

"You gonna take a swing at me, Victor?" Rapp egged the big man on. He was ready to end this thing right now. "What's wrong . . . your mom the neighborhood slut when you were growing up . . . she didn't hold you enough when you were little? She let every guy she met suck on her tit except you?"

"You got a big mouth," Victor snarled, barely able to contain his rage.

"Just trying to figure out what's wrong with you, Victor. You been shooting your mouth off all day. Acting like a world-class prick. We're all getting sick of it."

"I'm going to kick your ass!" Victor howled as he hopped from one foot to the other like a boxer.

Rapp didn't say a word. He moved to the middle of the mat and motioned for Victor to join him.

Victor started whooping and hollering as he danced circles around Rapp. He was throwing shadow punches and explaining in detail what he was going to do to Rapp, when suddenly one of the instructors reappeared in the doorway.

"What in hell are you ladies doing?"

Victor fell silent, but it was too late.

"That's it, you dumb-asses. If you've got enough energy to fight then you've got enough energy to run. You've got sixty seconds to muster your worthless asses outside on the line. Put your running gear on and move it!"

Everyone sprang into action, and while they were putting on their gear the other five men made their displeasure known through a mix of looks and verbal complaints. Rapp did not respond, while Victor seemed to relish it. He turned the taunts back on the other men and invited any of them to take a shot at him just as soon as one of them grew a set of balls. Rapp put on his shoes and sprinted for the door. He was the first one on the line, and while he waited for the others, it occurred to him that something wasn't right. If this program was so secretive and elite, what in hell was a loudmouth like Victor doing here?

CHAPTER 7

CAMP PERRY, VIRGINIA

TOM Lewis took the call on the secure line. He listened patiently to the person on the other end relay a seemingly benign message about a meeting that was to take place in Washington, D.C., the following afternoon. To anyone with the ability to breach the secure system, which of course included the internal security people back in Langley, the conversation would have seemed so ordinary as to not warrant a second thought. In the third sentence, however, an adverb was used that caused his right eyebrow to shoot up a quarter inch. Lewis thanked the person on the other end and said they would talk at the meeting the next day.

The clinical psychologist slowly placed the phone back in its cradle and tapped his pen on a generic desk blotter. Everything in the office was generic; all standard-issue government furniture, the kind that was purchased in massive quantities every year by the behemoth federal government. The desk, bookcase, and credenza were all made from particleboard coated with a thin plastic veneer that was supposed to look like wood, but didn't. The chairs were black plastic with coarse charcoal fabric seats that could render a pair of dress pants useless in just nine months. Lewis was amazed at how ubiquitous this type of furniture had become in Washington, which in turn led him to the conclusion that the maker of this substandard furniture was more than likely headquartered in the home district of the chairman of the House Appropriations Committee.

Lewis detested such poor craftsmanship, but nonetheless made no attempt to add a personal touch to this office. His private office was in the District and every square inch of it had been meticulously decorated. With what he charged for an hour of therapy he could not only afford the fine trappings, but even more, his clients expected it. In a rather short period of time he had built up a very profitable practice. His patient list was a virtual who's who of Washington's power elite. Lobbyists, lawyers, and CEOs made up the bulk of his business. He treated only a smattering of politicians, but dozens of women who were married to powerful senators and congressmen came to see him every week and poured their hearts and minds out. If he were unscrupulous he'd be able to use that information to his benefit, but he had never been tempted.

The thirty-six-year-old Lewis had both the passion and the natural inclination for his work. He had obtained an undergraduate degree in economics and math from Pomona College and a graduate degree in clinical psychology from the University of Pennsylvania. The latter was paid for by the government, which required him to serve four years in the army upon graduating. That stint in the army more than anything was what pulled Lewis into this current situation, in a windowless, crappy office on a base that very few people even knew existed. It seemed he had a knack for spotting mental deficiencies, which when he was in the army was something that greatly interested at least one flag officer and a couple of colonels down at Fort Bragg. He'd spent three years helping the Joint Special Operations Command tighten up their selection process and develop a new system for game theory.

Lewis took a moment to collect his thoughts and figure out how the call would affect his evening. The camp had a bachelors' quarters of sorts for the various employees and consultants who traveled back and forth to D.C. When a new class was on the post he normally stayed one or two nights a week so he could observe how they interacted. He had planned on staying the evening and spending some time with one of the recruits who was showing some troublesome signs, but the phone call was more pressing.

Lewis looked down at his World War II Elgin A-11 U.S. military watch. His father had given it to him on his deathbed three years earlier. Lewis had replaced the worn strap and kept the watch in near-perfect shape. It was seven-fourteen in the evening.

Nothing on his desk was that urgent, and besides, it was a perfect evening to get out on the open road and clear his mind. He collected the two open files and spun his chair around to face a gray metal safe, which was already open. Lewis placed the files in the proper slot, closed the safe, and spun the dial. He left the office door open, as there was nothing other than the contents of the safe that needed to be protected.

His motorcycle was parked in the first space in front of the building. Lewis took off his sport coat and tie and carefully folded and placed them on the seat. He unlocked one of the saddlebags of the BMW 1200 motorcycle and retrieved a gray and black leather riding jacket and pair of chaps. He never rode his bike without them. Even with the thermometer pushing ninety degrees. Imprinted on his brain was the road rash a friend had received when he'd been forced to lay his bike down on a hot California afternoon. The jacket and tie were placed in the saddlebag and he put on his gray helmet. The motorcycle hummed to life and Lewis climbed on. Sixty seconds later he tipped his visor at the sentry standing post at the main gate and blew past him. A minute after that he was rocketing up the entrance ramp onto Interstate 64 and on his way north. The drive would take a bit more than an hour, which Lewis didn't mind in the least.

No phones, no one knocking on his door wanting him to listen to his problems. Lewis was finding it increasingly difficult to find the time to clear his mind and focus on the task at hand. A big green sign informed him how many miles he had to travel to reach Richmond, but he barely noticed. He was already thinking of their new recruit. That had to be why she had called. Lewis set the cruise control at 70 mph, adjusted himself on the seat, and checked his mirrors. He considered how much work he had put into this one candidate. The man was as close to perfect as anyone they'd come across in the almost two years he'd been working on the program. Lewis leaned into a turn and wondered if it was possible for Hurley to run the kid out in one afternoon. Unfortunately, he knew the answer to that question, because he'd seen him do it on more than one occasion.

CHAPTER 8

LAKE ANNA, VIRGINIA

IT was a moonless night sky and all but a few of the exterior lights were off so as to not attract bugs. The mutts had just finished their run and another hundred up-downs and a few more exercises designed to fatigue little-used muscles and maybe get one or more of them to quit so they could get down to the serious stuff. Unfortunately, all seven were now filing into the barn in a manner not much different than that of cows returning from a day grazing in the pasture. Their heads were down, their pace was slow, and their footing unsure, and fortunately the arguing was over. The only thing they could think about at the moment was sleep.

Hurley took a sip of bourbon and looked out across the lawn. Despite the fact that it was his seventh in the past three hours, he was not drunk. When it came to booze, and a lot of other things, the spook had the constitution of a man three times his size. Tonight, however, his normally unshakable confidence was a little wobbly. Hurley was feeling a nagging indecision that to the average person was a daily occurrence, but to a headstrong, decisive man like him was rare. The shiner on his eye and his throbbing headache were nothing more than a nagging physical symptom. A few more glasses of Maker's Mark and they would be thoroughly dulled.

The problem was between his ears—a crack in his psyche that had put him in a rarely visited but increasingly familiar place. It was gnawing at the back of his head, trying to crawl into his brain stem and take him down. The signs were all there: tight chest, quick breath, a sudden desire to get the hell out of Dodge and go somewhere, anywhere but here. For a man who was used to being in control, used to being right all the time, it was the most unwelcome feeling he could imagine. He'd rather get kicked in the head until he was knocked unconscious than try to wrestle with this crap.

The fix, Hurley knew, involved something he still wasn't used to. He'd spent years burying his problems, patching them, hiding them under anything he could find. His job was too important, there were too many enemies to confront and not enough men willing to do it. There was too much to do, the stakes were too high for him to sit around and feel sorry for himself. He was after all a product of the Cold War. While the children of the sixties cut loose and got in touch, Hurley cut throats and got as out of touch with his feelings as was possible. He darted around Europe in the late fifties and early sixties and then Southeast Asia in the midsixties. The seventies brought him to South America, the early eighties to Central America, and then finally, for the biggest shit show of all, he landed in the Middle East. The entire thing was a gigantic multidimensional chess match with the Soviets, a continuation of what had happened at the end of World War I and then the aftermath of World War II.

Getting in touch with his thoughts or feelings, or whatever they were, was not something Hurley relished. There was right and there was wrong, and in between an abyss filled with society's whiners, people who had inherited the luxury of safety and freedom, while having done nothing to earn it. He had never heard these opinions pass the lips of his mother or father. They didn't have to. He was born during the Depression, but they had lived through it. They'd moved from Chicago to Bowling Green, Kentucky, with their five kids, to escape the long food lines and massive unemployment of the inner city. Hurley had come of age not knowing any better. His lot in life seemed just as good as the next kid's. He'd taken that stoic demeanor and joined the army. After serving his stint, he enrolled at Virginia Tech on the GI Bill and graduated with decent marks. That final spring a man from the federal government who was extremely interested in his military record asked him if he'd like to see the world. Asked him if he'd like to make a difference. Hurley bit.

Officially, he'd spent the last twenty-one years darting in and out of war-torn countries and doing his part to create a few wars, too. Unofficially, it had been longer than that. He'd been on the very edge of the conflict between the Soviets and America and had no illusions about which side was the more noble of the two. All a person had to do was spend a little time in Berlin to understand the effects of communism and capitalism. Talk about a tale of two cities, East Berlin and West Berlin were living, breathing examples. Posters for the governments who had run them since the end of World War II. One side was a vivid Kodachrome film and the other a grainy old black-and-white pile of crap.

Hurley had never been more proud than when that damn wall came tumbling down. He'd spilled his own blood in the battle and had lost a few friends and more sources than he could count or wanted to remember, but they'd won. Unfortunately, there wasn't a lot of time to enjoy their victory. Hurley and a few others already had their eyes on the jihadists. He'd come across them when he was helping bleed the Soviet Union of cash, equipment, manpower, and eventually the will to continue its despotic experiment. It had been in the Khyber Pass, and at first he saw nothing that made him nervous. These people wanted their land back and the Soviets out. The problem started with the religious zealots who were being shipped in from Saudi Arabia, Yemen, and a handful of other crappy little countries.

Hurley loved to swear, drink, and chase women, which put him on a collision course with the puritan, fun-sucking, Wahhabi jihadists from Saudi Arabia. He almost instantly developed a special dislike for them, but didn't understand back then that they would want to spread their jihad beyond the jerkwater mountains of Southwest Asia. That came later, when he started to see them meddling in the affairs of the Palestinians. It was starting all over again. The Soviets had been contained and beaten, and now this new enemy was out pushing its agenda. Hurley had a bad feeling about where it was headed, and on top of that, for the first time in his life he felt tired. This threat was not going away, and he suddenly wasn't sure he could find, let alone train, the next batch of kids who would be needed to meet the threat. He needed help. Unfortunately, asking for help was not something Hurley was good at.

He heard one of the dogs bark and then the sound of a motorcycle drifted through the pines. It was not the rumble of an American-made motorcycle, rather the purr of a Japanese or German bike. Hurley breathed a small sigh that was part relief, part resignation. It was the doc. He realized Kennedy must have called him.

A single beam of light slashed through the trees and a moment later the motorcycle coasted round the corner. The bike was so quiet, Hurley could hear the tires on the gravel driveway. The bike rolled its way up to the house and the rider eased the kickstand into the down position and then killed the engine. After retrieving a flat piece of wood from one of the molded saddlebags, he put it under the kickstand and then took off his helmet.

Thomas Lewis ran a hand through his shaggy blond hair and looked up at Hurley. He immediately noticed the swelling over the eye, but he was more concerned with a look on the man's face that he had only recently grown to understand. "Tough day?"

Hurley tried to laugh it off. "No easy days in this line of work. You know that."

Lewis nodded. He knew all too well the toll that their business could inflict on a person, and not just the body. The physical injuries were fairly straightforward. They could either be mended or not. The assaults on the mind and soul were an entirely different matter.

CHAPTER 9

BEIRUT, LEBANON

THE battered, dusty Peugeot slowed to a crawl. The driver leaned out over the steering wheel and looked left and then right down the length of Hamra Street. His friend in the passenger seat did the same, but in a more halfhearted fashion. There was no stoplight, nor was there a stop sign, but habits formed during war died hard. Samir was the youngest of four brothers. Three of them had died in the civil war that had destroyed this once-beautiful city. His closest brother, only thirteen months his senior, had been killed by an RPG while crossing this very intersection. To the Westerners who covered the bloody civil war, Hamra Street was better known as the Green Line. Ali and his friends called it no-man's-land.

It was the street that divided East and West Beirut and, to a certain degree, the Muslims from the Christians, or more accurately the Shiite Muslims from the Maronite Christians. There were neighborhoods on each side of the line where you could find pockets of Sunnis, Armenians, Greek Orthodox, and Druze. Some of these outposts were more exposed than others, and they had all but disappeared during the lengthy and savage civil war, while a few of the more entrenched ones were now rebuilding. The civil war in many respects resembled the mob warfare of Chicago in the 1920s, but with much bigger guns.

With the war officially over for almost two years, virtually every part of the city was showing signs of life. The Christians to the east were rebuilding at a blistering pace, and the Muslims to the west were struggling to keep pace. Construction cranes dotted the skyline, and you were now more likely to get killed by a dump truck or a bulldozer than by a sniper. At least in certain areas. Hamra Street was not one of those areas. The buildings were still gutted shells, perfectly suited for a sniper to lie in wait.

Samir scanned the building across the street to his left while his friend Ali, who was sitting next to him, did the same thing to their right.

"Still cautious," the man in the backseat said in a coarse voice.

Samir looked sheepishly in the rearview mirror. "Sorry."

Assef Sayyed nodded and took another drag from his cigarette. He remembered that Samir's brother had been killed not far from here. A lot of good men had been killed along this godforsaken stretch of road. Sayyed, however, did not make small talk with his men. Such familiarity led to their getting ideas. Ideas were not good. They only needed to follow orders. He also had no desire to get too close to the all-but-disposable men who worked for him. It was far easier to mourn the loss of someone you didn't know well than the loss of a close friend.

Once Samir received the go-ahead from Ali, he gunned the engine and tore across the broad street, over the abandoned trolley tracks, and into a canyon of half-demolished buildings on the other side. A year or two earlier he would have never dreamed of taking this shortcut. The car continued for two blocks, dodging piles of rubble, and then hung a sharp left turn. Building by building, block by block, things got better. The first sign was that the roads were clear of debris. Scaffolding and cement mixers were the next positive sign, and then finally they came upon a row of buildings that actually had windows, although the stone facades were pockmarked from artillery shells and small-arms fire.

Two young men stood in front of a roadblock, AK-47 assault rifles at the ready. Samir slowed the car to a stop and looked at the young face of the man who was pointing the barrel of his rifle at his head. They were all young these days, or old, but there were very few in between. An entire generation had either fled the country or been killed. Samir jerked his thumb toward the backseat and watched the guard's eyes open wide as he recognized the ruthless Assef Sayyed. The young man gave a quick bow of respect, and then ordered his colleague to move the barricade.

The block was sealed at both ends. Some had started to question the manpower and effort that went into this, but all Sayyed had to do was flash them one of his withering stares and they were silenced. The Syrian intelligence colonel was of the mind that this peace was more of a lull in the fighting, and the second they let their guard down they would pay for it dearly. He continually advised the other militias to reconstitute, to find new recruits and to train them diligently, and to use this lull in the fighting to stockpile arms and ammunition. With each passing month it was becoming increasingly difficult to convince them to direct their resources to the next battle. To the men under his command, however, there was no questioning his orders. Sayyed had made certain of that by putting a bullet through the forehead of one of his aides at a staff meeting just two months earlier.

Sayyed tossed his cigarette in the gutter and entered the office building. Extension cords ran along the floor and the wall to bring power to various levels. The place had been functional for just two weeks, and Sayyed did not plan to use it for more than another few days at the most. The greatest vulnerability for his side was a complete lack of air power. If some dog in Israel found out where he was, he could have jets scrambled and dropping bombs on him in less than twenty minutes.

He took the stairs down to the basement level. The smell of raw sewage was an instant reminder that the city was still suffering the ills of almost fifteen years of fighting. Two men were in the hallway standing next to a kerosene lamp. They were still without power in the basement. Without having to be told, the men moved away from the door. The older of the two snapped off a distinctly British salute.

"Colonel, it is good to see you."

Sayyed ignored the greeting. "Where is Colonel Jalil?"

The man jerked his head toward the door. "He is inside with the prisoner."

Sayyed motioned for him to open the door.

The guard extended his hand. In it was a black hood. "To hide your identity."

Sayyed gave him a disdainful look, and the man put the hood away and opened the door. A man sat naked in the middle of the room tied to a metal chair. One man was standing beside him, another in front. Both were wearing black hoods. Sayyed entered the room and walked directly to the prisoner. He grabbed him by his hair and yanked his head up so he could see his face. Sayyed stood there searching the man's features for half a minute. So far he only had a trickle of dried blood on his upper lip. Other than that he looked untouched.

"Who are you?" Sayyed asked.

"My name is Nihad Wassouf."

Sayyed stared at him for a long time and finally said, "I think you are a liar. In fact I think you are a Jew."

"No!" the man protested vehemently. "I am a Syrian."

"I doubt that."

"I would not lie about such a thing. Check with the names I have given you."

Sayyed was already doing just that, but this man seemed like a rat to him, and those lazy fools back in Damascus could be tricked. Without warning, Sayyed walked over to a small cart. A variety of tools were lying on the surface. His hands danced from one to the next. He did not want to do anything that would require medical attention at this point. Finally, he settled on a pair of pliers. Sayyed walked back to the man and held the pliers in front of him. "I am not as nice, nor am I as patient as these two men. I will ask you only one more time . . . what is your real name?"

The man stammered for a second and then said, "Nihad Wassouf."

Sayyed reached out and straightened the prisoner's forefinger on his left hand. He clamped the pliers down on the quarter inch of nail that extended beyond the tip of the finger and rocked it back and forth a few times. The prisoner began to squirm. A line of crimson blood appeared at the edge of the nail bed. "Tell me your real name."

"I already have . . . I swear."

"Why are you looking for the American?"

"I was sent here to negotiate his release."

"By who?"

"His company."

"I think you are lying."

"No . . . I am not. Call my friends in Damascus. They will vouch for me."

"I do not believe you."

"Please. I am only a messenger. They are willing to pay a great sum of money."

"What if you are a spy?"

"I am not."

"Liar!" And with that Sayyed tore the man's fingernail completely out of its bed.

CHAPTER 10

LAKE ANNA, VIRGINIA

THE doctor peeled off his leather riding gear and stood on the porch listening to Hurley recount the afternoon's events. He did so as passively as possible, even though his concern grew on several fronts. Interrupting, he'd learned with Hurley, was a bad approach. It was best to let him get it all out. Questions or comments could be perceived as a personal attack, which in turn would elicit a spirited counterattack, all of which the doctor knew was very counterproductive.

Lewis had met the spook five years earlier. The Department of Defense had shipped his ODA team off to Pakistan to help the black ops boys from Langley who were trying to train and equip the mujahedeen in the treacherous border region between Pakistan and Afghanistan. Hurley, in his typical gruff manner, had expressed his amusement that the vaunted Green Berets were now attaching shrinks to their units. He wondered if Lewis was similar to the political commissars who were attached to Red Army units, which was not exactly a compliment, since the communist officers were political appointees and in charge of Communist Party morale among the troops. They were also known to ship off to Siberia anyone who did not show absolute devotion to the party. They were feared and despised by their own men.

Lewis had read clean through the rough bravado of Hurley, and rather than take offense, he laughed along. As the weeks passed, however, Hurley began to consult the shrink with increasing frequency. Hurley soon learned the good doctor was a valuable asset to have around. Lewis, he found out, had a gift. He could read people. The doctor was a walking, talking polygraph.

When Hurley was finished giving the afternoon's play-by-play he did not stop to hear the doctor's opinion or let him ask questions. He moved headlong into what he thought needed to be done. "I want you to sit down with him and run him through the wringer. Clear your calendar for the rest of the week if you have to. I want to know what the deal is with this kid. He's hiding something and I want to know what it is."

As was his habit, Lewis pursed his lips and stared off into the distance while he thought about other possibilities. He respected, liked, and felt a sense of loyalty to Hurley, but he was not exactly a well-balanced, mentally healthy adult male. Kennedy, on the other hand, was possibly one of the most measured and thoughtful humans he'd ever had the pleasure of working with. Before he did anything he wanted to hear her side of the story.

"I'll clear my schedule for tomorrow," Lewis said, agreeing without really agreeing. "Let's head inside. I'm starving and I need to use the bathroom."

After Lewis had relieved himself and washed his face, they found Kennedy at the kitchen table reading a file and picking at a plate of noodles. Lewis looked at the uninspired pasta and frowned. One of his passions was cuisine, and it pained him to watch his colleagues put so little effort into something so important. Without saying a word he began searching the cupboards for something, anything that he could use to create a passable meal. Kennedy and Hurley shared a brief smile.

Lewis stuck his nose into the refrigerator, and without bothering to turn around, said, "Stan, would you be so kind as to fetch a bottle of wine from the basement? A Chateau Dominique would be fine." He took out a package of chicken and closed the door. Moving to the sink he paused for a brief moment and then said, "You might as well grab two." When Hurley was gone, Lewis looked over his shoulder at Kennedy and motioned for her to join him at the sink.

"So," he said, "Stan's not exactly thrilled with your new recruit."

"He's not the easiest man to please."

Lewis turned on the water and began to rinse the chicken. With a wry smile he said, "He thinks you set him up."

Kennedy rolled her eyes.

"This is the one you told me about? The kid from Syracuse?"

"Yes."

Lewis splayed the chicken open and let the water run through the crevices. "You never said anything about his fighting abilities."

Kennedy sheepishly shrugged her shoulders and said, "I didn't know he had them."

"That's a pretty big thing to miss." Lewis glanced up at her. "I'm not judging."

"I'm not proud that I missed it, but in the end isn't it a good thing?"

"Maybe . . . maybe not."

Kennedy explained what she knew about Rapp, which admittedly wasn't a great deal, but she pointed out yet again that a blank slate was not necessarily a bad thing. That they could mold him into the man they needed. She finished her verbal report as Hurley made it back up from the basement. Lewis asked her to prepare a small salad while he went to work boiling noodles and slicing up the chicken and preparing a creamy white sauce. Hurley was left to open the red wine.

While Lewis put the finishing touches on the main dish, Hurley and Kennedy started up again. They volleyed back and forth, each one putting forth his or her version of what had happened and how the other one had screwed up. Like any good shrink, Lewis was a good listener, and he played his part. It helped that these two were rarely boring. Hurley was a once-in-a-lifetime patient, the kind of man who was so outrageously entertaining that you sometimes felt you should pay him rather than the other way around. Sure, there was a flourish of exaggeration here and there, but Lewis had witnessed several of his exploits firsthand and knew the stories to be for the most part accurate.

Kennedy was very different. There was no cussing, or anger, or animated hand gestures accompanied by thespianlike facial contortions. There was just a calm, analytical, intellectual way about her that put you at ease. Her answers were never rushed and almost always thoughtful. She did not participate in personal verbal attacks or attempt to sway opinion by exaggeration. Wildly different in almost every way, they did share a few qualities that served to exacerbate the situation. Both were deeply suspicious of everyone they encountered and did not find it easy to admit they were wrong. On top of that, their long history and familiarity served to bring both the best and worst qualities to the surface in a very raw way. Lewis would never admit this to them, but it had become one of his great clinical joys watching these two argue: It was verbal combat at an Olympian level.

The table was set, the wine poured, and the food dished up. Kennedy picked at her salad while Hurley and Lewis devoured both the salad and the chicken and tomato fettuccine. Lewis ate in near silence while he watched the two joust. He interrupted on three occasions, but only for clarification. When he'd cleaned his plate and poured himself a second glass of wine, he pushed his chair back and was ready to give them his take on the matter. One of the things they had decided at the formation of the group was that they wanted Lewis to have full operational input. Hurley was in charge, but there was some apprehension in Washington over his cowboy attitude. Hurley, to his credit, understood that he had certain weaknesses. Rather than cop an attitude about Lewis's role expanding beyond weeding out the whackjobs, Hurley had told him, "I don't want any bullshit, PC, shrink stuff. You're paid to voice your opinions. Not give me an endless stream of what-ifs."

With that in mind Lewis put his glass down and said, "Two mistakes were made and you both know what they were."

Kennedy nodded, while Hurley said, "I can think of one. Her not doing her due diligence. What's the second one?"

"You can't think of a single thing you did wrong today?" Lewis asked.

"I'm not perfect, but this one's not my fault." Hurley pointed at Kennedy. "I am busier than shit trying to see which one of these boys has the right stuff. I'm not responsible for the turds she dumps in my lap."

Lewis was suddenly resigned to the fact that he would have to box Hurley in a little tighter. Clearing his throat, he said, "We're left with two options. Either this kid is really good or you're losing a step." Lewis took a drink and asked, "Which one is it?"

Hurley's jaw tightened. "I haven't lost a step!" In a slightly embarrassed voice he added, "I just underestimated him, that's all."

"And that's what worries me the most," Lewis said in an accusatory tone.

"Don't worry . . . I won't let it happen again."

"I'm afraid that's not good enough."

Hurley lit a cigarette and casually said, "Let's not make this into something bigger than it needs to be."

"Bullshit!" Lewis said with genuine fury.

"Come on . . ." Hurley said, trying to shrug the whole thing off.

"Don't 'come on' me—you fucked up today, and you fucked up big-time."

Kennedy leaned back, her eyes wide, unable to hide her surprise at Lewis's strong condemnation.

"Let's not overreact," Hurley said easily, trying to take some of the heat out of the conversation.

"Overreact." Lewis leaned forward. "I'm not sure it would be possible to overreact to this situation, and what is really bothering me is that you know it, but you're too pigheaded to admit it."

"It's not the end of the world."

Lewis's indignation was growing with each denial. "You're supposed to be infallible. These guys are supposed to fear you, loathe you, hate your fucking guts, but the one thing they are never supposed to do is lay a shiner on you." Lewis pointed at Hurley's swollen eye. "And they definitely aren't supposed to beat you . . . especially not five minutes after they've walked through the gate."

"He didn't beat me," Hurley growled.

"Well . . . that's debatable. From what I've heard

he had you beat and the only way you got out of it was by cheating."

"Yeah . . . well, life's not fair."

"At this stage, Stan, these guys are like young pups. You know that. When we lay down the rules we can't break them. It sends the wrong signal."

Hurley leaned back and stubbornly folded his arms across his chest. "I was suckered into this thing."

"I'm not sure you were, but for a moment, I'll go along with you." Lewis paused briefly and then said, "You're not supposed to get suckered. You're supposed to run these dogs until they're so tired they can barely stand. You're supposed to watch them go after each other . . . get a sense of what they're capable of, and then you're supposed to bring them into that barn and smack them down, just like when you and I went through boot camp. This is delicate work, God dammit, and you know it. There's a reason why we do things the way we do them, and your ego has no place in the decision process."

"My ego has nothing to do with this," Hurley shot back with a sour look on his face. "I just let my guard down. That's all."

"No," Lewis shook his head, "I'm inclined to agree with Irene on this one. You still see her as a little girl, and you don't give her the credit she deserves. She shows up with this new recruit and because he doesn't fit into your little box of where these recruits are supposed to come from, you decided to skip steps one, two, and three, kick his ass, and send him packing." Lewis sat back, took a drink of wine, and then in a calmer voice asked, "Does it mean anything to you that Thomas signed off on this?" Lewis was referring to the deputy director of operations.

Embarrassed, Hurley said, "I didn't think of that."

"Do you understand the situation you've created?"

Hurley didn't react at first and then very slowly he began to nod.

Kennedy was feeling better about her position, but she wasn't entirely sure what they were talking about and asked Lewis, "What do you mean by situation?"

"These things have a way of spinning out of control," Lewis said. "One recruit has some success putting a shiner on an instructor and all of the sudden the rest of them think that maybe they can take a shot. That these guys are human. Throw in the fact that Stan here had to cheat to avoid losing, and we now have a potentially dangerous situation."

"How so?" Kennedy asked.

"Do you think it's in our best interest to train your boy, send him off, and have him decide that when things get tough, the rules don't really matter?"

Kennedy now saw the point.

"Fuck," Hurley mumbled to himself. "What do you want me to do?"

"You're going to get the hell out of here for about five days. I want you to heal up. You let me and the others run these guys down . . . I'll get a better sense of this Rapp kid and his full potential."

"And then?"

"You come back here and you head into the barn with him and you beat him fair and square."

"And if he can't beat him?" Kennedy asked.

Lewis and Hurley shared a look. They were in uncharted waters. Lewis finally looked at Kennedy and said, "That would be a nice problem to have."

CHAPTER 11

THE first night didn't go so well, at least as far as sleep was concerned. Victor had kept all of them up telling outrageous stories of his sexual conquests, each one more graphic and bizarre than the already twisted story he'd just finished. After an hour or so he ran out of steam and called them all a bunch of faggots for not reciprocating. Victor then proceeded to launch into a symphony of unabated flatulence for a quarter of an hour before eventually falling into a deep, snorting slumber.

Rapp placed his pillow over his head and tried to block out the noise, but it didn't work. It was in those much-needed, sleepless hours just after midnight that Rapp began to explore the idea of getting rid of Victor. At first he considered getting up and throttling the idiot, right then and there, but knew it would only result in further punishment from the instructors and disdain from his fellow recruits.

Still, the thought of spending the next six months with the lout was something that presented a very real problem. A guy like Victor could easily drag someone down with him, and Rapp had an undeniable feeling that the two men were on a collision course. And not one of those collisions that could be avoided if one or both of them changed their behavior. It was inevitable. It was the kind you needed to brace yourself for. Either drop your hips, lower your shoulders, and make the other guy feel more pain than you, or he would do the same to you and you were toast.

There was something undeniably odd about the man. The idea of his participating in a covert op was preposterous. If he could ever walk among the enemy undetected it would be a miracle. Rapp wanted this new vocation with every fiber of his body, although he was smart enough to know that saying he would never quit and actually never quitting were two very different things. He also knew he would be tested in ways he'd never imagined. He'd be pushed to the full extent of his physical and mental abilities, and it was likely that at some point, when he was really in the hurt bag, that pang of doubt would creep into his mind. Could Victor create a climate in which, at his lowest point, he might consider quitting?

Rapp didn't want to find out. Somewhere in the middle of the night, as he was lying on his back watching bats dart around the rafters of the barn and listening to the snorting Victor, Rapp decided the moron would need to quit, and if he didn't do it on his own, and do it quickly, Rapp would have to find a way to subtly nudge him in the right direction.

They were up before the sun. Two of the instructors came in and cursed, yanked, kicked, and slapped them out of bed. Luckily for Rapp, he was half awake and heard the door open. His feet were on the floor before the DI could dump him out of his cot. He'd guessed this was how the morning would start, but the yelling was nonetheless unsettling. In between the barking and smacking, Rapp tried to make out exactly what it was that he was supposed to do. Somewhere in the middle of it he heard the words *line* and *PT*. He threw on his workout gear and running shoes and was out the door like a shot. The lawn was covered with a thick morning dew and the sun was only a gray veil in the east. They weren't allowed watches and there were no clocks in the barn, so Rapp guessed that it was somewhere in the vicinity of 5:00 A.M. The air temp had to be in the midseventies and the humidity was pasty. It would be another hot one.

As Rapp came to a stop on the line he was aware that he was the first and only one out the door. He figured to start with, there were certain things where it was smart to be first and others where it wasn't. Getting out of bed and getting on the line was an area to be first. Hand-to-hand combat and fighting drills he would never hold back on, but the endurance stuff like running and PT he would. He needed to stay healthy and hold some things in reserve. These guys didn't need to know he could run like the wind.

As he waited for the others, he caught a whiff of coffee and turned to look at the house. There, standing on the porch, was a new face, a blond-haired guy who looked to be in his midthirties. The man was staring intently at Rapp. Rapp returned the stare and even at a distance of several hundred feet noted the blue eyes. The guy was in a pair of jeans and a T-shirt. He was leaning against one of the porch columns sipping his coffee and making no effort to conceal his interest in Rapp. There was something different about the guy. Rapp could tell he was in shape, but he was way more relaxed than the other DIs who were marching around and that sadistic little cuss who'd tried to neuter him.

One by one the guys trickled out of the barn and fell in. Victor was last, which was becoming a common theme. Sergeant Smith was walking quickly beside him giving him an earful in a hushed voice. They had all been warned that there would be no yelling on the line. This wasn't the only place on the lake, and voices carried across the water. Inside the barn with the door closed, however, the decibel level went through the roof. Victor fell in at the far end from Rapp.

Sergeant Smith stepped out in front of the seven recruits and with a clenched jaw said, "You puds better get your shit together, or I'm gonna start knocking some heads. I've seen Cub Scouts do better than this. This is damn sloppy. It shouldn't never take you morons more than sixty seconds to get your ass out of bed, dressed, and on the line. When you go to bed, you make sure your shit is ready. You lay it out on your footlocker so it's ready to go. We start PT at five every morning."

Rapp watched the DI's eyes shift to the opposite end of the line. He leaned forward and saw Victor had his arm raised.

"Sarge, when are we supposed to take a piss? I gotta go so bad I'm about to drown."

Sergeant Smith walked over to Victor and got in his face. "Maybe if you had gotten your lazy ass out of bed when I told you to, you would have had time to piss." He stepped back and looked down the line. "We're going to do a quick warm-up. As much as I hate you idiots, the powers that be don't want you ladies getting hurt until they see if you've got some potential. I have tried to dissuade them, as you are the biggest collection of shitlickers I've seen come through here in some time."

"Sarge, I gotta go real bad," Victor whined.

"Then piss yourself, you big idiot." His head snapped to the group. "If you can't take care of your business and get out here in sixty seconds, I'm going to have to treat you like a bunch of toddlers . . . so go ahead and piss yourself, Victor. The rest of you who need to go I suggest you wait until we head out for our run. You can pull over on the trail and take care of business. Now drop and give me fifty, and if I see any of you pussies cheating we'll start over."

They did the fifty push-ups, followed by one hundred sit-ups, fifty up-downs, and then a few minutes of scissor kicks and a couple of stretches, and then Sergeant Smith led them into the woods. Eight of them in a nice neat line, with Victor trailing. Rapp guessed they were moving at just under a six-minute pace. He could keep a five-minute pace for ten miles, so he was feeling good. They finished the five-mile run and found themselves standing in front of an obstacle course in the middle of the woods. The place looked like a relic from an abandoned Renaissance festival. Sergeant Smith had his stopwatch out and was clocking them.

Rapp positioned himself fifth in line, carefully placing one man between himself and Victor. He wanted to see how these other four guys navigated the course, guessing that they'd all done it when they'd gone through boot camp. His idea kind of fell apart when Sergeant Smith started sending guys at thirty-second intervals. The course started with a low wall. It was a ten-foot-tall wooden, moss-laden wall with two telephone poles stuck in the ground in front of it. The first telephone pole stuck out of the ground about a foot and a half and was four feet in front of the wall. The next telephone pole was two feet in front of the wall and stuck out of the ground three feet.

Rapp watched as the first recruit headed for the wall, picking up speed. Right before the telephone poles he did a quick stutter step and then as nimbly as you could imagine, he placed his left foot on the first and shorter telephone pole, using it as a step. His right foot then landed on the second telephone pole and he launched himself up and onto the wall, grabbing the top with both hands and pinning his knee to the wall just a few feet from the top. It was like a controlled collision. The recruit was up and over, dropping to the soft ground on the other side.

The second guy did it the same way, and the third tried something slightly different that involved doing a pull-up. After the low wall was a forty-foot dash to a fifteen-foot-high wall with ropes hanging on the face. There was nothing fancy about this one. You just grabbed the rope, put your feet on the wall, and walked your way up. Next in line was barbed wire. Again, pretty straightforward. Dive under, keep your butt down, and do an infantry crawl to the other end. After that was a forty-foot cargo net strung between two towering pines. Beyond that was a set of logs set up in a zigzag pattern about three feet off the ground. They acted as a sort of footbridge to test your balance.

Rapp didn't have a chance to see what came after the balance logs because it was his turn to start. He quickly dried the palms of his hands on his shorts, and then when Sergeant Smith gave him the signal, he ran toward the short wall, mimicked the exact steps of the first recruit, and threw himself up and at the top of the wall. He caught it, pulled himself up and over, and landed with ease on the other side. The second, taller wall was easy enough to navigate, and the barbed wire was about as primal as it got. If a guy couldn't grasp the simplicity of crawling he should just quit and go home. The cargo net proved to be the first real challenge. About a third of the way up Rapp realized there was too much slack in the middle so he moved over to the side. After that it was easier. The balance logs were a breeze, the tires were nothing, and the transfer ropes were playground 101.

Then he came across something that looked like a set of uneven parallel bars, like the kind female gymnasts use. He paused, not sure how to attack the two horizontal telephone poles, and then almost on cue, one of the DIs was right there barking orders at him. Telling him what to do, and to do it quickly. Based on what the DI was telling him, it sounded like a great way to break a rib, but Rapp could see no other way, so he launched himself into the first pole and then the second and then it was more tires and a thing called the Burma bridge. After that there were more logs, ropes, and walls to negotiate and a sprint to the finish.

When Rapp crossed the line Sergeant Smith was staring at his stopwatch and shaking his head. He glanced at Rapp, contempt on his face, and said, "You suck."

Rapp was doubled over with his hands on his knees, acting more tired than he was. He wanted to smile but didn't. He couldn't have done that badly. The guy in the number-six position had yet to finish. Rapp turned to see how the last two were doing. At the edge of the course, about fifty yards back, he saw the blond-haired guy he'd seen on the porch earlier in the morning. The man was standing at the edge of the woods staring straight at him, again making no effort to conceal his interest.

CHAPTER 12

LANGLEY, VIRGINIA

KENNEDY parked in the east lot and entered the Headquarters Building at exactly eight-oh-three. She'd used the hour-and-a-half drive up from Lake Anna to try to prioritize her ever-increasing list of responsibilities, both official and unofficial. Much of her job was off the books, and that meant no notes and no files. She had to keep it all organized in her own mind, and every time she came back to HQ she needed to have her story straight. When the elevator doors parted on the sixth floor one of her bosses was waiting with a deeply concerned look on his face.

Max Powers nudged her back into the elevator and said, "Problem."

Powers was the Near East Division chief. It had taken Kennedy a while to get used to his style. Powers was famous for speaking in one-word sentences.

His colleagues who had worked with him over the years called him Musket Max.

Kennedy stepped back and asked, "What's wrong?" Her immediate fear, as it was almost every time she entered the building, was that her black ops program had been uncovered.

"Beirut," Powers said, offering nothing more.

Beirut could mean a lot of things, but on this hot August morning Kennedy was aware of one thing in particular. "John?"

"Yep."

"Crap," Kennedy mumbled under her breath. John Cummins was one of their deep-cover operatives who had snuck into Lebanon three days earlier. An American businessman who worked for a data storage company had been kidnapped the previous week. This company, it turned out, was run by a Texan with big contacts in D.C. The owner was old-school, former army, and over the past thirty years he had freely and enthusiastically kept the CIA and the Pentagon abreast of all the info he and his people happened to pick up in their international dealings. A lot of very important people in town owed him, and he decided now was the time to call in a few of his IOUs.

The Pentagon had zero assets in the region and the CIA wasn't much better. They were still trying to recover from the kidnapping, torture, and death of their Beirut station chief half a decade earlier. Langley did, however, have assets in Jordan, Syria, and Israel. Cummins, who had lived in Syria for the past three years, was the best bet. He'd built up some great contacts by passing himself off as a counterfeiter of U.S. currency and smuggler of American-made goods that were embargoed in the region.

From the jump Kennedy argued against using him. He was by far their most valuable asset inside Syria, and Beirut, although safer than it had been in the eighties, was still pretty much the Wild West of the Middle East. If anything went wrong Cummins would be lost. Someone with a much bigger title had overruled her, however.

"How bad?" Kennedy asked.

"Bad."

The doors opened on the seventh floor and Kennedy followed Powers down the hall to the office of Thomas Stansfield, the deputy director of operations. The door was open and the two of them breezed through the outer office, past Stansfield's assistant, and into the main office. Powers closed the soundproof door. Kennedy looked at the silver-haired Stansfield, who was sitting behind his massive desk, his glasses in one hand and the phone in the other. Stansfield was probably the most respected and feared man in the building and possibly the entire town. Since they were on the same team, Kennedy respected but did not fear the old spy.

Stansfield cut the person on the other end off, said good-bye, and placed the phone back in its cradle. Looking up at Powers, he asked, "Any further word?"

Powers shook his head.

"How did it happen?" Kennedy asked.

"He was leaving his hotel on Rue Monot for a

lunch meeting," Stansfield said. "He never showed. He missed his check-in this afternoon and I placed a call to my opposite in Israel. Mossad did some quiet checking." Stansfield shook his head. "A shopkeeper saw someone fitting Cummins's description being forced into the trunk of a car shortly before noon today."

Kennedy felt her stomach twist into a wrenching knot. She liked Cummins. They knew all too well how this would play out. The torture would have commenced almost immediately, and depending on how Cummins held up, death was the likely outcome.

"I remember you voiced your opposition to this," Stansfield said, "but know there are certain things that even I wasn't told."

"Such as?"

The ops boss shook his head, letting her know he wasn't allowed to talk about it. "The important thing now is that Schnoz's Syrian contacts back his cover story. If they don't step up to the plate for him, this will end badly." Cummins was half Armenian and half Jewish and had a nose to make a Roman emperor jealous; hence his unofficial cover name was Schnoz.

"Double down," Powers chimed in. "Get the Texas boy on a plane with a couple suitcases filled with cash."

"It's a possibility that I already floated with the White House. They're getting nervous, though, and for good reason."

"They should be," Kennedy said. "They just

burned one of our most valuable assets trying to do a personal favor that as far as I can tell has nothing to do with national security."

"Bingo," Powers said.

Stansfield was quiet for a moment. "I have a back channel I can use with the CEO. He wants this employee back, and I think when I explain to him what happened to our man, he'll offer to pay for both. It should help cement the idea that Schnoz was working as a freelancer."

"It better happen quick," Kennedy said. "We never know how long someone will be able to hold out. If they break Schnoz . . ." She stopped talking and shuddered at the thought of the damage that would be done.

"I know," Stansfield sighed.

"Rescue op?" Powers asked.

Stansfield looked slightly embarrassed. "Not going to happen. We knew it going in. Beirut is still radioactive."

"What if we get some good intel?" Kennedy asked.

"That's a big what-if."

"But if we do," Kennedy pressed her point, "we need assets in place."

Stansfield sadly shook his head.

"Corner office or Sixteen Hundred?" Powers asked.

Kennedy understood the shorthand question to mean, was it the director of the CIA who was freezing them out or the White House?

"White House," Stansfield replied.

"Our friends at the Institute." Powers offered it as a suggestion. "They're in the loop?"

Stansfield tapped the leather ink blotter on his desk while he considered the Israeli option. The Institute was the slang Powers used to refer to the Institute for Intelligence, or as they were better known, Mossad.

"I'm told they knew before we did."

"Maybe let them handle the cowboy stuff . . . if it comes to that."

The fact that it had not occurred to him to have Mossad handle the rescue spoke volumes about the complicated relationship. "If something concrete comes our way I'll consider it, but . . ."

"You don't want to owe them the farm," Powers said.

"That's right. They would more than likely demand something that I'm either unwilling or unable to give them."

"May I say something, sir?" Kennedy asked.

Stansfield wasn't sure he wanted to hear it, but he knew he needed to let his people vent. He nodded.

"This problem is never going to go away until we send these guys a very serious message."

"I assume you mean the kidnapping?"

"Yes."

"I told the director the same thing five minutes before you walked in the door, but it seems we lack the political will, at the moment, to take a more aggressive approach."

"Pussies," Powers muttered, and then looked at Kennedy and said, "Sorry."

"No need to apologize." She paused and then decided this was the right time to push her agenda. "You know what this means?"

"No."

"It's yet another example of why we need to get Orion up and running. How in hell can we expect our assets to operate in this environment? It's bad enough that we won't get tough with these guys . . . it's inexcusable that we won't even consider a rescue op. He's one of our own, for Christ's sake!"

Stansfield was not surprised that she'd brought it up. He would have done the same thing if he was in her place, but during a crisis like this it was a common mistake to hurry things that needed time. "I want this to happen as badly as you do, Irene, but it can't be rushed. If we send a bunch of half-baked assets into the field, we'll end up spending all our energy trying to pull them out of the fire. Trust me . . . I saw it firsthand back in Berlin. Just try to be patient for a few more months. If a couple of these guys can prove that they have the stuff, I'll green-light it, and support you every step of the way."

Kennedy took it as a promise but couldn't get her mind off Cummins and what he was enduring. Her thoughts for some unknown reason turned to Rapp. She hoped he was the one. The weapon they could turn loose on these murderous zealots.

CHAPTER 13

LAKE ANNA, VIRGINIA

THEY each ran the obstacle course three more times and then double-timed it back to the barn for breakfast. They stuffed their faces with eggs and pancakes, then were given thirty minutes to digest their food and make sure their bunks were squared away. Rapp was somewhat relieved that Victor used this time to pester someone else. Then it was off to the pistol range, which was a two-mile hike back into the woods. It was not a leisurely hike, however. They were given twelve minutes to get to the range and were told that anyone who was late could pack his bags. Rapp was starting to get the idea that they would be doing a lot of running, which was fine by him. He kept a pace or two off the lead and made it look as if he was struggling to keep up, but he wasn't.

The range was adjacent to the obstacle course. It was twelve feet wide and one hundred feet long, and was as bare-bones as you could get. Basically a tractor had scooped out a ten-foot-deep trench that ran between a row of pines. It was lined with old car tires and covered with camouflage netting, which in addition to the tree branches made the light pretty weak. There were three shooting stations made out of pressure-treated plywood and lumber. Silhouette targets were already hung at twenty feet and silenced 9mm Beretta 92Fs were loaded and ready to be fired. The first three guys stepped up, and when Sergeant Smith ordered them to commence firing all three methodically emptied their rounds into the paper targets.

Rapp swallowed hard when they were done. The first two guys punched soup-can-sized holes through the chests of the black silhouettes. The third target had a nice neat hole about the size of a silver dollar in the center of the face. There was not a stray shot among the three. Rapp was impressed, but the thing that really surprised him was the reaction of Sergeant Smith. The instructor had a smile on his face.

Sergeant Smith stood beside the last shooter and said, "Normally I don't like you SEALs, but goddamn! They sure do teach you boys how to shoot." He gave the recruit a rough slap on the back and ordered the next three up. The results were similar—at least as far as the first two were concerned. They had both punched nice neat holes in the chests of their targets. Rapp's target, however, looked a little rough.

Rapp lowered the pistol and took in his handiwork. He'd only started shooting a few months earlier, and without any actual training from an instructor, the results were lacking. The target looked like a piece of Swiss cheese, with holes from the chest all the way down to the groin. He set the heavy Beretta down on the flat plywood surface and grimaced as the instructors fell in, one on each shoulder.

"Definitely not a SEAL," Sergeant Smith said.

"Nope," Sergeant Jones replied. "Not a D Boy either. Might be a gangbanger, though. That's how those little fuckers shoot. Just spray it all over the place and hope they hit a vital organ."

"Definitely not the way we do things around here," Sergeant Smith said.

"Son," the taller of the two said, "where the fuck did you learn how to shoot?"

Rapp cleared his throat and admitted, "I don't know how to shoot, Sergeant."

"You mean you've tried and suck, or you've never been taught?"

"Never been taught, Sergeant."

There was an uncomfortable pause while the two instructors tried to figure out what to do. Unfortunately, Victor took the opportunity to throw in one of his asinine comments. "He shoots like a girl."

Underneath Rapp's bronzed skin his cheeks flushed. He had known that, due to his lack of training, shooting would be one of his weaknesses. Still, it embarrassed him that the others were so much better. Rapp looked to Sergeant Smith and asked, "Any pointers?"

The shorter man looked up at Rapp and regarded him for a moment before nodding and saying, "Let's see you do it again." Sergeant Smith handed him a fresh magazine.

Sergeant Jones yelled, "All right, Victor, you jackass. Get up here and show us what you can do."

The other five stood back and watched in silence while two fresh targets were put up. Sergeant Smith stood at Rapp's side and quietly issued instructions. He watched Rapp squeeze off one shot and then reached in to adjust his grip, elbow position, and feet. With each shot the instructor issued corrections and the grouping of shots grew tighter. This time the holes were still loose, but at least all of them were in the chest area, as opposed to all over the entire target.

Rapp heard someone giggle and he looked over at Victor's target. The clown had shot eyes and a nose in the target and five more shots made a downturned mouth. The remainder of the shots were concentrated in the groin area.

"Victor," Sergeant Jones said, "what in hell are you doing?"

"Long-term strategic planning, Sarge."

"I doubt your pea-sized brain could attempt any such thing."

"Population control," Victor said, spitting a gob of chew on the ground. "Shoot the nuts off all the hajis and no more baby terrorists. Twenty years from now we declare victory. Brilliant, if I say so myself."

Sergeant Jones put his hands on his hips. "Put

the weapon down, Victor, and step back." The big man did so, and then Sergeant Jones continued in a disappointed voice, "Since all of you appear to be decent shots and Victor here thinks this is a joke, we're going to head back over to the O course where I'm going to run all of you until at least one of you pukes. Our earnest, yet respectful virgin will stay here with Sergeant Smith and attempt to learn the basics of pistol shooting." The big sergeant eyed the group and when no one moved he said, "Well, I guess you ladies would like to do some push-ups first." In a gruff voice he shouted, "Assume the position."

All six men dropped to the ground and got into the plank position. They were told to start and no one said a word except Victor, who continued to complain as they counted out their punishment.

While they worked through their push-ups Sergeant Smith began instructing Rapp on the finer points of marksmanship. Rapp listened intently, digesting every word. Sergeant Smith told Rapp to aim for the head this time. He slammed a fresh magazine into the hilt and hit the slide release.

"When you have a fresh magazine in and hit the slide release, a round is automatically chambered." The sergeant offered Rapp the weapon and said, "The hammer's back. So she's hot. Not every gun is like that, but that's how the Berettas work. Also that red dot right there . . . red means dead. So don't point it at anything you're not going to shoot at and always keep that finger off the trigger until you're ready to fire. Got it?"

Rapp nodded.

"All right, show me that stance. Keep those feet just so. You're a lefty, so put your right foot a few inches in front of your left. Create the power triangle with your arms and place that dot right in the center of the head. Some guys get all hung up on breathing in versus exhaling, but I don't want you to think about that crap. You're going to need to learn to shoot on the run, so breathing in or out ain't going to work. The main thing right now is how you squeeze that trigger. Notice how I didn't say pull. Don't pull it. Squeeze it straight back and put a round right through the middle of the head this time."

Rapp did everything he was told and the bullet spat from the end of the suppressor. The muzzle jumped and when it came back down Rapp was staring at a perfectly placed shot.

"Do it again," Sergeant Smith ordered.

Rapp squeezed the trigger and the bullet struck the target half an inch to the right of the first one.

"Again."

The third shot bridged the first and second. Rapp fell into a rhythm. He didn't rush it, but he didn't take too much time either. It took him less than twenty seconds to empty the rest of the magazine, and when he was done all of the rounds were within a six-inch circle—a jagged hole punched through the face of the paper target. Rapp breathed a sigh of relief.

Sergeant Smith clapped him on the shoulder and said, "You're coachable, kid. Nice work. Let's try this a few more times."

Rapp was in the midst of reloading the weapon when by chance he turned his head and looked over his left shoulder. About sixty feet away, in the shadows of a big pine, a man was watching them. With the poor light Rapp couldn't be certain who it was, but he thought it might be the guy he'd seen on the porch earlier in the morning. Rapp turned back to Sergeant Smith and was about to ask him who he was when he thought better of it. It would be a mistake to confuse a little one-on-one instruction with friendship.

CHAPTER 14

DR. Lewis walked into the office, offered a faint smile to his visitor, and closed the door behind him. He'd been watching the new recruit intently for the past three days. At twenty-three he was the youngest project they had attempted to run through the program, and from what he'd seen the last few days the man showed a great deal of promise. Before sitting, Lewis glanced down at the notepad and pen sitting in the middle of the desk. Next to them sat a file with Rapp's name written in large black letters. It was impossible to miss and intentionally so. They knew surprisingly little about the man, but then again how much could you really know about someone this young—this untested? If he listened to the irascible Hurley, inexperience was a curse, and if he listened to the more pragmatic Kennedy, it was a blessing. Lewis didn't know who was right, but he had grown tired of listening to them bicker.

Moving behind the desk, Lewis sat in the worn leather and wood desk chair and leaned back. The chair emitted a metal squeak. The doctor ignored it and moved his eyes from the subject to the contents sitting on his desk. There were many tools in his trade—little tricks that could be used to test the people he was assigned to evaluate. Some were subtle, others more overt, but all were designed to help him get a better glimpse into the minds of the men they were recruiting. The file on the desk had been a test. Lewis had spent the last five minutes in the basement watching the recruit via a concealed camera. Rapp had sat sphinxlike in the chair. He had glanced at the file only once and then adopted a relaxed posture that spoke of boredom. Lewis didn't know him well enough to gauge whether it was sincere, but there was something about this Mitch Rapp fellow that suggested great possibilities. There was a casualness on the surface that helped mask something far more complex.

Lewis considered reaching for the notepad and pen. It was a way of establishing authority, and creating stress for the subject. Making him feel the pressure of possibly giving incorrect answers. Lewis decided against it. From what he'd witnessed over the last three days, it was highly unlikely that the ploy would fluster this one. Nothing else had so far.

Going on a hunch, Lewis clasped his hands behind his head and casually asked, "You know what you're getting yourself into?"

Rapp looked at him with his dark brown eyes

and shrugged as if to say it wasn't worth acknowledging the obvious.

"I don't read minds," Lewis said, only half serious. "I'm going to need you to verbalize your answers."

"Hopefully, you're going to turn me into a weapon . . . a killer."

Lewis considered the straightforward answer and then said, "Not me specifically, but in essence, yes, that is what we are going to do."

Rapp gave a slight nod as if that was just fine with him and continued to look right back into the bright blue eyes of the man who had been watching him from a safe distance.

"Do you have any reservations?"

"Not really."

Lewis placed his palm on the desk, and after staring at the back of his hand for a long moment said, "It would be normal if you did."

Rapp cracked a thin smile. "I suppose it would."

"So do you have any reservations?"

It was a pretty vague question, and Rapp didn't like vague. "In terms of what?"

"This is a big commitment. Most of your friends are probably taking jobs with Kodak or Xerox."

More than a few of them were, but Rapp simply nodded.

Lewis noted that Rapp was not jumping out of his chair trying to please him with earnest answers. Nor was he displaying the open disrespect that many of the candidates would employ as a defense mechanism. He was striking the perfect balance.

Lewis decided to skip his standard twenty minutes of preamble and get to the heart of the matter. "Have you ever wondered what it's like to kill a man?"

Rapp nodded. He had spent more time wondering about it than he would ever admit to this guy, or anybody else.

"Do you think that's healthy?"

This time Rapp let out a small laugh.

Lewis noted the classic deflection technique, but didn't want to seem judgmental, so he smiled along with Rapp. "What's so funny?"

"I can answer your question six ways, and depending on your mood, you might find all of the answers acceptable, or none of them."

"How do you mean?"

"It's all in the context."

"Context is important," Lewis agreed. "Give me an example."

Rapp thought about it for a moment and then said, "If I'm lying awake at night thinking about killing the guy who broke into my car and ripped me off, it's probably safe to say that I have some anger issues, and a poor grasp of what constitutes just punishment." Rapp put his tanned arm over the back of the chair and looked out the window for a second, wondering how much he should admit. "But if I lie awake at night thinking about sticking a knife through the eye socket of a terrorist who's killed a couple hundred innocent civilians," Rapp shrugged, "I think that's probably not so far out there."

Lewis appreciated the blunt answer. Wanting a

deeper reaction, he asked, "Do you miss your girl-friend?"

Rapp gave Lewis a disappointed look and shook his head.

"What's wrong? Did I say something that offended you?"

"No . . . not really . . ."

"From the look on your face it would appear that I did."

"I volunteered for this, but I hate playing all these games."

"Games?" Lewis asked with an arched brow.

"You're a shrink, right?" Rapp didn't give him a chance to answer. "You've been watching me for the past three days. I've noticed that you seem to be paying a lot of attention to me. More so than the others. You choose your words carefully, and you've undoubtedly read that file that's sitting on your desk. You know why I'm here."

Lewis hid his surprise that Rapp had guessed his profession. "It's my job to ask questions."

"But why would you ask if I miss her? Don't you think that's pretty obvious?"

"So that's why you're here?"

"I'm not here because I miss her. I miss my father, who died when I was thirteen. I miss my grandparents, and someday I'll miss my mom when she dies, and maybe if I get to know you, I'll miss you, too. That's part of life. I'm here for a very obvious reason. One that I'm sure you're already aware of."

Lewis noted how he had taken charge of the

conversation, but was willing to let this play out. "Revenge?"

"I prefer retribution, but it all depends on the definition you choose."

Lewis was pleased that he'd made the distinction. He was intimately familiar with the difference between the two words. "I'd like to hear your definition."

"Revenge is more wild, less calculated . . . deeply personal."

"And retribution?"

Rapp thought about it for a moment and then answered in a very clear voice. "Retribution is a punishment that is morally right and fully deserved."

"And the men who conspired to bring down Pan Am 103?"

Rapp leaned forward, placing his elbows on his knees, and said, "Every last one of them deserves to die."

Lewis looked at the file on the desk and asked, "You're Catholic?"

"Yes."

"So how do you square this with your Lord? Your idea of retribution doesn't exactly conform to the turn-the-other-cheek preaching of Jesus Christ."

"Nice try." Rapp grinned.

"How do you mean?"

"I'll tell you a little secret about me. I'm not the most patient guy. I have a lot to learn, and I'm eager to learn it, so when you start to hit me with selective theology you might get my back up a bit."

"Selective?" Lewis asked.

"Yeah. I've never understood the intellectual dishonesty of people who say the Bible is the word of God and then choose to pull verses only from the New Testament, for example. Turning the other cheek is one of their favorites, and they use it, while ignoring a dozen Old Testament verses and a few New Testament verses that say the men who brought down that plane deserve to die."

Lewis conceded with a nod. "So, if it comes to it . . . you don't think you'd have a problem taking another man's life?"

"That depends."

"On what?"

"Who the guy is, and more important, what he's guilty of."

CHAPTER 15

WHEN the sun rose for the fifth day they were one man short. It was Dick. Rapp didn't know the guy's real name, much less where he was from or where he was going, so it was hard to feel too bad when the guy stepped out of formation during a grueling set of up-downs in the hot afternoon sun. He simply approached one of the instructors, announced his intention, and the two men shook hands. Just like that the guy was done. Free of the pain, the sweating, the burning muscles, the tired eyes, and the battered ego. It all seemed too easy, and that's what scared the crap out of Rapp.

It made him briefly wonder if he was capable of pussing out. All it would take was a down moment. A bad spell, a cold, or a fever or another sleepless night. One misstep and he could be the one shaking hands and packing his bag. While falling asleep that night, Rapp focused on the positive. There was one man fewer to compete with. They kept saying it wasn't a competition, but Rapp wasn't so sure. If it wasn't a competition, why did they count or clock everything they did? The image of the fellow recruit bowing out after five days put Rapp on guard against a moment of personal weakness. It refocused him by showing just how rapidly this journey could come to a very unsatisfying end.

Rapp awoke tired but ready to push ahead. He was the first one on the line and was stretching his neck and shoulders waiting for the others when he noticed the two instructors having what looked like an unpleasant conversation. When everyone was finally on the line, Sergeant Jones stepped forward and with a disappointed look on his face said, "One of you screwed up real bad last night."

Rapp began racking his brain trying to think of any mistakes he'd made.

"We have rules for a reason. At this point you don't need to understand these rules, you just need to follow them." He paused to look each of them in the eye. "You have all been repeatedly warned to not divulge any personal information. Now . . . we're realistic enough to understand that you boys will discover certain things about each other. Some of you have a slight accent, so it's pretty easy to figure out what part of the country you come from. As far as prior military experience, we haven't busted your balls over debating the healthy rivalry between the services, but last night, someone crossed the line." He stopped and looked at the ground. In a disappointed voice he said, "The one thing you are never supposed to do is tell someone your real name."

Rapp heard someone farther down the line mumble something under his breath, but he couldn't tell who it was, and considering the mood of the two instructors, he didn't dare look.

"You are all smart enough to know this, and you were all warned what would happen if you slipped up on this one. This isn't a fucking summer camp. This is serious shit," Sergeant Jones said in a disappointed voice. He looked to the far end of the line and said, "Bill, pack your shit. You're gone."

The man they called Bill, whom Rapp had pegged as the hot-shooting Navy SEAL from Texas, took one step forward and shook his head at the harsh punishment he'd just received. He looked as if he was going to say something and then caught himself. Sergeant Jones started moving and told Bill to follow him back to the barn. Sergeant Smith stepped in to lead them in PT, but before he could start Bill turned back to the group.

"Victor, you're a real asshole. I told you I didn't want to talk, but you just wouldn't leave it alone." Looking at Sergeant Jones, he asked, "Why isn't he getting the boot as well?"

"Keep moving. We'll talk about it in the barn."

"This is bullshit. He told me who he was and where he was from. Same as me," Bill complained.

Victor laughed. "I gave you a fake name, you stupid hick."

"Why the hell would you do that?" one of the guys farther down the line asked Victor.

"Asshole," someone else grumbled.

"You guys should all be thanking me," Victor said in an easy voice. "One less guy to worry about."

Sergeant Smith silenced all of them with a growling order to assume the position. "The next one of you who opens his piehole is gone. Now push 'em out."

Rapp dropped his chest down to the dewy grass and pushed straight up, quietly counting out each push-up as he went. He'd done so many in the past five days that they were becoming second nature—almost like breathing. Somewhere past number forty and before number fifty, Rapp began feeling some serious ill will toward Victor. If only the big jackass would stumble and break an ankle. He was too risky to have around. For the rest of the morning, as they ran from one thing to the next, Rapp couldn't shake the feeling that he and Victor were on a collision course. With Dick quitting and Bill getting the boot, that meant two fewer people to run interference. Victor could focus more of his time on pestering Rapp.

The long run was actually nice, since Victor was the slowest of the group. They were spared his running mouth. When breakfast rolled around they all gave him the cold shoulder. It didn't matter to Victor, though. He stayed chatty, continuing to dole out insults and the occasional wise-ass comment that the instructors seemed to take better than they should have. They spent an hour on the obstacle course and another hour on the pistol range before heading back in for lunch. The attitude among the

recruits was decidedly sour. It was as if they had a
traitor in their midst. After lunch they went over
field-stripping various handguns, and then it was
announced that they were heading into the barn for
a little hand-to-hand combat.

For Rapp it was his first time back on the mat
since the day he'd arrived. He had wondered where
the mean old cuss had gone, and had almost asked
Sergeant Smith, but the guy wasn't exactly keen on
sharing information. Jones and Smith paired the
men up. Since there were five, someone had to be
the odd man out and it turned out to be Rapp. The
rules were simple: no blows to the head or groin.
Choke holds were encouraged, but they warned the
men to be careful not to crush anyone's larynx. If
you wanted out all you had to do was tap the mat.
Right before they started the blond-haired shrink
quietly slipped into the barn.

The first two men up were Roy and Glenn. Rapp
hadn't figured out where either of them was from,
and wasn't about to ask. Like all of them, the two
men were dark-featured, with black hair, brown
eyes, and tan skin. Roy was five-ten and Glenn was
perhaps an inch taller. Rapp guessed they were both
around twenty-seven. He was not overly impressed
with their fighting styles. They both used standard
judo techniques. Lots of holds and throws, but nothing that could be used to incapacitate an enemy in
one quick flurry. Technically, they were sound, and
they were both tough enough, and in good enough
shape, to draw out a lengthy, tiring, boring match.

After about four minutes they ended up in a

sweaty tangle in the middle of the mat and Sergeant Smith stepped in. Victor and Fred were up next. Fred was six feet tall and about 175 pounds, and had done a really good job of keeping to himself. He finished in the top three on every run, handled the obstacle course with ease, and was the top marksman after Bill. Victor, at six-two and 220 pounds, was by far the biggest of the group. His neck was nearly as thick as his thighs, which meant, as Rapp had noticed when he met him, that he would be really hard to knock out with a shot to the head. From all of the talking he'd done, Rapp half expected to see the second coming of Muhammad Ali.

Victor bounded across the mat, shadowboxing as he went. "You ready to get your ass kicked, Freddy?"

Fred said nothing. He walked to the center of the mat in his bare feet and took up his fighting stance. Rapp pegged him for a wrestler by the way he moved. Victor was such an oversized peacock that it was impossible to tell what he was capable of. Most guys his size were not boxers, but he did move pretty well on his feet. Sergeant Smith dropped his hand and the two men charged at each other. Fred went low just as Rapp expected him to. Victor tried to sidestep him, but his right leg got looped by his opponent. Fred hooked onto Victor's knee and pulled it tight to his chest. He stayed low and kept driving with his legs, trying to tip the bigger man over. Victor hopped back on his left leg and started delivering punches to Fred's back. The first few were misplaced and lacked power. Rapp watched Victor lose his balance and begin to go down. He changed his tactic and smacked Fred in the back of the head with a closed-fist punch. Fred appeared to slow for a split second, but he didn't lose his grip.

Victor went down and rolled immediately onto his stomach. He flared his arms and legs out so he couldn't be flipped. Fred scrambled over the top of him and shot his right arm under Victor's neck. He wrenched the bigger man's head back and placed his left forearm across the back of Victor's head. The hold was commonly known as the sleeper hold, and if it wasn't broken in short order it performed as advertised. Victor got hold of a couple of Fred's fingers and twisted with everything he had while turning in to the man. Victor used his strength to reverse out of it. At first it looked as if he was getting the upper hand, and then Rapp saw what Fred was up to. He had allowed Victor to think he was initiating the move, but in truth it was Fred's idea. Once on his back, Fred wrapped his legs around Victor's waist and clamped down with a vicious scissor lock. Victor only made things worse by trying to pull himself up and away.

As Rapp had learned the hard way, the best way to get out of that hold was with a well-placed elbow to the inner thigh. Earlier in the summer, his instructor had put him in the same scissor lock and made him pay dearly. By pulling away you stretched out the torso, which allowed the person initiating the hold to clamp down even tighter. Then you emptied your lungs to take in a big breath, and the person squeezed even tighter. The next thing you knew you were desperately in need of oxygen, writhing in pain and genuinely concerned that you were about to end up with a broken rib or two.

Victor made that mistake, and it was obvious by the worried look in his eyes that he knew he was in trouble. He swung hard, trying to hit Fred in the solar plexus, but the blow was blocked. Next he tried to twist away, which only allowed Fred to tighten his hold a few more notches. Victor's face was beet red. Rapp knew it would last only a few more seconds, and he was silently hoping to hear a few ribs pop between now and then. It looked as if Victor was going to quit. He started to wave his left hand, and then just as Fred relaxed a touch, Victor brought his big right fist smashing down. The blow hit Fred square in the face. His head bounced off the mat, and he released his legs. Then blood began to pour from his misshapen nose.

Rapp took a step forward, ready to kick Victor in the head. He was on the verge of delivering the blow when Sergeant Smith stepped onto the mat and began barking orders. Rapp took a step back and watched as Victor rolled off Fred, flopped onto his back, and began laughing.

CHAPTER 16

SERGEANT Jones was attending to Fred's broken nose. Roy and Glenn were talking quietly and shooting Victor daggers. Rapp looked to the door and noticed the shrink studying him. Twice now, Rapp had seen the rules of engagement broken, and so far, there had been no punishment handed out. Not that the old codger could be punished, but Victor was one of them, and if he could get away with it then Rapp could as well. It got Rapp thinking that maybe it was time to bend the rules a little bit. While he was working out the details of what he wanted to do, Sergeant Smith ordered him onto the mat and then pointed at Glenn.

"I would rather fight Victor," Rapp said.

"Well, you're not running the show around here," Smith snapped.

"He's doing you a favor," Victor said, still out

of breath. "A little pussy like you wouldn't last five seconds against me."

Rapp stayed calm, but there was something unmistakably ominous just beneath the surface. "Let's find out," he said evenly.

"Suicide," Victor retorted.

"I think you're afraid."

"Shut up, all of you," Sergeant Smith said. "Glenn, get your ass on the mat."

Rapp moved to his left, cutting off Glenn. He stayed facing the wiry instructor and said, "I'm confused. Do rules matter around here, or does Victor get to do as he pleases?"

"We have rules, dammit! Now get in the middle of the mat and shut up."

"No disrespect, Sarge, but this is bullshit. How are we supposed to trust each other . . . how are we supposed to trust you when he keeps doing whatever the hell he wants without getting punished?"

"You think there's any rules out there," Victor laughed, "in the real world? Hell no!"

"But in here . . . we should just let you do whatever you want?"

"Sarge," Victor said as he got to his feet, "I got this one. Don't worry. I can take care of this little college puke with one arm tied behind my back."

Sergeant Smith looked as if he was about to lose it, but the blond-haired shrink stepped in and said, "Sergeant, I think we should allow Victor and Irving to have a go at it."

The sergeant's head snapped around. Rapp noticed a brief exchange of thoughts between the men before the sergeant retreated. "All right," he grumbled, "both of you, center of the mat, square off, and on my mark you start."

"Do we bother with rules this time, or should I assume Victor will break them?" Rapp asked, stone-faced.

"The head and neck are off limits, dammit!"

"I appreciate the effort, Sarge, but I'd prefer no restrictions," Rapp said.

"I don't care what you prefer. I make the rules."

Rapp hesitated. He wanted clarification on this point, and he'd rather not have to worry about Victor cheating. "And if Victor accidentally punches me in the face?"

"God dammit!" the sergeant boomed. "This isn't a debate club. Do you ladies want to go for a nice long run?"

Rapp silently moved to the center of the mat, satisfied that he had made his point, but nonetheless wary that Victor would do whatever it took to win. A strategy was already forming in his head. Victor had shown that he was a fairly one-dimensional fighter. Against the uninitiated he could probably hold his own on the mat, but boxing was his preference. That was plain enough to see.

Victor was all smiles as he slapped one fist into the fleshy palm of the other. "I'm gonna kick your ass, you little puke."

Rapp brought his fists up close to his face like a boxer, elbows in tight. "And if you can't, Victor?"

"Oh! . . . there's no doubt. You're going down."

Rapp drew him in. He feigned that he was out

of position and allowed Victor to initiate the first salvo. Two slow left jabs were launched straight for Rapp's face. Rapp blocked them with his right hand and then ducked under a big hook that would have knocked him off his feet if it had connected. Rapp noted that three punches had been thrown by Victor and all three had been directed at his supposedly off-limits head, and more important, Sergeant Smith didn't seem to care that Victor was breaking the rules yet again. That would make things easier for Rapp. He changed directions and bobbed back to his left as Victor threw two hard right jabs. The first one Rapp dodged and the second one hit him in the left shoulder. The blow was solid, but Rapp played it up, intentionally stumbling to his right as if he were in trouble. Victor took the bait and charged in, his left hand trying to push Rapp's hands out of the way so he could deliver a knockout blow with his right.

As Victor brought his fist up by his right ear, Rapp sprang forward with such quickness that he caught Victor completely off guard. He grabbed the bigger man's left wrist with his right hand and threw up his left arm to block the coming punch. Rapp launched himself at Victor, his head arching back and then whipping forward. His hard forehead slammed into the soft cartilage of Victor's nose, making a sickening crushing sound. Before Victor could counter, Rapp wrapped his hands around the back of the big man's neck, pulling him down and in. Rapp delivered two harsh knee strikes to the big man's sternum before releasing him. Victor staggered back, blood pouring from his nose, gasping for air.

"Sorry about that, Victor," Rapp said, egging him on. "I didn't mean to break your nose."

"I'm going to fucking kill you," Victor screamed.

Rapp simply motioned for Victor to bring it on.

The big man charged. Rapp expected the bull rush. He feinted to his right and then back to his left, and as Victor lumbered by, he hit him with a punch to the kidney, which stood him up. Victor pivoted to meet the next blow, and rather than gain distance, Rapp engaged, moving in and wrapping his left hand around the back of Victor's neck and his right hand around Victor's biceps. Victor reared his head back and was prepared to deliver a head butt of his own, but before he could strike, Rapp did something that none of them expected. He jumped up in the air, swung his left leg under Victor's right armpit and then his right leg around Victor's neck as he allowed himself to fall to the mat. Rapp was now upside down hanging on to Victor's left arm and pulling him down on top of him. Rapp raised his hips, and the pressure toppled Victor to the mat. Rapp had him in a version of the same arm bar that he had put the mean old cuss in on the first day, except that Rapp wasn't looking for submission this time.

Rapp grabbed Victor's wrist with both hands. He twisted and pulled the arm until the elbow socket was on top of his right hip bone, and then he raised his hips while pulling down as hard as he could with his hands. Rapp did not stop, even when

Victor started to scream. The entire thing took just under two seconds. There was a loud pop, and then Rapp released the arm, which was now bent at a very unnatural angle.

Rapp got to his feet and looked down at Victor. The man was moaning, his entire body rigid with pain. Rapp didn't smile or gloat. There was a touch of guilt over what he'd just done, but Victor was a bully and a jerk. Fred was sitting at the edge of the mat with cotton shoved up his nostrils and an ice pack on his nose. Fred nodded to Rapp and flashed him the thumbs-up. Roy and Glenn wandered over, each man quietly congratulating him for solving their problem. Sergeant Smith was too busy attending to Victor, who was flopping around writhing in pain. Rapp had no idea whether he was in trouble. He looked over at the shrink, who was watching him intently. The man's lips were pursed in thought as if he appeared to have drawn some conclusion about Rapp. The only problem was, Rapp couldn't tell if it was admiration or disappointment.

CHAPTER 17

L EWIS made the calls late in the afternoon, after he'd had an hour to put his thoughts and observations down on paper. As darkness approached, they descended one by one on the house by the lake in southern Virginia. Kennedy was the first to arrive, then Deputy Director of Operations Stansfield, and finally Hurley. Stansfield's bodyguards remained on the porch. They were two of his most trusted and knew to be very selective about what they saw, and more important, about what they remembered. Stansfield suggested in his typical quiet way that they all adjourn to the basement. It was not a suggestion. It was an order.

The four of them walked downstairs and proceeded to a free-standing room that sat in the middle of the basement. It served as the surveillance/communications shack for the property. The inside walls and ceiling were covered with an egg-carton-

gray foam that absorbed sound. A bank of monitors and two listening stations occupied the wall on
the right, and an oval conference table for six sat in
the middle. When everyone was seated, Stansfield
closed the soundproof door and threw the bolt.

The number-three man at Langley took the
chair at the head of the table and loosened his tie.
He looked the length of the short table and said,
"Doctor."

Lewis was leaning back in his chair, his hands
steepled in front of his face. "We've had an interesting development."

"I'd say so," Hurley interrupted, unable to contain himself. "I heard one of my instructors is out of
commission for six months. Three titanium pins in
his arm. For Christ's sake. He was one of my best."
Hurley held up the appropriate number of fingers to
punctuate his point. "Three pins."

The doctor's bright blue eyes locked in on Hurley with the kind of all-knowing stare that could be
flashed only by a spouse or a therapist. The message
was clear. *I know you better than you do yourself.
Shut up and let me speak.*

"Sorry," Hurley apologized halfheartedly.

"Irene's recruit has proven himself quite capable." Lewis directed his comments at Stansfield.
"You heard what he did to Stan earlier in the week?"

"No." Stansfield turned his inquisitive gaze on
Hurley. "The bruising on your face . . . that was
caused by this Rapp fellow?"

The swelling was down, and the bright red
bruising had turned dark purple with a yellow tinge.

Hurley shrugged his shoulders. "I made a mistake. It won't happen again."

"You got thumped by a college kid with no military experience," Kennedy said. "I still can't get over it."

Lewis interceded before Hurley could blow his lid. Looking at Stansfield, he said, "Let me give you the narrative." Lewis explained in detail what had transpired during the opening minutes of Rapp's arrival at the complex. Hurley tried to interrupt twice, but Lewis shut him down with an open palm. Stansfield, for his part, listened in total silence. Kennedy had nothing new to add and knew how Stansfield hated too many people talking, so she kept her information to herself. In situations like this, Hurley was more than capable of scuttling his own ship.

"Now to Victor," Lewis said, turning his gaze from Stansfield to Hurley. "I have made it very clear from the outset that I am not onboard with your methods of deception."

"I know you have," Hurley said, "and in your theoretical world I'm sure your points have merit, but this is where the rubber meets the road. I don't have all day to dick around with these kids. I need to know who has the goods, and the sooner I find out the better."

"And using your system, how many men have you found thus far?" Kennedy asked, unable to resist.

"My concerns," Lewis said forcefully, "are centered on building a relationship of trust, and if we introduce deceit into the training—"

"It's not training," Hurley said with a scowl. "This is selection, and besides, this is what we do for a living. We deceive people. If these kids don't understand that, they have no business signing up with us."

"There is a major difference between deceiving each other and deceiving our enemy. Again, strong relationships are built on trust. We can work on the deception part later."

"This is bullshit," Hurley said defensively. "You two come and go as you please, but I'm the guy down here twenty-four-seven playing nursemaid. I don't pretend to know how to do your jobs . . . do me a favor and stop trying to pretend you know how to do mine."

"You are so thin-skinned," Kennedy said with a tone of open contempt.

"Yeah, well, young lady, this is serious shit. It ain't amateur hour. We recruit our candidates from the best of the best and that means Special Forces and Spec Ops guys. It doesn't mean some amateur who doesn't know the right end of a rifle from his ass or how to navigate his way through the woods in the dead of night or a thousand other things."

"Are terrorists living in the woods these days?" Kennedy asked, making it clear she was mocking him. "The last time I checked they were urban dwellers, so I'm not so sure knowing how to start a fire with a knife and belt buckle qualifies you to hunt terrorists."

"Don't talk to me about training. You have no idea what it takes to turn these guys into killers."

"Apparently, you don't either."

"Well, at least I know how to recruit, which is more than I can say for you."

"And what exactly is that supposed to mean?"

"It means you didn't do your job. I did a little reconnaissance of my own the past few days. Do you know where your boy spent the last few months?"

"He was staying at his mother's house in McLean."

"Yeah, and spending his days hanging out at a dojo in Arlington."

"And what, pray tell, would be wrong with that? I told him he would need to be in shape, and it would be a good idea to start taking some judo classes."

"Yeah, well . . . I spoke to his sensei."

"You did what?" Kennedy was irked that he had gone behind her back.

"I went in and had a conversation with his sensei. After going a round with him on the mat, I could tell something wasn't right."

Kennedy looked to Stansfield for help. "He had no right to do that. It's my recruit. I have worked almost two years on bringing him in, and I haven't left a single trail. No one in his life knows that we're interested in him."

"And they still don't," Hurley said dismissively.

"Really . . . how in hell did you introduce yourself?"

"I told him I was a trainer from Richmond. Said I went a round with this young kid named Rapp and was very impressed. I wanted to ask his sensei what he thought."

"And?" Lewis asked, suddenly very interested.

"The kid doesn't pass the smell test. His sensei says he came in three months ago and claimed he had almost no experience. Within a month and a half he had throttled everybody in the dojo except the sensei."

"Brazilian jujitsu?" Lewis asked.

"Yeah . . . how'd you know?"

"I saw him take Victor down today. The style is hard to miss."

"So he comes in here and almost bests me and then he snaps Victor's elbow . . . I'm telling you, the kid isn't who he says he is."

Stansfield's patience was wearing thin. "Be more specific."

"I'm not sure, but it doesn't feel right."

"What . . . you think he's a plant . . . a spy?" Kennedy asked in a mocking tone.

"I'm not sure. I'm just telling you he doesn't pass the smell test. You can't get that good that quick."

Kennedy looked at Stansfield. "Let's cut to the chase. He doesn't like him because he's my recruit." She sat back and folded her arms across her chest. "He's a misogynist."

"I don't like him because I don't know who the hell he is. We need to know everything there is to know about these guys before we bring them in. That's why military experience is a must. That way we know exactly what they've been doing for a minimum of four years."

"And how is that working out for us, Stan?" Kennedy shot back. "We don't have a single operative in the pipeline, and we've been at this for almost two years."

"I am well aware that I have failed to produce. Painfully fucking aware, but that doesn't mean I'm going to rush things and have something this important blow up in our faces."

Lewis, in a neutral tone, asked, "Stan, what is your problem with Rapp?"

He took a while to answer and finally said, "I can't put my finger on it. It's more of a feeling. A bad feeling."

"Do you know what I think it is?" Kennedy asked. "Two things. First . . . I think you have major control issues. You can't stand the fact that you weren't involved in recruiting him. And second . . . you feel threatened."

"What?" Hurley's face was twisted into a mask of confusion.

"He's you. He's the man you were forty years ago, and it scares the crap out of you."

Hurley shook his head dismissively. "That's bullshit."

"Really . . . well, I can say the same thing about your gut feeling. It's bullshit. What, do you think the PLO planted him in a D.C. suburb twenty-three years ago, raised him Catholic, and sent him off to Syracuse to play lacrosse? Or do you think it was the KGB before the Soviet Union collapsed and now he's a rogue deep-cover operative? Ridiculous." Kennedy dismissed the ludicrous idea with a flip of her right hand. "You're clutching at straws."

No one moved or spoke for five seconds, while

Kennedy's stinging remarks set in. Lewis finally said, "She has a point." He pushed back his chair and stood. "I'd like to show you something. I sat down and talked with him before all of you arrived. I think you will find this very interesting." Lewis approached the surveillance control board and pressed a few buttons. A black-and-white image of Rapp appeared on the screen. He was sitting in the office on the first floor. Lewis's voice came over the speakers. He was offscreen to the right.

"That was unfortunate, what happened this afternoon."

Rapp sat still for a few seconds and then nodded.

"Do you feel bad at all about what you did to Victor?"

It took him a long time to answer, and then he said, "We're all big boys here."

"So you feel no remorse?"

"I wish it hadn't happened, but Victor isn't exactly the nicest guy."

"I see. Is it possible that you intentionally broke his arm?"

"*Intentionally* is a strong word. We were sparring and one thing led to another."

"The thing that led to the other was you snapping his arm before he could tap out."

"I'm not sure he would have tapped out."

"You could be kicked out for what happened."

"Why?"

"Sergeant Smith thinks you intentionally broke Victor's arm."

"I don't see how that would be fair. No one said anything about what holds we could use or not use. We were supposed to stay away from the head and the groin. That was it."

"If you intentionally broke another recruit's arm that would be grounds for dismissal."

Rapp looked at the floor for a long moment and then said, "I don't like playing all these games."

"Games?"

"Yeah . . . games."

"How do you mean games?"

"You know what I'm talking about."

"I'm not sure I do."

"That file on your desk the other day." Rapp pointed to the clear surface. "The file with my name on it."

"What about it?"

"You were testing me."

"Really?"

"Yes," Rapp said in an easy tone. "I've seen the way you monitor what's going on around here. You study everything." Rapp gestured at the desk. "You're not the kind of guy who leaves sensitive files lying around unless there's a reason. I'm sure this place is wired for video and sound." Rapp motioned toward the bookshelf and then the overhead light. "When you asked to see me a few days ago and I was left sitting in here by myself for fifteen minutes, you were probably sitting up in the attic or down in the basement watching me. Testing me to see if I would open the file and read what was in it."

Lewis could be heard clearing his throat and

then saying, "Even if that were true, I don't see it excuses your breaking Victor's arm."

"I never said it excused anything. What I said is that you are playing games with us. You leave files lying around, tell us one set of rules and then let Victor break them. You were in the barn, how was it okay for Victor to punch Fred in the face?"

"We will deal with that separately. This is about what you did."

"I saw the way you reacted when Victor punched Fred in the nose." Rapp paused and looked down at his hands. "Do you know what I think . . . I think Victor doesn't fit in."

"How so?"

"Based on what I've seen since I've been here, there are just two logical conclusions where Victor is concerned. Either Victor is a recruit just like the rest of us or he's part of your evaluation process."

"Part of the process?"

"He works for you guys. He's one of the instructors."

"And why would we do that?"

"So you could get a closer look at us. You put Victor in with us, and his job is to tempt us into making mistakes. Ask us who we are and where we're from. Try to get guys to screw up so you can get rid of the guys who don't have the discipline."

"Interesting."

"Either way it isn't good. If I understand this program correctly, Victor is not the kind of guy you're looking for. So if he is a recruit, and you guys can't see that, I'm not sure I want to work for people who can't grasp the obvious."

"And if he is one of the instructors?"

"It's a pretty fucked-up way to train disciplined men."

"Let's assume you're correct for a second. Knowing all of that . . . you decided to break his arm."

Rapp shook his head. "I had my suspicions before, but I wasn't sure. After I broke his arm, I saw the way you and the other instructors reacted, and I pretty much knew he was one of you."

There was a good five seconds of silence and then Lewis asked, "Do you think you have a good moral compass?"

Rapp let out a small laugh. "Here we go with your vague questions."

"I know, but please try to answer this one."

"You mean do I understand the difference between right and wrong?"

"Yes."

Rapp hesitated. "I would say pretty much yes."

"But?"

"Here . . . at this place . . . it seems like that line keeps getting moved."

"Can you give me an example."

"That angry old cuss . . . the one my recruiter warned me about . . . well, I'm not here five minutes and the two of us end up in the barn . . . He's telling me to quit and save all of us the effort. I tell him no and suggest we should find out if I have what it takes. He very clearly tells me that the head and groin are off limits while we spar. We lock horns and twenty seconds into it I have him beat. He was about two seconds from blacking out when he grabbed my nuts and practically turned me into a eunuch. He never said anything to me about it. In fact I haven't seen him since. Then you have Victor running around here breaking every rule he wants while the instructors are all over the rest of us. Again, we go in to spar today and the instructors clearly tell us the head and groin are off limits, and what does Victor do . . . Fred is within seconds of beating him and Victor punches him square in the face. I saw the look on your face, but the other two didn't say boo. It's screwy. I don't know how you expect the rest of us to follow any rules. And here I sit . . . technically I didn't do anything wrong, and I'm being threatened with the boot."

"I didn't threaten you."

"You said Sergeant Smith thinks I should get the boot. I'd say that's a threat."

Lewis hit the stop button and turned to face Hurley. With arms folded, he said, "That was one of the more difficult sessions I've conducted. Do you know why?"

Hurley shook his head.

"Because I agreed with virtually everything he said."

CHAPTER 18

STANSFIELD stood at the end of the dock, looked up at the moon, and ran through the list of transgressions. Although he didn't show it, and he never did, he was livid with what was going on down here. He had allowed Hurley far too much latitude, and while much of his anger was directed at the snake eater, more of it was directed back at himself. How had he not seen the signs earlier? This place, this operation, all of it was his responsibility. Kennedy had tried to warn him as respectfully as she could, but his days were filled with a hundred other pressing issues of national security. And he had a blind spot when it came to Hurley. Especially on the operational side of things. He'd known Stan longer than anyone at the company. He knew his long list of talents, and his short but potent list of faults.

There'd been a few bumps over the years, occasions when Hurley had let him down, but even the great Ted Williams struck out every now and then. They had met in Budapest in the summer of 1956 just as everything was heating up in the unwilling Soviet satellite. Stansfield was in his thirties and was quickly rising through the ranks of the fledgling CIA, while Hurley was in his early twenties, fresh out of training and thirsting for a fight. Stansfield saw firsthand in the run-up to the Hungarian Revolution that Hurley had a real aptitude for mayhem. He was talented, and wild, and a lot of other things, some good and some bad. But one thing was undeniable. He knew how to get at the enemy. Engage them, upset them, bloody them, and somehow make it back with nothing more than a few bumps. In the espionage business it was easy to fall into a safe daily pattern. Begin the day at your apartment, head to the embassy for work, a local café for lunch, back to the embassy, maybe a cocktail party at another embassy in the evening, a stop at a local café for a nightcap, and then back to your apartment. You could safely move about a foreign capital without ever risking your job or your life. Not Hurley. When he landed in a new place he headed straight for the rough part of town. Got to know the prostitutes, the barkeeps, and most important, the black-marketeers who despised their communist overlords. Hurley fed him daily reports about the rising contempt among the citizenry and proved himself to be a first-class field operative. He became Stansfield's indispensable man.

Tonight, however, Stansfield was having his doubts. Budapest had been a long time ago. Sooner or later all skills diminished. The obvious transition was to move him behind a desk, but that would be like asking a racehorse to pull a plow. It would kill him. Stansfield looked back up at the house. He had silently left the meeting and walked down to the lake on his own. A simple hand gesture was enough to tell his bodyguards to wait at the top of the small hill. Hurley would know to come find him. He did not have to be asked.

Stansfield could tell his old colleague was well aware that he had disappointed him. He was as down as he'd seen him in many years, and it could have been because of a variety of factors. At the top of the list was probably that shiner on his face. Stansfield had to bite down on the right side of his tongue when he'd found out that Kennedy's recruit had been the one who'd painted him. Hurley's fighting abilities were unmatched by any man he'd ever encountered. His tolerance for pain, his quickness, his mean streak, his Homeric ability to find the weakness of another man, no matter how big or strong, had become the stuff of legend at Langley.

Looking back on it now, Stansfield could see where the mistakes had been made. He had allowed Hurley to create a cult of personality down here. His own little fiefdom of Special Operations shooters. All of them were extremely talented and useful, but as a group they had the ability to create a toxic stew of contempt for anyone who had not walked in their shoes. Even Doctor Lewis, a snake eater himself, had voiced concern. Kennedy had repeatedly attempted to nudge him in the right direction. She had the gift—the ability to glimpse where it was all headed. She knew they needed to adapt, change course and tactics, and she had been trying to get Stansfield's attention. The problem was, as the deputy director of operations, he was in charge of it all. Every valuable operative they had in every major city all over the globe and all of the support people who went with them. Virtually all of it was compartmentalized in some way, and a good portion of it wasn't even put to paper. It was a never-ending chess game that was played in his head every day, all day long.

Stansfield heard the soft footfalls on the stairs coming down to the lake. He turned and made out the image of Hurley in the moonlight. The platform swayed as he stepped onto the L-shaped dock. Hurley approached his boss without a word and pulled out a pack of Camels. He offered his old friend one, knowing that he liked to reacquaint himself with his old habit when he was away from his wife. The two men stood facing the lake, looking up at the starry night sky, puffing on their cigarettes for nearly a minute before Hurley finally spoke.

"I fucked up."

Stansfield gave no reply. Just a simple nod of agreement.

"Maybe it's time I call it quits."

Stansfield turned his head a few degrees to look at Hurley and said, "I will tolerate a lot of things from you, but self-pity is not one of them. You've never been a quitter and you're not going to start now."

"I got my ass beat by a college puke."

"You got your healthy ego bruised is what happened."

"You don't understand. It should have never happened. I still can't explain *how* it happened. I'm not getting any younger, but even on an off day I'm still better than ninety-nine point nine percent of the guys out there."

"I know math was never your strong suit, but the answer is pretty obvious."

"What the hell is that supposed to mean?"

"If you can beat ninety-nine point nine percent of the guys out there and he bested you that means he's in the point one percent."

Hurley shook his head. "I don't see how it's possible. Not enough training."

"You don't see it, because you don't want to. I did a little checking on my own. Irene's find is an exceptionally gifted athlete. He's considered a bit of a freak of nature in the world of lacrosse. Did you know he's considered to be one of the greatest college lacrosse players of all time?"

"What in hell does that have to do with fighting?"

"A great athlete can learn almost anything, and do it a lot quicker than an average athlete," Stansfield said firmly. "Your big problem, though, is that you allowed your personal disdain for anyone who hasn't worn the uniform to cloud your judgment."

"Still—"

"Still nothing," Stansfield cut him off. "The boy is a three-time All-American and national champ. You got thumped by a world-class athlete."

"Who has no real training."

"You yourself said he's been taking classes."

"Rolling around some mat at a strip mall is not training."

Stansfield let out a tired sigh. It was his way of releasing pressure so he didn't blow. Some people you could gently tap with a finishing hammer a few times and they would get the point. Not Hurley, though. You had to hit the man square in the forehead with a sledgehammer repeatedly to get your point across.

"Sorry," Hurley said meekly. "I'm still having a hard time buying this kid's story."

"You are possibly the most stubborn person I have ever met, and that's saying a lot. You have used that to your advantage many times, but it has also gotten you into a fair amount of trouble, and before you get all sensitive on me, this is coming from the guy who had to get you out of all that trouble over the years. I've called in a lot of favors to pull your ass out of the fire. So hear me when I tell you that this issue is moot. The kid beat you, and quite honestly I don't care how he did it, or where he learned how to do it. The fact is, he did it, and that makes him a very desirable recruit."

Hurley finally got it. "What do you want me to do?"

"Fix it."

"How do I fix it if I'm not even sure where I fucked up?"

"Stop being so conveniently modest. You know where you made mistakes . . . It's just not in your nature to confront them, so dig a little harder and they'll turn up. And by the way, I made a few mistakes of my own. Ultimately, you are my responsibility." Stansfield glanced back up at the house. "That last hour in there was one of the most embarrassing of my career."

Hurley was too embarrassed himself to speak.

"We're supposed to know better," Stansfield continued. "We're the veterans, and we just had two kids point out something that we both should have caught. There was a day when I knew better. To put it mildly, you are an organizational nightmare. You belong in the field. I think this," Stansfield held his arms out and motioned at the nature around them, "lulled me into thinking that you were in fact in the field, but you're not. You're too corralled down here."

"Then let me go active again," Hurley said in an almost pleading voice.

Stansfield mulled the thought over while taking one last puff. There were any number of sayings that could be applied to the espionage trade, but few were as appropriate as the phrase "nothing ventured, nothing gained." At some point you had to jump into the game. Stansfield had grown weary of receiving secure cables telling him that another one of his assets had been picked off by these radical Islamists. It was time to start hitting back.

"Stan, these Islamists aren't going away."

"I've been telling you that for ten years."

"Looking at the big picture, they've been a minor irritation until now, but I sense something bigger. They are organizing and morphing and spreading like a virus."

"You can thank the damn Saudis and the Iranians for that."

That was true, Stansfield thought. Very few people understood the bloody rivalry between the Sunnis and the Shias. Each sect was growing more radical—more violent. They couldn't wait any longer. Stansfield lowered his voice. "Stan, in six months' time, I want you operational. Stop trying to run these kids down like it's a Special Forces selection process. Irene's right, I don't really care if they can survive in the forest for a week with nothing more than a fingernail clipper. I want them ready for urban operations. I'm going to task Doc to you full-time. Listen to him. He knows what he's doing."

"Okay . . . and after six months?" Hurley asked with a bit of optimism in his voice.

"I'm going to turn you loose. We need to hit these guys back. At a bare minimum I want them lying awake at night worried that they might be next. I want you to scare the shit out of them."

Hurley smiled in anticipation. "I know just what to do."

"Good . . . and one last thing. You're almost sixty. This is a young kid's game. Especially your side of the business. Our days are numbered. We need to start trusting these kids more. In another ten years they're going to take over, and we'll probably be dead."

Hurley smiled. "I'm not going down without a fight."

CHAPTER 19

BEIRUT, LEBANON

SAYYED mopped his brow with a rag. The front of his white T-shirt was splattered with the blood of the man who had just confessed to myriad sins. The basement was warm and damp, and he'd been at it for most of the day. He couldn't remember the last time he'd had to work so hard to get a man to talk. He was thirsty and hungry, but both needs would have to wait. They were gathered upstairs, nervously waiting to hear what he'd discovered.

Sayyed dropped the pliers on the metal cart. The device bounced and fell open, the serrated clamps releasing a bloody fingernail. There were eight total, strewn about the stainless-steel surface, sticky and gooey with blood and tissue. Sayyed admired his work for a second. Every man was different. For some, the mere threat of physical pain was enough to get them to admit their deception. Others, like this Jewish pig, took a little more work.

He'd employed many different methods to get at the truth, but he preferred fingernails and toenails for the simple reason that there were twenty of them. And they grew back.

Sayyed had seen torture practiced in a wide variety of forms. Most sessions were brutish and conducted without forethought or planning. Slapping and kicking was the most common method, but employed against a man who had been desensitized to such things, it was more often than not useless. There were stabbing and slicing and shooting, and although they worked, they also required medical care if you were going to continue to interrogate the individual. There was degradation, such as shoving a man's head into a bucket full of human excrement, sticking things in orifices where they didn't belong, and a long list of things Sayyed found distasteful. Electrocution was the only other form that Sayyed would use. It was extremely effective and clean. Its only downside was the potential for heart failure and long-term brain and nerve damage. Sayyed liked to spend time with his subjects. To truly debrief a prisoner took months.

Sayyed could never understand why people would so casually throw away such a valuable commodity. Killing a subject after he admitted to his lies was foolish. As an interrogator you had barely scratched the surface. An admission of guilt was just that and often nothing more. The truly valuable information lay buried in the subject's brain and needed to be slowly and carefully coaxed to the surface. And to do that you needed time.

Sayyed wiped his hands on a blood-smeared towel and said to one of the guards, "Clean the wounds and bandage the fingers. I don't want him getting an infection."

He put on his black dress shirt and left the interrogation room. He continued past the guards and up one flight of stairs. There were a dozen men milling about the lobby. Most were in plain clothes, a few wore fatigues, but all were armed with rifles and sidearms. Sayyed continued up another flight of stairs to the second floor, where he found more armed men milling about the hallway.

He frowned at the sight of them. The presence of so many men was bound to draw attention. His colleagues were far too one-dimensional. They were still thinking of their struggle as a ground battle between vying factions. Car bombs, snipers, and assaults must always be taken into account, but the bigger threat at the moment was the jets flown by Jews and the Americans. These men had not walked here, which meant there were far too many cars parked in front of the building. Sayyed traveled with a light contingent of bodyguards for this very reason. Three or four were usually more than enough. The others were either too paranoid, too proud, or too stupid to see the folly of traveling in such large motorcades.

Eight guards were standing in the hallway outside the office at the back of the building. Sayyed approached one of the more recognizable faces and said, "I pray for the sake of our struggle that no more than six vehicles are parked in front of this building."

The man looked in the direction of the street and without answering took off at a trot.

Sayyed was pleased that at least one of these morons knew how to take orders. He opened the door to the office and found four faces instead of the three he had expected. Mustapha Badredeen, the leader of Islamic Jihad, was at the head of the table. To his right was the leader of Islamic Jihad's paramilitary wing, Imad Mughniyah, and then Colonel Amir Jalil of the Iranian Quds Force. He was Iran's liaison between Islamic Jihad and Hezbollah. The last man, Abu Radih, was not welcome, at least not as far as Sayyed was concerned. He was the representative for Fatah, the extremely unreliable band of men who claimed to speak on behalf of the approximately five hundred thousand Palestinians living in Lebanon. In Sayyed's conservative opinion, they were nothing more than a gang of organized mobsters who stumbled from one confrontation to the next leaving a trail of havoc in their wake. They were only good for two things: to use as a buffer against the Jews to the south or as cannon fodder against the Christian militias to the east.

"Well?" Colonel Jalil asked.

Sayyed ignored the Iranian and turned instead to Mustapha Badredeen. "CIA."

"I knew it!" Radih said, excitedly.

Sayyed glanced at the imbecile who had created the problem and said, "You knew no such thing."

"I did so," Radih said defensively.

"How could you have possibly known? What

evidence did you have in your possession that pointed to the fact that this man was CIA?"

"I have my sources."

Sayyed laughed at him. It was an empty claim and everyone in the room knew it. "And the businessman you kidnapped last week, what has he told you?"

"He admitted that he is an American agent."

Sayyed was dubious of the claim, but the fool had just painted himself into a corner. "In that case I will need you to turn him over to me."

Radih realized his mistake. "Well . . . he has admitted to a lot of things. My men are not done interrogating him."

Sayyed stared at him with a look that told everyone in the room that he didn't believe a word of it.

"I will give you a report in a few days," Radih said.

Sayyed dismissed him with a look of contempt and addressed the other men. "The man downstairs is an employee for the CIA who has spent the better part of the last four years in Damascus. My government will want to assess the damage he has caused. To do that thoroughly, I will need Radih to transfer his hostage to me. I'm afraid this point is not negotiable."

"But he is my hostage," Radih said, half yelling. "It was my operation."

"An operation that was not approved."

Radih ignored the point and said, "He is extremely valuable. He has told us his company will pay a large sum to get him back."

"Not if he is an American agent." Sayyed shook his head sadly and scratched his thick black beard. "As we know all too well, the Americans do not negotiate for hostages. Especially the CIA." Pointing at the ceiling he added, "They are far more likely to track him down and drop a bomb on all of us."

The other men shared nervous looks. "The other American, the one you grabbed in front of his hotel last week," Badredeen said to the Fatah leader, "he has told you implicitly that he is an agent?"

"It is my suspicion," Radih said, thankful for the breathing room.

"What was he doing in Beirut?"

"He works for one of their big telecommunications companies."

Radih blathered on about his prisoner, but Sayyed was only half listening. The CIA man in the basement had verified the fact that the other man was a legitimate businessman, but Sayyed did not feel like coming to the aid of the twit from Fatah. He would know for certain only after spending months interrogating the men. Sayyed looked at Mughniyah and said, "Some men are very good liars. It takes a skilled hand to discern the truth from these Americans."

Mughniyah nodded and spoke for the first time. "I don't like the coincidence. We should turn him over to Sayyed. He will get to the bottom of it."

Sayyed was quietly pleased. Mughniyah had a reputation for killing those who crossed him. Radih would not want to defy him.

"The entire thing gives me great concern," the Iranian chimed in.

Sayyed could barely stand the man. He was a self-proclaimed intellectual who was part of the rabble who had helped bring down the shah and bring about the Islamic Revolution of Iran.

"It cannot be a good sign that the Americans are back," Jalil said, as he caressed his bottom lip with the forefinger of his right hand. "Nothing good can come from them poking around in our business."

"I will find out what they are up to," Sayyed said confidently.

The three men exchanged looks, ignoring Radih, who was growing more agitated by the second. Badredeen spoke for the group. Turning to Radih he said, "Please transfer your hostage to Sayyed as soon as is possible."

"That means tonight," Sayyed said, not wanting to give the man an inch.

"That is impossible," Radih said, as if they were asking him to fly to the moon. "This man is too valuable. I am more than capable of finding out his true identity." With a casual flip of his hand he said, "I will give all of you a report within a few days."

"That will not work." Sayyed held his ground. "I want him tonight."

"I will not give him to you. He is my prisoner."

Mughniyah leaned forward in his chair and glared at the representative from Fatah. The temperature seemed to drop a few degrees. "I don't remember your seeking our permission to conduct this operation in the first place."

"And when was the last time any of you came to me to ask permission to launch an operation?"

With an icy voice Mughniyah said, "I do not need your permission."

"That hardly seems fair."

"You are invited to these meetings as a courtesy . . . nothing else."

"The rest of you have taken hostages for years and have profited greatly while the rockets of retaliation rained down on my people and I did not complain to you. Now all I am asking is that I be allowed to share in the spoils of war. You have not allowed me to partner on any of your other business ventures, so I must take what is rightfully mine." With a look of sadness he added, "I have given nothing but loyalty and this is how you treat me."

Mughniyah threw his arms up in frustration. He looked at Badredeen and Jalil. "Talk some sense into him before I shoot him."

Sayyed didn't let it show, but he was enjoying every minute of this.

Badredeen sighed heavily and said, "This is only temporary. Hand the man over to Sayyed. He is without question the best man to do the job. When he is done, if the man is in fact a businessman, he will turn him back over to you and you can then negotiate a ransom. That is fair."

Radih shifted nervously in his chair. He did not want to give up the man, but he could not defy these four. Any one of them could have him killed before the sun rose again. He could see what Sayyed was up to. The hostage could be worth as much as several million dollars if he did in fact work for the telecommunications company, and once the man was out of his hands, he would be lucky to get half of the ransom. Still, half was better than being dead. With great reluctance he said, "Fine," and then glancing sideways at Sayyed, he added, "you can interrogate him at my camp."

Sayyed laughed. "Nice try."

"Why not?"

"Because I said so. I do not need to explain such things to you."

"He is being unreasonable," Radih said to the other three.

Before they could answer, Sayyed said, "I need to inform Damascus of this situation, and I need to continue my discussion with the American agent. I expect Radih to have his prisoner here by ten o'clock tonight so I can get to the bottom of this, and I suggest you all leave as quickly as possible." He glanced at the ceiling. "The four of us," he said, intentionally leaving Radih out, "are far too tempting a target, and with the American in the basement, who knows what they are up to these days. They may have other spies in the area." Moving toward the door, he said with absolute finality, "I will have more answers for you tomorrow."

PART II

CHAPTER 20

ISTANBUL, TURKEY

OF all the changes Rapp had to make over the six months of his training, adjusting to the solitude had been the most challenging. As he became increasingly immersed in his new trade, he drifted further and further away from his friends. The big change was not that he did not see them as much. It was a mental detachment. With each new level of training they had less in common. His new life was far from social.

Rapp's childhood had been fairly normal. He'd grown up in a nice upper-middle-class suburb of Washington, D.C., and pretty much stayed out of trouble. He did well in school, although some subjects, like French, were far easier than math and science. He excelled at every sport, which guaranteed a certain level of acceptance among his peers. There had been just one setback, and it was a pretty big one.

When Rapp was thirteen, his father dropped dead of a massive heart attack. It was a heavy blow, but Rapp didn't go into a complete free fall, nor did he retreat into a shell. The truth was his dad wasn't around much. He was a workaholic who golfed on the weekends. He was in no way a bad father. He was fair and honest with his two boys, and as far as Rapp could tell he had been faithful to his mother and treated her with the respect she deserved. It was neither bad nor good, it just was.

Rapp had a tight group of friends in the neighborhood, and his father had been wise enough to take out the right amount of life insurance, so very little on the home front changed. The awkward moments came at the sports banquets where he was the only one without a father, and the holidays when the memories of his father inevitably bubbled to the surface, but through it all he was more concerned about his little brother and mother.

There was one area where it definitely changed him. He wanted stability in his personal relationships. His friends became more important than ever. Not that they hadn't been before, it was just that he had never had to think about it. All he had to do was walk out his front door, get on his bike, and within a block or two he couldn't help but stumble onto a basketball or stickball game. More than anything, though, his father's death taught him that the clock was ticking. Everyone was going to die. Some a lot sooner than others, but in the end there was no avoiding it, and since he wasn't a Hindu, he pretty much figured he'd better make the best of his one shot. This drove him with amazing intensity and focus on the fields and courts of his youth.

And then there was Mary. Rapp met her when he was sixteen. He was playing baseball and she was running track. He didn't know if it was love at first sight, because he hadn't a clue what love was, but it was unlike anything he'd ever experienced. It was like every great emotion he'd ever felt all rolled into one euphoric wave and it scared the crap out of him, because he instantly knew he was not in control. Fortunately, she was, and she had the sense and stability to not jerk him around too much. Her father was a captain in the navy and a huge lacrosse fan. With three daughters of his own, he enthusiastically attended Rapp's lacrosse matches. Rapp and Mary dated all through high school and then headed off to Syracuse together, where Mary ran track and eventually landed in the Newhouse School of Public Communications. Her ambitious plan was to become a sports announcer. On a chilly December night in 1988 Mary was returning home from a semester abroad when her plane was blown out of the sky, killing 259 passengers and crew and 11 more innocent souls on the ground in Lockerbie, Scotland. The terrorist attack that became known as Pan Am Lockerbie hit Rapp like a hammer blow.

They had planned their entire life together. They'd discussed kids, ambitions, and fears, but never once did they think that one of them would be taken. If he'd made it through the death of his father relatively intact, the opposite was true this time. He crumbled. He was already home for Christmas break and planning on picking Mary up at Dulles after she'd connected through JFK. Strangely enough, when he received the news he never questioned it, never challenged it, never asked for proof. The downing of the plane was all over the news and there was no doubt that she was on it. She'd called him from Heathrow right before she'd boarded.

He was a wreck for the first week. He refused to see a soul, including Mary's parents, and then on the morning of her funeral he emerged from the basement shaved and wearing a suit and tie. His mother and his brother, Steven, accompanied him to the funeral, where he sat stone-faced in a state of bewildered shock. Midway through the service, though, something happened. The shock, the pain, the agonizing self-pity over the fact that he would never see her again, never hold her, never smell her, the list went on, and on, and on like some pounding surf that threatened to drown him.

Sitting in that pew that morning, listening to all of the crying, witnessing all of the pain and loss, made him want to make a break for it. He did not want to share his heartache with these people. None of them knew her the way he did. It was his dreams that had been dashed. His life that had been turned upside down and wrecked. Self-pity was something he had never experienced before, and it sickened him.

Rapp took his pathetic self-absorbed emotion and shoved it as far down in his gut as it would go, and he plugged it with the first and only thing he had available—anger. That anger slowly metastasized into a suit of armor. For the first time since the news had hit him, he saw a way out. A faint light at the far end of the cavern. He wasn't sure what it was, but he knew he had to head toward it. It was the only thing that offered him hope. The rest of these people could sit around and feel sorry for themselves and each other, but not him. He wanted to hurt someone. He wanted to make someone pay. He didn't know for certain that he would achieve his goal, but he knew with absolute certainty that he wanted to kill the men who were responsible for bringing down that plane. Rapp didn't know if it was right or wrong, and he didn't care. All he knew was that the anger kept the pain at bay.

Rapp and Hurley had developed a hate-hate relationship. The shrink had told him it didn't really matter as long as they were united in their hatred for the enemy. It had been a strange six months, and looking back on the journey, Rapp was amazed that he'd made it through without any serious injury. He was young enough going in to be fearless, but coming out on the other end, looking back at what he'd been through, was another story. It was a little like being told not to look down while on the high wire. You just take it one step at a time, and when you get to the other side, and reality sets in, you think you must have been off your rocker to ever try it in the first place.

Rapp could point to a specific date and time when the physical hell and mental abuse had all but vanished. It was replaced by eighteen-hour days that were structured to the minute and more academic

than grueling. There were still long runs and lots of
push-ups and pull-ups, but they were designed to
keep them in peak shape, not to try to get them to
quit. The low point was the day after he'd broken
Victor's arm.

For the first week they were rousted at five every morning. Rapp didn't need an alarm. He was
on his feet as soon as the door was opened, but on
the morning after the incident with Victor, Rapp
found himself thrown from his cot and rolling
across the dusty floor. After landing with a thud, he
came up swinging. It was still dark and his muscles
were tight and he never saw the blow that came out
of the darkness. It hit him in the solar plexus, and
as Rapp doubled over from the first strike another
punch hammered his left eye. Rapp hit the floor
and lay there gulping for air like a largemouth bass
flopping around on a dock.

The lights suddenly came on, and with them
the insults came raining down from the mouth of
the mean old cuss. He stood over Rapp, his fists
clenched, a look of smug satisfaction on his face. If
Rapp had had a gun at that moment he would more
than likely have killed the man. The four remaining
recruits were ordered outside and for the next four
hours were forced to endure unimaginable tortures.
One man collapsed from exhaustion and another
simply quit. It was now down to just Rapp and Fred.
That was when the bastard turned all of his attention on Rapp. By noon they were down to one. It was
an unwarranted slap to the back of the head that did
Rapp in. As calmly as possible, he turned to face the

old man and told him, "If you ever slap me again, I'm going to put you in the hospital."

The old man ordered Rapp into the barn and they went at it again. This time Rapp lost fair and square. Or so he thought at first. As he lay there on the mat, bloodied and exhausted, he realized what had happened. The old man didn't think he could take him fair and square, so he ran Rapp into the ground first. He dumped him from his cot at 4:00 A.M. and spent the next eight hours wearing him down and tenderizing him. Rapp never had a chance. The old prick had made it personal, and in Rapp's mind that did not reflect well on the organization he thought he was joining. The whole thing was starting to look and smell like a shit show. Rapp got to his feet, told the old bastard exactly what he thought of him, and quit.

Rapp packed his stuff and was almost to the gate when the shrink caught up with him. He tried to talk Rapp out of quitting and when that didn't work he outright asked him to stay. Rapp still didn't budge, so Lewis put all the cards on the table. He formally introduced himself and admitted that Victor was in fact one of the instructors. He explained that he had vigorously protested using him to infiltrate the recruits. Rapp asked him for the old cuss's name, but Lewis refused. "If you stay and make it through the rest of the training you will find out who he is, but short of that, I cannot oblige you."

When Rapp held his ground, Lewis told him only that the old man was not the most likable guy, but he assured Rapp that he was exceedingly good at his craft. He assured Rapp that the nonsense was over and that from this moment forward they would be focusing on tradecraft. Rapp still wavered. He simply couldn't see how it was possible for the old cuss to change his behavior. Lewis, sensing Rapp's indecision, said, "You're one of the best I've ever seen. We could really use you. In a way that might explain why he's so hard on you."

Rapp finally relented. It was down to just him and Fred. They still began every day with a workout, but the rest of the time was spent either in the classroom, in the barn, on the pistol range, or on field exercises to Richmond and then to Atlanta. They employed their skills against random targets—unwitting businessmen. They followed them, surveilled their every move, and looked for the right opportunity to dispatch them. Everything was analyzed and critiqued by Lewis and the old man.

While at the lake house they were allowed to speak only Arabic. They honed their fighting skills with virtually every conceivable weapon. They focused on knives and guns for the most part, but they were also taught to inventory every room they entered for objects that could be used to defend or kill. A day didn't go by where the old cuss didn't remind them of the endgame—he was turning them into killers. They studied physiology until they had an intimate understanding of the best ways to either dispatch or incapacitate an opponent. They became expert marksmen with a variety of pistols, shooting with both left and right hands. They were taught escape and evasion techniques, explosives, and the tricks of the countersurveillance trade.

As a final step, Rapp and Fred were told that if anything went wrong they were on their own. Embassies and consulates were off limits. The United States government didn't know they existed and it sure as hell wasn't going to claim them if they landed in hot water. The mean old cuss asked them if they accepted this. If they didn't, they could walk away right now, no questions asked. After only brief consideration, both men said they fully understood the need for plausible deniability. They were in.

Hurley then formally introduced himself and told Rapp and Fred they were now free to reveal to each other their real identities. Rapp and Fred had already done this several months earlier, but they went through the motions as if it were the first time. After that they were forced to memorize a lengthy list of addresses and phone numbers across Europe and the Middle East. A day did not pass without Hurley's reminding them that the United States government had no knowledge of their existence. If they were caught doing something illegal in a foreign country they were on their own. There would be no cavalry or diplomatic effort to gain their release. As often as Hurley brought it up, Rapp did not dwell on it, for the simple reason that he did not plan on getting caught.

CHAPTER 21

As planned, Rapp was the first one to arrive in the former capital city of the Byzantine Empire. He'd been given a long list of orders, and one of them was to stay away from the safe house until it was dark. It was February and the temperature was in the midfifties. Rapp took the tram to the Beyoglu District, found a men's room, retrieved a few objects from his luggage, and then deposited the suitcase in a locker and set about exploring the area, which he'd already memorized by map. He was immediately taken by the scope of the city, as well as its rich history. He'd traveled to London and Paris previously, and Istanbul rivaled them in every way. The images of London and Paris were well known throughout the Western world, but Istanbul, far more rich in history, had in a way been forgotten by people in Europe and America.

After stopping for a quick bite at a café, Rapp

made his way toward the Galata neighborhood, where their target lived. Hurley had given him specific orders to stay clear of both the target's apartment and his office. Rapp had not made a conscious decision to defy the order; it more or less just happened. As he turned onto Bankalar Daddesi, or Banks Street, he couldn't help but walk past the target's place of work along with several hundred other people who crowded the sidewalk. Rapp passed on the opposite side of the street and noted the bank guard standing next to the front door. With that done, he decided he might as well take a look at the man's apartment, which was six-tenths of a mile from the office. It was on a tree-lined street that reminded Rapp of a much smaller version of the Boulevard Montmartre in Paris. It was a wealthy enclave, and as in all such enclaves in cities the world over, the occupants were protected from the riffraff by security guards, ornate fences, and iron bars on the first-floor windows. At first glance, neither the office nor the apartment looked like the ideal place to strike.

When the sun finally set, Rapp found his way to the two-bedroom flat via a back alley. He went by once without stopping to check and see if there were any surprises and then circled back. In the poor light he threaded the worn key into the lock and held his breath. The first attempt did not work. Rapp jiggled the key a bit and then tried again. This time the dead bolt released. He stepped into the room, barely breathing, and closed the door behind him. He stood statuelike, all of his senses on high alert. This apartment was the only definitive link to him in the entire city of twelve million people. Hurley had warned him that this was the second-most-dangerous moment when conducting an operation. Rapp asked him what was the most dangerous, and the old man had replied with a devilish smile, "When you engage the target."

After dropping his bag, he locked the door and found the wall switch. Two small wall sconces cast a yellow light over the room. He fished a large rubber doorstop from his suitcase and wedged it under the door. He couldn't help but smile to himself as he thought of Hurley's rules. The man even had rules about how to go to the bathroom. Some of them, like the rubber doorstop, made complete sense, while others, like which stall to choose, and why, seemed a bit much. Rapp checked the windows next. They had bars, which were padlocked. There was only one way in and out—the door he'd just come through. That was not the best situation should the police come looking for them. Rapp made sure the shades were pulled tight on the two garden-level windows that faced the alley and then he went straight for the bedroom.

At the bottom of the armoire, under an extra blanket and pillow, he found what he was looking for. Rapp placed the tattered leather suitcase on the bed, dialed in the combinations, and popped the clasps. Inside was a shrink-wrapped file, a small arsenal of pistols, silencers, ammunition, knives, and a surveillance kit. Rapp snapped on a pair of latex gloves and retrieved a Beretta 92F from the foam cutout. He checked the slide, the chamber, the firing pin, and then the trigger. The gun had been cleaned by a pro. After screwing a silencer to the end, he took one of the fifteen-round magazines and inserted it, chambered a round, and checked the safety.

Rapp then set about doing a complete examination of the apartment. He retrieved the electric razor from his shaving kit, pressed two buttons, waited for the light to blink. The shaver was actually a scanning device used to detect bugs. Hurley had explained that the flat had been rented by a freelancer, which in this case was code for a retired Agency employee. The man was to sanitize and stock the flat, but Rapp had been ordered to go over the entire place again from top to bottom just to make sure. It took him the better part of an hour to go over the entire apartment.

When the jet lag finally caught up with him, Rapp was too tired to make anything to eat, so he took a quick shower and then tore the shrink wrap from the file. He had been given a full briefing on Hamdi Sharif back in the States, but this file, he was told, would be far more target-specific. The target was fifty-eight years old. He was a Turkish national, and according to press clippings, had made his money in real estate. What the clippings left out was that the majority of his wealth had come from supplying arms to various regimes throughout the Middle East and Southwest Asia. British, French, and American intelligence agencies all had his number, but Sharif was in bed with the Russians, which made him a bit of a sticky situation. None of the allies wanted to risk upsetting the Russians, so they tolerated him.

Rapp frowned as he reviewed the section on Sharif's ties with the tangled web of former Soviet generals and Ivan-come-lately millionaire businessmen. All but a few were thugs and Mafiosi, and the legitimate businessmen were being dropped and squeezed out of their holdings on a weekly basis. Russia had become the Wild West, and the sheriff was in on the fix. The KGB brutes had new business cards, but other than that, not much had changed. The allies, for some reason, couldn't see that the more they turned a blind eye the more brazen these men were becoming. Rapp could give a rat's ass about the Russians and who they used to peddle their arms, so long as those arms didn't end up in the laps of terrorists. Unfortunately for Sharif, that was precisely what he had been doing, and in ever-increasing shipments.

Most of the file was a summary of what Rapp already knew, such as his ties to Hezbollah, but there were a few new snippets about a Marxist outfit called Dev Sol. In the past year the group had targeted the overseas offices of fifteen U.S. corporations in Istanbul. The bombs were all military grade, and the Brits were saying Sharif's outfit had supplied the goods. Sharif was a Muslim and an ardent supporter of Hezbollah, Hamas, and Fatah. How he had ended up in business with a bunch of leftist, God-hating communists was a real head-scratcher. The file didn't draw any conclusions, just gave the facts. Rapp was left to venture guesses on his own. He supposed it was money first, and then the old saying—my enemy's enemy is my friend.

The Dev Sol wrinkle gave Rapp pause, however. He got the sense that this might be about more than just Pan Am Lockerbie, or at least that certain important people stateside don't care so much when innocent civilians get killed, but by God, if the day-to-day operations of a couple of Fortune 500 companies were disrupted, it was time to send a message. Those corporations contributed a lot of money to the coffers of important politicians in Washington. The more Rapp thought about it, the more he realized it didn't matter. It was like Sharif supporting Dev Sol. As long as he and the corporations were going after the same enemy, it didn't much matter.

Rapp finished the file and stuffed it under the mattress. He lay there for a long moment with his eyes open thinking about the detailed report. It was written in English, but it had not been written by an American. The choice of words was distinctive and the sentence structure more formal. Rapp concluded the Brits had put the report together, and that they had taken a long, hard look at solving the Sharif problem. They had conducted careful surveillance on the arms dealer. His daily routine was detailed down to the minute. The report didn't say how long they had watched him, but he got the impression it was for several weeks. Rapp remembered that the shrink back at the lake house had told him you could discern patterns in almost any person's life. In reading Sharif's file, those patterns jumped off the page. And one in particular was almost impossible to ignore. Rapp's mind began to wander down a path that he should have steered clear of, but he found it impossible to resist.

After a few minutes he set the alarm on his watch, turned off the bedside lamp, glanced at the loaded pistol, closed his eyes, and began to drift away. Hurley's orders couldn't have been more clear, but it would be two more days before he arrived in the city. Rapp began to imagine how he would do it. The act of his first kill played out in his mind like a movie. As he drifted off to sleep, he decided he would go for a nice long run in the morning. And he would break another one of Hurley's rules.

CHAPTER 22

RAPP awoke rested and went through the motions of his morning routine without coming to grips with what he had for the most part already decided. He shaved, drank a glass of orange juice, and mixed some granola and yogurt into a small bowl. He read the file again while eating. He started with the summary and worked his way back to see if he'd missed anything. After reading it a second time he was even more convinced that it had been prepared by the Brits, which led to a very obvious question. Why had they decided not to act? It could have been as simple as Hurley, or someone at Langley, offering to solve the problem for them.

Rapp had been trying to decipher the organizational structure of the team that was centered on the Lake Anna house for some time now. There had to be more people involved than the handful of operatives he'd met. After Rapp had proved himself worthy of joining their endeavor, the veil of secrecy was lifted a notch. His recruiter gave him her real name, although he had no way of knowing if it in fact was her real name. Irene Kennedy was the only person in the small group who actually worked at Langley. According to her, everyone else was a contractor. Rapp asked the obvious question: "What am I?"

Kennedy thought about it for a second and said, "Does it matter to you?"

"Maybe."

"Technically you don't work for the CIA."

"But I work for you."

"That's correct. The important thing is that you have no record of ever working for the federal government, and we'd like to keep it that way."

Rapp thought long and hard about what he was about to say. "So I'm a hired gun."

Kennedy's squinting eyes showed that she wasn't exactly in love with the label. Rapp surprised her even more by what he said next.

"How about assassin?"

She frowned. "No."

"By my estimate, I've fired around twenty thousand rounds of ammunition since arriving here."

"And you've become quite the marksman."

"And what's the point of all of this training? To keep shooting paper targets . . . or to eventually sink a bullet into a target's head?"

"You know the answer."

He did. "Remember the first time we met?"

She nodded.

"You told me there are people in Washington

who think that we need to take a more aggressive approach with these terrorists."

"Yes."

"But they don't have the courage to say so publicly."

"It would be foolish for them to do so. We live in a civilized society. They would be thrown out of office."

"And a civilized society would never condone assassination, even in instances where it involved national security."

"Not unless we were at war, and even then it would be tricky."

Rapp digested that for a moment and then said, "I'm not into semantics. Private contractor, hired gun, operative . . ." he shook his head, "killer . . . The point of all of this is to go out, find the enemy, and put a bullet in his head. Right?"

"I suppose that is an accurate definition. I suppose the answer is yes."

"So I'm an assassin."

"Not yet," she offered with a sly smile. "You haven't killed anyone."

Rapp looked in the mirror at his reflection and wondered if he really knew himself. The college athlete looked back at him with the innocence of youth. The public face in no way jibed with the thoughts of retribution that filled his head. Inside he was a much older man. A jaded, hard man who was now a trained killer. He thought again of his conversation with Kennedy and his new profession. He was ready. Eager really, but not in a reckless way. More methodical perhaps than at any time in his life. He asked himself again if he should proceed with his plan. The answer came back a resounding yes.

Rapp secured the silenced Beretta in a shoulder holster and covered it with a lightweight blue and silver reversible running jacket. He stuffed one of the surveillance kits into a fanny pack and strapped the pack to his waist. He put a dark blue Nike baseball hat on his head and checked himself in the full-length mirror on the inside door of the armoire. There was a slight bulge under his right arm where the 9mm was holstered. As a last measure he grabbed a white towel from the bathroom and looped it around the back of his neck. He stuffed the ends inside the running jacket, zipped it up, and checked himself in the mirror. The bulge was no longer noticeable. Rapp lowered the zipper, turned to the side and stuck his left hand inside the jacket. He gripped the Beretta and attempted to aim the weapon. The silencer caught on the jacket. He tried again, this time partially drawing the weapon, but keeping it hidden inside the jacket. He found it worked best if he raised his right arm as if he were checking the time on his wristwatch. Rapp practiced the move fifty more times until he was completely comfortable with it. Finally, he checked the alley and then left the apartment, locking the door behind him. He decided to skip stretching before the run. No sense in giving the neighbors time to observe him.

Whenever possible, reconnaissance is best done on foot. A satellite can't give you the smells and sounds of a neighborhood, and it can't see what might be lurking behind a window or under the awning of an apartment building. A car isn't bad, but then again cars usually travel at fairly high speeds, placing them in the area of concern for a few seconds at most. Often they were the only choice, but in this situation, walking the neighborhood was the best option. Or in Rapp's case, running it.

He took off at a trot. From studying the file, Rapp knew there was a park a block down the street from Sharif's apartment. The previous night he'd found a low wall that offered a decent vantage point where he could stretch and keep an eye on Sharif's building without drawing too much attention to himself. It was a mile and a half to the park. After one mile Rapp stopped at a public phone and punched in an international calling card number using the knuckle of his forefinger. When he heard the dial tone he punched in the number for the phone service. Five seconds later he heard the prerecorded greeting. At the beep he left a coded message in Arabic that told Hurley everything was proceeding according to plan, which technically was the case, but probably not for much longer.

Rapp carefully placed the phone back in the cradle and took off for the park. He circled the entire area twice and saw nothing that would lead him to believe that there was any surveillance. There were a few doormen who were out sweeping, a couple of early morning exercisers, and some people walking their dogs, but no police. Rapp entered the park at seven-forty-one and settled in by the wall. He started stretching his calves; first his right for thirty seconds and then his left. He'd positioned himself so that he had a clear view of the front of Sharif's apartment building. There was no wind and Rapp guessed the temperature was in the high fifties. According to the Brits, Sharif's apartment was one of two on the fifth floor. It was a big place, totaling forty-five hundred square feet. His mother, his wife, and one of his daughters lived with him.

Rapp started on his calisthenics and kept track of the people entering and leaving his corner of the park. Every minute or so a pedestrian passed just outside the park. None of them paid him an ounce of attention. It was the same the world over. Most of these people had been sound asleep thirty minutes ago and they were now off to start their daily grind. They would be lucky if they were fully awake by the time they reached their offices.

Rapp did fifty push-ups, followed by fifty sit-ups, and then stretched some more. At eight he checked the apartment door and his pulse quickened just a touch. At eight-oh-five he frowned and started to doubt the accuracy of the surveillance report. Then at eight-oh-seven the apartment building's doorman stepped outside and held the door open for a plump man and a little brown Dachshund. The man was wearing sunglasses and a long black trench coat. He had his collar turned up against the morning chill. The sunglasses, coat, and dog all matched the photos from the surveillance report. It was Sharif.

Rapp glanced at the open park bench about

eighty feet to his left and started doing more sit-ups. Every time he rose, he could look over the wall and see Sharif moving closer with his dog. Every time he lowered himself to the ground he thought of his orders. The plan was for Rapp to arrive two days early and conduct countersurveillance to make sure they weren't being watched. He would then call the service and flash them the all-clear. Hurley and Richards would arrive on the third day and they would begin direct surveillance on the target for a minimum of five days. If all went well, they would then make their move.

Rapp let out a slight grunt even though the sit-ups were easy. Sharif was almost to the bench. Rapp lowered himself to the ground and rested for a second. The entire operation seemed far too complicated. Far too many moving parts, as his college coach liked to say. Too many places where something could go wrong. Rapp began another set of twenty-five sit-ups. Sharif was just arriving at the bench. The man bent over, undid the dog's leash, and tossed a small blue ball into a grassy area. The little brown sausage took off after it. When Rapp came up the next time, Sharif had a mobile phone out and was punching in a number. Kennedy had played a tape to Rapp and Richards two weeks earlier on which Sharif implicated himself in a number of illegal dealings with known terrorist organizations. Rapp asked her where she got the intel, and she politely told him it was classified information. Rapp guessed it came from these morning chats on his mobile phone.

Rapp did another sit-up and thought of Dr. Lewis, the shrink. The man must have asked him in every conceivable way how he thought he would cope with taking another human life. Rapp had answered that question so many times he finally said to the shrink, "Well . . . I guess I won't know until I kill someone."

"That's right," Rapp muttered to himself. The whole idea behind the Orion Team was that it would have a small footprint. It would cut through all the bureaucratic BS and get things done in a more expeditious manner. And of course deniability was paramount. Rapp finished the set of twenty-five and lay flat on his back for sixty seconds, playing the entire thing out in his mind's eye. The longer they were on the ground in Istanbul lurking around Sharif's apartment and office, the greater the chance they'd be noticed. He didn't like that one bit. He also didn't like the idea of dragging this thing out when the solution was so obvious. He thought of how mad Hurley would be and dismissed the thought almost immediately. The man was always mad about something.

Rapp thought of the past three years. All the sleepless nights when he had yearned for the opportunity to meet just one of the men behind the downing of Pan Am 103. When he had imagined down to the most minute detail what he would do to them. And now he had the man who had supplied the plastic explosives and military-grade fuse and detonator sitting in his sights. He'd waited long enough. When the best course of action was staring you in the face you should take it. Rapp hopped to his feet and did a couple of side bends before walking over to a tree. He stretched one thigh and then the other, stealing a glance at Sharif as he did so. The man was too busy yapping on the phone to notice Rapp.

Rapp did a few more stretches and took a quick inventory of his surroundings. He counted four people within two hundred feet. The closest had just passed by on the sidewalk. Rapp waited to give the woman a good head start and then stepped out from behind the tree. His feet fell silently on the dirt jogging path that ran in front of Sharif's bench. He unzipped his jacket a foot and slid his left hand inside. His thumb found the safety. He flipped it up. Rapp then pulled his hand out of his jacket and kept moving toward the target, who had yet to notice him. Twenty feet away Rapp's pulse was as steady as it had ever been. His eyes narrowed a bit and he took in a deep breath. He could hear the man clearly now. It was the same voice he'd heard on the tape Kennedy had played for him. He was talking about an extremely valuable shipment.

Rapp never flinched, never wavered for a second. He was only ten feet away when Sharif finally looked up. Rapp gave him a friendly nod and then raised his right wrist to look at his watch. A split second later his left hand slid between the folds of his jacket and found the grip of the Beretta. He swung the gun up, the holster acting as a sling, the blue fabric of his running jacket bulging just slightly.

Rapp's finger was prepared to squeeze the trigger when he changed his mind. He wanted to look into Sharif's eyes. He wanted to confront the man. The two men locked eyes for a second. Rapp smiled at him, and then changed directions, took two steps, and casually sat down on the bench next to the arms dealer. Rapp leaned forward and jabbed the end of the silencer into Sharif's ribs.

A look of panic washed over the Turk's face. His mouth was agape, the mobile phone held in his right hand a half foot from his face. A man's voice could be heard squawking from the tiny speaker. Rapp elevated the silencer a few inches and squeezed the trigger. The bullet pierced the fabric of the running jacket, leaving a small hole, and then a millisecond later it shattered the cell phone. Sharif let out a yelp, dropped what was left of the phone, and clutched his bloody hand.

Rapp jabbed the silencer firmly into the man's ribs and in a menacing voice said, "How do you sleep at night?"

"What?" Sharif asked in total confusion.

"You heard me, you piece of shit. How do you sleep at night? Do you think of all the innocent people you've helped kill? Do you think of their faces?" Rapp poked him hard with the silencer. "Do you think of their final seconds . . . how they react when a bomb goes off in the cargo hold of a 747 at thirty-one thousand feet?" Rapp saw the recognition and then fear in the man's eyes.

"I don't know what you're—"

"Shut up," Rapp commanded. "I know who you are, and I have no desire to listen to your lies."

"But—"

This time Rapp jabbed the silencer so hard into the man's ribs that Sharif let out a small cry. "I only want to know one thing," Rapp said. "Do you ever think about them? Have you ever felt an ounce of guilt over all the people you've helped kill?"

Sharif shook his head slowly and parted his lips to speak.

Rapp didn't want to hear his lies. He squeezed the trigger and sent a bullet into Sharif's chest. The Turk grunted and clutched his chest with both hands. Rapp stood, lifted his right arm again, as if he were checking the time, and squeezed the trigger three times in quick succession. The bullets spat from the end of the silencer, all three of them striking the arms dealer in the nose. The hollow-tipped rounds were designed to pancake on impact and triple in size. A pink mist exploded from the back of Sharif's head. A good portion of the man's brain was now in the bushes behind the bench. Rapp flipped the safety into the up position and moved off down the path without even the slightest bit of remorse.

CHAPTER 23

LANGLEY, VIRGINIA

THE Counter Terrorism Center was tucked away in the basement of the Old Headquarters Building at CIA. It was underfunded, understaffed, under decorated, underground, and pretty much isolated from all the major players in the building by both geography and attitude. Eight diligent souls worked there, and that was counting an overworked administrative assistant and Irene Kennedy, who was loosely attached to the group as an expert on all things Arab and Islamic.

Kennedy had spent her youth moving from one diplomatic post to the next, all of them in the Middle East and all of them save one in Arabic-speaking countries. Her father had diplomatic credentials but in fact worked for the CIA. Kennedy was reviewing a particularly bad translation that had been kicked downstairs by someone on the intel side of the building. The translation was so poorly done that Kennedy finally sat back and looked at her colleague Andrew Swanson. The tall, blond-haired Dartmouth grad was leaning against the wall of her cubicle tugging at his curly hair. He'd been up all night trying to make sense of the intercept.

"You keep pulling your hair like that and you'll go bald," Kennedy said without looking up.

Swanson pulled his hand away and tried to stand still. After a half minute he couldn't take it any longer and said, "The thing doesn't make any sense."

"That's because the translation is wrong." Kennedy scratched a few more notes in the margin.

"I knew it."

Kennedy closed the folder and tapped it with her pen. "I'm going to need the tape."

Swanson groaned in frustration. "Shit."

She looked at the designation on the folder. "What's the problem?"

"It's frickin' NSA."

"I see that."

"I'll be lucky if I get the tape before the Fourth of July."

Kennedy grabbed a Post-it note and wrote down a name and number. She stuck it to the front of the folder and handed the whole thing back to Swanson. "Call Kathy. Tell her I said she owes me and ask if she can messenger the tape over this afternoon."

"And if she tells me to get in line like everyone else?"

Kennedy's phone rang. She looked at the small, rectangular, monochrome screen and saw that it was Stansfield's extension. "She won't. I promise. Now run along and bug someone else. I need to take this." Kennedy grabbed the handset and said, "Good morning, sir."

"Good morning. Would you please come upstairs. There's something we need to discuss."

Kennedy instantly recognized the touch of intensity in her boss's voice. The average person would not have noticed, but she knew him so well that she was instantly alert. "I'll be right up." She hung up her phone, locked her desk, and started for the door. On the elevator ride up she reviewed the various operations that she was currently running or involved in. There were fourteen active operations that she was associated with to one degree or another. It could be any one of them, or something entirely new. She really hoped it wasn't anything new. She didn't know if her marriage could take much more of her job. She barely saw her husband as it was.

Kennedy passed through Stansfield's outer office. His assistant Meg was on the phone and motioned for her to go in. Kennedy entered and closed the door behind her. Stansfield was standing at the map table behind his desk reviewing a document. The corner office was devoid of any personal touch, with the exception of a family portrait of his wife and kids that he kept on his desk, and even that faced away from visitors. As Langley's top spy, he was very cognizant of those who collected information and ferreted out secrets. Kennedy had done some digging three years earlier and came up with a long list of medals, citations, ribbons, and awards that Stansfield had received dating back to World War II. Not a single one of them was displayed, either here or at home. Thomas Stansfield was an intensely private man.

"Please sit," he said without turning around. "There's tea on the table. Help yourself."

Kennedy went to the leather couch, opened the bamboo box, and selected a green tea. After tearing open the package she dropped the bag in a cup and filled it with steaming hot water. Stansfield crossed the office, a piece of paper in hand. He sat in the chair to Kennedy's right, slid the sheet of paper across the cherry-inlaid coffee table, and clasped his hands in front of him.

Kennedy stopped dunking the tea bag and looked at the very top edge of the sheet. As someone who was on the operations side of the business, she was intimately familiar with what she was looking at. It was a secure cable. These sheets came in all day long from U.S. Embassies and Consulates the world over. They were sent using some of the most secure and classified encryption software mathematicians could design. The designation across the top told her not only the sensitivity of the information but where it had originated. This particular piece of paper had come from the U.S. Consulate in Istanbul. Kennedy swallowed hard as her eyes raced through the body of text. Hamdi Sharif was dead. Gunned down in a park across the street from his house.

"Is my memory failing me," Stansfield said, "or was I misinformed about the operational timetable?"

Kennedy read the cable again and went over the dates in her head. Finally, she looked up at her boss and said, "To the best of my knowledge Stan and Richards aren't even in the country."

"Where are they?"

"Greece."

Stansfield sat back and ran his right hand over his black-and-blue-striped tie. "Where is Rapp?"

"In-country."

He thought about that for a second. "When did he arrive?"

"Yesterday afternoon."

"You're sure."

She nodded. "He checked in last night and then again this morning."

"His time or ours?"

"It would have been around midnight our time."

Stansfield looked out the window for a moment and then removed his black glasses. He set them on his lap and rubbed his eyes. Jumping to conclusions wouldn't do him any good. Anything, of course, was possible when it came to a character like Sharif. He had made more than a few enemies over the years, but the notion that two separate camps had decided to go after him at the exact same time was a tough one to swallow.

Before Stansfield could say what was on his mind, his office door burst open. Max Powers, the Near East chief, strolled in without offering an apology. "Big news."

"What now?" Stansfield asked.

"Our favorite arms dealer is no longer with us."

Out of the corner of his eye Stansfield saw Kennedy withdraw the secure cable and fold it in half. "Which arms dealer would you be referring to?"

"Sharif, that fat Turk," Powers said with a satisfied grin. "Someone blew his head off in Istanbul this morning."

"His entire head?" Kennedy asked, taking the comment literally.

"The back of it at least." Powers placed the palm of his right hand on the back of his head and tapped his bald spot several times. "I have a good source who works for Turkish NIO. Says someone plugged him up close. One in the heart and they're not sure how many in the face, but more than one. Right here." Powers tapped the space at the top of his nose between his eyes. "Tight grouping. Very professional. Blew the back of his head off."

NIO was Turkey's National Intelligence Organization. "Do they have any idea who carried it out?" Kennedy asked.

"Not a clue, but the rumor mill is already working overtime."

"Candidates?" Stansfield asked.

"Usual suspects . . . Jews, Frogs, Iranians, Iraqis, Syrians, and us, of course."

"Russians?"

"My guy said they were thick as thieves. Also said he got a call from your old friend at KGB."

"You mean SVR," Kennedy reminded him of the Russian Intelligence service's new name.

"Yeah, but, he referred to them as KGB. Same assholes as before. Just a new name."

"What did Mikhail want?" Stansfield asked, referring to Mikhail Ivanov, the deputy director of Directorate S, perhaps the most ruthless outfit in the espionage business.

"Not happy," Powers said with an emphatic shake of his head. "I guess he made some pretty heavy demands."

"Such as."

"He wants to know who did it, and he expects full cooperation. Said he's going to make life very hard for anyone who doesn't cooperate fully. Pushy bastard."

"Any witnesses?" Kennedy asked.

"Not one," Powers said with a grin. He looked at his watch. "The Turk's been dead for five hours. It looks like it was professional. Five hours means the guy who pulled the trigger is long gone. They're screwed."

"Guy?" Kennedy asked.

Powers shrugged. "Just my guess. No offense, but it's pretty much an exclusively all-men's club."

Kennedy smiled to let him know she wasn't offended.

Stansfield asked, "Your source . . . he's good?"

"Great. Very dialed in."

"Loyalties?"

"To the almighty dollar, but he prefers to do business with people he likes. We can trust him."

"Keep me posted. I want to know what Mikhail is up to. If he starts swinging his velvet hammer, we

might be able to win over a few more hearts in Ankara."

"Good idea."

"Anything else?"

"I'll have my gang put together a full workup
for you."

"Thank you." Stansfield looked to the door,
letting Powers know he wanted to get back to his
meeting with Kennedy.

As soon as the Near East chief was gone, Kennedy was on her feet. She made a beeline for Stansfield's desk and grabbed the handset of his secure
phone. She started punching in numbers, pausing
for prompts and then hitting more numbers. After
an interminable twenty seconds she accessed the
voicemail. Kennedy listened intently to Rapp's brief
coded message and then slowly hung up the phone.

Stansfield twirled his glasses in his right hand
and asked, "Well?"

Kennedy nodded, cleared her throat, and said
in near disbelief, "It was him."

CHAPTER 24

THE handsome young man loosened his tie and nudged his bag toward the Customs desk at John F. Kennedy Airport. He casually yet carefully studied the face of every officer who was checking passports and clearing people through Customs. He had a U.S. passport and thus was spared the more stringent and crowded queues that were serving foreigners seeking to visit the United States. He chose this particular line, not because it looked like the fastest, but because the officer manning it looked to be the oldest and most uninterested of the six currently on duty. When it was his turn he stepped to the elevated desk and slid his passport across the cheap blue laminate surface.

The officer, a fifty-some-year-old gray-haired man, gave him a serious look and then glanced at the passport. He was all business. In a voice devoid of real interest he asked, "Did you have a good trip, Mike?"

The man gave a relaxed shrug and said, "Business."

"What do you do?"

"Computer software. Workforce management stuff."

The man asked a few more standard questions before getting back to his second one. "Workforce management . . . what's that?"

"Sorry . . . scheduling software. They tell me workforce management sounds more cutting-edge."

The officer let out a small laugh while he applied the appropriate stamps. He closed the passport, slid it back across the surface, and said, "Have a nice day."

"Thanks, you too." The software salesman headed for the main door and a connection to one of the domestic terminals. He was just another man in a blue suit, white shirt, and burgundy tie trying to earn a living. Other than the fact that he was tanned and fit, there was nothing that made him stand out. He found a stall in the men's room outside the Delta ticketing desk. He carefully pulled back the magnetized liner on his black Travelpro carry-on bag. He deposited the passport for Mike Kruse along with a wallet stuffed with matching credit cards, a Maryland driver's license, a bent and tattered UVA college ID, and a brand-new Blockbuster card.

He extracted a thin money clip with just one credit card, a Virginia driver's license, and eight hundred dollars in cash. After closing the suitcase, he left the men's room and proceeded directly to the Delta ticket counter, where a very enthusiastic young woman with a Southern accent asked how she could be of service.

"I'd like to purchase a ticket on your next flight to Dulles." He placed his driver's license on the counter.

The woman was already pecking away at her keyboard. She nodded at her screen and then looked at the license. "Well, Mr. Rapp, we have a flight that leaves in one hour and forty-eight minutes."

She went on to give Rapp the time of arrival and cost of the ticket plus tax. He simply smiled and slid four hundred-dollar bills across the counter. Three minutes later he was on his way with his change and ticket. He'd spent the last three days traveling across Europe pretending to be someone else. He was relieved to be back on U.S. soil, but was not naive enough to think that his problems were over.

He'd taken a roundabout way back to the flat after he'd executed Sharif, and he'd forced himself to run at a much slower pace than he was used to. A man running a sub-five-minute mile in any city of that size would look as if he were running away from something. Back at the flat, Rapp snapped on the latex gloves and wiped down and disassembled the Beretta. He placed the magazine, slide, and frame back in the worn leather suitcase along with the surveillance kit. He locked the case and put it back in the armoire under the pillow and blankets. The barrel and firing pin were tightly rolled up inside the running jacket and placed in a brown grocer's bag. The rest of the clothes that he'd worn to the park, including his shoes, were placed in a second grocer's bag.

Rapp took a fast shower and put on his suit. After taking two minutes to walk through the flat and make sure he wasn't missing anything, he stuffed the two paper bags in his black duffel and attached the duffel to the top of his black, wheeled carry-on suitcase. Forty-one minutes after executing Sharif, Rapp locked the apartment and headed for the tram. The closest stop was three blocks away and Rapp had two major decisions to make.

The first was to find the right place to dispose of the two brown bags and to do it quickly. The second decision involved getting out of the country. Three different plans had been researched. The first was to simply fly out of the country, the second was to take the train, and the third was to rent a car. Rapp did not like the car rental as an option unless it was to be used to drive to Ankara, eight hours away, where he would leave it at the airport and grab a flight. Using the car to cross the border would create a different set of problems that he wanted to avoid. It put a name in a system that the police could trace. It would be a fake name, of course, but even the false identities that they had manufactured were to be protected. Heading straight for Istanbul's airport would be the faster way out of the country, but it would also involve standing in close proximity to a large number of police, who he didn't think had a description of him, but he couldn't be sure.

A half block from the tram stop he ducked into

a bakery and purchased a coffee, newspaper, and breakfast roll. He paid in liras and took the coffee black and in a to-go cup. Outside he removed the lid, blew on the hot coffee, and watched a nearby public garbage can. He had enough credits left on his tram card that he didn't need to worry about buying a new ticket. The digital readout above the stop told him he had two minutes before the right tram arrived. Rapp put the lid back on his coffee and partially opened the black duffel bag. He extracted the more damning of the two paper bags and stuffed it under his left arm.

The hum of the approaching tram caused everyone to look, and that was when Rapp moved. He headed toward the flock of passengers who were waiting to board, pausing for a split second near the garbage can. He released the suitcase, grabbed the bag and stuffed it in the big circular receptacle. The tram stopped, the throng moved forward in unison, and ten seconds later they were all on their way to Sirkeci Station.

When they pulled into the grand old home of the Orient Express, Rapp searched the crowd for police officers who were showing unusual signs of alertness. There were none to be seen, which he took as a good omen. He exited the train and went straight to the nearest kiosk. Rapp had the departure times for Greece and Bulgaria memorized and knew that the express trains for both countries left in the evening. Hanging around the busy transportation hub for the rest of the day just to grab an express train was foolish. It was better to start working his way toward the border. A train was leaving for Alpullu in fifteen minutes. Rapp bought his ticket and made a quick stop at a bank of pay phones. He punched in the long series of numbers and then, in Arabic, left the coded message that would tell Richards and Hurley to not bother coming to Istanbul. Then, threading his way through the busiest part of the terminal, he slid past a trash bin and got rid of the second paper bag that contained his running gear.

After that he found the right platform, boarded his train, and took his seat. He pretended to read the newspaper, while keeping a close eye on the platform. When the train finally pulled out of the station, Rapp relaxed a touch with the comforting thought that he was putting distance between himself and the crime. Distance, he had been taught by Hurley, was your greatest ally and your number-one objective after taking someone out. As the train rolled through some of Istanbul's less desirable neighborhoods, he thought of Hurley. The man would lose it when he retrieved the message.

Rapp spent the rest of the afternoon hopping westbound trains until he crossed the Greek border at two in the afternoon. The Greeks and Turks did not have good relations, diplomatic or otherwise, so for all intents and purposes he was safe. He was sick of riding in trains and listening to other people yammer, so he decided to rent a car. It would be returned at the Macedonia International Airport in Thessaloniki, and as long as he didn't kill anyone in Greece, no one would care that an American by the name of Mike Kruse had rented a crappy little red, four-cylinder Fiat.

Rapp pointed the tin can south and headed for the coast. As he neared the ocean he cracked the window and smelled salt air. The landscape before him didn't look anything like the travel brochures he'd thumbed through back at the rental agency. The city of Alexandroupolis lay before him, an industrial fishing village with a few archeological sites of significance. Istanbul it was not. It was gray and brown and dirty and dead and it didn't affect his mood one bit. Rapp was not the kind of person who allowed geography or climate to depress him—as long as he didn't have to stay in one place too long. He rolled through Alexandroupolis just before sunset and continued up the coast for another fifteen kilometers until he found a small light blue seaside hotel. It was off season so the place was not busy and the rate was cheap. Rapp wheeled his bag straight into the reception area, which also doubled as the bar and dining room.

A heavyset, older gentleman waved to Rapp from behind the bar. Rapp walked over and the two of them worked out the details in broken English. The proprietor then held up a bottle of liquor and asked Rapp if he would like a drink. Rapp wondered for a brief second what Hurley and Richards were doing in Athens, and then decided that a drink was a great idea. He ordered a beer. The barkeep placed a bottle of Mythos in front of him along with a full bottle of ouzo and two shot glasses. He filled both glasses and slid one closer to Rapp. It was the beginning of a long night.

Three beers, and as many shots, into the evening, Rapp looked at the house phone and considered calling Hurley at his hotel. He dismissed the idea as a bad one and ordered some dinner. Fortunately, two college kids from England showed up and the bartender now had to divide his attention among the three of them. Four beers and a few more shots later, Rapp looked up and caught a reflection of himself in the mirror. It was at that exact moment that he realized a killer was staring back at him. He studied the reflection for a long moment and then held up a shot glass filled with ouzo. He toasted the man in the mirror and went to bed. He did not awaken until almost noon the next day.

CHAPTER 25

VIENNA, VIRGINIA

THE world headquarters for International Software Logistics, Inc., or ISL, was located in a new office park on Kingsley Road. The campus, as the developers called it, consisted of five buildings. They were all made of brown brick and reflective glass. Three of the buildings were strictly office space while the other two were a mix of office and industrial. The developers were an LLC out of the Bahamas who had quietly set aside the southernmost building for Software Logistics. It was at the far end of the office park and it backed up to a ravine. Nice and private. The building had twenty-two thousand square feet of space. The front quarter was built out with a reception area, six offices, a conference room, an area for cubicles, a break room, and a bathroom. The warehouse occupied the remainder of the space and for the most part sat vacant. There were plans, however, to do some expansion.

Stansfield looked at the building through the windshield of a Dodge Caravan and suppressed his concern. These front companies were laborious to set up. The LLC he was part of had directed legitimate funds into the development of this piece of land. The other owners were like-minded men of his era who had made millions and now in that final season of their lives were suddenly very concerned with where their country was headed. All five of them had fought in World War II under the command of Wild Bill Donovan, who ran the Office of Strategic Services. After the war they went on to have successful careers in defense, politics, finance, and in Stansfield's case, espionage. He went to great lengths to make sure they were protected should the Orion Team ever be exposed. But they all understood that if you were going to run an effective clandestine operation you actually had to lock horns with the enemy and possibly get your hands very dirty.

Kennedy told him she could handle the meeting, but he had his doubts. It wasn't that he didn't think her capable. While it was perfectly fine to send people off with messages, words had a funny way of being interpreted differently by different people, often in a way that gave them the outcome they were seeking. And there was a very real chance that his old friend would steamroll her. Even so, his desk was full and he did not want to go through the deceptions it would take to actually get to the meeting.

Kennedy left his office and Stansfield began to

systematically move through the stacks on his desk and map table that required his close attention. As the afternoon ticked away he periodically found himself staring out the window thinking about the new recruit. There was something about this Rapp fellow. He hadn't seen any of his people this fired up about anything in a long time. The kid was either a diamond in the rough or a disaster waiting to happen, depending on who you listened to. Kennedy was possibly biased by the fact that he was her find and Hurley was surly on a good day and an intolerable bastard on a bad day, so it was hard to see who was right. Lewis was steady, analytical, and unfortunately had no desire to run things. He had no doubt that Kennedy was right for the job, but she needed a few more years under her belt before she would be ready.

Stansfield stewed over their personalities for a good five minutes and then decided he needed to go to the meeting. The outcome was preordained. Hurley had never liked this Rapp fellow, and while Kennedy and Lewis were formidable, Hurley would wear them down with his bombastic, stubborn ways. And in truth, it was his call. As the person in charge of field ops he needed to be able to trust his men without question. Stansfield became stuck on the team concept for a second. Through all of the bickering and managing of egos, they had lost sight of one very important fact—the new recruit had not only succeeded, but had done so on his own. He arrived in Istanbul and less than twenty-four hours later he had successfully removed a very nasty thorn in America's side. There were a number of allies who would be cheering Sharif's death as well, and Stansfield hoped that at least one of them would be blamed. As much as Stansfield would love to take the credit for the assassination of Istanbul's merchant of death, he couldn't. The Orion Team needed complete anonymity or they risked investigation and exposure, which would in short order render them useless. That was why these new recruits could have no link whatsoever to Langley.

But what was the sense of any of it if you didn't engage the enemy and make him bleed? Stansfield had to be cautious with his hopes, though. How much of this was wishful thinking? He had yet to meet the young man. Who was to say this Rapp fellow wasn't in reality an uncontrollable asset who would eventually blow up in his face? Lewis didn't think so, and that was worth something, but still Stansfield realized he needed to meet this fellow and find out for himself what he was made of. If he was as good as some of them were saying it would be a tragedy to throw him away.

Stansfield asked his security detail to prepare for the vehicular version of a shell game. Langley kept a number of nondescript, windowless vans in the motor pool for just this type of thing. As the Operations boss, Stansfield did not have to inform anyone of his needs. His security detail only had to show up and take what was available. The detail had access to extra license plates and a variety of magnetized decals to help facilitate the deception. At seven-oh-four they left the back service gate at

Langley in a white van with the Red Carpet Linen Service logo on the sides.

They headed for Tyson's Corner and once inside the busy parking structure, Stansfield was moved to a Ford Taurus. Fifteen minutes later, he found himself standing alone, under a tree next to the main entrance of George Mason University. The Dodge minivan was parked across the street. Stansfield waited for five minutes and then the vehicle flashed its brights. After climbing into the backseat he handed Joe, head of his security detail, a piece of paper with an address on it. The driver memorized the address and handed the paper back to his boss. He briefly consulted his road atlas and then put the car in drive. Five minutes later they were at the office park.

"Joe," Stansfield said, leaning forward, "take us around back. There's a call box and a code for the door."

When they reached the back of the building Stansfield got out and punched in the code. He trusted Joe, but the fewer people who had the numbers, the tighter the circle remained. Stansfield motioned for Joe to pull in and then pressed the big red button to close the door. Four cars and a motorcycle were already parked inside. To the right, shelves, like the kind you'd find in a library, jutted out from the near wall. They were filled with software titles that were legitimately being shipped overseas. To the left were pallets and boxes and then a sea of darkness.

Stansfield headed for the offices and asked Joe to stay with the car. There was a cipher lock on the door. He punched in the four-digit code, leaned into the door, and was immediately aware of loud shouts coming from just ahead.

Stansfield frowned and wondered first and foremost why the conference room hadn't been soundproofed. He also wondered why these supposed professionals were incapable of keeping their tempers in check. As he stepped into the room, he almost didn't notice the man sitting at the break table reading a magazine.

"They've been at it like that for almost an hour."

Stansfield recognized the face instantly. "Mr. Rapp, I presume."

CHAPTER 26

RAPP didn't know who the man was, but there was something about him that instantly garnered respect. The gray hair, charcoal suit, shiny wing tips, discerning eyes, and the fact that he'd just walked unannounced into the secure building told him he was standing before someone who more than likely had an office on one of the top floors at Langley. After he gave him the once-over, he couldn't help but think the man reminded him of a more slender version of Spencer Tracy. Rapp decided he'd better stand. He offered his hand and said, "Yes. And you are . . . ? "

Stansfield gave him a grandfatherly smile. "George."

Rapp studied him with suspicion. "That's not your real name, is it?"

"No," Stansfield said.

After a moment Rapp said, "Any chance you're the guy running this show?"

Stansfield gave him a relaxed smile. "When you get to my age you better be running something, or it's time to retire. Please sit." He motioned with his right hand toward the chair Rapp had been sitting in. Rapp returned to his seat. Stansfield smelled coffee and found a pot on the counter. He helped himself. "Would you like some?"

"No thanks."

After joining him at the break table, Stansfield blew on his coffee and said, "I hear you've been making waves again."

Rapp wasn't sure how much he should say, so he shrugged his shoulders and kept his mouth shut.

"Would you care to walk me through your decision?"

"What decision would that be?"

"Why you decided to act on your own in Istanbul?"

Rapp's dark eyes narrowed. He studied the old man for a few seconds. He was in enough hot water for breaking their damn rules. He wasn't about to break another. "I'm afraid I don't know what you're talking about."

Stansfield grinned. "I'm afraid you do."

"I'm at a bit of a disadvantage. If you're who I think you are, you know I can't discuss any of this with someone unless they give me the green light." Rapp jerked his head toward the conference room door.

"Good point. You don't know me, and that's for good reason, but I know you."

Rapp gave him a dubious look that changed

into a humble one as the silver-haired man recited his life story, including date of birth, Social Security number, parents' names, a long list of athletic accomplishments, and his relative strengths and weaknesses. It wasn't until the last part, though, that Rapp began to feel vulnerable.

"Three days ago you used a 9mm Beretta pistol to execute a man at point-blank range. Here and here." Stansfield touched his heart and then tapped the bridge of his dark glasses. He looked at the door to the conference room and said, "You have one avid supporter, another who thinks you have great potential, and one very forceful detractor. They are in there deciding your fate right now. If you want to continue on your current career path, I am more than likely your best hope. So if you have anything you'd like to say, now is the time to do it."

That this man knew so many details about his life and was able to recite them, chapter and verse, without a single note, told Rapp all he needed to know. "You seem to have most of the facts." He carefully turned the question back on George by saying, "I'm sure you've formed some opinions."

Stansfield sat back and crossed his left leg over his right. "I'm hearing conflicting stories. That is why I decided to meet you in person."

"What are the conflicting stories?"

"You appear to be a man who is possibly uniquely suited for this line of work. You also appear to have a hard time following rules, and that, young man, can be a dangerous thing."

Rapp nodded. It was becoming apparent that

Spencer Tracy's little brother really was the guy who ran this entire show, which meant he needed to get him in his corner, and do it before Hurley sank him once and for all. "Sir, would I be totally off the mark if I guessed that at some point in your career you spent some time in the field?"

Stansfield grinned but did not answer the question.

"And when you were in the field, did things always go as planned?"

Stansfield saw instantly where he was headed. "There's a big difference between adapting and disregarding orders."

Rapp nodded and was sullen for a split second. That was exactly what Hurley had screamed at him, with a few colorful words thrown in to boot. If Doc Lewis hadn't been there, Rapp was pretty certain they would have come to blows.

"To be fair," Stansfield continued, "I use great caution when I evaluate a decision that someone has made while operating in a high-stress environment."

The man's choice of words gave Rapp pause. He considered them carefully and then said, "High-stress?"

"Yes."

"I'm not sure I'd call it high-stress, sir."

Stansfield's eyes sparkled with amusement. "You snuck into a foreign country using a false identity, killed a man at close range, and then made it out of the country all on your own. You didn't find any of that stressful?"

"The getting-out part . . . maybe a little, but really only getting out of Istanbul. After that the odds of getting caught were pretty low."

"Why did you decide to act on your own?"

"I didn't go to Istanbul thinking that I would handle the job on my own. It happened. It evolved. I saw the opportunity and I took it."

"What do you mean you saw the opportunity?" Stansfield was keenly interested in the young man's next words.

"I read the surveillance briefing that the Brits gave us . . ."

Stansfield held up his hand and stopped him. "Who told you the Brits gave us that report?"

"No one."

"Then why did you say the Brits gave it to us?"

Rapp shrugged as if to say it was obvious. "I could tell by the way it was written."

Stansfield nodded for him to continue and made a mental note to revisit the subject later.

"I read the report and there it was . . . it jumped right off the page."

"There what was?"

"The opportunity. The report said that the target took his dog to the park every morning. He sat on a park bench and talked on his cell phone while he threw a ball to his little dog." Rapp turned his palms up and said, "How does it get any easier than that? No bodyguards to deal with, no drivers or armor-plated cars, no security cameras . . . very few witnesses, and the few who are around are busy living their own lives."

"And it didn't occur to you to pass this information on to Stan?"

"It did, but it also seemed like it was too good to pass up."

"If you'd brought it to Stan, you wouldn't have been passing it up."

"You're not serious."

"Completely."

"If I had brought my idea to Stan he would have called me a moron and told me to shut my mouth."

The young recruit was probably right. "Stan is very good at this type of thing. This is not his first dance."

"So I've been told," Rapp said, unimpressed.

"You have some problems with Hurley, I hear."

"Who doesn't?"

The point was more accurate than not. "Still . . . he has a lengthy resume."

"I'm sure he does, but the entire thing was more complicated than it needed to be. The whole idea here is that we are supposed to get in, get it done, and get out without anyone noticing we were there. If we'd stuck with Stan's plan, we would have followed the guy around for five days and come to the same conclusion that was right there in the Brit report, and our odds of screwing up somewhere . . . being noticed . . . would have increased fivefold at least."

He was probably right, but Stansfield didn't tell him so. He would have to deal with Hurley later. "When did you read the report?"

"When I got to the safe house."

"That first night."

"Yes."

"And you decided that night that you would handle it on your own?"

"No . . . I saw the possibility, that was all."

"And when you decided to go to the park armed the next morning?"

"I thought there was a chance. I wanted to see with my own eyes and then decide."

"But when you left the safe house you were prepared to kill him if the opportunity presented itself?"

Rapp hesitated and then admitted the truth. "Yes."

Stansfield took a sip of the coffee and slowly set the mug on the table. "Any other reason why you chose to act on your own?"

"How do you mean?"

Stansfield gave him a knowing grin. "I was your age once . . . a long time ago. I was asked to do certain things for my country, and until I actually did them, I wasn't sure I had it in me."

Rapp looked down and studied the pattern in the gray-and-black carpeting. It was not in his character to be this open with someone he'd just met, especially on a subject like this, but there was something about this guy that made it difficult to be anything but forthright. "I wanted to kill him," he finally said.

"Revenge?"

Rapp shrugged his shoulders in a noncommittal way.

"Remember . . . we recruited you for a reason. I know what you went through. I know how you were affected by Pan Am Lockerbie."

"Revenge, justice . . . I don't know. I just know when I left for the park that morning I wasn't sure, and then as soon as I laid eyes on him I wanted to kill the bastard. I was sick of all the planning and talking. It made no sense that it had to be so complicated."

Stansfield took off his glasses and looked at Rapp with his gray-blue eyes. "Any other reason that may have pushed you over the edge?"

Rapp looked at the carpeting again. He hadn't even admitted the next part to himself. At least not fully. Without looking up he said in a soft voice, "I was afraid I wouldn't have the guts to do it."

With the understanding of someone who had walked the same path, Stansfield gave him a sympathetic nod. It had been a long time since Stansfield had killed a man, but he remembered the doubt that gnawed at him until he pulled that trigger for the first time. "How do you feel now?"

"How do you mean?"

"Now that you have taken a human life?"

Rapp gave a nervous laugh and checked his watch. "Do you have a few hours?"

"You know laughter is often a defense mechanism used to deflect."

Rapp thought of Doc Lewis. "I've heard that somewhere else recently."

"This isn't a good time to deflect."

Rapp noticed the concern on the old man's

lined face. He fidgeted with his hands and then said, "This isn't exactly a topic I'm used to discussing."

"No . . . you're right about that." Stansfield himself had never spoken to a soul about the men he had killed. It simply wasn't his way. There were others, though, whom he had worked with over the years, who were quite different in that regard. Some spoke with an intensity that was more academic, as if they were simply trying to perfect their craft for the sake of perfection. Others took a more lighthearted or twisted approach to their play-by-play analysis of how they had killed a man. The best ones, Stansfield had always felt, were the ones who kept it to themselves.

"This is very important," Stansfield said. "How are you up here?" The old man tapped his temple.

"I think I'm fine."

"No problem sleeping?"

"No, in fact I've slept better than I have in years."

"Good. I want you to understand something very important. Hamdi Sharif chose to get into the arms business, and he knowingly sold weapons to terrorist groups that were going to use those weapons to kill innocent civilians."

"I know."

"I am every bit as responsible as you for his death."

Rapp frowned and gave him a look that said he wasn't quite buying it.

Stansfield had expected that. "Who do you think sent you on that operation?"

"I don't know."

"I did. I was the judge and the jury. You were merely the executioner. Never forget that." He spoke with intensity for the first time in the entire conversation. He was almost pleading for Rapp to grasp the gravity of what he was saying.

Finally Rapp nodded, even though he wasn't sure he fully grasped the man's meaning.

Stansfield stood and said, "Why don't you go home now?"

"What about their decision?"

"Don't worry. I'll smooth things out. Just try not to cause any problems for the next few months."

CHAPTER 27

"THANK God," Lewis announced upon seeing Stansfield enter the room. "I can't spend another minute trying to talk sense into these two."

With pure disappointment, Stansfield glared down the length of the table, first at Hurley, who was on the left, and then at Kennedy, who was directly across from him. They were both on their feet. "Sit," he commanded. Kennedy sat. Hurley remained standing. "The first person who raises his voice is being sent to Yemen for the rest of his career."

"You can't send me anywhere," Hurley snarled.

Stansfield directed his full attention to Hurley and communicated his resolve with an icy stare that silently communicated the fact that he could do a lot worse than sending his ungrateful ass to Yemen. Of the three, Hurley was the only one who had seen this look before. It had been nearly three decades ago but Hurley still remembered that his stupidity had almost cost him his life, and if it hadn't been for Stansfield's magnanimous attitude he would have died that day. Hurley slowly sank to his seat.

"Have I failed you two so poorly that it has come to this?" Stansfield said in a calm but disappointed voice. "You scream at each other like children trying to bully their way to victory." He cocked his head in Kennedy's direction. "I expect far more from you. What did I tell you about losing control of your emotions?"

"That it's a weakness."

"Correct. And how has it worked for you this evening . . . screaming at one of the most hotheaded men in all of our nation's capital? Did your logic become more clear? Did your points carry more weight? Did you somehow persuade him to see things your way by shrieking at him like some wild banshee?"

Kennedy shook her head, her embarrassment complete.

Stansfield turned his icy gaze on Hurley. "And you . . . are you happy that you have succeeded in getting young Irene to finally sink to your depths?"

"That's bullshit. She's a grown woman. She can fight her own battles. I resent the fact that every time she doesn't like what I'm doing she goes running to you." Hurley pointed at him. "You know the rules as well as I do. I'm in charge in the field. What I say goes. I'm God and that too-smart-for-his-own-good college punk wandered so far off the reservation he's lucky I don't put a bullet in his head."

"That's our litmus test these days? When an operator doesn't follow orders to the letter, we put a bullet in his head?"

"You know what I mean. He went way beyond his operational parameters. He basically threw them out and flew off the handle."

"And succeeded. Let's not forget that part."

"Shit," Hurley scoffed at the point. "Even a blind squirrel finds a nut once in a blue moon."

"This is how you would like to argue with me . . . by mixing squirrel and moon metaphors?"

"You know I'm right."

"You are partially right, and you have also become an intolerable bully whom I'm not so sure I can keep around."

"Say the word and I'll resign. I'm sick of this bullshit."

"And then what will you do, Stan?" The deputy director of operations leaned over and placed his hands on the table. "Become a full-blown alcoholic. Another bitter, discarded spy who closes himself off from an ungrateful citizenry. You're already halfway there. You drink too much. You smoke too much. You piss and moan like some miserable woman who's mad at her husband because she's no longer young and beautiful. And there's the meat of the problem, isn't it, Stan?"

"What's the meat of the problem?"

"I think you may have heard this before. He reminds you of yourself."

"Who? The college puke?"

Stansfield nodded slowly. "And he might be better than you. That's what really scares you."

"That's bullshit."

Stansfield should have seen it sooner. He stood up abruptly and said, "So, your recommendation is that I cut him loose?"

"Absolutely. He's too much of a loose cannon. Sooner or later he's going to cause you a lot of problems."

"And who do you have to replace him?"

Hurley waffled. "A couple of decent candidates."

Stansfield looked to Lewis, who was at the head of the table. "Doctor?"

Lewis shook his head. "Neither of them have his skill set. Even if we worked with them for a year I don't think they could match him."

"That's not true," Hurley said, while looking as if he'd just taken a bite out of a lemon.

"Irene?" Stansfield asked.

She didn't speak. Just shook her head.

Stansfield pondered the situation for a moment and then said, "Here is my problem. We are flying blind in Lebanon and Syria. The director and the president overruled me and sent Cummins in to negotiate for the release of that Texas businessman." Stansfield stopped speaking for a second. He couldn't get over the stupidity of that decision and all of the damage that had been done after Cummins himself had been taken hostage. "Our assets have been getting picked off one by one for the past six months. Our network, that we worked so carefully to rebuild, is now in shambles. This situation has to be turned around, and I need men in the field to do it. I need shooters on the ground. We've all spent enough time over there to know that weakness breeds contempt. That stops today. I want these guys looking over their shoulders wondering if they're next. I want the leadership of Islamic Jihad and Hezbollah afraid to pop their heads out of their holes for fear that they might get those heads blown off. I want them on notice that if they're going to grab one of our assets who is negotiating in good faith and torture him for months on end . . . dammit, we are going to come after them like crazed sons of bitches." He turned his attention back to Hurley. "I don't want to lose you, but I need this kid. He's too good to just throw away. He knows how to take the initiative."

"Initiative? That's what you want to call it?"

"Oh, for Christ's sake, Stan, could you please get hold of your ego and hypocrisy and listen to me. This is bigger than you. We have a gaping hole in our operational abilities. A big nasty neighborhood in the Middle East that is breeding terrorists like rabbits, and we have nothing. I need to get back in there."

"You're calling me a hypocrite?"

"You have an extremely convenient short-term memory. Tell me, Stan, how many times in your first two years did you get yourself into trouble by ignoring orders or running off and launching your own operations?"

"It was a different time back then. We were given far more latitude."

"And you still got in trouble." Stansfield shook

his head as if trying to reconcile an irreconcilable thought. "Does the truth matter to you at all, or do you just want to go round and round all night until you wear everyone down? You don't remember all the times I had to go to bat for you and bail your ungrateful butt out of trouble, and now you're coming down on this new kid as if you were some saint."

Hurley started to speak, but Stansfield cut him off. "I'm not done. If the kid had screwed up, we wouldn't be having this conversation. He'd be gone. But he didn't screw up, did he? He made all the right decisions. He took care of our problem and didn't leave a speck of evidence and made it back here all on his own. He's a natural and you want to throw him away."

Hurley stubbornly shook his head.

Stansfield was done arguing with him. "Irene," he said, turning his attention to Kennedy, "what about running him on his own? Break him off from the team. Let Stan and Richards work together."

Hurley didn't hear Kennedy's answer because he was too busy reliving all the various times he'd landed in hot water with a station chief or someone back at Langley. There were too many to even begin counting. That was part of the reason why Stansfield and Charlie White had set him up as a freelancer almost twenty years ago. He'd worn out his welcome at every embassy from Helsinki to Pretoria. Simply put, he wasn't good at following rules, so White and Stansfield had removed him from the system. They had gone to bat for him against Leslie Peterson, that Ivy League prick who wanted to gut the Clandestine

Service and replace it with satellites. He liked to say, "Satellites don't get caught breaking into embassies." Yeah, well, satellites can't seduce an ambassador's secretary into working for the CIA or kill a man. At least not yet anyway. Hurley grudgingly saw the plain truth—that he was an ingrate.

"I can work with him," Hurley announced. "And if I can't, I'll turn him back over to Irene, and she can run him."

Stansfield was speechless for a moment. Kennedy and Lewis were thunderstruck.

"Don't look so surprised," Hurley grumbled. "No one hates these fuckers more than I do."

CHAPTER 28

MOSCOW, RUSSIA

SAYYED stood just inside the glass doors. He looked through the frosted window as a gust of wind whipped up a cloud of dirty snow. It moved like a ghost through the dark night and caused a shiver to run up his already frigid backside. He did not like Moscow, had never liked Moscow, and would never like Moscow. Not in summer and definitely not in winter. His warm Mediterranean blood found it to be perhaps the most inhospitable place he had ever visited. He could practically feel his skin cracking.

With voyeuristic awe, he watched an abnormally round woman waddle by. She was wrapped from head to toe in the dark fur of some animal he couldn't quite pinpoint. Why did these people live here? He would endure a hundred civil wars if he could avoid ever coming here again. A vehicle entered his field of vision from the left. The handler reached out and touched his elbow. He gestured to the waiting SUV and grunted the way big Russian men do.

Sayyed was fairly certain he'd smelled vodka on the man's breath when he'd met him at the gate. That was another thing about these Russians, they all drank too much. Sayyed was not the kind of Muslim who ran around telling everyone what they could or couldn't do. He enjoyed a glass of wine from time to time, but never in excess. They would want him to drink tonight. He knew it. He didn't want to drink and he didn't want to go outside, but he had no choice. He had been summoned, and his bosses in Damascus had eagerly offered him up. With great effort he clutched his long black coat around his neck and stepped into the cold Moscow night.

The bite of the cold wind snatched at his ears and cheeks. His eyes filled with tears, and he could have sworn the hair in his nose had turned to icicles in under a second. He opened his mouth narrowly to catch a breath, but his teeth ached from the sub-zero temperature, so he lowered his head and shuffled toward the car. He'd learned that the hard way on the last trip. You never ran on a Moscow sidewalk in winter. No matter how cold it was. You shuffled. Half skating. Half walking.

It wasn't until he was in the backseat that he realized he was sitting in a brand-new Range Rover. Apparently capitalism had been very good to the SVR, the KGB's bastard offspring. The man who had fetched him from the gate tossed Sayyed's suitcase in back and jumped in the front passenger seat.

"I take it you don't like the cold?" a voice asked in decent yet accented English.

Sayyed had his head shoved so far down into his jacket that he hadn't noticed the diminutive man sitting next to him. "How do you people live here?"

The man smiled, popped a shiny cigarette case, and offered one to his guest. Sayyed grabbed one. Anything that would provide a scintilla of warmth was to be taken advantage of. After he'd taken a few long drags and had stopped shivering, Sayyed sat back and said, "I do not think we have met before."

"No, we have not. I am Nikolai Shvets."

Sayyed offered his hand, "I am Assef."

"I know," the boyish-looking man replied with a smile.

"I take it you work for Mikhail?"

"Yes. The deputy director is a very busy man. He will be joining us later."

That was fine by Sayyed. Mikhail Ivanov, the deputy director of Directorate S, was not someone he looked forward to dealing with. Sayyed had done everything in his power to get out of the trip, and then to delay it when he was told he had no choice. Two days ago Ivanov had called his boss at the General Security Directorate in Damascus and told General Hammoud he would consider it a personal insult if Assef Sayyed was not in Moscow by week's end. The last the general had heard, the meeting had already been scheduled. He was not a happy man, and he made sure Sayyed understood just how unhappy he was.

"The deputy director is very much looking forward to speaking with you. He has been talking about it for some time."

Sayyed couldn't pretend happiness over seeing the old spider, so he said, "It's too bad you did not travel to Damascus. It is very nice there this time of year."

"I would imagine." The man glanced over his shoulder and looked out the back window. "Your Mediterranean blood is too thin for our Moscow winters."

The boy man made idle conversation as they worked their way around one of the ring roads that circled the big metropolis. Sayyed barely glanced out the window even though it was his habit to be constantly alert for surveillance. It wouldn't matter in this iceberg of a city at this time of night. Streetlights and headlights were amplified by the white snow, blinding him every time he tried to see where they were. This truly was a miserable place. No wonder communism had failed. How could any form of government succeed if everyone was depressed?

They finally stopped in front of a hotel in the heart of old Moscow. A doorman in a massive black fur hat and red wool coat with two rows of shiny brass buttons yanked open the door, and Sayyed felt a blast of cold air hit his ankles. With a second doorman shuffling along with him, he walked through the front door of the hotel and did not stop. Cold air was still whistling through the doors and he wanted to get as far away from it as possible. Eight steps into the lobby he found himself drawn in the direction of heat and then finally spied a roaring fire on the far side of the lobby. He actually smiled and shuffled over, his brain not realizing the lobby was ice free.

"What do you think?"

Sayyed parked his backside directly in front of the flames. He took in the opulent lobby and nodded. It was much nicer than the dump he had stayed in the last time he was here. "Very nice."

"It has just reopened. It is Hotel Baltschug. Very historic. Very expensive." Shvets left out the fact that his boss owned a piece of the hotel. He owned a piece of most things in Moscow these days. At least the nice things. A group of Russian, Austrian, and Swiss businessmen had purchased the hotel just after the collapse and had tried to renovate. After a year of getting turned down for permits and dealing with theft and workers not showing up, one of the Russians went to Ivanov for help. The problems disappeared almost overnight. All they had to do in return was sign over 10 percent of the hotel.

Sayyed did not want to leave the fire, but he had to get ready for dinner. He was finally convinced to move when they informed him that his room had two fireplaces that were both lit and waiting for him. The room was as nice as the lobby, with gilded plaster and hand-painted murals on the ceiling, tapestries on the walls, and a commanding view of the Kremlin and Red Square. It was fit for a pasha.

That was when it hit him. Ivanov the spider never did anything nice unless he wanted something in return, and he was being extremely nice. Sayyed took a steaming-hot shower and wondered what the man was after. He'd heard stories lately that the SVR was worse than the KGB. That once they sank their talons into you, they owned you for the rest of your life. He suddenly longed for the bombed-out rubble of Beirut. There, he was a lion. Here, he could end up being someone's lunch.

CHAPTER 29

SAYYED had just one wool suit. It was black and was worn for special occasions. He was wearing it tonight because it was his warmest suit, and also because to a man like Ivanov, appearances were exceedingly important. He lectured his people about taking care of themselves and was known for firing people who put on too much weight or women who wore too much or too little makeup. Sayyed had carefully trimmed his beard and slicked his black hair back behind his ears. At forty, he was still in decent shape, or at least he wasn't out of shape. The black suit and white shirt and tie helped hide those few extra pounds he'd put on over the last couple of years.

As he walked toward the restaurant he immediately picked out the men from Ivanov's security detail. There were four in the lobby, one by the front door, one by the elevators, and two bracketing the entrance to the restaurant. The boy man suddenly appeared from behind a large plant. His cigarette was hanging from the side of his mouth and he was smiling. Sayyed had been in such a rush to avoid the cold earlier that he had failed to notice that Nikolai was extremely handsome. More pretty, really. In kind of a movie star way. There were none of the usual rough edges that were standard with the lackeys in the Russian state security services. His skin was fair, his eyes a greenish blue, and his hair a light enough brown that he would probably be blond if he lived in a warmer climate.

"Your room is nice . . . Yes?" Shvets asked.

"Very."

Shvets popped his cigarette case with one hand and offered one to his guest. Sayyed took one, as well as a light.

"Director Ivanov is waiting for you at your table. I hope you are hungry."

"Yes. Very much so."

"It is the cold weather. Please follow me."

The restaurant was decorated in deep reds and sparkling golds, most of it in velvet. It was typical Russian. Heavy-handed and desperate to impress. This backwater behemoth knew nothing of understated class. Sayyed was no snob, but he was proud of where he came from. The Ottoman Empire had lasted for more than six hundred years. After fewer than one hundred years these brutes had gone from one of two superpowers to a mob state.

A haze of blue-gray smoke hung in the air. Every table was occupied. There were easily several hundred people in the restaurant, and they all appeared to be in various states of inebriation. It occurred to Sayyed, for the first time, that the Russians were loud people. Especially when they laughed. Sayyed didn't recognize any faces, but he guessed they were all very important. That was the Russian way. Even during the height of the great workers' paradise, the ruling elite had lived an opulent life, separate from the workers. They enjoyed luxuries that the little people never dreamed of.

Two towering men stood watch near a booth in the back corner. Red velvet curtains were pulled open and fastened with tasseled ropes to marble columns. Sayyed glimpsed Ivanov sitting between two young beauties. The man was nearing sixty and was showing no signs of slowing down. He was a consumer of all things that interested him. In a way he was the perfect man to run an intelligence service, assuming his interests were in line with those of the state.

Sayyed had been told that Ivanov's power had grown significantly in recent years. In the days of the Politburo, the black market was tolerated but never flaunted. During the transfer from centrally controlled markets and government plans to pseudocapitalism, no one was better positioned to take advantage of the new wealth than the men at the KGB. They had the guns, the enforcers, and the spy-craft to break, blackmail, or frame any man who did not welcome them to the buffet. And Ivanov had an insatiable appetite.

Ivanov saw him coming and yelled his name. He

tried to stand but was stuck between the two girls, so he gave up and sat back down. "Assef, it is good to see you." The Russian threw out a large hand with rings on the forefinger and pinky.

"And you, too, Mikhail," Sayyed lied. He reached across the table and clasped Ivanov's hand.

"If you had turned me down one more time I was going to send my men after you," Ivanov said with a hearty laugh, although his eyes weren't smiling.

Sayyed laughed and tried to play along. The comment was without a doubt meant for him to re-member. And keep remembering every time Ivanov called on him. Sayyed so badly wanted this evening to end, and it had only just begun.

Ivanov ordered an expensive bottle of Bordeaux and introduced Sayyed to the girls. The blonde one was Alisa and the redhead was Svetlana. The redhead was suddenly very interested in the spy from Syria. That was how Ivanov had introduced him—as a spy, of all things. The Russians might have found the moniker intriguing, but to Sayyed it was an insult, one of many he was sure he would be forced to endure on this cold winter evening.

More wine was ordered, along with plate after plate of food. Sayyed was full by the time the main course was served. Ivanov steered the conversation away from anything serious, and Svetlana steered her hands toward Sayyed's groin. Sayyed had no illusions about his ability to woo women. He was handsome enough, but not enough to garner the at-tention of a twenty-year-old runway model. Ivanov had undoubtedly ordered her to take care of him.

Sayyed wondered if she would be beaten after he turned her down.

When the plates were cleared, Ivanov nudged Alisa out of the booth and ordered Svetlana to follow. He told the girls to go to the bar and order dessert. As they walked away, he slapped each girl on the ass. They turned around, one giving him a dirty look, the other pouting. Ivanov laughed at them and watched them hold hands all the way to the bar, and then as if a switch had been flicked, he turned all business. After whispering something in one of his bodyguards' ears, he plopped back into the booth and moved around so that he was sitting a mere foot from Sayyed. The drapes were pulled shut, and they were alone.

"You have been avoiding me."

He'd said it with a crooked smile, but that menacing glint in his eye was back. Sayyed deflected by saying, "I do not enjoy travel, and the cold weather is something my body is not used to. I meant no offense."

"Ah . . . I know what you mean. In the summer I find Damascus to be unbearable. But don't worry, I wasn't offended," Ivanov said, lying to himself more than Sayyed. "I just wish it hadn't taken this long. We have many important things to discuss."

"Yes, I know," Sayyed said, trying to be agreeable.

Ivanov took a gulp of wine and asked, "How long have we known each other?"

"A long time," Sayyed said, looking into his own glass. "Twelve years, I think."

"Thirteen, actually. And we have fucked with the Americans like no one else." Ivanov made a fist and shook it. "Every time they have tried to stick their nose in your business, we have sent them running away like a scared dog."

"That is true," Sayyed said, making no mention of all the times the Russians had stuck their long snouts into his business.

"And now they are back again."

Sayyed was still looking at the expensive French wine in his glass. He could feel Ivanov watching him with intensity. He shrugged and said, "Not really."

"That is not what I have heard."

"What have you heard?"

"I have heard you captured one of Langley's deep-cover operatives."

Sayyed's mind was swimming with thoughts of murder. The idiots in Damascus, no doubt, had passed the information to the Russian. Did anyone in his government know how to keep a secret? Knowing he was trapped, he said, "We caught one of them snooping around. I'm not sure he was an agent of any particular importance."

Ivanov smiled. "I think you are being modest."

Sayyed didn't know how to answer so he took a drink of wine.

"I am told this man worked in their Directorate of Operations. That he reported directly to Deputy Director Stansfield. That he worked in Berlin and Moscow for a time."

Someone in Damascus really did have a big mouth. "As you know from experience, these men are trained to lie. I cannot say with any certainty that his claims are truthful."

"They usually try to understate their importance, not overstate it."

That was true. "The important thing is that we have bloodied them yet again, and as you know, they do not have the stomach for this kind of thing."

Ivanov gave him a dubious look. "I'm not so sure these days."

Sayyed was. "Do not worry yourself with such little fish."

"This might be a bigger fish than you think," Ivanov said, with a hint of inside knowledge.

"What have you heard?"

"Things . . . rumors here and there. Nothing concrete, but I've been in this business long enough to smell a rat."

"What things?"

"Hamdi Sharif."

Sayyed thought of the recently deceased arms dealer. "Yes. I knew him well."

"Who do you think killed him?"

Sayyed had heard two rumors. "Mossad more than likely, but there was something else I picked up."

"What?"

Sayyed was not afraid to repeat the rumor. A man like Ivanov would take it as a compliment. "That he was stealing from you and you had him killed."

Ivanov looked at him with unblinking focus, but did not respond.

"If that was the case," Sayyed said, "then that was your right."

Ivanov shook his head. "If he was stealing from me I would have known, and I would have killed him. But he was not stealing from me."

"So it was the Jews."

"No . . . I don't think so."

"Who then?"

Ivanov sat brooding for a half minute and finally said, "I would like to speak to the American rat you are keeping in that basement in Beirut."

He had not told a soul in Damascus where he was keeping the CIA man, which meant either that Ivanov had obtained the information from one of Sayyed's supposed allies or that it was a good guess. Whichever was the case, he would need to move the American as soon as he got back. "You are more than welcome to speak to him. You are welcome in Beirut anytime. You know that."

Ivanov began shaking his head at the mention of Beirut. "I cannot. There are far too many things happening here in Moscow. Things that need my urgent attention."

Sayyed tried to deflect by saying, "So you think the Americans are trying to get back in the game?"

"I don't think so, I know so."

Sayyed looked skeptical. "How?"

"Because Thomas Stansfield is finally in charge of their clandestine activities."

"You think one man is capable of turning that mess around? They don't have the stomach to get back into Lebanon. This man I caught . . ."

Ivanov pounded his fist on the table, cutting him off. "Let me tell you something about Thomas Stansfield. I had to go up against him early in my career. The man plots on more levels than you or I are capable of comprehending. He is a master of deception operations. He gets you running around like a dog chasing your tail." Ivanov circled his hand around his wineglass faster and faster. "You become obsessed with traitors in your midst and you forget to do your job. You see shadows everywhere you turn, and you become completely defensive, and that is just one facet of the man. There is another side, where he is more Russian than American."

Sayyed had no idea what he meant. "More Russian than American?"

"He is the last of a breed of Americans who knew how to be every bit as dirty as the dirtiest enemy. Don't let his grandfatherly image deceive you. The man is a street fighter with a big set of Russian balls."

Sayyed wasn't sure why the man's balls were Russian. Beyond that, he thought Ivanov was overreacting. "The Americans haven't bitten back in years," Sayyed scoffed.

"I know, and that was because we had the CIA in a box and Stansfield didn't have the power. But he is in charge of their clandestine service now, and I'm telling you he is going to stick his nose in our business, and we can't allow that to happen. Trust me. If he gets so much as a toehold, we will be in for the fight of our lives."

Sayyed still wasn't convinced.

Ivanov leaned forward, then grabbed the Syrian's hand. "I am asking you this one time. I will only ask it once. Will you give me the American, so I can find out what he knows? I know your Iranian friends want him, but I will make sure you are compensated."

This was why Sayyed did not want to come to this godless frozen city. There was nothing in it for him, especially since he was not done dissecting the mind of Agent John Cummins. Unfortunately, there was no way out. If he did not bend to Ivanov's wishes, he might not make it out of the country in one piece. With a heavy sigh he told Ivanov that he could have the American.

CHAPTER 30

HAMBURG, GERMANY

THE Hamburg operation was significant for a number of reasons, not the least of which was that certain people began to take notice. A single murder can be an accident or an aberration. Two murders in as many weeks, separated by time, but connected by relationships, is a tough one to swallow for people whose job it is to be paranoid. The second reason it was significant was that Rapp finally realized Stan Hurley was extremely good at what he did. Hurley had given them five days to get their affairs in order. They were going on the road and would not be coming back to the States for several months.

The old clandestine officer announced with a gleam in his eye, "We've been kicked out of the office by management. They don't want to see us back in Washington until we have some results to show for all the money and time that's been spent on your sorry asses."

Rapp was not given all the details, but he got the distinct impression that Langley was upset about something. Hurley's attitude had changed even before they left the States. They were to engage the enemy and make them bleed, and the prospect of finally getting back in the game had transformed Hurley. This time Rapp and Richards went in together. Or at least their flights arrived the same afternoon. Rapp arrived second. He saw Richards waiting for him on the other side of Customs. Rapp was carrying an American passport on this trip, and he handed it to a nice-looking older gentleman, who flipped through the pages with German efficiency. The backpack, jeans, and beat-up wool coat must have been enough to tell the man he was not here on business, because he didn't ask that standard question, "business or pleasure." He applied the proper stamps and slid the passport back. Not a glance or a question. Rapp laughed to himself. If only it was always this easy.

The two men shook hands and made their way to ground transportation, where they took a cab to the harbor promenade or Landungsbrücken, as it was known to the locals. A big cruise ship was coming into port. Tourists lined the sidewalk gawking at the massive ship that looked completely out of place so close to all the old brick buildings. Rapp and Richards did not gawk. They were on the move toward the warehouse district, where Hurley was waiting for them.

They passed a prostitute working the riverfront. Richards turned to Rapp and said, "Isn't this where the Beatles got their start?"

Rapp cracked a small smile. He liked Richards. The guy was quirky in a normal way. They were in Hamburg to kill a man and Richards wanted to talk about the Beatles. "Never heard that," Rapp said.

"Pretty sure they did. They played some strip club for something like two months straight." Rapp didn't say anything. "I'd like to see it while we're here."

Rapp cocked his head and gave Richards a long look before he couldn't help himself and started laughing.

"What?" Richards asked.

Rapp lowered his voice and said, "We're here to kill a man, and you want to go hang out at some strip club where the Beatles played thirty years ago?"

"What's wrong with that? That we do what we do for a living doesn't mean we can't do what normal people do?"

Richards had a much easier time transitioning between their two worlds. "You have a point. I can't wait to see the look on Stan's face when you ask him."

"Ha . . . you watch. If it involves booze and strippers, my bet is he's all in."

"You're probably right."

The flat was located in one of the hundred-year-old warehouses that had been converted into condominiums near the river. It was damp and cold. A lot like London. Hurley informed them that the majority of the units in the building were as yet unsold. The one they were using was owned by an American company that had purchased it as an executive apartment. Rapp didn't concern himself with certain details beyond the target, but Richards was more curious. He tried to find out which American company the unit belonged to and if it was a former spook who let them use it. Hurley said if there was something he needed to know he'd tell him. "Otherwise . . . don't worry about it."

Rapp and Hurley hadn't exactly made peace. It was more of a truce. After the night he'd met George, or whatever his real name was, Rapp, Richards, and Hurley had gone back down to the lake house to begin prepping for the Hamburg operation. Hurley from time to time still looked at Rapp as if he were mentally retarded, but he had cut back on his yelling and cussing. Rapp took this as a sign of détente.

After five days Hurley asked Rapp to take a walk. "Have you gone over the last op in your head?"

"You mean Istanbul?"

"How many ops have you been on?" Hurley asked him with a wake-up expression on his face.

"Sorry," Rapp said. "Yeah . . . I've thought about it."

"Anything you would have done different?"

Rapp stared at the ground while they walked. "I'm not sure I know what you mean."

"The fact that you acted on your own is behind us. I already told you that. Part of my job is to make sure you get better. What I'm asking you is a tactical question. When you look back on what happened in the park that morning, once you decided to kill him, is there anything that you would have done different?"

"I don't know," Rapp answered honestly. "It all just kind of happened."

Hurley nodded, having been there before. "That's good and bad, kid. It might be that you're a natural at this. Ice in your veins, that kind of shit. Or . . . you got lucky. Only time will tell, but there's one thing you did that jumps out as being pretty stupid."

"What's that?" Rapp asked. Hurley had his full attention.

"I read the police report."

Rapp didn't know why he was surprised, but he was.

"The shot to the heart . . . it was point-blank. Literally. The report was conclusive. The muzzle of the weapon was in direct contact with Sharif's coat."

Rapp nodded. He was there. He remembered it well.

"Why would you do that?"

"Because I wanted to kill him."

Hurley stopped and faced him. "Kid, I've seen you shoot. You're not as good as me, but you're damn good and you keep getting better. You don't think you could have popped him from say ten feet?"

Rapp didn't answer.

"Why did you sit down next to him?"

"I'm not sure."

"Bullshit," Hurley said with a smile. "You allowed it to get personal, didn't you?"

Rapp thought back to that morning, not even a week ago. The feeling came back. That split-second decision to sit next to Sharif so he could look into his eyes. He slowly nodded. "Yeah . . . I guess I did."

Hurley's jaw tightened while he processed the admission. "I'm not going to stand here and tell you there haven't been times . . . times that I took a certain amount of joy in sending some of these scumbags to paradise . . . but you have to be really careful. Pick the right environment. Never in public like you did. He could have had a gun, somebody could have seen you sitting next to him . . . a lot of things could have gone wrong."

"I know."

"Remember, in public, the key is to look natural. That's why I showed you the shoulder holster technique. That's why we practice it. You look at your watch and no one thinks twice about it. You're a guy checking the time. You sit down on a park bench that close to another guy and someone might notice. Just enough to cause him to look twice, and that's all it might take. The next thing you know the carabinieri are chasing you down the street shooting at you." Hurley gave him a dead-serious look. "Trust me, I've been there." Hurley shuddered at the memory.

"What?" Rapp asked.

"You ever been to Venice?"

"Yeah."

"The canals." Hurley made a diving motion with his hands.

"You dove into one of those canals?" Rapp asked while recalling their putrid shade of green.

"And this was thirty years ago. They're a lot cleaner now than they were back then."

The condo was raw exposed brick with heavy timber beams secured to each other by sturdy iron brackets with big bolts. The floors were wide plank, more than likely pine, stained light to add a little brightness in contrast to the dark mud-red bricks. The furniture was utilitarian. Grays and blues. Wood and metal frames. Long sleek lines and the kind of fabrics that could be cleaned. Pure bachelor efficiency. It was a corner unit, so it had two small balconies, one off the master bedroom and another off the living room. There was a second bedroom and a loft space with a desk and pullout couch. When they arrived Hurley had everything prepared.

The dining-room table was covered with a sheet. Hurley carefully pulled it back to reveal what he'd pieced together in three short days. The target was a banker by the name of Hans Dorfman. He looked innocent enough, but then again, to Rapp, most bankers did. Dorfman's crime, as Hurley stated it, was that he'd decided to get into bed with the wrong people.

"You're probably wondering," Hurley asked, "why a well-educated man, who was raised a Christian, would decide to help a bunch of Islamic whack jobs wage terrorism."

Richards looked down at a black-and-white photo of the sixty-three-year-old banker and said, "Yep."

"Well, officially it's none of your goddamn business. When we're given an assignment it's not our place to question . . . right?"

Both Rapp and Richards gave halfhearted nods.

"Wrong," Hurley said. "I don't care what anyone tells you, HQ can fuck up and they can fuck up
big-time. Beyond that, you'll run into the occasional
yahoo who doesn't have a clue how things work
in the real world. When you get a kill assignment,
you'd better question it, and you'd better be damn
careful. We don't do collateral damage. Women and
children are strictly off limits."

Rapp had heard this countless times from Hurley and the other instructors. "But people make
mistakes."

"They do," he agreed, "and the more difficult
the job, the greater the chance that you'll make a
mistake, but if you want to make it out of this one
day with your soul intact, follow my advice on this.
Question the assignments they give you. We're not
blind—or robots."

Richards was still looking at the photo of the
banker. "Stan, are you trying to tell us this guy isn't
guilty?"

"This guy?" Hurley waved his right hand from
one side of the table to the other. "Hell no. This Nazi
piece of shit is guilty as hell. In fact, guys like this
piss me off more than the ones who shoot back. This
prick lives in his fancy house, takes two months off
every year, goes to the nicest places, and sleeps like a
fucking baby every night. He thinks it's no big deal
that he helps these scumbags move their money
around. No," he shook his head, "this is one of those
times when I will enjoy pulling the trigger."

CHAPTER 31

HURLEY explained to them that the process wasn't so much about finding the best option as it was eliminating the bad ones. That is, if you had the time to go through all the alternatives. After two days together, Hurley made the decision and they both agreed. Sunday night was the perfect time to make their move, and it would happen at the house. It was located thirty-five minutes outside of Hamburg, a nice wooded one-acre lot. Rapp was pretty sure Hurley had known from the get-go that this would be the appointed hour, but he wanted some pushback. He wanted Rapp and Richards to tear into his plans and make sure there wasn't a better time to go after Dorfman. For two days that's pretty much all Rapp and Richards did.

For Rapp, one of the more enlightening exchanges happened when he asked the salty Hurley, "What about the dogs?"

"Dogs," Hurley said with a devilish smile, "are a double-edged sword. Take this fuck stick, for example." Hurley pointed to Dorfman's black-and-white photograph. Hurley had taken a black marker and drawn a Hitler mustache on him the night before. "He's an anal-retentive Nazi prick if I've ever seen one. Wants complete order in his life, so he gets two poodles . . . why?" He looked at Rapp and Richards.

"Because they don't shed," Richards answered.

"Exactly. Hans is a neat freak. Wants everything just so . . . wakes up the same time Monday through Friday, and Saturdays and Sundays he allows himself one extra hour of sack time. He thinks he's too smart for the religion his parents raised him on, so on Sundays instead of going to church, he reads two or three newspapers, studies his Value Lines or whatever it is that a German banker studies, and he takes his dogs for a walk along the river and comes back and takes a nap. He has pot roast, mashed potatoes, and green beans for dinner, watches some crappy TV on the couch, and then lets the dogs out one last time at ten o'clock and then it's lights out."

Richards looked at the surveillance info. "How do you know all these details? I don't see any of it here."

Hurley smiled. "This isn't my first banker."

Rapp set that thought aside for a second and asked, "But what about the dogs?"

"Oh, yeah. The dogs. The dogs run the show. They need to be let out four times a day. Every morning at seven on the dot, a couple more times during the day, and then one more time before they turn in. What does he have to do every time before he lets them out?"

"Turn the alarm off," Rapp answered.

"You two see any alarms at the lake house?"

"No," Rapp answered.

"That's because they can make you lazy. You ever see me lock my hounds up?"

"No."

"What good does a dog do you if he's locked in his kennel?"

"If he's a guard dog, not much."

"That's right." Hurley looked at Rapp and said, "I bet I can guess your next question. You think we should take him while he's walking the dogs by the river?"

"The thought occurred to me."

"There's three reasons why I would prefer to avoid that option. The first is that it's harder to control things in a public setting. Not to say we couldn't do it. We might get lucky and have no witnesses like you did in Istanbul, but that can't be guaranteed. But two and three are why the park won't work. I need to talk to him and a public park is hardly the place for the kind of conversation we're going to have."

This came as a complete surprise to Rapp and Richards. Richards asked, "Why?"

"I'll explain it later."

"What's the third reason?" Rapp asked.

"We can't let anyone know he's dead before 9:00 A.M. Monday."

"Why?" Richards asked.

Rapp answered for him. "He'll tell us when we're done."

The Dorfman file was shredded and burned late Saturday night. By Sunday morning the ashes were cool enough that they could be scooped into a bag and thrown down the garbage chute. They spent two hours that afternoon sanitizing the condo. If they had to come back they could, but Hurley wanted to avoid doing so if possible. At eight in the evening they packed the last of the gear into the trunk of the rented four-door Mercedes sedan and left.

Rapp was the wheel man for the evening. Hurley and Richards were going in. It occurred to him that he was being punished for taking the initiative in Istanbul, but what could he say? Someone had to stay with the car. On the drive down the E22 Hurley went over the plan one last time. Every minute or so, he threw a question at Rapp or Richards asking them how they would react if this or that thing did not go as planned. Traffic was almost nonexistent, so they made it in just thirty minutes.

It was a dark, cold, windy night with temperatures expected to dip near freezing. They were all dressed in jeans and dark coats. Hurley and Richards also had black watch caps on their heads. The neighbor behind Dorfman was a widow with cats, but no dogs. The plan was to access his property from her backyard. At nine they did a final radio check and then at nine-fifteen Rapp turned the silver Mercedes onto the winding country road. The dome light was set to off. Rapp downshifted and coasted to a near stop several hundred feet from the widower's house. Richards and Hurley stepped from the slowly moving vehicle, carefully nudged their doors closed, and then disappeared into the trees. Rapp continued. A little less than a minute later he turned onto Dorfman's street and did a slow drive-by. The house was set back from the street about seventy-five feet. The front of the house was dark, but faint lights could be seen beyond what they knew was the living room and dining room.

Rapp pressed the transmit button on the secure Motorola radio, "All's clear up front."

Hurley and Richards found their way through the overgrown property of Dorfman's neighbor with relative ease. This was not Hurley's first trip, and he didn't feel the slightest bit guilty for not telling the new recruits. They did not need to know everything. He had personally put together the surveillance package on Dorfman eight months earlier. The stuff about the dogs he knew from many years of experience, and as far as bankers being anal retentive, it was a fairly accurate statement. The stuff about Dorfman having left the church that his parents raised him in and being a Nazi prick, he'd learned by keeping an eye on the man for close to two years.

To run an effective organization you need money. Hurley and Kennedy had been working overtime trying to map out how these various groups moved their money around the globe, and they had decided Dorfman was the key. In this, the ultimate asymmetric war, where they could not use even a fraction of the might of the United States military, they needed to get creative. If they couldn't openly bomb the terrorist training camps in the Bekaa Valley, then maybe there was another way to hurt them.

Hurley and Richards took up position near the back door at nine-thirty. If they had missed him somehow, Hurley was prepared to cut the phone line and break in. That option presented two problems, however. If he busted the door in, the security system would be tripped, and although an alarm would not be received at the monitoring station, the house's siren would begin to wail and would likely arouse the attention of one of the neighbors. Dorfman also owned a pistol, a shotgun, and a rifle. That Dorfman might react quickly enough to stop the intruders was unlikely, but Hurley didn't like unlikely.

The back light, above the kitchen door, was turned on at ten-oh-one. Hurley was crouched closest to the door on one knee and Richards was right behind him. From where he was positioned, Hurley could hear the chimes on the keypad as the digits were entered. The door opened, and the two standard poodles bounded out the door and onto the patio. Hurley had to trust Richards to do his job and stay focused on his. He sprang from his position and put his shoulder into the door before it could be closed. He hit it with enough force that it bounced back and hit an unsuspecting Dorfman in the face.

Over his shoulder he heard the dogs begin to growl. He grabbed the door by the edge and, looking through the glass, came face-to-face with a stunned Dorfman. The growling had turned to barking and Hurley resisted the urge to turn around to see how close they were to taking a bite out of his ass. Instead he pulled the door toward him and then smashed it into Dorfman's face. There was a scramble of nails and paws on the brick patio and then the welcome sound of compressed air forcing a projectile down a muzzle. One shot and then a second, each followed by short yelps and then some whimpering. Hurley saw the light switches to his left. There were three of them. He raked his silencer down the wall, knocking all three into the off position and relegating them to semidarkness. Quickly, he slid through the door, partially closed it, and stuffed the silencer into the shocked and open mouth of Dorfman.

CHAPTER 32

THE Mercedes was the same color and model as the one Dorfman drove. Rapp cruised the neighborhood listening to Hurley and Richards with one ear and the police scanner with the other. His German was nonexistent, but as Hurley had pointed out, the only thing he needed to listen for was a car being dispatched to Dorfman's address. No car was dispatched, so Rapp pulled the rented Mercedes into the driveway and turned around in the small car park so it was facing out. Hurley reasoned that if any of the neighbors saw the car they would assume it was Herr Dorfman's.

Rapp walked around the side of the house to the backyard and helped Richards carry the second poodle down to the basement. A small dart with red fins was still stuck in the animal's rib cage. It rose and fell with the animal's heavy breathing. Rapp had been tempted to say something to Hurley two days earlier when he informed them that they were going to use a tranquilizer gun to take out the dogs, but he kept his mouth shut. He knew that Hurley loved his dogs, but still, they were going to kill a man tonight. From a big-picture standpoint, it didn't make a lot of sense to him. Hurley's way was going to take a little more effort and would not silence the dogs as quickly. Hurley knew what Rapp was thinking and noted that the surveillance report said that the dogs usually barked when they were let out of the house. Especially at night. It wasn't as if they were storming a terrorist stronghold. It was just a German couple in their fifties, so Rapp kept his tactical opinion to himself.

Rapp was now looking down at one of the Germans. Frau Dorfman was blindfolded, gagged, hog-tied, and shivering from fright. He glanced at the knots Richards had made. They were well done. Her wrists and ankles were bound and attached with a length of rope. The only reason Rapp knew anything about them was that his little brother had been fascinated by many things as a child, but knots and magic were the two that became his passion. After their father died, Rapp saw it as his duty to take an interest in Steven's various hobbies, even if they weren't his.

The basement had been finished as a rec room with a bar and a small pool table. Richards had been nice enough to deposit the big German woman on an area rug. Rapp saw a blanket on the back of the couch. He grabbed it and paused. On the wall behind the couch was a poster-sized photo of Dorfman and his two dogs. He was holding a trophy and the two dogs were licking his face. Rapp covered the woman with the blanket. It was going to be a long night for her, and an even longer morning, but unlike her husband, she would live. Rapp grabbed the phone next to the couch and yanked the cord from the wall. He quickly coiled the cord around the phone as Richards reappeared from the utility room flashing him the all-clear sign. They were not to speak a word in front of the woman. Rapp climbed the stairs to the first floor, turned off the basement lights, and closed the door.

Per the plan, all of the lights had been turned off on the main floor except for the single light over the kitchen sink, as was the Dorfmans' habit upon going to bed. Rapp walked through the formal living room, past Richards, who was keeping an eye on the front of the house. The French doors that led to the study were cracked an inch. Rapp pulled his black mask down to cover his face, entered, and closed the door behind him. Dorfman was on the floor in his light blue pajamas. His comb-over hair was all askew and his nose was bleeding. A leather reading chair had been tossed to the side and the rug pulled back to reveal a floor safe.

Dorfman looked up at Rapp with tears in his eyes. Again, Rapp didn't understand German beyond a hundred-odd words, but he could tell the whimpering idiot was asking about his dogs and not his wife. Rapp looked around the office and counted no fewer than ten photos of his dogs. There was one five-by-seven of the wife and two kids that had to be fifteen years old. Rapp counted seven trophies and a dozen-plus ribbons.

Dorfman was still desperately asking about his "Hunde." Rapp raised his silenced Beretta and said, "Shut up!"

Hurley squatted down on his haunches and tapped the dial of the safe with the tip of his silencer. His German was perfect. He ordered Dorfman to open the safe. Dorfman closed his eyes and shook his head. They spoke for another twenty seconds, and still he refused. Hurley looked up at Rapp and said, "Go get his wife."

Rapp shook his head.

Hurley frowned.

"Let me take a shot at this. What do you say I grab one of your dogs and put a bullet in his head?" Rapp saw the flicker of recognition in the banker's eyes. "That's right, you idiot. I'm going to get one of your dogs and bring him up here." Rapp reached into his coat and pulled out a tactical knife. He bent over and stuck the tip in front of Dorfman's face. "I'll do you one better. I'm going to lay your *hund* at your feet and then I'm going to cut out one of his eyes and force-feed it to you."

"*Nein . . . nein.*" Dorfman looked truly frightened.

"If you don't open the safe, I'm going to start with your pooch's eyes, and then his tongue, and then his nose, and then his ears, and if you still haven't opened it by then, I'm going to shove all of it down your throat, and then I'll start in on the second dog, and if that doesn't get you to do it, then I'll start in on you."

Dorfman closed his eyes as tight as he could and shook his head in defiance.

Patiently waiting for Dorfman to decide to open the safe wasn't in the cards. Rapp flipped the knife up in the air and caught it, reversing his hold. He then slammed the tip of it down into Dorfman's thigh. The banker's entire body went rigid with pain and he opened his mouth to scream. Hurley gave him a quick backhanded chop to the throat, successfully choking off the shriek of agony.

Ten seconds passed before Dorfman was calm enough to talk to. "Last chance. Open the safe," Rapp said.

Dorfman was now slobbering, muttering something, and shaking his head.

"Fine," Rapp said as he moved to the door. "We'll do it your way." Rapp went back into the basement, turned on the light, and stood over the two poodles and the wife. He wasn't sure which one to grab, so he picked the one on the left. Rapp cradled it in his arms and went back to the office. Richards opened the door for him. Rapp gently laid the pooch at his master's feet. The sight of his precious dog in the arms of the masked maniac sent Dorfman into a near-apoplectic state. Hurley slapped him hard and once again pointed at the safe. At least this time Dorfman didn't shake his head.

Rapp retrieved his knife and held the tip in front of the dog's face. "Left eye or right eye? You choose."

Dorfman was now bawling like a child, reaching out for his dog.

Rapp wasn't sure he had the stomach for this, but what the hell else were they going to do? He glanced at Hurley, whose dark eyes, alert with uncertainty, framed by his ski mask, seemed to be pleading with him to stop. Rapp got the impression that Hurley would rather torture the banker than harm the dog. Rapp cradled the dog's head in his arms and slowly started moving the blade toward the poodle's left eye. He was within a centimeter of piercing the outer layer when Dorfman finally relented. He literally threw himself onto the safe and began spinning the dial. Rapp waited until he'd entered the correct combination and then released the dog. Dorfman crawled to his dog and pulled him in, kissing him on the snout and the top of his head.

"What the fuck," Rapp muttered to himself, and then asked Dorfman, "You care more about that damn dog than you do your wife . . . don't you?" Dorfman either didn't hear him or chose to ignore the question. Rapp looked at Hurley, who was emptying the contents of the safe.

"I told you," Hurley said as he pulled out three objects and held them up for Rapp to see. "An SS dagger and insignia. Nazi prick."

"A poodle-loving Nazi who helps terrorists. Great." Rapp started to raise his gun but stopped. "Is it in there?"

Hurley held up some files, computer disks, and an external hard drive. "I think so." He leafed through the files quickly. "Yep . . . it's all here. Jackpot!"

"Dorfman," Rapp said as he pointed his gun at the banker's head. "I bet if those damn terrorists were running around killing dogs you would have thought twice about helping them."

"Please," Dorfman said, "I am just a businessman."

"Who helps terrorists move their money around so they can target and kill innocent civilians."

"I know nothing of such things."

"You're a liar."

"That's for certain," Hurley said as he stood with the bag full of files and disks. He placed the rug back over the closed safe and while moving the chair back said, "You have their names, their accounts." Hurley shook the bag. "You knew exactly who you were dealing with."

"I was doing my job . . . for the bank."

"Like a good Nazi." Hurley gave him a big smile and pointed the Beretta at Dorfman's head. "And I'm only doing my job." Hurley squeezed the trigger and sent a single bullet into Dorfman's brain. The man fell back against the hardwood floor with a thump that was louder than the gunshot. A puddle of blood began to seep out in all directions. Hurley looked at Rapp and said, "Let's get the fuck out of here. We need to be in Zurich by sunrise."

"What's in Zurich?"

"Same thing that's always in Zurich . . . money and assholes."

CHAPTER 33

MOSCOW, RUSSIA

IVANOV carefully lowered himself into his chair at SVR headquarters in the Yasenevo District of Moscow. Last night had been a wild one. He had closed a very lucrative business deal. A group of foreign investors were looking to pick up some natural gas contracts and were willing to give Ivanov a seven-figure retainer and a nice piece of the action if he could guarantee the acquisition. Now all Ivanov had to do was talk some sense into one of his countrymen who had already made a nice profit on the fields. And if he couldn't talk some sense into him he would have Shvets and a crew of his loyal officers pay the man a call and make him an offer he couldn't refuse. Ivanov smiled as he thought of his favorite movie, *The Godfather*. He would very much like to meet Francis Ford Coppola someday. The man had captured the essence of power perfectly.

That was what Russia was all about in the wake

of the collapse of the Soviet Union. The two systems were not, at the end of the day, all that different from each other. Both were corrupt to the core, and both systems served to line the pockets of the powerful. Under the old Soviet system, the inefficiencies were ridiculous. People who had no business holding a position of authority did so often, and their inability to make smart decisions doomed the communist experiment from the start. There was no motivation for the talented to rise to the top. In fact, it could be said that there was the opposite motivation. If you dared criticize the foolish systems put into place by some imbecile who held a post because he was the brother-in-law of an important official, you were more likely than not to get your meager pay cut. Everyone wallowed in that subaverage world except the lucky few.

Today things were dynamic. Money was to be made everywhere, and lots of it. Start-up companies were popping up at an incredible rate and foreign investors were lining up to get into the game. The game, though, was a treacherous one. Remnants of the Soviet system were still in place, sucking off the system and causing a huge drain on the efficiency of the new economy. And then there were the corrupt courts, police, and security services. It was *The Godfather*, the Wild West, and 1920s gangster America all rolled into one.

These bankers and businessmen could either wallow in that inefficiency and red tape for months, costing them valuable time and money, or they could come to Ivanov and he could make their problems go away. Unlike the army of Jew lawyers who had descended on the city, who claimed they knew what they were doing, Ivanov could actually follow through on those claims and deliver real results to his new partners. And they were always partners. Depending on the deal, Ivanov would sometimes lower his fee, but never his percentage. The 10 percent ownership stake was non-negotiable.

He was not alone in this, and that was yet another parallel to the Academy Award–winning movie. There were others in Moscow and across the vast country who were doing the same thing, although, Ivanov would argue, not as well. Ivanov was not shy about touting the importance of his role in this brave new world, and defended it as a natural extension of his state security job. Someone needed to keep track of all these foreign investors and make sure they weren't stealing the Motherland's natural resources. After all, he was far more deserving of the profits than some twenty-five-year-old business-school graduate. At least that was what he told himself.

Shvets entered the office looking far too rested and handsome, which had the effect of worsening Ivanov's mood.

"Good morning, sir." Shvets remained standing. He knew better than to take a seat unless he was ordered.

"Get me some water," Ivanov grumbled.

While Shvets poured a glass he asked, "You look like you stayed out all night. Would you like some aspirin as well?"

"Yes." He snapped his long tanned fingers to spur his assistant to move faster. He could feel his headache passing from one temple to the other and then swinging back, as if he were being scanned by an irritating beam. He downed the three pills and the water. For a split second he thought of adding vodka. It would definitely help with the headache, but it was too early to surrender. Shvets and the new breed would take it as a sign of weakness.

"I heard you got them to agree in principle to the partnership."

"Yes," Ivanov moaned.

"Would you like me to have Maxim bring the contracts over?"

"Yes . . . and so, I want to know when you are leaving for Beirut and who you're bringing with you."

"Tomorrow, and I'm bringing Alexei and Ivan."

Ivanov thought about that. Alexei and Ivan were two of his best. Former Spetsnaz, they'd fought with valor and distinction in Afghanistan but had gotten in trouble when their regiment's political officer had turned up with his throat cut one morning. They had more than likely done it. Political officers were notorious for being assholes, and in those final days of the USSR more than a few of them simply disappeared. Ivanov was always looking for men who were good with their hands, and these two were better than good. "Why Alexei and Ivan?"

"Because they're from Georgia and they look like they could be Lebanese."

That was true, but Ivanov didn't like having his two best gunmen leaving his side. In Moscow these days, the only thing you could count on was that sooner or later someone would try to take you out. It was just like the American mobsters. The vision of Sonny Corleone being mercilessly gunned down at the tollbooth, betrayed by his own brother-in-law, the snake, sent chills down Ivanov's back. He shuddered and then decided he would keep Alexei and Ivanov close. They were his Luca Brasi times two. "Take Oleg and Yakov."

Shvets frowned.

"Why can't you just follow my orders?"

In a calm voice, Shvets said, "When have I once failed to follow your orders?"

"You know what I mean. Your face. I am in no mood for it this morning." Ivanov lowered his big head into his hands and groaned.

"I might as well go by myself."

"That is a brilliant idea. Travel to the kidnapping capital of the Mediterranean by yourself so they can snatch you off the street and hold you for ransom. Brilliant!"

"Is it my fault that you stay out drinking and screwing until sunrise?"

"Don't start."

"I am half your age, and I can't keep up with you."

"You are half my size, too, so we're even."

"You need to slow down or there will be problems."

Ivanov's head snapped up. "Is that a threat?"

"No," Shvets said, shaking his head, with a pathetic disappointment in his boss. *Why must my loyalty always be questioned?* "I am talking about your health. You need to take some time off. Go someplace warm. Maybe come to Beirut with me."

"Beirut is a hellhole. It was once a great place . . . not anymore. You will see."

"I heard it's coming back."

"Ha," Ivanov laughed. "Not the part where you'll be going. The famous Green Line looks like Leningrad in 1941. It's a bombed-out shell. Our friends are trying to reconstitute it before the Christians take it over. It is not a nice place."

Before Shvets could respond there was a knock on the office door. It was Pavel Sokoll, one of Ivanov's deputies, who worked exclusively on state security financial matters. And if his ghostly complexion was any hint, he was not here to bring glad tidings. "Sir," Sokoll's voice cracked a touch. It did that when he was afraid he was going to upset Ivanov. "We have a problem."

"What kind of problem, God dammit?"

Sokoll started to explain, and then stopped, and then started again when he realized there was no good way to spin the bad news. "We have certain accounts that we use to move money overseas. For our various activities, that is."

"I'm not an idiot, Sokoll. We have accounts all over the place. Which ones are you talking about?"

"The ones in Zurich . . . specifically the ones"— he glanced at his notes—"at SBC." He closed the file and looked at his boss.

Ivanov glared at the pasty man. They had 138 accounts with the Swiss Bank Corporation. "Which accounts, dammit!"

Sokoll opened the file again. Rather than trying to read the numbers, which even he didn't understand, he reached across the desk and handed the paper to his boss.

Ivanov looked down at the list of accounts. There were six, and he was intimately familiar with whom they belonged to. "What am I supposed to learn from this? There is nothing. Just account numbers."

"Actually, sir"—Sokoll pointed nervously at the sheet—"on the far side those are the balances of each account."

Ivanov's eyes nearly popped out of his head. "This says these accounts are empty!"

"That's right, sir."

"How?" Ivanov yelled as he jumped to his feet.

"Swiss Interbank Clearing executed the order at nine-oh-one Zurich time this morning. The money was emptied out of these accounts electronically."

"I know how it works, you fucking moron, where did it go?"

"We don't know, sir."

Ivanov made a fist, as if he might come over the desk and bash his deputy over the head. "Well, find out!"

"We can't," Sokoll said, fearing for his life. "Once the money is gone, it is gone. There is no way to trace it. Swiss banking laws—"

"Shut up, you fool," Ivanov yelled. "I am well

aware of Swiss banking laws, and I don't give a shit. You'd better find a way around them or you are going to be either dead or looking for a job."

Sokoll bowed and left without saying another word.

The vodka was on the sidebar. It was always on the sidebar. Five different kinds. Ivanov could barely see, his head hurt so much, and he really didn't care which bottle he was grabbing, vodka was vodka at this point. He poured four fingers into a tall glass, sloshing a bit over the side. He took a huge gulp, clenched his teeth, and let the clean, clear liquid slide down his throat. No one was supposed to know about those accounts, let alone have the ability to drain them of their funds. This could seriously jeopardize his standing within not just the Security Service but the entire government as well. It could potentially destroy all of his investments. Without the power that came with his office, he would be worthless to his partners. The long list of enemies that he'd made over the years would think nothing of coming after him. His hand started to shake.

Shvets finally asked, "How much money?"

Ivanov had to take another drink to gain the courage to speak the number. "Twenty-six million dollars . . . roughly."

"And it belonged to . . . ?"

It took Ivanov a moment to answer. "Our friends in Beirut."

Shvets thought of the different militant terrorist groups. "Their money or ours?"

"Both . . ."

"Both?"

"Yes! Think of it as a joint venture."

"We invested money with those zealots?" Shvets asked, not bothering to hide his surprise.

"It's control, you idiot. I don't even know why I bother explaining sometimes. We put in money so we would have a say in how it was used. Think of it as foreign aid." It was more complicated than that, but Ivanov didn't have the time or clarity of mind to explain the complicated arrangement this morning. Or the fact that approximately ten million of it was KGB money that had been siphoned off over the years.

"Foreign aid to terrorists? Lovely."

"Stop with your judgments. You know nothing. They put money in the accounts as well. In fact, most of it was theirs." Ivanov had helped them find new revenue streams by peddling black market items such as drugs, guns, and porn. The drugs and guns were shipped all over the Middle East and North Africa and the porn was smuggled into Saudi Arabia.

"If the majority of the money was theirs, why did we have control of it?"

Ivanov gave an exasperated sigh as it occurred to him that he would have to go upstairs and tell the director. He tolerated these side business deals, but only to a point. This he would not like very much. In fact, there would be a great deal of suspicion that Ivanov had stolen the money for himself, if for no other reason than that they could all imagine themselves doing it.

Shvets repeated his question, and Ivanov said, "It was part of the deal. If they wanted our help, we wanted to know what they were doing with it, and we wanted them to put their own funds in as well." It was only a half truth, but Ivanov did not feel the need to go into details with one of his deputies.

"I'm assuming the twenty-six represents the bulk of their assets."

"Yes." Ivanov took another gulp. The vodka was starting to lubricate the gears in his brain. He began to make a list in his head of who he would need to talk to.

"Who had access to the account information and pass codes?"

"They did and I did. Any withdrawal of more than twenty-five thousand had to be authorized by each of us separately."

"So you had one pass code and they had the other?"

"Yes." Shvets was asking too many questions.

"Who had access to both sets of pass codes?"

"No one." The headache was starting to come back, although this time it was in his neck. He began rubbing the muscles with his left hand while he took another drink of vodka. "It was intentionally set up so that neither party would have both pass codes."

Shvets considered that for a moment and then said, "Someone had to have both codes. Someone at the bank. How else could the codes be verified and the money moved?"

Ivanov stopped rubbing his neck. Why hadn't

he come to the same conclusion sooner? "Dorf-man."

"Who?"

"The banker." Ivanov looked up Dorfman's office number and punched it in as fast as his fingers could move. It took more than two minutes, three people, and a string of threats to get an answer that told him things were not good. Dorfman had not shown up for work, and they had been unable to reach him. Ivanov hung up the phone and laid his head down on the desk.

Shvets opened the office door and asked the secretary to bring them coffee. He then walked over to the desk and took the glass of vodka. Ivanov tried to stop him.

"This is not helping," Shvets said in a paternal voice. "I am tied to you whether I like it or not, and if we are going to avoid being interrogated by our colleagues in the Federal Security Service, we need to clear your head and get you thinking straight."

Ivanov's entire body shuddered at the thought of the FSS goons dragging him into the basement of Lubyanka, the once-feared grand headquarters of the KGB. He knew all too well what went on in those prison cells in the basement, and he would kill himself before he ever allowed that to happen.

CHAPTER 34

SOUTHERN GERMANY

THE trip was uneventful, in the sense that they pointed the hood of the big Mercedes south and stopped only twice before reaching the Swiss-German border. For eight hours they cruised at an average speed of 120 kilometers an hour down the smooth, twisting autobahn. Near some of the larger towns they had to slow, and when they neared the mountains to the south the winding, rising road slowed their progress only slightly. They were thankful that there was no snow.

They skirted Hannover, Kassel, Frankfurt, Strasbourg, and a blur of other towns, while Hurley pored over the treasure trove of information he'd retrieved from the banker's safe. Richards fired up the laptop and used the decoding software to uplink the information on Dorfman's disks via the satellite phone. Kennedy had a team assembled in D.C. who were translating and filtering the information.

Richards was done sending the information by the time they reached Kassel. He slept for the next two hours. Rapp listened to the snippets of conversation coming from the backseat and wondered what the next move would be. Hurley liked to operate on a strictly need-to-know basis, and Rapp and Richards rarely needed to know, at least as far as Hurley was concerned.

Halfway through the trip, Hurley ordered Rapp to pull over and switch with Richards. They topped off the gas, used the men's room, and Hurley bought coffee and some snacks for him and Richards. Rapp didn't mind driving but Hurley was insistent. An hour or two of downtime was crucial. One never knew when things would get interesting. As was often the case, though, Hurley did not listen to his own advice and continued to work at a feverish pace. Rapp climbed into the backseat, and after a few minutes of silence he asked Hurley, "What are we doing?"

Uncharacteristically, Hurley laughed. "I'll explain before we cross the border. Right now I need to figure this shit out."

It occurred to Rapp that the man was punch-drunk, but he didn't dwell on it. Within minutes the hum of the tires rolling at high speed on the concrete surface of the autobahn sent Rapp into a trance. He rolled up his jacket, wedged it in between the door frame and his head, and fell asleep. For the next few hours he drifted in and out of sleep, the shrill ring of the satellite phone interrupting dreams of poodles, bad comb-over hairdos, and trussed-up, plump

German women. At one point he was drifting off to sleep and wondered what Frau Dorfman would do with the dogs now that her husband was not of this world. For some reason that made him think of the expanding pool of blood under Dorfman's head. How far had it stretched? Would it begin to dry in the arid winter air? How much blood was actually in a human head? One pint? Before he could decide on an amount he drifted off.

Hurley never slowed. He reviewed every document, every file, Post-it note, and receipt. He'd filled close to an entire notepad with the most pertinent information. At 5:00 A.M., they stopped at a roadside motel outside Freiburg and got two connecting rooms, where they cleaned up and changed into suits and ties for the border crossing. Hurley ordered them to pack their weapons in the hidden compartments inside their suitcases. By six they were back on the road with fresh coffee and rolls. And Hurley was ready to explain what they were doing. Unfortunately, he chose the wrong military campaign to illustrate his point.

"You two familiar with Sherman's march to the sea?"

Rapp was behind the wheel. Having been raised in northern Virginia, he didn't really consider himself a Southerner, but he was a proud Virginian, and that meant he knew his Civil War history. To a true Southerner like Richards, who had been raised in Covington, Georgia, the mere mention of William Tecumseh Sherman was enough to start a fight.

"Total war," Hurley said. "Just like Sherman. If

our enemy won't come out and meet us on the field of battle, we need to bring the war to their doorstep. We need to destroy their capacity to fight. We need to spook them into maneuvering in the open so we can crush them."

Rapp could see both men's faces in the rearview mirror. Hurley was oblivious to the revulsion on Richards's face.

"Are you trying to tell me," Richards said, "that we're Sherman?"

"I sure as hell hope so," said Hurley, in a state of near elation. "He won, didn't he?"

Rapp couldn't take it anymore and started laughing.

"What the hell's so funny?" Hurley asked.

When he got control of himself he said, "You're sitting next to one of Georgia's finest. It's like singing the praises of Andrew Jackson to a bunch of Indians."

"Oh," Hurley said as he realized his mistake. "No offense intended. We'll have to debate that one over beers one night. Sherman was a badass." Throwing him a bone, he added, "And Lee and Jackson were two battlefield geniuses. Can't deny that." Then he changed tactics and asked, "You've hunted birds, right?"

"Yeah."

"Why do you bring a dog into the field?"

"To get the birds up."

"Exactly," Hurley said. "These guys have done a damn good job keeping their heads down the past ten years while Langley's been focused on Central America and avoiding those dickheads up on Capitol Hill. I told you about our operative that got snatched off the streets of Beirut a few months back . . . well, that's not the first time that's happened. We got soft in the eighties and let these assholes get away with way too much shit." Glancing at Rapp's face in the mirror, he said, "April of '83 our embassy gets hit . . . sixty-three people killed. Langley lost eight of its best people that day, including our Near East director and station chief." Hurley left out the fact that he had been in the city that day. That he could have easily been one of the victims. He also left out the fact that Kennedy's dad was one of the men they'd lost. It was not his place to share something so personal. If she wanted to tell them one day, that was her business. "Our response . . . we send in the Marines. October of '83 the Marines and French forces get hit by a couple of truck bombs. Two hundred and ninety-nine men wasted, because a bunch of fucking diplomats conned the command element into thinking too much security would send the wrong message. Mind you, not a single one of those dilettante pricks ever spent a day in that godforsaken city. Our response after the barracks bombing . . . we say we're not going to leave, we drop a few bombs, and we leave."

Hurley swore to himself. "And they get it in their heads that they can fuck with us and get away scot-free. March of '84 they grab my old buddy Bill Buckley, our new station chief, Korean and Vietnam War vet. Amazing guy." Hurley looked out the window for a moment with sadness in his eyes. "They tortured him for almost a year and a half. Flew him over to Tehran. The bastards taped it. I've seen parts." Hurley shook his head as if trying to get rid of a bad thought. "They sucked every last drop of information out of him, and then they sold it to the Russians and anyone else who was interested. Bill knew a lot of shit. The info they got from him did a boatload of damage. I can't even begin to tell you how many nights I've lain awake wondering how I would have handled it. They brought in a so-called expert. A Hezbollah shrink by the name of Aziz al-Abub. Trained by the Russians at the People's Friendship University. The names these assholes come up with just boggles the mind. Al-Abub pumped him full of drugs and poked and prodded. The word is he had two assistants who helped him. They turned it into a real science project. Bill's heart eventually gave out, but not before they extracted some of our most closely held secrets.

"One by one assets started to disappear. Highly placed sources in governments around the region and beyond, and how did we react? We didn't do jack shit, and the result was they became more emboldened. Qaddafi, that quack, then decides to plant a bomb in a disco in Berlin, and finally we decide to hit back and drop a few bombs on his head. Unfortunately, we missed, and then in July of '88 that cowboy captain of the *Vincennes* decides he's going to start racing all over the Strait of Hormuz chasing ten-thousand-dollar fiberglass gunboats with a half-billion-dollar Aegis guided missile cruiser."

Hurley had to stop and close his eyes as if he still couldn't believe that ugly piece of history.

Rapp finished it for him. "Iran Air Flight 655. Two hundred and ninety civilians."

"Yep," Hurley said, realizing that having lost his girlfriend later that same year, Rapp would know the story. "Not our proudest moment. I don't care what anyone tries to tell you, that one was our fault. Instead of owning up to it, and using it as an opportunity to show the Iranian people that we weren't out to get them, we denied the entire thing. Went so far as to blame it on them. Now, they weren't without fault, but that captain had two choppers on board to deal with those gunboats. The strength of the Aegis cruiser is distance. You don't close with the enemy to use your World War II–era guns. If there's really a threat, you back off and fire one of your missiles."

"And that's what led us to Pan Am Lockerbie," Rapp said.

Hurley nodded. "It's a little more complicated than that, but in a nutshell . . . yeah."

"So," Richards said, "we fit in how?"

"Let's just say some people in Washington have seen the error of their ways. This terrorism, especially the Islamic radical shit, has some people spooked, and it should. They saw what happened last time when we allowed someone like Buckley to get snatched without lifting a finger. It gives people the wrong idea. Now the Schnoz has been grabbed, and it's starting all over again. I'm not supposed to tell you guys this, but what the fuck . . . five of our sources have been killed in just the last few months. We've had to recall another dozen-plus. We're flying blind. And once again, by doing nothing, we've reinforced the idea that they can do whatever they want to us, and we won't lift a finger."

"And the stuff you've been working on all night. How does that fit in?" Rapp asked.

"Let's suppose for a second that you have five million dollars sitting in a Swiss bank account. That money represents years of extortion, drug and gun running, counterfeiting, and a host of illegal scams. You've worked yourself to the bone squirreling away this money. What would you do, if you woke up one morning and found out that account, your account, was empty?"

Rapp looked at the winding road and said, "I'd flip."

"You think you might pick up the phone and start demanding some answers?"

"Yeah."

"Damn right you would. Right now these pricks are sleeping soundly in their beds, thinking their money is safe in Switzerland. At some point in the next twenty-four hours they're going to find out that their ill-gotten gains have vanished, and they are going to pick up the phone and they are going to go absolutely apeshit. And when they do"—Hurley pointed skyward—"we will be listening."

CHAPTER 35

ZURICH, SWITZERLAND

A s promised by Hurley, the border crossing was uneventful: dour, serious Anglos in nice suits, in a nice car, crossing from one efficient European country into an even more efficient European country. They continued to wind their way toward the banking capital of the world as the sun climbed in the sky and Hurley explained in more detail what they were up to. After another forty minutes they arrived on the outskirts of Zurich. Hurley told Rapp which exit to take, and where to turn. A few minutes later they pulled up to the gates of an estate.

"What's this, an embassy?" Rapp asked.

"No," Hurley said, smiling. "The home of an old friend."

The car had barely come to a stop when the heavy black-and-gold gate began to open. Rapp eased the sedan slowly up the crushed-rock drive. The garden beds were bare and the manicured arborvitae wrapped in burlap to protect them from the heavy, wet snows that were common this time of year. The place must have been magnificent in the summer. The house reminded him of some of the abodes of foreign ambassadors that dotted the countryside west of D.C. Hurley had him pull the car around the back, where one of six garage doors was open, the stall empty, anticipating their arrival.

Carl Ohlmeyer was waiting for them in his library. The man was tall, thin, and regal. At first glance, he was more British-looking than German, but his thick accent washed that thought from Rapp's mind almost as quickly as it had appeared. He was dressed impeccably in a three-piece suit. Hurley had given them the man's brief history. They had met in their twenties in Berlin. Ohlmeyer had been fortunate enough to survive World War II, but unfortunate in that his family farm was twenty-one miles east of Berlin rather than west. He had received his primary education at the hands of Jesuit priests, who had drilled into him the idea that God expected you to better yourself every day. Luke 12:28 was a big one: "For of those to whom much is given, much is required." Since Ohlmeyer was a gifted mathematician, much was expected of him. When he was sixteen the Russian tanks came down the same dirt road that the German tanks had gone down only a few years before, but going in the opposite direction, of course. And with them, they brought a cloud of death and destruction.

Two years later he enrolled as a freshman at the prestigious Humboldt University in the Russian-controlled sector of Berlin. Over the next three years he watched in silence as fellow students and professors were arrested by the Russian secret police and shipped off to Siberia to do hard time for daring to speak out against the tenets of communism. The once-grand university, which had educated statesmen like Bismarck, philosophers like Hegel, and physicists like Einstein, had become nothing more than a rotted-out shell.

Buildings that had been partially destroyed during the war sat untouched the entire time he was there. All the while in the West, the Americans, British, and French were busy rebuilding. Ohlmeyer saw communism for the sham that it was—a bunch of brutes who seized power in the name of the people, only to repress the very people they claimed to champion. Hurley recited for them Ohlmeyer's stalwart claim that *any form of government that required the repression, imprisonment, and execution of those who disagreed with it was certainly not a government of the people.*

But in those days following the war, when so many millions had been killed, people were in no mood for another fight. So Ohlmeyer kept quiet and bided his time, and then after he received his degree in economics, he fled to the American sector. A few years later, while he was working at a bank, he ran into a brash young American who hated the communists even more than he did. His name was Stanley Albertus Hurley, and they struck up a friendship that went far beyond a casual contempt for communism.

Ohlmeyer, upon seeing Hurley, dropped any pretense of formality and rushed out from behind his desk. He took Hurley's hand in both of his and began berating his friend in German. Hurley gave it right back. After a brief exchange, Ohlmeyer looked at the other two men and in English said, "Are these the two you told me about?"

Hurley nodded. "Yep, these are Mike and Pat."

"Yes . . . I'm sure you are." Ohlmeyer smiled and extended his hand, not believing their names were Mike and Pat for a second. "I can't tell you how exciting it is to meet you. Stan has told me you are two of the best he has seen in years." Ohlmeyer instantly read the looks of surprise on the faces of the two young men. With mock surprise of his own, he turned to Hurley and said, "Was I not supposed to say anything?"

Hurley looked far from enthused over his friend's talkativeness.

"You will have to excuse my old confidant," Ohlmeyer said, putting a hand on Hurley's shoulder. "He finds it extremely difficult to express feelings of admiration and warmth. That way he doesn't feel as bad when he beats you over the head."

Rapp and Richards started laughing. Hurley didn't.

"Please make yourself comfortable. There is coffee and tea and juice over there on the table and fresh rolls. If you require anything else, do not hesitate to ask. Stan and I have some work to do, but it shouldn't take too long, then I suggest all of you get some sleep. You will be staying for dinner tonight . . . no?" Ohlmeyer turned to Hurley for the answer.

"I hope."

"Nonsense. You are staying."

Hurley hated to commit to things. "I'd like to, but who knows what might pop up after this morning?"

"True, and I will have my plane ready to take you wherever you need to go tomorrow morning. You are staying for dinner. That is final. There is much we need to catch up on, and besides, I need to tell these two young men of our exploits."

"That might not be such a good idea."

"Nonsense." Ohlmeyer dismissed Hurley's concern as completely inconsequential. He looked down at the briefcase in Hurley's hand. With a devilish look he asked, "Did you bring the codes?"

"No . . . I drove all the way from Hamburg just so I could stare at your ugly mug. Of course I brought them."

Ohlmeyer started laughing heartily before turning to Rapp and Richards. "Have you ever met a grumpier man in your entire life?"

"Nope," Rapp said without hesitation, while Richards simply shook his head.

While Rapp and Richards retired to the other end of the forty-foot-long study to get some food, Ohlmeyer and Hurley were joined by two men whom Rapp guessed to be in their midforties. They looked like businessmen. Probably bankers. The four of them huddled around Ohlmeyer's massive desk while the silver-haired German issued explicit instructions in German. Forty minutes later the two men left, each carrying several pages of instructions.

At nine-oh-five they received the anticlimactic call that the seventeen accounts had been drained of all funds, but that was just the beginning. Over the next three hours the computers continued to execute transfers. Each account was divided into three new accounts and then split again by three, until there were 153 new accounts. The money had been flung far and wide, from offshore accounts in Cyprus, Malaysia, and Hong Kong, and across the Caribbean. Each transfer ate away at the balance as the various banks charged their fees, but Hurley didn't care. He was playing with someone else's money. The important thing was to leave a trail that would be impossible to untangle. With all the different jurisdictions and separate privacy laws, it would take an army of lawyers a lifetime to slash through the mess. By noon the number of accounts had shrunk to five with a net balance of $38 million.

CHAPTER 36

BEIRUT, LEBANON

SAYYED'S lungs and thighs ached as he climbed the crumbling concrete stairs. His week had gone from miserable to intolerable, starting with his trip to Moscow and ending with his superiors in Damascus issuing one of the most idiotic orders he had received in all of his professional career. With the cease-fire finally looking as if it was going to take hold, the cursed Maronites had decided to accelerate their land grab. Their focus, it appeared, was the historically important area known as Martyrs' Square in Beirut's Central District. Damascus ordered Sayyed to get to the square, plant his flag, and plant it as quickly as possible. Like some battlefield general who had been ordered to hold a piece of land at all costs and then given no support, Sayyed was left to sort out the how.

Fifteen years in this city had taught him the importance of keeping a healthy distance between himself and the other factions. Rifles and machine guns were nasty things, and placed in the hands of teenage boys they were extremely unpredictable. The idea of taking up one side of the square while the Maronites grabbed the other made his skin crawl. One errant shot, one young, crazy Eastern Catholic, who wanted to avenge the death of a brother or the rape of a sister, could plunge the entire city back into war. Orders, unfortunately, were orders, and as much as he would have liked to, he could not ignore them. So Sayyed sent Samir and Ali to choose an adequate building. And while he was contemplating how to fill it with enough men to deter the Maronites, he was struck with an ingenious solution.

Shvets would be coming from Moscow to collect the CIA agent in just a few days. That would leave him with the American businessman Zachary Austin. He was not an agent of any sort, Sayyed was sure of that. The only question that remained was how much they could get for him, and how that money would be split with that fool Abu Radih. The Fatah gunman had been crying like a little girl over the fact that he'd been forced to surrender the telecommunications executive. If Sayyed brought him in, it would be seen as a great gesture of maturity and goodwill by the others. And maybe he could negotiate it in such a way that he could get the Fatah rats to come hold the entire western end of the square.

The two had sat down over tea the previous afternoon. Radih had brought no fewer than twelve men—a ridiculous number for the current level of tension. Sayyed first explained the situation with the Maronites moving into Martyrs' Square. He was hoping that the emotionally charged piece of land would spur Radih to action, and he was not disappointed. The man was so eager to show his passion for the cause that he leaped at the chance to hold the western half of the square. Without so much as seeking a concession in return, he pledged fifty men to the operation.

The number surprised even Sayyed, and he was tempted to hold back his offer to hand over the American. Radih was an emotional fool to commit so much without gaining a single concession, but Sayyed had a problem. He couldn't very well hold the west side of the square and leave the two Americans in the basement of the office over on Hamra Street with only a few men guarding them. He had served three years in the army before joining the General Security Directorate, and he recalled something they'd told him in infantry school about consolidating your forces. It would be for only a few days, until the Russians could pick up the CIA spy. After that, Sayyed didn't really care what happened to the businessman, just so long as he got his share of the ransom.

Sayyed looked across the small bistro table and said, "I have finished interrogating the businessman from Texas."

"So is he a spy?" Radih asked.

"No. I am certain he is in fact a businessman."

"Good. Then I can commence negotiations for his release."

Sayyed did not speak. He waited for Radih to make him an offer—the same arrangement they'd had in the past.

"I will guarantee you 20 percent of the ransom."

Sayyed was tempted to ask for fifty. The others would likely back him, but he needed Radih's help with the Maronite problem. "I think thirty would be fair . . . considering everything else." Before Radih could counter, Sayyed said, "I will bring him to the new building tonight along with the other American. It can be your new command post for a few weeks." It was an honor Radih would never be able to refuse. He would be considered the vanguard in the struggle to reclaim the city from the Christians.

The building itself would have to eventually be destroyed. It listed at a five-degree angle toward the square and looked as if a strong wind might topple all seven stories into the street, but it was built out of sturdy concrete and would have to be blown up before it would fall. Of all the buildings that bordered the square it was perhaps the second-strongest position. Unfortunately, the Maronites had the best position, no more than three hundred feet directly across from them.

Radih had already made one mistake, and Sayyed blamed himself for it. The self-promoter had left his sprawling slums near the airport in a ten-vehicle convoy and arranged for the peasants to send him and his men off as if they were valiant Muslims on a mission to evict the Crusaders. Instead of a quiet arrival, they had pulled into the square flying the bright yellow Fatah flag. The chances for escalation were now ripe.

That was not Sayyed's preference. The last thing he needed with Shvets coming to pick up the CIA man was open conflict. The prisoners had arrived the previous evening, transferred in just two cars. The proper way. Very low-key. And then for the next few hours, men and supplies were slowly transferred over from the office on Hamra Street. They had successfully moved the bulk of their stuff without tipping their hand, and then in one fell swoop, with a gesture of egotistical grandeur, Radih had announced to the entire city that they were staking out their turf. While that might accomplish the short-term goals of Damascus, it also might plunge the city back into chaos.

As Sayyed reached the roof, he realized that it also might get him killed. He peered around the corner with his left eye and looked across the street. The Maronite building was one story taller, and with a glance he counted no fewer than five heads and three muzzles along the roof line. It had just been reported to him that they were filling sandbags and barricading the windows and doors on the first floor. Of course they were. That's what he would do, and was in fact doing. It would be really nice if they could get through this little standoff without a shot being fired, because if just one shot was fired, the entire square would erupt in a fusillade of lead projectiles. He'd seen it happen before. Literally thousands of rounds would be exchanged in minutes. He would have to remember to tell the men to keep their weapons on safe.

Sayyed found Samir around the other side of the blockhouse at the top of the building. It was the place most shielded from the position across the street. Samir handed Sayyed the satellite phone that Ivanov's effeminate deputy had given him before Sayyed left Moscow. "Hello," he said as he placed it to his ear.

"My friend, how are things?"

Sayyed frowned. It was Ivanov, and he sounded as if he was drunk. It was only midafternoon. "Fine," Sayyed said, as he stole a quick look around the corner. The sun had reflected off something across the street, and he got the horrible feeling it was the front end of a sniper's scope.

"How are things in your fine city?"

Sayyed pulled the phone away from his ear and looked at it with skepticism. Something was wrong with Ivanov. The man hated Beirut. He sighed and put the phone back to his ear. "A little tense at the moment, but nothing I can't handle."

"What is wrong?"

"Just a land grab by one of the other militias. It has created a bit of a standoff."

"Fellow Muslims?"

"No," Sayyed said, irritated by the implication. Ivanov liked to get drunk and lecture him on history. Specifically, that Muslims loved nothing more than to kill each other, and the only time they stopped killing each other was when they decided to kill Jews, Hindus, or Christians. "Maronites."

"Ah . . . the wood ticks of the Middle East. Haven't you been trying to exterminate them for a thousand years?"

"What do you want?"

"My package," Ivanov said, slurring the words. "Is it ready? You haven't decided to negotiate with the Persians, have you?"

"I am standing by our deal. When can I expect it to be retrieved? I assume you are still sending someone."

"Yes . . . although I am considering coming myself." There was a long pause and then, "You did offer . . . didn't you?"

"Oh," Sayyed said, surprised that Ivanov was taking him up on his insincere offer. "Absolutely."

"Good. I will be there in three days. Maybe sooner."

"Fantastic," Sayyed lied. "I will have everything prepared. I must go now. There is something urgent I need to attend to. Please call if you need anything else." Sayyed punched the red button and disconnected the call. He looked around the desolate landscape, with its pancaked and shelled-out buildings, and wondered how he could ever play host to Ivanov in this pile of rubble.

Then as he turned to go down the stairs he came face-to-face with Imad Mughniyah, the coleader of Islamic Jihad. Mughniyah, not known for levity, looked as if he was ready to kill someone. "Imad," Sayyed said, "what is wrong?"

Mughniyah looked back into the stairwell and motioned for his two bodyguards to give him some privacy. "Who was that?" he said, looking at the phone. "I heard you talking."

"Ivanov."

"What did he want?"

"To insult me, I think, but I did not take the bait."

"Anything else?"

"He was going to send one of his men to pick up the spy. Now he's changed his mind and he's going to come himself."

"He just changed his mind . . . right now?"

"Yes," Sayyed said, wondering what all the questions were about. "What is wrong?"

Mughniyah again looked over his shoulder to make sure no one would hear him. In a raspy voice he said, "My bank accounts . . . in Switzerland . . . they are empty."

"What do you mean empty?"

"Empty . . . gone . . . nothing."

Sayyed knew there must have been a mistake. "Impossible."

"I have checked three times already. And it is not only the two Islamic Jihad accounts. My personal account you helped me set up is also empty." There was a hint of accusation in his words.

"This can't be. There has to be a mistake. Have you called Hamburg?"

Mughniyah nodded. "My cousin tried six different times today."

"Did he get hold of Dorfman?"

He shook his head. "Herr Dorfman is dead."

"Dead!"

"Killed in his own home last night."

Sayyed's knees felt weak. He was the one who had suggested Dorfman to Mughniyah and the others.

"You are the only one of us who knew this banker. You specifically said we would never regret investing our money with him."

Sayyed could see where this was going. They would need to blame someone, and he was the easiest target. "Are you sure he's dead?"

"As sure as I can be from here."

Sayyed didn't like the way the Islamic Jihad's heavy was looking at him. "We will get to the bottom of this. I promise you I had nothing to do with this. Come with me," Sayyed said, wanting to get off the roof lest Mughniyah decide to throw him off. "We'll go to my bank here in town. I'm sure there has been a mistake. I had money with him as well."

"Tell me again . . . what is the connection with Dorfman?"

Sayyed had already reached the first landing. He stopped dead in his tracks and looked at Mughniyah. "Ivanov introduced me to him six years ago."

"And he just called you and mentioned none of this?"

"Not a word."

"Fucking Russians . . . always scheming."

CHAPTER 37

ZURICH, SWITZERLAND

RAPP and Richards missed most of the excitement. With the time change and lack of sleep over the past few days, both of them took Ohlmeyer up on his offer of a room. Rapp had just enough energy in him to slip out of his suit and pull back the covers, but not enough to brush his teeth or anything else. He didn't even bother to close the curtains. He did a face plant on the big king-size bed and was out cold. He could do that sometimes. Just lie down on his stomach, close his eyes, and it was good night, Irene. The only problem came when he woke up. Lying on his face like that caused his sinuses to drain and blood to pool around his eyes.

His arms were pinned beneath him. He cracked one eye and thought of the ultimate yin and yang— life and death. He wondered if it was normal to think about it so much or if he should bring it up to Lewis when he made it back stateside. That was if he made it back. That thought brought a smile to his face. He had no idea why he found it amusing that someone might kill him, but he did. Probably because there was a better-than-even chance that whoever the man was, he had no idea the kind of fight he was in for. Rapp didn't discuss it with anyone, not even Lewis or Kennedy, but he was good at this kind of work and he was getting better.

At twenty-three he was already intimately familiar with death. There was his father and then Mary, and now less than a week ago he'd stared into the eyes of a man and pulled the trigger. And as life drained from the man's face, he had felt nothing. At least not guilt, or sorrow, or nerves. It was as if a calm had passed over him. And then last night, the bizarre home invasion of Herr Dorfman. When he'd signed on with Kennedy, he hadn't had that type of thing in mind. Killing a man in the manner that he'd killed Sharif, he'd dreamed of at least a thousand times. Dorfman, never. Never once had his fertile imagination predicted that he would see a man shot in the head while he clutched his prized poodle.

Without warning, or any real conscious decision, he jumped out of bed, assumed the position, and started doing push-ups. He thought of the old saying: If you're not busy living, you're dying. It felt good to be living. He ripped through fifty push-ups, flipped over, and did fifty sit-ups, and then decided he needed to take a run. He dug out his gear. It was four-thirty-seven in the afternoon. His running shoes were virtually brand-new, as the last pair had been stuffed in a garbage can in Istanbul. With a house this big, Rapp assumed they had to have a workout room. He was right. A staff member must have heard him coming down the stairs and met him in the foyer. He escorted Rapp back upstairs, down the hallway past his room to the far wing of the house. The room had windows on three sides, a treadmill, a bike, and a rowing machine, as well as a universal machine and some dumbbells.

Rapp got on the treadmill, picked the mountain course, and hit start. For the next thirty minutes the ramp rose and fell, and all the while he kept a six-minute pace. When the digital readout told him he'd run five miles, he punched the red stop button and jumped off, his chest heaving, sweat dripping from his face. He didn't even have enough left for a cool-down. As he stood hunched over, his hands on his knees, he wondered for a brief moment if he might vomit. And that was when she walked into the room. Rapp stood up straight, a pained look on his face, and tried to take in a full breath.

"Here you are," she said in near perfect English. "I have been looking all over for you."

Rapp could hardly conceal his surprise. Here, standing before him, was possibly the most attractive woman he'd ever laid eyes on, and she was looking for him. Still out of breath, he started to speak but stopped. The nausea came back and he decided rather quickly that he needed to open one of the windows or he really was going to vomit in front of this beauty. He held up a single finger and said, "Excuse me."

Rapp cranked one of the windows open and took in the fresh cold air. A couple of deep breaths later the nausea began to pass. "Sorry," he said as he turned back around. "I'm a little out of shape."

The blond beauty placed a hand on her hip and gave him an appraising look. "I don't see anything wrong with your shape."

Rapp laughed nervously and, not knowing how to respond, said, "You look great . . . too, I mean, you don't look like you need to work out . . . is what I mean." That's what came out of his mouth. Inside his brain he was screaming at himself. *You're a moron.*

"Thank you." She flashed him a perfect set of white teeth.

That was when Rapp noticed the dimple on her chin. Her overall looks had knocked him so off-kilter that he was just now getting around to categorizing her individual features: blue eyes, platinum blond hair pulled back in a high ponytail, prominent cheekbones, like some Nordic goddess. *Weren't these people all related somehow?* A tiny little upturned nose. The dimple on the chin, though, that had caught his attention for some reason.

"My grandfather sent me to find you."

That was where he had seen it. Herr Ohlmeyer had that same dimple, or cleft, or whatever it was that they called it. Somehow it looked much better on her. Rapp smiled and offered his hand, "I'm Mitch . . . I mean Mike." *Get ahold of yourself,* his brain screamed at him.

"Greta. Pleased to meet you."

The smile made him a bit wobbly in the knees. *Of course you are,* Rapp thought to himself. The image of Greta in pigtails and lederhosen with a white blouse and ample cleavage, holding a couple of beer steins, flashed across his mind. *What the hell is wrong with me?* He noticed her face muscles tighten a bit and then she looked down at their still-clasped hands. "Oh, I'm sorry," Rapp said as he released her hand. He hustled over to the shelf where the towels were and grabbed her one. Instead of giving it to her, he began mopping her hand. "I'm so sorry."

She laughed nervously and took the towel from him. "My grandfather wanted me to tell you, drinks are being served at six sharp in the library. Jacket and tie are required. His rules, not mine."

"Okay," Rapp replied, and then, feeling some irrational need to keep talking, he asked, "What are you wearing?"

She crinkled up her nose and said, "You are funny."

And then she was gone. In stunned silence Rapp watched her leave. He didn't know how it was possible, but she looked every bit as good from behind. She was in a pair of jeans that were tucked into brown leather riding boots. The door closed with a click that snapped Rapp out of his trance. He slapped himself in the head twice. "What are you, fifteen, you moron?"

He tried to finish the workout, but his mind wasn't in it, so he went back to his room, took a cold shower, and thought about Greta. Romance, companionship, call it whatever you want, it was not something he had put a lot of thought into since losing Mary. He'd had a few flings here and there, but they were purely physical. They all wanted to fix him. That was the problem. They knew who he was, and that he'd lost his high-school sweetheart in the attack that had so devastated Syracuse. Being the captain of a national championship lacrosse team, at a school that was crazy about the sport, virtually guaranteed that a certain number of women would end up in his lap. Unfortunately, they eventually wanted to talk about his feelings, about how he was coping with the loss and heartache. Nothing could have been more unappealing to him. His feelings, his personal agony, were no one else's business.

It had been almost four years now. Maybe that was what was going on. Time really was healing the wound. Or maybe it was Sharif and Dorfman. Maybe tossing their bodies down that big hollow pit in the back of his mind had helped stay the pain. Or maybe it was simply the fact that Greta was so stunning, she'd blinded him into forgetting his past for a moment. *No, that couldn't have been it. At least not all of it.* He'd met plenty of gorgeous women the past few years, and none of them had hit him with this kind of lightning bolt.

Rapp knotted his tie in the mirror and decided to leave the question there. It was a riddle. An unsolved problem, more than likely all the above, or some of the above. And what did it really matter? He'd felt something he hadn't felt in years and wasn't sure he would ever feel again. The spark of a crush, or love at first sight, he had no idea. He had a hard time buying the latter. More than likely it was simple lust. Two young, attractive people, their pheromones in overdrive. Was there a chance she felt the same thing? He recalled the look she'd given him as she gave him the once-over.

Staring at his reflection, he asked, "What does any of it matter? I'm leaving in the morning. Going on safari." Rapp cinched the Windsor knot just so and decided to enjoy the evening. He would forget about yesterday and tomorrow, the pain and the obligations, and just try to live like a normal person for one night.

CHAPTER 38

MOSCOW, RUSSIA

VANOV placed the handset back in the cradle and reached for the glass of vodka. It was snatched from his grasp a split second before his hand got there. His fingers closed and found air. He blinked several times before looking up and seeing Shvets holding the glass. "Mine," was all he could manage to say.

Shvets wanted to tell him he spoke like a toddler when he was drunk, but it would do no good at this point. "What did he say?"

"He has no idea."

"You're sure?" Shvets should have listened on the extension. When his boss got like this he was extremely unreliable.

"What's there to be sure about?" He pushed himself away from his desk and leaned back in his high-back leather chair. "The man is a camel jockey. He is not smart enough to steal this money from us."

Shvets would have loved nothing more at this exact moment than to tell his alcoholic boss that Sayyed was smarter than him, but he'd seen him shoot people for such insolence. "I should go to Hamburg?"

"No. I need you here. Send Pavel."

Now, there was an idiot, Shvets thought. Pavel Sokoll was fine with numbers and balance sheets, but borderline retarded when it came to everything else in life. Sending him to Hamburg would get them nowhere. "We need answers, and I'm afraid sitting here will not get us any. Sending Pavel will only add to the confusion. You won't allow me to discuss this with anyone other than you or Pavel, so getting those answers is going to be very difficult."

"But I need you here."

"There will be no 'here' in a few days," he said with some force. "Once word gets out that the money is missing, the phone will start ringing and sooner or later it will be kicked upstairs, or worse, across town, and once that happens, they will pull you in."

"Us! You mean us!" he half screamed. "Your wagon is hitched to mine."

"Trust me, a minute doesn't pass that I don't think of it."

"And I have been good to you."

"Yes, you have," Shvets said halfheartedly.

"And I will continue to take care of you. We just need some answers."

"What we need is money," he said, trying to get Ivanov to see the fundamental problem. "Answers might lead us to the money, but we will not get those answers sitting here in Moscow."

"Stop speaking in riddles."

"Just let me go to Hamburg and see what I can find out. I will fly out tonight, and if all goes well, I'll be back on the first flight in the morning."

"And what am I going to do?"

Shvets's solution was suddenly very clear. "Go out and get drunk. Order up some women and go to Hotel Baltschug."

Ivanov frowned. He was in no mood to socialize.

"You must keep up appearances. You know how this town is. If rumors start that you are in trouble and no one sees you in public they will believe the rumors. If they see you out acting as if everything is normal they won't believe the rumors." Shvets was willing to say almost anything to convince him. Sitting here in this office was getting them nowhere. He'd seen his boss in these funks before. Usually only for a day or two. Always a pity party, but somehow the heaps of despair and recrimination eventually focused him, and he came out of it like a bear ready to charge. And when that happened, Shvets had better have a better understanding of what had happened, or he could end up being the casualty.

He suggested, "Bring Alexei and Ivan. They will make sure you are taken care of."

Yes, Ivanov thought. *My two Luca Brasis. No one would dare challenge me with them as my companions.* Ivanov felt better just thinking of his two loyal soldiers, and besides, some flesh might be the remedy for his dismal attitude. And he wanted a drink. "Fine," he relented, "but I want you to call me as soon as you hear something."

Shvets turned tentative. They'd done enough talking on the phones today, and in this new era of electronic surveillance, there was no telling who was listening. "I promise," he lied as he started for the door. "And remember . . . act like nothing has changed tonight."

CHAPTER 39

ZURICH, SWITZERLAND

RAPP entered the study a few minutes before six and found Hurley alone, a phone in his left hand and a drink in his right, staring out the French doors at the snow-capped mountains in the distance. Hurley glanced casually over his shoulder, the phone pressed against his left ear, to see who it was, and then went back to what he was doing. Rapp glided across the room, stepping from the hardwood floor onto a large Persian rug. The library was on two levels. The second floor consisted of a catwalk that accessed the stacks of books lining the four walls. There wasn't a dust jacket on a single book.

A large wood-paneled door to Rapp's left opened with a click. Herr Ohlmeyer appeared, a warm smile on his face. He held up one of his long fingers and silently motioned for Rapp to join him. Rapp glanced at Hurley to see if the man wanted to discuss anything, but he was still on the phone, so he followed Ohlmeyer into a much smaller windowless office.

Something about the room felt different. Off in some way. When Ohlmeyer closed the door, there was a click of finality and then near total silence. Only the faint hum of a CPU. Rapp became aware of his own breathing and then realized the room was soundproof. The floor was elevated a few inches, and the walls and ceiling were built-in and covered in fabric. Behind the desk with the triple screens was a bank of black-and-white security monitors three high and five across. In front of the desk was a small conference table maybe forty-eight inches across. It had four bland wood chairs. The room was such a stark contrast to the rest of the house that Rapp couldn't help but take notice.

Ohlmeyer could see the younger man's interest and said, "In my business one must take certain precautions." He pulled out one of the chairs, told Rapp to sit, and then grabbed a file from his desk. Placing it on the conference table, he said, "I admire what you are doing. This is not an easy life you have chosen."

Rapp nodded in a noncommittal way, but other than that did not respond.

"Do you have any regrets so far?"

Without hesitation, Rapp said, "No."

"No problems sleeping . . . no second thoughts?"

"I'm not a big sleeper."

Ohlmeyer smiled and scratched the dimple on his chin. "Your type rarely is."

"My type?"

"Yes. The hunter. It is imprinted in your genetic code. Almost everyone has it, dormant for thousands of years. In many there isn't enough of it left to do them any good. They spend their days in sedentary jobs that challenge them neither physically nor mentally. They do not have your abilities and your drive, of course."

Rapp supposed there was a good deal of truth in his words; he simply had not put a lot of time into thinking about it.

"I have some documents here," Ohlmeyer said as he tapped the file. "Stan knows about this, but he does not want to know the details."

"Details?" Rapp asked, wondering what Hurley was up to now.

"You are in a very dangerous line of work. You are but a small vessel in a harbor packed with giant supertankers. Those supertankers bump up against each other sometimes, causing little harm to themselves, but to you it is the end." He clapped his hands together, signifying the destruction of Rapp's boat. "In your work, you need a special kind of insurance, and do you know why?"

Rapp could hazard a guess but he got the idea Ohlmeyer would prefer to do the talking. "Not really."

"Because those supertankers don't really care about you. They may lament your misfortune, but only briefly. The tanker, the ego of the captain, all comes before you. Think of it as the ship of state, if you will. You are young, and if you are lucky your career will last for another four decades. During that time your handlers will come and go and the political winds of change will reverse directions more times than you will be able to count, and sooner or later it is likely that someone within your own government will begin to think of you as a problem. Ships of state do not like to be embarrassed, and if that means sinking a small vessel every once in a while . . . well, that is a price they are willing to pay."

Rapp had a bad feeling. He looked at the file and said, "What's that all about?"

"It is your insurance policy." Ohlmeyer opened the file and clipped to the first sheaf of documents was a Swiss passport. "Stan has assured me that your French is perfect."

Rapp nodded.

"And your Italian, German, and Arabic?"

"My Italian is good, my German is weak, and my Arabic is pretty good."

Ohlmeyer nodded. That matched with what Hurley had told him. "I have prepared three separate legends for you. Swiss"—he slid the set of documents out of the file, followed by two more. "French, and Italian. You will need to memorize everything in these files and, most important, you will need to visit Paris and Milan in the coming weeks."

"Why?"

"You now own a safety-deposit box in each city, and one in Zurich, but I will take care of that one for you. You will want to place certain things in these safety deposit boxes. Things that will help you survive should you need to go underground, as they say."

Rapp frowned. "Does Stan know about this?"

"It was his idea. Mine as well, but we did the same thing for him years ago." He slid over a blank sheet of paper with three names on it. The first two were French and the third was Italian. "Please practice signing each of these a few times before I have you sign the signature cards."

Rapp took the pen and began practicing the name Paul Girard. "Why isn't Stan handling this?"

"He does not want to know the details."

"Why?"

"Because every man in your profession needs a few secrets."

"Even from his own boss and government?"

"Especially from your boss and your government."

Rapp was wondering how he was going to keep all of these different aliases straight. Hurley had already given him two, and here were three more. He practiced a few times on the other names and then signed the cards.

"In each box," Ohlmeyer said, "will be twenty thousand dollars in cash, various documents, such as birth certificates, in case you lose the passport, and a matching set of credit cards and driver's license. As I said, you will want to add certain things to each box, but you should talk to Stan about that. There is also a numbered account here in Switzerland that I will be administering."

"A numbered account," Rapp said, barely able to conceal his surprise.

"Yes, Stan has requested that as well, and told

me that it is up to my discretion to release the funds."

Rapp was tempted to ask the size of the account, but instead said, "May I ask you a personal question?"

Ohlmeyer nodded, with a smile, as if he already knew the question.

"Why are you doing this . . . helping us?"

"We will discuss it over dinner tonight, but the short answer is that I believe in freedom."

"Freedom," Rapp said as he turned the word over in his mind for a second. "That's a pretty vague term."

"Not really, but if it helps you understand my motivation, you'll need to understand that I grew up in East Germany. I saw what the Soviets were really like."

Rapp's mind was filled with a menagerie of black-and-white atrocities, courtesy of the *World at War* shows he saw as a kid. "So you hate the Russians."

Ohlmeyer gave a little laugh and said, "Let's just say I believe in good guys and bad guys."

CHAPTER 40

HAMBURG, GERMANY

BY early afternoon they learned that Dorfman was dead. The news sent Ivanov into a fit of rage. He went on for a good five minutes, ranting that he had never trusted the man, which caused Shvets to silently ask himself why the fool had let a man he didn't trust handle such a large sum of money. After that, Ivanov, whose job and nature was to be paranoid, spewed out no fewer than a dozen conspiracy theories in as many minutes. He was convinced that Dorfman had gotten drunk and whispered secrets in the wrong person's ear. That this person had then decided to bump Dorfman off and take the money for himself. But then again, there were supposed to have been safeguards in place, so the criminals had to have had a certain level of sophistication.

Ivanov had a long list of enemies that he ran through. There was a Cuban general he'd screwed over in an information swap five years earlier. How that man could possibly fit into this scenario was beyond Shvets, but he'd asked for the list of possible suspects so he simply listened and let Ivanov purge the information from his vodka-soaked brain. There was a German industrialist whom he'd fleeced a year earlier, a Spanish tycoon as well, and then there were a host of Jews and Bolsheviks who had been out to get him for years. None of it appeared to be useful, but then again maybe it was.

Shvets took the information and boarded a Lufthansa flight to Hamburg. Before leaving he'd called their man at the consulate and told him to work his contacts with the local police and get him a copy of the crime scene report. When he arrived at five-thirty-six that evening, Petrov Sergeyevich was waiting for him, the report in hand. Shvets had met Petrov briefly a few years earlier. After a polite exchange, Shvets told him to drive him to the bank. He sat in the passenger seat and read the report. Herr Dorfman had been stabbed in the thigh and shot once in the head. His wife was found bound and gagged and locked in the basement. She reported two men wearing masks entering the house at approximately ten in the evening. She did not hear them speak and could not give police a description other than the fact that they were roughly the same size.

The dogs, strangely enough, were unharmed. One was locked in the basement with the wife and the other was found wandering around the first floor. At some point the latter dog stepped in the pool of blood by Dorfman's head and then tracked it around the first floor. There was no sign of forced entry and none of the neighbors had seen a thing. Shvets found it interesting that the wife and dogs were unharmed. That more than likely ruled out the vying factions in Moscow, although if Shvets was advising them, he would have tried just this thing to throw off a man like Ivanov. Whoever they were dealing with was very professional.

Shvets finished the report, closed it, and decided it was nearly useless. Anything was possible. Dorfman could have told someone about the money and that someone could have gotten the idea in his head to steal it. Twenty-six million dollars could do that to certain people. Shvets had thought about it himself. He had the skill set to make it work. It would have been so much easier if Dorfman had stolen the money and tried to disappear. They would have tracked him down. They always did. The fools habitually ran off to some beachside resort where they naively thought they would blend in with the locals and tourists.

They reached the bank shortly after six-thirty and Shvets weighed the benefits of having Sergeyevich accompany him into the building. He decided against it. There was no need for muscle. At least not yet, he hoped, and besides, the fewer who knew about Ivanov's vulnerable position the better. The bank was typical. Tall, covered in glass, and imposing, all meant to give the impression of stability and security. It was one of many things Shvets was counting on.

The armed guard who tried to stop him in the

lobby told him the bank was closed, but Shvets assured him that he did not wish to make a financial transaction. He was tempted to add that that was, of course, unless the guard could somehow refund the $26 million that had been stolen from Shvets's employer and associates, but Shvets was fairly certain that this man was incapable of making that happen, so he instead asked to see the head of security.

When the security guard hesitated, Shvets said, "Of course this has something to do with Herr Dorfman's death."

That changed things significantly, and in less than a minute Shvets had been escorted to the top floor, where he came face-to-face with another, much older security guard. Same white shirt with black epaulets and black pants. Shvets flashed his SVR credentials and told the man secrecy was of the utmost importance. He was then told that the bank president was extremely busy.

"No doubt meeting with the board of directors." The uncomfortable look on the man's face gave him the answer he was looking for. "I will wait no more than two minutes. Tell him now, and tell him that it involves Herr Dorfman. There are some very influential people in Russia who require some immediate answers."

Shvets sent the man off to deliver the message. Less than a minute later, the guard came back down the hall with a well-dressed man who looked as if he had been through a difficult day. The guard stood awkwardly nearby while the bank president said, "I am Herr Koenig. How may I help you?"

"I am Nikolai Shvets. I am with the Russian government." He again flashed his gilded badge and then, nodding toward the receptionist, said, "Is there a place where we can have a word in private?"

"Yes," the banker offered, nodding enthusiastically. "Please follow me."

Shvets was disappointed when they ducked into a glass-walled conference room instead of the man's office. There was nothing to learn from this bland space. No photos of loved ones. Not a single hint of personal information. He would have to ask Sergeyevich to look into the man's life for some leverage.

Koenig remained standing, obviously impatient to get back to the board. "What is it you wish to discuss?"

"I understand," Shvets said, "that Herr Dorfman had a very unfortunate evening last night."

The man nervously cleared his throat. "The police have advised me not to discuss matters surrounding the murder of Herr Dorfman."

"Would you like me to inform the police that $26 million of Mother Russia's money went missing this morning, or would you like me to go straight to the press with that announcement?" Shvets was well aware of his lie, but he could hardly tell the man the money belonged to various terrorist groups and the head of the SVR's feared Directorate S.

The banker's gray pallor deepened, and he steadied himself against the back of a nearby chair while he mouthed the number.

"I do not wish to go to either the police or the press, but that is up to you, Herr Koenig."

"What would you like to know?"

"How much money is missing?"

"Counting your twenty-six million . . . forty-seven. But none of the money was actually in our bank," Koenig said defensively. "In fact, we are trying to sort out what Hans has been up to for all these years."

"What do you mean the money was not in your bank?"

"The deposits were all in Swiss banks or offshore accounts in the Caribbean and Far East."

"But Herr Dorfman managed the accounts in his official capacity as a vice president of this bank."

Koenig raised a cautionary finger. "We are not sure on that point. So far we have found no official records of any of these accounts in our system."

Shvets wasn't so sure he believed the man. "Up until a minute ago you were thinking your exposure was roughly twenty million. It has now more than doubled. What makes you think it won't double again before tomorrow?"

"I disagree with your use of the phrase 'your exposure.' As best we can tell, Herr Dorfman was in no way acting as an officer of this bank while he managed these various accounts."

"Herr Koenig," Shvets said with a sad laugh, "you and I both know that will not stand up. Those deposits may not have sat in your vault, but you had an officer of this bank who was managing on a daily basis a minimum of forty-seven million, and quite possibly more. This bank earned fees off that money . . ."

"But—"

"Please let me finish, Herr Koenig. I am not here to assign guilt. I am here to catch whoever took this money so we can get it back to its rightful owners."

Probably for the first time since midmorning, a touch of color returned to Koenig's face. "As there always is in these situations . . . a financial forensic investigation is under way."

"How long will it take to complete?"

"It could take some time."

"Please be honest with me. I am going to head back to Moscow tomorrow and the men I work for . . . they are not nice. They could never have a conversation like this. They would much prefer to strap you to a chair and attach things to your testicles, so I suggest you tell me what you know." Switching to a friendly tone, he added, "Then I can go back to them and tell them you are a reasonable man. Someone we can trust."

Koenig struggled with what he was about to say and then blurted it out. "I'm afraid we will never find that money."

"Why?"

The banker threw his arms out. "It has been spread to the wind. I have never seen anything like it in all my years. The initial round of transfers was executed via fax in three waves. They came from all over the world."

"Where?"

"Hong Kong, San Francisco, New York, London, Berlin, Paris, Istanbul, Moscow, New Delhi . . ."

"Moscow?"

"Yes."

"I would like to see the faxes."

The banker shook his head.

Shvets sighed, "Ohhhh . . . why must we do this the hard way? Herr Koenig, I know where the accounts were held. Your branch in Geneva. You are not as innocent as you would like me to believe. You will show me those faxes, and if you don't, some people will come visit you in the middle of the night and do to you what was done to Herr Dorfman."

Koenig swallowed hard. "I think I can make that concession."

"Good. Now why do you say we will never find the money?"

"My legal counsel has informed me that not a single bank that we transferred the money to today has consented to our request for information."

"Certainly there's a way."

"It would involve years of lawsuits, and even then you would be lucky to track down a fraction of the funds."

"Well, maybe you need to turn up the pressure." Koenig watched as his words seemed to have the opposite effect from the one he'd intended.

Koenig stiffened. "I should warn you that a faction of the board feels very strongly that this is dirty money."

"Dirty money?" Shvets asked, as if the accusation were an insult.

"There are rumors that Herr Dorfman was an agent for the East German Stasi before the wall fell."

"Rumors are bad things."

"And there is another rumor that he worked for your GRU as well. That he helped certain people launder money."

Shvets gave him a wicked grin. Dorfman had, in fact, been a spy for the KGB, not the GRU. "Where have you heard such things?"

"From people who know such things," Koenig answered cagily. "Would you like to talk to them?"

Shvets suddenly got the feeling that he'd lost the upper hand. He needed to say something to fluster Koenig. "Back to these banking laws for a moment. I assume these very same laws could be used to conceal gross incompetence of your branch in Geneva . . . or better yet, that one of Herr Dorfman's colleagues at the bank helped himself to millions of dollars that did not belong to him. Don't they say that most bank heists are inside jobs?"

"That is pure, unfounded speculation."

"As is your gossip about Herr Dorfman being a GRU spy." Checkmate.

Koenig squirmed for a moment and then offered, "Would you be willing to talk to the people who have sworn that Herr Dorfman was a spy?"

"Absolutely," he said, even though he had no such intention, "but I would like to see those faxes first. Especially the one that originated in Moscow."

Koenig studied him cautiously for a moment and then said, "I will have copies of the faxes made for you. Give me a minute." He left the room, glancing back over his shoulder with a frown.

Shvets paced while he waited. This was starting to look like a big mess. Once these thieves in suits confirmed that Dorfman had worked for the KGB, they would not be the slightest bit inclined to repay a single dollar. The Germans hated the Russians almost as much as the Russians hated the Germans. Koenig came back a few minutes later. He had two other men with him this time, and Shvets knew the jig was up. Koenig handed over the stack of faxes. They were blank, except for the sending and receiving fax numbers. The man might as well have written "Fuck you" in large letters across the top sheet. Still, it was better than nothing.

CHAPTER 41

ZURICH, SWITZERLAND

THEY had drinks in the library, although Rapp thought of it more as shots like he had done back in college, except instead of a smelly bar in upstate New York he was in a mansion on the outskirts of one of the most refined cities in the world. Herr Ohlmeyer did not believe in ruining fine spirits with anything other than ice, so the liquor was served either up, on the rocks, or neat, which Rapp learned was basically naked, meaning nothing but the booze. Rapp chose a glass of sixteen-year-old Lagavulin single malt scotch and asked for it on the rocks. Ohlmeyer liked playing host and told Rapp it was a fine choice. Rapp took the glass, smiled, and said, "Thank you."

Greta had not made her entrance yet, so Rapp took the opportunity to corner Hurley, who was standing by the massive granite fireplace speaking with one of Ohlmeyer's two sons. He approached

Hurley from behind and tapped him on the shoulder. "We need to talk."

Hurley said something to Ohlmeyer's son in German that Rapp did not understand, and after he had walked away, Hurley turned to Rapp and asked, "What's up?"

Rapp jerked his head in the direction of the small soundproof office. "What was that all about?"

Hurley's jaw clenched as was his habit when he didn't want to talk about something. Reluctantly he said, "It's part of the deal. Don't worry. Just listen to Carl, he knows what he's doing."

"Does Irene know about it, or Spencer Tracy, that guy who I'm not supposed to know?" That was how Rapp referred to the man he had met briefly at the offices of International Software Logistics, the man who, he assumed, was running the show. The question caused the veins on Hurley's neck to bulge, which in turn caused Rapp to take a step back. That particular physical cue was often a precursor to Hurley's blowing his top.

Hurley felt the older Ohlmeyer's eyes on him and told himself to take a deep breath through his nose and exhale through his mouth. It was a trick Lewis had taught him. It helped him center himself. Ohlmeyer despised public outbursts. "Listen, kid . . . this is a tough business. There's certain things they don't need to know about, and quite frankly, don't want to know about."

Rapp considered that for a second before asking, "Can it get me in trouble?"

"Pretty much everything we do can get you in trouble with someone. This is about taking care of yourself. No one else needs to know about this other than Carl and his two boys."

Rapp took a sip of his scotch and was about to ask another question, but thought better of it. *Don't look a gift horse in the mouth.*

Hurley wished he could say more, but the kid would have to figure it out the hard way, as he himself had had to do back in the day. He took a big gulp of bourbon and thought about how much easier it would have been if someone had just pointed a few things out to him. Hurley changed his mind and decided to let it fly. "Kid . . . you're good, and that's no small thing coming from me. My job is to find faults and try to beat them out of you. At some point in this line of work . . . I don't care how good you are . . . I don't care how just your cause . . . sooner or later you're going to land yourself in a big pile of shit. It might be your fault, although more than likely, it'll be some asshole back stateside out to make a name for himself so he can advance his career. He'll put a target on your back, and trust me on this one, even though you're going to want to stand and fight, you need to run. Run and hide . . . lie low . . . wait for things to blow over."

"And then what?"

"You live to fight another day, or maybe you just disappear for good." Rapp frowned, and Hurley knew exactly what he was thinking. "We're not that different, kid. The idea of running away for good isn't in our veins, but it's nice to have options. You bide your time, you find out who it is who's out to get you, and then you go after them."

Rapp absorbed the advice and looked around the courtly library. "When are we shipping out?"

"Tomorrow morning. I was going to tell you guys later."

"Where to?"

"Back to the scene of the crime."

"Beirut?" Rapp whispered.

"Yep." Hurley held up his glass. "Although I might have a small job for you first."

"What kind of job?"

"We might have a lead on someone."

"Who?"

"I don't want to say yet."

"Come on!"

"Nope . . . no sense in getting your hopes up. Irene is flying over in the morning to brief us. If she's verified it, I will send you on a quick one-day detour, and then you can join up with us in Beirut."

"And the intel on Beirut?"

"It's good . . . really good. These guys have been singing like birds all day."

The men spent another thirty minutes in the library. Ohlmeyer took the time to introduce both of his sons to Rapp and Richards. The older one was August and the younger was Robert, and both were vice presidents at the bank and held positions on the board. The patriarch of the family assured the two young men that they could trust his sons, and Hurley seconded the opinion. Ohlmeyer knew that they would be leaving in the morning and suggested that they reconvene at the earliest possible time to work out the protocols and to make sure that each man understood the details of his various legends.

CHAPTER 42

SHORTLY before seven they moved from the library to a sitting room that was decorated in the French Baroque style. The white, carved flowers, leaves, and shells on the furniture and molding were in stark contrast to the deep natural woods of the library. Sitting on one of the room's four sofas was Greta. Next to her was an older woman whom Rapp took to be her grandmother, and thus Carl Ohlmeyer's wife.

Greta smiled at him from across the room. Rapp, in control of his faculties this time, flashed her a crooked grin and walked over, shaking his head. "Good evening, ladies." Rapp offered his hand again. This time it was dry. "Greta, you look lovely."

"Thank you, Mitch . . . I mean Mike."

Rapp laughed, "You're good."

"I'd like you to meet my grandmother, Elsa."

Rapp offered his hand. "Very nice to meet you,

Frau Ohlmeyer. You have a lovely home." Rapp thought he noticed something wrong with her eyes when she smiled. A certain disconnect. Her grip was also a bit weak, and he wondered if she might be ill.

Herr Ohlmeyer was suddenly at Rapp's side. "Michael, I see you have met Greta."

"Yes, we bumped into each other this afternoon."

"And my wife." Ohlmeyer placed a hand on her shoulder.

"Yes."

Looking back at his granddaughter, he said, "Greta is our pride and joy."

"I can see why. She is very sharp."

"Yes, and so far the only one of my grandchildren who has shown any interest in getting into the banking business."

For the next five minutes, Rapp got the family history. Carl and Elsa had two boys and two girls. One daughter was married and lived in London and the other was divorced and in Spain. August's and Robert's wives were currently on vacation with their sister-in-law at her Spanish villa. There were eleven grandchildren, of which Greta was the third-eldest. Elsa did not speak, although she did smile a few times. Richards, Hurley, and the two brothers were at the opposite end of the room, no doubt discussing matters of far greater importance, but Rapp didn't beat up on himself too badly. Standing this close to Greta was worth it. Every chance Rapp got he stole a look. Her high ponytail had been changed out for a loose clip in the back that made her look much more mature than when he'd met her earlier in the day. She was wearing a cobalt-blue silk blouse and a black skirt with gray tights. He thought Herr Ohlmeyer caught him at least once ogling her and he had no idea what Elsa was thinking. She just kept smiling at him with that faraway look in her eyes.

The Ohlmeyers were kind enough not to ask him any personal questions about his own family, as he would have been forced to tell them a lie. Herr Ohlmeyer decided it was time to sit for dinner. He asked for his wife's hand, but before she stood, she pulled her granddaughter close and whispered something in her ear. Greta giggled, while her grandmother pulled away and flashed Rapp an intriguing smile, before pulling her granddaughter close again. She whispered another few lines before finally taking her husband's hand and standing.

Elsa took a step toward Rapp, and to his surprise, she reached out and gently patted him on the cheek. She gave him a warm smile and then walked away without saying a word.

Rapp turned to Greta. "You have a very interesting grandmother."

Greta reached out and grabbed his arm, pulling him close and walking him toward the dining room, but in no rush to catch up with the others. "Granny Elsa is an amazing woman. Unfortunately, she is not well."

"What's wrong?" Rapp said, as his stomach did flips over Greta's touch.

"She has Alzheimer's."

"I'm sorry."

"No need to be sorry. These things happen. Such is life."

"I suppose," Rapp said, turning toward her. She smelled so good, he wanted to bury his face in her mane of shiny blond hair.

"She has no regrets. She led a very active life up until just a year ago. I am living here now and working at the bank. This way I can spend time with her . . . while she still remembers me."

"That's nice."

"We spend our evenings going through letters and photos. There is so much family history that only she knows. My grandfather is a brilliant man, but he has a hard time remembering the names of his own grandchildren."

"Not yours. You can tell, he thinks the world of you."

"Well . . . I work for him. I would hope he remembers my name."

As they entered the dining room, Rapp said, "Do you mind me asking what your grandmother whispered in your ear?"

Greta gave him a nervous laugh and rested her head against his shoulder before releasing his arm. "Maybe after a few drinks."

Rapp followed her like a puppy dog down the right side of the long table. There were chairs for twenty but they were only eight, so they clustered at the far end with Carl at the head of the table and Elsa to his left, followed by Greta and Rapp. Hurley was to Carl's right, followed by August, then Richards, and finally Robert.

The wineglasses were filled and conversations that had been going continued while new ones were started. Richards got Rapp's attention at one point and gave him a you-lucky-bastard shake of his head while darting his eyes at Greta. Rapp for his part struck up a rather boring conversation with Greta's uncle, who was sitting directly across from him. When Greta had finished her glass of wine Rapp leaned over and asked, "So can you tell me now?"

Greta slid her hand over and patted his thigh. "One more glass, I think." She held up her glass and one of the servants filled it. "So how does an all-American boy such as yourself end up in this nasty line of work?"

"We get recruited like any other profession."

"So your background is military?"

Rapp shook his head and smiled. "I'm a fine arts major with a minor in poetry."

Greta's face lit up in surprise for a moment and then she caught herself. "You are teasing me."

"Yes, I am."

"Why?" she asked playfully.

"Because you know I can't talk about my past . . . and I tend to tease people whom I like."

"So, you like me?" she said with an approving nod.

He didn't know why he decided to say it. Maybe it was the wine, maybe it was his newfound confidence that he was finally making a difference, that he was part of something important, but he did nonetheless. Rapp leaned in close so only she could hear and said, "I don't know what it is about you, but I've had a hard time thinking of anything but you, since we met this afternoon."

She smiled at him, her cheeks flushing just a touch. "You are different. Not so guarded."

Rapp laughed. "I'm probably the most guarded person you'll ever meet. Just not with you, for some reason."

"Is that good or bad?"

"I think it's good. At least it feels good." Rapp looked into her blue eyes. She was smiling back at him. He was about to really open up when Herr Ohlmeyer tapped his wineglass with his knife several times and stood. Ohlmeyer raised his glass and started giving a toast. Rapp turned his chair slightly so he could face him, and his right knee moved to within a few inches of Greta's thigh. Then her left hand slowly slid over from her lap and found his knee. From that moment on, Rapp didn't register a single word that came out of Herr Ohlmeyer's mouth. Nor did he hear anything Hurley said when he rose to make his toast.

The main course arrived. It was a braised beef of some sort, served with mushrooms, potatoes, gravy, and vegetables, the kind of meat-and-potatoes meal Rapp loved. There was only one problem. He had just stuffed a forkful of beef in his mouth when Greta leaned over and told him what her grandmother had whispered in her ear.

"My granny thinks you are extremely attractive. She told me I should sleep with you."

Rapp would have been fine if it had ended there, but it didn't. As he tried to swallow the meat Greta leaned over once more.

"She said that if I don't she will."

Rapp froze, his eyes bulged, and a piece of meat got stuck in the crossroads of his throat. His brain's autopilot kicked in and the hunk of meat came flying back up as fast as a major-league fastball. The only thing that saved it from pelting Richards in the face was Rapp's quick hands. A fit that started out as a cough morphed into eye-watering laughter. Greta smacked him on the back a few times and had to hold her napkin over her mouth to conceal her own laughter and amusement that she had set the chain of events in motion. Conversation ceased and all eyes settled on the young duo.

Greta saved them by announcing, "I am sorry." She dabbed at her eyes. "I told him a bad joke."

Rapp finally got hold of himself and everyone went back to their conversations. Rapp noticed Hurley giving him a few cautious looks, but other than that no one appeared to notice the flirting. Shortly after dessert was served, Elsa tapped Greta on the arm and told her she was tired. Everyone stood while the two women made their exit, and then Ohlmeyer suggested they retire to the library. Hurley disappeared into the small soundproof office, and it was Rapp's turn to talk with the two uncles. They gave Rapp a message service to call if he needed to contact them. He was never to call the office directly, especially if he was in trouble. Rapp kept looking over his shoulder, hoping to see Greta, but she did not return. About an hour into it the brothers thought they had made enough progress and agreed they would sit down again when Rapp came through town again in the coming weeks.

It was just before ten when the two brothers left. Rapp thanked Herr Ohlmeyer for an interesting evening and headed upstairs with one thing on his mind—Greta. He stood in the long hallway outside his room for a moment, loitering, hoping she would suddenly appear. He had no idea where her room was, but suspected that the guests were in this wing and the family's rooms were in the other wing of the house. After another fifteen seconds of standing there feeling stupid, he gave up and opened his door.

Rapp peeled off his suit coat and tie, draping both over the back of the desk chair. With the water running, he started brushing his teeth and unbuttoning his white dress shirt. He walked back into the bedroom and was dropping the dress shirt on top of the tie and coat when he thought he heard a sound at the door. He froze, hoping it was Greta. A few seconds later he heard the footsteps of someone walking away. He walked to the door and listened for a few seconds before checking the hallway. It was empty. Rapp closed the door and stood there resting his head against the door. After nearly a minute he decided he was acting like a fool. He twisted the lock from midnight to three and climbed into the big bed, wishing Greta was next to him.

He yawned and rubbed his eyes. He was tired after all. Rolling over, he extinguished the bedside lamp and thought about tomorrow. The side trip that Hurley had alluded to had his interest. He wondered who the target was, and if he'd had a direct role in the Pan Am attack. The happy thoughts of ending that type of man's life sent him drifting off toward sleep, and then suddenly there was a faint knock on the door.

Rapp threw back the blankets and rushed to the door. The knocking grew a bit louder. Rapp twisted the lock and opened the door a crack. The sight of Greta's blond hair put an instant smile on his face. She pushed through, not wanting to be discovered in the hall, closing the door behind her and locking it.

Rapp opened his mouth to speak, but she put a finger on his lips and a hand on his chest. She pushed him back toward the bed, and then, rising to her toes, she kissed him on the mouth. Rapp responded with a soft gasp and pulled her close, wrapping an arm around her waist. Hands started to roam and the kissing became intense, and then Rapp pulled her head back and rested his forehead against hers. He looked into her eyes, but before he could speak, she gave him a wicked smile and pushed him back onto the bed.

Rapp watched as Greta undid her robe, letting it fall to the floor. She was naked. He reached out for her, and she slowly climbed onto the bed. He pulled her close, kissing her neck and running a hand down her perfect, smooth, naked backside. A low rumble of approval passed his lips as he nibbled on her ear and then other parts. Holding her tight, he took control and rolled over. Rapp held her exquisite face in his hands and looked into her eyes. At that moment there was nothing beyond the here and now. There was no yesterday, or tomorrow. He hadn't felt this alive in years.

CHAPTER 43

BEIRUT, LEBANON

THEY were to meet two hours after sunrise. Sayyed asked Mughniyah why two hours, and he told him it was because the cowardly Americans attacked only with the cover of darkness and the Jewish dogs with the rising sun at their backs. Sayyed had seen the Jews attack at all hours of the day but he wasn't going to argue with Mughniyah, at least not considering his current mood.

Sayyed looked down at his little CIA guinea pig. The man was not doing well. None of the nails had grown back enough to use the pliers, so he'd been forced to drill a hole through one of the agent's nail beds to try to get him to respond to his questions. Instead the man had passed out. There were parameters in these situations, but they were only parameters. You could never tell when you had an outlier. On that note, Sayyed still wasn't sure about Cummins. Given the less than sanitary conditions, it was entirely possible that he was seriously ill. Aziz al-Abub had taught him how a subject could become sick to the point of the nervous system shutting down. Once that happened, the only thing you could do was nurse the subject back to health and then start over.

Unfortunately, Mughniyah and the others wanted answers that were simply not here. At least not in Cummins's head. They were distrustful of Ivanov and his constant plotting, but there was still a deep-seated hatred of the Americans and Jews, and they wanted to know if this man knew anything about their missing money. Beyond that there was a fundamental problem that they had overlooked, which was not unusual for the collective group. They were far too one-dimensional and always looked at a situation as if it were a street battle in Beirut. Attack, retreat, dig, and fight—this was the extent of their military repertoire. In the espionage business Sayyed had to analyze in three dimensions and project possible outcomes. This John Cummins was going to eventually end up in the hands of Ivanov, if for no other reason than that Ivanov was used to getting his way. Sayyed had to be very careful what type of questions he asked, with an eye to the fact that the subject would eventually inform Ivanov of what he'd been asked.

Sayyed would have to start the subject on a cycle of antibiotics. The others could talk all they wanted about not handing Cummins over, but Sayyed was done with him. There was nothing more to learn and he did not wish to be put in the middle of this fight. He wiped the small splotch of blood on the front of the white butcher's apron and wondered what he should tell Damascus. They would want to be fully briefed on the situation, but they did not have to deal with all of these crazy Palestinians.

That was the paradox of Lebanon in general and Beirut specifically. The Palestinians were supposed to be in Palestine, not Lebanon. The Palestinians had upset the balance that the Turks had kept for centuries. Their displacement by the Jews shattered the fragile peace and plunged the country into civil war. And now more than fifteen years later, that civil war was over and the Palestinians were growing cocksure. With relative peace, Damascus was losing its sway over how all these vying factions conducted themselves. Damascus, for its part, was slow to realize what was plain to see. The child was now an adult and did not appreciate, much less need, the consent of the parent. Fortunately for Sayyed, he was more like an uncle—a very nonjudgmental uncle. Especially this morning.

Sayyed knocked on the metal door and waited for it to be opened by the guard. He stepped into the hallway and closed the door behind him. Looking at the two guards, he said, "He will need medical attention. Pass the word to the others. I want him treated like a baby. No more kicking or punching."

The two men nodded and Sayyed moved off down the hallway, still struggling with what he should tell Damascus. He could hardly share the details of the past few days. The Swiss accounts that had been so carefully set up were now empty. Damascus had contributed zero to the accounts, but they were aware of their existence. They did not know, however, that Sayyed had set up an account for himself with the aid of Sharif and Ivanov. He took a cut of every arms shipment that came into the country by helping assure that the various Syrian factions would leave the merchants be. Damascus needed to be kept in the dark as long as possible.

He stopped in the small sandbagged lobby on the first floor. The door was completely blocked and the floor-to-ceiling windows on each side were now nothing but small portholes, just enough to allow a man to take up a rifle position. Oh, how he wished those pesky Maronites would go away. He climbed to the second story and followed the extension cords and phone lines to the makeshift command post. Once again the hallway was filled with armed men, but this time they did not upset Sayyed. He needed them to deter the Christians from doing anything stupid.

They were living in abject squalor. There was no running water, electricity, or phone service. The men were relieving themselves in the basement in random rooms and corners. No wonder Cummins was sick. Electricity and phone service would have to be brought in from three blocks away, via a series of patched cords and lines that had been spliced into the service of an apartment building.

The guards stepped aside so he could pass, and he entered the command post. The men were standing around a sheet of plywood that had been placed on top of two fifty-gallon oil drums—Mughniyah and Badredeen from Islamic Jihad; Jalil, who was Sayyed's Iranian counterpart; and Radih from Fatah. Each man had benefited handsomely from his association with the Turkish arms dealer and now they were once again paupers.

"Close the door," Mughniyah commanded.

Sayyed did so, and joined the men at the makeshift table.

"Well?" Mughniyah asked.

"Nothing."

"Nothing?" Radih asked, obviously dubious.

Sayyed looked at the little toad from Fatah and said, "I have been informed that some of your men have taken certain liberties with my prisoner over the past few days."

"Your prisoner?" Radih shouted. "He is my prisoner!"

"The prisoner," Sayyed said, "has been kicked and brutalized by your men and due to the lack of sanitary conditions from your men defecating all over the basement like a pack of wild dogs, it appears *the* prisoner is now ill."

Badredeen made a foul face and said, "Really . . . you should institute some basic hygiene. At least have the men go on the roof. The sun will take care of it for you."

"Do you want to walk up seven flights of stairs to go to the bathroom?" Radih asked.

"Enough," yelled an impatient Mughniyah. He looked from one end of the table to the other, making it clear to all that he was not in the mood for petty arguments. "Someone has stolen millions of dollars from us and you want to argue about where the men should shit?"

"I was only—"

"Silence!" Mughniyah screeched. With his fists clenched he turned on Radih. "I am sick of it . . . all of the complaining and fighting, the bickering, and for what . . . it gets us nowhere. Millions are gone, Sharif is dead, our banker is dead, and that vulture Ivanov is now talking about coming to Beirut for the first time in years. Am I the only one who finds this a bit disconcerting?"

"He told me he had nothing to do with Sharif's murder," Sayyed offered.

"And since when do you believe anything that comes out of a Russian's mouth?"

"I have no trust in the man, but on this point, he did seem to be upset that someone had killed Sharif."

"Maybe someone else did kill Sharif, and that was when Ivanov decided that with our Turkish friend gone it was the perfect time to take all of the money."

Sayyed considered that one for a moment. It was possible. Ivanov had proven many times that he could be ruthless.

"Add to that these damn Christians deciding to make a show of strength." Mughniyah gave a swift shake of his head. "I like none of it. Something is very wrong and we know far too little."

"Why would Ivanov want to visit Beirut?" Badredeen asked.

"Land."

All eyes fell on Colonel Jalil of the Iranian Quds Force. "Explain," Mughniyah ordered.

"There is a great deal of valuable land here in Beirut, and many are saying that with war finally behind us, there are huge sums of money to be made."

"Why can't these people leave us alone?" Mughniyah asked no one in particular.

"What about the Americans?" Radih asked. "We have one of their agents in this very building."

"Who was sent here to negotiate the release of the businessman you kidnapped." Sayyed's tone suggested what he thought of the idea.

"That is the story he has given you."

Sayyed turned his head to look at Radih. "You doubt my ability to get the truth out of people?"

"None of us are perfect."

"So you think the American is holding back on us? That his coming here is all part of a master plan by the Americans to take over Beirut?"

"I did not say that."

"You did, in so many words." Looking back toward the leaders of Islamic Jihad, he said, "We do not have enough information to know what is actually happening. It could be anyone at this point, but based on what we do know, we have to assume that Ivanov is the front runner."

"So what should we do?" Badredeen asked.

Sayyed thought about it for a moment and then said, "Let him come to Beirut. Keep our eyes and ears open and see what we can find out."

Mughniyah was scratching his beard thinking

about what had been said. "Beirut is our fortress. Spread the word to our people at the docks and the airport. I want to know of anything that looks suspicious. Americans, Russians, Jews . . . I don't care."

"And we should alert our allies," the Iranian said. "Everyone should be extra careful until we know exactly what is going on."

"I agree," Mughniyah said. "Quietly spread the word to our people in Europe. Especially anyone who has a connection to Sharif. Let them know of our concerns . . . that someone might be targeting us."

It was the right decision, but Sayyed needed to add something. "No mention of the money, though. At least not yet." One by one they all nodded as he knew they would. To a man, they were too proud to admit that they had been duped out of such a large sum of money.

CHAPTER 44

ZURICH, SWITZERLAND

THE Gulfstream 450 landed at Zurich International Airport and proceeded to the fueling pad rather than Customs. The flight plan stated that the plane was stopping for fuel before continuing to Kuwait. The truck was waiting, and while one of the men began to unwind the hose, a second man in blue coveralls approached the plane's fuselage, opened his hand, and slapped the side of the plane three times. A second later the hatch opened and the stairs lowered. The man bounded up the steps and hit the button to pull the stairs back up and close the hatch. He checked to make sure the cockpit door was closed and proceeded into the cabin.

Hurley took off the baseball cap and sat in one of the two open chairs across from Irene Kennedy. They were separated by a table. "Good morning." Hurley tapped the thick file that was sitting in front of the young counterterrorism analyst. "I assume that's for me."

Kennedy pulled the file closer to herself and said, "Before we get to this, there are a few things we need to discuss."

"Well, let's make it quick, because I have a schedule to keep, and we need to get you back up in the air before Customs comes poking around."

She nodded as if to say fine and then asked, "What was the final dollar amount?"

"For?"

"You know damn well what for."

"Oh . . . the thing." Hurley looked around the cabin as if he was trying to add it all up in his head. "I suppose somewhere in the neighborhood of . . ." Hurley flashed her a four with one hand and a five with the other. "Roughly, of course. A lot of it gets siphoned off along the way. Fees and whatnot."

"You're sure?" Kennedy asked, fairly confident that he was lying to her.

"Irene, to be frank, it's really none of your business. This is between Tom and me."

"Well, Thomas wanted me to ask you face-to-face, since you're so paranoid about using phones."

"He knows damn well why I don't use phones. The same reason he doesn't."

"True . . . but he still wants to know."

"Why?" Hurley asked.

"Because he thinks you're holding back on him."

Hurley laughed. Stansfield knew damn well Hurley would never give him an official accounting.

To handle all the black-bag stuff they threw his way, he had to have access to piles of cash. "Darling niece, I think you are either bending the truth or trying to bluff me. Which one is it?"

Kennedy studied him with a crooked frown, none too happy that he had figured out what she was up to. "A little of both, I suppose."

"And why are you trying to stick your pretty little nose where it doesn't belong?"

"Because someday, not too soon, I hope, you and Thomas are going to die and somebody will need to make sense of the tangled web you've left behind."

"If anything happens to me in the next few days, tell Thomas I said to visit our old friend from Berlin who now lives in Zurich. He'll have the answers you need."

Her bluff called, Kennedy grabbed a file sitting in the seat next to her. Unlike the bland manila one on the table, this one was gray. Kennedy placed it in front of Hurley and opened it to reveal a black-and-white photograph of a man exiting a car on an unknown city street. "Look familiar?"

Hurley glanced at the photo and lied. "Not really."

"This is Nikolai Shvets . . . Name ring a bell?"

"A soft bell. I have a lot of Russian names floating around in my head. It's hard to keep them all straight. Kind of like reading *War and Peace*."

"Sure," Kennedy replied, not buying a word of it. "Care to guess where this photo was taken?"

Hurley glanced at his watch. "We don't have

time to play Twenty Questions, young lady, so let's get on with it."

"Hamburg. A certain bank that drew a lot of interest yesterday. Any idea why one of Mikhail Ivanov's top deputies would show up yesterday, of all days?"

Hurley shook his head.

"He threatened the bank's president about some missing funds." Kennedy searched his face for some recognition. "And if your answer is still no, I won't bother playing you the tape of your old friend Ivanov talking to a certain terrorist that we've been looking for."

Hurley frowned. He didn't like being forced to answer this kind of question by someone so junior.

"Thomas told me," Kennedy said, "that you would be reluctant to talk about this, but nonetheless, I have been ordered to get an answer from you."

"What kind of answer?"

"How many people did you piss off yesterday, other than the ones we know about?"

"It was a thick file." Hurley shrugged. "Some accounts had names attached to them . . . others were just numbers."

"So your earlier estimate might be a little light?"

"Get to your point."

"It looks like you've pissed off some people in Moscow, and you know how they can be when they're upset. They don't play nice. If they get so much as an inkling that we were behind any of this . . ." She shook her head. "We'll be in serious trouble."

"So you want me to confirm what you don't want to hear?"

"I just want to know the facts so I can go back and brief Thomas. He needs to tell our embassy people, if they are in danger of reprisals, and anyone else who might get stuck in Ivanov's crosshairs."

Hurley swore under his breath and finally said, "Yes, I took some of the bastard's money, and with any luck it'll be the beginning of the end of him."

Kennedy took the news without comment and placed a small tape player between them. "Now . . . you will be very interested to hear this brief conversation."

Kennedy pressed play and the slurred voice of Mikhail Ivanov could be heard asking, *"My package . . . Is it ready? You haven't decided to negotiate with the Persians, have you?"*

"I am standing by our deal."

Kennedy pressed the stop button. "You recognize the first voice?"

Hurley nodded. "Ivanov."

"Correct. The second voice?"

"No."

"Colonel Assef Sayyed."

Hurley was impressed. "What the hell are they doing talking on an open line?"

"They weren't, but you didn't hear that from me."

"Then how'd you get it?"

"I can't say." Kennedy pressed play again.

"When can I expect it to be retrieved? I assume you are still sending someone."

"*Yes . . . although I am considering coming my-self. . . . You did offer . . . didn't you.*"

"*Absolutely.*"

"*Good. I will be there in three days. Maybe sooner.*"

Kennedy hit stop. "There's more. Tapes of Iva-nov and Sayyed and others as well. You'll want to listen to all of them, but Thomas does not want you bringing the tapes into Beirut."

"Understood. Did you happen to pick up Badre-deen or Mughniyah?"

"Unfortunately, no, but we have a few others that I think will please you." Kennedy retrieved another folder from her briefcase and laid it before Hurley. "Tarik al Ismael."

"Music to my fucking ears. Please tell me you ID'd the prick."

"Hiding right under our noses a few kilometers down the road."

"Where?"

"He's been working at the UN office in Geneva. Attached to the Office for the Coordination of Hu-manitarian Affairs, if you can believe it. He lost a few pounds, cut his hair and beard, and ditched his contacts for eyeglasses. You have to admire his tradecraft." Kennedy fingered the old photo from his days when he was running operations for the Libyan intelligence service, and then the new photo. "It's a pretty good effort."

"You sure it's him?"

"Ninety percent on the photo and ninety-nine point nine on the voice ID. And he was calling about money missing from his account. If we hadn't had the big ears focused on these banks, I don't think we would have ever caught him."

Hurley thought of their conversation last night and frowned. "So you want to send Rapp after him?"

"Not just me. Ismael is near the top of Thomas's list."

"I don't know, Irene," Hurley said with obvious reluctance. "Ismael could bite back. He's not some fat arms dealer. He's a real killer."

"In a perfect world, Thomas would send all three of you after him, but we don't have that luxury right now."

"Why? Let's put Beirut off for a few days."

Like a Vegas dealer, Kennedy slid the gray file off to the side and moved the manila file front and center. "In the transcript, you heard Ivanov ask if his package was ready?"

"Yeah."

"He asked Sayyed if he was going to negotiate with the Persians instead . . ."

"Yeah."

"Remember what they did to Buckley?"

"Remember—I think about it all the time. I was just telling Mitch and Bobby Richards about him."

"Well, Thomas thinks the Schnoz is the package they are referring to."

Everything stopped. Hurley didn't so much as twitch for a good ten seconds. He'd known the Schnoz for close to twenty years and there was a running shopping list in his head of all the operations he'd been involved in. After a quick assessment of the potential damage, he leaned back and dropped the F bomb. Cummins had worked in Moscow before Damascus. If the Russians got their hands on him, they would be screwed in some of their most sensitive operations. He shook his head to get over the shock and said, "We can't let that happen."

"Thomas agrees. He has a source that says Schnoz is still alive. Emaciated and battered, but still alive."

"Shit."

"That's why he wants you and Richards to get to Beirut ASAP. As we discussed last night, Rapp will join up with you tomorrow or the next day. In the meantime, you two start poking around. If you can't find anything in forty-eight hours, Thomas wants you to use some of the new funds to negotiate for the Schnoz's release. Very quietly, though."

"Of course." Hurley was still trying to calculate the damage. "What about backup?"

"He's agreed to send a SOG team, but doesn't want to put them in-country until you have something solid."

"Understood." SOG stood for Special Operations Group. There was a good chance Hurley would know the men. "Air cover?"

"If you need it he'll get it. Last resort, though."

Before Hurley could comment, there was a banging on the side of the plane and he realized it was time to go. Kennedy passed him two files. "Those are for you. This one," she said as she handed him a third, "is for Mitch. Make sure he knows to destroy it before he makes contact with Ismael."

"Will do." Hurley stood. "Anything else?"

Kennedy joined him in the aisle. She didn't want him to go, but he was a good soldier, so there was no stopping him. So much of their shared sorrow revolved around that once-beautiful city on the eastern shore of the Mediterranean.

Hurley could see that she was concerned, and he knew why. He gave her a hug and said, "Don't worry. Everything will be fine."

"Yeah," she said, not really believing it herself and holding back the tears. "Beirut's still a nasty place." She stayed strong for him. There was no turning back now that he knew. The only thing to do was support him. She kissed him on the cheek and said, "Be careful."

CHAPTER 45

GENEVA, SWITZERLAND

WHEN it was all done Rapp would swear that he felt the zip of the bullet as it passed his left temple. It was that close. The only thing that saved him was the awkward movement that the Libyan made as he drew his pistol. The fake was weak. He looked over his left shoulder a bit too dramatically and then swung back to his right, drawing his gun, his long overcoat flaring like a matador's cape. The other reason Rapp didn't fall for it was that mean old cuss Stan Hurley. It was the first time Rapp could honestly say he was grateful for all the shit Hurley had heaped on him. All of that damn methodical, shitty training paid off in the split second it took Ismael to draw his gun and turn on him.

The fact that Rapp didn't want to kill the wrong man also contributed to the harsh reality that he was now cowering behind a Swiss mailbox, rounds of an undetermined caliber thudding into the metal receptacle at an alarming rate. And Hurley had been right, of course. He had told them that there were two ways to win a gunfight. Either land the first shot or find cover and conserve your ammunition. Hurley had put them in a situation so similar to this that it was now damn near calming to listen to his opponent mindlessly fire one shot after the next into a four-sided box of steel that had survived every change of season for the past fifty years.

Back in the woods of Virginia the idea was to find cover while Hurley fired live shots at you. And mind you, he didn't fire them safely over the horizon. He liked to hit things close to you. Not rocks or anything hard enough to cause a life-ending ricochet, but soft things like dirt, sandbags, and wood. The object of the lesson was to teach you what it felt like to be shot at, so you could keep your head when confronted with the real thing. As a bonus, you learned to count not just the number of rounds you fired, but the number of rounds your opponent fired as well. At first, the exercise was unnerving, but after a while, as with most things in life, you adapted and got the hang of it.

Rapp squatted, his back pressed firmly against the mailbox, and counted the number of shots, which had been eight so far. He was waiting for the inevitable calm in the storm. There was a problem, however. While Rapp's pistols were equipped with silencers, the Libyan's gun was not. Eight extremely loud gunshots had rung out in a city with one of the lowest murder rates in the entire industrialized world. It might as well have been an artillery barrage.

There was no telling how many extra magazines the Libyan had in his possession, but he doubted the man could match the seventy-two rounds Rapp carried. Rapp released the grip of his still-holstered Beretta and stabbed the big gray button on his Timex digital watch. Just as Hurley had taught him, it was set for stopwatch mode. The average response time for a police car in a city of this size was roughly three minutes. And that was assuming there wasn't one nearby. There were rules that were flexible, and there were rules that couldn't be broken, and killing a police officer was one of those unbreakable rules. Hurley had told them, "If you kill a cop I will kill you before they do."

The first eight shots had come in rapid succession. By the sound they were 9mm or maybe .40 caliber at the most. Rapp never heard where the first one landed after it flew past his head, but the second shot had blown out the driver's-side window of the white BMW parked a few feet away, which was now chirping and beeping like a car with Tourette's syndrome. The next six had hit the mailbox. Not a smart move unless he had a second gun, and he was closing on him. Rapp thought that unlikely. Ismael was spooked and on the run, which in itself bothered Rapp.

The drive from Zurich had been easy. Just under three hours, counting a quick stop to call the answering service and confirm that the target was at his place of work. The file was straightforward. They were monitoring the calls he made at work, they knew where he lived and the make and model of his car. Hurley gave Rapp specific instructions. Tail Ismael after work and follow him to his apartment. If he comes out for an errand or an evening stroll and there's an opportunity, take him. If not, wait until morning and shoot him while he's getting into his car. Rapp had followed the instructions to the letter, and when Ismael bowed out of his apartment at ten-oh-nine that evening, Rapp watched him round the corner and then pursued on foot.

A block later Rapp noticed that Ismael had a duffel bag slung over his left shoulder. It was at that point that the wheels started to turn in Rapp's head. He asked himself if it was normal to leave your apartment on a crisp winter night when you should be getting into bed. It wasn't unheard of for someone to head out after ten, but it was far from common. Especially on a Tuesday night. Throw in the overnight bag and you now had someone who might be running. That was pretty much what Rapp was thinking when Ismael pulled his lame matador move. That, and wondering if he could rush him at the next intersection, shoot him in the back of the head, and be in France before midnight.

Now, because he had failed to heed Hurley's warnings, he was crouched behind a mailbox, counting bullets and wondering if Ismael had one or two guns. One more shot thudded into the mailbox and then there was a two-second pause. Rapp stuck out his gloved hand to see if he could draw a shot. He pulled it back as a tenth bullet whistled harmlessly past. It sparked off the stone sidewalk and skipped down the street. Rapp thought he heard the clank of a slide locking in the open position, but he wasn't sure. A split second later he heard the heavy footsteps of someone running. That was it. He was either reloading or out.

Rapp drew the silenced Beretta from under his right arm and bolted between the two parked cars to his left. He stayed low, glancing over the roofs of the cars. He caught a glimpse of the Libyan as he took a left turn at the next corner. That put a smile on Rapp's face. *Run all you want,* he thought. The more distance we can put between us and those ten muzzle blasts the better.

Rapp rounded the corner wide and fast, trying to keep the parked cars between himself and Ismael. They were on the Left Bank, or Rive Gauche, and Ismael was headed toward the Rhone. They had just turned off a street that was purely residential and onto one that was a mix of retail and apartments. The shops were all closed and fortunately the sidewalk was deserted. Rapp stayed in the street and broke into a full sprint. Geneva, because it was wedged between two mountain ranges on one end and a lake on the other, was even more cramped than your standard European city. The streets were barely wide enough for two small cars to pass. An American SUV was out of the question.

Ismael was a good hundred feet in front of him. Not an easy shot standing still, let alone running and aiming at a moving target. Rapp kept the pistol at his side. Long black coat, black pants, black shoes, and a black gun. Black on black. Nothing to see. He was gaining on Ismael with every stride, staying low, the top of his head just barely visible over the roofs of the vehicles. And then Ismael saw him as Rapp passed from one car to the next. There was now no more than seventy feet of separation. Just over twenty yards. Either the man was really slow or Rapp was really fast, or probably both.

Sixty feet and closing was the best Rapp could figure when they locked eyes. Rapp started to raise his pistol to fire, but before he had it leveled, Ismael was swinging the bag around and then all hell broke loose. The bag exploded, spitting red-orange flashes on the dark street. Rapp turtled, dropping behind a nice piece of German steel. Counting shots was not an option with whatever it was in the overnight bag. The rate of fire told Rapp that it was probably an Uzi or a MAC-10. To the uninitiated, a gun was a gun, but in his new line of work, caliber was every bit as important as rate of fire. Since the Mercedes had no problem stopping the rounds, Rapp concluded it was a 9mm Uzi. If it had been the MAC-10 he would have felt the punch of the .45 caliber rounds as they penetrated the body and rattled around the interior of the car.

Rapp glanced at his watch as glass rained down on him from the blown-out windows. He could picture, in his mind's eye, the Libyan backing up as he laid down fire. The Uzi he was firing used either twenty-, thirty-two-, or forty-round magazines. The forty was unlikely because it probably wouldn't fit in the bag, and if it was twenty he would be done already, so that meant it was thirty-two rounds and he was almost out. And once Rapp heard the click it would be over. There was no way the guy could pull a weapon like that out of a bag and reload it before Rapp was on him.

The bullets stopped, the noise replaced by a half dozen car alarms that were now chirping and beeping and screeching and flashing. Rapp came up with his weapon this time, his finger on the trigger, ready to fire. Ismael was gone. Rapp caught a glimpse of him farther down the block and tore off, again staying in the street so he could use the cars for cover. The clock in his head was marking time as he pressed his advantage. He closed again to within sixty feet. Ismael looked over his shoulder, raised the bag, and let loose another burst. Rapp went into a crouch behind a car but kept moving. Rapp couldn't be sure if it was a four- or five-round burst, but it had stopped and Ismael was on the run again. Rapp, thinking the gun was out of bullets, or close to being out, ran tall now, more worried about speed than cover.

Ismael made it to the corner and turned left. Rapp stayed wide again, and when he cleared the corner, he came upon the unwelcome sight of Ismael standing there with his left arm wrenched around a woman's throat. Rapp didn't look at her. He didn't want to look at her. Old, young, fat, skinny, none of it mattered. Ismael's right hand was still in the duffel bag, gripping the Uzi, which might or might not be out of bullets. Ismael started screaming at him to drop his weapon or he would kill the woman. Rapp continued to close as he had been taught. His pistol was up, directly in front of his face, an extension of his left eye, which was attached to his brain, which was still counting the seconds and telling him to finish this and get the hell out of there.

The woman was now screaming, and for the first time Rapp noticed she had a small dog on a leash that was yipping and snapping at Ismael's legs. He had no doubt that Ismael would kill the woman, but what purpose would it serve? If Ismael had any bullets left in that gun he would turn it on Rapp right now and zip him with a nice burst to the chest. If he shot the woman, he was a dead man, and he didn't want to die, as he had proven very loudly over the last half minute. His only way out of this was to kill the man who had been chasing him. He was nicely shielded by the woman. All he had to do was swing the bag around and unload. Rapp stopped at twenty feet and decided that since Ismael hadn't taken aim at his chest, he was bluffing.

In the end, it was the dog that tilted things in Rapp's favor. Ismael wisely tried to create some distance between them by stepping back. What he didn't know, because he hadn't bothered to look down, was that the little yipping dog had run a couple of circles around them, and his leash had formed a nice little lasso around the Libyan's ankles. Ismael stumbled and jerked to his left to catch himself. For a brief second, the side of his head was clearly visible. Rapp was now only twenty feet away. He squeezed the trigger once, and that was all it took.

CHAPTER 46

BEIRUT, LEBANON

HURLEY stepped onto the roof, a bottle of Jack Daniel's in his hand, his thoughts already traveling back in time. The hotel was in a neighborhood called Bourj Hammoud. It was controlled by the Armenians, which was why Hurley had decided to stay here for the night. The Armenians were one of the few factions that had managed to stay neutral during the civil war. There had been a few shots fired between the Armenians and their Maronite neighbors, but no major battles.

It had been a strange day—the meeting with Kennedy, the briefing with Rapp before sending him off, and the analysis of the intercepts. There was nothing like stealing a man's fortune to get him riled up. Voices they hadn't tracked in years had popped up. Beirut was going to be a very target-rich environment. Before they could leave, though, they had to look the part. He dragged Richards to one of Zurich's secondhand clothing stores, where they purchased some ill-fitting suits and dress shirts, well-worn shoes, and some beat-up luggage. Hurley added some gray to his hair and both men skipped shaving. They boarded a flight for Paris and then on to Beirut, just two men in a sea of travelers.

They arrived as the sun was setting on the far end of the Mediterranean, feeling a mix of anticipation, anger, and apprehension. That's what Beirut did to Hurley. He'd spent time in the city before the civil war, back when it was a thriving mecca of Christians and Muslims living side by side, socializing, raising families, enjoying life, and for the most part getting along. Then the PLO began to radicalize the slums and demand a say in how things were run. The Maronites had no intention of sharing rule with these gypsies, and the battle lines were drawn. No one, not even Hurley, had thought the disagreement so egregious that it would plunge the city into a fifteen-year civil war, but it did. More than a million had fled, 250,000 were killed, hundreds of thousands of people were wounded and crippled, and the economy and much of central Beirut were laid to waste. That such a great city could be so thoroughly destroyed was enough to shake the faith of even the most optimistic.

At the airport there were a few signs that things were headed in the right direction. The part of the terminal that had been severely damaged during the Israeli shelling of 1982 was now torn down, and reconstruction was under way. Hurley and Richards trudged down the metal stairs with their fellow passengers. Tired and bored Lebanese militiamen flanked the travelers and directed them toward Immigration and Customs. The last time Hurley had been here, Immigration and Customs consisted of a single portly bureaucrat sitting behind a metal desk on the tarmac. His job had been less about border security than about collecting the bribes needed to enter the country. Now they filed into the airport, where there were posterboards announcing ambitious rebuilding plans.

They threaded through the Customs lines, trying their best to look tired and bored. Richards passed with barely a glance. He handed over his cash that they called a fee, but was more of a bribe, because it never saw its way into the Treasury. Hurley had to answer a few questions from the Customs official, but nothing that was too alarming. He thought he caught one of the supervisors standing behind the three Customs agents paying him a little too much attention, but that, after all, was his job. In the end it was nothing to worry about. The man did not intervene or follow them to baggage claim.

They collected their luggage and stood in line once again. This time they were both searched. Then, outside at the cab stand, Hurley slipped the man a twenty-dollar bill and told him in Arabic that he wanted to pick his own cab. For no reason other than the fact that it was random, Hurley chose the fourth cab in line. They took it to the under-renovation Intercontinental Hotel, where they went inside and bought a drink. This was also where Hurley persuaded the bartender to sell him the bottle of Jack Daniel's. From there, they found another cab, skirted the central business district, and had the man drop them off three blocks from the Mar Yousif Inn.

Hurley would have preferred to have had the safe house ready, but there was no getting around it. Not if he wanted to use someone he could absolutely trust. Besides, there was only so much he could control. Setting up a new base of operations was never easy, and was even more difficult in a town like this, with shifting battle lines.

Hurley looked out across the skyline. He couldn't swear, but there seemed to be quite a few more lights than there had been a few years earlier. Perhaps progress was being made. He heard some voices and stepped around the top of the blockhouse that encased the stairs. A few of the hotel workers were clustered around a folding table, sitting in plastic chairs. They waved to Hurley. He flashed them a smile and walked to the far edge. Beirut was like most densely packed cities, in that the inhabitants used roofs to try to escape the claustrophobic feeling of being shut in. There was another plastic chair in the corner where he was standing, but he didn't feel like sitting. He looked north, over the rooftops, at the ocean. Way out there on the horizon to the northwest he could make out the glow of the lights on Cyprus. Back to the south the airport was lit up, receiving its last few flights for the day.

A not-so-welcome memory started to bubble up. Hurley gripped the bottle tightly, held it to his lips, and took a swig of Jack with the hope that he could drown it out. After a minute he started up a heater and tried to remember the last time he'd been in the city. He wasn't counting his last trip two years earlier, as he had been in and out in less than a day. Hardly enough time to look up any of his old contacts. The city brought back so many memories. A few good, a lot bad.

He took another swig but it didn't work this time. His gaze was drawn to the west where the old embassy had stood. He'd been here that day—here being the Bourj Hammoud district. Hurley had met one of his contacts for coffee that morning, a man named Levon Petrosian, the Armenian crime boss who kept things working during the civil war. In addition to making sure the neighborhood had power, water, and food, Petrosian handled all of the gambling and prostitution, and of course collected a pretty penny in protection money. After their meeting, Hurley decided to take the crazy Armenian up on his offer to sample some of the merchandise. Hurley had been in bed with two women from the Armenian Highlands of Eastern Turkey when the explosion rocked the room.

His worst fears were realized when he'd scrambled onto the roof, still pulling on his pants. Bombs were becoming increasingly common back in 1983, but this one was much bigger than the average mortar round or RPG. The plume of debris and smoke was close enough to the embassy that Hurley was certain it had been the target. The only question was the amount of damage done. Hurley raced back to the bedroom to collect the rest of his stuff and then down to the street, where his driver was asleep behind the wheel of the company Jeep. Hurley bumped him out of the driver's seat, started the Jeep, and tore off down the street.

When he arrived and looked up at the seven-story building his heart was in his throat. The front entrance was gone. A gaping hole from the seventh floor all the way to the first. A big gash between the main part of the embassy and one of the wings. Strangely enough, the roof, for the most part, was intact. He remembered something about its being reinforced to handle all the communications gear they'd put up there. As the dust settled, the first of the survivors began to crawl out of the building. Hurley was still holding on to hope at that point.

It would be two full days before they grasped the extent of the damage. By then, the hope that Hurley had felt in those moments after watching the first survivor come out of the building was entirely gone, along with one of his best friends, Irene Kennedy's father, and sixty-two others. As was standard for the Lebanese civil war, the locals took the brunt of the blast, but in terms of American personnel, the CIA took the heaviest toll. Eight Agency employees were killed, and the Near East Section was decimated.

Stansfield had been associate deputy director of operations at the time, and he had rushed over to assess the damage. The guilt Hurley felt was over-whelming. He tried to resign, but Stansfield would hear none of it. He didn't care that Hurley had missed a one o'clock meeting at the embassy. There was some speculation about that. Was Islamic Jihad lucky in their timing, or did they have inside information that Langley's top people would be meeting at that time, and if so, some had spoken out loud that it was very convenient that Hurley missed the meeting. Hurley was placed under a microscope by a few higher-ups, but Stansfield covered for him.

His operative was meeting with Petrosian the Armenian, and the meeting had gone longer than anticipated. That was as much as anyone needed to know. The fact that he was in bed with two hookers while the van crashed through the gate was inconsequential. They had already lost enough good people, they didn't need to lose another because of his vices—vices that Stansfield was well aware of.

Hurley knew Stansfield was right, but that didn't mean he could simply ignore what had happened. He was an operational wreck for those next few months. Stansfield received a report that Muslim men were turning up dead in areas of the city that were known to be relatively peaceful, completely randomly and at all hours of the day. One man was shot while reading the paper on his small terrace, another was strangled in the bathroom of a public restroom, another killed leaving a nightclub. All three men had loose connections to Islamic Jihad. Stansfield called Hurley back to D.C. to ask him if he knew anything about the murders, and to his astonishment Hurley admitted to the killings.

Stansfield could not allow one of his oldest friends and best operatives to go running off half-cocked killing whomever he wanted, even if the targets were somewhat legitimate. As Hurley had pointed out, Islamic Jihad had declared war on the United States; he was simply obliging them by participating in the war. There was a bit of logic in his thinking, but Langley couldn't afford any more scrapes with the press and the politicians at the moment. The solution was easy. Things were heating up along the Afghanistan-Pakistan border, and Hurley knew the Russians better than anyone. So Stansfield shipped him off to Peshawar to help train and equip the mujahedeen.

And now, almost ten years later, here he was full circle. Right back in this stew of religious fascists who all fervently believed they, and they alone, knew what God wanted. Hurley had been trying to warn Langley for years that these Islamic wack jobs were the next big problem. He'd seen both fronts up close. Beirut and Afghanistan and the Afghanis made these guys look like pikers. Any culture that swaddles its women from head to toe and refuses a drop of booze while exporting opium around the globe is seriously screwed-up. Another of Hurley's rules was to be extremely distrustful of anyone who didn't drink. Afghanistan was an entire society that didn't drink, and it scared the piss out of him.

Hurley took a pull from the bottle and shook out another cigarette. He lit it, blew the smoke up into the ocean breeze, and thought about tomorrow. The safe house should be set up and equipped by then, and the backup would be ready by early afternoon. He'd have to see what kind of info the Agency guy had, and if it wasn't enough, he'd go pay Petrosian a call. Hurley had heard he owned more than two thousand apartment units in the neighborhood. That would generate a lot of income, but a guy like Petrosian could always use more money, and that was one thing that Hurley finally had a lot of.

What he didn't have was time. If they were going to save the Schnoz they would have to work fast. Sometimes working fast could be used to your advantage, but you had to mix it up, and they'd been moving at a pretty good clip for about a week. Sharif, Dorfman, and by now Ismael. They might as well stay on the attack for a few more days.

Hurley looked at the bottle of Tennessee whisky and wondered if he'd come back to Beirut to die. All the times he'd cheated death, all the men he'd killed over the years, all the gods, real or imagined, that he'd pissed off. If it was anyone's time it should be his. Looking skyward, he said, "Don't piss off the gods." He poured some of the whisky down his gullet and smiled. If it was his time, so be it.

CHAPTER 47

MARTYRS' SQUARE, BEIRUT

SUNDOWN was shortly after five in the evening and sunrise shortly after six in the morning. With limited power in the building, and no curtains on the windows, there wasn't much to do after sundown, so Sayyed had gone to bed early. Loyal Samir had scrounged up a mattress and a lantern and set up a room for him on the fifth floor away from all of the men and most of the noise. He'd checked on the two prisoners briefly to make sure they were following his orders. The businessman was faring much better than the spy. Sayyed had brought a doctor in to take a look at Cummins and the prognosis wasn't good. Due to the beatings, poor diet, and unsanitary conditions, the doctor feared he was suffering from liver failure.

The news upset Sayyed. He had been warning the guards for several weeks to lay off the prisoners. But they somehow couldn't get it through their thick heads that the two men were worthless to them if they were dead. Add to that the stress of the missing money and Ivanov coming to town and it was enough to make Sayyed's temper flare out of control. He gathered the men in the basement and told them he would execute the next man who dared lay a hand on either prisoner. He caught one of the men rolling his eyes at the order, and before the imbecile knew it Sayyed had the muzzle of his Markov pistol pressed firmly against his forehead. The others finally got the point.

Sayyed went to bed wondering if they would rebel or follow his orders. It was just another thing to add to his general discomfort. He did not sleep well. His dreams, vivid and bizarre, taunted and tortured him. He was running. He must have been on the beach, because no matter how fast he told himself to run, his legs plodded along as if they were stuck in deep sand. There was a dense fog, so thick that he could see no farther than the end of his hand. Jets were overhead, screeching and dropping deafening bombs in the distance. Bright flashes erupted through the marine layer, the noises of the big bombs muted by the moisture in the air. Why was he running toward the bombs? What was he running from? He woke up with a start, his heart pounding out of his chest, covered in sweat.

Sayyed looked around the office where he'd decided to spend the night. A soft moonlight spilled in from the blown-out window. There was a pile of garbage in the corner where Samir had swept the glass and debris. Scavengers had taken everything. The furniture, even the carpeting, had been pulled up, leaving only the bare concrete floor and the dried glue that had been used to hold the carpeting down. The whole thing was depressing. The geniuses in Damascus should all be forced to live like this for a night.

Sayyed decided to get some air. He pulled on his shirt but didn't bother to button it up. He climbed two flights to the roof and with a murmur greeted the two men standing watch. All was quiet across the street. He lit a cigarette and wondered what Ivanov was up to. The man was always plotting. Given the choice between making a fortune the honest way and stealing it from someone, he was convinced, Ivanov would prefer to steal it. He was a thief at heart. It was in no way a stretch to think of him plotting to kill Sharif, and then with the Turk out of the way, killing Dorfman and taking everything for himself.

Sayyed sighed. He wished he could skip ahead a day or two. Be done with this mess and go back to Damascus for a few weeks. His two girls were grown and married and had very little to do with him, and that was fine. He didn't particularly care for their husbands. Beyond that, he had never been around when they were growing up, so there was no real connection. His wife—they barely spoke. The women in life weren't the draw. Civilization was the draw. Running water, and functioning toilets, and sleeping in a clean bed without fear of two thousand pounds of steel and high explosives being dropped on your head. That's what he needed. A VCR and a stack of movies and some sleep. He needed to recharge.

If he could run, he would. Walk out of this hell-hole of a city and leave it all behind. He'd considered it many times as his pot of money grew with Herr Dorfman. Another year or two and he would have made it. He could have gone back to Damascus, retired, and used the money he had stashed away in Switzerland to invest in opportunities as Beirut stabilized. He could have lived like a wealthy sheik. All of those years of hard work gone in an instant. It was almost impossible to bear.

He finished his cigarette and looked at the stars. He did not like having to stay in one place like this, especially a place so primitive. The food was horrid and infrequent, the conditions ripe for illness, and he couldn't sleep, and if he couldn't sleep he would make mistakes. Mistakes were not something he could afford these next few days. He did not want to go back to the depressing room with the soiled mattress, but he had to, at least to close his eyes and rest.

Sayyed plodded down the steps and into the dark room. He took his shirt off, setting it on the floor, and then lay back down on the dirty mattress, trying to ignore the stench. The crux of the problem was the money, and it was a bigger problem than any of them realized. They were all lamenting their loss of personal wealth, but the dire situation lay in their inability to pay their people.

There were a few mentally unstable militants who would work for free, but the bulk of the foot soldiers would walk away. They were paid in cash every week, and payday was Thursday. They would be able to scrape together enough to get through this week, but then they would be bankrupt. The following week they had to pay their monthly bribes to the police, politicians, bureaucrats, and spies in the other camps. There would be hundreds if not thousands of hands extended, waiting for the money, and behind them families, waiting to put food on the table. If they did not rectify this situation quickly it could be a major disaster. The Maronites and the other factions would swoop in and pick up territory it had taken them years and thousands of men to gain.

Everything they had worked for would unravel. He would have to tell Damascus, and of course leave his personal loss out of it. They were likely to punish him by banishing him to Yamouk, the bleak Palestinian refugee camp on the outskirts of Damascus that was teeming with the pushy tribe in search of a permanent home. He heard footsteps down the hall and then some voices. They sounded as if they were going from room to room. Looking toward the open doorway, he saw the beam of a flashlight. Sayyed grabbed his pistol and sat up.

"He's up here somewhere," he heard a voice in the hallway say.

"Who is it?" Sayyed asked.

"It's me. I've been looking all over for you."

Sayyed recognized Radih's voice and lowered his gun. "I'm in here."

Radih appeared in the doorway. Three other men were behind him. "Assef, you are not going to believe the news I bring you." Radih clapped his hands together.

Sayyed looked for his watch, but couldn't find it. "What time is it?"

"Nearly two in the morning. You must get up. I have amazing news."

Sayyed sighed. He half rolled off the mattress, looking for his watch. He found it, strapped it on, and then grabbed his shirt. "It better be good. I need some sleep."

"You will not be disappointed."

Sayyed felt like crap. He needed water and then coffee and then some food, in that order, and then maybe he could think clearly. He motioned for Radih to get on with the story.

Radih told his men to leave and in a hushed voice said, "Do you remember an American who went by the name Bill Sherman?"

Did he remember him? The man had purportedly killed Sayyed's predecessor while he was enjoying his breakfast one spring morning. "Of course."

"My spies at the airport . . . one of them says he saw Sherman tonight."

"At the airport?"

"Yes. He came in on a flight from Paris, along with another man."

Sayyed was dubious. There had been rumors here and there that Sherman had been back to the city. In fact, anytime someone met his end at the hands of an assassin, Sherman's name somehow became attached. "How can you be so sure? It has been many years since anyone has seen him."

"My man says he has aged. His hair has gone gray, but the eyes"—Radih pointed to his own—

"he said they are those same eyes. Eyes of the Devil. He said he remembers him as a very nasty man with many vices."

Sayyed's lips felt unusually parched. He found the jug of water that Samir had left in the corner and took a drink. *Why would the Americans send Sherman to Beirut after all these years?* The most obvious answer was in the basement of this very building. They wanted their agent back. *But why send an assassin like Sherman?* The man was a harbinger of death, not a negotiator. Turning back to Radih, he asked, "Did your spy happen to know where he was headed?"

With a self-satisfied grin, Radih said, "I put out the word yesterday, after our meeting. I told everyone to be on the lookout for anything suspicious. My people know how to do their jobs. They followed him and the other man to the Intercontinental."

"And?"

"They had a drink at the bar, and he bought a bottle of Jack Daniel's from the bartender and then got into a cab, one of ours. He had the cabbie drop him off in front of a hotel on Daoura. After the cabbie was gone, they walked three blocks to a different hotel."

"Which one?"

"The Mar Yousif Inn."

"And he is there right now?"

"Yes. They got two rooms for one night. I just spoke to the manager. They are still there."

"Are you sure?" Sayyed asked skeptically. "The Bill Sherman I remember would never allow himself to be followed."

"My men are good. We have trained them to use radios. They have a system set up at the airport. When they see someone who might be a fat target they follow him and pass the word to me. We then swoop in and grab them. I have men heading to the area now. There's only one problem."

"What?"

"The hotel is in Bourj Hammoud."

Sayyed needed to wake up. Normally he would never ask such a stupid question. The Sherman he remembered was tight with the Armenians. This would have to be handled delicately. "If we get in a gun battle in Bourj Hammoud, we might not make it out alive."

Radih did not disagree. "We can wait and follow him. If he leaves the Bourj we can grab him."

They had been lucky enough to stumble across him. That luck would not hold with a man like Sherman. He would see them sooner rather than later, and then he would kill whoever it was who was watching him and disappear. "Tell your men to hold."

Radih seemed relieved. "And then what?"

"The chief of police owes me a favor. They can operate in Bourj Hammoud without too much trouble."

This time Radih shook his head. "I'm not so sure."

"Normally you would be correct, but there are some things that you are unaware of. Some influential Armenians owe the chief a few favors. As long as we aren't going in to take one of their own, we will be fine."

"If a single shot is fired . . ." Radih winced at the thought.

Sayyed finished it for him. "The entire neighborhood could erupt." Such was the reality of Beirut. The city was always one gun battle away from plunging back into chaos and civil war.

CHAPTER 48

WHEN he hit the midway point of the last run of stairs that led to the small lobby, Hurley noticed the man sitting in the chair with his back to the door. It was probably nothing, but then again Hurley had survived all these years by noticing the little things. If enough of them piled up, they usually led to trouble. There was a couch and three chairs. The man was in the chair the farthest to Hurley's left—the same seat he would have chosen if he was to keep an eye on any guests coming down. Hurley watched him intently as he crossed the red-tiled floor. The man slowly closed his eyes and went back to dozing. Rather than head straight out, Hurley stopped at the desk. No one was there. He looked through the open door of the small office and couldn't see anyone, but could hear a TV. Looking back over his shoulder, he checked to make sure the fat man in the chair was still in his position. He had his eyes closed again and appeared to be dozing. Hurley checked him off his list.

The pay phone was behind the man in a quaint, claustrophobic alcove. Rather than use it, Hurley decided to head outside and take in the lay of the land. When he reached the front door he paused to see if there were any goons loitering. If there were, he would head back up to the room, grab Richards, and they would head to the roof. They could make it two buildings in either direction by hopping from one roof to the next, and then use any of the adjoining apartment buildings to make their escape. The sidewalk in front of the hotel was empty, so he stepped outside, tapped out a Camel, and fired it up. He casually looked up and down the block. He counted eight cars that he had seen the night before and one new one, and it was only a small two-door hatchback. Nothing to be alarmed about.

Right or left? It was funny how often that's what it came down to—a flip of the coin. He chose left. It was slightly uphill, not that it mattered, but he remembered seeing a small market in that direction the night before and it had a pay phone out front. He flipped the butt of his heater into the street to join the menagerie of discarded brands and started moving. It was before eight and the street wasn't busy. It was empty, in fact. He saw two cars drive through the next intersection, moving from right to left, and then a man with a briefcase hustled across the street. Hurley couldn't remember if it was normal or abnormal for a city like Beirut to be so slow at this time. Every city had a different pulse. Some were bustling by seven, but most Mediterranean cities were a little slower-paced. Especially one that had endured as much trauma as this one.

There was a boy standing in front of the market. Hurley guessed him to be about eight. As Hurley approached, the boy held out a paper and started giving him his pitch. Hurley smiled at him. He didn't care where he was; you had to admire a kid who got his ass out of bed to sell something. He reached into his pocket to grab some money, and right about the time he had a firm grip on his wallet alarm bells started going off. There was movement to his left, from the market, two or three car engines turned over, and then there were footfalls. Hurley looked left, then right, and then noticed that the cute little kid was backpedaling to get out of the way.

Two men came out of the supermarket—big, burly guys in uniforms who stopped just out of his reach. Car tires were now squealing and engines were roaring as vehicles closed in from three directions. Hurley turned, with the idea of running back toward the hotel, but there were two more men hoofing it up the sidewalk. One of them had a big German shepherd on a leash. *That's new,* he thought, never having seen a police dog in the city. In less than five seconds he was surrounded by ten men and three sedans. Six of the men were wearing police uniforms and four were in civilian attire. The civilians had pistols drawn. They could be either part of a militia or detectives, or worse, Syrian intelligence officers. The uniformed police were wielding wooden truncheons.

Interesting, Hurley thought to himself. Not a single one of them attempted to lay a hand on him. Hurley calculated the odds while he slowly reached for his cigarettes. Even if he had had a gun, he wasn't sure he could have gotten himself out of this jam. They all looked nervous, which in itself told him something. Someone had prepped these guys. Told them to keep their distance, which was not standard operating procedure in this part of the world. Normally it was club first and ask questions later.

Hurley lit his cigarette with the steady hand of a brain surgeon. He greeted the men in Arabic and asked, "What seems to be the problem?"

"Good morning," announced a smiling man in a three-piece suit who appeared just beyond the phalanx of men. "We have been waiting for you, Mr. Sherman." He glanced ever so slightly at the two men behind Hurley and gave them a nod.

Hurley turned and blocked the first blow with his left hand, wrist to wrist, and then delivered a palm strike to the man's nose. He ripped the truncheon from the man's hand and ducked just in time to miss the blow from his partner. The man was out of position from swinging so hard and had left his ribs exposed, so Hurley rammed him with the truncheon and sent him to the ground. Just as he turned to face the others he was cracked across the head and then the back. He dropped to one knee and then to the ground as the batons and feet came crashing down. As they took the fight out of him, Hurley lay bleeding and hoping that Richards had enough time to run.

CHAPTER 49

RAPP rocked the clutch of the little silver Renault Clio and closed the gap between himself and the next car waiting to get through the checkpoint to Beirut proper. It was his third checkpoint since the Syrian border. The little 1.2-liter engine was about as big as the one on his dad's old John Deere riding mower. If he had to run from the authorities it would be a very short chase. He'd been in line now for about fifteen minutes, inching his way forward a few feet at a time. The car didn't have any air-conditioning so he had the windows rolled down.

Rapp slapped his hands on the steering wheel to the beat of some atrocious techno music that he'd picked up at the airport. The title of the album was *Euro Trash,* and he agreed. He would have preferred a little U2, or maybe some Bob Seger, but the idea here was to make them think he was French, not some American assassin on safari. Third in line now, he leaned out the window to get a better look at the teenager holding the AK-47 assault rifle. Rapp had no idea which faction he belonged to, but the kid seemed calm enough. The first checkpoints were manned by the Syrian army, and then as he neared the city the militias were in charge.

He'd found a pay phone at a gas station along the way and called in to check on things. The automated voice told him his room was ready and gave him the address and the location. Rapp wrote it down, memorized it while on the road, then crumpled it up and threw it out the window. The file told him to expect four checkpoints, counting the border. Each one would cost him between five and twenty dollars. So far whoever had put it together was right on the mark.

The line snaked ahead and Rapp yawned. It was finally catching up with him.

After sinking a hollow-tipped parabellum into Ismael's head, Rapp had steadily retreated, keeping his gun leveled at the woman, who was temporarily frozen with shock. Rapp wasn't going to shoot her and wasn't worried that she would shoot him. He kept his weapon raised to conceal his face and to deter her from looking too closely at him. People in general did not like to look down the barrel of a loaded gun. When the woman finally glanced down at the man who had threatened her life only moments before, Rapp turned and ran.

He didn't turn the corner because he did not want to head back down the street where Ismael had just fired the Uzi. Half the block was likely to be looking out their windows, and a few of them would be on the phone with the police. So he ran straight, at an all-out sprint, for two blocks, the gun at his side. Then he took a hard right turn and stopped. His breathing was heavy but under control. He holstered the pistol while he looked for a place to reverse his jacket. Twenty feet ahead on his right there was a stoop that would offer some concealment. Rapp ducked into the shadows, tore off his overcoat, and turned it inside out. He tossed the clear black-rimmed glasses to the ground and mussed up his slicked-back hair before emerging from the shadows wearing a khaki trench coat. He headed back to the corner he'd just rounded. The distinctly European police klaxon could be heard screeching in the distance.

Rapp calmly crossed the street, looking to his left. He could just barely make out the woman. She had been joined by three or four people. Rapp acted as if he didn't notice. After he cleared the intersection he picked up the pace, but not so much as to draw attention. He looked like a man out for a brisk walk. The Rhone was now only a block and a half in front of him. With each step the sirens grew in force, but Rapp wasn't worried. They would go to the body first and then they would check the damage caused by the Libyan's Uzi and then they would begin to look for a suspect.

Rapp reached the river, which at this point was fairly wide. He turned right and after looking up and down the block to make sure no one was watching, he casually slid his left hand between the folds of his jacket and grabbed the Beretta he'd used to kill Ismael. Rapp waited until he was in the shadows between two streetlights and then drew the gun. He flipped it casually a good twenty feet into the ice-cold water and kept moving. A block after that, he disposed of the second gun, then had to make his first big decision. Just on the other side of the river, one mile away, was Geneva International Airport. If he hustled, he might be able to catch the last flight out to Paris.

Airports made him nervous, though. There were always cameras and police, and if you were going to get on a plane you had to buy a ticket and show a passport, and that left a trail. His legends were to be cultivated and protected, not used for convenience' sake. So he turned back for the rental car and rehearsed what he would tell the police if they stopped him. Fortunately, the story was never needed. Police were flooding the area, but they were still headed to the crime scene. On his way back he didn't see a single police car heading out to look for suspects. When he climbed behind the wheel of the rental car he checked his stopwatch. Four minutes and thirty-seven seconds had elapsed since he'd taken refuge behind the mailbox. Not bad.

Once behind the wheel he had a lot of options. The primary plan was to cross the border into France and then drive to Lyon, but he was too pumped-up, and with the border crossing so close, they might be looking for a man of his general description. Again, there was no longer any hard evidence that could tie him to Ismael's death, but why push it?

Rapp wasn't sure he could calm his nerves for the border crossing. The reality of what he'd just been through was setting in. There was no queasiness or feeling of nausea. He was simply pumped, the feeling very similar to the way he felt after scoring a game-winning goal, but better. He cranked the music and headed back for Zurich. Greta was on his mind, but there wouldn't be time. He'd have to grab the first flight to Paris or Istanbul and then on to Damascus.

He made it to Zurich just before four, parked in the rental car lot, and tried to grab a few hours of sleep before things opened at six. It didn't work, though, and he sat there with his seat reclined, playing it over and over in his head until he had analyzed every second of what had happened with Ismael. Each mistake was noted and alternatives explored, but as his old high-school coach liked to say, "A win is a win. It doesn't matter how ugly it is."

Strip it all down and that's what it was. Rapp won and Ismael lost. As the sun started to rise, Rapp looked out from the concrete parking structure and realized that one day he might be in Ismael's shoes. He'd pretty much spent the rest of the morning thinking of ways to prevent himself from ending up with a fate similar to that of the Libyan intelligence officer. From Zurich to Istanbul, and then Damascus, and all the way down this hot, dusty road to Beirut, he played a game of chess with himself. What should Ismael have done, and how should he have reacted if Ismael had done something different?

Exhaustion was finally catching up. Rapp let out a long yawn and then the kid motioned him forward. Rapp greeted the kid in French. He couldn't have been more than sixteen. Rapp smiled while he tapped out the techno beat and chomped on his gum.

"What is your purpose?" the kid asked with a lack of enthusiasm you'd expect from someone who was expected to stand in the sun all day sucking on emissions and asking the same question over and over.

"Business."

"What kind of business?"

"Software."

The kid shook his head. "What's that?"

"Computer stuff." Rapp reached over and picked up the flashy color brochure they'd ordered from a French company. He showed the kid, who was by now bored with their conversation.

"I like your music."

"Really?" Rapp said, surprised. "Are you here every day?"

The kid nodded.

Rapp looked over at the kid's dusty boom box and then reached over and ejected the tape. He slid it into the case and said, "I've been listening to it for a week straight. Knock yourself out. I'll pick it up when I drive back out in a few days."

The kid was excited and lowered his rifle. "Thanks . . . for you . . . half price today." He flashed Rapp five fingers.

Rapp paid him, smiled, slipped the little car back into gear, and drove away. It took him another twenty minutes to find the safe house. Based on the stories he'd heard from Hurley, he was surprised that during that time he didn't run into any more armed men. As per his training, he did a normal drive-by and barely glanced at the building. All he wanted to do was go to sleep, but it had been drilled into him that these were the precautions that would save his life, so he continued past and then circled back, checking the next block in each direction.

It was a five-story apartment building among four-, five-, and six-story apartment buildings. Rapp was too tired to care if it had any architectural characteristics beyond a front and back door. He parked the car, grabbed his bag, and entered the building. He didn't have a gun on him, at least not yet, so there was pretty much only one thing to do. Climb the stairs. If it was a trap, he'd have to throw his bag at them and lie down and take a nap. No one was waiting for him when he got to the fifth floor. There were three doors on the left and three on the right. They had the two on the right toward the back. Or so he thought. After checking above each door he came up empty, so he checked the ones across the hall and found two keys. That was when he remembered he was supposed to enter from the back of the building.

That snapped him out of it a bit. That and the lesson that he might be Ismael someday. He told himself to slow down and stop rushing things. He checked his watch. It was two-eleven in the afternoon. He hadn't slept in more than a day, and the day before that only a few hours. He opened the door and closed and locked it behind him. He could barely keep his eyes open, but he still dug out the doorstop and wedged it under the door. Not bothering to check the rest of the place, he went into the bedroom and opened the closet. There on the floor was a suitcase that looked a lot like the one from Istanbul. Rapp placed it on the bed, opened it, and found three Beretta 92Fs with silencers and extra magazines. It was the same suitcase.

Rapp loaded one of the guns and put the suitcase away. With his last bit of strength, he stripped down to his boxers and climbed under the covers of the twin bed. He shoved the pistol under the pillow and wondered who the person was who went from city to city dropping off their tools of the trade. Would he ever get the chance to meet this mystery man or woman? Probably not. As Hurley liked to say, they were on a need-to-know basis and there wasn't a lot they needed to know. Rapp began to drift off to sleep even though he knew that Hurley and Richards would probably be there in a minute. He figured any sleep was better than none.

CHAPTER 50

THE bag they'd placed over his head offered a mix of putrid smells—feces, vomit, snot, and blood all mixed together with the sweat of all the men who had worn it before him. And it wasn't the perspiration of exertion, it was the ripe sweat of fear, an all-out assault on his olfactory system, designed to make him pliable to whoever it was who would walk through the door and begin asking questions. Hurley had no idea where he was, other than the fact that he was in a basement. He'd felt the stairs as they'd dragged him from the trunk of a car and into the building.

It was the second car he'd been in that morning. In the midst of his pummeling by the police he blurted out the only name that he thought might help. "Levon Petrosian! I am a friend of Petrosian!"

The clubbing and kicking stopped almost immediately, and then one of the men asked him what he'd said. Hurley could tell it was the portly one in the three-piece suit, even though he couldn't see him. The man ordered him cuffed and placed in the backseat of one of the cars. They were not gentle, but Hurley did not expect them to be, so it wasn't too bad. That was when they placed the first hood on his head. It wasn't too bad, really. It could have used a good cleaning, but at least it didn't smell like a bowl of shit.

He marked the time in the back of the car, counting the seconds and trying to make sense of the noises beyond the glass windows. The metal cuffs were biting into his skin. He twisted his wrists around and tried to see if he could get out of them, but it was no use. Twenty-seven seconds later, the car doors opened. Hurley couldn't be sure, but he thought two men got in the front seat and one man joined him in the back. He felt something hard jabbed into his ribs.

"Don't move, or I will kill you."

Hurley couldn't be sure if the object at his side was a gun or a truncheon. "Fuck you." The object was jabbed even harder into his side.

"You shouldn't talk to a policeman like that."

The voice came from the front seat. It was the older pudgeball. "Policeman," Hurley said with open disdain. "If you're cops, what am I being arrested for?"

"For striking a police officer. One of my men has a broken nose."

"You mean the one who was going to crack me over the back of the head with his stick? I have a great idea. Don't bullshit me, and I won't bullshit you."

"Striking a police officer is a very serious matter."

"Yeah . . . so is kidnapping, so why don't you just pull over and let me go and I'll make sure no one puts a price on your head."

"Are you threatening us?"

"Just telling you the truth. I make it a habit not to kill cops . . . that is, unless they are corrupt."

Hurley doubled over as the man next to him delivered a stinging blow with whatever it was that he was holding. Hurley recovered and said, "I can't wait to tell Petrosian about this . . . the first thing I'm going to do"—Hurley turned to his right as if he could actually see the man next to him—"is take that stick of yours and shove it up your ass. Although you'd probably like that, wouldn't you?" Hurley expected it this time and folded his arms up quickly, locking the object between his right biceps and forearm. Then he reeled his head back and smashed it in the general direction of the other man's head. They hit forehead to forehead, like two pool balls. A loud, resounding crack. Despite the pain that Hurley felt he started laughing wildly and kicking and thrashing.

That was when they decided to pull over and put him in the trunk. Not long after that, maybe ten minutes, they stopped, pulled him out of the trunk, and stripped him down to his birthday suit. Hurley endured this part without comment. He had a sinking feeling where this was all headed, and it was bleak, to say the least. He held out hope, though, that

Richards had been able to get away. They wasted no time tossing him into the trunk of a second car and speeding off. It was a bumpy ride, and it must have been an older car, because the fumes grew so strong that Hurley started to think he would suffocate. It occurred to him that that might be the best possible outcome. Fall asleep and die from carbon monoxide poisoning. He could skip all of the degradation and take his secrets with him.

Unfortunately, he had survived, and they had dragged him into this dank basement that smelled like an outhouse. They'd switched out the hood that the police had used and put this disgusting burlap bag on his head. Hurley took in shallow breaths through his mouth and focused his mind. Throwing up under this thing would be extremely unpleasant, but then again there was a really good chance that he was about to endure the most repugnant degradation the mind could imagine, so why worry?

The mind, Hurley knew, could take only so much before it simply opened up and let the secrets spill out. They said everyone eventually broke, but Hurley didn't think of himself as everyone. He was a mean, nasty man who might have lost a step, but he was still very much in control of his mind. Under the smelly hood he smiled at the challenge ahead of him. He went through the long, nasty list of the things they would do to him. He committed himself to fighting them every step of the way, and if he was lucky they'd either intentionally or accidentally kill him. And that was a victory he would take in a heartbeat.

Hurley sat there for at least an hour. He was bored, because he knew what they were doing, and he'd just as soon get on with it. Isolation was a standard interrogation/torture technique, and while it worked on most people it was useless on Hurley because of the simple fact that he really didn't like people all that much. There were a few here and there that he'd met over the years who could hold his interest, but most others were either boring or irritating.

There were noises on the other side of the door. Footsteps, some talking, but nothing he could make out, and then the door opened. Hurley tried to count the different steps. His best guess was three or four men. They spread out around him. Someone approached him from behind and Hurley resisted the impulse to flinch. The man grabbed the burlap bag and yanked it from his head. Hurley blinked several times and took a look around the room. An industrial lamp hung from the ceiling, a brown extension cord snaking its way to the door. Hurley looked at the three men he could see. Two were familiar.

"Gentlemen, there must be some misunderstanding here," Hurley announced in an easy tone. "I thought hostilities in Beirut were over."

The two men in front of Hurley shared a brief smile. The older one said, "Mr. Sherman, I have been looking forward to this for some time."

"So have I, Sayyed."

"So you know who I am?" Sayyed asked with a raised eyebrow.

"I sure do. You're the GSD goon here in Beirut."

"And you, Mr. Sherman, are a CIA assassin."

Hurley looked as if he had to think about that for a second, and then he nodded and said, "That would be correct. I kill people like you for a living. In fact, I killed your boss, Hisham."

Sayyed nodded. This was going to be very interesting. "It really was a shame that you weren't at the embassy that afternoon. We planned the entire operation with the hope that you would be there."

"Yeah . . . it was a real shame. Although I've tried to make up for it over the years by killing as many of you assholes as I can."

Sayyed gave him an affable smile. "It looks like your killing days have come to an end."

"Possibly." Hurley surveyed the dank room. "Things don't look so good, but I'm always up for a challenge."

"This is a challenge you will not win, and you know that."

"I'm afraid I don't. You see I'm a fucked-up guy. I'm not okay in the head, and I pretty much hate you limp dicks more than I love life, so this is gonna be a tough one."

"Really, Mr. Sherman, your false bravado is so American . . . so Hollywood."

Hurley winced at the word *Hollywood*, as if it pained him to be associated with the town. "No false bravado here, Sayyed. I am going to fuck with you until I take my last breath. I'm going to feed you so much disinformation, you won't know what to believe. You'll be killing your own people before it's all over. You won't sleep at night, and when you do you'll be dreaming of traitors around every corner. Spies in your own camp. This is going to be a blast."

"Really?"

"Yep." Hurley gave him a nod to confirm his conviction. "The two of us are going to take a little trip into the bowels of my sick mind, and trust me, you won't make it out unscathed."

"Ha," Sayyed laughed. This was a first. "Fine. I think we should begin our journey. Don't you?"

"Absolutely! The sooner the better . . . that's my motto."

"Why have you decided to come back to Beirut after all these years?"

"You know why I'm here."

"Let's not assume I know your motives."

Hurley smiled. "You have something I want."

"And what would that be?"

Hurley had thought about this while he had sat under the putrid hood. Ivanov was due to show up the day after tomorrow and he would be desperate. They were all desperate because Hurley himself had drained their little secret bank accounts. He just hoped they hadn't gotten their hands on Richards, and if they had, that he would be smart enough to leave Hamburg out of his interrogation. He needed to make this seem to be about exactly what it was without the money coming up. "I am here to negotiate the release of John Cummins."

"And why would I give him to you?"

Hurley tilted his head back and looked up at the ceiling. "Well, let's think about that. If you give him back to me, I won't kill you."

This elicited laughter from all, including Hurley.

Sayyed stopped laughing abruptly and snapped his fingers. He looked at one of his men and pointed at the door. The men left and came back a few seconds later wheeling the small stainless-steel cart. Sayyed took it from him and positioned it next to the subject. He smiled at Hurley and picked up the pliers, opening and closing them.

"Manicure?" Hurley asked.

"I like to call it Twenty Questions."

"You're so clever, Sayyed," Hurley said, his voice dripping with mock admiration. "Kind of like a game show. I can't wait to get started."

"Good. Let's start with your real name."

"Jack Mehoff," Hurley offered, straight-faced.

"Jack Mehoff," Sayyed repeated. "That is your real name?"

"Of course it isn't, you fucking moron. Jack Mehoff . . . jack me off. Come on, let's go. Off with the first fingernail. You win. I lose. Let's go."

Sayyed searched the subject's face for a sign of stress. He had never had a prisoner ask to have his fingernail torn off. His demeanor would change in a second, though. Sayyed chose the forefinger on the left hand and wedged the grip of the pliers in under the nail bed. "Last chance. Your first name?"

"Don't change the rules on me. Very confusing for your subjects. You said Twenty Questions. I blew the first one, come on, let's go," Hurley said with a smile.

Sayyed clamped down hard on the pliers and began to rock the nail back and forth.

"Oh, yeah," Hurley announced. "Let's get this party started."

Sayyed gave it one good yank and ripped the entire nail off.

"Holy Mary mother . . ." Hurley unleashed a string of swear words and then started laughing. "Damn, that stings. If that doesn't wake you up nothing will. This is great!" His laughing grew to the point where he couldn't control it. He was shaking so hard his eyes started to tear up. "Oh . . . I can't wait for the next one. This is fucking great."

Sayyed remained undeterred. "Your name?"

"Bill Donovan."

"Really?"

"Nope."

"Really, Mr. Sherman, what is the harm in your telling us your first name?"

"Probably nothing at this point, but it's my nature to fuck with guys like you."

"I will ask the question again." Sayyed stayed steady. "What is your real name?"

"Ulysses S. Grant."

"You are lying?"

"Of course, you fucking idiot. Don't you read history?"

Sayyed moved in for the second fingernail. He wedged the pliers under the nail bed, wiggled it again to make sure he had a good enough grip, and then looked into Hurley's eyes. He didn't like what he saw. It was the wild-eyed look of a crazy man.

"Do it. Come on," Hurley egged him on. "What

are you waiting for? You're not turning into a pussy on me, are you?"

Part of Sayyed knew he should stop and come back later when he could control the situation. The men were here, however, so he needed to pull this second nail, and then let this lunatic sit and stew for a while. Probably come back and use electricity. He tightened his grip and yanked the second nail free.

Hurley howled again with the laughter of a madman. The shrieking turned to cackles and then uncontrollable laughter. His eyes were filled with tears as he yelled, "Eighteen more to go! Heeee haw-www!"

Sayyed dropped the pliers on the cart. "That's right. We'll give you a little rest before we start with the others." He started for the door.

Hurley looked at the other man who was standing in front of him. "Is that you Abu . . . Abu Radih? I haven't seen you in years. I heard you have your own little terrorist group now . . . Fatah. Look at you . . . all grown-up," Hurley said admiringly.

Radih smiled and shook his head. He clearly thought the American insane.

Hurley tilted his head to the side as if trying to recall some distant memory. "I bet you weren't more than four feet tall when I used to fuck your mother. Did you tell your friends that she was a prostitute?" Hurley craned his head to look at the other two men. "His mom could suck cock better than any whore I ever met, and trust me, I've been with a lot of whores."

The smile left Radih's face in an instant. He

lashed out with his right fist, hitting Hurley in the mouth. Hurley's head rocked back from the blow, and then, before Radih could throw another punch, Sayyed grabbed him from behind.

"No," Sayyed ordered. "Do not let him get to you."

Hurley shook the sting and fog from his head and came up smiling. One of his top middle teeth had been knocked out and his mouth was filling with blood. "Look!" Hurley yelled, showing them the gap in his top row. "Look, you knocked my tooth out." Radih and Sayyed stopped struggling for a second, and that was when Hurley unleashed a gob of blood and the one busted tooth from his mouth. The bulk of it hit Radih in the face. With his arms tied behind his back and his legs taped to the chair, Hurley started bouncing the chair an inch at a time toward the two men, snapping his teeth and barking like a dog.

CHAPTER 51

MOSCOW, RUSSIA

IT was almost noon, and Ivanov was still in bed. He claimed he wasn't feeling well. Moaned something about the snow and the cold and the gray, depressing Moscow sky. Of course it had nothing to do with all of the vodka and wine and heavy foods he'd consumed until well past midnight. Shvets would have liked to throw him in a cold snowdrift and shock him back to the here and now. The young Russian didn't understand depression. He couldn't see how people allowed it to get so bad that they couldn't get out of bed, was unable to understand that the drinking and the sleeping were all intertwined like a big sheet wrapped around your body until you couldn't move. And then you started sinking. Stop the drinking, get out of bed, and work out. Have a purpose in life. It was not complicated.

Shvets crossed from one end of the parlor to the other, glancing at Alexei, who was one-half of his boss's favorite bodyguard duo. They were in a corner suite on the top floor of Hotel Baltschug. He looked out the big window across the frozen Moscow River at the Kremlin, Red Square, and St. Basil's Cathedral. Shvets had never understood why the Bolsheviks had let the cathedral stand. They were so anticzar, so antireligion, why let this one church remain while they destroyed so many others? The answer probably lay in their own doubts about what they were doing. The people had risen up and helped them grab power, but the people were a tough beast to tame. Shvets thought they probably feared it would bring about another revolution.

Frost had built up around the edges of the window. It was minus twenty degrees Celsius, and the wind was blowing, whipping up clouds of snow, but so what? That was February in Moscow. Only a weak man allows the weather to affect his mood. Shvets let out a long exhalation, his breath forming a fog on the window that froze within seconds. Ivanov was about to drag him down, take him under like some fool walking out onto the melting March ice of the Moscow River. These weren't the old days of deportation to a Siberian work camp, and executions against the back wall at Lubyanka, but the government was by no means just. The new regime was just more astute at PR. They could still be beaten senseless and be forced to sign false confessions of crimes against the state and whatever else they decided to trump up. Then they would be taken to the woods and shot, far away from the ears of the people and the new press.

Ivanov would of course try to save his vodka-soaked hide. That was his nature. He would blame anyone but himself, and since Shvets was the person most directly in the line of fire, the only person other than Ivanov who had actually met Herr Dorfman, he would be the scapegoat. Gripped with an unusual fear, Shvets had a sudden urge to flee. He paced from one end of the parlor and back, trying to calm himself, but he couldn't. The idea of running was suddenly in front of him, like a big flashing road sign warning the bridge is out. Turn now or crash.

But he had a wife and two boys—not that he saw them very much, or really loved them, or more precisely her. The boys were too young to judge. His wife, on the other hand, had been a mistake. She'd gotten fat and lazy, and Shvets spent as little time with her as possible. He could certainly live without them, but could he live with himself if anything happened to them? He wasn't sure about that one, so he set it aside. Starting over was the other problem. As Ivanov's top deputy, he was poised for lofty heights within the SVR, and like his boss, he could leverage that for personal gain in the not-so-distant future.

That was something he did not want to give up without a fight, but the rumors were starting, and by next week they would be undeniable. He had either to run or turn on Ivanov, go to SVR headquarters and ask for a face-to-face with Director Primakov. Even as he thought about it, he knew it would be far riskier than running. It was easy to trick himself into thinking they would reward him for doing the right thing, but the SVR was not all that different from the old KGB. You were rewarded for plotting, conspiring, and crushing your political and professional opponents, not for doing the right thing. If he turned on Ivanov in such a manner he would not be rewarded, he would be punished. Not right away, but eventually. They would send him away. No one would want to look at him, because he would be a reminder of their failures.

He didn't even consider going to the federal counterintelligence service. The FSK would jump at the chance to embarrass their flashy sister agency, especially if it meant taking down someone as big as Ivanov, but Shvets had no desire to be branded a traitor for the rest of his days. The men who turned against the security service had an extremely high occurrence of suicide.

Shvets was pragmatic to the core, but this sitting around could only spell disaster. Some type of action had to be taken. He turned away from the window and looked at Alexei, the thick-necked bodyguard. "Alexei, do you trust me?"

The bodyguard lifted his heavy head and looked at Shvets. He shrugged in the way a man shrugs when he finds a question not worth answering.

"Do you know what is going on with our boss?" Another shrug.

"You know he's in trouble, yes?"

This time big Alexei nodded.

"He's in a great deal of trouble, and he doesn't want to admit it. He would prefer to drink himself silly and shut himself in with the hope that the problem will simply go away. The problem isn't going to go away. In fact, it is only going to get worse." Shvets was tempted to tell him what was going on, but wasn't prepared to go that far. "I need your help, Alexei. I need to get him out of bed and sober him up enough so that he can defend himself. Do you understand that?"

"Yes."

"Good," Shvets said, satisfied that he had gotten somewhere with the man. "Now don't shoot me or break my neck, but I'm going in there to wake him up."

Alexei pursed his big lips while he thought about that one. "He told me. No one. Including you."

"Your job is to protect him, right? Well, if he put a gun to his own head, would you try to stop him?"

"Yes."

"That's what he's doing right now. By getting drunk and sleeping the day away he's killing himself as surely as if he put a gun to his head and pulled the trigger. You need to help me save him."

"What do you want me to do?"

"Nothing. Just sit here . . . and don't hurt me." Shvets didn't wait for an answer. He went to the bedroom door, knocked twice, and then opened. The bed was huge, and with all the pillows and blankets and two prostitutes and poor light he couldn't tell what was what, so he went to the window and yanked open the heavy velvet drapes. Gray light poured into the room and Shvets heard Ivanov moan. He searched the tangled mess and still couldn't find the man's head.

"Sir," Shvets announced, "Director Primakov is here to see you."

A flurry of activity erupted from under the blankets. One or both of the girls screamed as Ivanov dug his way out, all elbows and knees. His red face appeared midway down the length of the bed. "What?" he asked, a mask of horror on his face. "You can't be serious."

"No, I am not, but if you don't get out of bed and do something about this situation, he will show up sooner than you think. Or maybe you would prefer Director Barannikov to show up with the FSK boys and drag you downtown."

Ivanov pulled his head back under the covers. "Go away."

"No, I will not. You have been pouting for three days now. We need to come up with a plan of action, or we are doomed."

"We are worse than doomed ... We are fucked."

"Stop being such a baby."

"Be careful what you say to me, Nikolai, or I will get out of this bed and throw you out the window."

"Not a bad way to go when compared to what the FSK will do to me. Unfortunately, you have neither the strength nor the courage to throw me out the window, so it looks like I will be tortured in the basement of Lubyanka." He looked over at the bed, but there was no movement or reply. "Please, boss! I beg you to do something ... anything. Defend yourself. Tell Director Primakov the money is gone."

"You are a fool. I will be put under an examination that I won't be able to withstand."

"Then place the blame on the dirty Palestinians. You know how Primakov hates them. Tell him they killed Sharif over a bad business deal and took all of the money. Blame the Americans, the Brits, the French, the Germans . . . I don't care. Just blame someone and start investigating. What you are doing . . ."

"What was that?" Ivanov snapped as he popped his head back out.

"Blame someone and start investigating."

"Before that . . . at the beginning."

"Blame the Arabs."

"You are right . . . Primakov does hate them. But my money . . . what about that?"

Shvets was pleased with his small victory. Now he needed to bait the hook. "I have some ideas about that as well." He started walking toward the double doors. "I suggest you get out of bed and shower. I will order an extremely late breakfast. We can discuss your finances over coffee and eggs."

CHAPTER 52

BEIRUT, LEBANON

RAPP was in his boxers, pistol at his side, staring at the door of the apartment and trying to decide what to do. It was dark and he had no idea how long he had slept. Whoever was trying to get into the apartment had picked the lock. Rapp raised the pistol and took aim. Either that or he had a key. He eased his finger off the trigger. Maybe it was a nosy landlady, or Hurley was testing him. No, it wouldn't be that. If they were still in training it would be something he'd gladly try, but not in the thick of it like this. For all he knew, Rapp might use it as an excuse to shoot him.

Rapp stayed in the hallway that led to the bedrooms so he could use the wall as cover. The door started to move and then stopped. The rubber stop he'd placed underneath it was doing its job. The door opened a crack and Rapp heard someone saying something, whispering as if they were talking to someone else. But then Rapp heard, "Hey . . . Open up," in English.

Part of the problem was that he had no idea how long he'd slept and consequently what time it was. He had awakened with a start as he heard some soft knocking on the door, followed by the sound of metal on metal, and now whoever was out there was talking to him and getting louder.

"Hey, shithead . . . Open the damn door. We've got big problems."

The contraction of *we have* was what caught his attention. It was not Hurley or Richards so the *we* thing threw another level of mystery into the equation.

"I know you're in there. Open this fucking door, so I don't have to break it down."

Rapp quietly crossed the room on the balls of his feet. The door was cracked about an inch. "Who is it?"

"Fucking Goldilocks. We've been compromised. Open the door. I need to get you the hell out of here."

Rapp's heart started trotting. *Goldilocks . . . compromised . . . What the hell was going on?* "What's the password?" Rapp heard the word *shit* followed by a heavy sigh.

"I'm not part of your merry little band. I don't know the password." There was a pause and then, "There's a leather case in the bedroom closet with a few handy things in it. You're probably holding one of the silenced Berettas right now. I'm the guy who put it there."

Rapp frowned. "Were you in Istanbul a week ago?"

There was a pause and then, "Yeah . . . was that you?"

"Nice little garden flat with alley access."

"Case was in an armoire."

"With a pillow and blanket on top," Rapp said.

"Bingo."

"Let me close the door first and then I'll let you in."

"Roger."

Rapp pushed the door closed and kicked the doorstop out of the way. With his pistol in his right hand he opened the door and then stepped back, holding the gun in a two-handed grip. The guy entered the room and closed the door behind him. He was wearing brown pants, brown shirt, and brown baseball hat. Where had Rapp seen that outfit before?

The visitor dropped the box he was carrying and raised his hands. "Kid, could you lower the gun. If I was a terrorist I would have blown the damn building up."

Looking over the iron sights of the Beretta, Rapp said, "A few more questions. What's going on?"

"You've been compromised. I was ordered by Washington to come get you."

"Who?"

"Irene."

Rapp lowered the gun. "Why?"

"Follow me," the man said as he picked up his box and started for the bedroom. "Stan and your other buddy were picked up at their hotel this morning."

"This morning?" Rapp asked, dumbfounded. "What time is it?"

"Almost six-thirty. They were grabbed by the cops and then handed over to those assholes from Islamic Jihad."

Rapp stopped moving. "Say that again."

"Don't stop moving, kid. They could be on their way here right now, and I don't think we want to be standing around talking when they show up." He opened the box and pulled out clothes that matched his. "Here . . . put these on. I'll grab your shit." He tossed the clothes on the bed and went to the closet, retrieving Rapp's suitcase as well as the beat-up leather case.

Rapp's mind was swimming upstream trying to process what he'd just learned. "But . . ."

The man turned on him, a frightened, wild look in his eyes. "No buts," he hissed. "No questions, no nothing. We need to get the fuck out of here, and I mean now."

Rapp nodded and began putting on his clothes. This stranger was right, of course. He quickly put on the brown uniform and stuffed his clothes in his suitcase, while the stranger wiped down the door-knobs. In just under two minutes they were out the door and on their way to the street. The stranger went out first and after casually looking up and down the street motioned for Rapp to follow. They threw the suitcase and empty box in the back of a simple white minivan, then left. Rapp glanced at his rental car and almost said something, but thought better of it. They had bigger problems.

CHAPTER 53

MUGHNIYAH refused to come to Martyrs' Square, so they had to go to him. Sayyed could hardly blame him. He couldn't wait for the standoff to end, and the hostages to be out of his care. He was tied to them like a mother to her breast-feeding brood. Still, there was something very exciting about the work that lay ahead. Bill Sherman was a once-in-a-lifetime experiment. The American intrigued and horrified him at the same time. Sayyed had participated in close to a hundred interrogations, and he'd never seen anything even close to what he'd witnessed today. The other man, the younger one, was fairly straightforward. A few threats, some punches and kicks, and one fingernail was all it took to get him talking. He'd gotten a name out of him. Several, actually. It was possible that they were both fake, but he didn't really care at this point.

The important thing was that the great and powerful America had once again failed. They had tried to interfere in the affairs of tiny Beirut and he had beaten them at their game yet again. And this one would hurt. Cummins was one thing, but Bill Sherman would have secrets to tell. Secrets that Moscow would have to pay for.

They were in the cellar of a bistro on General de Gaulle Boulevard—the west end of town, just a block from the ocean. The civil war followed the same patterns as any war, but on a much smaller scale. Two blocks either side of the Green Line were virtually destroyed, buildings blown to pieces from high-explosive artillery shells and mortar rounds. Nearly every building had the pockmarks of small-arms fire, but beyond the Green Line you could find a street devastated by the war, yet there would be one building untouched. That one would survive while six or eight in either direction fell made no sense, but it was an undeniable fact of war that some men, and some buildings, seemed to have an almost invisible shield around them. Farther away from the Green Line, entire neighborhoods had made it through the war with far better success, losing only a building or two from the random shelling. Mughniyah loved these buildings. He noted them and used them for his most important meetings.

This restaurant was that kind of lucky building. Sayyed had been initially irritated by all of the extra security measures. They were brought to three different locations and forced to switch cars before they arrived at the bistro. Mughniyah was the most paranoid of the group by a long shot. They found him in the back room with Badredeen. Plates of hummus, *ackawi,* roasted nuts, kibbeh, baba ghanouj, and spiced fish were waiting. After the last few days Sayyed could barely contain himself. He dug in, using the flatbread to scoop up the hummus and then some olives and cheese.

Mughniyah watched with interest as Sayyed devoured the food, and Radih sat sipping his water. He had heard of the deplorable conditions at Martyrs' Square. He'd spent the better part of his life living in abject poverty, so it wasn't that he was above slumming it with the men. And he despised the Maronites as much as, or more than, any of them. It was the American prisoners who kept him away. Those men would attract too much attention. The Americans would be looking for them, and if they got lucky—well, the building would be leveled with everyone in it.

"Radih," Mughniyah asked, "why aren't you eating?"

"I'm not hungry."

Mughniyah could tell there was something else bothering him, but he was extremely unsympathetic to the problems of others. He stabbed out his cigarette and asked, "Can we be sure he is the same Bill Sherman who escaped the embassy bombing in '83?"

Sayyed nodded while he washed some baba ghanouj down with a glass of water. "It's him."

"And did you learn anything from him today?"

"We should kill him," Radih said. "He is the

devil himself. We should not tempt fate a second time. Give me the word and I will kill him tonight."

Mughniyah had no idea what had precipitated such a drastic statement from a man who loved to barter for the lives of hostages. He turned to Sayyed. "And what do you think?"

"Mr. Sherman is an interesting man. A professional liar and provocateur, for certain, but he is also an extremely valuable asset."

"The man is a curse on all of us," Radih proclaimed. "I am telling you we should rid ourselves of lies and kill him tonight."

Thinking it would be a good idea to change the subject, Sayyed asked, "Where is Colonel Jalil?"

"He will not be joining us." Mughniyah turned and shared a knowing glance with Badredeen.

They had been conspiring. That was plain enough to Sayyed, and if it meant leaving the Iranian out, that was fine with him. Sayyed watched as Mughniyah's mood turned dark. He'd seen it before, and when he was sour like this he could be prone to violence. Like some fifteenth-century sultan, he could on a whim ask for someone's offensive head to be separated from the rest of his body. No hierarchy had ever been established for the group, but there was nonetheless a natural order to things. Mughniyah sat atop the food chain for the simple reason that he was the most ruthless among a group of men who were no strangers to violence.

The key, Sayyed had learned, was to think very carefully before answering him when he was in one of his exceptionally surly moods. "What do you have in mind, Mustapha?"

Before he could answer, Radih said for the third time, "I think we should kill him." He did not bother to look at the others. His voice was eerily devoid of his normal youthful passion. "I think the man is the Shaitan himself. We should take him out to the statue tonight and disembowel him. Leave him to a slow death. He can howl his lies at the moon. Let him be an example to the Americans and anyone else who wants to send their assassins to Beirut."

Sayyed held his breath. His eyes darted back and forth between the upstart and the lion. Radih was not a deeply religious man, and his proclamation that the prisoner was the devil was likely to give the duo from Islamic Jihad pause, but then again Mughniyah did not like being interrupted.

"Assef?" Mughniyah asked Sayyed.

Sayyed pulled in a quick breath and said, "I'm not sure I would go as far as to call the man Satan, but on the other hand there is undeniably something very wrong with Mr. Bill Sherman." Glancing at Radih he added, "I can appreciate why Abu might think that would be a good idea, but I'm afraid we would be destroying a very valuable commodity."

Mughniyah grinned knowingly. They were of the same mind.

"Before we decide on something so brash," Badredeen said in his easy tone, "we need to assess a few things. Such as our finances."

Mughniyah held out his hand and said, "We will get to that in a second, but first, I want to talk about Sherman . . . Why is he back after all these years?"

Sayyed straightened up. "He says he is here to kill us, but it is unwise to listen to much of anything that comes out of his mouth." He glanced at Radih and gave him a reassuring nod. What Sherman had said about the young man's mother did not have to be repeated. "His associate, though, is far more truthful, and he says they are here to negotiate the release of Agent Cummins."

Radih was rubbing his swollen knuckles. "I do not believe either of them."

"You don't think they are here to negotiate the release of Agent Cummins?" Mughniyah asked.

"I don't believe anything that comes out of their mouths."

Sayyed could see Mughniyah's legendary temper begin to simmer. "Do you understand the term *unintended consequences*?"

The young leader of Fatah shrugged as if he couldn't care less.

"How about luck . . . as in good or bad luck?"

Radih nodded this time.

"Well, let me explain to you why your mood is starting to upset me. Six months ago, you decided to kidnap an American businessman, who, as it turns out, is just that. He is not a spy. You kidnapped him without coming to us for approval. For that reason alone I could have you shot. That single kidnapping has set in motion a series of events. Agent Cummins was then sent to try to negotiate the release of this businessman. You decided to then grab Cummins rather than negotiate a fee and end it. Fortunately, or unfortunately, we found out that Mr. Cummins is a CIA spy."

"How could that be unfortunate?" Radih proclaimed more than asked.

Mughniyah sat back and gripped the armrests of his chair, almost as if he were trying to hold himself back. "I am in a rather bad mood tonight, so I suggest you keep your interruptions to a minimum, Abu, or I might lose control and snap your scrawny little neck." He let a moment pass, and when he was sure that he had the younger man's attention, he continued. "Where was I? Yes, as it turned out, Mr. Cummins was not who he said he was. He is in fact an American spy. Now, when we are a few days away from handing Cummins over to the Russian, the notorious Bill Sherman and another CIA lackey show up. Are you following me so far?"

Radih nodded.

"All of this was set in motion by one event. Your kidnapping of the businessman. These are what we would call unintended consequences. How many more unintended consequences are going to pop up? Are there any more Americans in the city, or on their way to the city? Will the four of us survive the week? These are the questions that we will not know the answers to until this thing plays itself out. Your heart is in the right place and you are eager, but you need to understand that your actions have consequences. Have I made myself clear?"

"Yes."

"Now the unfortunate thing is that the Americans appear to have learned their lesson after they let us ship their old station chief off to Tehran, so we could thoroughly interrogate him and then dismantle their network of spies. This time it appears they are going to try to get one of their own back. The only surprise is that they didn't try to do it sooner, but now that we have the legendary Mr. Sherman, I think the stakes have been raised considerably."

"How so?" Radih asked, trying not to sound confrontational.

"Mr. Sherman is a particularly nasty man, who no doubt has many nasty secrets bottled up in his sick little head. The CIA will not want those secrets to get out, so I am afraid they will try to get him back as well."

"So," Badredeen said, picking up the conversation, "we must move quickly and carefully to rid ourselves of all these Americans."

"And that is where the Russian comes in." Mughniyah stared at Sayyed. "Assef, when was the last time you heard from the Russian?"

Sayyed wiped the corners of his mouth. "Yesterday. I was not able to get hold of him today."

"Has he mentioned anything about Dorfman and the empty accounts?"

"No."

Mughniyah and Badredeen looked at each other and nodded in agreement. Badredeen spoke. "Don't you find his silence on the subject a bit strange?"

"I do."

"There are three possibilities." Badredeen held up one finger. "The first, the Russian has no idea our banker was murdered in his home on Sunday and that the very next morning, millions of dollars were emptied out of accounts that he himself helped us set up. Does anyone believe for a second that the Russian is that clueless?" When they were all done agreeing, Badredeen moved on to his second point. "The Russian, being the greedy man that he is, killed Dorfman and took all of the money for himself."

Mughniyah held up two fingers and said, "I am going with option two."

"What about option three?" Sayyed asked.

"Someone unknown to us killed Dorfman and stole the money. The only problem with this theory is that Dorfman was very secretive about his clients. The man had no social skill. He cared only for his dogs."

"Still . . . someone . . . an enemy could have found out." Sayyed tried to keep the options open.

"Let me ask you," Mughniyah said, leaning forward, "can you think of anyone you know who has a reputation for cheating people out of their money?"

"I don't want to be in the position of defending Ivanov, but I think we need more evidence before we settle on him as the thief."

"You didn't answer my question."

Sayyed nodded. "You are correct. Mikhail Ivanov is not exactly the most honest man I know."

"And let's not forget the little falling-out he had with our Turkish friend," Badredeen added.

Sayyed was the one who had passed on the information he'd picked up from Damascus. Hamdi

Sharif, the arms dealer whom they had worked with for close to a decade, had reportedly had a fight with Ivanov over a business deal. A month later, Sharif ended up assassinated on a park bench in front of his house. He had asked Ivanov about it, but of course the man had denied any connection.

Mughniyah placed his big hairy right hand on the table. He tapped a thick finger and said, "Moscow is a den of thieves. I warned all of you about this years ago. The collapse has turned it into a free-for-all where the most brutal simply take what they want."

Sayyed could not argue with what he had said. "So what do we do?"

"You say the Russian will be here Friday?"

"Yes."

"Good. We are going to have a little auction."

The word seemed to wake up Radih. "What kind of auction?"

"The kind where we sell the American spies to the highest bidder."

"What bidders?" Sayyed asked.

"Don't worry," Mughniyah cautioned. "Just make sure the Russian is here, and I'll take care of the rest."

"What about Damascus? I must report this missing money."

Mughniyah shook his head. "Not yet. Give me a few days and then you can tell them."

CHAPTER 54

RAPP stepped out into the hot afternoon sun and looked over the edge of the veranda. The narrow street that snaked its way up the hill was barely wide enough for a single car to pass. Down at the bottom, maybe a hundred yards away, he could see the Toyota pickup truck blocking the street. The houses on this little goat hill were all flat-roofed. Clotheslines were strung up and shirts and pants and other garments flapped in the breeze. Beneath him, in the tiny courtyard, three vehicles were packed in with no more than a few feet in between. The ten-foot wall had a ring of razor wire strung from one end to the other. He looked to his right and found a stack of green fiberglass crates. Stenciled on the side in black letters were a string of numbers and letters that he didn't understand, then a few that he did.

Each crate contained multiple M72 LAW antiarmor weapons. Next to those were a crate of rounds for an M203 grenade launcher that was leaning against the wall. Above that, affixed to the wall, was a hand-drawn laminated map that marked the distance and elevation to certain landmarks up to a mile away. Rapp was wondering what all this stuff was for when he heard the voice of the man who had pulled him out of the safe house the night before.

"We call this the sky box . . . not anymore really, but during the height of the war we would sit up here and watch it all unfold."

Rapp turned around to find Rob Ridley sipping on a bright red can of Coke. "Sky box?"

Ridley approached the edge of the balcony, pointed toward the ocean to the north, and then drew his hand south. "See that big, ugly scar that runs from the north to the south?"

"Yeah."

"That's the famous Green Line. We'd sit up here and watch them fight, like a football game. That's why we called it the sky box."

Rapp pointed to the stack of U.S. Army crates. "Looks like you guys did more than watch."

"That shit is more for self-defense, although I saw some badass snipers roll through here. That's the unwritten story about this little war . . . the snipers. They did most of the damage. We found that they were getting a little close." Hurley pointed up at the overhang. "They started sending rounds in here on a daily basis. We put up sandbags, and then after one of our guys got killed, we put in a request for a couple of those badasses from Fort Bragg. Two of them showed up five days later." Ridley pointed at the map on the wall. "They put that thing together. In six days they had thirty-one recorded kills, and that pretty much solved the problem. Kinda like bringing in an exterminator." Ridley laughed and then added, "That's classified, so don't go around telling that story to just anyone."

"How long have we had a presence up here?"

"You'd have to ask Stan that question. I was still in the Marine Corps when they blew our barracks up." Ridley pointed to the south. "Right over there. I showed up in '88. That was when we started rotating sniper teams through here. They loved it. In fact this is where the D Boys battle-tested the first Barrett .50 cal. He shot a guy just over seven thousand feet away."

"That's more than a mile."

"One-point-three and some change." Hurley looked off toward the Green Line. "Strange breed, those snipers. Pretty quiet lot . . . kept to themselves for the most part, but that night they got shitfaced and naked. I guess seven thousand feet is a pretty rare club. At any rate I think we've been up here since '85."

"I thought we pulled out," Rapp said.

"Langley never pulls out . . . or at least rarely. Shit, this little outpost is what stopped this thing from being a complete disaster. We knew everything Damascus was up to. We helped blow up supply convoys, target the occasional asshole who wandered too far away from his home turf. We even taught these guys how to use indirect fire and the other side knew we were here, too. That's why they sent those snipers after us."

"So this is where you're based?" Rapp asked, thinking it didn't make a lot of sense.

"No." Ridley shook his head. "Not for over a year. Things are too quiet around here now."

"So what exactly do you do for Langley?"

"I'm kind of here and there. I guess you could call me a floater."

Rapp had no idea what that meant and got the distinct impression that Ridley wasn't going to enlighten him any further. Rapp let out a yawn. His nights and days were upside-down. After their mad dash from the apartment, Ridley had filled in some of the blanks. The problem was that beyond the obvious fact that Hurley and Richards had been picked up, Ridley had very few details. Rapp had pressed him hard, wanting to know what Langley was doing to find them. Ridley had to admit not much of anything. Langley was sending a small six-man SOG team, and they were actively trying to collect any intel that would aid in a rescue.

Ridley worked his sources well past midnight, but every single one of them seemed to have conflicting information. Finally at 4:00 A.M. he sent Rapp to bed and told him to get some rest. He assured Rapp he'd been through more than a few of these abductions, and they tended to progress slowly, especially for the first few days. Rapp had a hard time falling asleep. He couldn't stop himself from imagining what Hurley and Richards were going through. As part of his training, he'd spent two days tied to a chair. Guys would come in randomly and smack him around. They even gave him some low-voltage shocks from a small engine battery. There was nothing remotely enjoyable about the experience, and Hurley had cautioned them that it paled in comparison to what they would go through at the hands of a sadist or a skilled interrogator. Finally, around sunrise, he had dozed off.

"Listen, I know what you're going through."

Rapp gave him a sideways glance. Ridley was a few inches shorter and a decade or so older. Rapp couldn't quite figure out if he was an optimist or a pessimist. He seemed to kind of float back and forth between the two.

"I've known Stan for six years. I'd do anything to try to save the guy. But we need to get some good intel before we can even consider lifting a finger."

Back in training, if someone had asked him to lay down his life to save Stan Hurley, he would have laughed at him, but now he wasn't so sure. "Any idea where they are?"

Ridley pointed east. "The other side of the big ugly scar. Indian country."

"You ever go over there?"

Ridley gave him a nervous laugh. "I try not to."

"So you've been?"

"Occasionally. It's nowhere near as bad as it was back when the shit was really flying." He searched Rapp's face, wondering what he was thinking. "It's still a nasty place for a stranger like you, kid."

Rapp nodded even though he really wasn't listening. "So it wouldn't be such a good idea to wander over there and start asking questions."

"That would be about the dumbest thing you could do, kid." Ridley could see the upstart wasn't listening to him. He reached out and grabbed his arm. "I've been to that little lake house down in southern Virginia. I've seen the way Stan takes badasses and grinds them up and spits out little pussies, so I'm guessing if you made it through his selection process you've got some serious skills. Am I right?"

Rapp looked at Ridley's grip until he released his arm. "What's your point?"

"I don't care how good you are. Going over to Indian country on your own is a suicide mission. We'll end up looking for three of you instead of two."

"Well . . . I'm not good at sitting around, so somebody better come up with a plan and come up with it quick."

The triple beep, beep, beep of a car horn caught their attention and they both looked to the base of the hill, where a three-car convoy had just pulled up to the roadblock.

"Finally," Ridley said.

"Who is it?"

"A local who knows more about this hellhole than anyone."

CHAPTER 55

MOSCOW, RUSSIA

SHVETS anxiously checked his watch. They'd been in there for more than an hour, and each passing tick of the clock only added to his apprehension. For starters, he didn't like sitting in the waiting room of Director Primakov's office on the top floor of SVR headquarters. Any trip to these lofty heights would test a man's nerves, but considering the events of the past few days, Shvets worried that he might be leaving the building in shackles. He doubted that Primakov knew about the missing money, or the other mistakes that were piling up. The SVR was an entrenched organization with thousands of operations, and Ivanov was regarded as a daring man who knew when to be ruthless and when to smile, and in the years between Stalin's violent mood swings and the collapse of the CCCP, that would have been more than enough. Now, he wasn't so sure.

This was a brave new world. The money grab was in full swing. Oligarchs were popping up and riding the wave of decentralization, but not without problems. The peasants were growing dissatisfied with what they saw as unbridled greed and corruption, and the one thing every Muscovite feared more than even a tyrant like Stalin was the rage of the mob. The mob was like some ancient god who needed regular sacrifices. The men in charge knew that, and in order to satisfy that mob and keep it from bubbling over into the streets, they would look for a few bodies to throw them. One or two public executions would go a long way toward calming the hordes.

It was Shvets's plan. After he'd forced some real food into Ivanov's gullet the previous afternoon, he began to sketch out their strategy. It would be centered on Primakov's distrust of Islamic Jihad and its sister organizations. The missing funds would be laid at their feet, along with the assassination of the banker. As Ivanov's devious brain began to work, he hit upon the idea of blaming them for Hamdi Sharif's murder as well. Shvets wasn't so sure. He was from the new generation. Ivanov was from the old, whose motto was, If you are going to lie, lie big.

The tricky part was this agent they were offering up. They had confirmed through one of their sources inside the CIA that John Cummins did in fact exist and that he had worked in Moscow before being stationed in Damascus. If Ivanov could deliver someone like that, Primakov might be willing to forget the missing funds. The only problem was coming up with the money to pay off the Palestinians. Ivanov would have to convince Primakov to give him the funds necessary to complete the transaction.

And then this morning Sayyed called and things became infinitely more interesting. He explained that he was now in possession of two more Americans, who had been sent to try to buy the release of Agent Cummins. One of the men was nothing more than an underling, but the other was the catch of a lifetime. When pressed, Sayyed refused to give details, saying he would only discuss the matter in person, when they arrived in Beirut. Still, there was no mention of Dorfman and the missing money.

Sayyed's continued silence over the missing funds had caused Ivanov to rethink the issue. What if Islamic Jihad and Fatah no longer feared him? What if they thought Russia too disorganized to care? There had been plenty of heated feuds between the various Palestinian factions over the years, and Sayyed was the man who had profited the most by peddling arms to all sides. What if that thug Mughniyah had decided to take what he wanted? Kill Dorfman, take all the money, solidify his position, and thumb his nose at Ivanov?

That thought had caused Ivanov to reach for the vodka, but Shvets had stopped him. He was scheduled to meet with Primakov in less than an hour, and he needed to be sober. The problem had become clear to Shvets as well. Why else would Sayyed stay quiet over the missing funds? If his money was gone as well, he would be demanding answers. The only logical reason for his silence was that they had taken the money and they were daring Ivanov to bring it up.

Ivanov had to assume they had every last shred of damning information that Dorfman had kept. All of the various accounts, and how Ivanov had bilked his own government out of millions on the arms shipments by playing the middleman with Sayyed. That information alone could sink him. Ivanov's hands were tied, at least for now. That was how Shvets had counseled him. Go along with this ruse. Go to Beirut and look the liars in their eyes, and then ask them where the money had gone. Bring a show of force that will make them think twice about stealing from you.

Ivanov liked the idea. As he walked into Prima-kov's office he turned and told Shvets to wait out-side. Shvets knew his boss too well to think he was anything other than a duplicitous snake. As he ner-vously checked his watch, the minutes ticking by, he figured out what Ivanov was up to. He was in there right now, blaming him for the missing funds. He'd probably already ordered someone to begin creating a false trail between him and Dorfman. That way, when it really did blow up, Ivanov could step back and blame his inept deputy Shvets. Shvets didn't know if he was more upset with Ivanov or with him-self for not seeing it sooner. He should have left him in bed and gone to Primakov and taken his chances.

When the door finally opened, Ivanov appeared with a stoic look on his face. He never broke stride as he headed for the elevator. As he walked past his deputy he snapped his fingers for him to follow. Shvets hopped to his feet and buttoned his jacket, hustling to catch up.

Once in the elevator, Shvets asked, "Well?"

"It was good. He understands what must be done."

Shvets started to ask another question, but Ivanov shook his head in a very curt way that told him this was not the place to talk. When they entered Ivanov's office less than a minute later, the director of Directorate S went straight for the vodka. Shvets did not try to stop him this time. It was approaching midafternoon, and he took it as a victory that he'd kept him sober this long. He waited for his boss to consume a few ounces.

When Ivanov looked relaxed enough, Shvets asked, "What did he say?"

Ivanov yanked at his tie. "He sees things our way. He knows the true character of those Palestinian carpet monkeys."

Shvets was used to his boss uttering racist slurs, so he paid them little attention. He also knew that his boss was paranoid enough in general, but especially today. He was worried his office was bugged. "So what is the plan?"

"We leave in the morning."

"Alone?" Shvets asked, honestly scared.

"No." Ivanov had a huge grin. "The director has been quite generous. He is sending along some Spetsnaz. One of the crack Vympel units."

Shvets wasn't sure if that was good or bad news.

The Vympel units specialized in assassination and sabotage, among other things. "Why a Vympel unit?"

"Because he's sending us with cash."

"How much?"

Ivanov smiled and held up five fingers.

"Really?" Shvets's surprise was evident on his face.

"Don't be so shocked. I have no doubt it will be counterfeit. Probably being printed as we speak."

Shvets had heard rumors about the old KGB printing presses that could turn out francs, deutsche marks, pounds, and dollars on demand. "Will they be able to tell?"

"If the Americans can't tell, how will the Palestinians be able to tell?"

Shvets wasn't so sure but he went along with it.

"Don't look so nervous." Ivanov came over and put an arm around Shvets's shoulders. "I told him how useful you have been to me. I have no doubt that when we return with these mystery Americans you will be given a nice promotion."

Shvets smiled, even though he didn't feel like it. The truth was, there was probably a better than even chance that he'd be given a dirty, dank cell.

CHAPTER 56

BEIRUT, LEBANON

ACCORDING to Ridley, it was very poor spycraft to meet a source at a safe house, but for this particular source they made exceptions. The reason was fairly straightforward. The source owned the house. Levon Petrosian had the complexion of someone who was born further north, but had lived long enough in the sun-baked city that his skin was deeply lined and had taken on the appearance of a permanent sunburn. His white hair had receded almost to the midpoint of his head, and he was a good fifty pounds overweight. He entered the house out of breath, a cigarette dangling from his lips, his four bodyguards moving in tandem, two in front and two behind. The bodyguards were young, big, and fit. Two looked like locals and two had Petrosian's northern complexion.

Petrosian walked over to Ridley, grabbed him by the shoulders, and kissed the American on both cheeks, and then, refusing to let go, he stared into Ridley's eyes and spoke to him. His face didn't so much as twitch. His eyes didn't blink. Only his lips moved. After the intense one-sided exchange, the Armenian gave Ridley one more hug and then his eyes lifted and settled on Rapp. He released Ridley and asked, "Is this the one?"

Ridley nodded.

Petrosian sized Rapp up and then announced, "I must shake your hand."

The man spoke perfect English, but with one of those clipped heavy Russian accents. Rapp couldn't come up with a single good reason why this man would want to shake his hand, but he stuck his right hand out as a polite reflex.

In a voice only the two of them could hear he said, "I have hated that Turkish pig Hamdi Sharif for almost twenty years. I want to thank you for putting a bullet in his black heart. When I heard he was dead I wept tears of joy."

Rapp's own heart began to beat a little faster. How in hell did this man know he had killed Sharif? Rapp tilted his head to the left so he could get a look at Ridley. The man shrugged his shoulders as if to say he was sorry. So much for secrecy.

"I am very sorry about Bill."

Rapp had to remind himself that to these people, Stan Hurley was Bill Sherman. "Thank you. Have you found any information that may help us?"

He winced as if disappointed in himself. "I'm not sure if it will help, but maybe. I confirmed that it was the police that picked our friend up in front of his hotel this morning. In fact it was the police chief, that pig Gabir Haddad."

"Haddad is not a bad man," Ridley said for Rapp's benefit. "Just extremely corrupt. He works with us sometimes."

"He works with anyone if they have enough money," Petrosian said.

"Levon, anything to drink?"

"No, thank you. My stomach is upset today."

"So this Haddad," Rapp said, "who gave him the order?"

"I am fairly certain it was your friends from Islamic Jihad, but I will know more later. I am having dinner with Haddad this evening."

"His idea or yours?" Ridley asked.

"His . . . He is afraid he has offended me, which he has, of course. He knows he cannot simply come into my neighborhood and grab my friends. It would have been nice if you had told me Bill was coming. All of this could have been avoided."

"I know . . . I already told you I was sorry. He was planning on seeing you today. He didn't want word getting out that he was back."

"And how did that work out for him?"

"I know . . . but just be careful with Haddad. We can't afford to lose you."

"I am always careful. It will be at a restaurant of my choosing, and I will make sure the street is blocked off. Trust me . . . he's the one who needs to be nervous."

"That's what worries me. What if he's desperate?"

"He has always been a desperate little man. He knows what he did this morning was wrong. He will be full of fear, and I will play on that fear to get every last piece of information from him."

"Any idea where they took him?" Rapp asked.

"That is the question, isn't it? Where did they take him?" Petrosian shuffled across the stone floor and out onto the veranda. "Beirut is not a small city. It is not like your New York or Chicago, but it is not small. Have you figured out how they found him?"

"No," Ridley said. "He flew in last night shortly after nine. That's all we know."

"I have talked to the people at the hotel, and I am satisfied that they did not know who he was. Somebody must have spotted him at the airport. From the old days. He made a big enough impression in certain circles, and those little Palestinian rats do all the dirty work at the airport. Baggage and fueling . . . cleaning the planes and the terminal. They treat it like their own little syndicate," Petrosian said with contempt. "I have heard rumors that some of the cab drivers are involved in a kidnapping ring."

"Would they have any pull with Haddad?" Ridley asked, thinking of the police chief.

"No," Petrosian answered as he flicked a long ash over the edge and onto the cars below. "That would have to be someone much higher up. My guess is the same people who grabbed your other man . . . the Schnoz . . . Isn't that what you call him?"

"Yes. You mean Islamic Jihad?"

"Correct . . . with the help of a few others."

"Anything else?"

"Little things here and there." Petrosian paused and chewed on his lip for a moment. "Have you heard about this standoff at Martyrs' Square?"

"I heard a little something yesterday, but not much."

"It is a funny thing," Petrosian said while looking off into the distance.

"What are you talking about?" Rapp asked.

Ridley pointed to the north. "Follow the scar to the sea . . . one block short, you can see an open area. That's Martyrs' Square."

"Before the war it was a beautiful place. Full of life," Petrosian said in a sad voice.

"It was the scene of some of the heaviest fighting during the war," Ridley added. "The buildings are all empty shells now."

"Now that the cease-fire has held, certain groups have gotten the idea that it is time to grab land while they still can. The Maronites started earlier in the week and they began occupying the buildings along the east side of the square. The Muslims got word and started moving their people into a building on the west side."

Rapp looked at the spit of land. He guessed it was around two miles away. "Does that mean a fight is brewing?"

"Part of me wishes they would all just kill each other so the rest of us can pick up the pieces and get back to where we were before this mess started, but I know that this is not the answer. We need the peace to hold."

"And how does this Martyrs' Square situation figure into our other problem?"

"It might not, but then again manpower is an issue."

"Manpower?" Rapp asked, not understanding.

"These groups are like any organization. They have limited resources. They have to collect garbage, collect taxes, man their roadblocks, punish those who aren't behaving . . . the list goes on and on. The point is, if they are forced to hold the west end of Martyrs' Square they will be weak in other places."

Rapp wondered how he could use that to his advantage. As the sun moved across the afternoon sky he got the sinking feeling that they were losing an opportunity. That if they didn't act, didn't do something bold and do it soon, Richards and Hurley would share the same fate as Bill Buckley.

CHAPTER 57

HURLEY had lost track of time. After the fingernail incident, they'd left him alone. Turned off the light and shut the door. He sat in the chair, his arms duct-taped to the armrests and his ankles to the two front legs. His chest and shoulders were also taped to the chair back. Big loops of silver tape, as if he were a mummy. For the first few hours he tried to catalogue everything he'd seen, said, and heard. Abu Radih was what he'd expected—a thin-skinned overwrought child in a man's body. If he was lucky, he could provoke the man into killing him. That was the first priority. He had to enrage the man to the point where he defied the orders of the others. Go down fighting. He dozed off thinking of his own death. What a beautiful death it would be if he could pull it off. Exercise his will over a free man. Inflict enough mental pain on Radih to get him to do something he himself knew was wrong.

The thought brought a smile to his swollen lips, and then he let his chin rest on his chest and went to sleep. He awoke some time later. It could have been an hour, three hours, or half a day, and what did it really matter? The stink in the room was horrendous, but it was far better than the hood. He needed to go to the bathroom, so he whizzed right there, letting it splash over the seat of the chair onto the concrete floor. That helped him relax a little bit, but his fingers were starting to really sting, so he started talking to God to take his mind off the pain.

Hurley had no illusions about his potential for sainthood. He pretty much knew where he was headed when it was over, and yes, he did believe in the man upstairs and the man downstairs. He'd seen too much nasty shit in his life to think for a second that there wasn't both good and evil in this world. Where he fit into that paradigm was a little more complicated. One of his favorite aphorisms involved sending Boy Scouts after bad men. Good people needed men like Hurley even if they couldn't bring themselves to admit it. Maybe God would take pity on him. Maybe he wouldn't.

Hurley bowed his head and asked for forgiveness for any of the innocent people he'd killed over the years, but that was as far as he was willing to go. The assholes, he would not apologize for. He then nodded off to sleep again. He awoke later to the sounds of a man screaming. He knew instantly that it was Richards. What they were doing to him, Hurley could only imagine. The screams came and went, rising and falling like waves crashing into the rocks. And then Hurley could tell by the steady rhythm what they were doing. They were electrocuting him and they weren't bothering to ask questions. They were just trying to wear him down. Listening to the pain of one of his own men was the most difficult thing of all.

Hurley bowed his head again and asked God for the strength to kill these men. It went like this for four or five cycles. He tried not to obsess over the time. When he was awake, he tried to prepare himself for what would come next. With an almost endless string of awful possibilities, there was one in particular that had him worried, and when the door finally opened, it was as if his captors had read his mind.

A man entered, plugged in the cord for the light, and there in the doorway was a bloodied and battered Richards. Two men were at his sides, holding him up. His wrists were bound in front of him with duct tape. The red marks on his chest confirmed what they had been doing, although it wasn't all. Richards's face was beaten and swollen—one of his eyes completely shut.

Sayyed entered the room, a man following him with a chair similar to the one Hurley was in. He showed the man where to place it and said to Hurley, "How are you feeling today?"

"Great!" Hurley said with enthusiasm. "You guys really do a nice job of making people feel comfortable."

"Yes." Sayyed smiled. "I'm sure you would show us the same hospitality if we were in your country."

"Slightly better," Hurley said, flashing the new gap in his teeth. "You know how competitive we Americans are. We didn't put a man on the moon by making our women walk around in sheets all day and blowing ourselves up."

"We all know that was faked."

"Sure it was," Hurley said agreeably as they placed Richards in the other chair. One of the men produced a knife so he could cut Richards's duct tape. Hurley wanted that knife, and in Arabic asked, "Where's my buddy Radih? Either of you boys ever get a blow job from his mom?" Hurley then launched into an invective-filled description of the sex acts that Radih's mom used to perform for him.

Sayyed would never admit it, but this American's descriptive abilities were in a league of their own. In fact, the descriptions were so detailed that even he wondered for a second if it could be true.

Hurley read the unsure looks on the faces of the two goons and said, "You really didn't know Radih's mother was a whore? You should try her sometime. She's getting a little up there in age . . . not quite as tight a fit, if you know what I mean." Hurley winked at them as if they were of the same mind.

"That will be enough," Sayyed said. He ordered the men to finish taping Richards's wrists to the chair. When they were finished he told them they could wait outside.

Hurley smiled at them and waited until they were at the door and then shouted, "Don't forget to ask Radih about his mother. Dirtiest piece of ass I've ever had."

The door closed with a click. Sayyed placed his hands on his hips and let out an exasperated sigh.

"It's true," Hurley said, punctuating his words with an emphatic nod. "The woman was a sex machine. She should have paid me."

Doctrine told Sayyed he should ignore the comments, but he felt that he needed to say something. "You are a very interesting man, Mr. Sherman. You must be very unsure of yourself."

"Why do you say that, Colonel?"

"It is so obvious. Do I really have to say it?"

"Well, unless I've learned how to read minds since we last saw each other, I suggest you spit it out."

"You are afraid you won't be able to stand up to my methods, so you are trying to enrage my colleague to the point where he kills you."

Hurley screwed on a confused look. "Colonel, you give me way too much credit. I'm not that smart. I'm just a horny bastard who's slept with a ton of prostitutes . . . one of whom just happens to be Radih's mom."

Sayyed laughed at him. "You are an unusual man."

"What do I have to do to get you guys to take me seriously? I'm going to lie to you about a lot of shit, but I am dead serious about Radih's mom, and I'm not knocking the woman, she was amazing. And besides, you can't blame a woman for trying to put some food on the table. Can you?"

Sayyed thought about that for a second and simply shook his head. It was time to take charge again. He wheeled his little cart over and checked his instruments. When he was ready he broke open some smelling salts and stuck them under the other American's nose. Richards snorted and opened his eyes. Turning back to the foul-mouthed older one, he said, "Your friend, Mr. Richards, was kind enough to give us his name."

"Never heard of him."

"Yes . . . well, let's see if we can jog your memory. This is what we are going to do." Sayyed picked up the tin snips and said, "I will ask you a question. If you refuse to answer or lie I will cut off one of his fingers."

"Cool." Hurley straightened up as much as the tape would allow. "I'd like to see you cut one off right now. Go ahead . . . let's get started."

"Mr. Sherman, what is your real name?"

"Come on, cut his finger off. Cut his wrist off . . . that would be really awesome."

Richards was awake now, a panicked look in his eyes. "What the hell?"

Sayyed said, "He has already told us your name, but I want to hear you say it."

"Fine . . . William Tecumseh Sherman. Are you happy now? Can we go home?"

"No. That is not the name he gave us."

"I think I'd know my own name."

"Last chance." Sayyed placed the tin snips around the first knuckle on Richards's left hand.

"William Tecumseh Sherman."

"Wrong answer." Sayyed pushed the two red handles together and there was a quick snip and the pinky fell to the dirty floor. Richards started screaming, and Sayyed quickly moved the snips over to Hurley's pinky. "Your turn," he yelled. "Name?"

Hurley had already turned his head away, as if he couldn't bear to watch what was going on. He started to move his lips and mumbled a name.

"Louder . . . I can't hear you."

Hurley slowly turned his head, made eye contact with Sayyed, and then looked down at his pinky. The distance was about right. He pretended he was starting to cry while again mumbling, and when Sayyed moved just a touch closer, offering up his good ear so he could hear better, Hurley lunged forward, tilting his head to the right. He caught the top third of the man's left ear between his teeth and clamped down with all of his strength, grinding and chewing and growling and then yanking his head back.

Sayyed screamed and broke free, his hand clamped around his bloody ear. He stumbled away and then turned to look at his subject. What he saw horrified him. Bill Sherman had a chunk of his ear hanging half out of his mouth. The insane American smiled at him and then started chewing on the ear, crunching it like a potato chip.

CHAPTER 58

RAPP looked out across the city. Night had fallen and that scar known as the Green Line now looked like a wide, formidable river, a black swath of darkness that cut the city in half. But travel two blocks in either direction and there were signs of life. Buildings lit up with inhabitants, traffic moving about the city, horns blaring, and under-powered engines revving—all the normal sights and sounds of a city. But not in that desolate corridor. Only twice in the last hour had he seen a car dare cross no-man's-land. It appeared the cease-fire was activated as they usually are, by segregating the various factions. He could not see the east-west streets to the north, and it was likely that more cars had crossed in that sector, but not enough to change what was obvious. This was literally a city torn asunder.

The problem as Rapp saw it was fundamental

geography. He was on this side and they were on the other side—the *they* being Hurley and Richards. The only way to save them was to go over there, but Ridley had explained to him that going over there was a very bad idea. Going over there would result in his being captured, tortured, and then killed, in that order.

Rapp's response to Ridley was, "So you're pretty much admitting that Stan and Bob are going to be tortured and killed."

"I'm admitting no such thing."

"The hell you're not," Rapp said, his frustration finally boiling over.

Ridley shot back, "I know you're the new wonder boy, so this might be hard for you to understand, but there are things that are going on that you have not been read in on."

"Like what?"

"Things that are way above your pay grade, rookie." Ridley caught his mistake and tried to temper his words by adding, "Listen, I don't make the rules. There are certain protocols that I have to follow. Langley tells me who I can share things with. If you're not on that list my hands are tied."

"Like Petrosian, for instance. I'm sure you cleared that with Langley. You telling a foreign national that I was the man who killed Sharif." Rapp watched as Ridley looked away. "Are you fucking kidding me? There's no way in hell you got approval from Irene to give him that information."

Ridley sighed. "We need Petrosian on this one, and the man does not trust strangers, so I gave him a little piece of information that I knew would please him. He hated Hamdi Sharif more than any person on the planet. It goes back to the beginning of the civil war here. They were both arms dealers and they agreed not to sell weapons to Fatah. Petrosian lived here, and he felt that a militarized Fatah would only prolong the fighting. About six months into the war he found out that Sharif had broken their agreement and was selling weapons to the radical Palestinians. Petrosian was right. It prolonged the war, destroyed the city, killed thousands more, and Sharif became a very wealthy man. Petrosian vowed to kill him, but Sharif never set foot in the city again."

"Fine . . . so you used what I did for your own benefit, which means you owe me. I deserve to know what in hell is going on." Rapp could see Ridley was at least thinking about it, so he pressed him a little harder. "That could have just as easily been me that got picked up. I deserve to know what Langley is doing to try to get them back."

"They're working on different levels. Signal intercepts, applying pressure where they can, calling in favors . . ."

"What in hell does all that mean?"

"It's complicated, is what it's supposed to mean, and on top of that, Stan, your friend Bobby, and you aren't even supposed to exist. How the fuck do you expect them to go to the State Department with that one . . . Excuse me," he said in a falsetto, "two of our black ops guys, who don't actually exist, were kidnapped in Beirut. Could you help us get them back?"

"Bullshit."

"Bullshit . . . what in hell is that supposed to mean?"

"It means it's bullshit. If you think the State Department is the answer to our problems, if Langley thinks they're our solution, we're fucked."

"I didn't say they were the only game. I told you it's complicated. And what the hell would you know? You're a damn rookie."

"A rookie who's smart enough to know this is bullshit," Rapp yelled. "You know what the solution is . . . you just don't want to say it because you"— Rapp pointed at him—"and all of the other pussies back at Langley don't have the balls to follow through on it."

"Please, enlighten me, boy wonder. What's the solution?"

"We do what the Russians did."

"What the Russians did?" Ridley mocked him.

"Yeah . . . back in the mideighties . . . after four of their diplomats were kidnapped."

Ridley's gaze narrowed. "Where'd you hear that story?"

"Stan."

"For Christ's sake," Ridley muttered, obviously not happy that Hurley had told Rapp the story.

"Two diplomats and two KGB guys get snatched by one of the Palestinian factions. One of them happens to be the KGB's station chief here in Beirut. The Russians know what happened to the CIA's station chief when he got kidnapped, because they paid for the information that the Iranians sucked out of him. They don't want to see all of their operations exposed, so they send in a joint force of Spetsnaz and KGB goons and they start whacking people."

Ridley was shaking his head. "That's not the answer."

"Really . . . since you appear to know the story, tell me how it ended."

Ridley shook his head. "Nope."

"One was killed and the three were released," Rapp said. "And how many Russians were kidnapped after that?"

"Zero," Ridley reluctantly admitted.

"That's right, and how many Americans?"

Ridley shrugged. "Not zero."

"So what's the lesson to be learned?"

"We're not the Russians."

"That's your answer."

"Listen . . . I know you're frustrated. *I'm* frustrated, but I am telling you this is way above both of us. There are a lot of really important people who want this cease-fire to last. They will never allow us to go around shooting people like the Russians did."

"But the Palestinians can keep kidnapping *our* people?" Rapp waited for Ridley to give him an answer that wasn't coming anytime soon. "Like I said . . . this is bullshit."

That had been more than three hours ago. Rapp and Ridley had not exchanged words since then. Rapp had dumped his anger into studying maps of West Beirut, reading the intelligence reports, and trying to come up with some way to prevent this disaster from following the course of the previous hostage negotiations. Anyone who didn't understand where this was headed was either deluding himself by ignoring history or just too stupid to connect the dots. Out of this frustration came the realization of what it would all mean to his own future.

He'd spent years thinking of little more than how he would make the other side hurt, and now after all of his training, right when he was getting started, it would be derailed. Hurley and Richards would end up telling them everything they knew about him. His career would be over. The anger welled up inside him, and as he looked out across the city, he could feel himself drifting further and further away from the people pulling the strings in D.C. Their half measures and dithering disgusted him. It was like Hurley had told them on the drive down from Hamburg: "We got soft in the eighties and let these assholes get away with way too much shit." Apparently Washington still hadn't learned its lesson.

Ridley joined him on the veranda. He was holding two beers. He set one in front of Rapp and took a swig out of the other.

Rapp eyed the beer and then said, "I'm not in the mood."

"Shut up and drink. And listen for a change. I've been doing some thinking. This thing isn't going to end well. Cummins was bad enough . . . Stan . . . the shit that guy has in his brain . . . the stuff he's seen over the years." Ridley shuddered at the thought of the enemy getting their hands on all that information. "I can't even begin to calculate the damage." He paused, took a swig of beer, and shook his head. "Someone needs to do something and you seem like just the kind of crazy asshole that would volunteer for a mission like this, although it's actually not a mission. There's nothing official about it. In fact, I'm going to get so pissed tonight that I pass out. And then when I wake up in the morning, and you're not here, I'll call Langley and tell them you've gone AWOL."

"And where will I be?" Rapp asked.

"Petrosian will be here in one hour. He has arranged to take you over to the other side. The police chief, no less, is taking you."

Rapp was surprised. "The same asshole who snatched Stan?"

"One and the same."

"Can I trust him?"

"Absolutely."

"How?"

"Because this time he has given Petrosian his word that nothing will happen to you."

"And I should be impressed by that?"

"Yes, you should. The chief will drop you off at a small hotel a few blocks west of Nijmeh Square, and then you're on your own. My advice is you spread some cash around, telling the hotel manager and the vendors that you would like to meet with Colonel Assef Sayyed. They will claim they've never heard of him, but they all know who he is. They will tell him you are looking for him and he will have someone collect you before the day is out. Then it will go one of two ways." Ridley took another drink and organized his thoughts. "He will either sit down and negotiate with you, in which case Petrosian has agreed to bankroll you to the tune of one million dollars."

"You're kidding me."

"No, he is a man who likes to show his gratitude, and besides, you just eliminated one of his top competitors. He's bound to pick up a few more contracts."

"Will a million do it?"

"Doubtful, but it will let them know we are serious, and they all know Petrosian is not a man to be fucked with."

"So if it's not enough money . . ."

Ridley waved him off. "I'm going to be working on getting more."

"Langley?"

"Maybe, but we have some other options. I just need to see if I can pull it off."

Rapp thought about the money that Hurley had taken from the Swiss bank accounts. He almost told Ridley but decided to keep it to himself for now. "That's option one. What's option two?"

"They throw you in the dungeon and they torture you and eventually kill you."

"But I'm a rookie, so how much harm can I really do." It was a statement, not a question.

"Something like that. A pawn for a bishop." Ridley shrugged. "Maybe you even get lucky and take a few of them down with you." Ridley drained his beer and looked to the west. "There's one last thing. The story about the Russians."

"Yeah."

"Stan didn't tell you the whole thing. The Russians . . . they wiped out a couple of families . . . women and children included. Fucking butchers." Ridley shook his head, trying to get rid of the bad memories. "We're not the Russians. We don't kill women and children. At least not intentionally. Never forget that."

CHAPTER 59

SAYYED held the small mirror in his hand, turned his head to the right and checked his bandage, carefully fingering the edges. The morning sunlight came through the window of his room, providing ample light. There was no hope of reattaching the jagged hunk of cartilage and skin—at least that's what the doctor had told him, although Sayyed suspected that the man was not well versed on the most recent medical advances. When all of this was over, which he hoped would be very soon, he would have to go to Paris and see if there was a plastic surgeon who could do something about the nub that was now his ear.

Growing his hair out would help, but Sayyed did not want to live the rest of his years with such a permanent reminder of his time spent with Bill Sherman. That was still the only name he had to go on. The other man, Mr. Richards, had told them he did not know his boss's real name. As to whether he was telling the truth, Sayyed would only know that after a few more sessions, and depending on how the bidding went, he might not get that opportunity.

One thing was certain: Mr. Sherman's sanity was no longer up for discussion. In the nearly twenty years that Sayyed had been doing this, he had never encountered anyone close to this animal. The man was clearly insane. How else could you explain biting off someone's ear and then chewing it? The all-too-fresh memory caused Sayyed to shudder. He'd never experienced anything so strange in his life. The pain had been bad, excruciating at the time, but it had faded. The image, though, of another person chewing on his ear had only grown stronger. He did not like it one bit, and it made him all the more anxious to get through this day and be done with this Bill Sherman or whatever his real name was.

Sayyed finished buttoning the fresh white shirt that Ali had fetched for him and then put on his suit coat. He heard footsteps coming down the hall and turned to see Radih standing in the open doorway.

"You wanted to see me?"

"Yes. How are our neighbors across the street?"

"Nothing new. We estimate they have between thirty and fifty men."

"And us?"

"Thirty-two."

Sayyed nodded, and thought the number enough to handle a problem should one arise. Changing subjects, he said, "You have heard about this new American? The one who is staying at the Shady Cedar?"

Radih nodded. "Two of my men have been following him this morning." He held up a two-way radio. "They have sent me regular updates. They say the man is a fool."

"A fool?" Sayyed said, finding the word an interesting choice.

"He is wandering around the streets, asking merchants for information about kidnapped Americans and mentioning your name. He's handing out money and telling people where he is staying. Telling them he is here to negotiate their release."

Sayyed was not surprised that his name was being mentioned. Chief Haddad had told him everything. The fact that Petrosian was sticking his nose into their business did not surprise him. He had known when he sent the chief into the Bourj to grab the two Americans that there would be repercussions. That was why he had to pay Haddad such an outrageous sum.

Sayyed could tell something was bothering Radih, so he asked, "What is wrong?"

"I am worried that some other faction will grab him. In fact, I will be amazed if he makes it to lunch, and if someone else gets him . . ." He made a pained expression and a clicking noise.

"It could complicate our negotiations."

"Yes."

Haddad had told Sayyed that the new American was young, inexperienced, and very nervous. Radih was right. If one of the other factions grabbed him, they would try to ransom him, which would make things more complicated, especially if he wanted to complete the entire transaction today. There was another angle that he had just considered, but could not share with the others. If the Americans were serious about bidding, they were likely to drive the price far beyond what he was hoping to get. In the end it was unlikely that Mughniyah and Badredeen would agree to hand them back to the U.S. government, but it was worth a try. The smart thing to do was to take this new variable out of play and see what the Americans were willing to offer. "Why don't you pick him up, but be very careful. You know how sneaky the Americans can be. Take him someplace first and strip him down. Make sure he isn't carrying any tracking devices. Then bring him here and show him the rabid dog in the basement . . . find out how serious they are about making an offer."

"You are not seriously considering handing them back to the Americans?"

Maybe not, but Sayyed was at a minimum willing to consider his options. America was a very wealthy country. Maybe they could make up all of their lost funds and then some. Sayyed could put himself back on the road to a life of opulence. Knowing how unhinged Radih was about the American, Sayyed knew he would have to keep these thoughts to himself. "No, I am not, but I would like to see if the Americans can help drive the price up a bit."

Radih stared at him for a moment and said, "You should let me kill him. Remove all temptation."

Can I trust Radih with these prisoners today?
was the question Sayyed asked himself yet again.
It would be nice if he could convince Mughniyah
to come keep an eye on things, but he wanted to
be part of the negotiations at the airport. Sayyed
understood his colleague's anger, but he could not
understand his persistence. The man simply did
not understand what was at stake here today. He
supposed a great deal of it was due to his youth. He
could crawl back to Sabra and Shatila and rely on his
black market trades and the payoffs he received from
all of the impoverished refugees. He had many years
ahead of him and many opportunities to rebuild his
wealth and he did not have to answer to Damascus
for missing funds. Still, none of these points would
matter to him. His judgment was clouded by his hatred. Normally, he would chastise Radih or humili-
ate him, but not this time. They just needed to get
through today and then things would return to normal. He decided on a more mature approach. Not
wanting to argue with him, he said, "I understand
your anger, but you are better than this, Abu."

Radih shook his head. "I do not think so. My
heart is filled with nothing but hatred for this man.
I will not sleep until I have killed him."

"And that is understandable, but you must take
comfort in the fact he will die a thousand deaths at
the hands of whoever buys him today. He will experience more pain than we can even begin to imagine."

"None of that matters to me. I must kill him
with my own hand."

A compromise occurred to Sayyed, one that he would never have to honor, but one that might be enough to keep Radih from ruining their chances of refilling their coffers. "I promise you, Abu, that whoever buys him today, I will make the transaction contingent on the other party agreeing that when they are done with Mr. Sherman you will be given the honor of killing him." Sayyed watched the Palestinian turn this idea over in his hate-filled mind. He could see that he was not quite convinced, so he said, "And I will allow you to spend some time with him today, so he can be taught a proper lesson before he leaves."

A thin smile creased Radih's lips and he said, "I would like that very much."

"Good," Sayyed said, placing his hand on his shoulder. "Now go get this other American, and make sure no one is following you. Bring him back here and we will see what he has to say, and then I will give you some time to take out your frustrations on Mr. Sherman."

CHAPTER 60

RAPP sat on the edge of the hotel room's bed, tapping his foot. It was ten-oh-nine in the morning, and he was having a hell of a time trying to calm his nerves. All he'd brought along was a small duffel bag that Ridley had helped him pack. Petrosian had come back to the safe house after his dinner with the police chief to go over the plan. He was not optimistic that Rapp would succeed, but agreed that doing nothing was a worse alternative. So, shortly before midnight, Rapp was shuttled from Petrosian's armor-plated sedan to the Beirut police chief's four-door Peugeot. Rapp was not thrilled about the idea at first, but when Petrosian explained that the chief was eager to make amends for his lack of judgment the day before, Rapp went along with it. Petrosian also knew that the chief would tell the right people that another CIA man had shown up and was looking to negotiate the release of his colleagues.

They made it through the checkpoint fine, but Rapp had to resist the urge to shoot the smug little turd of a police chief and both of his men. It would have sent a nice message, but ultimately the wrong one, considering his final objectives. And besides, he had a role to play, so as they neared the hotel Rapp fired off one anxious, paranoid question after another. The chief did his best to calm his guest, but Rapp played the inconsolable nervous wreck better than he could have hoped.

They reached the Shady Cedar Hotel at twenty minutes past midnight. Ridley had handpicked the hotel because it was smack dab in the middle of Indian country. All three men escorted Rapp into the lobby. The chief asked to have a private word with the manager, and the two men disappeared behind the closed door of the small office behind the reception desk. The other two policemen stood chain-smoking by the door, while Rapp stood at the front desk and did his best to look nervous as hell, which was no easy thing considering the fact that he really wanted to kick down the door and pistol-whip the double-dealing police chief.

After five minutes Chief Haddad appeared, stroking his mustache and assuring Rapp that everything was taken care of. The little kiss-ass hotel manager joined in, telling Rapp that all would be fine. Rapp got the distinct impression that all would not be fine, and that both of these men would look to make money by turning him in to Islamic Jihad, but that was the point of the whole crazy exercise. So Rapp anxiously shuffled his feet and kept rubbing his neck as if he was a wreck.

Pointing toward the door, Rapp asked, "Can't one of your men stay the night?"

"I'm afraid that is not possible. Besides, you will be safe here."

Rapp acted even more worried, but truth be told, he didn't have a worry in the world. He could sleep in peace and then in the morning he could begin to ask around for information. The idea that the chief wouldn't tell the very people who had asked him to grab Hurley was ludicrous, but Rapp played dumb.

The elevator was out of order, so he took the stairs to the fourth floor. He closed and locked the door to the room and wedged the rubber doorstop into the small gap at the bottom. Next he opened the curtains to see what kind of exit the window might provide. It was a good twenty-five feet to the street. Ridley had sent him off with a grab bag of things, including a thirty-foot coil of rope. Rapp tied one end to the foot of the bed and left the rest of it coiled by the window. Then he took out his silenced Beretta and Motorola radio. He set the gun on the nightstand and keyed the transmit button on the radio.

Ridley's voice came over the radio a few seconds later. Rapp told him he'd made it to the hotel and was in his room. The radios weren't secure, so they kept the conversation vague and short. Rapp confirmed that he would check in at eight and then every two hours after that. If he missed any of the check-ins, Ridley should assume Rapp had made contact. After that, it was anyone's guess how things would turn out. Rapp brushed his teeth and lay down on the bed with his clothes on. He didn't expect to sleep, but if he did, all the better.

He lay there in the dark with his eyes closed, going over all of his options. In his mind's eye he could see how things were going to proceed, and if he had any chance at all of making it back alive, he would have to stay calm and seize the opportunity if and when it presented itself. *When* it presented itself, he amended. Petrosian had said it himself. The Fatah and Islamic Jihad factions had grown thin during the cease-fire. Men were leaving their ranks and finding jobs. It was very possible that they would make a mistake. It was simply up to Rapp to see it coming and make his daring move.

Rapp did fall asleep. He had no idea when he had dozed off, or for how long, but it was enough to recharge his battery. He checked in with Ridley at the appointed hour, and then, not wanting to lose his nerve, he left the hotel and proceeded directly to Maarad Street a few blocks away. The vendors were manning their tents, selling all kinds of produce and food. Rapp worked his way up and down both sides of the street, speaking English and playing down his French when he had to speak it. He continued to play the role of the dolt. Almost to a man, people shunned him as soon as he asked about Colonel Sayyed. There was one man, though, who had opened up. He was selling electronics, small radios, tape players, and two-way radios like Rapp's Motorola.

Rapp stepped into his small tent and said hello. There was a polite exchange and then Rapp asked him, "Do you know anything about the two Americans who were picked up a few days ago?"

The man pointed to two radios and loudly asked Rapp, "Which one do you like better?" And then in a much quieter voice he said, "Yes, I know of the Americans." He then stuck out his hand for cash.

Rapp peeled off seven one-hundred-dollar bills. The man pocketed the bills and picked up a small alarm clock radio. He began to explain its various features. In between lauding the various components he lowered his voice and said, "There is a rumor that the Americans are being held in the basement of an old building on the west side of Martyrs' Square."

Before Rapp could ask another question the man was stuffing the alarm clock in a bag and sending him off. That was when Rapp noticed the two guys with stern faces and distinctive bulges under their jackets. He went straight back to the hotel. He wanted to pass on this nugget of information before he was picked up. As he reached the street that the hotel was on, he turned left, which was the wrong way. He took two steps, and then, acting as if he'd just realized his mistake, he turned left again and saw the two men halfway down the block just standing there, staring at him. Rapp kept moving so as to not let them know that he was onto them. It was not lost on him that the two men following him had made no effort to conceal their interest.

Rapp hustled up the next block, and when he entered the hotel he noticed a new manager behind the desk, who gave him a very unpleasant look. Rapp supposed the man thought someone might blow up the hotel just because of his presence. As he climbed the stairs to the fourth floor he realized you could hardly blame the guy. He was like some saloonkeeper in one of those old western movies where the troublemakers were all gunning for the new sheriff.

When Rapp got up to the room he sat on the edge of the bed and collected his thoughts, trying to prioritize the various bits and pieces. The vendor was the only real highlight, and even that might be worthless. Was it a wild rumor or was it fact? Rapp knew that unless he had a chance to talk to the man he would never be able to figure it out. The two men trailing him had him worried. Were they on their way up to his room right now, preparing to kick his door down and drag him off?

Rapp thumbed the transmit button and said, "Curly, this is Moe, over." The Three Stooges monikers was Ridley's idea.

"I'm here, Moe, what's up?"

"I just got back from the market. Two guys tailed me back to the hotel."

"Not a surprise. How was the market?"

"Pretty much treated me like a leper . . . just like you said."

"Yeah . . . bad part of town. They haven't seen a gringo around there in some time. I'm sure you were a big hit."

"I did pick up one piece of information." Rapp paused, trying to figure out the best way to pass it along without giving too much away on an open channel. "Remember last night . . . when our Armenian friend talked to us about the manpower issue."

There was a slight delay and then, "Yep . . . I remember."

"He referenced a local standoff . . . a land grab . . . kind of a standoff at the OK Corral."

"I'm with you."

"There was one vendor . . . cagey fellow. Told me on one side of the corral, the guys are keeping some things in the basement."

"I think I copy. Can you give me more on the source?"

"He sold electronics. Boom boxes, small radios, clocks, that kind of stuff."

Ridley asked for a description of the man and his stall and Rapp gave it to him. Then Ridley said, "I'll pass this on to the American and see what he's heard. Anything else?"

"No," Rapp said as he crossed over to the window and pulled back the curtain. The two men who had followed him had taken up positions directly across the street. "Those guys I mentioned have decided to camp out in front of the hotel."

"Not a surprise. You sure you still want to do this?"

Rapp had just been asking himself the same question. But like his high-school lacrosse coach used to say, you can't score unless you shoot. "I'm fine," Rapp said into the small radio. "If I don't check in at noon, you'll know I'm either dead or in the middle of negotiations."

"Let's hope it's the latter."

"Roger that. Over and out." Rapp took off his khaki sport coat and went into the bathroom to splash some cold water on his face. He patted the drops of water with a towel and looked at himself in the dusty, cracked mirror. Rapp eyed his fractured reflection; his thick head of black hair, the beginnings of a beard, his bronzed olive skin and his eyes so dark that they were almost black. He could walk among the enemy without getting so much as a suspicious glance, but that would all change if he didn't do something. Very carefully he patted his hair and then, using his index finger, he probed a little deeper. He could barely feel the small section of metal. Ridley had taken a flexible fourteen-inch bandsaw blade and cut it down to a neat little three-inch piece. An eighth of an inch thick and only a half inch wide, the black metal section was then threaded into his dark head of black hair.

Rapp played Ridley's words over again in his head. "We know from debriefings that these things follow a certain pattern. It usually starts with a whack across the back of the head, but not always. You're then tossed in either the backseat or the trunk, taken somewhere and stripped naked, and then moved one or two more times. There's a good chance you'll never be in the same building as them. Then again . . . they might be two doors down and you'll never know they're there unless you get free."

Rapp stared at his reflection and questioned his sanity. "Are you fucking nuts?" Rapp couldn't remember if he'd ever talked to himself out loud like this in the mirror. Maybe drunk, but never sober. It all flashed before him in that moment. He could slip out the back door and find his way back to the other side of town. Like Ridley had told him last night, "If you get cold feet, no one will judge you." Except for himself, of course. Rapp did not want to live the rest of his life that way. This wasn't like making a mistake in the heat of battle. This would be making a conscious decision to run from the field of battle. And not just to run, but to desert two of his fellow soldiers and leave them for dead. Rapp knew himself well enough to understand that a failure of this magnitude would haunt him for the rest of his days.

He pushed himself away from the mirror before he lost the courage. He checked the window again. They were still down there and had possibly been joined by another guy who was standing at the far end of the block. Rapp looked over at his gun, which was on the night table. It had been suggested that, to complete his performance, he should leave the gun in the room, but he didn't like that idea. He'd rather walk out of the hotel buck-naked than leave the gun. He could explain it away as a precaution. Everyone else in this town walked around with a gun, so why shouldn't he? The radio was the only other thing to decide on. He chose to bring it with him. If he didn't get picked up right away, he might need to call Ridley with an update. As a precaution, he changed the channel and turned it off.

Rapp quickly scrawled a note and left it on the small desk in the corner, then put his sport coat back on and checked all the pockets. Everything was where it should be. Lifting the back of his jacket, he wedged the Beretta into his waistband and gathered his sunglasses, the map, and a large wad of cash and headed for the door. He hesitated for a split second, then told himself not to think.

"I'd rather go down swinging," he muttered as he shut the door. If he survived this little ordeal he'd have to ask Lewis if talking to yourself was a symptom of losing your mind.

Rapp moved quickly down the four flights of stairs to the lobby. There was a new man behind the front desk and he looked nervous as all hell, which Rapp took as a sign that someone had talked to him. This was it. Showtime. Rapp continued out the front door into the blazing daylight and held his map above his head to block the sun while he looked up and down the street. Looking out from behind the sunglasses, he pretended not to notice the duo from Islamic Jihad. With his face buried in the map, he turned to the right and started heading east as if he was going back to the market.

Within half a block, Rapp's nervous system began sending his brain alarms, each more frantic than the previous one. Now he was talking to himself again, but this time it was in his brain. The conscious, here-and-now, higher-functioning part was talking to the ingrained lower-functioning part like a jockey talks to a thoroughbred as it's being led into the starting gate. *Easy*, he repeated to himself over and over. It took every ounce of control to override his training and millions of years of basic survival instincts that were embedded like code into the human brain. Up ahead, Rapp recognized a black car that was parked across the street. Earlier in the morning the car had been empty. Rapp ignored the man behind the wheel and turned down a narrow side street. Just thirty paces ahead a rough-looking man was stationed in front of a shop. His left leg was straight and firmly planted on the pavement and the other bent up behind him and placed against the side of the building. His big frame was resting against the wall while he took a long drag off his cigarette. The man had dusty black pants and a white dress shirt with sweat-stained armpits, and there was something vaguely familiar about him. Rapp wondered if he had been in one of the photos Ridley had shown him.

The street was otherwise empty. The survivors of the bloody civil war could smell trouble, and they had wisely decided to stay indoors until the morning's sideshow was concluded. Rapp heard the men behind him, their thick shoes pounding out their progress and pace on the sidewalk. Suddenly a car engine revved, and the pace of his pursuers quickened. With every step Rapp could feel them closing in from behind. His brain ran through options and avenues of escape and he denied each one, willing himself to stay the course like a deranged ship's captain headed for the shoals at full speed.

They were close now. Rapp could feel them. The big fellow up ahead threw his cigarette to the ground and pushed himself away from the building. He smiled at Rapp and produced a leather truncheon from his back pocket. It was at that moment Rapp realized who the man was. Rapp dropped the map in feigned surprise and turned to flee. The two men were exactly where he expected them to be, guns drawn, one pointed at Rapp's head, the other at his chest.

The sedan skidded to a stop just to his right, the trunk and front passenger door swinging open. Rapp knew what was next. He closed his eyes and clenched his jaw as the truncheon cracked him across the back of the head. Rapp stumbled forward, his sunglasses clattering to the pavement. He fell into the arms of the two men with pistols. He let his legs go limp, and the men struggled with his weight. He felt the arms of the big man wrap around his chest and yank him upright. His 9mm Beretta was pulled from the back of his waistband and he was dragged the short distance to the car's trunk. Rapp landed headfirst with a thud. The rest of his body was folded in on top of him, and then the trunk was slammed shut.

The engine roared and the rear tires bit through a layer of sand and dirt until they found asphalt. Rapp was thrown back as the vehicle shot away. He slowly cracked open his eyes, and as expected, found himself enveloped in darkness. His head was throbbing a bit from the blow, but not too badly. There was no fear on his face or doubt in his mind, though. Just a smile on his lips as he thought of his childhood friend Cal Berkley and his pet snake. Cal's pride and joy was his pet boa constrictor, Buckeye. When they were bored during the hot summer months they'd go over to Cal's house and watch him feed rats to Buckeye. Well, one day Cal came home from school to find Buckeye dead, with a hole in the side of his body and a bloody white rat still alive in the tank. Apparently, Buckeye had gotten lazy and swallowed the rat before it was dead. Once inside, the rat had then chewed its way out.

Rapp couldn't help but smile at the thought of doing the same thing to these assholes. This was either going to be the most spectacular success of his life, or the end of it. Fear and debate no longer had a place in his thoughts. There was no turning back. No more hand-wringing. This was all about deception and action. The game had started. He was descending into the belly of the beast. The only question was, would he be able to eat his way out?

CHAPTER 61

THE Aeroflot Tupolev Tu-154 was cleared for landing on Beirut International Airport's only operating runway. Ivanov's bullish attitude was back. Primakov was backing him all the way on this little excursion. These Palestinian dogs thought they had everything figured out, but as usual Ivanov was three steps ahead of them. Ivanov blamed himself for just one mistake during this entire mess. Why hadn't he thought of killing Dorfman first? All of that money could have been his. How could he have missed such an opportunity? Ivanov supposed he had been blind out of necessity. In his world a talented banker who knew how to skirt laws and hide money was absolutely essential. That was another problem he now had to deal with. Where was he going to find another man with those capabilities? He would have to fly to Hamburg soon after he delivered the Americans to Primakov. He would sit down with Dorfman's boss, Herr Koenig, and make him see that certain reparations were in order.

Shvets had come up with that idea. Get Koenig to authorize a few loans to shell companies that were in Ivanov's name and were run out of Switzerland. Loans that would never be repaid. Shvets explained that a bank of this size wrote off more than a hundred million dollars a year in bad loans. If handled the right way, he could bleed Herr Koenig out of several million dollars a year. This opened up a whole new avenue of possibilities for Ivanov. He could apply the same principle with a few of the new bankers in Moscow. In only a few years he could have all his money back and then some. That Shvets was a smart boy. Maybe too smart.

Ivanov watched Shvets exit the cockpit and close the door. As his deputy sat in the aisle seat next to him, he noted the way Shvets glanced at his glass of vodka, barely able to hide his contempt.

"We will be on the ground in less than a minute," Shvets announced while he fastened his seat belt.

"Good. I am eager to get this over with and get back to Moscow."

Shvets wondered what kind of man wished to be gone from a place before he'd arrived.

Glancing out the window, Ivanov asked, "Do you think we could persuade Herr Koenig to visit us in Moscow early next week?"

"Doubtful," Shvets said with a shake of his head.

"Well, try, and if he won't come to us then I will go to him. As always, though, I would like to try to do this the civilized way first. Two businessmen exploring an opportunity."

"In some countries they call it a shakedown."

Ivanov drained his glass and gave Shvets an unhappy frown.

Shvets realized the sulking Ivanov was gone and the ruthless one was back. "Sorry."

Ivanov did not reply at first. He had picked up on the man's growing insolence over the past year, but it seemed to have grown exponentially over the past week. Maybe it was time to replace him. The question was with whom. The private sector was exploding with opportunity, and the SVR no longer had the pick of the litter. He decided he shouldn't give up on him so easily. A good lesson or two might restore the proper attitude, and if that didn't work, he'd think about having him shot. Cutting him free would be foolish. Shvets knew too many of his secrets.

The plane landed on the relatively short runway and braked hard. While they taxied to the designated area, Shvets leaned over and asked, "What is our plan if the bidding goes over five million dollars?"

Ivanov laughed. "It won't."

"How can you be so sure?"

"Because I am smarter than these dogs."

Shvets was intrigued. "What have you been up to, sir?"

"Let's just say I made a few calls to my friends in Tehran and Baghdad."

"And?"

"They have agreed that it would be foolish to pay for something that I am willing to give them for free."

Shvets was dubious. "Are you sure you can trust them?"

The plane stopped in front of an old, rusty hangar. The doors were open and light streamed into the interior from the holes in the roof. Sayyed stepped from the shadows and waved at the plane. Ivanov laughed at the sight of him. "There are two things you need to know to understand the Middle East. The first is that they all hate the Jews. The second is that they have nothing but contempt for the Palestinians."

CHAPTER 62

IT couldn't have been more than five minutes. The trunk opened and they were on him. Rapp couldn't tell how many, but it was more than two and fewer than five. They punched, grabbed, and pulled, finally yanking him from the space and throwing him to the floor. Rapp tried to block the blows as best he could, but they were coming from too many directions, and besides, the goal was not to show them how skilled he was at fighting, it was to play possum. To that end, Rapp started screaming and begging them to stop. The ass-kicking did stop, but only because they began stripping him.

When they were done, Rapp lay on the hard, dusty floor, whimpering. As best he could tell, they were in some type of bombed-out building. All of his clothes and possessions were thrown into the trunk of the car that he had just been yanked from. The vehicle started up again, and then the driver floored the gas and sprayed Rapp with loose gravel. The four men who were standing around him all started laughing.

A fifth man walked into the circle. Rapp recognized him as the one who had been leaning against the building. He was a senior member of Fatah. "Why are you doing this? I have been authorized by my government to negotiate with you."

Radih squatted on his haunches. He held out Rapp's Beretta. "Why do you need this to negotiate?"

Rapp shrugged. "This is a dangerous town . . . I don't know."

Radih slapped him hard across the face. "I think you are a liar."

"Sorry."

"Shut up!"

"But the money . . ."

Radih slapped him again and Rapp started to whimper.

"I'm just a messenger."

"And what do you have to offer?"

"Money. Lots of it."

"How much?"

"A million dollars."

Radih roared with laughter. "I think it will cost you a lot more than that."

"Maybe I can get more money?" Rapp said hopefully.

"And maybe we will sell you to the Russians with the others."

"I can get you the money."

"I don't care about the money. And besides, you do not seem like you would fetch a very good price." The other men nodded and laughed. Radih was suddenly curious about this man. He had to be very low-level. "Why were you chosen to negotiate their release?"

Rapp shrugged and didn't answer.

Radih slapped him and one of the other men kicked his legs and screamed, "Answer him."

"I volunteered. Please don't hit me."

"And why would anyone volunteer for something like this?"

Rapp spoke softly into the floor.

"Speak up!"

"I said I am related to one of the men."

"Related? To who?"

"Stan Hurley."

"We don't have a hostage named Stan Hurley."

"Yes, you do. Hurley is his real name. You probably know him as Bill Sherman. That's why I volunteered. Please don't hurt me," Rapp pleaded. "I mean you no harm, I just want to get these men released. I promise we will not bother you again—"

"How are you related to this Stan Hurley?"

"He's my dad."

Radih could hardly believe his luck. He might not be able to kill Bill Sherman, but Sayyed had said nothing about his son. Radih stood. "Let's go," he announced to his men. "Tape his wrists and toss him in the trunk."

Rapp was as passive as he could be while they wound the duct tape quickly around his wrists. He counted ten times and noted that they didn't bother to tape his ankles.

"I can make you guys rich," Rapp pleaded as they tossed him in the trunk of a different car. The trunk was slammed shut and then they were off. He had no idea where they were to begin with, so the twenty-odd-minute drive that they went on through the city was unnecessary. Just before they stopped, however, things became noticeably quieter. Almost as if they were in the country. When the trunk popped again, Rapp was hit with a blast of sunlight. He glimpsed a building that looked like it was slated for demolition. Two big men yanked him roughly from the trunk. Rapp's bare feet hit the rough ground and he realized they were in an alley. The buildings on each side were riddled with pockmarks, and not one of them had a window. Two blocks away he caught a glimpse of blue. Before he could take in anything else he was rushed into the building and down a flight of stairs. He was immediately hit by the smell of raw sewage. He almost gagged, and this time it wasn't for effect.

The hallway was ten feet wide with rooms on each side. They were all missing doors except three rooms at the midpoint on the right. He noted the two guards with bandannas tied around their faces. They were the first men who had tried to conceal their faces, and then Rapp realized it was the smell. The men who had him by the arms yelled ahead to the guards to open the first door. They removed the padlock from the latch and swung the door open.

With a good enough head start Rapp thought he might be able to bust the latch off.

"Please," Rapp pleaded with the men. "I'm only an analyst. I can't do this. Please give me my clothes back and let me call Washington. I'll get you your money."

They tossed Rapp into the room like a rag doll. He tumbled to the floor, begging them to listen to him. Then the door was closed, and he was again enveloped in darkness. Rapp began to whimper, softly at first and then a little louder. For some strange reason, this room smelled better than the hallway, almost as if it had been cleaned with bleach. He recalled the landscape in the alley and remembered the thin strip of blue on the horizon only a few blocks away. It was the sea for certain, and with all of the bombed-out buildings it fit the general description of Martyrs' Square. The merchant must have been right. Rapp rolled onto his side and started digging through his thick hair. The fact that they hadn't covered his head with a hood worried him. He found the small blade and placed one end in his teeth. He set the blade against the top edge of the tape and began slowly moving his hands back and forth.

CHAPTER 63

THE stairs at the tail of the Russian plane were lowered and Sayyed watched the soldiers in black fatigues file down the steps. He counted thirty. All heavily armed. All Russian special forces. Sayyed had no doubt they were intended as both a show of force and an insult.

Sayyed raised the radio to his lips and said, "You were right."

Mughniyah's voice came back, "How many men?"

"Thirty Spetsnaz. Heavily armed."

There was a long pause and then, "I will be there in five minutes."

Sayyed attached the radio to his belt and watched as the elite Russian soldiers spread out to cover the area. Finally, Shvets appeared and then Ivanov. Both men were in suits and wearing sunglasses to protect their delicate Moscow eyes. As they approached, Ivanov yelled at Sayyed from across the tarmac. The big Russian threw out his arms and walked the final ten paces as if it had been far too long since they had last seen each other.

Sayyed was not going to be a rude host, so he held out his arms as well, and despite his misgivings, he greeted Ivanov with a smile. As much as he distrusted the man, there was something likable about him.

"Assef, my friend, how are you?" Ivanov practically picked the Syrian up in his arms.

"I am well. Thank you for coming."

Ivanov pushed the Syrian intelligence officer away and held him at arm's length. "What happened to your ear?"

Sayyed gently touched the bandage and said, "Oh, nothing. Just a little accident."

"Other than that you are well?"

"Yes."

Ivanov peered over the top of his sunglasses at the hangar and the surrounding landscape—the bombed-out hangar, an airliner with only one wing, and another with no engines. "I see Beirut hasn't changed much."

"Things are getting better." Sayyed pointed back toward the construction equipment at the main terminal. "We thought privacy would be best for this meeting." He motioned toward the hangar, saying, "I promise it will be worth your effort."

"Yes, but what is this nonsense? I have to compete for my information like some rancher bidding on heads of cattle?"

They started walking toward the shade of the hangar. Sayyed followed the script that Mughniyah had given him. "Yes . . . well, if it was up to me it would only be you. But I am not the only one with a voice in this."

"Mughniyah?" Ivanov asked.

"Yes."

"I have warned you. He is in love with the religious zealots in Iran, and we both know they will never be the answer to a lasting peace in Beirut."

"I know . . . I know," Sayyed said, patting Ivanov's arm as they entered the hangar, "but there is only so much I can do."

"And you have been a staunch supporter. Do not think that has gone unnoticed." Ivanov took off his sunglasses. "Now, where are these Americans that we are all so interested in?"

Sayyed pointed to their left. In the shadowy recesses of the hangar next to a rusty, broken-down truck, a man wearing a black hood sat in a single chair.

"But I thought there would be three?"

"There are," Sayyed said. "Think of this one as a sample."

Ivanov was not happy. "I have flown all this way and you play games with me. I do not like this, Assef."

"No games," Sayyed lied. "Security is very important. One of these Americans is such a big fish that we must be extra careful."

"What is his name?"

"I cannot say just yet."

"Why?"

"We must wait for the others."

Ivanov looked around the empty space. Shvets and the Spetsnaz commander had wisely stopped twenty feet away to give them some privacy. Where were the representatives from Iran and Iraq? Turning back to Sayyed, he asked that exact question.

"They will be here any minute."

Ivanov checked his watch and huffed. His instincts told him something else was going on here. "I do not like this. I do not like this one bit. I am on time. I have important business to attend to back in Moscow."

"I am sorry, Mikhail."

"Sorry will not work." Ivanov leaned in close so he was eye to eye with Sayyed. "When you come to Moscow, I treat you like a prince. I come here, and we meet in this." He waved his hand around the dilapidated space.

"Mikhail, I am sorry. We do not have your resources."

"And that is something you would be wise to remember. I do not deserve to be treated like this."

"I am sorry," Sayyed could only say again.

"If you are so sorry, you will stop playing games with me and tell me who this big fish is. And if you do not want to stop playing games, then I will be forced to start playing them as well. Maybe I will get on my plane and fly back to Moscow. You can conduct your little auction without me."

"Mikhail, I am—"

"Don't say it again. If you are truly sorry you

will tell me who the mystery American is. If not, I am done playing games and I will leave."

Mughniyah had specifically told him not to divulge that information until he was there, but Sayyed was growing weary of the man's paranoia. He did not trust Ivanov, but he couldn't see what harm could be caused by telling him about Bill Sherman. "I will give you a sneak peek, but you have to play dumb when Mughniyah gets here." Turning, Sayyed said, "Follow me." As they walked over to a folding table, he said, "This American is rumored to have been heavily involved in some of the CIA's most sensitive operations. Including operations directed at your country." There were three files on the table. Sayyed picked up one and handed it to Ivanov.

Ivanov had been preparing himself for this for the past twenty-four hours. He had expected to see the man in person, but in a way it would be easier for him to downplay his reaction this way. He opened the file, looked at the Polaroid photo of the American spy, and nearly gasped. Ivanov hid his emotions and tilted his head as if he were trying to place the face, even though he knew with absolute certainty who the man was. He and Stan Hurley had tangled back in Berlin a long time ago. Hurley had become such a problem that he had sent two of his best men to kill him one night. Neither came back. Their bodies were found floating in the Spree River the next day. The day after that, Hurley marched into Ivanov's office in broad daylight and put a gun to his head. Hurley explained the rules to him that morning, rules that Ivanov already knew, but had none-theless ignored. The Americans and Russians were not supposed to kill each other. It was all part of the new détente of the Cold War, the easing of tensions in the early seventies brought about by Nixon and Brezhnev. The American then gagged him, blind-folded him, tied him up, and pilfered his files.

When Hurley was done, he loosened the ropes on Ivanov's wrists a bit and whispered in his ear, "You should be able to wiggle your way out of these in a few minutes. By then I'll be gone, and you'll be faced with two options. You can scream your head off and try to chase me. If you do that your bosses and everyone else back in Moscow will know that you let an American waltz into your office in the middle of the day, tie you up, and steal your files. You will be an embarrassment to the KGB, and we both know how much the KGB likes to be embar-rassed. Your other option . . . well, let's just say I hope you're smart enough to figure it out."

Ivanov was smart enough, and he had never told a soul about that day. He coughed into his hand and turned to Sayyed. "I have heard of this man. What else can you tell me about him?"

Sayyed thought it best to not be too forthright on this point. Telling him that the American was the toughest, craziest man he'd ever encountered would not be good for the negotiations. Fortunately, he was saved by the sounds of approaching vehicles.

CHAPTER 64

HURLEY dangled in the air from a hook that was tied to his wrists. His toes hovered only a few inches from the floor. His shoulders ached like nothing he had ever experienced. This had been his punishment for taking a bite out of Sayyed. They also decided to tape his mouth shut, but he thought that had more to do with silencing his insults than with their fear of being bitten. The only nice thing to come of it was that they'd left him alone. Not that hanging by your wrists a few inches off the ground was a nice thing, but it was certainly preferable to having your fingernails ripped out and being electrocuted.

There was a noise at the door. A second later it opened and the light turned on. Hurley blinked a few times before he could see it was Radih. The Fatah leader crossed over and exhaled cigarette smoke into Hurley's face. Hurley inhaled the smoke and thought he might apologize for all the nasty things he'd said about Radih's mother if only the man would offer him a heater.

Radih reached up and tore the tape off the American's mouth. "I have a surprise for you."

"We gonna try the rubber hose today?"

"No, something much better."

"Great," Hurley said with feigned enthusiasm. "I can't wait. Hey . . . about that stuff I said about your mom—"

Before Hurley could get the rest of it out, Radih smashed his fist into Hurley's stomach. "I have had enough of your lies. I am going to make you feel more pain than you have ever imagined."

"Good," Hurley coughed. "I hope you kill me, because Mughniyah will kill you for it. Nothing could make me happier than making sure you went down with me."

"Don't worry. I'm not going to kill you," Radih said, smiling. "But I am going to kill your son."

Hurley laughed. "What the fuck are you talking about?"

Radih turned to his men. "Get him."

"My son?" Hurley asked. "You must be off your rocker, unless you mean one of your bastard brothers I fathered with your mother."

"Yes . . . keep talking. We will see how tough you are in a moment."

The two men returned, each with one arm looped under Rapp's armpits. Rapp was shuffling along trying to keep up and blabbing incessantly about the money he could get them.

Rapp saw Hurley and yelled, "Dad. Don't worry, we're going to get out of this. Washington is going to pay for your release."

Hurley looked at Rapp and said, "What the fuck are you talking about? Have you lost your mind?"

Radih was finally having some fun. "This is beautiful. You are right. I can't kill you, but I can kill your son. A big American fuck-you." Radih snapped his fingers and pointed at the floor. "Bring him here." The men dumped Rapp on the ground at Radih's feet. "I will handle him," he said as he drew the American's silenced Beretta from his waistband. "Hold the father's head and make sure his eyes are open."

The two men left Rapp and took up positions on the right and left side of Hurley. They grabbed his head and dug their thumbs into the skin just under his eyebrows and pulled up.

"Make him look," Radih commanded as he grabbed a fistful of Rapp's hair. "Over here."

"Why are you doing this?" Rapp wailed in a panicked voice. "Our government will pay you."

Radih bent over and said, "They will pay for him, you idiot. You are worthless." He straightened and looked at Hurley. "Are there any other lies you'd like to spew about my mother?"

Hurley didn't offer a reply.

"How does a man of your considerable though twisted talents sire such a stupid child?"

Rapp looked up, only half listening to the insults. His focus was on a beautiful 9mm suppressed Beretta. Radih kept waving the gun back and forth, sticking it in Hurley's face and then pointing it at Rapp's head. Rapp followed it like a tennis volley. Radih's finger was on the trigger and the red dot above his thumb told Rapp that the safety was off and the gun was hot. The man settled into a rhythm with his insults. He was now saying something about Rapp's mother, the woman he presumed to have slept with Hurley. The Palestinian stuck the tip of the suppressor under Hurley's nose and ordered him to beg for his son's life. As Hurley started to speak, the gun began its slow-motion arc back to Rapp.

Rapp made his move. He'd sawed most of the way through the tape around his wrists while he was back in the holding cell. Now, not sure the tape would break, he went for a two-handed grab around the barrel of the gun. His hands clamped down on the steel while the gun was still swinging Rapp's way. Rapp stood, driving the gun straight up so a misfire wouldn't bury itself in Hurley's chest. At the top, he pivoted to his left, bringing the gun up and over the top of his head, before pulling it back down on the other side, effectively putting Radih in an arm bar. In this position the Palestinian couldn't move unless he let go of the gun. Rapp delivered a quick knee strike to Radih's face, and a bullet spat harmlessly into the cinder-block wall.

Having dazed him, Rapp ripped the gun free. He swung the pistol back, cracking Radih across the forehead with the heavy metal grip. The blow sent him to the floor. Rapp tried to wrench his wrists free of the remaining duct tape but it caught. The other two men were finally starting to move. Hurley, realizing that one of the men might yell for help, started screaming at the top of his lungs as if he were being beaten. Rapp took a step back to get a better angle and yanked again, but the last bit of tape held, so he flipped the gun up in the air and caught the grip with both hands. The man on his left was no more than four feet away when he fired the gun twice, hitting him both times in the chest. The man collapsed at Rapp's feet.

Rapp swung the gun around on the other man, who was caught between the door and Hurley. He was never going to make it, so he stopped and put his hands up in the air.

"Shoot him," Hurley ordered in a raspy voice.

Rapp squeezed the trigger and buried a bullet in the man's forehead.

"Get me down . . . quick," Hurley hissed.

"What about him?" Rapp asked, pointing the gun at Radih, who was showing signs of life.

"Get me down first."

Rapp ripped through the last bit of tape while he ran over to the wall and untied the makeshift pulley. Hurley dropped the short distance to the floor, landing on his feet. He wavered for a second and then caught his balance.

"Give me that gun," Hurley ordered, "and check the right thigh pocket of that second one you shot. He should have a knife."

Rapp placed the gun in Hurley's hands and went off to search for the knife.

Hurley walked over to Radih, whose arms were starting to flop around as if he was waking up from a deep sleep. Hurley stomped on his stomach, and the Palestinian's eyes popped open. Hurley bent over and pressed the suppressor against Radih's chest. Looking into his eyes, he said, "You should have killed me when you had the chance, you piece of shit." Hurley pulled the trigger.

CHAPTER 65

TWO of the sedans pulled into the hangar and three more stopped just outside. All of the doors opened at roughly the same time and a dozen well-armed men fanned out, creating a barrier at the door, effectively sealing Ivanov off from his Spetsnaz escort.

Ivanov looked at the commander with extreme disappointment.

Mughniyah approached with a confident grin on his face. Four of his bodyguards trailed a few paces back. "Mikhail, welcome to Beirut."

"I would hardly call this a welcome."

"You will have to excuse all of this, but I am not in a good mood today."

"And why is that?"

"Because I just found out that you have been scheming behind my back yet again."

"What are you talking about?"

"You will notice that our Iraqi and Iranian friends are not here."

"Why?" Sayyed asked, alarmed by the news.

"Because I found out that Mikhail had made a deal with them. Didn't you, Mikhail?"

Ivanov tried to laugh the question away as if it was a harmless maneuver.

Mughniyah turned his attention back to Sayyed and said, "He set the ceiling at five million. The others were going to bow out and let him win."

"What did you do with them?" Sayyed asked.

"For the moment they are my guests. I will decide if I am going to kill them later."

Ivanov clasped his hands together and laughed. Mughniyah was proving to be much smarter than he had given him credit for. "You have outsmarted me, Imad. That does not happen very often. Would you like me to leave, or would you like to discuss business? Negotiate some terms, perhaps?"

"I will negotiate nothing with you. I am going to name a price and you are going to pay it."

"Really?" Ivanov said. "And what if I decide I don't like your price?"

"Then we will have a big problem."

Ivanov nodded as if he found the game amusing.

"Before we get to that, though, I need you to return all of the money you took from our Swiss bank accounts."

"Money that I took!" Ivanov's eyes nearly bulged out of his head. "I did no such thing."

"I think you did."

"As a matter of fact I want my money back from *you*."

"Your money?"

"Yes, my money." Ivanov's face was blazing red. "The money that you took. You don't think I suspected you at once? You never liked Sharif. You did nothing but complain about his prices. You called him a rat and a traitor to the cause for charging his inflated prices."

"I did not kill Sharif," Mughniyah denied flatly.

"And why should I believe you?"

"Because I am a man of honor. Someone who fights for what he believes in . . . not a thief like you."

"Honor! This is beautiful. You, of all people, speak of honor. Imad Mughniyah, the hijacker of civilian airliners, the kidnapper of professors, the man who shells entire neighborhoods filled with women and children. You speak of honor. That is laughable." Ivanov literally spat the last word at his accuser.

Mughniyah reached for his gun, but the Spetsnaz commander beat him to the draw and pointed the barrel of his Markov pistol at the side of Mughniyah's head. All of a sudden it appeared as if everyone had a gun. Slides were being racked and hammers cocked.

"Enough," Sayyed shouted. "Your disdain for each other has blinded your judgment."

"And you are a fool," Mughniyah yelled.

Sayyed approached him, and in a voice loud enough for only Mughniyah to hear said, "And you are broke. How are you going to pay all of your men next week and the week after that? Get control of your hot temper and let me handle this." Speaking to the group, he then said, "Everyone, lower your weapons." He motioned with his hands and repeated himself two more times until finally all of the weapons were either holstered or pointed in a safe direction.

"I know that Imad did not steal the money, and I do not think that Mikhail did so either."

"How can you know?" Mughniyah angrily asked.

"Tell me. Why would he come here today if he had stolen our money?"

While Mughniyah pondered that question, Shvets stepped forward. "I can assure you that my boss had nothing to do with the stolen funds. I visited Herr Dorfman's boss in Hamburg last week. More than fifty million dollars was stolen. It appears we were not the only targets." Shvets wanted to get out of here with his life, so he quickly added, "We are following several leads, including one that the money was stolen by an organized crime element out of Prague."

"And I can promise you," Ivanov added quickly, "that when we find these people, we will get our money back, and we will punish the people who took it."

"Thank you," Sayyed said. "Right now, we have something very important to negotiate. We have three Americans. John Cummins, who served four years in Moscow and the last four in Damascus, another relatively young man by the name of Robert Richards, and the infamous Bill Sherman." Sayyed grabbed the file off the table and handed it to Ivanov, giving him a second to study the photo again. "Now, how much would your government be willing to pay for these three men?"

Ivanov unconsciously licked his lips. A prize like Stan Hurley would virtually guarantee him the directorship. Primakov was getting old and lacked the ruthless animal instinct that it took to run the SVR. He could control the interrogation and filter what information he passed on. The thought of keeping that asshole Hurley in the basement of one of his secure sites like some exotic animal was almost too much to take. He reminded himself that this was still a negotiation and his funds were not unlimited. "I am confident that my government would pay five million dollars for these three."

"That is not enough," Mughniyah complained before anyone had had a chance to absorb the offer.

Thus started the back and forth, with Ivanov coming up three million in his price. They were stuck there for a few minutes while Mughniyah kept saying that he would only accept an offer of sixteen million. Ivanov, as well as Sayyed, tried to explain to him that the issues of the stolen money and the value of the American spies had nothing to do with each other. Ivanov raised his offer to ten and was prepared to walk away when Mughniyah finally countered at fourteen. Thirty seconds later they had agreed on twelve, and everyone breathed a sigh of relief, no one more so than Sayyed.

They were only halfway done, though. Mughniyah wanted all the money in their possession before they would turn the men over, and Ivanov wasn't going to release a red cent until he laid eyes on Stan Hurley.

Sayyed broke the stalemate by saying, "You need to call Moscow, correct?"

"Yes."

"Why don't I retrieve the prisoners? They are not far from here. You can make the arrangements to have the money transferred, and when we get back we can complete the transaction."

Ivanov, who wanted to get as far away from this horrible place and these horrible people as quickly as possible, leaped at the chance to expedite his departure. "That is a wonderful idea." Turning to Shvets, he said, "Nikolai, go with Assef and bring the prisoners back here."

The last thing Shvets wanted to do was leave the relative security of this hangar and drive into downtown Beirut. He considered asking if he could bring a few of the Spetsnaz with him, but he knew the request would be denied. As he followed Sayyed and his men to their car, he wondered how much longer he could continue to work for Ivanov.

CHAPTER 66

R APP found the knife, dug it out of the man's pants, and crossed the room. He took his gun back from Hurley and stuck it under his armpit while he cut the tape from Hurley's wrists.

The tape peeled free and Hurley said, "Give me the gun."

Rapp held out the knife. "Get your own."

Hurley grumbled and took the knife.

"There are two guys in the hallway." Rapp started dragging one of the bodies across the room and placed it by the wall with the door. "I'll open the door, you try to sound like Radih. Yell for them to get in here and I'll pop 'em."

When the bodies were piled out of sight, Rapp placed his hand on the door handle. Hurley stood behind him. Rapp nodded and yanked the door open. Hurley muttered something about a mess and ordered the two guards to get in there. Unfortunately, only one appeared. Rapp shot him in the back of the head while pulling the door open farther and swinging his left arm around, searching for the second man. The tip of the suppressor ended up less than a foot from the man's face. Rapp squeezed the trigger and shot him in the nose, pink mist exploding out into the hallway. Stepping over the body, he looked left and right. The hallway was empty.

Rapp dragged the guard into the room. Hurley was already stripping the first guard of his pants, shirt, and boots. Rapp did the same with the second guard and told Hurley to grab the man's bandanna. When Rapp found the radio he asked Hurley, "Do you know where we are?"

"No."

"I think I might. What about Bobby and Cummins?"

"Bobby should be here, but I think they took Cummins to the airport. They're trying to auction off our asses."

"We'll get Bobby in a second, but I need to call Ridley first." Rapp dialed in the right frequency and hit the transmit button. All he got was static.

"Bad reception down here," Hurley told him. "We'll have to get out of the basement."

"All right . . ." Rapp looked around the room. "I assume Bobby is naked, too."

"Yeah . . . Let's grab him some clothes."

Rapp scavenged up a set while Hurley collected two ammo pouches with eight extra AK-47 magazines. When they had everything, they tied the bandannas around their faces and Rapp checked the hallway. It was still empty, so they ducked out, closing the door behind them and locking it. The next door over was padlocked, so Rapp shot the lock off with his Beretta. Hurley opened the door and froze. There, dangling from the hook in the middle of the room, with a rope wrapped around his neck, was Richards.

"Motherfuckers," was all Hurley could manage to say.

Rapp considered checking for a pulse, but Richards's skin was chalk white. He'd been dead for hours. "Should we bring him with us?"

"No." Hurley shook his head.

Rapp closed the door to Richards's cell and told himself he would process it later. They ran down the back hallway, but when they got near the stairs they heard some voices. Hurley started making hand gestures, but Rapp waved him off, pulling him back away from the stairs.

Whispering in his ear, Rapp said, "I have an idea." Rapp handed him the two-way radio. "Try Ridley again. Tell him I think we're at Martyrs' Square. I'm gonna run down to the front of the building and see if I can start a little something." Rapp started to move, but Hurley grabbed him.

"What are you talking about?"

"Just wait here. If I'm right, you're gonna hear a shitload of gunfire in about a half minute. Then we'll make our break." Rapp pointed at the radio. "Just try to raise Ridley. I'll be right back."

Rapp tore off down the hallway, slowing when

he was fifteen feet from the stairs at the front of the building. He stopped and listened for a moment, but heard nothing. Then there was the sound of a foot scraping along the floor and a faint voice. Rapp couldn't tell if it was coming from the first floor or farther up. He considered going back to Hurley. He could use his silenced Beretta to take out whoever was at the back of the building and then try to make a run for it. Fundamentally, though, there was a problem. They were on the wrong side of town and severely outgunned. They needed a diversion to get out of here.

"Full speed ahead," he muttered to himself as he started up the stairs, his silenced pistol in his left hand and the AK-47 in the right. Midway up the steps he got his first glimpse of a small lobby off to the left, maybe fifteen by fifteen feet. Rapp counted two heads and then three. The main entrance was sandbagged, as were the windows on each side, although they'd left two holes in the sandbags to fire from—exactly what Rapp was looking for.

When he hit the landing he noticed two more men lying on the floor. One was standing, looking out one hole in the sandbags, watching the street, and two more were sitting in folding chairs, playing a board game. Rapp walked straight for the man who was on his feet. He kept his pace casual and started shaking his head as if he was going to tell them just how crappy things were downstairs. One of the men started bitching in Arabic. The best Rapp could figure was that the man was telling him he had another hour before he had to pull a watch in the toilet. Rapp laughed and then raised the suppressed Beretta. He had had eighteen shots to start with and was down to twelve.

The guy who was standing got it first, a nice little shot from ten feet right in the left eye. The two guys playing the board game—one got it in the back of the head and the other in his open mouth. Rapp never stopped moving. It was another nice thing Hurley had taught him. When you have the advantage, close with the enemy. He was no more than eight feet away when he shot the two nappers. The first one was clean, but with the second guy, he was off a bit on the first shot, so he had to fire one more to put him out of his misery.

Six shots left. Rapp glanced to his left. The hallway had been barricaded with scraps of broken office furniture. The stairs going up were empty. He walked over to the little one-by-one-foot hole in the sandbags and looked across the street. Sure enough, about two hundred feet away was a similar building. This had to be Martyrs' Square. Rapp slung his AK-47 over his right shoulder, stuffed the Beretta in his waistband, and picked up the dead lookout's AK-47. He gripped the rifle firmly, flipped the selector switch to full automatic, and sighted at the building across the street. He didn't want to kill anyone over there, but he did want to make sure he got their attention, so he chose a position on the second floor and let it rip. The bullets shredded the afternoon calm, thudding into the sandbags across the street and then the building itself as it climbed.

Rapp emptied the entire magazine and dropped the weapon.

Without hesitating, he moved to the peephole on the other side of the front door and took aim with the other AK-47. This time he sprayed the entire building down, firing in controlled bursts. Twenty or so rounds into the magazine, the building across the street erupted in gunfire. Rapp hauled ass down the stairs as he heard bullets smacking into the building and gunfire being returned.

Hurley was standing at the other end, waiting for him. "What in hell did you just do?"

"I gave the big FU to Washington and got us a little diversion." Rapp looked up the stairs. The men were gone. "Come on. Let's get the hell out of here."

They climbed up the stairs, and when they reached the landing a heavyset guy in green fatigues came running down from the floor above and started ordering them to the upper floors to return fire. Hurley pointed out the back door with his rifle, and when the man looked in that direction, he deftly stuck a knife through his carotid artery. Blood came cascading out, pulsating through his fingers.

Hurley followed Rapp out the back door just as a sedan skidded to a stop between two piles of rubble. The two men in the front seat jumped out of the car, yelling and asking what was going on. Rapp couldn't hear them over the gunfire, and since they weren't pointing a gun at him he wasn't in any rush to kill them. All he wanted was their car. Two more men exited the rear of the car, one Caucasian and the other Middle Eastern. Both looked vaguely familiar, which made Rapp think he'd seen them in some of the photos Ridley had shown him.

Hurley said, "Merry fucking Christmas," and then shot the two men in front.

Rapp raised the Beretta and took aim at the fair-skinned guy on the left.

Hurley yelled, "Don't kill the little Commie. Crack him over the head and stuff him in the trunk. I've got the other one."

Rapp and Hurley rushed the two men, their weapons leveled.

Hurley swung the butt end of his rifle and cracked Sayyed across the temple. As the Syrian dropped to his knees, Hurley said, "Sayyed, old buddy. I can't wait to play Twenty Questions with you."

EPILOGUE

ZURICH, SWITZERLAND, FOUR DAYS LATER

THOMAS Stansfield sat on the park bench and looked up at the Rietberg Museum. He loved Zurich—the lake, the unique pace, the beauty of the mountains, but most important the safety it afforded a man of his profession. This city, and the small country it was part of, had managed to stay out of World War II, even with war raging just beyond its borders in every direction. And in the years after that, it had continued to offer respite for Cold Warriors like himself and the man he was about to meet, a place where they could lower their guard, not completely, but enough to enjoy life a little, and occasionally meet face-to-face to discuss mutually beneficial opportunities, or in this instance, conclude vital transactions.

Stansfield saw the two black sedans enter the park and glanced at his watch. The meeting would start on time, which was a nice surprise. The man he was meeting was notoriously late. Stansfield watched the sedans stop thirty feet behind the two vehicles in his entourage. Every detail had been agreed to in advance so as to not make either party unduly skittish. Two men in dark overcoats and sunglasses exited the first car. They looked like Eastern European versions of the two men who were standing a respectful thirty feet behind the CIA's deputy director of operations.

A man with unusually large ears and puffy eyes exited the second car and buttoned his blue, double-breasted suit coat. One of the men approached with a wool overcoat, but the older man waved him off, which brought the hint of a smile to Stansfield's face. He had spent six years in Moscow. To a Russian, forty degrees in Zurich this time of year would feel like summer. Yevgeny Primakov motioned for his men to stay by the car and walked over to the bench.

Stansfield did not stand and Primakov did not expect him to. Neither were handshakes offered. These were two men whose entire jobs revolved around seeing through other people's deceptions.

"Did you bring my man?" Stansfield asked.

"Yes. Did you bring mine?"

"That was not part of the agreement."

"It should have been," Primakov said gruffly.

"There would have been a slight problem there, Yevgeny."

"What?"

Stansfield turned so he could face him. "My man wants to come back to America. Your man." Stansfield shook his head. "He doesn't want to go back to Russia. What does that tell you?"

"How can I know that? You have not allowed me to talk to him."

Stansfield pulled a manila envelope from inside his jacket. "I gave you the highlights on the phone. His boss, one of your deputies, has stolen more than twenty million dollars from Mother Russia and her fine citizens. That money is currently sitting in various accounts around the world. How do you think Deputy Shvets would be treated if I were to hand him over to you?"

Primakov did not answer the question.

"Yevgeny, you do realize I could have given this to the White House? They would have shared it with your president when the time was right, and you would have been put under suspicion along with that thug Ivanov."

Primakov couldn't bring himself to say thank you, so he asked, "Why the courtesy?"

"Because I don't like my people being kidnapped and treated like a science experiment. You did bring Mr. Cummins?"

"Yes." Primakov stuck out his hand for the envelope.

"Not until I see my man."

Primakov motioned to his men, and they opened the back door of the first car. The bodyguard had to help Cummins out of the sedan. He was incredibly thin, but it was him. Stansfield looked over his shoulder and snapped his fingers. One of his bodyguards took off at a trot to help with the transfer.

"The package."

Stansfield handed it to Primakov, who immediately tore it open. He flipped through the twenty-odd pages and asked, "And how do I know this isn't all made up?"

"Check it yourself. The access codes are all there. The money is still in the accounts, although trust me, I thought about using it for a few of our more creative programs."

Primakov considered that for a moment. He finally managed to say, "Thank you."

"You're welcome," Stansfield said as he stood. "Just do me a favor, Yevgeny. Let's stick to the old rules. You stay away from my guys, and I'll stay away from yours."

Stansfield walked away with his other bodyguard close behind. He stopped at the first sedan to check on the Schnoz, and then got into the backseat of the second car. The bodyguard closed the door and then went around the other side and climbed in the backseat. As soon as they were out of the park the bodyguard took off his sunglasses and asked, "Did he buy it, sir?"

Stansfield looked over at Mitch Rapp and said, "One hundred percent."

Rapp looked out the window, thinking that Hurley had truly lived up to his reputation as the biggest SOB on the block. It had been pure evil genius to pay Ivanov's money back into his accounts and have Shvets inform on him. "So what's going to happen to Ivanov?"

Stansfield looked down and straightened his tie. "I think Mikhail Ivanov is going to spend the next few months being thoroughly interrogated by the SVR's goon squad."

"And then what?"

"He won't be able to deny the money, will he?"

"No."

Stansfield nodded. "You're a smart kid. Fill in the blanks."

"Couldn't happen to a nicer guy." Rapp shrugged as if he didn't care. "What about Sayyed?"

"Some questions are better off not asked."

Rapp frowned. He didn't like not knowing.

"Listen," Stansfield said, "I can't release a guy like Sayyed. He'll just go back and torture more of our people." Stansfield shook his head. "The man will get what he deserves."

"Sir, I hope you know I don't give a crap what happens to him."

"Good."

"What about Shvets?"

"Shvets will be fine as long as he continues to cooperate. In a few years we'll cut him loose and let him start a life of his own."

They drove in silence for a while, and then Rapp finally asked, "Sir, why did you want me to come along for this? Being your bodyguard is not exactly my area of expertise."

Stansfield had been wondering when the rookie was going to get around to asking the question. He grinned to himself and asked Rapp, "You think Stan Hurley is a son of a bitch?"

"The biggest one I've ever met, sir."

Stansfield laughed. "Now you know he's not big on compliments?"

Rapp nodded.

"Well, he had some pretty amazing things to say about you when you got back from Beirut. Ridley as well. Irene has been telling me for close to two years that she thought you might have the goods, and I guess you proved to all of us last week that you most certainly do."

"Thank you, sir."

"So I guess I wanted to have a closer look at you . . . and show you that despite what you may have thought in Beirut, I will go to great lengths to get my people back."

Rapp nodded. He supposed Ridley had passed on his blistering critique. "I know that now, sir."

"Good. Now I think you should take a week off. You've earned it. I don't care where you go as long as it's west of here. Seven days from now report to Stan. I've got something else I want you two to work on."

Rapp was tempted to ask, but decided he didn't want it weighing on him while he was trying to recharge.

"Any idea where you're going to go?" Stansfield asked. "In case we need to get hold of you?"

Rapp looked at the snow-capped mountains and thought of Greta. With a smile on his face he said, "I think I'm going to stay right here in Zurich."

EMILY BESTLER BOOKS / ATRIA
PROUDLY PRESENT

#1 *New York Times* bestselling author
Vince Flynn's Mitch Rapp,
"a Rambo perfectly suited for the war on terror"
(*Washington Times*), in

KILL SHOT

A Thriller

Turn the page for a preview of *Kill Shot*. . . .

PRELUDE

THE man flew through the air, propelled by one of the other recruits. CIA handler Irene Kennedy watched from inside the house with casual interest as he failed to tuck and roll. He hit the ground flat and hard— the kind of impact that more than likely knocked the wind out of him, maybe even bruised a rib. Kennedy pursed her lips and calculated his odds of making it through the remaining eight weeks of the training program. She'd seen so many men roll through here that she could handicap them like a Vegas bookie. This one she gave a less than 10 percent chance.

Kennedy's thoughts, however, were not really with this batch of recruits. She was more concerned with a certain man who had waltzed through the rigorous training program a little more than a year ago. Mitch Rapp had been her rookie, and in the year since they had unleashed him on the purveyors of terrorism, he had left a steady trail of bodies from Geneva to Istanbul to Beirut and beyond. His record to date was perfect, and that in its own way added to Kennedy's tension. No one was perfect. Sooner or later, no matter how much talent they had, the mighty got tripped up. To complicate the odds, Kennedy had pushed to allow him to operate on his own. No backup. Just an advance team to scout things out and then he moved in all by his lonesome to do the dirty work up close and personal. No team members to bail his ass out if things went south. Rapp had argued that a small footprint would mean less chance of being caught.

Instinctively, Kennedy liked the simplicity. She'd seen more than her fair share of operations that had become so cumbersome in personnel and scope that they never got off the ground. Rapp had successfully argued that if he failed he was just one man with a foreign passport who could never be traced back to Langley. Hurley, the hard-assed spook and trainer, had pointed out that his little game worked only if he was dead. If they took him alive, he'd talk, just like everyone did, and then their exposure would be horrible. Theirs was not a risk-free business, however, and in the end Thomas Stansfield was willing to roll the dice on Rapp. The young operative had proven himself very resourceful and Stansfield needed to cross more names off his list of most wanted terrorists.

This mission was different, though. The stakes were considerably higher. It was one thing when Rapp was lurking about some Third World country practicing his craft, but at this very moment, he was about to do something very illegal, and unsanctioned in a country where he could not afford to make even the slightest mistake.

So intense was Kennedy's concentration that she hadn't heard the question from the man sitting behind the desk. She brushed a strand of her shoulder-length auburn hair behind her ear and said, "Excuse me?"

Dr. Lewis had been studying her for the last few minutes. Kennedy was a complex, confident, and extremely guarded professional. It had become an occupational obsession for Lewis to find out what made her tick. "You're worried about him."

Irene Kennedy's face remained neutral despite the fact that she was irritated by her colleague's ability to read her thoughts. "Who?"

"You know who," Dr. Lewis said, his soft blue eyes coaxing her along.

Kennedy shrugged as if it was a small thing. "I worry about every operation I'm in charge of."

"It seems you worry more about the ones he's involved in."

Kennedy considered the unique individual whom she had found in Upstate New York. As much as she'd like to deny it, Lewis's assessment of her concern over Rapp was accurate. Kennedy couldn't decide if it was the man, or the increasingly dangerous nature of the operations they'd been giving him, but in either case, she did not want to discuss the matter with Lewis.

"I've found," Lewis said in a carefree tone, "that I worry about him less than most. Always have, I think."

Kennedy flipped the comment around in her head. She could easily take it two ways—maybe more. "It's a lot easier when you're sitting on that side of the desk." Kennedy flashed him a rare smile. "I'm his handler. I put him in these situations, and I'm his only lifeline should something go wrong. I would think that clinically"—she raised an eyebrow, mimicking one of Lewis's overused facial expressions—"even you would understand that."

The shrink stroked his bottom lip with his forefinger and said, "Worrying about someone, or something, can be normal . . . and even healthy, but if taken too far . . ." Lewis shook his head and made a sour face. "Definitely not good."

Here we go, Kennedy thought to herself. This was not an accidental conversation. Lewis had been thinking about this for some time, plotting his line of questioning. Kennedy knew from experience that to try to run from the tête-à-tête would only make it worse. Lewis was patient and tenacious, and his reports were given serious weight by the deputy director of operations. The doctor would zero in on a problem and pepper you with questions until he was satisfied. Kennedy decided to lob the ball back onto his side of the net. "So you think I worry too much."

"I didn't say that," the doctor said with an easy tone and a soft shake of his head.

"But you implied it," Kennedy said.

"It was merely a question."

"A question that you asked because you think you've noticed something and you're worried about me. And since you initiated it, I would appreciate it if you would explain yourself rather than treat this like one of your therapy sessions."

Lewis sighed. He'd seen Kennedy get this way, but never with him. Usually it was with Stan Hurley, who was exceedingly adept at getting under people's skin. She was always calm and analytical in her dealings with Lewis, so the fact that she was so quick to anger now was proof that his concerns were valid. "I think when it comes to a certain operative . . . you worry too much."

"Rapp?" Kennedy asked.

"Correct."

"Please don't give me some psychobabble that you think I'm in love with him." Kennedy shook her head as if anything so humdrum was beneath her. "You know that's not how I work."

Lewis dismissed the idea with the back of his hand. "I agree. That is not my concern."

"Then what is?"

"That you do not give the man his credit."

"Credit? Credit for what?"

"Let's start with the fact that he came down here a little more than a year ago, without any military experience, and bested every man we put in front of him, including your Uncle Stan. His ability to learn, and do so at an incredibly rapid pace, is unlike anything I have ever seen." Lewis's voice grew in intensity. "And he does it in every field of discipline."

"Not every field of discipline. His marks in geopolitics and diplomatic affairs are dismal."

"That's because he sees those fields as an utter waste of his time, and I don't necessarily disagree with him."

"I thought we wanted well-rounded people to come out of this place."

Lewis shrugged his shoulders. "Mental stability matters more to me than well-rounded. After all, we're not asking him to negotiate a treaty."

"No, but we need him to be aware of the big picture."

"Big picture." Lewis frowned. "I think Mitch would argue that he's the only one around here who keeps his focus on the big picture."

Kennedy was a woman in the ultimate man's world, and she deeply disliked it when her colleagues treated her as if everything needed to be explained to her. "Really," she said with chaste insincerity.

"Your man has a certain aptitude. A certain ability that is heightened by the fact that he doesn't allow extraneous facts to get in the way."

Kennedy sighed. Normally she would never let her frustration show, but she was tired. "I know you think

I can read minds, but today that skill seems to have left me. Could you please get to the point?"

"You do look more tired than normal."

"Why, thank you. And you look like you've put on a few pounds."

Lewis smiled. "No need to hurt my feelings, just because you're worried about him."

"You are a master at deflection."

"It is my job to observe." He swiveled his chair and looked at the eight men and the two instructors who were putting them through the basics of hand-to-hand combat. "Observe all of you. Make sure no one has a mental breakdown and runs off the reservation."

"And who watches you?"

Lewis smiled. "I'm not under the same stress," the doctor said as he spun back to face Kennedy. "As you said, he is your responsibility."

Kennedy mulled that one over for a second. She couldn't disagree, so she kept her mouth shut. Plus the good doctor excelled at compartmentalizing the rigors of their clandestine operation.

"I'm looking out for you," Lewis said in his understanding therapist tone. "This double life that you've been living is not healthy. The mental strain is something that you think you can manage, and I thought you could as well, but recently, I've begun to have some doubts."

Kennedy felt a twist in her gut. "And have you shared these doubts with anyone?" Specifically she was thinking of Thomas Stansfield.

"Not yet, but at some point I am bound to pass along my concerns."

Kennedy felt a sense of relief, even if it was just a brief reprieve. She knew the only way to avoid a bad personnel report was to allay Lewis's concerns. And the only way to do that was to talk about them. "This aptitude that you say he has, would you care to share it with me?"

Lewis hesitated as if he was trying to find the most delicate way to say something that was brutally indelicate. With a roll of his head he said, "I have tried to get inside Rapp's mind, and there are days where I swear he's so refreshingly honest that I think I know what makes him tick, and then . . ." Lewis's voice trailed off.

"And then, what?"

"There are other days where I can't get past those damn dark eyes of his and that lopsided grin that he uses to defuse anyone who goes poking around in his business."

"That's the aptitude that puts you at ease? His lopsided grin?"

"No," Lewis scoffed. "It's far more serious than his ability to be open one moment and then impenetrable the next, although that may have a hand in how he deals with everything. I'm talking about the very core of all of this. Why are we here? Why have we secretly funneled over fifty million dollars into this operation? I'm talking about the fact that he is a one-man wrecking ball. That he has methodically, in a little over a year, accomplished more than we have accomplished in the last decade. And let's be brutally honest with each other." Lewis held up a finger. "The 'what' that we are talking about is the stone-cold fact that he is exceedingly good at hunting down and killing men."

Kennedy did not look at Lewis, but she nodded. They had all come to the same realization months ago. That was why they had turned him loose and allowed him to work on his own.

"I'm here," Lewis continued, "to observe and make

sure we have the right people and that their minds can handle the unique stress of this job. I have stress, you have stress, but I doubt ours compares to the stress of operating alone, often behind enemy lines, and hunting down a man and killing him."

"So you're worried that he's going to snap on us."

"Not at the moment. In fact, I think he has coped extraordinarily well with the rigors of his new job. I've kept a close eye on him. When he's back here, he sleeps like a baby. His head hits the pillow, sixty seconds later he's out and he sleeps straight through the night."

Kennedy had wondered about this same thing. Not every operative handled the taking of another human being's life with such ease. "So how does he deal with it . . . the blood on his hands?" she asked.

"He is a linear creature, which means he doesn't allow a lot of ancillary issues to muddy the waters of his conscience. These men . . . the ones we target . . . they all decided of their own volition to get involved in plots to kill innocent civilians. In Rapp's mind—and this isn't me guessing, he's expressed this very clearly—these men need to be punished."

Kennedy shifted in her chair. "Simple revenge."

"He says retribution. The distinction is slight, but I see his point."

"Given the loss of his girlfriend, I don't find that particularly troubling. After all, this is a job that requires a unique motivation."

"Yes it does, but his runs deep. He thinks if these men go unpunished, it will only embolden them to kill more people. To screw up more people's lives," Lewis answered.

"You'll get no argument from me. Nor from our boss, for that matter."

Lewis smiled. "There's one more thing, something that adds a unique twist."

"What's that?"

"He wants them to know he's coming after them."

"Theory or fact?"

"A bit of both. He knows that he can make them jumpy. Keep them up at night worrying when he's going to show up. He wants them to fear his existence."

"He told you this?" Kennedy asked, more than a bit surprised.

"Parts of it. The rest I pieced together," Lewis said with a nod.

"And why didn't you tell me?"

"I'm telling you right now."

Kennedy moved to the edge of her chair. "I mean, why didn't you tell me when you first learned about it?"

"I told Thomas," Lewis said, covering his bases.

"And what did he say?"

"He thought about it for a long moment and then said making these guys lose a little sleep might not be the worst thing."

"For Christ's sake." Kennedy pressed her palm against her forehead. "As his handler, don't you think you should let me in on stuff like this?"

"I'm not sure I understand your concern. I think he's fine, and Thomas does as well."

Kennedy pinched the bridge of her nose in an effort to stifle the headache she felt coming. "This isn't the NFL. We don't trash-talk. We don't taunt the other team in order to throw them off their game. My men need to be ghosts. They need to sneak into a country, quietly do their job, and then disappear."

"Irene, I think you are exaggerating your concerns. The enemy knows something is afoot. Bodies are piling up at an unusual clip, and if the fear Rapp is generating causes some of these men to be a bit jumpy"—Lewis shrugged—"well then, so be it."

"So what in the hell are you trying to tell me . . . that you're okay with Rapp, but you're worried about me?" Kennedy asked, the suspicion in her voice obvious.

"I'm okay with both of you, but I do think you worry too much."

"I'm worried about him because he's about to kill a high-ranking official in the capital of one of our closest allies and if he screws up, the blowback could be so bad every single last one of us will end up in front of a committee on Capitol Hill, be indicted, and then end up in jail." Kennedy shook her head. "I don't know what your shrink books have to say about all of this, but I think a fear of going to jail is a healthy thing."

"My point, Irene, is that Rapp is good. Maybe the best I've ever seen, and his target is a lazy, overfed bureaucrat. Tonight will go fine. That's not what I'm worried about."

"Mr. Rapp is unique. He has already proven his penchant for autonomy. He bristles against control, and so far, Thomas has been willing to ignore all of these little transgressions because the man is so damn good at what he does."

"But?"

"Our country, as well as our beloved employer, has a glorious history of throwing those men who are at the tip of the spear under the proverbial bus when things get difficult. If they do that to a man like Rapp . . ." Lewis winced at the thought.

"Our country and our employer don't even know he exists."

"I know that, Irene. I'm looking down the road, and

I'm telling you there is a real danger that at some point we might lose control of him."

Kennedy scoffed at the idea. "I haven't seen a single thing that could lead you to that conclusion."

"Irene," Lewis said in a far more serious tone, "strip it all down and what we have is a man who has been taught to kill. Kill people who have harmed innocent civilians or threatened the national security of this country. Right now, his mission is clearly focused. He's out killing bad guys who live in foreign countries. What happens if he wakes up one day and realizes some of the bad guys are right here? Living in America, working for the CIA, working on Capitol Hill."

"You can't be serious?" Kennedy said, shocked by the theory.

Lewis folded his hands under his chin and leaned back in his chair. "Justice is blind, and if you train a man to become judge, jury, and executioner . . . well, then you shouldn't be surprised if he someday fails to see the distinction between a terrorist and a corrupt, self-serving bureaucrat."

Kennedy thought about it for a moment and then said, "I'm not sure I'm buying it."

Lewis shrugged. "Only time will tell, but I know one thing for certain. If there comes a time where you need to neutralize him, you'd better not screw up. Because if he survives, he'll kill every last one of us."

ALL THINGS ARE NOT AS THEY SEEM

"There's been talk of strange things coming out of Faerie; looks like we just killed one of them." Ahira gestured toward the wolf-like thing lying on the ground.

I was going to say something, but Andrea's eyes widened, and her mouth opened. The wolf-like creature rose, its formerly dull eyes now glowing.

"It's mine," Andrea said, her quiet voice piercing through the shouts and growls.

"Be gone; you will not harm me or mine," she chanted. "Be gone, now and forever, I tell you twice!" Strands of light played through her fingers as the animal crouched for a leap.

"Be gone, I tell you a third and last time!"

The animal was gone in a flash of flames, and suddenly above Andrea a cloud of darkness hovered.

"Be gone, it is done," she said a last time.

"For here and now," the cloud spoke, its voice deep. "But you have ruined my fun. Perhaps I shall ruin yours sometime. . . ."

BUY A ROC STAR TITLE AND GET A SPECIAL ROC BOOK FREE!

THE ROC STAR TITLES

JULY **REAPER MAN** Terry Pratchett	**OCTOBER** **RATS AND GARGOYLES** Mary Gentle
AUGUST **BAZIL BROKETAIL** Christopher Rowley	**NOVEMBER** **THE ROAD TO EHVENOR** Joel Rosenberg

SELECT FREE ROC BOOK FROM THIS LIST

_____0-451-45069-8 THE BEST SCIENCE FICTION STORIES OF ISAAC ASIMOV, Isaac Asimov

_____0-451-45002-7 PROJECT SOLAR SAIL, Arthur C. Clarke

_____0-451-45108-2 RED IRON NIGHTS, Glen Cook

_____0-451-45050-7 THE COPPER CROWN, Patricia Kennealy

Send in proof of purchase (register receipt & xerox of UPC code from books) with this coupon and $1.50 for handling and postage (Check or money order payable to Penguin USA. No cash)

ROC STARS/Penguin USA Offer
375 Hudson Street
New York, NY 10014

NAME _____

ADDRESS _____ APT. #_____

CITY _____ STATE _____ ZIP_____

Employees and family members of Penguin USA are not eligible to participate in THE ROC STARS promotion. Offer subject to change or withdrawal without notice. Offer expires December 31, 1992.

RS

JOEL ROSENBERG

THE ROAD TO EHVENOR

A Guardians of the Flame Novel

A ROC BOOK

ROC
Published by the Penguin Group
Penguin Books USA Inc., 375 Hudson Street,
New York, New York 10014, U.S.A.
Penguin Books Ltd, 27 Wrights Lane,
London W8 5TZ, England
Penguin Books Australia Ltd, Ringwood,
Victoria, Australia
Penguin Books Canada Ltd, 10 Alcorn Avenue,
Toronto, Ontario, Canada M4V 3B2
Penguin Books (N.Z.) Ltd, 182-190 Wairau Road,
Auckland 10, New Zealand

Penguin Books Ltd, Registered Offices:
Harmondsworth, Middlesex, England

Published by Roc, an imprint of New American Library,
a division of Penguin Books USA Inc. Also available in a Roc hardcover edition.

First Printing, November, 1992
10 9 8 7 6 5 4 3 2 1

This one is for
Mary Kittredge

Acknowledgments

I'm grateful for the help and advice I've gotten with this one from:

—the others in the workshop: Bruce Bethke, Peg Kerr Ihinger, and Pat Wrede;

—David Dyer-Bennet;

—Harry F. Leonard;

—my copyeditor, Carol Kennedy;

—my agent, Eleanor Wood;

—my editor, John Silbersack;

—my wife, Felicia Herman;

—Diane Duane, for the hiccup cure;

—Beth Friedman, for the last-minute poorfreading, er, proofreading;

—and, particularly, for some ongoing research assistance on the subject of fatherhood, my daughter, Judith Eleanor Rosenberg.

Prologue:

The Dream Is the Same

THE NIGHTMARE IS always the same:

We're trying to make our escape from Hell, a whole crowd of us running through the slimy corridors. Everybody I've ever loved is there, along with strange faces, some of which I know should be familiar.

Behind us, there's a screaming pack of demons, some in cartoony shapes, some that look like misshapen wolves, all of whom have me scared so bad I can hardly breathe the scalding, stinking air. The walls keep trying to close in on me, but I push the hot, slime-covered surface away.

The exit is up ahead, a gash in the wall, and the crowd starts to push through. I can't tell who's gone through, but I can only hope that my kids are among them. Please.

Some have made their escape, but there's no way for the rest of us: the demons are approaching too quickly, and they're going to catch us.

And then I see him: Karl Cullinane, Jason's father, stand-

ing tall, face beaming, his hands, chest, and beard streaked with blood and gore.

"We're going to have to hold the corridor," Karl says. "Who's with me?" He smiles, as though he's been waiting his whole life for this, the fucking idiot.

Figures push out of the crowd, all of them bloodied, some of them bent. I guess I notice Kościuszko and Copernicus first, although both of them are shorter than I thought they'd be.

A buddha-faced Chinese steps forward, his face shiny with sweat that he doesn't seem to notice. "A boddhisattva," he says, "is one who pledges not to attain heaven until the rest of humanity does."

Another man stands tall, lean as a sword, not seeming to notice that the right side of his chest is cut open, slashed to the grayish liver. "Of course," he says, taking his place next to a slim, hawk-faced woman in what looks like a burial robe. Her robe is burning so hard I can hear her flesh crackle, and she winces in pain, but it doesn't stop her.

"Moi aussi," she says.

Two nondescript men push forward together. "Once more, Master Ridley," the first says, his accent clipped and British.

The other shakes his head and smiles wearily. "I'd thought—but no: once more, then."

A heavy-bearded, heavy-set man, still wearing his hangman's noose, his eyes wide in madness, pushes forward, shoulder to shoulder with Georgie Patton himself.

Humanity streams by us, and it's all I can do not to be swept along with it.

The corridor has always seemed tight, maybe twenty feet across, but the line of them—thousands of them, arms linked tightly—can't quite stretch across it.

They need one more to close the ranks, or it's all for nothing, and the demons are fast approaching.

One more. They always need one more.

Karl looks at me—they all look at me: Brown, Ridley, Joan, Ahira, Horatius, all of them—his bloody face puzzled. "Walter? What are you waiting for?"

Then I wake up.

2

PART ONE

HOMEWORK

CHAPTER ONE

In Which I Spend a Morning at Castle Cullinane

If you don't think that sex is violent, next time try thrashing around a bit.

—WILL SHETTERLY

My name is Walter Slovotsky.

As near as I can figure, I should be turning forty-three in the next tenday or so, and maybe it's time I grew up. I've spent the past couple of decades as, variously, a hero, a trader, a farming consultant, a thief, and a Jeffersonian political fanatic. Oh. And a killer. Both retail and wholesale. I'm sort of a jack of all trades.

In addition, I've managed to father two daughters (that I know of; I, er, get around a bit), generate a few hundred interesting aphorisms, and sleep with an even more interesting variety of women than I did in college (see above), including my second-best-friend's wife-to-be (we weren't all that friendly at the time. When he found out about it he almost killed me, but we all ended up as friends) and, some years later, his adopted daughter (he never found out about it; I'm not sure how that turned out, not yet).

But here I am, getting on in years, about to make some

major changes in my life, and I thought I'd do it this way. May as well start with food.

Food's an important part of my life.

The early morning crowd, plus me, was gathering for breakfast.

Settling into a new castle makes for long hours and hefty appetites. I've always had the latter, anyway, hangover or no.

"Please pass the bacon," I said. I don't miss the taste of nitrites; they do good things with smoking pig parts in Bieme. Just the thought of beans and hocks, Biemestren style, makes my mouth water.

"In a hurry?" Jason Cullinane gestured with an eating prong. "Father used to say that death is always willing to wait until after breakfast." He looked disgustingly fresh for this pre-goddamn-dawn hour of the morning: face washed, dark brown hair damp and combed back, eyes bright. I wouldn't have been surprised if he sprouted a bushy tail.

My mouth tasted of bile and stale whiskey, and my head ached. I'd had a bit too much to drink the night before, but only a bit, I decided: my head was only thumping, not pounding.

It's a sin to let good food go to waste, and I like to pick my sins carefully—I chomped into a thick piece of ham, then washed it down with a swallow of milk from a glazed mug. The milk was fresh, but not nearly cold enough. Milk should be cold enough to make your teeth hurt.

"Kid," I said, "your father stole that line from me. Like most of his good ones."

I was rewarded with a flash of teeth, the sort of smile that his father used to have.

Despite the tenday's growth of beard darkening his cheek and chin, it was hard to think of him as an adult. He looked so damn young.

His gaze went distant, as though he was thinking about something, and just for a moment a flash of the other side of his father crossed his face, and there was something distant and cold in his expression. But the moment passed, and he looked about fifteen again, even though he was a couple of years older. Good kid.

Jason Cullinane favored his mother, mainly. I could see Andrea's genes in his cheekbones and the widow's peak, and in the warm dark eyes. But there was more than a little of Karl Cullinane visible—in the set of his chin and shoulders, mainly. I'd say that it frightened me, sometimes, but everybody knows that the great Walter Slovotsky doesn't frighten.

Which only goes to show that everybody doesn't know a whole lot.

"The bacon?" I gestured at the platter.

Tennetty finally passed it. "What's the hurry this morning?"

"Who said there's a hurry? I'm hungry."

The first time I'd seen Tennetty, years ago, when Karl and I were running a team of Home raiders, she had just staggered out of a slave wagon, a plain skinny woman of the sort your eye tends to skip over. No character lines in her face, no interesting scars.

Even from such a start, Tennetty hadn't worn well as the years had gone by; her bony face sagged in the morning, and the patch fit loosely over her empty left eye socket. She rubbed at the scar that snaked around her good eye, then tossed her head to clear her bangs from her eyes—well, *eye*. Tennetty was getting sloppy, maybe; in the old days, she wouldn't have let her bangs grow that long.

The old days. The trouble with old people is that they always talk about the old days like they were the good days. I don't buy it. Maybe because my memory is too good—there were too many days out on the road, sleeping on rocks, never sleeping fully, because there's always trouble ahead. Hell, we were looking for trouble, then. Part of the plan.

"So?" Jason said. "What are you up to this morning?"

"I've got a date with a bow and some rabbits, maybe a deer," I said. Or maybe not. More likely, my date was with the limb of an oak tree. No, not to hang from it—to put some arrows into it.

Tennetty nodded judiciously. "You and the dwarf?"

I shouldn't have been surprised. Even after twenty years, Tennetty still hadn't noticed that Ahira didn't like to go hunting. Not for food, unless absolutely necessary; not for sport, ever.

"Not his cup of tea. Ahira's still asleep."

7

There had been many late hours of late, and the sun wasn't quite up. I didn't blame it. The time before dawn is when I like to start staggering toward a bed to sleep in, not staggering out of it. It was uncharacteristic of me to be awake at this hour, but one thing I learned a long time ago is to do things that are uncharacteristic—keeps you young, maybe, and alive, sometimes.

Or maybe I'm just kidding myself. I've never been good at consistency. Maybe I was up because of the damn dreams, and because of Kirah.

I poured myself another cup of tea. I don't know what U'len was putting in the mix, but it had a nice nutty smell that I had gotten very fond of. Not the sort of thing I'd dare have on the road—you can smell it in the sweat for a day or so; when you're on the road, eat what the locals eat, or keep it bland—but very nice.

Jason eyed me quizzically over his mug. "Are you feeling okay?"

"Just fine," I said, easily. Lying always comes easy to me. I had been having a lot of trouble sleeping of late. Not the only kind of trouble. After several years of getting better, Kirah was getting worse. Some things even time doesn't cure. Some things just lie beneath the surface and fester.

Damn it all. It wasn't my fault.

Back before I met her, before Karl and I freed her, Kirah had been ill-used. One of her owners was worse than simply brutal, and while there were no scars on her body—believe me; in happier days, we explored that matter *very* thoroughly—the scars on her mind had festered over the years.

A miracle was needed, and I didn't have one handy.

We Other Siders have seemed to work wonders at times, but it's only a matter of seeming to—we've just used the skills we brought with us, or acquired in the transition. Of the original seven of us, I was an ag major; Karl a dilettante; James Michael Finnegan a computer science major; Andrea, English; Doria, home ec; Louis Riccetti, engineering; the late Jason Parker (R.I.P.; he didn't make it through even twenty-four hours on this side), history.

The real treatment for what was ailing Kirah wasn't available on This Side and whether it was available on the Other

Side was debatable, if you like debating useless questions. Psychotherapy can help, but it can't work miracles.

The real treatment for what was ailing *me* could probably, as of last night, be found two rooms down from Kirah's and mine—in the bed of Jason's adopted sister, Aeia. Assuming, of course, that Aeia wanted to pick up where we left off.

Alternately, it was time to go out on the road.

I didn't like either option much. Resuming my relationship with Aeia would be dangerous, and it made sense to stay put in Jason's new barony for the time being, keeping in shape, waiting to hear some word about Mikyn.

I also didn't like the idea of Bren, Baron Adahan being under the same roof, whether he really was there to help the family settle in or to pay court to Aeia.

Most of all, I didn't like the fact that the universe doesn't appear to give a fuck what I do and don't like.

Jason speared the last piece of bacon and set it on my plate. "We could use some more food out here," he called out, not getting an immediate answer. Service was less than wonderful.

Tennetty shook her head. "Not like the old days at the castle. Used to be you could hear a servitor jump."

He made a be-still motion. Unsurprisingly, it worked, at least for now. After years as Karl's bodyguard (that's the nice word for it) Tennetty had fallen into the same pattern with Karl's son.

It was just the three of us alone around the small round table in what had been the old cook's nook in the castle, a small room between the kitchens and the formal dining room, its mottled glass windows covered with bars on both inside and outside.

The table and room could handle as many as eight or ten people, so Jason had coopted it as a breakfast room for the family three weeks—pardon me: two tendays—before, when we'd arrived to take over what had been Castle Furnael and now was Castle Cullinane.

Over the clatter of cups and saucers out in the kitchen, I could hear U'len berating one of the younger cooks, her voice rising in simulated anger, then falling into real, grumbled curses.

Pick your theory: if you assume that what you need in staff is experience with the people living there, I would have been tempted to do a complete staff switch with Thomen Furnael—excuse me, with the Emperor Thomen. Plan A: screw it—pay the two dollars. Plan B would be to keep almost everybody in place, under the theory that experience with the local facilities is the main issue. The baronial keep didn't need a quarter the staff that the castle did, after all.

Either way would have been reasonable, either way would have worked, but nobody was asking Walter Slovotsky's opinion. Ahira and I were teaching the boy about what we tend to call the family business, but running a castle has never really been part of that, and we'd kept our opinions largely to ourselves.

Unsurprising, really, that Jason had settled on an untheoretical compromise: bring in a few of his own people, keep on all but a few of the locals, and let them bump into each other all over the damn place.

Which is why the rolls were blackened on the bottom, my rooms hadn't been swept out in a week—although the flowers were changed daily—and hot baths were just plain not available without special arrangement and a lot of effort.

Tennetty gave a quick glance at Jason; he nodded, and she turned back to me. "Need some company?"

"Eh?"

"Need some company? Hunting?" She cocked her head to one side. "We were talking about hunting, no?"

"Yeah. And not really, no company needed," I said, then changed my mind. "Well, come to think of it, if you've got nothing better to do, sure." Unless you're burdening yourself like the White Knight, it's just as well to carry an extra weapon, and that's what Tennetty was. Pretty good one, too.

She smiled. "Nothing to kill here but time."

I would have been a lot happier if she hadn't meant it. I was going to spend the morning bowhunting, in part to stay out of trouble, but mainly for practice, and effect. I don't mind killing my own food—back when I was majoring in meat science, I slaughtered and butchered more than a lot of cows—but it doesn't give me any thrill. It did give Tennetty a lot of pleasure, which is why I was nervous about going hunting with her.

Frankly, I'd just as soon have skipped it all. Playing with weapons is an inadequate Freudian substitute, no matter how big and manly the bow is, or how far and fast it can shoot.

Jason frowned. Sometimes I can almost read minds: giving Tennetty permission had been easy, but it was harder for him to decide whether his sense of duty prevented, permitted, or demanded that he go along.

He finally came down on the side of having fun, although from which angle I wouldn't have wanted to bet.

"I haven't been hunting in a long time," Jason said, tossing the weight of the world from his shoulders for a moment. He relaxed, just a trifle.

I was tempted to turn this into a lesson about not assuming an invitation, but decided to let it pass. Ever since Jason had traded the silver crown of the Emperor of Holtun-Bieme in on the barony, he hadn't had a lot of time to relax, and he deserved a morning off.

"Sure," I said. "Come on."

"Good morning," Aeia Cullinane said as she walked into the breakfast room, my daughter Janie at her side, the two of them complicating my day while they brightened it.

"Morning, Daddy. Morning, all." Janie bent to kiss me on the cheek. Short black hair and bangs that always try to cover the eyes, thin limbs fleshing out almost daily, mannish leather breeches covered by a muslin shirt belted tight to show slim waist and slender curves: my teenage daughter. Sixteen, barely, but This Side sixteen, not Other Side sixteen. They seem to grow up faster here than I remember them doing there.

"Morning, sweetness," I said.

She slipped into the chair next to Jason and reached for a hunk of bread while Aeia struck a pose while pretending to decide where to sit. I didn't mind; I was enjoying the view.

There's a sharp mind behind the bright eyes that have just a touch of a slant to them. Part of her sunbleached hair was bound behind her in a ponytail, leaving the rest to frame her face, wisps of hair touching at high cheekbones. She was dressed, to the extent that she *was* dressed, in a short white

11

silk robe, its hem cut diagonally, about knee-length on the left side, mid-thigh on the right. It was a great view, but a bad idea, probably; the guards were a rough lot.

Jason frowned at his adopted sister. "Do me a favor?"

She tilted her head to the side. "Depends."

"Put some clothes on before you come out of your room, eh?" The master-of-the-house voice didn't quite fit, not yet, but it was getting better.

"What do you call this?" she brushed a hand down one side.

"Trouble. I don't know what you've been doing in Biemestren, but that doesn't go here."

"Oh," she said, dismissing the point rather than acknowledging it. She smiled at me as she sat down next to me, resting warm fingers on my arm for a moment as she pressed her leg up against mine. Not teasing, just touching.

Explain something to me: why are women two degrees warmer than men are?

And why do I keep getting in trouble over women?

It's real simple, most of it: I *like* the ones I sleep with, whether or not they've got their clothes on, whether or not they're willing to take them off. Add to that a certain amount of grooming and, er, charm, and subtract the sense of desperation that most men have around pretty women, and I do okay, or get into trouble, depending how you look at it.

Tennetty eyed her own fingernails. "I wouldn't worry. If there's anybody here who doesn't know what happens if he lays a hand on Aeia or Janie, I'll explain it—"

"Thanks much, Ten," Janie said from around a bite of bread, "but I can explain things myself."

"—and if I need help, Durine, Kethol, and Pirojil are always available." Tennetty considered the edge of a knife I hadn't seen her draw. Like I say, I'm too slow in the morning. "I don't think I'll need help."

Jason brushed the objection away. "That wasn't what I meant. I don't want to have Bren jumping up and down every time somebody looks crosswise at her."

"Not to worry." Aeia smiled, amused by the thought of Bren Adahan being jealous. "Maybe he'll be too busy watching me to put his hands on Janie's bottom. It's important to keep the menfolk busy, Janie told me last night."

She glanced over at Jason, then turned to me, to see if I noticed. I pretended not to, which only made her smile more.

Jason didn't quite blush. Janie, on the other hand, had a great poker face; she had taken the smile from her face by the time she had turned back to him.

I guess I was supposed to be upset, but there's part of being a parent that appears to have been left out of my makeup: the thought of my daughter having sex doesn't bother me. Sorry. Long as she visits the Spider or the Eareven priest twice a year and gets herself taken care of—something I made sure she did for the first year after menarche—I just hope she has fun.

Somebody trying to force her or hurt her would be different, but that's not sex, dammit. I'd do to that kind of slime the same thing I did to the last ones that raped her mother. (And no, I wouldn't do it slower. Doesn't make it any better, and it doesn't make them any deader.)

I wasn't supposed to know what was going on between Janie and Jason, though. It made things simpler. Jason and I already had enough to argue about.

Aeia went on: "But if I need any help with my social life, I'll be sure to let you know."

Jason didn't suspect anything; he wasn't good enough an actor not to glance from face to face if he knew. Janie didn't seem to pick up on it, either, which meant nothing.

I smiled back at Aeia in a sort of avuncular way, I hoped. We needed a long talk, her and me, and that would have to be orchestrated just right.

Forget the orchestra, though—what tune did I want to play?

A friend of mine who was an acting major used to say there was an old saying in the theatre: "Drunk and on the road don't count." We hadn't been drunk, but we had been on the road. And, if the truth be known, it had been awfully good, for both of us.

Compare that to a woman who didn't let me touch her anymore, who claimed that she loved me but never laughed or smiled in my presence, whose shoulders shook in the night with silent weeping. You tell me how you'd rather sleep next to *that* than to one who sleeps in your arms, her breath warm on your neck, her legs intertwined with yours, matching you heartbeat for heartbeat.

But you don't leave your wife of almost two decades because she's an emotional cripple, and you don't dump her for a younger woman just because when you touch her, it makes you feel twice as alive.

All that seems reasonable. I don't know what you actually *do*, though. That makes me feel awfully old.

When I was younger, I always knew what to do.

I pushed back from the table; that seemed right for the moment. The ground didn't open up and swallow me. Always a good sign.

"Jason, Tennetty, and I are going hunting," I said to Aeia.

She either didn't take the hint, or dismissed the idea. "Have fun." She made a moue as she reached for a sweetroll. "Bren up yet?"

I shook my head. "Haven't seen him."

I wondered for a moment if that was a red herring for my benefit, if she was sneaking off to sleep with Bren the way that Janie was to be with Jason, then decided that I wasn't going to get anywhere guessing. I don't care who plays musical beds, as long as I don't have to sleep alone. Which had been the trouble, of late. One of them.

Besides, there's Slovotsky's Law something-or-other: Don't accuse your mistress of cheating on you with her future fiancé.

To hell with it. I was spending too much time musing about musical beds. I stood up. "I'm out of here, folks."

Tennetty hacked off a fist-sized hunk of bread, dipped it in honey, and stood. "Let's go kill something."

The castle was quiet in the golden morning light, probably a holdover on the part of Karl's staff. He used to insist on—well, try to insist on—sleeping late, and U'len was probably keeping things quiet in his memory, or maybe just out of habit.

"Meet you at the stables," I told Tennetty and Jason.

She nodded and sprinted for the back staircase, while Jason maintained a dignified walk. I headed up to the two-room suite my wife and I shared. Well, maybe it was a three-room suite, if you included the secret passage to the room next door, although the room next door was unoccupied, and the passage was barred from our side. I like the idea of having a back way out; I'm cautious enough that I don't want anybody else to have a back way in.

Kirah lay stretched out on the bed, the blankets having slid aside, revealing one long leg almost to the hip. Sunlight splashed on her long, golden hair, her breasts rising and falling with her gentle breathing, her arms spread wide, her mouth just barely parted, all trusting and innocent and vulnerable and lovely.

I felt cheated: I wanted to reach over and hold her for a moment before I left, but I couldn't. Not while she was sleeping, ever. One of the rules. Not mine. Kirah has her own way of enforcing her rules. Call it passive-aggressive, if you like—but it *hurts* her when I push things.

Damn.

I exchanged my cotton trousers for leather ones—you can get cut by the brush—and after I'd buttoned the fly I shrugged into a hunting vest, and then the double shoulder holster that Kirah had made for me. I belted my shortsword around my waist, tucked an extra brace of throwing knives never mind exactly where.

An oak box with a trick catch—you have to push down on the top of the box while you press up on the latch—held my two best pistols, loaded, oil-patched, and ready to go; I slipped them into the holster. A nice design: it held one pistol a bit too high, but the other, held in place by a U-shaped spring hidden in the leather, was held slantwise under the armpit, butt-forward. Draw, cock, and bang.

Me, I'd rather store most of my guns safely unloaded, and eventually I'd be able to. Jason's twin sixguns were the first on this side, but they wouldn't be the last. With Jason's revolver and speedloader, it's flip, slip, slam, and blam—flip the cylinder out, slip the Riccetti-made speedloader into place, slam the cylinder shut, letting the outer shell of the speedloader fly where it may, and then *blam*. And that's worst-case; most of time, I'd keep the revolver loaded, trusting Lou Riccetti's unlicensed modification of the Ruger transfer-bar safety to keep the gun from going *bang* unexpectedly.

On the other hand, it takes more than a minute to load a flintlock, and I've never, *ever* been in a situation where I've said to myself, "Gee, it'd be nice to have a loaded gun in about a minute."

Never. It's either *nah*, or it's *now*.

A small gunmetal flask of extract of dragonbane sat on the bureau, carefully sealed with wax, secondly because I don't like the reek of the gooey stuff, but mainly because a good friend of mine is highly allergic to it, being a dragon. While creatures with the sort of magical metabolisms that can be harmed by dragonbane had long been driven away from the Eren regions—humans and magical creatures tend not to get along—there had been rumors about things coming out of Faerie, and out on the Cirric Jason had seen a few creatures he couldn't identify.

So I slipped the flask into my vest.

Last but not least, I tucked two Therranji garrottes into their separate, leather-lined pockets. Vicious things—the slim cables were made with springy barbed wire, the barbs canted backwards so that the garrotte could only be tightened. Just tuck the handle through the loop, then slip the barbed-wire noose over a head, give the wooden handle one hard jerk, and let go—in order to get it off, the poor slob would have to remove the handle, then slip the loop off the butt end.

Can't get it over the head? No problem—whip it around the neck, put the handle through the loop, and pull. Trust the Therranji to come up with a weapon that mean—elves can be nasty—and somebody like me to carry two of them on his person.

Still, peace is nice. You don't have to take a lot of precautions before going out for a simple walk in the woods.

I wanted to take one last look at Kirah sleeping, and I wanted not to take one last look at her, so I hung a quiver from my shoulder, grabbed my best longbow and a couple of spare strings, and headed down to the stables.

Jason was already in the saddle of a huge red gelding—another one of Carrot's foals, I think—and the stableboy was finishing saddling a stocky roan for Tennetty. I picked a small-ish piebald mare and saddled her myself, earning a broad, gap-toothed smile from the stableboy, touched that the great Walter Slovotsky would handle his own horse.

Well, it didn't hurt for him to think that.

Water and field rations are always kept ready in the stables. Until they string the telegraph to Biemestren and out to Little Pittsburgh, there's no way to know when a messenger will have to be dispatched in a hurry. I slipped a canteen over the saddlehorn, and a pair of saddlebags in front of it.

We rode out through the main gate and into the day.

The gently rolling land around the former Castle Furnael, now Castle Cullinane, had been cleared at least a mile in each direction, in part to give the baron some farmland of his own, I suppose, but mainly to prevent any large force from sneaking up on the castle. The western road cut through at least two miles of wheat fields before it swung north toward the woods that countless Furnael barons had used as their private hunting preserve. That was down the road almost two miles away, just enough distance to warm the horses.

Hooves clopped quietly on the unpaved road, while above, soft white clouds scudded across a deep blue sky, something that only soft white clouds ever do. Below, waist-high stalks of young green wheat bowed gently in the breeze. The air was still cool from the night, with none of the after-noon tang of sunbaked fields, but the day was young.

"Nice day," Jason said.

"That it is," I said, hitching at my holsters. Nice days make me nervous.

Jason had one of his twin revolvers in a holster on the left side of his chest, the butt facing forward, just about even with his left elbow. Not a bad placement, actually—it would be a bit clumsy to get at it with his left hand, but it could be done.

I envied him the weapons. If a messenger from Home didn't show up soon with a pair for me, I'd have to ride over and have a word with Lou. After all, I was the one who built the first flintlock on This Side, and seniority should count for something, no?

Tennetty chuckled. "Always ingratiating yourself with the help, eh?"

"Eh?"

"The horse," she said. "You saddled it yourself." She snorted. "That dung-footed stableboy looked at you like you were, I don't know, something special."

"Well . . ." I shrugged, as modestly as possible, under the circumstances. "I am, Tennetty."

She was disposed to leave it be, but Jason couldn't. "So why did you do it?"

I shrugged. "I used to trust other folks to saddle my horse, but I've found that I take a more active interest in my cinch straps than any stableboy possibly can."

Tennetty nodded. Jason frowned. We set off in a fast walk down the road.

"So," he finally said. "You think we're settled in enough, yet?"

I nodded. "Sure. You're going to have to let the staff problems sort themselves out, but looks like everything's okay here. You itchy to get back on the road?"

He nodded. "Ellegon's due tomorrow, or maybe the day after. I think we'd best go find Mikyn's trail. I'm worried about him."

Mikyn was a good kid, but he was on his own, as far as I was concerned. Yes, he was one of Jason's childhood friends, but it was more important to me that he was a *gotterdammerung* looking for a place to happen, and I've been around enough of those in my time. No rush, thanks. Besides . . .

"Let's hang on for a while," I said. "Ahira had a word with Danagar before we left Biemestren—he's put some more feelers out."

Mikyn was somewhere, perhaps in the Middle Lands, perhaps elsewhere in the Eren regions, searching for the man who had enslaved his family. The odds were poor that Mikyn was on a warm trail; they were only fair that his disguise as a traveling farrier would hold up.

Odds wouldn't stop him from looking, the young idiot. Well, hell, odds wouldn't have stopped me, either.

Jason pursed his lips. "I should have done that."

"Maybe." Actually, it would have been a bad idea; the last thing that Emperor Thomen Furnael needed was for Jason to be telling his best field agent what to do. Thomen's seat on the throne was probably precarious enough as it was; his only title to it was as a gift from the usurper's son. I'm not condemning, mind; *usurper* is a technical term, and Karl was my second best friend.

"In any case," I said, "we're probably best off waiting until we hear something, then hitching a ride on Ellegon. It'll likely save time. Besides, truth to tell, I'd like at least a few more days of rest, food, and good light exercise before we go back in harm's way." Still, I wondered about Mikyn. "You know if he's any good with fire and iron?"

Jason nodded. "Better than me. Nehera gave a bunch of us the short course, a few years ago. I don't think anybody would confuse either of the two of us with a master farrier, but I could do a good, clean, quick job, and Mikyn was better."

"In any case, we wait. We'll hear soon enough." Or more than soon enough.

"Very well." He nodded. "Wouldn't we be better off waiting at Biemestren?"

Tennetty snickered. "Oh, a great idea." She drew her sword, a short, cross-hilted rapier, and gave a few tentative swipes through the air. "Why not just hack Thomen's legs off for real?" She slipped the rapier back into the sheath with a decided *snap*.

"Eh?" Jason was bright, but he was still young.

"Think about it," I said. "Imagine yourself riding up to the castle. In Biemestren. What happens?"

"What do you mean, what happens?"

"Just what I said. Tell me what happens. What's the first thing you do?"

He shrugged. "I'd pay a call on Thomen. I'd ride through the gate, and leave my horse out front."

"Right," I said. "You'd ride right through the gate. Without asking permission, because you spent most of your childhood living there, and it still feels like home to you, and nobody there would think of stopping you, right?"

He caught it. There was nothing wrong with Jason that a few years of growing up wouldn't cure, assuming he had the time to grow up.

His lips twisted. "And what his royal highness, the Emperor Thomen, formerly Baron Furnael, doesn't need is Karl Cullinane's son suggesting that the throne doesn't really belong to him."

"Exactly." I nodded. "You stay the hell out of Biemestren until and unless you're sent for, just like all the other barons. And when you go, you walk just a bit more humbly than they do."

He smiled. "And, say, occasionally flash a bit of temper, only to be silenced by a single look from the Emperor."

Tennetty laughed. "He catches on fast." She turned to him. "Now, in the interim?"

He raised his hands in surrender. "I guess we stay here, eh?"

"For the time being," I said.

"Good. —Now let's get some exercise." Without a polite word of warning, or even a curt one, Tennetty kicked her horse into a canter; it took a good half mile for the two of us to catch up.

Where the road swung north to give a wide berth to Benai Hill, a path into the forest broke through the plowed ground and met the road.

The path was well-maintained, even after it entered the forest—overhead branches were hacked off, some brush cleared by the side. I wouldn't have wanted to gallop down it in the dark, or even canter in the light, but it was perfectly fine for a nice, quick walk.

Kind of pleasant, really: stately oaks and elms arching high above, keeping things all cool and green and musty, even though the day was already heating up. My hearing's awfully good, for a human, but I couldn't hear any animal sounds over the clopping of the horses' hooves.

A nice quiet day.

Something rustled in the bush toward the side of the road.

I had a throwing knife in my left hand and a cocked pistol

in my right as a rabbit scampered across the path, losing itself in the woods.

Tennetty was only a little slower with a flintlock; Jason was third, his revolver, one of the only two that existed, carefully pointed toward the sky.

"What—?"

"Ta havath," Tennetty said. *Take it easy.* "Just a rabbit." Tennetty glared at me as she carefully holstered her pistol and slipped her rapier back into its sheath. "What was *that* about?"

I shrugged an apology as I reholstered my own pistol and slipped my throwing knife back into its sheath. "Sorry."

The two of them were kind enough to let the matter drop.

It was a nice day, so why was I coming close to jumping out of my skin at every sound? Yes, there were those rumors of things coming out of Faerie, but we were solidly in the Middle Lands, far from Faerie.

Not good enough. I mean, it was true, but it wasn't an excuse.

I could have argued that Tennetty and Jason were just as jumpy as I was, but that would have been just for the sake of arguing—the two of them were operating under the sound principle that when somebody quickly draws a weapon, he's got a good reason. Which I hadn't. A rabbit within shooting range is a good reason to draw a hunting weapon slowly, carefully, without alarming the rest of your party. It is *not* a reason to suggest by word or action that the shit's about to hit the fan.

We rode in silence and I kept my jumpiness under control as we followed the path in for maybe half an hour—remember, every step you take in has to be taken out—until we came to a small clearing, where I called for a break.

I dismounted, more stiffly than I liked, and rubbed at the base of my spine.

Getting a bit older every year, Walter.

Tennetty either didn't hurt or didn't want to show it. I wouldn't have bet either way.

"Leave the horses?" she asked, sliding out of the saddle as she did.

"Sure." I uncinched the saddle and set it on the spread-out horse blanket, slipped the bridle, and tied the horse to a tree, just the rope and hackamore to hold him there. Jason did the same.

Tennetty just slipped the bridle and dropped the reins. "Stay," she said. I guess that if her horse couldn't stay ground-hitched, she was willing for it to be her problem.

I slipped into my shooting gloves and leathers—I'll cut my fingers and scrape my arm when it's for real, but not when it's practice, thank you very much—then strung my bow, a fine Therranji composite that had cost me more than I like to think about. I'd have to show this to Lou; I doubted even he could have improved on it. Nicely, elegantly recurved, it was made from three pieces of almost black wood, a long strip of reddened horn sinew-bound to its belly, the whole thing covered with a smooth lacquer. The grip was soft, thick leather, gradually molding itself to my fingers with each use. About a fifty-pound pull—which is plenty, really.

"I've always seen you favor a crossbow," Jason said, stringing his own longbow. He slung his quiver over his head, then hitched at his swordbelt. He thought about it for a moment, then unhooked the swordbelt, leaving it around the pommel of his saddle.

I nodded. "Usually do," I said. "Hey, Jason?"

"Yes?"

"What would you say," I said, quietly, "if I told you that there's six Holtish rebels hiding behind those trees over there and that they're about to jump us?"

He started to edge toward his horse.

Tennetty snickered. "What you should say is, 'I'm sorry, Holtish rebels, let me drop my pants and bend over for you, so you can stick my sword up my backside,' that's what you should say." She jerked a thumb toward his horse. "Wear the sword."

He buckled the sword on with good grace. I've known people who take direction worse than Jason. Lots of them. I've seen one of them in a mirror, every now and then.

I fitted a practice arrow to the bowstring—I don't waste killing broadheads on trees.

Now, I like crossbows. You can fire them with one hand,

from the saddle, or from a prone position, three things that you can't do with a longbow. You can do two out of those three things with a short bow, but you give up range and striking power. Not a good compromise. A longbow has greater range than any crossbow without a good winding gear, and a much greater rate of fire.

The only trouble is that it takes a lot of practice to get good at it, and more practice to stay good at it.

Across the meadow, maybe twenty yards away, an oily crow sat on a limb, considering the silly humans below.

Well, let's see if I can still do zen archery. The trouble with being a stranger in a strange land is that you have to be your own zen master. I brought the bow up, keeping my form perfect, not aiming with my eyes, not exactly, and visualized the release, the string leaving my finger in perfect form— smoothly, evenly, instantly, not with a plucking loose.

I let go, and in less than a heartbeat, the arrow was quivering in the limb, a full three feet to the right of where the crow had taken flight.

Jason snickered. "Off by a full arrow's-length. Not too good, Uncle Walter."

Tennetty caught my eye; the corners of her lips were turned up. If it had been anybody else, I'd call the expression a smile. "See how close you can come to his arrow, Jason Cullinane. I'm curious."

Jason brought up his bow and loosed too soon, the string loud against his leathers. The arrow disappeared into the forest.

Tennetty laughed out loud, and Jason started to bristle, but caught himself.

"Well," he said, "let's say we start hunting in that direction."

"After," I said. "Let's fire some more practice arrows first."

Hunting, like fishing—and sex, for that matter—is one of those things where you really have to be there to understand it.

Except for the killing part, I like it, a lot. At least the way we did it. You stalk across the floor of the dark forest,

23

the comforting rot of leaves and humus in your nostrils, listening, watching intently—and without worrying about somebody jumping out from behind a tree and killing you. It's a good thing.

At my side were people I trusted, because I don't go hunting with people I don't trust.

There are other ways to do it. One of the best ways to actually catch food involves finding a good spot and waiting for the game to pass by. You sit, conserving energy, and wait. Eventually, if you've picked your spot right, your rabbit comes into view, or your deer, or antelope or whatever. But that's survival hunting.

This was more fun. Back on the Other Side, I never could move this quietly. I'm not complaining, mind, but being one of the big guys isn't all that it's cracked up to be. Trust me.

Besides, we weren't really hunting. What we were doing was relaxing, and by the time we'd worked our way into the forest, firing a few practice shots here and there, I'd managed to get rid of my jumpiness. For now.

Just as well. "Jason, you see that stump over there?" I asked, pointing to one about forty yards away.

"The one just behind that fallen tree?"

"Right. Bet I can put an arrow into that root, the one that bends up to the right."

He shrugged. "So can I."

"From here?" I raised an eyebrow. "A silver mark to who gets closer?"

He nodded. "Sure."

"Tennetty?"

"No, I don't need to donate to the cause," she said.

"No. We need a referee and judge."

"Yeah, sure." She took up a drill instructor's stance. "Awright. Nock your arrows. Draw your bows. Three. Two. One. *Loose.*"

It was a tricky shot, trickier than it looked, if I was right—the leaves from a lower branch of an old oak blocked the top of the parabolic flight of the arrow. You have to remember that your shot does not travel in a straight line, but in an arc. The trick was to aim so that the arrow's flight would take it through a gap in the leaves . . .

I released, smoothly. I was a bit off, but more lucky than off: it barely nicked a couple of leaves, not slowing it enough to make it miss. It *thwok*ed comfortably into the root, while Jason's arrow buried itself in the ground, easily a foot short.

"Pay me," I said.

"Put it on account," he said.

"Sure."

I retrieved my arrow, and nocked it, looking for another target.

"Er, Uncle Walter?" Jason frowned as he examined the head of his arrow, but I didn't think he was frowning at it.

"Yeah?"

"How come I get the feeling that we're not really after deer?"

Tennetty chuckled. "Maybe because we're too busy shooting up the trees?"

"There's a perfectly good archery range behind the barracks," Jason said.

"If you know anything more boring than spending a morning firing arrows at a bull's-eye, you be sure and don't let me know."

Me, I'd much rather pretend to go hunting and shoot up a few trees. I never really practice with my throwing knives—I just use them, every once in a long while, to assure me that I still have the Talent for it. But that's deeply imprinted. I don't have to practice that any more than a fish has to practice his scales.

My learned skills are different; if I don't put in at least a few hours with the longbow every tenday or so, I start to go real sour, and there have been more than a few times that would have been unfortunate. Unfortunate in the sense of Stash and Emma Slovotsky's baby boy getting himself dead. As Woody Allen would say, death is one of the worst things that can happen to somebody in our line of work, and many of us simply prefer to pay a small fine.

So I practice. I've spent far too much of my life practicing at how to shoot with some things and cut with some others, but there you have it. Part of the dues.

But you don't tell anybody everything.

"I like this better," I said. "Out on a nice day with some good company, clean air, maybe the chance of making a few marks . . ."

". . . off some sucker," Tennetty said, with a smile.

But it wasn't a nice smile, and it almost ruined the morning.

CHAPTER TWO

In Which I Discuss Some Family Matters

Chi fa ingiuria no perdona mai. (He never forgives those he injures.)

—ITALIAN PROVERB

MOST OF THE TIME, things go from bad to worse, but every now and then the human universe shifts for the better: it's clear that something bad's going to happen, but then something else entirely does, something gentler.

Sometimes it's nice; sometimes it's just something bad that declines to happen. Either is just fine with me.

The first time I remember it, I was about seven, I guess. My parents had gone out for the evening, and my brother, Steven, had a date, so they'd hired a baby-sitter. Mrs. Kleinman, her name was; she lived on some sort of widow's pension in a set of funny-smelling rooms in the red brick apartment building down the block from our house. Ugly old biddy, who really didn't like kids. Never wanted to play, or talk; all she wanted to do was turn on the television, take off her shoes, and fall asleep on the couch with one hand in a bowl of potato chips.

Well? What would you do? I'd done the obvious thing,

and there had been trouble when Stash and Emma got home. Whenever old Stash—it's an old Polish nickname, okay?—got angry, there was this tic in his right cheek; it would twitch with every pulsebeat.

He came into my room, the light in the hall casting half his face into shadow, his fists unclenching. Stash was a short, broad man, but he had huge hands, and they made huge fists.

He wouldn't have punched me, but he was going to spank me. His face was so red from the chin to the top of his balding that I thought he was going to blow up, and the tic was pulsing two to the second, the speed of a fast walk. I was worried about him more than me, I swear, as he loomed over my bed.

"Walter . . ." he always called me Cricket, except when he was angry at me, and he was furious.

And then he swept me up in his huge arms. I could smell the whiskey on his breath. Gales of laughter rocked me. *His* laughter.

"God, Cricket, I guess that old biddy *did* deserve to have her shoes nailed to the floor."

I guess that's why the smell of whiskey on somebody's breath doesn't bother me.

I was currying the mare when I heard Bren's footsteps behind me. The cleaning stalls at Castle Furnael—Castle Cullinane, that is—were well designed, with a low, calf-high open wooden box in the center of the stall. You stand the horse in the box, which inhibits it from moving around, and prevents you from getting kicked.

I wasn't worried about being kicked. There wasn't any good reason to be concerned about anything at all. One of the stableboys and two of the horse soldiers were just outside, reshoeing a stubborn gelding; the other stableboy was across the way, working on Jason's horse, and the house guard was within a quick shout. If we were going to have a problem, it wasn't going to be here.

Besides, Bren Adahan would hardly be here to give me a problem, eh?

"Hello, Baron," I said, turning slowly, resting my hand on the partition separating the cleaning stalls. It's reflex—ever since my first day on This Side, I've always looked for a place to run. I've always had a reason. I haven't always *had* a place to run, mind, but I've always looked for one. "Where've you been keeping yourself?"

"All over, Walter Slovotsky," he said. "I spent the morning at two of the tenant farms. Then I came in and did an inventory at the farm. Then the kennels, and now here."

"Inventorying the baron's livestock?" A good idea, and something I should have thought of. I tended to think of the walled keep itself as being Jason's new home, although really it was the keep and the huge chunk of land it sat upon, including the livestock managed at the clump of buildings down by the pastures, a couple of miles away.

"Somebody ought to," he said. He was in tan today, in a pale, almost snowy doeskin tunic and leggings, the effect picked up by an antler clip that held back the hair that otherwise would have fallen over his right ear.

Very stylish, but then again, Bren, Baron Adahan was always very stylish. I've always been more fond of substance, myself. No, that's not fair. I had been out in the field with him, and he had gotten as down and dirty as the rest of us. A good man to have at your back in a fight, something both Jason and I knew from experience.

Perhaps to remind me of that, he wore a very ordinary leather combo belt tight on his hips, his shortsword on the left, a dagger and a flintlock on the right.

"Have you a moment?" he asked.

"For you, Baron, I've always got a moment," I said, not meaning it.

He smiled, as though there was no hypocrisy in his voice, or in mine. "I'll be leaving tomorrow; there are matters in my barony that need my attention."

"Little Pittsburgh?" I said. There's always something happening in the steel town.

"Yes. Not just that, but yes." He nodded, and then, for no reason or other, it happened: we were friends again, even if only for the moment. "Let me give you a hand." He stripped off his tunic, then unbuckled his sword and hung it on a post. I had the brush ready for him before he had his hand out.

He stroked the harsh bristles with his thumb. "Ranella's

devoting her attention to the railroad, and somebody has to take care of the administration," he said, as he ran the brush down the other side of the horse, steadying her with sure fingers in her mane as she whickered and pranced just a little. "Something I was trained for, no?"

"Each to his own, Bren."

His smile was forced. "I'm going to ask Aeia to come with me."

"Don't blame you at all," I said. "I would, if I were you."

He was silent for a long time. We sometimes have to live on the silences. "Maybe she'd be better off here, with the others."

I nodded. "Maybe. She's going to have to decide for herself."

"There is that." He dropped the subject. "I see you didn't come back with any game today. Enjoy your hunt nonetheless?" he asked, taking up a firm grip in the mare's mane with one hand while he reassuringly stroked her neck with the other.

"It was pleasant enough."

"The doing, not the prey, eh?"

"Something like that." I tucked the hoof pick under my left arm, then stooped to pick up the mare's front hoof and scraped it out. It was packed full of horseshit and dirt, much like life itself. I would have liked to let it slide by—I am a lazy bastard, and there are standards to maintain—but all sorts of hoof diseases can get started if you don't clean them out properly.

Bren held out his hand for the pick. I handed it over and steadied the horse while he did the right front hoof, then moved back to do the rear one on that side. I finished with the final hoof, then gave the horse a solid pat on the flank as I closed the stall door.

"Leave her there, in the grooming stall, an' it please you," the stableboy called out. He was working on Tennetty's horse across the way. "I've got to muck out her own stall, and I'll do it just as soon as I finish with this horse, Walter Slovotsky."

"She'll need some fresh straw," Bren said.

"I'll get it, Baron—" the stableboy cut himself off; Bren was already partly up the ladder toward the loft. I swarmed up after him.

There was a skittering at our approach, but you almost never see the rats.

Stables are stables: bales, tied with twine, lay brick-stacked against the front wall, four rows deep. Bren hacked through the twine with a hayknife while I used the pitchfork to pitch it to the stone floor below.

"It's difficult," he said, standing at the edge, considering the edge of the hayknife, "to be a disciple of the late, great Karl Cullinane."

"So I hear."

"You have to change, you see." His smile wasn't friendly anymore. "In the old days, it would have been simple. Nobody not of my station would have thought to take, oh, anything I wanted. But if someone did, there wouldn't be a problem." He patted the spot of his belly where the hilt of his sword would have been. " 'All men are created equal,' eh? Didn't used to be that way. Anybody short of my class wouldn't have had the time to get as good with a sword as I was. Am."

He thought about it for a long time, then he turned and stuck the hayknife back in a bale, and vanished down the ladder. He had gotten some horsehair and sweat and dirt on his chest and breeches, I guess, which was why he left carrying his tunic in his hands, without looking back for a moment.

I looked at his retreating back for a long time, even after it wasn't there.

I went up to our rooms to find Kirah, but she was gone and hadn't left a note as to where she was going to be. I came to This Side illiterate in Erendra, and put in a lot of effort first changing that, then teaching my wife her letters. Damn inconsiderate of her not to even leave a note.

I probably should have gone looking for Kirah, but I looked for a couple of friends instead.

I found Doria with the dwarf and my younger daughter over in the blacksmith's shop, next to the bathhouse.

"Daddy!" My baby daughter's face lit up and she ran for me; a father is always a hero to his daughter, even if he doesn't deserve it.

I swept Dorann up in my arms. "Whatcha doin', kiddo?"

"Aunt Doria and Uncle 'hira are showing me how to smith," she said, suddenly becoming serious as she raised a finger. They're very serious at three and a half. "Now don't you touch the metal. It's *hot*."

"Okay, Dorann," I said, giving her a quick kiss on the top of her head. "I'll be careful." My daughters are always watching out for me. It's nice. I ran my fingers through her hair. "Isn't it about your nap time?"

"Don't need a nap," she said. Which settled that.

Both my daughters run to stubbornness, once they get their minds made up. Kirah used to claim that it came from me, and I used to claim that it came from her, and we used to argue about it constantly, if never angrily, until she finally gave up; so I guess I was always right, and the stubbornness *does* come from Kirah's side of the family.

"What's that in your ear, sweetie?" I palmed a piece of rock sugar from my pouch as I set her down. It was wrapped in a twist of paper, so it was easy to trap it with the back of my forefinger and middle finger as I clapped my hands to show that they were empty, then pretended to pull it from her ear. "You hiding candy again?"

Sleight of hand is related to pickpocketry, and the latter is one of my talents. It's never gotten me a jewel brighter than Dorann's white smile and squeal of delight as she popped it into her mouth.

Ahira had chased the smith out—or more likely, given him the day off—and was bent over the forge, doing some minor repairs to a mail shirt. Tricky work—you want to be sure to weld each ring tightly shut without welding any ring to the other. During the time we were working for King Maherralen over in Endell, he had picked up some of the art.

So had I, actually, although not as much as he had, which isn't fair, given my head start—back on the Other Side, before all this started, I spent a summer apprenticing at Sturbridge Village. It would say something about genetics versus environment, but with Ahira, it was pretty hard to decide what was what.

I'm not sure whether Doria was legitimately interested, or just being sociable. Dorann, on the other hand, was interested in everything.

I remember when Doria used to wear her Hand cloak: a big, bulky dull white thing that made her look old and shapeless. I hadn't seen her wear it since Melawei; she probably put it away with all of her other Hand memorabilia, and maybe memories.

Today, Doria had tucked the hem of a white cotton pullover shirt into her tight pair of Home jeans, and was looking fresh and immaculate as she held Doria Andrea's hand.

"Looking cute today, Dore," I said.

Doria and Ahira looked too young. He had stripped to the waist for the work, and the muscles beneath the skin of his hairy, barreled chest were like rope beneath the scars. One weal on his right shoulder still stood out, red and angry, and it looked like somebody clumsy had played tic-tac-toe with the point of a knife just under his left nipple. Which was pretty close to what had happened, so I understand. He didn't talk about it much.

If you ignored the scars, though, Ahira hadn't changed one whit in the years we had been on this side: while the top of his head barely came to the middle of my chest, the shock of thick brown hair—thick both ways—held no trace of gray. It probably wouldn't for a while; dwarves live long lives.

The fingers that held the tongs in the forge were thick and strong, the joints like walnuts. His face was flushed almost crimson from the heat, and sweat poured down his forehead and dripped down his cheeks; with his free hand he took a dipper of water from the cooling trough and dumped it on his head, to an accompaniment of giggles from Dorann.

Save for the eyes, Doria still looked like she was in her early twenties: her skin was still creamy smooth, her short blond hair shiny with youth. Beneath the mannish shirt, firm breasts bobbed invitingly. (Okay, I admit it: I like women. Sue me.)

Doria slipped her free arm around my waist. "A-*hi*-ra's

get-ting *twit*-chy," she sang, leaning her head against my shoulder. "Too much coming-out-of-retirement, I think."

"Too much above-ground, maybe." Shaking his head to clear the last of the water from his face, he pulled the tongs out of the forge, and considered the color of the glowing ring before clamping it into place and hammering it down. *Wham. Wham.* "Truth to tell, we haven't been making enough trouble of late."

Doria's eyes twinkled. "Not major trouble."

The dwarf smiled. "Oh, that. Well."

The phrasing and timing were off, just a trifle; they weren't hinting that they'd been sleeping together, but up to some innocent deviltry.

The major-trouble theory was Ahira's theory, not mine. He thought that Lou Riccetti, the Engineer, was the real revolutionary, that the technological advances coming out of the Home colony in the Valley of Varnath were the real challenges to the established order, that everything that the rest of us did was just a distraction, a diversion to keep everybody's mind off the real game. Karl had agreed.

I'm not sure. What put an end to slavery in the United States? Was it the Union army, or the industrial revolution?

Me, I don't know; I only *act* like I know everything. I like things complicated, a lot of the time, but not always. Far as I'm concerned, we should have been sticking to the original plan: kill off the slave traders, thereby raising the price of human chattels to the point where they become prohibitively expensive.

So far, so good. It gets harder every year, but slaves get more expensive every year, too.

Part of the plan is to make it look doable, and that means staying alive. I've always thought that my personal survival is the centerpiece of any good plan.

I laughed. "Hey, we got half the world thinking that Karl's still alive and out there, somewhere."

"True." The dwarf pursed his thick lips for a moment. "I guess it still makes sense, though, to wait around here until we get some word about Mikyn." His broad face split in a smile. "We dwarves are patient folks."

"Shows." Sarcasm is wasted on Ahira. I don't mean

that he doesn't get it—he does—but it doesn't bother him. "Still . . . Mikyn's bitten off a big chunk; he might need help chewing."

"Possibly, but I'm in no rush." Ahira picked up another piece of wire stock, about six inches long, and tossed it into the forge. "If Ellegon's available, though, we might want to hop over to the coast and snoop around Ehvenor." He said it casually, as though it was something he was just considering, but he and I had been friends for too many years for it to go over my head. Ahira wanted to investigate, and was going to try to talk me into it.

He looked at me, and smiled weakly, then rubbed at his shoulder.

Doria has the bad habit of asking questions when she already knows the answer. "Perhaps you want to look up whoever did that to you as well?"

He shook his head. "Life's too short."

For a moment, a dark cloud passed over his face, and I knew that something important had happened to him after we split up outside of Ehvenor, but one thing I learned long ago about James Michael Finnegan is that he will talk about his problems only when he wants to. I doubt that there's anybody he trusts more than me, but even I would hear about it some other time, if ever.

"Life's too short, and so are you." Doria's mouth twitched. "I'm not sure that whatever's going on near Ehvenor is any of our concern."

It could have been anything, or nothing. There had been stories of some strange killings closer to Ehvenor, of animal mutilations that reminded me of ones we had in the western states on the Other Side, of more dragons issuing from Faerie, of other large magical creatures, most of whom had been gone from the Eren regions since the coming of Man.

Some of the stories were probably true—Jason and his crew had killed some huge creature while they were in the Shattered Islands. It didn't sound like anything I'd ever heard of.

He looked up at me. "What do you think?"

"I think Doria's right; I think we have enough to do without biting off some magical problem."

And, besides, he wasn't thinking it through. A magical problem wasn't something that just he and I could look into by ourselves.

In the center of the city of Ehvenor has long stood a building that has been an outpost of Faerie in the Eren regions—probably the only outpost of Faerie in the Eren regions. I'd seen it a couple of times, from a distance, a huge, glowing white building that seemed to have a subtly different shape every time you looked at it. I hadn't tried to get close, and didn't want to. Call it the Faerie embassy, or the Faerie outpost, or whatever—call it whatever you want; it's nothing I had any need to rub up against. There's something about being around Faerie that drives people crazy, and the outskirts of Ehvenor are wild and crazy enough. Trust me.

I rubbed at the back of my left hand, at the place where a long-healed scar should have been, would have been, if I hadn't had a flask of healing draughts handy that last time.

He wasn't thinking it through—it wouldn't be just the dwarf and me. Add Jason, and we were still short. But enough of that for now. If we could put it off long enough, maybe we wouldn't have to do it. Let it be somebody else's problem.

"Think it over and let me know," he said.

"I can tell you now," I said. "It's none of our concern, and we have enough else to do."

"Perhaps," he said, Doria echoing him with a curt nod, Dorann holding out her arms for Doria to pick her up. It was a dismissal.

Doria, my baby daughter, and my best friend had been having a fine day without me.

I found Andrea Cullinane in her new workshop, unpacking.

Ideally, a wizard's workshop should have been built up against the wall of the keep, somewhere out of the way. I'd done that when Lou and I were laying out Home, and Karl and Andy had had something similar done in Biemestren, but Castle Cullinane was small, and most of the space within the walls was claimed.

Andrea had taken the last one in a row of continuous storerooms in the dungeon, a dank, cold end room of a series lit only by barred windows, simple unglazed openings at the juncture of ceiling and wall. The only way in was through the storerooms, weaving my way through musty stacked barrels of wine, past plump bags of grain, ducking underneath green-crusted hams hanging from ceiling hooks, walking through the sunlight-striped dark and damp.

I don't like basements. Back home, back when I was a kid, I could always hear the scrabbling of rats every time I went downstairs. I remember going after one with a baseball bat once, but I swear it reared back and hissed at me and chased me the hell upstairs.

Cellars and dungeons on This Side tended to be worse than home—some special efforts I'd taken to cut down on the Endell rat population long justified what King Maheralen of Endell used to pay me.

But there weren't any rats here. Or mice. Just musty, damp, cold silence.

I shivered.

I stopped at what passed for the door to her workshop: a sheet of undyed muslin hung across the opening, damp to the touch.

"Andrea? It's me."

A pause. "Just a moment, Walter," she said. I listened hard for the sound of syllables that I could only hear and not remember, but there weren't any. Just a rustling, as though of paper and then cloth. Then: "You might as well come in."

I pushed through the muslin, shuddering at the touch of it. The room was lit by several sputtering lamps in addition to the barred sunlight streaming down, although none of the light managed to dispel the gloom. Wooden boxes, some open, others still nailed shut, stood stacked on the stone floor or on tables. I don't care where you are—This Side, the Other Side—moving cuts into work seriously.

Skin damp from a sponge bath—some of the water was still heating in a blackened copper vessel over a lamp—she was just finishing buttoning her fly.

I would have been happy to help her with her clothes. On or off. Andrea Andropolous Cullinane: black hair, no longer salted with gray; high cheekbones; elegant nose; tongue playing with the lower full lip; slick black leather vest cut high and matching black leather jeans that looked like they'd been applied with a fine brush (I admit it: I imprinted young on women in tight jeans)—all tight at full breasts and trim waist, leaving her long midriff bare.

I could see vague lines of stretch marks on her flat belly if I looked real hard. Not that I minded looking hard; even so, she looked *good*. Maybe too good.

I fingered the amulet hanging from the leather thong around my neck. The diamond-cut crystal was pulsing through a superficially reassuring progression of dull green and amber. No red, no indigo, no bright colors.

Which didn't mean anything, not really. Andy had built all of our amulets, and could have defeated any of them.

"How's the work coming?" I asked, with just the slightest overemphasis on "work."

She smiled. "Unpacking gets you dirty. No sense in getting clothes dirty, too."

Even if that meant working naked in the cold and damp of a dungeon? Just maybe, catching a quick glimpse of herself from a shiny surface or two wouldn't bother her.

I reached for her crystal ball, stopped myself, and then continued the motion at her quick nod of permission. A neat bit of equipment: its stand was a brass snake, impaled on the pole.

Colder to the touch than it should have been, and heavier. Like life itself, don't you know.

I looked into the perfect crystal, but all I saw was my own reflection, widened and distorted. I hadn't expected anything more, and didn't get it.

Just as well.

"We could try to get him out here by way of having him inspect Little Pittsburgh," she said.

It took me a moment to realize that Andy had picked up our conversation from the night before, about how to get Lou Riccetti, the Engineer, out for a visit. Lou hadn't been out of the Home settlement in years and years, and it would probably do him some good to travel a bit, see the world. Her new idea was to invite him to inspect Little Pittsburgh, the steel-making town in Barony Adahan, the next barony to the east.

38

Not a bad idea, but I hate that sort of parenthetical leap, when she assumes that I'll follow the train of thought back to the previous conversation.

"Possible," I said. I wasn't going to try to change Andy, not over something just irritating. Better to change the subject. "What have you been up to?"

Her smile was a little too knowing. "Sleeping. Dreaming. Working. Unpacking. The usual, you know?"

Her voice was just a hair too light, too casual, or maybe my own bad dream had oversensitized me, which would be a first; nobody's ever accused me of even being sensitive.

"Dreams?" I asked.

"Dreams," she said. "You know: stories that you tell yourself when you fall asleep. Sausages chasing bagels through tunnels, stuff like that."

"Is that all?" Look: my dreams are just dreams, Jungian archetypes cut open and dribbled into the creases of my mind. But I deal with magic and a wizard's dreams as little as I can.

"No," she said, raising a hand to dismiss the subject, then letting it drop. "No, that's not all. I've been having dreams of running through endless streets, always lost, always looking for a way out. Not good." She sighed. "But they're just dreams." She looked down at a book and stroked a short nail against its plain leather cover. "I probably shouldn't drink wine before bed. It makes me dream too much." She looked down at the book again.

There is a way for a wizard to enter somebody else's dream. It's risky for both parties; it's also one of the classic ways for wizards to duel, for one to try to bend another's will.

She looked up at me. "What aren't you asking me?"

I pursed my lips. "I'm not sure whether you're worried about somebody attacking you through your dreams, or whether you're wishing there was another wizard around to dream with you."

Her smile might not have been irresistible, but I wouldn't have wanted to bet. "Neither. I'm wondering something else entirely." She fingered the book. "I'm wondering why I'm getting interested in location spells again, in direction magic. I was already pretty good at them, but lately I've had a real taste for the stuff." She toyed with a slim steel needle. "If you want to put this into a haystack, I can give you a good demonstration."

"Thank you, no."

That was not good; trying too hard to locate Karl—a wizard can bash his or her head against the wall of death as much as he or she pleases—was what had driven Andy to exhaustion, and she was just barely recovering. Alternately, perhaps it had driven her near madness, and she never would recover, but merely learn to hide it better.

I changed the subject. "Have you seen my wife today?"

She nodded. "She was somewhere around," she said, gesturing vaguely. "Is that why you're down here?" she asked. "What's going on?"

It felt like I was missing something, but I wasn't sure what. "I was just talking to Ahira. Just for the sake of discussion, how would you feel about a field trip?" I asked, hoping she would say no.

If we were going to look into whatever was happening on the edge of Faerie, we'd need somebody capable of working magic. If I could get Andy to turn us down, it shouldn't be a problem turning Ahira's notion off—there were perhaps half a dozen minor wizards in Holtun-Bieme, all of whom had the typical wizard's nervousness about going in harm's way, none of whom I'd trust anyway. That would leave Henrad, formerly Andy's apprentice, but Henrad had been out in the field with Ahira and me before; I suspected that he hadn't regained any taste for it. Things had gotten a bit messy for sensitive types like Henrad—and me, for that matter.

"Where?" she asked.

"Toward Faerie, maybe as far as Ehvenor."

"Check out the rumors?" she asked, just a touch too eager. At my nod, she smiled. "I'd love to." She reached over to her worktable and fingered a gem, working it between thumb and forefinger. "With some study, I could work up the spells that would let me take some readings and, just maybe, see what's going on. But it wouldn't be a good idea—I've been trying to cut down, and you know how that goes."

There Are Some Things Man Is Not Meant To Do. You can tell which they are because they're bad either for you or for somebody else. Nobody ever is better off by doing heroin, and doing magic seems to affect some people about the same way: they get hooked on it, go crazy for it. Stable magicians can hold themselves to a maintenance dose, but maybe Andy had overdone it, trying to Locate Karl. More likely grief—compounded by lack of exercise, food, and sleep—had overwhelmed her.

Still, she was looking good.

"You're wondering if it's a seeming," she said, standing hand on hip.

"No." Not if she had been working naked—a fascinating notion in and of itself. I didn't know enough about magic to know if her seeming would delude her as well as others, but it didn't matter. I knew Andrea: she wouldn't have been working without clothes if the sight of her real body bothered her, and even if she had put up a seeming, she would know what she really looked like.

I guess I didn't sound convincing: she shook her head, denying an accusation I hadn't made. "It's no seeming, Walter. Rest, food, exercise, and—"

"The hair didn't come from exercise."

"—and a bit of dye," she said, taking a step toward me. "I don't like the look of gray. Turns the men off." She reached up and touched my temple, just where I was going rather, well, handsomely gray. "It looks better on you."

I guess that was my cue to reach for her, but I'm not sure that either of us really wanted to. We'd been lovers—once, or twice, or five times, depending on what you're counting; I'd rather enjoy than count—almost twenty years before, and there was still something between us.

I was tempted, for a lot of reasons. Forget hormones for a moment—although I think I spend too much time thinking with my testicles for my own good. Andy and I had quite properly loved each other for years and years, and her husband, my friend, was dead, and maybe we needed to celebrate his life in a very private and personal way.

But not under the same roof as my wife.

It occurred to me that I was being noble, silly as that idea sounds, in trying to talk her into staying off the road. Both Andy and I knew what was likely to happen if and when we were out in the field together, and perhaps I had just persuaded her, albeit indirectly, to stay safely home.

I took her hand in mine, her fingers soft and warm, and brought them to my lips.

"Old friend," I said, "it's good to see you looking good."

Screw nobility. Just remember that Walter Slovotsky is somebody who cares about his friends. Andy was, apparently for the first time since Karl was reported dead, doing well. I wasn't going to fuck around with that. In any sense.

Well, when you don't know what to do, it's probably a good idea to take a nap, eat a meal, or go to bed with somebody you like. Some combinations work well, too.

Kirah's and my rooms were empty; I stripped to the buff and stretched out under the down comforter and fell asleep.

Interlude:

The Dream Is the Same

THE NIGHTMARE IS always the same:

We're trying to make our escape from Hell, millions of us streaming across the vast plain. Everybody I've ever loved is there, along with faces familiar and strange.

Behind us, stretching across the horizon, there's a screaming pack of demons, some in cartoony shapes, some that look like misshapen wolves, all of whom have me scared so bad I can hardly breathe the freezing air.

The exit is up ahead, the gold ladder up through the clouds, and already there are people climbing it, a steady stream that reaches up into the fluffy whiteness, and beyond. I can't tell who's gone through, but I can only hope that my kids are among them. Please let it be my kids.

Some have already climbed through the clouds, but there's no way that all of us are going to: the demons are approaching too quickly, and they're going to catch some of us.

And then I see him: Karl Cullinane, Jason's father, stand-

*ing tall, face beaming, his hands, chest, and beard streaked
with blood and gore.*

*"We're going to have to hold the perimeter," Karl says.
"Who's with me?"*

*He smiles, as though he's been waiting his whole life for
this, the fucking idiot.*

"I'm with you," somebody says.

Figures push out of the crowd, some bloodied, some bent.

*Jefferson and Franklin work their way through, accompa-
nied by a thick old black woman, her shoulders stooped from
too many years of hard labor, her hair bound back in a blue
kerchief. Or maybe it isn't Jefferson—his hair is kind of a dusty
red instead of white. Doesn't matter—he belongs here.*

*"Please, Madame," he says, his voice tight, "go with the
others."*

*She snorts. "I only spent thirty-seven years on my knees
scrubbing white folks' floors to put food on the table fo' six
children, and put those six children through school." Her fingers clench into fists. "Think I let them get at my babies,
motherfucker?"*

Franklin chuckles. "He begs your pardon, Madame."

Jefferson bows deeply. "Indeed, I do."

*Another man, massive brows looming over eyes that see
everything, his walrus mustache white as snow, bites his cigar
through, then discards it with a muttered oath. "We can hold
it," he said, his voice squeakier than I thought it would be.
But he sounds like himself, not Hal Holbrook. "But we need
more."*

*Karl looks at me—they all look at me: Jefferson, Twain,
Ahira, mad old Semmelweis, all of them look at me—his
bloody face puzzled. "Walter? What are you waiting for?"*

Then I wake up.

CHAPTER THREE

In Which Hiccups
Are Cured,
Dinner Is Eaten,
and an Excursion
Is Arranged

*The blazing evidence of immortality is our dissatisfaction with
any other solution.*

—RALPH WALDO EMERSON

*Wanting it doesn't make it so. If it did, we'd all learn to want
harder. I can already want quite vigorously, thank you very
much.*

—WALTER SLOVOTSKY

IT'S CALLED THE PATHET-
ic fallacy, but that's only the technical term; nothing pathetic
about it.

I remember when I started personalizing things—I was
about five, or six.

It runs in the family. Stash—I thought of him as Daddy,
then—still had the Big Car, the 1957 Buick Starfire 98 he had
bought in Las Vegas, on his one and only trip there. It was
among the last and absolutely the best of the standard American bigmobiles, a huge car pulled around by a three-hundred-
horsepower V8, easily enough for the job—a monster engine,

it would roar like a lion. Two-toned, black and yellow like a bumblebee, wraparound windshield, curved fenders, and a rear deck large enough to camp out on.

The Big Car had bench seats like a couch. It was big as a house, and when I rode in it, held down by the big-buckled seat belts Daddy and his friend Mike had spent a weekend putting in, I felt as safe as I did on a couch in my house.

Sometimes, people in Volkswagens would honk at us, derisively.

Daddy would just chuckle. "They don't get it, eh, Em?"

And then Mom would give out her sigh, the deep one that meant *here he goes again*, and then she'd say, "What don't they get?"

He'd say something like, "How this metal all around us protects us, how if we're in a crash with one of them little shitmobiles—"

"*Stash*. Shhh."

"—it's going to spray them all over the landscape, but old Beauty here's gonna protect us."

It was kind of a mantra for the two of them, although I doubt that either of them would have recognized the word.

They stopped repeating the mantra the day that some idiot in a blue Corvair plowed into us head-on as we were coming home, just about to pull into our driveway. We were jerked *hard*—windshield starred all over in an instant; full ashtray flung its contents into the air, blinding me until I could cry the ashes out; the buckle of my seat belt left bruises on my right hip that flared purple and yellow for weeks—but we were okay. The worst hurt of us was Steve, my brother—he had gotten bashed against the back of the front seat—and all he had was a bloody nose.

The idiot in the Corvair got taken away in an ambulance, so badly battered that I can't to this day decide whether it was a man or a woman.

Blood was everywhere, and the harsh smells of gasoline and smoldering oil hung in the air. Mom, one hand on the back of Steve's neck, had taken him inside the house, but nobody thought to chase me away.

I waited with Daddy while the man with the wrecker hauled away our car. Our car.

God, it was mangled. It wasn't just that the fender and hood had been crumpled, and the glass broken, but the front wheels twisted out at funny angles, as though the axle had been smashed, and the body overhung the frame on one side.

The wrecker man shook his head as he pulled the lever that lifted the front of the car up and into the air.

"Buy it new, Mr. Slovotsky?" he asked, over the futile protest of the metal.

"Stash," Daddy said, absently. "Everybody calls me Stash. Short for Stanislaus. And yeah," Daddy said. "I bought it new. Ten years ago." He patted the mutilated steel, then pulled his hand away as though embarrassed.

The wrecker man shook his head once, quickly, jerkily, as though to say, *It's okay. I understand.* "Yeah. Good machines. Wish they still made them," he said, starting to turn away.

"It's just a machine."

"Sure, Stash." The wrecker man smiled. He didn't believe Daddy any more than I did.

Or any more than Daddy believed himself. Stash ran blunt, gentle fingers through my hair. "I drove your mother to the hospital in this car when we were having you, Cricket."

"Can they fix it, Daddy?" I asked, still clutching at my side, rubbing at my hip.

He shook his head, tears he didn't notice working their way down through the five-o'clock shadow on his cheeks.

"No," he said. "It's broken too bad to fix. But you and Steve and Mom are okay, Cricket, and that's what matters. That's the only damn thing that ever matters." He gripped my hand tight.

"No, I'm not okay," I said, probably whining. "I'm *hurt.*"

"Yeah. Just hurt. Bruised maybe. And I'm real sorry about that, Cricket, honest I am, but we all could be dead, dead, dead."

Muttering something in Polish, he let go of my hand and gently stroked the car's metal flank as the wrecker pulled it

47

away from the curb. I never learned much Polish, and I don't remember the words, but I know what they meant.

They meant: "Thank you, thou good and faithful servant."

We watched until the wrecker turned the corner and the Big Car was gone, and then we just stood there and watched a long while longer, until our eyes were dry.

When I woke, Kirah was across from the bed, watching me.

I had already been vaguely aware of her, but, suspicious though it is, my hindbrain didn't want to wake me for that.

A bit spooky: she was sitting in an overstuffed armchair by the window, her legs curled up beneath her, the sun through the bars striping her face in gold and dark. Only one corner of her mouth was visible, upturned in a smile that could have been friendly or forced. I couldn't tell; my wife learned her dissimulation skills before she ever met me.

"Good afternoon, darling," she said. She was sewing: white cloth heaped in her lap, needle darting in and out.

I stretched, then wiped at my eyes. "Hi there." I took a pair of shorts from the bureau next to the bed and slipped into them before I levered myself out of bed and padded across the carpet to bend over—slowly, gently, carefully—and kiss her, careful to clasp my hands behind me. She couldn't help it; and I had to.

She tossed her head, perhaps for display, perhaps in nervousness; I backed off a half-step and was saddened at the way the tension flowed out of her.

"Sleep well?" she asked me, in her ever-so-slightly-halting English.

"Nah. I've never been very good at it," I said. It was an old joke between us. Sometimes, when the center falls apart, you hold onto the forms.

"You cried out a couple of times," she said. "I couldn't make it out."

That was just as well. "Bad dream," I said.

I went to the washbasin and splashed some water on my face and chest, then toweled off my face in front of the closet while I picked out some clothes for a semi-formal supper, quickly settling on a short, loose-cut jacket of brown and silver over a ruffled tan shirt, and taupe trousers with silver piping down the seam. I like my formal clothes comfortable, and besides, the cut of the sleeves kept the throwing knife strapped to my left arm handy. Not the sort of thing I've ever needed at a formal dinner, but you never know.

I buckled my formal sword belt tightly around my waist, decided that it fit fine, then unbuckled it and slung the belt over a shoulder.

"Where have you been keeping yourself today?" I asked.

She shrugged. "Around." She bit off a thread and slipped the needle into the cloth, then carefully set down her work before she stood and came to me, gathering her long, golden hair at the nape of her neck.

She stopped just in front of me, not quite touching.

It wasn't just the dress, although that was spectacular: Kirah was in a long gown of white lace over red silk, scooped low in front and cut deeply in back, revealing a lot of soft, creamy skin. I swear, my wife was more beautiful every year. There's a richness of beauty that can come on in a woman's thirties, after all the traces of baby fat and innocence have gone, but before the years have dragged the elasticity from her skin and muscle.

And it was all for show.

No, that wasn't fair. "Really, where were you?"

"I spent the morning helping Andrea."

So, that was what Andy had been keeping from me. I didn't like the sound of any of this, but kept my disapproval off my face, I hope.

Andy was *supposed* to be keeping her use of magic to a minimum, on Doria's orders. Andy had spent far too much energy in her obsessive need to try to Locate Karl, and it's not good for humans, wizard or not, to be around magic a whole lot. Power is dangerous, even when you think you're controlling it.

Now, my own opinion was that Doria was being a bit too much of a Jewish mother, something she was only half equipped for. But even if Doria was right about the danger, it should be relatively safe for Kirah: she couldn't read magic. A page out of Andrea's spellbook would be the same blurry mess to her that it was to me. If you don't have the genes for it, you can't do wizard magic; if you don't have the right relationship with the gods or powers or faerie, you can't do clerical magic, like Doria used to do.

She cocked her head to one side. "I was just starting to debate whether or not to wake you for dinner, or just let you sleep through." She smiled as she took a step back, then one closer, every move a step in a dance.

"Dinner soon?"

She shook her head. "Not for a while yet. But you always take so long to wake up."

I reached for her and felt her stiffen in my arms. "Sorry." I let my arms fall to my side.

She put her arms around me and laid her head against my chest. That's okay under the rules, sometimes. "No. I'm sorry, Walter."

"You can't help it." I started to bring my arms up, but caught myself. It wasn't her fault. I had to keep reminding her of that.

My hands clenched. It wasn't her fault. It wasn't her fault that if I held her, she'd tense, and if I reached for her she'd scream. But it wasn't mine, either. I've always done my best by her, but whatever I am, I'm not a healer of psyche and spirit. At best, I'm an observer of psyche and spirit.

" 'This, too, shall pass,' " she said, quoting me accurately, not Abe Lincoln inaccurately. I used to say it when she was pregnant, kind of as a mantra.

Kind of funny, really: I'm always politically incorrect. Here, for suggesting that women ought to have roughly the same rights as men; on the Other Side, for—only rarely, rarely, and usually with bad results—pointing out that pregnant women go crazy for about a year, or longer.

Maybe it's not their fault. Maybe nothing's nobody's fault.

"Sure." It could happen. I'm skeptical, mind, but it could happen.

Slowly, carefully, I put my arms around her, not quite holding her, and kissed her on the side of the neck. She took it well: she flinched, but she didn't cry out or push me away.

Some victory, eh? I let my arms drop. "I'll see you at dinner."

It hadn't always been this way. Back in the beginning we'd spent more time in bed than out, in my memory if not possible in reality.

Hell, our first time had been within a couple of hours after Karl and I had pulled her out of the slaver wagon and freed her, along with the rest of that bunch of slaves. Like I always said, this business has always had its fringe benefits.

Even in the early days, though, there had been hints—times when I reached for her in the night and she would shrink away, only to explain that she was just tired, other times when I would come up behind her and put my arms around her affectionately and she would stifle a scream, only to smile in apology for being startled so easily.

But those times had been few and far between, then.

It had come on slowly, few and far between becoming occasional becoming not infrequent and then frequent so gradually until I realized that we hadn't made love for almost a year, and that she couldn't bear to be touched.

I needed a drink.

I found a shiny gray ceramic bottle of Holtish brandy and a pair of earthenware brandy mugs in the sitting room on the second floor.

Well, the staff called it the sitting room—I thought of it as a brag room. The rug covering the floor was a patchwork of pelts, the walls decorated with heads of various beasts that various Furnael barons had killed: a few seven-point bucks, several decent wolf- and boar-heads, and one huge brown bear, its jaw opened wide, yellow teeth ready to chomp. I doubt that the teeth were as polished and shiny in real life as they were now.

Among all the predators, high up on one wall, was one small rabbit—the whole thing, mounted on a plaque sideways, stretched out as though frozen in mid-bound. I'm sure that there's a family story behind the last, but I've never found out what it is.

A spooky place, but not because the animals looked like they were ready to come alive. They didn't; Biemish taxidermy was substandard, and there's never been great glass-work in most of the Eren regions. Instead of glass eyes, there were the here-traditional white spheres of polished bone. It was like having a room full of little Orphan Annie's pets staring down at me. Takes some getting used to. Brandy helps.

Only trouble was, I had started hiccupping, and I hate drinking with the hiccups. Gets up the nose.

I had a fire going in the fireplace, and had settled myself comfortably into a low chair in front of the flickering flames when Doria tapped a fingernail against the doorframe.

She had dressed for dinner in a long purple dress made from a cloth I always think of as velour, although I know that's not the right name for it. The top was fitted tightly from low-cut bosom to her hips, where a pleated skirt flared out underneath a woven golden belt, the golden theme picked up by filigree on the bosom and arms of her dress and the strap of her pouch.

"Well?" she said.

"Nice," I said. "Pull up a throne."

She looked at the two brandy mugs warming on the flat stones in front of the fire.

"Expecting me?" she said, as I stretched out a lazy arm and gave each mug a half-turn.

I hiccuped as I shook my head. "Nah. But it doesn't cost anything to heat two mugs. You never know when a friend's going to stop for a drink."

"Or to cure your hiccups." She smiled as she folded herself into the chair and leaned her head against the high back.

"Yeah." I was a bit sarcastic.

She pulled what looked like a piece of quartz out of her pouch. "Suck on this for awhile."

I shrugged and popped it into my mouth. Sweet—"Rock candy," I said, from around the piece. Demosthenes, eat your heart out.

"Very clever, Watson."

I raised an eyebrow, as though to say, *And this is going to cure the hiccups?*

She nodded. "Ninety percent. Hiccups are caused by an

electrolyte imbalance in the blood; sends the diaphragm into spasms. Usually acidosis. Sugar or salt will push things the other way; if this doesn't work, it means you're alkalotic, and a bit of lemon will do. Hang on a moment."

I was going to argue with her, but the hiccups went away, probably of their own volition. "Where did you hear about this? From the Hand?"

"No. It's an Other Side thing. Friend of mine named Diane. Don't know if you ever met her."

"Mmmm . . . maybe. I don't know."

"Nah; you never met her." She smiled. "You'd remember. —How are the mugs?"

"Hang on a sec." The mugs were warm enough: just this side of too hot to hold, the ideal temperature for drinking Holtish brandy. I uncorked the bottle and poured each of us a healthy slug. I was going to get up and give hers to her, but she rose instead and settled herself down on the arm of my chair, her arm around my shoulders. She smelled of soap and flowers.

"L'chaim," I said, almost gargling on the Hebrew *ch*-sound.

That earned a smile. "L'chaim," she repeated, then drank. I did, too. The brandy burned my throat and warmed my belly. Not a bad trade.

"Something bothering you?" she asked.

"Just the usual," I said, keeping my voice light. "You're not the only one who worries, you know."

She chuckled. "What are you worrying about now? Your chances with the upstairs maid?" Her fingers played gently with my hair.

I faked a shudder. "Have you *seen* the upstairs maid?"

"Seriously."

I shrugged, gently enough not to dislodge her. "I shouldn't complain. Things are going well. Andy's looking a lot better, and the dwarf is pretty much healed up. Jason's a good kid. Greener than the Hulk, but—"

She silenced me with a finger to my lips. "We are going to get to Kirah, aren't we?"

I didn't answer.

Doria waited. She was better at waiting than I was.

"Not her fault," I said, finally. "What would you call it, post-traumatic stress disorder?"

She shrugged. "Two years of psychology classes, and you'd have me be the local psychiatrist?"

"I won't tell the AMA." I raised my little finger. "Pinky swear."

"Well, there is that." She considered the problem as she sipped, then dismissed it with a shrug. "It doesn't matter, Walter. Slapping a label on it doesn't mean you understand it, or know how to fix it. She's in bad shape . . . or at least your relationship is." Doria sipped, then sighed.

I raised an eyebrow. "I didn't know that it showed. You've still got enough power to detect it?"

"No." She shook her head. Had the Matriarch stripped her of all of her power, or were there a few spells left in the back of her soul, awaiting need? Doria wouldn't say. "But I always thought of spells as a way of augmenting other sensitivities, not as a substitute. How long has it been for the two of you?"

"Since what?"

One side of her mouth twisted into a wry frown. "Guess."

"Hey, I don't tell. Remember?"

"Yes." She smiled. "Usually."

I thought of the last time, and tried to forget it, remembering instead one wild, warm night at Home, years ago, shortly after Karl and I had gotten back from a raid. I think it was the second night—the first was Karl's Day Off, so it must have been. We'd left Janie, then just a baby, with Karl and Andy, and taken blankets away from the settlement, through the woods, and up the side of a hill. We had gotten incredibly drunk on a small bottle of wild huckleberry wine, and made love under the stars all night long.

I mean, really, no shit, my hand to God: all night long.

If I close my eyes, I can still see her, her hair floating in the breeze above me, framed in starlight. . . .

But that was a long time ago, in another country, and the wench would rather be dead than warm in my arms again.

I changed the subject. "Andy's looking a lot better, lately. I don't think it's a seeming."

Doria sat silently for a moment, then smiled, dropping the matter of Kirah and me. "It's amazing what a bit of exercise and food and general activity can do, eh? Not to mention laying off the magic."

"She—" I stopped myself.

"She hasn't given it up?" Doria shrugged. "I'm not surprised. The disease model never *quite* worked for alcoholism, and putting it all on magical addiction probably isn't exactly right."

I was surprised to hear her talk like that. Doria had been beating the drum for keeping Andy the hell out of her workshop, by anything this side of force.

"But it's *close*," she said. "I wish the rest of you would believe me. There's a seduction there, a constant temptation. I was an awfully chubby girl," she said, as though changing the subject, although she wasn't. "I finally managed to, most of the time, keep my weight down to something acceptable by controlling what and how I ate. Just so much—and always so much; if you starve yourself now, you'll binge later—and no more."

I took her hand in mine and kissed it. Gently, gently; you always have to touch Doria gently, and that's the way it's always been, and one of the things I've always liked about her. "You had other problems, but you've come a long way, kid."

She sighed. "One would hope so." Her fingers toyed with my collar and then with my mustache. "We'd better go down to dinner, eh?"

The trials of the life of the ruling class are something you learn to bear up with after a while, even if you're only a member of the ruling class by association. Everything's a trade-off. You tend to eat well, but you can be interrupted for or dragooned to help out on any of a number of things.

In this case, I was helping entertain two newly arrived village wardens on a formal visit. Not a bad idea, really, having the village wardens come in to be wined and dined; I'm glad I'd suggested it to Jason.

We took our seats formally around the table: Jason at the head; Andrea at the foot; Ritelen, the senior of the two wardens, at Jason's right; then Kirah, Dorann, and Janie down the side; Doria, me, Aeia, Bren Adahan, and finally Benen, the other warden, down the other, giving each warden a seat of honor at the right of either Jason or Andrea. It gave Kirah a chance to engage in some formal chitchat with Ritelen, a barrel-chested, walrus-mustached man, as only she and Jason were within quiet conversation range of him.

It looked silly, is what it did. The formal dining table was meant to seat thirty, and less than a dozen people were spread too thinly.

Personally, I would have liked to set us down in two clumps, one at each end. Four to six is about the right number for a dinner conversation. Any more and the group will tend to split into several conversations, and most people will have the deep suspicion that they're in the wrong one. (Not me, mind. The conversation with me in it is by definition the most interesting.)

Or it can turn into a monologue.

Naturally, it didn't turn into a monologue from either of the two village wardens; that would have been too sensible, and too interesting. I would have liked to hear more about the wheat rot they were having in Teleren village, and would have wanted to pitch both of the wardens on the value of mung bean sprouts as a nutritional supplement.

But it didn't work out that way. Over the soup course— a thick, meaty turtle soup, heavily laden with cracked pepper and pieces of carrot that were just barely firm to the bite, served with hot rolls, still warm, firm, and chewy-crusted from the steamer; U'len does good work—Bren Adahan was holding forth on some fine point of horsemanship.

"—the trick is to get the animal not to anticipate, but to react instantly. Any idiot can canter a horse at a fence and find himself taking it without wanting to; most good horsemen can anticipate early that the horse is going to want to go; but for the very best, nothing happens until you tell it to. I remember a time . . ."

Aeia and Janie paid very close attention, and all of the other women were listening almost as closely.

Except for Andrea. Gorgeous in a long dress of jet and

56

crimson, she tented her fingers in front of her mouth and barely pretended to listen.

I think I understand the connection between women and horses, but I don't care for it. It's almost sexual—or maybe I should drop the "almost," and no, I don't mean any crass joke about women and stallions. (In fact, all of the women I know have the sense to stay the hell away from stallions, as do I. An uncut male horse goes absolutely apeshit if he smells a mare in heat, or gets too close to a menstruating woman.)

Look: I don't have anything against horses. During the last twenty years I've walked thousands of miles and ridden easily twice as much, and I wouldn't want it the other way around, honest. I'd prefer cars, and I *much* prefer traveling on Ellegon when he's available, but I don't have anything against horses, not really.

On the other hand, they're remarkably dumb animals. They don't have any sense at all—you can ride them to death if you push them too hard, and you don't dare get too attached to them, because when it all hits the fan you *have* to be able to leave them behind. I once spent a full day hiding crouched in a rain barrel, breathing shallowly through a piece of tubing. I don't think a horse would have fit in there with me, and if I hadn't been willing to abandon my horse—a sweet little mare who used to nuzzle me affectionately, like a dog; I hope she found a caring owner—at a moment's notice, I would have been dead, dead, dead.

So don't talk to me about horses.

Particularly not about taking a fence when you didn't intend to. I almost broke my fucking neck.

Ahira's lips quirked into a smile. "Possibly we could talk about something else at dinner?" he asked, as U'len entered, bearing the next course on a silver salver.

"By all means, talk instead of eating my fine capons," U'len said. She was an immense woman, all sweat and fat and muscles, an almost permanent sneer on her face.

I'm not impressed with the local tradition of serving the meat course before the fish course, but I was impressed with the three birds resting on the huge serving plate: they were huge, plump, and brown, starred with cloves and bits of garlic and onion, crispy skin still crackling from the oven.

They smelled like heaven ought to.

"Take it easy on me," Jason said, easily slipping into his father's role as U'len's verbal sparring partner. "I know good food when I taste it. We'll see if this is."

"Hmph." She set the bird platter down in front of Jason, then began to wield the carving knife and fork herself.

Aeia was unusually lovely tonight in a ruffled blouse over a long, bright Melawei sarong that left her left leg bare from ankle to mid-thigh. She smiled over her wine glass at me, earning me a glare from Bren Adahan, but no particular glance from my wife.

Sit still, Bren, I thought. *You're going to make life difficult for all of us.*

"What do you think of the wine?" she asked.

I took another sip. "Not bad." It would have been nice to sit close to her, to feel her leg against mine, to feel a woman press harder against me instead of pull away.

I drank some more wine. A bit too tannic for my taste, but it was still young—the Biemish style of winemaking gives you wine that needs long cellaring, although the result can be worth it. Winemaking was one of the things Bieme had to give up during the war years, and almost all of what the Furnaels had put down had been drunk during the siege. In the whole country there was nothing really ready to drink.

U'len started carving. I don't know about you, but I've always had a fondness for watching anybody do just about anything they're good at.

Blade flashing in the candlelight, in less time than it takes to tell it she had the first bird cut up, Eren-style: skin cut into palm-sized squares, each topped with a spoon-molded hunk of stuffing; breast sliced into thick chunks; thigh separated from drumstick; top part of the drumstick neatly removed from the meat; back and the rest of the carcass on its way to the kitchen for soup stock, while a pair of her assistants brought in the turnip greens and chotte to accompany the birds.

While she started in on carving the second bird, Jason speared a piece of skin and stuffing, and took a tentative bite.

"Well?" she asked, not pausing in her slicing, no trace of deference or even respect in her harsh voice. "How is it?"

"Not very good," he said.

I thought Benen's jaw was going to drop off and fall on his plate, although Ritelen, having figured out what was going on, hid a smile behind his walrus mustache and napkin.

"It isn't, *eh*?" U'len set her massive fists on her even more massive hips.

He looked at her for a long moment. "Nah. We, er, can save everybody else the, uh, problem of eating this. I'll just take care of it all."

"Uncle Jason's ly-ing, ly-ing," Dorann chanted, silenced momentarily, a moment later, by a mouthful of stuffing. Kirah's timing is sometimes very good.

U'len had served out the fish course—stream trout baked in sorrel and cream; okay, but I know a much better way to cook fresh trout—and was in the process of serving dessert when Kethol, Durine, and Pirojil walked in.

Not exactly the three musketeers. Kethol: lean, raw-boned, red-headed; Pirojil, chunky and pleasantly ugly; Durine, a quiet bear of a man. They had been Karl's surviving companions in what was becoming known as the legendary Last Ride, and two of the three of them had been with Jason in the search for Karl, the one that had turned up, well, me.

Pirojil spoke for the three of them. "Baron, we got a peasant outside, says he wants to see you. There's been some trouble out toward Velen."

I guess it was the night for Benen to be shocked, first at three soldiers interrupting the baron's formal dinner without so much as a with-your-permission; second, at the reason they'd interrupted the dinner; and third, at the way Jason was already out of his chair, and buckling on his swordbelt as he walked toward the far entryway.

"Well, let's see what the problem is," he said. "Baron Adahan, please take my place."

I would have been impressed with Jason's courtesy to the Holt, but I sort of figured it was more an attempt to keep Adahan's nose out of the problem than to avoid getting it out of joint.

"Be right with you," Tennetty said from around a final bite of trout, seemingly unbothered; Tennetty's never been much for desserts. She stood, reflexively feeling for the hilt of her knife before belting her sword about her waist.

I wasn't disposed to accompany them—the three musketeers knew enough to search the peasant, and Tennetty was along. Besides, I was looking forward to U'len's raspberry tart, even though the seeds always get caught between my teeth. But Jason was leaving, and Ahira was following him, so I did, too.

I guess my own sense of egalitarianism would have called for inviting him in, but nobody had asked.

We met with him in the courtyard, under the watchful eye of the keep guard, a dozen flickering torches, and a starry night sky.

The peasant wasn't what I'd expected, although I should have thought it through. Velen was a good two days' walk away—the peasant farmer had sent a son, not gone himself. Yes, he was short, dirty, smelly, and not too bright, and not so stupid as to not be nervous. He knuckled his forehead incessantly as he spoke, grunting out his complaint that somebody or something had killed his father's cow.

He actually wept.

Yeah. A cow. Not a big deal, right? Wrong. To a one-plot, two-cow peasant family, it probably represented the difference between getting by and starving. A good milk cow would go a long way to keeping a small family fed, between the milk and a calf every year or two. Cows aren't a terribly efficient way to deal with edible grain—if you know enough about balancing proteins, vegetarianism is more efficient by an order of magnitude—but a lot of what they can get by on just fine isn't edible for humans.

Grazing rights on some of the baron's pasture wouldn't help out the peasant's family. Peasants don't eat grass.

"Sounds like wolves to me," Jason said. His lips twisted into a frown. "The population went way up during the war."

Ruling classes are good for something; keeping the number of other predators low is one of them. In Bieme, it's also one of the traditional jobs of the baron.

Tennetty shrugged. "We can handle wolves," she said. "The four-legged kind, or the two-legged. Shotguns all around?"

Durine nodded. "Not for chasing them down, but for chasing them away."

"Took the cow out of his paddock?" Ahira shrugged. "Possible." He looked at me and raised an eyebrow about halfway, spreading his palms just so.

I pursed my lips and shook my head. "Nah."

Ahira nodded.

"You don't think it's a wolf pack?" Jason was irritated.

I sighed. "You missed it. Ahira just asked me if I thought it was too likely to be a trap, or if we ought to go out and take a look at the corpse before the wolves finish it off."

"You did?" he said, turning to the dwarf.

Ahira nodded. "Actually, I did." He smiled. "Pretty disgusting, eh?"

Jason frowned; I smiled.

It happens with old friends: you spend a lot of time with somebody over a number of years, you have some of the same discussions over and over again. Then one day you realize that when you're doing some things, or talking about others, you're leaving out most of the words, or even all of the words. You don't need to guess how they're going to deal with a situation: you *know*. A gesture, a word, or even less than that—and it's clear.

But that's not something you can explain to a seventeen-year-old, even a very responsible, precocious seventeen-year-old. They won't believe you.

In this case, though, it was easy. It wasn't necessary for Ahira and me to involve ourselves in an ordinary wolf hunt, but if it was something else, it could be connected to those stories of things coming out of Faerie, and anything involving magic could involve Arta Myrdhyn, and us.

Look: I don't know why Arta Myrdhyn—yes, *the* Arta Myrdhyn of tale and legend—sent us across. It's even barely possible he did it so that we'd open the Gate for his return, as he claimed. Me, I'm skeptical. I guess it's partly that I don't like people I don't like pushing me around—my friends

61

do enough of that. I've never liked jigsaw puzzles, and like even less being a piece in one.

Or I'm afraid that the universe might do to me what I was always tempted to do: bash the piece into place, even if it doesn't quite fit.

Tends to be hard on the piece.

The trouble with life is that none of it comes with a manual, and you always have to decide what involves you and what doesn't. After more than twenty years of friendship, I knew that this was the sort of thing that Ahira would sleep better after checking out, and that he wouldn't want to sleep until we were closer to checking it out.

As usual, he was nagging me into doing something that I had misgivings about.

Well, we were trying to teach the kid about life and such, so I might as well continue the lesson.

"Equipment," I said to Ahira. "Tell him what I think we'll bring."

He nodded, and beckoned Jason over, whispering in his ear.

Actually, this might be a bit tough.

"Okay," I said. "Figure one flatbed wagon and a team to draw it." That was easy; everybody knows I prefer a padded bench to a hard saddle. "Rations, and standard road gear—just grab a couple of packs in the stables. But we'll take a quick run up to the supply closet and grab one net hammock each." They were of elven silk, light as a feather and strong. Given the right geometry, I'd much rather sleep a few feet off the cold, cold ground than on it. Or in it, for that matter. "Signal rockets, five fast horses—just in case. Boar spears, grenades, shotguns plus personal weapons for all. But I bet he forgot the sprouting box."

Ahira's smile widened. "A lot you know. I told him two."

"Fine." One of my less-than-crazy theories is that for people eating peasant food anywhere—which is largely pick-your-starch-and-beans—taking some of those beans and sprouting them is going to increase the nutrition they're getting significantly, at little effort and no extra cost.

Hence the sprouting box. Johnny Appleseed, eat your heart out. "That isn't all."

"So I told him." Ahira laughed. "Go on."

"All that's too utilitarian—you told him to be sure to throw a couple of extra blankets in the flatbed, so I don't have to rest my tender butt on a hard bench. Add a *clean* teapot, and some tea. And a bottle of Riccetti's Best." I don't tend to get drunk on the road, but an occasional swig of good, smooth corn whiskey before bed cuts the dirt real well.

Ahira nudged the boy. "See?"

Jason frowned. I think he was looking for the trick, but there wasn't one, other than twenty years of being friends. I'm tricky, honest, but I hadn't set this up.

Tennetty snickered.

The peasant wasn't following any of this, which was reasonable—a lot of the conversation had been in English, and he probably only spoke Erendra.

Jason turned to him. "You can show us where?"

"Yes, Lord, I think—certainly come daylight."

Jason beckoned to Durine. "Find Maduc dinner, and a place to sleep for the night, see that he's fed and ready to leave at dawn."

"Yes, Baron Fur—Cullinane."

"Yup," Jason said, with a smile. "Baron Furcullinane, that's me. Your other cow? How do you know it's safe?"

A good deduction: the peasant, young or old, wouldn't leave his only other cow endangered for the day and a half it had taken him to walk in.

"My father keeps it in the hut with them, Lord."

Ahira looked at me, spreading his hands. Durine led the peasant away.

"You'd better go get some sleep, Jason," I said. "Going to be a long day for you, tomorrow." Andrea was busy sneaking up behind us in the dark, trying not to be noticed, so I didn't notice her. Let her have her fun.

"You, too."

Ahira shook his head. "Nope. It's a bright enough night. Walter and I are heading out now."

"Missing a night's sleep," I said.

He shrugged. "Won't be the first time. We'll say good

night to the family and be off." He turned to Tennetty. "You coming along?"

"Sure." Tennetty sighed. "Probably won't be anything to kill." She turned to me. "How do you expect to find it in the dark?"

Ahira shrugged for me. "We won't be there before dawn, and by then it'll be well marked. Buzzards." He thought about it for a moment. "The three of us ought to do."

Jason cleared his throat. "And how about me?"

I smiled. "But you're leaving tomorrow, aren't you?"

He spread his hands. "Fine. I'm being taught a lesson. May one inquire as to what it is?"

"I thought it was obvious." Ahira sighed. "When we're *here*, you are Baron Cullinane, and we're guests in your house. Fine. No problem. But once we step outside that house, or even plan on doing it, we're not your guests, or your servants, or anything less than your partners."

"Make that 'senior partners,' " I added. "And add 'teachers.' The dwarf and I don't just have a few years on you; there's a lot of experience, too."

He stood silent for a moment, and I honestly wondered how it would go. I mean, when I was seventeen, I didn't take being chastened in public all that well.

Come to think of it, I still don't. I don't even much take to being corrected in private.

"Have a good trip," he said, turning and walking away.

Tennetty spat on the ground. "Asshole." I was curious about whether that was addressed to Jason or to Ahira and me, but I didn't ask. Don't ask a question if you don't want to hear the answer.

"Not fair," Andrea Cullinane said from behind me. "But thank you."

I jumped a bit, as though she had startled me. Tennetty cocked her head suspiciously, and Ahira didn't have to.

I chuckled. "I didn't do it so you could have him around a bit longer. I did it for my own tender skin. If Jason's going to be working with us, he's going to have to be reliable." Besides, he had the village wardens to keep entertained.

And maybe I was still remembering that the boy had once bolted when it counted—okay, right after it counted—

and that had brought a whole world of trouble down on a lot of heads.

She was in her new leathers again, covered by a matching black leather trailcoat, its surface dark without being glossy. She had a bag slung across one shoulder, and beneath the open buttons of the coat, a flintlock pistol was holstered on each hip, the one on the left hip butt-forward.

"What are you dressed up for?" I asked, as though I didn't know.

Her eyes went all vague and distant, a look I didn't like. "I need to get out of here; I'm going stir-crazy." She shook her head as though to clear it.

"There've been stories," she went on, "about things coming out of Faerie, about animals bit in half. And then there was that huge thing, whatever is was, that Jason and Tennetty ran into on one of the Shattered Islands. You may need me."

"Wolf pack sounds a lot more likely."

Magical creatures and humans don't tend to get along, and few at all remain in the Eren regions. There are always stories, but most of the time they're just stories. I've been in on the creation of enough legends to know what nonsense they can be.

She cocked her head to one side. "What if it isn't just a wolf pack? What will you do then?"

What the fuck did she *think* I'd do? "I'll run like hell, that's what I'll do."

I had worked this all through earlier in the day, and everything had come down on the side of leaving Andy out of it. Forget Doria's theories.

Look: given the world we live in and the situations we've been in, it's no coincidence that a lot of the women I know have been raped. Relative freedom from the likelihood of that kind of assault is a relatively modern invention—in most societies, the only question is who, other than the woman, has been affronted. (It's customary for us to talk about the Other Side as though everything worked right and well there, but in the country where I was born, assaults are a crime against the state, not the person, and it's the state that decides whether or not to prosecute it. Yeah, I know.)

Everything leaves scars. Kirah has her troubles; it turned

65

Tennetty into a barely controlled psychopath; Doria came damn close to ending up permanently between the lettuce and the broccoli, if you catch my drift; and while I think she's made the best adjustment of them all, there's a trace of madness around the edges of Aeia's eyes. Just like the trace around Andrea's.

No. One crazy, Tennetty, was bad enough on the field— even if we were only going to be chasing down a few skinny, scared wolves. We didn't need somebody else marginal, and we particularly didn't need a borderline magic addict. Okay, maybe she wasn't a magic addict; Doria is perfectly capable of being wrong.

But Andy had been out of the field for years and years, so after all my talk about how we can practically read each other's mind, I feel like an idiot for having to report that when Ahira said, "Okay. Let's say a quick goodbye and get out of here," it came as a complete surprise to me.

And not a pleasant one, either.

CHAPTER FOUR

In Which I Think Unwise Thoughts and Say Some Farewells

The course of true love never did run smooth.
—WILLIAM SHAKESPEARE

Nothing is more annoying than somebody who has a keen eye for the obvious.
—WALTER SLOVOTSKY

I MANAGED TO SAY goodbye to all my family, starting with the youngest one.

Doria Andrea takes after her father—she's a late-night kind of Slovotsky, like me and Stash, unlike Emma and Steve and her mother and sister—but when you're that age, staying up late means making it through a long dinner, and that's about all.

"Sleep well, little prosecutor," I said as I tucked her in, in a private joke that only the originals among us would have gotten, and nobody but me found even mildly funny.

D.A. wrapped her little arms tight around my neck as I leaned over. "Come back soon, Daddy. Please."

"Will do," I said, gently prying myself away. I rested my hand on her head for a moment, on the soft baby-hair that was getting more golden each day, like her mother's. "G'night, Sweetheart."

Janie was waiting for me out in the hall, leaning against the wall. She started to say something, but cut off when I put

67

a finger to my lips. I shut the door gently and followed her over to the landing.

"Trouble is, Daddy dearest," she said, ignoring my grimace, "you're getting *too* tricky in your old age."

"Oh?" I asked, trying to sound casual. I *hate* it when she calls me "Daddy dearest."

"You've managed to teach my boyfriend not to push you around—to not *try* to push you around. But it looks to me like you gave up a cheap little dry run that would have been good for the lot of you. Doesn't sound like a good trade to me." She shrugged. "If my opinion counts for anything."

Since that had been bothering the hell out of me anyway, I found it as hard to disagree with her as it would have been to admit that it was wrong, so I didn't do either.

"It counts, kid," I said, hugging her for only a moment.

She smiled. Why is it that my daughters' smiles brighten the whole world?

"Be good," I said.

Kirah was sitting in the overstuffed armchair, a lamp at her left elbow, her sewing set aside as she worked on some knitting or tatting or whatever; I don't know the difference and I don't much care.

"You're going," she said, her voice flat, as though to say, *I won't ask you not to go.*

"So it seems." I smiled. "Hey, not to worry. I know how to duck."

She forced a smile. Either that, or her real smile and her forced smile had started to look the same to me. I should have been able to tell, after all these years. I really should.

"That's good," she said.

It was getting chilly out, and it was already chilly in. I shrugged out of my finery and padded over to the closet, dressing quickly in undershorts, black leather trousers, blousy black cotton shirt, and—lest I look like Johnny Cash—a long brown cloak, fastened loosely at the breastbone by a blackened brass clasp. I took a rose from the vase on our nightstand, sniffed at it once, and stuck it in the clasp, examining myself in the dressing mirror.

I'm not entirely sure I liked the sharp-eyed fellow who looked back at me, although he was good-looking enough.

Pretty darned handsome, in fact, the features regular, and there was kind of a pleasant Eastern cast to his eyes. Nice firm jawline, and clever mouth under the Fu Manchu-style mustache. He was well into his forties, but there were only hints of lines at the edges of his eyes, although the touches of gray at the temple were pretty nice—too bad that the gray was as lopsided as the smile.

It was clear from that far-too-easy smile that he spent too much time being entirely too pleased with himself, but it wasn't clear to me that there was enough character in his face for that to be at all reasonable.

It was entirely possible that he was thinking about how he was going out on the road with a particularly attractive old friend of his, and how—what with her son having cleverly been talked out of joining him—he might arrange to get his ashes properly hauled.

It was also possible that he was thinking about how wrong it was to be thinking about that in front of his wife. I doubt it, though. Like I say, I'm not entirely sure I liked the guy.

"What are you thinking?" she asked, as though we were a normal husband and wife, the kind who could ask each other that kind of question and expect an honest answer.

Kirah, I thought, *what happened to us?* "Well," I said, putting on my reassuring smile, "I'm thinking I'm practically naked." Close enough.

I went to the dresser and put on my weapons: throwing knives properly stowed, pistols in their holsters, master belt holding both shortsword and my long, pointed dagger. I know that a bowie is a better weapon, but I like the dagger better. Tradition, and all that.

Besides, I'm used to it.

I rolled up my hunting vest and stuck it under an arm. The Therranji garrottes were in two of the pockets.

She put down her knitting or tatting or whatever it was and walked to the chifforobe in the corner.

"Here," she said, handing me a full leather rucksack. "Clothes, some dried beef, a few candies, everything you need." She smiled up at me. "Almost."

69

I stuffed the vest inside, then slung it over a shoulder. "Thanks." I kissed the tips of my fingers and touched the air in front of her.

She leaned toward my hand and swallowed once, twice, hard. "You'll be back soon?"

Of course, I should have said. *Don't worry.* "Do you want me to?"

"Yes." She nodded. "Oh, yes. I do."

"Then why not—good."

She waited expectantly, her face upturned. No matter how many times it went wrong, I always thought that if I moved slowly enough, gently enough, she would be okay. This time it would be okay.

Asshole.

"It's okay, Kirah," I said, putting my arms around her. For a moment, just a moment, I thought it would be okay, now that she could let me touch her again.

But she shook her head once, emphatically, and then again, violently, and then she set her hands on my chest and pushed me away. "*No.*"

I walked out of the room, ignoring the whimper behind me.

Dammit, it's not my fault.

There was a farewell committee waiting for us down in the stables: Doria, Aeia, Durine, Kethol, and Pirojil. Bren Adahan had been left to keep the village wardens company.

The riding horses had already been saddled, and the two-horse team hitched to the wagon.

I settled for just checking my cinch straps and finding a carrot for the dappled mare that Tennetty had picked out for me before hitching the horse to the back of the flatbed wagon. I was going to drive the flatbed, but I wanted a riding horse, too. You never know when you're going to need to get away quickly, or across country. Flatbeds and fields don't get along.

Ahira was already on the back of his small gray mare, and as I walked through the wide doors, Tennetty swung up to the saddle of a nervous black gelding with a white blaze across his face, and kicked him into a clomp past the lanterns and out into the dark of the courtyard.

Andrea folded a blanket neatly across, twice, and set it down on the flatbed's seat before climbing on. "Let's go," she said, patting the seat next to her.

Doria, still in her purple evening dress, looked at me, pursed her lips and shrugged. "Take care of yourself, Walter," she said. Her fingers kneaded my shoulders for just a moment, and then she kissed me gently on the lips. "Watch out, eh?"

"For who?" I shot her a prizewinning smile she didn't return.

"All of you," she said. "Particularly Andrea."

I didn't know how things were going to break with Aeia—hell, I didn't know how I wanted them to break—until I heard myself saying, "Walk me to the gate—the rest of them will catch up in a moment."

I caught the dwarf's eye; I spread the fingers of one hand wide for a moment. *Give me five minutes, okay?*

He repeated the gesture and nodded. *Not six*, that meant.

Aeia and I walked out of the stables and into the dark. I could almost feel hostile eyes on my back, and wondered what window Bren Adahan was looking down from. Torches ringing the keep crackled in the still air, sending clouds of dark smoke into the dark sky. Above, a gazillion stars stared back at us, hanging intently on our every motion, every word. Or maybe not.

She was still wearing the Melawei-inspired outfit she had worn to dinner; I mentally worked at the complicated knot at her left hip.

"You're scared about this," Aeia said.

"Always am." And that was true enough. "Wake up scared in the morning, go to bed scared at night."

She laughed, a warm, coppery sound like a carefully bowed cello. "You couldn't have persuaded me of that when I was a little girl. My Uncle Walter scared? Nothing could scare my Uncle Walter, any more than . . ." she grasped at the air, looking for the right analogy, ". . . it could scare my father."

I chuckled. "Well, half right. Karl was too dumb to be scared."

71

She took my hand and we walked in silence, holding hands like a couple of schoolkids. "Just a couple of days?"

I shrugged. "Probably. Could be a few more. Or things could really heat up and we might be gone for awhile. You never know." It was like in the old raiding days, when a team would head out on the road, looking for trouble, usually finding it in the form of a slaver caravan. Slavers have to move the property around, particularly new property. People have a tendency to form relationships with other people, even if they own them. Bad for their business.

I never really liked those days, back when I was seconding Karl. Yes, there was a certain something to them; the parts that Karl didn't participate in were often kind of nice. See, not all of the folks we freed over the years were men. Some of them, quite a few, were women, and some of those were more than a little attractive. It's amazing how grateful a woman can be when you've just freed her, and often spectacular how she'll show her gratitude. You could ask my wife about that.

Besides, the money was good.

But . . .

"Bren's asked me to go with him over to Little Pittsburgh," she said. "What do you think I should do?"

"Little Pittsburgh's an interesting place," I said. "A bit dirty and sooty, but interesting."

"That wasn't what I meant."

"I know." Her hand was warm in mine. "You meant that we're going to have to make a decision sometime," I said. "Bren won't wait forever. Kirah won't not-see forever. We're going to have to decide what we are."

She nodded. "You can add that I won't wait forever. But I wasn't asking for forever, I wasn't asking about eventually. I was asking for now. What are we to be now, Walter Slovotsky?"

I rubbed my thumb against the softness of her hands. "Friends, at least."

She stiffened and let go of my hand, and touched herself above the waist at the right side. The air between us chilled, and I remembered Aeia holding a rifle straight, cheek welded to stock, squeezing the trigger gently, ignoring the red wetness spreading across the right side of her waist.

"Comrades-in-arms," she said, her voice holding a trace of that Cullinane coldness. "At least."

"Of course." I gestured an apology. "Always," I said.

The coldness broke into a smile. "Better." She put her hands on my face and kissed me hard.

As we rode through the gate, Andy started to say something but caught herself. Just as well.

CHAPTER FIVE

In Which I Ride at Night, and Rediscover What a Pain in the Ass It Is

I will not give sleep to my eyes, or slumber to my eyelids.
—PROVERBS 132:4

RIDING DOWN A COUN-
try road in the dark was interesting at first. Ahead, the road curved and bent, twisting gently through fields and past villages, as the horses clopped through the dark, the rhythm of their hooves always in awkward syncopation; someday, I'm going to get a string of horses with matching strides.

It was dark, but not cloudy; the stars above shone their pale light over the landscape, turning it all delicate shades from the palest of whites to a rich, velvety black. The night was rich with sounds, from the distant hoot of an owl and the skritching of insects to the quiet *whisshhh* of wind through the trees. Night near a forest always smells vaguely of mint to me.

But it all palls quickly.

Ahead, the road did just what roads do: it went straight for awhile, then it bent, then it went straight again. The stars above shone their pale white light over the landscape, robbing it of all color except a hint of sickly blue, turning the night into something seen on an old black-and-white TV set.

And all the while, the horses just clopped on down the road, every once in a while relieving themselves, filling the air with the scents of manure and horse piss.

Rather have a Buick, thank you much.

Actually, just for the entertainment value, I would have settled for Ahira's eyes. Dwarves can see deeper into the infrared than humans can, and not only does that give them two colors the rest of us don't have, it's a huge benefit in the dark. (It's also why their warrens are usually lit by glowsteels rather than heat sources—a torch puts out a *lot* of IR.)

We kept quiet, generally. It really would have been perfectly reasonable to talk as we rode, except that I had a vision of somebody lying in ambush chuckling over how easy we were making it as we rode under a tree. Without the distraction of conversation, either Ahira or I might be able to pick up a stray sound, if there was some trouble ahead.

Now, if I'd really thought that there was going to be trouble ahead, we wouldn't have been out here; I would have been safely in my bed at the castle instead of sitting on the hard seat of a flatbed, each rut in the road bashing the back of the seat against my kidneys.

By the time we arrived in Velen, my eyes were aching from lack of sleep, the sun was hanging mockingly over the horizon, and there were buzzards in the air to the southwest.

CHAPTER SIX

In Which We Encounter Some Wolves

There are no compacts between lions and men, and wolves and sheep have no concord.

—HOMER

How come you can never find a dragon when you need one?
—WALTER SLOVOTSKY

BY THE TIME WE GOT TO the buzzards, it was well onto midmorning. The buzzards had settled down both onto the carcass and onto the cornfield surrounding it.

Heedless of the damage she was doing to the calf-high corn rows, Tennetty rode hard at the birds, scattering them into flight.

I guess they didn't know about her; they took her seriously enough to beat their wings lazily into the air, but half a dozen took up residence in a neighboring oak, squawking out complaints and verbal abuse. Middle Lands buzzards are smaller than I'd always thought Other Side buzzards are (I've never actually seen an Other Side buzzard, so I'm not sure)— about the size of a big crow, huge ugly wattles hanging under wickedly curved beaks. Hideous things.

Bones aching, I set the brake and climbed down from the flatbed.

What we had here was the typical local setup: a dirt road

ran diagonally across a vaguely rectangular piece of land, vanishing into the dark of the forest on either side. The woods could be only a strip of a few dozen yards, left mainly as a windbreak, or they could be much deeper.

The road was edged with a low stone retaining wall that raised it about two feet above flat ground level. I'd seen better-maintained retaining walls; this one was a bit fallen down. But that wasn't my problem. It was the baron's problem, and his tax collectors'—they were supposed to be sure that the farmer was maintaining his well and roads.

The house, such as it was, was a half-timber, wattle-and-daub shack next to the road. A hedged privy, a dubious chicken coop, and the ubiquitous stone well were the only other structures. There was some movement over in the crofter's shack, and that would have to be attended to, but I wanted to take a look at the cow first.

Or what was left of it. The wolves had done a good job, and the buzzards had been working hard to finish it. They—the wolves; buzzards don't eat take-out food—had dragged it about thirty feet through the field, doing even more damage to the young corn than Tennetty had.

The cow was a stinking, bloody mess, half-covered with flies.

I was kind of relieved. Back when I was majoring in meat science, I had to slaughter a lot of cows, and the part I hated most was the killing, and dealing with the fresh-dead. You have this pneumatic stunner—looks like a bull-barrel shotgun, sort of, connected by hose to a compressor—and you put it up against the cow's forehead and pull the trigger. The air pressure sends out the hammer—basically, just a piston—which gives the cow a sharp rap on the skull, hard enough to knock it unconscious at the least, break bones more often. At which point you hoist it, cut it, and let it bleed out.

Messy work, but within just a few minutes, you don't have something that looks like a cow anymore; you've got parts. Sides of beef, viscera, tongue. Skin flayed off, waiting to be tanned.

We had even less than that here. The wolves had eaten about half the cow. Actually, they had eaten or carried off the rear half of the cow, legs and all, leaving the front half more mutilated than eaten.

It didn't make sense. It was too neat—in too many places, the flesh had been bit through cleanly. Possible for a wolf, I guess, although he would have had to be trying hard to be neat. And why would that be? Who would teach a wolf to play with his food?

But it *was* wolves—their prints were all over the soft ground. The pack had headed off to the northeast, into the woods.

Ahira and Andrea had left their horses hitched to the wagon; they joined Tennetty over the bloody mess, the three of them waving clouds of flies away.

The dwarf's brow furrowed. "It looks like the rear half of this thing is gone, bitten clean away."

Andy raised an eyebrow. "You mean, like what Ellegon would do?"

Ahira didn't answer.

There was more movement inside the shack. Tennetty stalked over and pounded on the door with the hilt of her shotgun.

"Out. Everybody *out. Now.* We need to talk to you," she said. You can always trust Tennetty to know just the right way to put everything.

I would have sworn that the ramshackle building wouldn't have held more than a couple of people, but in a few minutes a family of seven stood nervously on the dirt, the mother holding a baby in her arms, the youngest daughter—cute despite the dirt; they can do cute real well at that age—holding a struggling chicken tightly.

Tennetty ducked inside. I wished that she would talk things over before she did them; these sorts of things can be death traps.

But she came out laughing—not just giggling, but laughing *hard*, one hand holding her stomach. I thought she was going to drop the shotgun. "Yeah," she managed to wheeze out, in between gales of laughter, "they've got a . . . cow in there. And a goat, and I think there's some, some chickens in the cellar."

Ahira and Andrea were over with the family, trying to

calm them down. I sort of got the impression that having a bunch of strangers with guns around wasn't either normal or comfortable for them.

On the other hand, when she turns on her smile, Andrea can charm bark off a tree.

"Greetings, all," she said. "We're just here to look into your wolf problem. The baron sent us."

"Old or new?" the woman asked, suspicious of us, if not of the notion of the nobility looking into predators.

"New," she said. "Baron Cullinane. We work for him. Tennetty, Daherrin, Worelt, and Lotana," she said, indicating us in turn.

I'd had a moment of nervousness. Andrea's always had an unfortunate tendency to honesty, and four of us have gotten fairly famous through the Eren regions. That can be handy, but more often it's a problem: more than a few idiots would like to see what holding onto the former Empress of Holtun-Bieme would get them. (Dead is what it would get them, I hope. But maybe they don't know that. Or maybe they don't care what I hope.) And lots of folks would like to find out if they're better with a shortsword than One-Eyed Tennetty or faster with a knife than Walter Slovotsky. (Yes, there are both; but you'll understand that I'd prefer not to demonstrate that.)

Andy's instincts were right on the money: she had picked out false names for the three of us, but not for Tennetty. Tennetty was fairly famous in her own right—women warriors weren't common, particularly one-eyed ones—and giving her a false name might be a clue that the rest of us were traveling under false colors.

The man ducked his head. "Begging your pardon, but—"

His wife shook her head, quickly. "No."

"I saw them," he insisted.

"How many?"

"Half a dozen, perhaps more. Wolves, yes, but . . ."

"But what?"

"There was something else," he said.

Andy's gentle smile broadened. I think she was trying to look reassuring, but she came off as amused. "And what might that be?"

He gripped at the air in front of him. "It looks like a wolf, just like a wolf, but it isn't." The words came fast, as though stumbling out. "I saw; I know. It isn't. It is larger, it moves strange, it isn't a wolf, it just looked like one."

I gave it a try. "What do you mean, it wasn't a wolf, but just looked like one?"

His fingers twitched in frustration. "It didn't *move* right. It bends in the wrong parts."

"A wolf that bends in the wrong places," Tennetty said. "Doesn't sound like a major problem to me." Tennetty dismissed them with a gesture; they filed back into the hut, although we could feel their eyes on us.

"It was a day and a half ago," Ahira said, *sotto voce.* "Wolves can cover a lot of territory in a day and a half. If they want to."

I wish I'd taken that zoology class. What was the dynamic of pack wolves? Did they have a territory, or—

Andrea knelt next to a pile of turds, one hand in her wizard's bag.

"Hang on a moment," I said, irritated. "I don't—"

"If you can come up with a better way to find them than with a location spell, Walter," she said, "then let's get to it."

"I'm a fairly good tracker," I admitted. Traditionally, it's the job of the nobility to protect the peasants, whether it's from invading raiders or wandering wolves. We weren't the local nobility, not really, but we were sitting in for him.

"Not good enough." Tennetty shook her head. "In a few days, if they're holed up and not on the move, you should be able to find them. In the meantime, not only do they fatten themselves on the local cattle, but we have to sleep during the heat of the day and hunt through the night."

"On the other hand, Andrea's supposed to keep her use of magic to a minimum. It's not healthy—"

"—for you to be talking about me in the third person," Andy said, her smile wide, but not particularly pleasant.

Ahira held up a hand. "We are all tired. But let's think it through." He ticked it off on blunt fingers. "We've got no problem with having wolves around, as long as they know enough to stay away from people. These don't." He added a finger. "They aren't going after cattle because other game is

scarce: it isn't. They have a taste for beef, and aren't frightened enough of humans. So they have to go. It's cool in the
woods—we'll duck off the road into the woods and pitch the
sleeping tarp, everybody gets some rest, and then a hot meal,
and then we hunt late in the afternoon."

He frowned. "With the location spell."

No point in putting it off any longer. The horses were saddled,
the guns loaded and lashed into place. My bow was only half-
strung, slung over my chest, two dozen widebladed hunting
arrows stuck into the quiver on my back. (Yes, stuck—you
don't want the arrows falling out if you take a fall.) A flask
of Eareven healing draught was strapped to my left calf—my
scabbard kept banging into it.

My hand was sweaty where it gripped the boar spear. It's
the best hand-to-hand hunting weapon ever invented: six feet
of shaft, grip points wound with leather and brass, topped by
a long, fist-wide blade. About two feet back of the blade was
the crosspiece. The classic crosspiece is just that: a piece of
brass intended to hold whatever you've just stabbed at arm's
length. Some genius—no, not one of us; we don't have the
patent on genius—had modified it into kind of a U-shaped
staple, points sharp, but unbarbed. The result looked like a
trident with a glandular condition.

Tennetty held four of the horses. They stood prancing,
waiting, while Andy, in a ring of torches, crouched over the
wolf shit. There was something in her expression that took
me way back.

Once, a long time ago, I saw a little corgi who had just
been hit by a car, about half a block from the vet's. My
brother Steve and I were walking home from school and just
came in at the end of it. Dr. MacDonald, a comically rotund
little man, came running, a black bag like a real doctor's in
his hand. He knelt over the little dog.

I don't remember much about the dog itself—I looked
away.

But I do remember the look in Dr. Mac's face as he
loaded the syringe: not only a kind of sedate compassion, but
a raging unhurried competence. I misread it, and I grabbed
for Steve's arm. "He's going to be able to save it."

Steve shook his head. "No. He's going to make the dog stop hurting."

There was that same something in Andrea's face as she silently knelt on the dust, oddments of bone and beak and feather spread out in front of her in the shape of a run-over bird.

With medical precision, she cleaned the ball of her left thumb, then pricked it with the razor point of a knife she had borrowed from Tennetty, letting one, two, three fat drops of blood well up, then fall into the dirt and the wolf turds.

The fire flared higher as she spoke, first in a quiet mumble, the volume growing steadily as her voice became clearer, uttering words that could only be heard but never remembered, smooth sibilants that vanished on the ear and in the mind. The torches flickered higher as she screamed out the vanishing syllables.

For a moment, just a moment, I thought that nothing would happen. There's a part of me that doesn't really believe in magic.

But then a feather twitched, and a piece of bone began to vibrate, and the twitching feather was joined by a white, ghostly one, as was the bone, and then another and another. Bits of feather and bone, both real and pale simulacrums, assembled themselves into bird, and flapped into the air.

Ahira and Tennetty were already on their horses, the butts of their spears resting in their stirrups.

Andrea rose, her face pale and sweaty in the firelight. "Quickly, now," she said, her voice a husky hiss. "The bird will try to keep itself halfway between me and the wolf. Let us hurry."

We cantered off toward the setting sun.

Just to show you what an asshole a kid from New Jersey can be, I used to think that riding a cantering horse was sort of like driving a fast car. Yes, I thought, you have to worry about bumping into stuff, but physically demanding, nah. Except on the horse.

Well, a lot I knew.

We clopped down roads, cut across fields—yes, careless of the damage to crops, but conscious of the damage a pack of wolves can do to the local livestock—avoiding cutting through the woods.

Ahead, the bird fluttered, barely visible, constantly slowing, but always flying just a little too fast, just a little too far for us to ease up on the horses. Riding a fast-moving horse is hard.

Yes, my mare would jump over a drainage ditch, but I had to hang on to her back as she leaped the ditch, and landing was every bit as hard on me as it would have been if I was doing the jumping. Not to mention the way the saddle of the usually-cantering and sometimes-galloping horse kept threatening to slam the base of my spine into the base of my skull.

I was about to call a halt, using as my excuse that I didn't think the horses could take it, when the bird stopped at the edge of a field, perched itself neatly on a gnarled limb, then dissolved into a shower of feathers and bones.

I looked over at Andrea.

She nodded; the spell had dissolved because we were close, not because it had run out of magic.

The woods blocked out the setting sun, loomed dark and menacing.

Ahira was already on the ground, his boar spear in his hand. He planted it solidly in the ground, then picked up his crossbow, quickly cocking it and slipping in a bolt.

"Tennetty, keep your spear ready, but get your rifles and bow out. Andrea, shotgun on the half-cock—"

I slipped from my saddle and started to string my bow.

Ahira shook his head. "Nope; Walter, you work your way around and drive them toward us." He tossed me a pair of grenades.

I chuckled bravely as I stowed the grenades in my vest. Well, it was supposed to be a brave chuckle, but it sounded forced to me; I just hope the others weren't quite as perceptive.

"And what if they decide to run toward me instead of you?"

He chuckled back. "Then I'd suggest you climb a tree. Quickly."

Skulking through the woods is partly art, but mainly craft.

It doesn't matter who or what you are: if you try to walk on the floor of a forest—twigs, dry leaves, and God-knows-what-else underfoot—you will make noise. The trick is to stick to hard-packed dirt, to flat rock and green grass. This can get a bit complicated when you're also being damn sure to stay within dashing range of a tree.

I circled around downwind of where the wolf pack should have been, making more noise than I would have liked, but not enough to carry very far. The idea was to spook them after all, and drive them in the direction of my friends.

Nice thing to do to your friends, eh?

Well, it was Ahira's idea, not mine. And it shouldn't be a problem—that's what the guns and the bow were for. Not that that was my problem, not now. My problem was keeping myself alive and unbit while I located the pack.

Hmm. If I were running a wolf pack, I'd have posted scouts some distance away from the body of the group. It would be an interesting mathematical problem—the farther away the circle of watchers, the more warning they could give, but the more of them you'd need. Probably susceptible to some sort of minimax solution, or game theory analysis, but I don't guess that wolves do either.

The other way, of course, would be—either instead of or in addition to posting scouts—to have some roaming watchmen making regular tours.

I don't know whether it was a hidden watchman or a roamer I'd missed that jumped me. With barely a rustling of leaves and twigs, two hundred pounds of coarse fur and awful stink lunged out of the dark brush for me, teeth unerringly aimed at my leg.

—Which wasn't there. Emma Slovotsky's baby boy doesn't wait around to get bitten by a wolf.

I danced out of his way and kicked him as he passed—it didn't hurt him, but it made his lunge carry him past me.

By the time he had spun around, I was already up the nearest tree, chinning myself on a thick branch, my stomach left somewhere behind me on the ground.

As I clambered the rest of the way to the branch, shouts

and shots echoed off in the distance, but they seemed less important than the way the wolf scrabbled at the bark of the tree as he tried to get at me.

He howled once, then went silent—he didn't snarl, didn't growl. The silence was more frightening than snarling would have been. The way he crouched down in preparation for a leap was even worse.

I know I'm supposed to be completely cool and calm at all times, but it's only in the job description—it has nothing to do with reality. My fingers trembled as I pulled a grenade out of my vest, and tried to strike the fuse on the patch of roughness on its side. From the shots and shouts off in the distance, it sounded like the other part of the fight had already taken off, but it still made sense to scare any remaining wolves in their direction.

Meanwhile, my new friend was eyeing me silently, in between leaps up the side of the tree that brought his awful yellow teeth within inches of my ankles. I thought about trying to pull myself up so I could stand on the branch instead of sitting on it, and decided that I could too easily lose my balance trying. I thought about kicking at his face, but I only thought about it.

It took three strikes until the grenade's fuse sputtered into life, and I pitched it hard in what I hoped was the direction of the pack, and then turned to deal with the lone wolf.

I wish I could report that I did something clever or heroic, but all I did was pull one of my brace of pistols, and cock it. The next time he gathered himself for a leap it gave me a stable enough target to aim at, and I gently squeezed the trigger. Shooting down is supposed to be hard, but that's only when you're shooting out and down—you tend to compensate for the distance to the target instead of the horizontal component of the distance.

But with wolfie ten feet directly below me, I just laid my iron sights low on his chest and pulled the trigger, rewarded by a bang, a cloud of foul smoke, and a gout of flesh and gore from the base of his neck.

He took a half dozen wobbly steps back, then fell over, watching me with glassy eyes as I clambered down.

It wasn't anything personal, not anymore. Wolfie was just

protecting his pack, the way I was protecting mine, and I'd happened to be equipped with weapons he wasn't genetically prepared to deal with. I'd say I was sorry about that, but I really wasn't.

What I was sorry about was that we were on opposite sides. He reminded me of an old friend as he growled at my approach, yellow teeth bared for one last try, wanting a last taste of an enemy's blood in his mouth.

I slipped one of my throwing knives into my hand and flung it hard, burying the point in his throat, slicing through the jugular. Blood wet his chest and darkened the ground.

He died quickly.

I know that the grenade had gone off sometime during all that, and I know I'm supposed to be able to pay attention to everything that's going on, but I honestly don't remember when it happened. Look: I'm no hero, but it wasn't cowardice that kept me there with the dead wolf for a long moment.

I guess what it was, was that I felt like shit.

I felt like giving the dead body a pat, but that wouldn't have done any good, so I ran off into the forest.

Thick brush clawed at me in the dimming light. My sense of direction is unerring, so I knew that I was just feet away from where the strip of forest broke on cleared land, but for the life of me I couldn't see it.

I broke through into soft dirt and a battlefield lit by the red and orange light of a setting sun.

It was still too light out for stars, but the faerie lights were already out in force. Under their pulsations, wolf bodies and parts of wolf bodies lay scattered across the ground, most with arrows protruding from their immobile sides, others chewed by leaden teeth. One had fought his way through the rain of lead and steel to reach Ahira; it lay on the ground, still struggling at the end of his boar spear.

Only one stood, squared off against Andy and Tennetty.

Ahira freed the boar spear with a wrench that sent the wolf into a final spasm, and turned to face the last wolf.

Except that it wasn't a wolf.

It *looked* like a wolf, all right, albeit an overlarge, gray one. I would have assumed it was just the alpha male—until it moved. It didn't bend at the joints, the way any animal did—it flowed, liquidly, legs snaking instead of bending as it moved.

Tennetty fired a pistol into its side, but either she missed or it didn't do anything important: whatever it was just shuddered and braced itself for a leap, no sound escaping through its bared teeth.

Andy brought up her shotgun, but she's never been much of a gunner: the blast dug up a spray of dirt to one side.

The wolf-thing lunged for her.

That was when Ahira, grunting with the effort, drove his boar spear down into its chest, shoving the tripartite head of the spear not only through the wolf-thing, but a full two feet into the soft dirt, pinning it to the ground like a bug on display.

Its legs squirmed like snakes, and ripples shook its body from nose to tail, until its bright eyes went dull and glassy, then dark, as the spasms subsided.

Ahira gave one last shove to the boar spear and then released it.

I had been running toward them across the soft ground, staggering more than once as I almost fell flat on my face, although God alone knew what I could do. Now I let myself ease into a slow walk. You don't have to run when the enemy's dead.

Tennetty let her swordpoint drop and wiped it on her leggings before putting it away in her scabbard. She walked over to where another boar spear protruded from the body of a dead wolf, set her booted foot against the wolf's side, and wrenched the spear loose. She leaned on the spear like a farmer leaning on his hoe.

"Shit, Walter," she called out. "You missed all the fun."

Things had gotten closer than they should have. The wolves should have just run away, and been picked off with bow and guns, not charged en masse. Ahira and his boar spear had been intended to be a sort of free safety, to pick off any problems that the guns and bow missed.

Ahira staggered away a pace or two. He squatted on the soft ground, then sat down hard, breathing heavy.

I stood over him. "A bit close, eh?" I offered him a hand, but he shook his head.

"Too close," he said. "They were working as a team; it was like that thing was directing them." He gestured at the wolf-thing lying on the ground, his spear still stuck through it.

Andrea smiled as she wiped her brow. "Now I remember why I've always let the rest of you do field work." She gestured toward the wolf-thing. "What *is* that?"

Ahira shook his head. "There's been talk of strange things coming out of Faerie; looks like we've just killed one of them." His mouth pursed into a line, then relaxed. It didn't matter what it was, now that it was dead.

I was going to say something, no doubt something clever, but Andy's eyes widened and her mouth opened.

"Ohmi*god.*"

The wolf-thing rose, its formerly dull eyes now glowing, its body flowing around the boar spear like water. It shook itself, like a dog, sending the boar spear tumbling end over end into the air. The spear left behind no mark in its dark fur.

Oh, shit.

It took a growling step toward Ahira, flattening itself for a leap.

Tennetty danced toward it with her own boar spear, but she overcommitted herself: a grizzled paw, moving bonelessly, slapped the spear out of the way and out of her hands. She was clawing for her sword when the thing leaped on her.

Ahira was too far away, and he was between Andy and the ground where the wolf-thing was savaging Tennetty; it was up to me.

The right thing to do, the only sensible thing for me to do, would have been to stand back and put a throwing knife in the right place. The only trouble with that plan was that the two of them were rolling around so fast that there was no way of doing that—I'd be as likely to put the knife into Tennetty as into it. Still, there was that flask of dragonbane extract in my vest; I could drip some down the blade, hoping that this was one of the creatures with the kind of magical metabolism that dragonbane screwed up.

In any case, the silliest thing to do would be to leap on its back and try to plant a knife in just the right spot, but only an idiot would try it, and I'm not an idiot. Karl was an idiot—that's the sort of thing he would have done.

Me, I'm too smart.

My reflexes, on the other hand, were stupid: before I quite knew what I was doing, I had pulled one of my Therranji garrottes from my vest and had leaped for its back.

Tennetty's arm, through deliberation or accident, was jammed in its teeth. It was the only time I had ever heard Tennetty scream. The creature had flattened its chest and torso, cupping Tennetty's waist, threatening to flow over and engulf her.

I flung one arm around its neck and clung to its back like a rider on a runaway horse, but it was like clinging to hard jello: there was no hard muscle, no bone against which to gain purchase. Somehow or other—damned if I know how— I was able to lock my ankles together beneath it as I tried to slip the garrotte around its neck, but Tennetty's arm was in the way.

"*Let go,*" I shouted. "FortheloveofGod, leggo."

Somehow, I managed to get the wire around the neck and to work the handle through the loop.

I jerked hard; the garrotte disappeared into the dense fur. Now it was supposed to writhe uselessly, trying to remove the garrotte from its neck, while it died, this time for keeps. But the wolf-thing didn't stop—if anything its struggles intensified, as it rolled over, slamming all of us hard into the ground.

Things got a bit vague there for a moment, but I tried to hang on as, with a hard shake, it dislodged Tennetty. The neck turned impossibly far around for me as we rolled around the ground together.

I *think* I remember slipping a throwing knife into my free hand, and then into the thing's side, but I don't think that would quite have been possible.

Somewhere in all that it managed to dislodge my dagger, but I managed to cling to its back . . .

. . . until a double-bending flip that a creature with a real spine wouldn't have been able to pull off flung me out and down, hard.

Some gifts won't ever leave me: I hit the soft ground with a proper slap-and-roll, my left arm numb from the shock. I staggered to my feet—

"It's mine," Andrea Andropolous Cullinane said, her quiet voice piercing through the shouts and growls.

She had dropped her smoking rifle. Now she shrugged out of her cloak, dropping it negligently to one side, ignoring the chill air as she faced the wolf-thing, the sun over her shoulder framing her in all the colors of fire. Ahira was at her side, his axe now in his hands, but he moved away at her gesture.

She faced off against the wolf-thing.

"Be gone; you will not harm me or mine," she said. "I tell you once." She tossed her head, clearing the hair from her eyes. Her tongue snaked out and touched her full lips once, twice, three times.

The wolf-thing took a hesitant, flowing step toward her.

Her smile was thin as she raised a hand, strong, slim fingers stroking the air in front of her. "Be gone, now and forever. I tell you twice."

A low thrumming filled the air as she thrust her arms out in front of her, fingers spread, but cupped forward.

The light of the setting sun started to take liquid form, threads of gleaming honey rolling across her fingers, splashing on the ground all about her. At the touch of the liquid light, sticks and bits of stray straw flashed into flame, and the earth itself began to smolder.

The heat flashing on my face was hotter than a forge.

"Move back, move back," the dwarf said.

His face red and sweaty, Ahira scooped up Tennetty in one arm and seized my waist, dragging me backwards, although I really didn't need any encouragement. Still, I couldn't turn my back.

Andrea took a smooth step forward, toward the wolf-thing, one foot swinging out and planting itself firmly in the dirt, her hips swaying, grinding with an intensity that was almost sexual. Or maybe not almost; I don't know much about magic.

She let the strands of light play through her fingers as it crouched for a leap.

"Be gone, I tell you a third and last time."

She lowered her voice and the stream of light began to darken, and at first I thought that the spell wasn't working, but no: the thrumming grew louder and higher, the volume and pitch and violence of the sound growing, until it screamed like a Jimi Hendrix guitar riff.

The sound pressed the thing back.

Andy spread her fingers wide, and gathered up gleaming strands of golden dusk. Deft fingers, inhumanly powerful and delicate, wove the strands into a stream of braided ruby light that flowed from her fingers, splashing hard against the wolf-thing. Where the stream touched the wolf-thing, it burned, spattering flaming gobbets of flesh off into the air.

I tripped Ahira and forced him and Tennetty down.

Andrea screamed harsh syllables that could never be remembered, as the sound grew louder, pressing down on the world, the light so bright I had to cover my eyes.

Just in time. Even with my lids squeezed painfully tight, the flash dazzled me, and heat washed over me in a wave.

Worst thing in the world is to be blind during a fight—I forced my eyes open.

Sweat streaming down her face, Andy stood on a mound of dirt that poked above one of two irregular puddles of lava. A cloud of darkness hovered above the other, already dissipating.

"Be gone," Andrea said, quietly. "It's done."

"For here and now," the cloud said, its voice deep, but airy. "But you have ruined my fun. Perhaps I shall ruin yours some time."

She muttered something, then looked up, expectantly. Nothing. "Who are you?" she said.

The voice laughed. It wasn't a nice laugh. "Not all your rules work on me, though some do. I'll not give you a handle with which to hold me, or turn me. Call me, oh, Boioardo, though that never was and is not now my name."

She muttered another spell, and started to raise her hand, fingers crooked awkwardly.

"Oh, let me have a few more moments," Boioardo said.

91

"Perhaps you'll appreciate it, should we meet in a Place with different rules."

Faerie? I thought. "No, Andy. End it now."

Tennetty was starting to come around; I gathered her up in my arms, ready to run. I'm better at running than the dwarf is—although if Andy couldn't hold the thing, we were all cooked.

"Ah. So clever, Walter Slovotsky of Secaucus. Will you be so clever in the Place Where Trees Scream, or the Place Where Only That Which You Have Loved Can Help You?"

"Of course." I forced a smile; bravado is always a cheap thrill. "I'll be even cleverer; it's part of my charm."

Perhaps it wasn't going to be a cheap thrill—the darkness started to move toward me.

"*No.* Be gone," Andrea said, straightening her fingers. She muttered another word, and wind blew the darkness away, into the light of the setting sun.

It was gone. We stood alone in the dusk, wisps of smoke rising from the field. Ahira was bent over Tennetty, dealing with her wounds; Andrea stood on the mound of dirt rising above the darkening pool of lava, her face reddened, her whole body beaded with sweat.

Smoothly she turned, balanced like a dancer. "I think, dear friends, I'll take an attaboy on that one." She leaped lightly across the puddle of lava, took three steps toward us, and fainted dead away.

CHAPTER SEVEN

In Which Ellegon Shows Up and Points Out an Obligation

I was gratified to be able to answer promptly, and I did. I said I didn't know.

—MARK TWAIN

I'd always liked Robert Thompson's idea of avoiding compromise, of letting the person with the strong convictions have his own way . . . and then I realized that encouraged people to have strong convictions when they don't have enough data.

—WALTER SLOVOTSKY

THERE WAS A BRIGHT golden haze on the meadow. The corn was as high as an elephant's eye—granted, it would have had to have been a small elephant, and maybe the critter would have had to squat a bit. And—no shit, I was there—it looked like it was climbing clear up to the sky.

"Fuck you, morning," I murmured, *sotto voce*. I hate mornings. Never cared for *Oklahoma* much, either.

Well, we needed to keep somebody on watch. Tennetty had been banged up, and she had been reluctant to waste more healing draughts on herself than necessary—that stuff is expensive. Certainly worth more than my night's sleep. Andy was drained, and, besides, she's never had the kind of alertness to her surroundings that the dwarf and I have.

By the process of elimination, that left the dwarf and me, and, as usual, left me pissed off. (I shouldn't complain; for once it didn't leave me in deep shit.) Ahira and I had split the night, and while I think I'd gotten the better of the deal, I'd not gotten much the better of it.

We were camped on the edge of the woods, a few telltales protecting us from somebody or something sneaking around behind us, a single watchman—me—protecting our front. Field work is an exercise in applied paranoia.

Time to sit, and watch, and think, as the dawn brightened into morning.

A lot to think about in the night. Too much.

Whatever was happening on the edge of Faerie was no longer just somebody else's problem. It had struck close to home. It's not that I don't care if magical monsters mess with people elsewhere, but it's a big world, and I'm only one person. But my wife and kids were in Barony Cullinane. Boioardo, whatever he/it was, had mucked about in Barony Cullinane. That made it personal.

Still, it wouldn't hurt to spend some time around the barony instead of rushing off into trouble. Let the castle settle down, keep our ears open for a bit of news; let Tennetty heal on her own instead of using up expensive and rare healing draughts. Let me spend some more time with bow, sword, and pistol. I'd rather sit than run, run than fight, but I'd rather fight than die, thank you very much.

Maybe there was some way out of it. Sometimes, if you leave a problem alone long enough, somebody else solves it for you—Reagan diddled and twiddled his thumbs over the Osirak reactor outside of Baghdad until the Israelis took it out for him.

I would have been perfectly happy if the equivalent happened this time. Magic and humans don't tend to get along, I think; it's one of the reasons that we developed in other ways on the Other Side, and why the mundane tended to drive out the magical in the Eren regions. There was an age of dragons, when, if you believe the tales, clouds of them darkened the skies.

I didn't see what Stash and Emma's baby boy could do to halt the return of that sort of thing, even if I did want to put myself in the middle of it. Like trying to stop an oil spill by sticking your finger in a four-foot hole in the pipeline.

Sometimes, if you leave a problem alone long enough, somebody else solves it for you.

Like Kirah?

You've been really fucking clever in leaving that *alone, Walter,* I thought.

What should I do? Drop her, in favor of Aeia? Right; that'd be guaranteed to be good for Kirah's mental health. Try to force the issue? I wasn't about to lay my hands on a woman who shuddered when I touched her, and if somebody doesn't want to talk about something, there's no way to make her.

I sighed. I didn't see any good way out of it.

Maybe, just maybe, if I left her alone, if I kept the pressure off, if I didn't make it a matter of public record and public discussion, she'd work things out herself.

It was, at least, something to hope for.

Sometimes you have to settle for that.

Far off in the blue sky, a distant speck stopped moving erratically, and started down toward us.

Ellegon? I thought, trying to shout with my mind.

If it was him, he was too far off. Karl and particularly Jason have always had an unusually tight bond with the dragon, and could mindtalk with him at fair distances, but he and I have never been that close. Not possible, really—Ellegon knew Jason before Jason was born.

If it wasn't Ellegon, then it was trouble. There was that flask of rendered dragonbane in my vest; I got it out and pried the top off.

"Okay, everybody, we've got something inbound," I said, getting to my feet. "Battle stations, people."

Fight-or-flight is always a fun decision to make. When it's just me, I tend to vote with my feet—he who fights and runs away lives to run away another day and all that. But I couldn't outrun something that flies, not without a lot more than a bikini-wide strip of woods to hide my privates in.

I dipped three arrows in dragonbane and laid them gently on the rock in front of me. I could fire them quickly, and then flee even more quickly, if necessary.

The speck grew.

The sleeping bodies, all of them, had broken into a flurry of motion—Ahira shrugging into his clothes and armor; Andrea reaching for a rifle; Tennetty, her left arm bound up in a sling, bringing a pistol to the half-cock and tucking it in the front of her belt.

A familiar voice sounded in my head. *Walter, I would take it as a personal favor if you'd be kind enough to avoid killing me.*

At this distance, I could make out the familiar shape: large, saurian, huge, leathery wings beating the air.

I could practically hear the twang of my anus unclenching.

"And it's good to see you, too, Ellegon," I muttered, knowing that a whisper was as good as a shout at this distance.

Always a pleasure to be near the center of the known universe.

Eh?

The center of the universe—that spot just behind your forehead. Or just south of your belt buckle. You keep changing your, er, mind.

Just wait until you hit puberty.

In another century or two I'll be just like you. Sure. Once every dozen years or so. If I can even find a female dragon.

I muzzled a comment about "did the earth move for you, too"—

Just as well.

—as I unstrung my bow and set it aside. Accidents can happen—a quick flaming in the campfire burned the drag-onbane from the arrowheads, without costing me the arrows. Good arrows are expensive.

I looked up; the sky was clear.

Where are you?

Behind you, on final approach—passengers don't like my hard landings.

I rubbed at my tailbone. *So I recall.*

Chickenshit.

A dark shadow passed overhead; leathery wings snapped in the breeze as Ellegon braked in for a landing, then slammed down hard enough on the road fifty yards away that I could feel the ground shake.

Ellegon: more tons than I care to count of gray-green dragon, the size of a Greyhound bus studying hard to become a Boeing 737; long tail at one end, alligator head at other, with the usual vague wisp of steam or smoke issuing from between the dagger teeth.

The huge, saurian head eyed me with cold, heavy-lidded eyes. I guess Ellegon hadn't liked the 737 thought-slash-comment.

Good guess. The head turned away. A brief gout of fire issued from the cavernous mouth, red tongues of flame licking the dirt road.

The dragon lumbered forward a step and slumped to the ground on the warmed spot—I couldn't tell whether in fatigue or to make it easier for his passenger to climb down from the rigging on his back.

It's purely out of consideration. As we all know, I am the most considerate of dragons. The fact that I've spent most of the past three days with my aching wings pounding the air has nothing at all to do with it.

The passenger, of course, was Jason Cullinane. Some things are eminently predictable. He waved genially as he walked across the field toward us.

"Good morning," I said.

We could have used you yesterday, I didn't say. He'd work it out by himself. Eventually.

He hitched at his swordbelt, and at the shoulder holster that held a gun butt barely visible under his short jacket. "I thought, maybe . . ."

Ahira shook his head. "Don't 'think maybe,' next time. Think for sure."

I couldn't have put that better myself. I gestured at the log where I'd been sitting. "In the meantime, have a cuppa."

Back when we were both college students, a friend invited me up to her dorm room one Thursday to sit in on her weekly electronic conversation on one of the electronic information services—I can't remember for the life of me whether it was CompuSpend or the Source, or whatever. We sat in front of her Osborne—cute little machine—typing at the bunch of other folks, people from all over the country who were sitting typing at us. We occasionally wondered if they were sitting there naked . . . too.

The thing I remember most about it—well, the thing I remember second-most; it was a pretty good evening—is that the best, the most interesting parts of the six- or ten-handed electronic talk were the ones sent privately, below the surface of the public conversation, from one user to another.

Having Ellegon in on a meeting is kind of like that, even if the meeting is taking place while you're breaking camp.

Ahira tucked a folded tarpaulin carefully into his rucksack, tied the rucksack shut, then pitched it over to me; I tossed it into the flatbed wagon.

Tennetty took a tighter grip on the reins of the harnessed horses, who were prancing, snorting, nervously pissing, and otherwise indicating that they weren't happy. Horses tend to be nervous around Ellegon, probably for the same reason that a hamburger would tend to be nervous around me. Which is why Andy had already taken the saddle horses down the road.

Jason was sitting on the ground, his back against the base of a tree, his knees up; he set his cup of tea gently down on the soft moss. "We do have to look into what's coming out of Faerie. Ehvenor, eh?"

The boy has a keen eye for the obvious.

You're being too harsh, Ellegon said, his mental voice taking on that extra clarity, that particular brassy timbre that told me he was talking to me only. *Although he does have his father's subtlety, such as it is.*

The dwarf pitched me another bag of gear, then picked up a gnarled stick and took a last nervous stir at the ashes of the campfire. "Somebody has to." He pursed his lips for a moment. "I don't like it. Magic." He shuddered.

I chuckled. "You complaining about magic?" If it wasn't for magic, Ahira would still have been crippled James Michael Finnegan.

"Sure," he said. "And back on the Other Side, I would have complained about nuclear weapons, antibiotics, automobiles, and all other mixed blessings, too."

He looked over at Andrea. "How close do you have to be to find out what's going on?"

She gestured at a spot on the log she was sitting on. "Put

somebody or something who knows right there, and I don't have to be any closer than this."

Ahira raised an eyebrow. "Some sort of mind spell?"

"No, I'd ask him." She smiled.

"Very funny. Seriously, how far away from whatever is happening would you have to be to figure out what it is?"

She shrugged. "That would depend on what *is* going on. I might be able to read it anywhere from, say, three days ride to, maybe," she said with a squint, as she held her thumb and forefinger together right in front of her eyes, "this far from it."

"No way to do it from here? No matter what it is?"

She snorted. "Sure there is, if what's going on is broadly focussed *and* powerful *and* highly kinetic *and* unsubtle *and* unshielded, plus a couple more adjectives that wouldn't mean anything to you. But if it was, you'd have half the wizards throughout the Eren regions already alerted to it, and there would be . . . manifestations of that. So it isn't. So, if I'm going to find out what's going on, I've got to go see. The closer we get, the less I have to push myself in order to find it."

Ahira nodded. "I'll think it over." He looked over at me.

I knew what he was asking, but it was the wrong question. He was asking *when* instead of *whether*.

I shook my head. "No need to rush off without thinking. If we give it a couple of days, not only will we have time to pack intelligently, but we might be in better shape to hit the road."

"You sound too persuasive." Tennetty took a sip of her tea, and spat it out into the fire. "Gone cold on me." Her lips twitched. "You're not eager to go," she said.

"I'm not convinced we should go," I said. I hadn't liked the way Boioardo had looked at me, but I wasn't in any rush to go haring off after him. I've never seen the point in galloping toward my appointment in Samarra. (Well, that's not quite true. I used to date a girl named Samarra Johnson, who was well worth a gallop or two, but I digress.)

Tennetty scratched at herself, grimacing at the way her

bruised body protested any movement. "I'll take the flatbed and the horses back, if the rest of you want to go by air."

Fair enough. I may as well eat the cubs, then?

"Cubs?"

I forget. Not only can't you hear with your mind, your ears are handicapped, too. The wolf cubs. A gout of flame pointed out a direction. *Thataway.*

I sighed. There *would* have to be wolf cubs, wouldn't there? Hell of a note. You can't even save some innocent peasants from a ravening pack of wolves without having to clean up after, and feeling guilty as all hell about it.

There were two of them, and they were cute as anything, hungry to the point of starvation, and smelly as a pail of shit.

The small burrow under the rock wasn't much of a den, but it had probably been the best thing that mother wolf could dig in a short while. The pack was moving, under the influence or control of Boioardo, and long-term dens would have to wait.

The dwarf wasn't going to let me off the hook. "Well, you could always leave them to starve to death and just feel bad about it later."

Jason looked over at him. "That's the stupidest idea I've ever heard."

Andy crouched down and reached out to stroke one. It nipped at her, then nuzzled at her hand, probably trying to nurse. "Or you could slit their throats."

Tennetty knelt down beside the rock. "I'll do it. Not fair to leave them to starve." She drew her bowie and reached for the nearest of the cubs.

Jason grabbed her wrist. "What's your rush?"

"They're hungry." She shrugged her hand away. "They're no enemy of mine; I don't need to see them suffer."

He held up a hand. "Just put it away for a minute. Let's think this out."

I already had. Damn, damn, damn.

Sometimes, coming from the background I do is a burden, and it looked like Jason had inherited some of it from Karl. In a primitive society, people don't tend to be suckers for cute animals; interspecies empathy is a luxury, and people

100

who are scratching for existence can't afford it. You can't, say, raise all the puppies that your bitch breeds, and you don't have the expertise to spay her. So you have to either drown in litters of pups, or drown most pups.

Look—I've *had* to be hardhearted at times; there's situations where it's necessary to say that something's just natural, that there's nothing you can do about it. Cute baby animals die all the time out in the woods, and in a lot of cases it's just part of nature. And I've run into a lot worse than that.

But this wasn't part of nature. Boioardo had brought the mother of the cubs down out of the hills, and we had killed the pack, and that left the orphans with us. With me.

Ellegon's bulk loomed off in the distance, through the trees. *It would be awfully convenient if we had to take to our heels now.*

It would also be convenient if we had a proper canine milk source back at Castle Cullinane.

"Jason," I asked, "any chance there's a nursing bitch in the kennels?"

"No." He shook his head. "Not mine. Bren insisted on showing me the inventory, and that didn't mention it. On the other hand," he went on, "there's got to be a village warden somewhere around with one. You ever know a warden not to keep dogs?"

"There's the cows," Ahira said. "Cow milk might be worth a try."

Tennetty spat. "Silly idea. Just make it quick; that's the best you can do."

Jason shook his head. "I don't think my father would have, do you?" A thin smile played across his lips for just a moment. He reached into the den and scooped up one of the cubs. It nipped and wriggled as he handed it to me. It wasn't interested in sitting still.

He grabbed the other one and, ignoring its yipping and wriggling, headed down the path toward Ellegon. "Anybody who wants to come with me had better move it; we're heading back to the castle, on the double."

I looked down at the pup in my hands. Its fur was harder, denser than I would have expected a puppy's to be, and its eyes were glassy with hunger and thirst.

Shit, shit, shit. "Let's roll it."

"Okay." Ahira shrugged his pack onto his shoulders. "Let's give the boy a hand."

"I thought you wanted to leave them to starve to death and worry about it later."

"No, you didn't."

By the time we got back to Castle Cullinane, Aeia, Bren, and their entourage had left for Little Pittsburgh.

CHAPTER EIGHT

In Which, Surprisingly, Neither My Wife Nor I Are Urinated Upon

To sleep, perchance to dream.
—WILLIAM SHAKESPEARE

Bill, your mother swims after troop ships.
—WALTER SLOVOTSKY

THE COMPLEX PROBLEMS sometimes have simple, easy solutions—it's the simple problems that drive you crazy.

Like feeding the wolf cubs. The complex one was *What the hell do you feed them?*

The way I'd figured it, there was a huge chance that we wouldn't be able to find the cubs enough to eat, and that we'd have to put them out of their misery. I wasn't looking forward to that, mind, but it would have made things simpler.

But it turned out that what to feed adopted wolf cubs was already a solved problem, and so was taking a shot at domesticating them. It had been done before, in the old days, and the methods had been passed down by the dogkeepers. Some of the literate ones—and, in the old days, dogkeeping was a respectable profession, often taken up by petty nobility—had kept notes on the subject.

It was Fred (don't blame me; that's his name, okay? It's a variant of Fredelen, a common Holtish name) the

103

dogkeeper's firm belief that the Nyphien sheepdog was a mixture of the blood of wolf and the large Holtish dog called a *kalifer*, the oversized canine I always think of as a hairy mastiff.

Still, there were differences. According to Fred, a dog bitch would have done for the first few tendays, but after that, the pups would have savaged the poor thing's teats. Takes a mother wolf to keep baby wolves in line.

The standard baby wolf food was goat milk and whey, with the addition of one part bull blood for every ten of milk, and some herbs that Fred wouldn't identify.

. . . and more attention than a newborn human baby gets. If you want them coexisting with humans, you'd better have them smelling them constantly.

The next ten days were not fun.

The nightmare is always the same:

We're trying to make our escape from Hell, billions of us pushing our way through the damp curtains that hang down from infinity, obscuring the endless surface.

Everybody I've ever loved is there, along with faces familiar and strange.

Behind us, sometimes visible down the endless rows of curtains, the screaming pack of demons pursues. I don't want to look at them, and I don't have to, not anymore. We're almost out, almost safe.

But almost is never good enough.

The exit is up ahead, clearly marked with glowing green letters. And some are pushing their way through, thankfully. I think I see my wife and kids go through, and out.

I hope so.

The demons are approaching too quickly, and they're going to catch some of us. And then I see him: Karl Cullinane, Jason's father, standing tall, face beaming, his hands, chest, and beard streaked with blood and gore.

"We're going to have to hold them back," Karl says. "Who's with me?"

He smiles, as though he's been waiting his whole life for this, the fucking idiot.

"I'm with you," somebody says, and he waves whoever it is into his place next to Clint Hill and Audie Murphy.

"It's your turn," Karl says, turning to me. He's covered with blood, some sort of yellow-green ichor, and wolf shit.

He tosses his head to clear the blood from his eyes. "Your turn, Walter."

"Your turn, Walter," Jason said. He shook me again.

I woke up slowly, half in the here and now, half in the nightmare, still watching Karl's face superimposed over his son's.

Didn't like that at all—somebody in my line of work is supposed to wake up quickly, and before being touched at all. I don't care if my hindbrain thought me safe in bed next to my wife; the door was open, and an armed man had gotten in and next to me.

Not good, Walter.

Fast asleep, Kirah lay on the far side of the bed, curled under her blankets into a fetal position, her feet poised to push me away.

A dirty, smelly woolen shirt and pants lay on the floor next to me. Clothes to feed wolves in. Shudder. I levered myself out of bed, and shrugged into my wolf-feeding clothes—they were still vaguely moist with wolf drool—and a few oddments of weaponry before following Jason out into the hall.

My mouth had the metallic taste it gets when I don't get enough sleep. For some reason, I hadn't gotten enough sleep in the tenday we'd been back. Funny about that.

I stopped at the top of the stairs to look out the window.

Ellegon lay on the cold stones in the courtyard below, sleeping, his massive legs tucked underneath his body, his huge head resting on the cold stone, like a cat. Cute as a bus.

Too bad. I could have used the company. Being up and alone at night isn't any fun.

Jason handed me one of his two lanterns. The castle tradition, probably going back to the siege, was to keep too few wall lanterns burning in the middle of the fucking night, and everybody had to carry his own light sources with him.

"How are they doing?" I asked.

He shrugged. "Nora's been hiding under the stove; Nick's been eating enough for three of them." He raised a hand in farewell. "And I've got to get some sleep," he said, padding down the carpet toward his room, not bothering to throw a glance over his shoulder.

I made my way down into the inner ward, and the shack we were using as a wolf-kennel.

"Back-back-*back*, you vicious beasts," I said, as I unlocked the wire-mesh door and hung the lantern on the hook.

Obediently, the two pups bounded out of their hiding places, Nora almost making it through the door before she bounced off my foot and ran, yipping, back into the shed; Nick snuffled around my feet silently as he wagged his tail.

The locked cabinet held a fresh jug of Fred's foul-smelling wolf-baby food mixture; I took down a clean wooden bowl, and poured some for Nora. Nick hadn't gotten the idea of lapping out of a bowl as quickly as his sister; by the time I got some into one of the feeding bottles and a rag half-stuffed into the mouth of it, he was whimpering.

Another week or so and he'd be able to eat out of a bowl.

Or I'd wring his thickening neck.

I plopped myself down on a pile of straw—stupidly but harmlessly (this time) trusting Jason to have cleaned out the place before he left. The little monsters could have—and certainly would have—dirtied it up, if they'd gotten around to it.

Nick couldn't keep himself still; I had the usual trouble getting the pup tucked under one arm and getting the bottle to his mouth.

He ate greedily, like he hadn't been fed in minutes.

Basically, as Fred had explained it, the way you have a fair chance with wolf cubs or wild dogs is to catch them young enough—which he thought we did—and to spend all your time rubbing against them.

Make them members of your family, he'd said. Imprint them, he might have meant.

We'd see how it went over the long nights.

I understood why Fred didn't want to have to do it—

the smell of the pups scared Fred's dogs shitless. I was beginning to think that a spray bottle of wolf urine would be a wonderful invention for marking a territory as offlimits to domestic dogs.

I'll tell you, this would have been the perfect time for young Baron Cullinane to exercise a bit of baronial authority and tell one of the scullery girls she had a new job, as nurse to a pair of cubs.

But the Cullinanes are a stubborn breed—this was additional work, not expected, and Jason wasn't going to dump it on the castle staff, not if it wasn't absolutely necessary. No, that was for those of us who had taken on the responsibility: him, Ahira, his mother, and me.

Look: I like dogs, I like playing with dogs, I like hanging out with dogs for a few minutes now and then. Throwing a stick and having a dog fetch it is one hell of a lot of fun, the first couple of dozen times you do it.

But I didn't like spending six hours out of every day endlessly feeding and petting a couple of puppies, mucking out their kennel, and missing sleep.

Shit.

I had until dawn; Ahira would take over then. Hours of misery ahead.

Still, they were kind of cute.

I leaned back against the wall. Nora, always the less affectionate, retreated back into the shadows when she finished eating, while Nick kept sucking and licking at the bottle and the rag until he whimpered a bit, and fell asleep on my lap.

A long shift lay ahead, with nothing much to do but reflect on how the universe sucked.

Where had I gone wrong with Kirah? Was it something in how I touched her that had ruined sex for her? I don't mean to brag, but I've had relatively few complaints over the years. It isn't always unmeasurably wonderful or anything, but I'd always thought that I had more than a vague idea about what-goes-where.

No, I was being silly.

I rubbed at Nick's head, and he stirred for just a moment, then fell back asleep.

107

It's amazing how the same life can look good during the day and like a black cesspit in the middle of the night.

During the day, it was more important that I was living and working with friends who I cared for, and who cared for me; that the work we did was important to more than ourselves; that I had two beautiful, healthy daughters, both of whom were fond of me; that I was in good health and managed to keep up good spirits . . .

. . . and, at night, all I could think about was that my wife wouldn't let me touch her.

I guess I fell asleep, but I came awake suddenly. Nick, awake in my lap, had stiffened into immobility.

The drill is always the same: you get yourself armed and ready, and then you decide whether or not you're going to have to use it. I dumped the pup to one side and had my dagger out of its sheath—

"Walter?" It was Kirah's voice.

"Yeah." I slid the knife back in its sheath. "Just me," I said, bending to give the puzzled puppy a pat.

Balancing a serving tray on the palm of her one hand, she let herself in and knelt in front of Nick, who decided that she was okay, and demonstrated by wagging his stubby tail vigorously, then nipping gently at her face when she picked him up with her free hand.

"Hi there. What are you doing up?"

"Feeding you." She handed me the tray: half a loaf of U'len's garlic bread, in slices thick as my thumb; a huge mound—easily a pound—of cold, rare, roast beef, sliced thin enough for carpaccio, accompanied by a white clay mortar (as in ". . . and pestle") of freshly ground mustard and horseradish sauce; a wedge of blue-veined goat cheese surrounded by apple slices (try it!); a mottled brown pot of steaming herb tea, with two mugs.

My wife knows how to scrounge in a kitchen.

"I couldn't sleep alone." She smiled, aware of the irony. "I missed you, I guess."

"What time is it?" I asked, spreading a huge dollop of mustard and horseradish sauce on one slice of the bread, then heaping a restrained half of the beef on top of it before setting the tray up on the table. I'd leave some for her. At least until I finished my sandwich.

"Half past first hour." She set Nick down, and he immediately started chasing his tail.

"Pull up a seat," I said. I'd come on at midnight. "I've only been on for a bit more than an hour." Enough time to get seriously depressed, that was all.

I bit into the sandwich. The horseradish brought tears to my eyes, but it was worth it. There's something to be said for cold roast beef, thinly sliced, seasoned with just a little bit of salt, some cracked pepper, and mustard and horseradish sauce, served on coarse brown bread with little bits of garlic scattered through it . . . but I'd much rather eat it than say it.

Kirah seated herself just out of my reach, then leaned back, tugging at the hem of the light cotton robe she wore over blousy pants and slippers.

Nick went hunting for Nora, who just huddled deeper into her improvised nest in the far corner of the shack. Kirah started to get up, but desisted at my head-shake.

"Leave her be," I said, from around another mouthful. "Won't do any good to go chasing after her; she'll come out in her own time. Or not."

When something that can't be helped is bothering you, one cure is to think of something else that can't be helped that bothers you.

So I wished for a good Other Side reference book. Common sense and old records can only go so far. I remember something about most wolves deferring to alpha males, and that the way a human successfully deals with them is by persuading them that he's sort of a super-alpha male, but how did you do that? Growl and nip at them? Slap them on the snout? Pin them down with one arm and make them behave? Or was gentle firmness the way to go?

Common sense doesn't make it; all animals—homo sap definitely included—have their ways, and you violate them only at your peril. Doesn't matter how much you reason, or threaten—you can't get a cow to walk down stairs, a cat to point out game, or a horse to fetch.

I did remember from an ag ecology class that wolves

mainly live off rodent pests, and that farmers who hunt them aren't doing themselves any favor. Back when I was working for King Maherralen in Endell, I'd stopped the dwarf wolf-hunt cold. (Okay, okay: I strongly recommended to the King that he stop it, which he did.) There were much better things for the king's people to do, no matter how much bad blood there was between dwarves and wolves.

Would it be possible to return these guys to the wild? Damned if I knew.

Nick came over and started nuzzling and nipping at my hand. I tried to pet him into quietness, but it didn't work— he just kept at me. Sharp little teeth. "*No*. No biting."

Kirah giggled. "That's exactly the way you used to say it to Jane."

I laughed back. "I probably did." I gestured at the tray with my free hand, offering to make her a sandwich.

She shook her head. "No. I made it for you. —What do you think this Boioardo of yours was?" she asked.

I shrugged. "Something from Faerie. Something dangerous."

She pulled Nick over to her; he settled down in her lap and went promptly to sleep.

I raised an eyebrow.

"You just have to know how to talk to them," she said. She tossed her head to clear the hair from her eyes.

I spread a blob of goat cheese over a slice of apple and bit into it. It's one of those combinations that seem ridiculous until you try them, like prosciutto and melon, or raw oysters and hot sausage—the sweetness of the apple softened the bite of the ripe cheese, and the crunch of the apple complemented the gooeyness of the cheese.

I made another one, and offered it to Kirah, who surprised me by accepting it.

"I was talking to Andrea about it, about him," Kirah said, licking at her thumb for the last of the cheese.

"Nick?"

"No. The fairy."

Sometimes, I know just what to say to a woman: "Oh? She have any ideas?"

"No." Her look said that one of us was an insensitive

idiot who would probably need both guesses to figure out which. "*I* do."

"Well? What do you think?" Gee, maybe I could have sounded a bit more stilted, a little more condescending, if I'd tried. I don't know. When a relationship goes sour, there's nothing right to say.

"Hmm. You talked about how he moved sort of like a wolf, but sort of not, like he wasn't bending in quite the right ways, at the right places."

She had been listening closely. I nodded. "Yeah."

"Well, it reminded me of something. I was just watching Dorann this afternoon, and she was down on all fours playing with Betalyn—Fona's daughter? They were playing horse."

I smiled. "Who was on top?"

For once I'd said something that wasn't wrong: Kirah smiled too. "Betalyn—Dorann wanted to be the horse. But she wasn't bending in the same places that a real horse would. And when she reared back, she didn't toss her head the way a real horse would—she was playing at it."

Analogy is tricky. It can lead you to a useful truth, or right past it, and onto a landmine. "So, you think Boioardo is a baby fairy, out playing at being a wolf?"

"What do you think of the idea? Is it possible?"

I don't know why my wife cared so much about what I think, but she was watching me like everything hung on my next words. "Maybe. You could easily be right." Which she could have, although that's not why I said it.

Her shoulders eased; I hadn't noticed how tightly hunched together they were; I miss a lot.

"I'm not sure what good that does," she said. "But I thought . . ."

"It's worth sharing." But who knows about Faerie? What would that mean? Were all these rumors of magical outpourings from Faerie just the equivalent of a vicious kindergarten class out on recess? "I don't know if it does any good, mind," I said with a smile, "but it's worth sharing."

There were two obvious places to find out—Pandathaway and Ehvenor. Ehvenor, because Ehvenor was the only Eren-region outpost of Faerie. Pandathaway, because if there was any movement out from Faerie, no matter how subtle, the Wizards Guild would surely be looking into it, sooner or later.

I didn't like either choice, particularly Pandathaway. There was still a price on my head on Pandathaway—with a bonus if it was delivered in small slices.

That left Ehvenor. I never much liked Ehvenor. It's an outpost of Faerie, and the rules of the Eren region don't entirely hold there. It's not too bad out near the edge of the city—I've been there, and come out with nothing worse than a nervous tic that went away after a while. But they say that the further in you go, the more the fluctuating, positional rules of Faerie apply, and the less the solid ones of the rest of the universe do.

There was a solution that worked for a lot of problems: let somebody else handle it.

That looked like the best one to me. I'm not bad at what I do, but I'm not a magician, I don't like magic, and I've found it far healthier to stay out of the way of magic, no matter what the source.

"It scares you, doesn't it?"

I don't mind my wife thinking I'm not an idiot. "You *bet* it does," I said. "Anyone can get a reputation for being invincible. It's easy: to start, you go into harm's way and survive. Repeat, and you've got a reputation; do it a few more times, and you're a legend. But reputation doesn't make you invulnerable the next time. It doesn't matter how good you are, either; there's always a chance you're going to get unlucky. If you keep rolling the dice, eventually you're going to roll snake eyes too many times in a row."

"Like Karl did."

I nodded. "Like Karl did, like Jason Parker did, like Chak did, like . . . like we all will, eventually. Maybe."

We had been ignoring Nora too long; she came out from her hiding place and started chewing on my shoe.

"This is how the whole problem started, you know," I said, playfully—very gently—kicking at her. She responded by seizing the toe of my shoe between her teeth and shaking it back and forth, like a dog with a rat.

"Oh?"

"Slavery." I reached forward and took the pup by the scruff of the neck and held her firmly for a moment. "When you fight with another tribe—doesn't matter who starts it—and you win, what do you do with the survivors? Kill them to the last man, the way Chak's people would? Let them go, nursing a grudge—"

"Which they may have a right to."

"Sure. But it doesn't matter." I shrugged. "Right or wrong, if you just let them go, you're buying trouble. So, do you kill them—do you kill them all? Or do you take them in?"

And if you do, can you take them in as citizens or tribesmen, or whatever you want to call them? Of course not—even assuming you're willing to play that game, it takes two.

Slavery wasn't the only choice, of course; there were all sorts of ways short of that—colonization springs to mind. Karl had coopted Holtun, after Bieme had won the war. The difference was a matter of permanence and scale; he had taken the Holts in with the promise of earning co-equal status in the Empire, eventually.

"So, you're saying that the slavers who burned my village and took me when I was just a girl were just a bunch of nice people. Misunderstood. Did I ever tell you about the time that six of them, that *six* of them—"

"Shh." I started to reach for her, but stopped myself. "Come *on*, Kirah." I shook my head. "Not talking about what it became; I'm talking about how it started." I patted the pup. "Maybe out of the best of intentions, eh?" Maybe, in the long run, it would have been kinder to let Tennetty simply put them out of their misery.

That wasn't enough for Kirah. Her lips pursed into a thin line, and then she turned away. Damn her, she was always turning away from me.

"Kirah," I said, "I don't ever forgive anybody for ever hurting you. Deliberately or not." I wanted to reach out and take her in my arms and tell her that I'd make everything all right, but that's the kind of lie you can't tell a woman who screams if you hold her.

For a moment, I didn't know how it was going to break. Anything could have happened, from her taking a swing at me to her coming into my arms.

But she just picked Nick up, letting his lower legs dangle.

"Sure," she said, coldly, dismissing me. "Go away, Walter." There was a tremble in her voice, but I was listening carefully for it. "I'll handle things here. You need some sleep."

The perversity of my sleep patterns tends toward the maximum—I couldn't get back to sleep.

CHAPTER NINE

In Which We Leave on a Trip

I am always at a loss to know how much to believe of my own stories.

—WASHINGTON IRVING

Slovotsky's Law Number Nineteen: When telling a story, effect trumps truth.

—WALTER SLOVOTSKY

STASH USED TO SWEAR that it really happened, but lying runs in the Slovotsky family. Me, I don't believe it.

Story goes like this:

Once, when I was real young—three or so—Stash put me on a kitchen counter, and held out his hands.

"Jump, Walter, jump," he said. "Don't worry; I'll catch you."

"No, you won't," I said. "You'll let me fall."

"Jump, Walter, jump. Really—I'll catch you. Honest."

We went back and forth for awhile, him holding his huge hands out for me, me scared, knowing that this was some sort of test.

I jumped. And he stepped back and I fell on the floor, hard.

I lay there crying. "But you *said* you'd catch me."

"That will teach you not to trust anybody," he said.

I've thought about it, over the years. I've thought a lot

about it. Doing it would have been cruel, and my father would have cut his hands off before being cruel to me. But pretending that he had done it, maybe that's different. What he was telling me was true: guaranteed, if you live long enough, and trust people even casually, somebody you've trusted will let you down.

They're only human; everybody's fallible, including me. Particularly me.

Is it better to learn that through a childhood calamity that maybe never really happened or to risk learning it when it really matters?

Don't tell me that lies are always cruel.

Jason found me down in the fencing studio, a large room at the east end of the barracks annex. A light and airy place: one wall consisted mainly of shutters open to the daylight, the other wall was regularly whitewashed.

I'd taken out a practice saber and a straw dummy and—after a good stretch; you need those more and more as the years go by—I was practicing some lunges, working my thigh muscles so hard they practically screamed.

As a friend of a friend used to say, "After forty, it's patch, patch, patch." The maintenance costs on the physical plant keep going up, but the infrastructure keeps wearing down. My right knee had developed what was looking like a long-term ache, although it only got real bad when I overdid things. Still, not good. I thought about ice, and I thought about heat, and I thought a lot about traveling over to Little Pittsburgh to see the Spider, and find out if he could put some whammy on my cartilage.

"Mind if I join you?" Jason asked. He was dressed in a white cotton tunic with matching pantaloons bloused into the tops of his boots: good workout clothes.

"Why? Am I falling apart?" I gestured at the rack of practice weapons. "Sure. Pick a toy."

"Thanks." He selected a pair of mock Therranji fighting sticks and gave a few practice swats at my favorite sparring partner: a wooden pillar, covered with hemp matting that ran floor to ceiling. He blocked an imaginary blow, parried another, then hammered out a quick tattoo against the covered wood. *Thwocka-thwok-thwok-thwok-thwok.*

"Want some free advice, worth what you pay for it?" I asked, taking up an on-guard stance opposite him.

He nodded. "Sure." He moved one stick back defensively, and thrust the other one out tentatively.

"Don't try to be able to do everything. Balance yourself between overspecialization and not being able to learn anything." I moved in and gently parried an experimental thrust, beat his stick hard aside, then withdrew.

"Nice," he said. He tried a complex maneuver that I didn't quite follow, which probably foreshadowed an attack against my sword arm; I parried easily and moved to the side, letting his lunge take him by me, blocking his attempted slash with his left stick.

"Thankee much, young Cullinane." I faked a slash at his right wrist, then turned the movement into a thrust that would have skewered him through the chest except for two things: one, we were using practice weapons; two, Jason blocked—too nicely by half!—with his left stick.

It had taken me too long to figure out what he was doing—he wasn't trying real Therranji stick play. He was fighting two-swords style, using his left stick as though it was a dagger, his right like a saber. Close in, the dagger is a killing weapon—if you go corps-a-corps against a two-swords man, you'd best not already have something interesting to do with your free hand. At normal fighting distance, it's a decidedly annoying additional blocking device and threat, particularly the ones with the pronged hilt that can trap your blade.

The classic one-sword solution to the two-sword problem is straightforward, in both senses. You maneuver your opponent into taking a square stance—all attack and little defense—while you're in a three-quarters or side stance, very effective on defense. Block hard on the long sword, then attack the long-sword arm, hit it hard, withdraw enough to be sure that he's lost the weapon—that's not the point to get eager—then skewer him.

Forget fencing targets, forget one-cut finishes. All those pretty lunges in an attempt to get through to the body aren't worth half as much as a good, deep cut down the forearm, a

117

slice through muscle and tendon that leaves a weapon dropping from a bloody hand.

I was thinking about too much theory, I guess; Jason worked his way through my defense and gently bounced what I was thinking of as his blocking stick off my head.

"Damn." I backed off, rubbing at the sore spot. It hurt.

He smiled. "Another point?"

"Nah."

He set the fighting sticks back in the rack, then turned to face me. "You don't think much of the idea of sniffing around Ehvenor, do you?"

"No, I don't." I shook my head. "I don't like messing around with magic."

He nodded. "I understand that. I agree. But a messenger just arrived. Seems there's other things going on near Ehvenor, too—there's been a 'Warrior lives' killing in Fenevar."

Complete with note. In English, apparently.

I hadn't heard from the dragon for hours.

"Mikyn?"

He shrugged. "Possibly not. It's our only lead."

Now, that was something reasonable. I mean, handling an outpouring of the magical was out of my league, but following a clue toward a lost friend was something I could handle.

"One party or two?" he asked.

Two parties was the obvious solution. One to look into Faerie, one to chase after Mikyn. One party to contain me, one not. But, still, what would we do when we caught him? Arrest him? For what?

Mikyn, you're under arrest for suspicion of being crazy because we haven't heard from you for too long.

Nah. On the other hand, if he had gone over the edge . . . well, it needed somebody relatively senior and trustworthy. There was a shortage of those. "I dunno. Let me talk it over with Ahira."

Jason nodded. "Sure. Let's go."

"Now?"

"Is there some problem with now?"

———————

The dwarf was in the darkened smithy, again, his finished mail shirt hanging from a frame on the wall. Light from the coals reflected from his eyes, making them all red and demonic. He had a piece of work going in the forge. It looked like the start of something: a piece of thumb-thick bar stock about the length of my forearm, with another, shorter piece welded perpendicularly onto it, about a quarter of the distance from one end.

"What's that going to be?" I asked.

He smiled as he slipped the joint back into the forge, and worked the bellows, hard. Heat washed against my face in a solid wave, while rivulets of sweat worked their way through the hair and the scars on his naked chest. He had been at it for some time; the thick hot air in the smithy was filled with the not-unpleasant reek of fresh sweat.

"Don't you remember those newfangled nightsticks the police were starting to wear, back on the Other Side? I figured I'd give one a try." He tapped the hammer gently against the end. "The handle's supposed to spin—I've got Kayren whittling a collar for this. I'll slip it over, then flare out the end just a trifle."

"I remember them," I said, "but those were made of wood."

Ahira smiled. "I figure I can handle the extra weight." He was silent for a long moment. "You're trying to decide whether or not it's one party or two."

Jason looked disgusted. "Oh, come *on*."

"Hey, kid," I said, "you have a friend for more than twenty years, and spend most—"

"Too much, anyway," the dwarf put in.

"—of your waking life with him, and he'll read your mind, too."

Trouble was, Ahira was only close, this time. I was more thinking about keeping the hell out of the Faerie matter than I was about who would be looking into it.

The dwarf shrugged. "It's pretty obvious. The Faerie matter is more important, but the likelihood that it's something we can affect, one way or the other, is small. On the other hand, Mikyn is one of ours, and so is the Warrior myth we created. We have to look into that." He was silent for a moment. "One party," Ahira said. "Mainly to check out Ehvenor; that takes priority over looking for Mikyn."

"That seems awfully clear to you," I said. I can't always read his mind—Ahira's smarter than I am. But sometimes I can divert him.

"Andrea's necessary for Ehvenor," he said, ignoring the objection, "and I'm not going to let her wander around without us."

"Is that an issue?"

He pursed his lips for a moment. "Yes. She's going, she says, and Tennetty's going with her. Tennetty is dangerous without proper supervision—so that means at least one more of us."

Jason cocked his head to one side. "How about two parties? We've got more people available. Durine, Kethol, and Piro, for a start."

"We could let you take Kethol and company and go haring after Mikyn," Ahira said, as though considering it.

"Well, yes."

"Bad idea," the dwarf said. "I want them around, keeping an eye on the family." That's how Ahira referred to my wife and daughters: *the* family, as though none other mattered. I understand that. "If Daherrin was here, we could get some help from his team, but he's not. We don't have enough for two parties." He smiled at Jason. "The lesson begins: pick the party."

Jason made a fist, and stuck out his thumb. "Me."

"Who's going to take care of the pups?" I asked. "I thought you were going to take responsibility for them."

Jason smiled weakly. "I guess I have to add the job to the scullery maids' roster—and Jane says she'll take a turn."

I grinned back at him. "Handy to have a bit of rank, eh?"

"I *tried* to handle it without delegating it to them. Okay?" Not waiting for a smartass answer, Jason added the index finger. "Second is Mother—you're right that we have to have a wizard in on this, if we're going to look into the Faerie matter." He was missing the point: Andrea was already insisting on checking out Ehvenor. The only question was who would go with her, not whether or not she would go. "Then there's you two." He rubbed at the side of his nose with his middle finger. "You don't like the idea of trying to do two things at once, do you?"

I snorted. "I sometimes have enough trouble doing one thing at once." I cocked my head to one side. "Don't you have any misgivings about taking your mother along on this?"

She had handled herself well in Velen, and I'd been watching her closely since. She looked fine, not much different at all, although maybe there was a bit more of a rosy glow to her cheeks than usual. But going out in harm's way wasn't something Andrea had been doing, not since the very beginning. And if it required magic?

Again, it was all academic—Andrea was going, and that was that—but Ahira and I were teaching Jason; "academic" doesn't mean "irrelevant."

"No," Jason said. "I don't." Jason's expression wasn't one of unconcern; it was a cold and distant look, the expression of a chessmaster who knows the value of his pieces, and will push them around the board into the right place, no matter whose face the piece wears.

"It's necessary," he said. He added his little finger. "Tennetty." He held out his hand, fingers spread. "Five of us. Small enough not to draw unnecessary attention, small enough to hide with a little cover, large enough to handle some trouble. Ellegon to drop us off and pick us up. Just outside of Ehvenor, I'd think."

"No," Ahira said. "If there's something really sticky going on there, we don't want to drop right in on it. Better to work our way up to it, and sniff around as we go. The locals may have done some of the looking into things for us."

Better, yes. Best was to keep the hell out of it. I didn't say as much, but I guess my face showed it.

Ahira turned to Jason. "Give us a minute, will you?"

"But—"

"Now will be fine," he said, gesturing to the door of the smithy. "You can get my saddle from the stable. I want to put a few more equipment rings on it."

He stood in the doorway, watching the boy walk away, then turned back to me.

"Give it up, Walter," Ahira said. "You don't have to go,

nobody's going to hold an axe to your throat. But you know you're going, just as well as I do." His chuckle was hollow in his barrel chest. "Three reasons; take your pick. First," he said, "because while this whole thing about creatures coming out of Faerie was distant, as of about ten days ago it became local, it became personal. Your wife and kids live in this country, in this barony, and you're no more going to leave that kind of menace uninvestigated than I am."

He looked up at me. "Second reason: Jason, Andy, Tennetty, and I are going. You're not going to let us go into this alone," he said, as though daring me to dispute it.

"Noble guy, aren't I?" I smiled.

He didn't take the bait, not directly. "One last reason," he said, not looking me in the eye. "Your wife won't let you touch her, and if you can get away for awhile, you won't have to deal with that. You can put off handling that for as long as we're on the road." He turned back to the forge.

I wanted to be angry, to be furious with him for mentioning it. If he'd said it in the presence of anybody else, I know I would have been.

But he was right. On all three counts.

Damn, damn, damn.

Jason walked through the doorway, a saddle slung over his shoulder. "Where do you want this?" he asked.

"Just dump it on the floor," Ahira said. "You'd best go pack. We leave in the morning."

As we walked away, Jason's brow furrowed. "What was that all about?"

"What?"

He gestured clumsily. "Ahira. It was like he was . . . I don't know. Not there. Angry, maybe. Was it something I said?"

"Nah. It's not you. Game face," I said.

"Eh?"

"Never mind."

He frowned.

I thought about explaining that even when you look at the football game as a job, as a way to pay for school, you get yourself psyched up for it, and that when you trot out on the field, your heart pumping hard, the ground springy beneath your feet, ready to, say, grab a quarterback and slam him down so hard that his descendants will still ache, there's a kind of glare you wear, whether or not you intend to. And then I thought about how he probably didn't have the background to appreciate it, and how I didn't feel like explaining football to a This Sider.

And then I thought about how if I kept saying "Never mind" to the kid every time he asked a question, he was going to slip a knife into me someday, so I just smiled.

"Honest," I said. "It's not important."

I'd said goodbye to the kids, and to the pups, so I went over the list one more time. Weapons, clothes, food, money, miscellaneous. Miscellaneous was, as always, the largest category. I was packed for running, if necessary—the most important stuff was in either my belt pouch or my small rucksack.

Grab and run, if I had to. When the shit comes down, you grab your friends, and—if time—your essentials. Leave the rest be.

There was a gout of fire below in the courtyard.

They're waiting for you. So am I.

So wait a bit longer.

My big rucksack was packed solid; I took it to the window and tossed it down to Ahira's waiting hands. *Thunk.*

I turned back to Kirah. "Like the old days, eh, old girl?" I asked, smiling.

She didn't smile back. "I don't want you to go."

Walter Slovotsky's advice to wives whose husbands are packing for a trip: be nice. Let problems lie.

Look—trivial problems can wait, or you can solve them yourself while your spouse is gone. That's why we call them trivial, eh? They're not important. You can't solve anything serious between the time he takes his rucksack down out of the closet and when he heads out the door. That's not the time to try.

All it can do is screw up his mind while he's gone. So leave it be. This wasn't a time to be discussing that; it wasn't the time for either of us to be discussing anything.

The obvious thing, the right thing for me to do was to ignore what she'd just said.

"Right," I said. "And you don't want me to stay, either. You can't stand to have me touch you, remember?"

"Please. Don't blame me for that." She faced me in the doorway. "It's not my fault, Walter. I try, but every time you touch me, it's like . . ." she raised her hand in apology, as a shudder shook her frame. "I'm sorry."

Walter Slovotsky's advice to husbands leaving on a trip is ever the same . . .

I gripped her arms tightly, ignoring her struggles. "It's not my fault, either, Kirah. I didn't do that to you, and I won't be blamed for it. I won't—" I started, then stopped, and let her go. She gripped herself across the middle and turned away. Her shoulders shook as she fell to her knees.

"No." *I won't live my life in penance for harm others have done to you,* I didn't quite say.

It's neither of your fault, if you want my opinion, Ellegon said, his voice pitched only for me.

Thanks. I think I needed that.

All part of the service. Should we get going, or do you want to have a few more tender moments with your wife?

I kissed the tips of my fingers and held them out toward her back. "Goodbye, Kirah."

Ah, parting is such sweet sorrow . . .

The sun had shattered the chill of the earliest morning, but clouds were moving in, and the sky to the east was slate gray and threatening. Time to get going—flying through rain is no fun at all.

Jason and Andrea had already climbed up and fastened themselves into their seats on the rigging we'd lashed to Ellegon's broad back, while Ahira was under the dragon's belly, giving the knots a last check. I'm as safety-conscious as anybody else, but riding Ellegon isn't like riding a horse—he'll let you know if things start to give.

Alternately, if I do have it in for you, a few strands of rope aren't going to make a difference. The dragon snorted, startling the honor guard of soldiers who had gathered to bid us good journeying.

Doria was taking her duties as Steward seriously—she had a list of things to do sticking out of her blouse pocket.

"Going to have this place in good shape by the time we're back, eh?" I asked, with a knowing smirk.

She smiled and shrugged. "I lost my old profession when I defied the Mother; I'd better find something else I can do." She knew better. If nothing else, there was always a job open at the Home school, teaching English, civics, and pretty much anything else; besides, Lou Riccetti would be glad to have her around.

"Home ec majors," I sniffed. I gave Doria a quick squeeze goodbye, then climbed up and belted myself into the saddle behind Tennetty.

She turned in her seat and gave me a quick glare. "You took long enough."

"Leave it be." Andrea frowned her into silence.

"Everything okay?" Ahira asked, as he levered himself into his seat and belted himself in, too firmly; dwarves dislike flying almost as much as they do traveling by boat.

Jason felt at the butt of his revolver, from where it projected under his jacket. "All set."

Tennetty folded her arms in front of her chest and leaned back against the pile of gear lashed between the two of us. "Fine."

Andrea gestured in impatience. "Let's go."

"Ducky," I said. "Let's get the fuck out of here."

Hang on . . .

PART TWO

ROADWORK

CHAPTER TEN

In Which We Reach Fenevar, and the Trail Heats Up

'Tis the men, not the houses, that make the city.
—THOMAS FULLER

Health hint for the traveler: Don't throw rocks at guys with guns.
—WALTER SLOVOTSKY

I'VE ALWAYS TAKEN THE ideas from where I could get them. Hey—I'm not as inventive as Lou; I do the best I can.

I got the "Warrior lives" notes from my big brother, Steve. It was one of the few Vietnam stories he ever told me. (When he wasn't drinking, that is. Two beers and he'd start with the stories, and wouldn't stop with either the stories or the drinking until he was totally wasted.)

It wasn't something he'd done—he had spent most of his time in Vietnam as a door gunner on a sort-of-unarmed helicopter, what they called a slick—but it was a habit that some of the ground soldiers had: they would leave the ace of spades, the death card, on dead enemies. The way he explained it, it supposedly started when somebody had a short deck of cards on him, and thought it kind of funny. Eventually, a lot of the outfits had their own cards printed up, with the name of their unit on them.

"Now, let me understand this," I had said. "They'd expect Charley—"

"You weren't there," he had said, softly. "Call them the Vietcong, or the NVA, or the enemy."

"—they'd expect the enemy to run across dead bodies of their own people, and get spooked because they had a *playing card* on their heads?"

He'd shrugged. "I didn't say it made sense. I said that's what they did. But it did make sense. It made the whole thing more personal. There was a way to make it even more personal," he had said. "But we didn't do that most of the time."

"I thought you flew all the time," I said. If he was going to reproach me . . .

"Just flew *most* of the time," he had said. And then he wouldn't say any more.

The ideal place to have Ellegon take us would have been as far away from Ehvenor as we could get, if you asked me; the right thing to do would then be to make tracks in the opposite direction from Ehvenor.

That, however, wasn't the plan. The plan was to be dropped off down the coast from Ehvenor; Fenevar seemed about right. It would have been convenient to be dropped off behind some outcropping near the rocky shore of Fenevar. The only trouble was, there wasn't a rocky shore.

The land near Fenevar was flat and at water level, more swampy than lakeshore. There wasn't much forest or other cover; as was true of much of the arable land around the Cirric, farmers had long cleared and planted well up to the edge of the freshwater sea, and beyond, growing tame wild rice in the shallow, swampy water.

The dragon had to leave us back up the road, in the rolling foothills, a good half-day's walk down to the city.

As we had learned back in the old raiding days, the danger when Ellegon touches down is directly related to two things: how isolated the area appears, and how long he is on the ground. We did the best that we could with both.

How's it look? I asked, as Ellegon banked hard in a tight circle.

The wind beat hard against my face, pulling tears from my eyes. I could barely make out the hill below in the gray predawn light, but Ellegon's eyes were better than mine; he had spotted the road that bisected it neatly, cutting through the dense wood.

Nobody around, as far as I can tell. Coming in.

Air rushed by as the dim ground rushed up. Ellegon, his wings pounding the air hard, slammed down on the dirt road.

Their safety straps already off, Jason and Ahira slid to the ground below, while Tennetty and I pulled straps loose and tossed packs and rucksacks down. I lowered Andy down to Ahira's waiting arms, then slid down a loose strap to the ground.

Ellegon took a few steps down the road, then leaped into the air, climbing in a tight spiral before flapping off into the sky.

I'll start checking rendezvous points in a couple tendays. Until we meet again, be well, he said.

White light flared as Ahira pulled a glowsteel from his pouch. He already had his huge rucksack on his back. "Let's go, folks. We've got a full day's march to Fenevar."

Tennetty, shrugging into her own rucksack, nodded. "And nothing more than sour beer to look forward to at the end of the trip."

While a modified direct approach—distract, grab, and go—is one way of getting something specific, it's a lousy way to try to find any information.

There's any number of strategies to use when you're snooping around for intelligence—and I can always·use some more intelligence.

One of the best is also one of the simplest. Any town along a trade route—and, for obvious reasons, we've always tended to work around trade routes—has at least one travelers' inn. If it's a sizable town, usually more. Travelers—no matter what they trade in—almost always like to talk. Not always honestly, mind. Then again, who am I to complain about a bit of dishonesty?

All we got out of the first two inns we tried was a mild buzz.

The talk in the Cerulean Creek Inn, the third inn of the

evening, flowed like the sour beer; it tended to slop over on the floor and turn it into mud.

The general practice along that part of the coast is to sell ale by what they call a pitcher, although it's barely half the size of a common water pitcher. Some drink right out of the pitcher; others use a mug. I poured Tennetty another mug full, then tilted mine back, barely wetting my mouth.

She took a long pull. "Well?" she asked.

"Well, what?"

"What brilliant things have you found?"

I had debated bringing Tennetty along this evening. There were plenty of problems: women warriors were rare in the Eren regions, and she was relatively well known. She was moderately famous as Karl Cullinane's one-eyed bodyguard, her temper was never fully under her control, and she scared me.

On the other hand: her glass eye was in place, visible and entirely convincing under a fringe of hair, and nobody would have mistaken me for Karl, either in truth or in legend.

She was the obvious choice for this, despite the minuses—she could be counted on to keep her mouth shut, unlike Jason; she wouldn't look out of place in the drinking room of an inn, unlike Andrea; she wouldn't draw the wrong sort of attention, unlike Ahira.

Maybe I would have been better bringing Ahira along. He wouldn't have stood out: over in the far corner, a dwarf and his human companion sat, sharing a loaf of almost black bread and a bowl of thick stew of unlikely ancestry. By the cut of his leather tunic, I decided the dwarf was from Benerell—the Benerell style has always been for clothes that barely fit. The human could have been of any origin, although you'll find more of that wheaty blond color in Osgrad than elsewhere.

Changes happen, even while you don't look for them. Or maybe particularly when you don't look for them.

I hadn't answered Tennetty. I turned to her, raising my voice ever-so-slightly.

"I don't know, either," I said. "That . . ."—the line called for a long pause—"*thing* we saw this morning was one of the strangest things that has ever reached Tybel's eyes, and that's a fact."

The broad-faced fellow down the bench from me pricked up his ears.

I picked up our empty pitcher and turned it over, empty. I'd buy more in a moment, unless somebody took the hint.

"Yeah," Tennetty said, not helping much.

I don't know about her, sometimes. This was the third time we'd tried this routine, and her side of it was no more polished than the first.

I'm afraid I glared at her.

"That it was," she added, chastened, trying a bit more. "Really, strange."

It was all I could do not to raise my eyes toward the ceiling and implore the help of the gods, or of heaven.

"Very strange."

"Begging your pardon, traveler," the fellow whose attention I had caught said, "but did you talk of seeing something strange?" He half-rose, courteously gesturing with his own, full pitcher.

Several times, I thought. *And pretty darned clumsily.*

"I guess I might have," I said, beckoning him over. I guess if a fish is hungry enough, he'll bite a hook with a plastic bug on it.

He splashed some ale into each of our mugs, then politely sipped at his pitcher.

"Lots of strange things been seen of late," he said. "More and more over the past few years. Travelers report many things, although tales do grow in the telling."

I nodded. "That they do. But this was something that didn't grow. It was a wolf that wasn't a wolf."

We were gathering an audience, or at least some company; the drinking room of a tavern isn't the place for those who prefer solitude. The dwarf and human pair wandered over as I launched into a seriously edited version of our encounter with Boioardo and the wolf pack: I cut out the fight, had him eating a deer instead of a cow, and placed it outside of Alfani rather than back in Bieme. I've always been a stickler for details, just never for accurate ones.

The obvious way to find out something is to go around and ask questions, but that invariably raises the question of who you are and what you're after. Given that there is a price on my head—the Pandathaway Slavers Guild is no more fond of me than I am of them—I'd rather not answer honestly, most places I go.

So the obvious way was out. Another way is to talk about something interesting, something related to what you're interested in, and let everybody else impress you with what they know about it.

A little bald man, a trader in gems and gold who had given his name as Enric (and who must have been a lot tougher than he looked, given his admitted profession and lack of a bodyguard) ordered a round for the table. "It's coming from one of the Places of the other ones, perhaps, they say. Or from," he made a sign with his thumb, "*there.*"

"Places of the other ones?" I tried to look puzzled. "There? You mean—"

"I mean just as I say, traveler. It's an old belief that it is dangerous to mention either by name. My grandfather, long dead though he is, used to talk of them as only *them*, and while I thought that strange, he did live to sixty years."

Another man spat. "Faw. Just a superstition."

"Maybe it was, and maybe it wasn't. Maybe they know when their names are spoke, and maybe they don't. What with strange things happening, with something or other having wiped out that little village up near Erevale, I'm not one to take chances." He turned to me. "What do you think, Tybel?"

I shook my head. "I've never been one to take chances, either." Without a damn good reason. Wiped out a village? I hadn't heard about that.

"A wise man," he said. "And with the Warrior about, turning visible only to kill? I used to own a servant, had her for ten years—Venda, her name is. Stout as a stoat, and loyal as a good dog. But with the Warrior about—and there are many who say it's Karl Cullinane—murdering honest men who own such, I'll tell you that I sold her, for quick coin and without apology."

Tennetty frowned. "One moment. The way I've heard it is that Karl Cullinane and his people will leave alone all but slavers, and Guild slavers in particular."

Enric shook his head. "That's the way it used to be, for

sure. For years and years. I've met some of the Home raiders and traders—I even camped for an evening with a bunch of his men one night, in Kuarolin, up along the edge of the Katharhd? Tough-looking bunch, but I felt perfectly safe among them, and they were welcome in most towns—nobody thought they'd be hunting for any but slavers, and slavers are none too popular anyway.

"But there's been word of it changing. There was a hostler murdered in Wehnest, for nothing more than having a bought servant."

"Not just off in Wehnest, either." A burly man slapped his fist down on the table, causing mugs and pitchers to dance. "Just outside our own Fenevar, not forty days ago, Arnet and his brother were murdered in their beds, and one of those notes left behind. Englits all over it, they say." He shuddered. "Dangerous language, I hear—they say that you don't have to be a wizard to write spells in it."

"That's nonsense. Pfah." Another spat. In Fenevar, you can tell the locals by their habit of spitting as punctuation.

"You have to be one of their wizards to do it, to make their gunpowder."

I listened with more than half an ear for the next hour, buying just a bit more than my share of the rounds. That's the key to being inconspicuous. You don't have to be average—you just have to seem like you're typical.

I guess I drank too much. But I do remember hearing a fragment of a phrase from Reil the baker, one I didn't want to inquire into too closely.

"—and that's what Alezyn said. You know, the new farrier, the one who was through about five tendays ago?"

Bingo. Alezyn was Mikyn's father's name. It was possible, of course, that there was a real farrier going by the name of Alezyn, but I don't believe in coincidences—somebody with that name near a killing.

It all made sense. Many smiths—most, easily—and a lot of hostlers did some shoeing on the side, but like anything else, shoeing horses is something you get a lot better at if you do it regularly. On the other hand, outside of the largest cities, there simply wasn't enough work for a full-time farrier, and it was a respectable and likely profession for a smith or horseman to take up, if he had a bit of money for tools, and the taste for the road.

Didn't take much in the way of tools, either. A small anvil and maybe a portable forge if you were extravagant, although you could build a firepit for that kind of work. Hammers, tongs, various trimming knives and clippers, plus some bar stock, and you were in business. You could put all of it on the back of a packhorse, if you were pressed, although you'd probably want a wagon.

Home raiding teams usually carried at least one traveling farrier's rig with them. It always was a good idea for a raiding team to send scouts out, and one of the best covers we had used, back during the raiding years, was that of a farrier.

Mikyn had separated from the rest of the team, taking the traveling farrier rig with him.

We were getting warm, perhaps. Possibly we could wrap up the Mikyn matter quickly, before investigating Faerie. Not a bad idea, all things considered. We had a double objective, after all, if we could manage it: sniff around Ehvenor to see if we could find out what was happening with Faerie, and see if we could track down Mikyn.

Which was more important? Okay, Ehvenor. Fine.

Which was more urgent, though? That was another thing.

Maybe a better question was: which could we handle better?

And why ask questions when there was beer to be drunk. Er, drank?

Enric refilled my mug. "You're decidedly good company, Tybel," he said. "It's been a pleasure meeting you."

"That's because I listen well."

Somehow or other, Tennetty got me back to our rooms.

I don't remember dreaming that night, although I do remember getting up once to puke into the thundermug next to my bed. (If I hadn't, the smell would have reminded me.)

In the morning, I had the godfather of all hangovers.

Anything for the cause, eh?

CHAPTER ELEVEN

In Which I Have a Hangover

It is only the first bottle that is expensive.

—FRENCH PROVERB

Mrmf. Gack. Urpffff.

—WALTER SLOVOTSKY

TRYING TO GET SOMEthing decided over a hangover is no fun at all. Trying to do anything over a hangover is no fun at all.

I couldn't see it, not with my eyes closed, but there was a thumb-sized flask of Eareven healing draughts at my elbow as I lay stretched out on the settee in our common room. Tennetty had placed the filigreed brass flask there when she and Ahira had hauled me out of my room and set me up on the settee. A damp cloth lay across my eyes, easing the dry burning of my eyeballs to mere agony.

Sadistic bitch. She knew that I wouldn't take it, not for something like this. Healing draughts are for emergencies.

"You okay, Walter?" the dwarf asked.

"Peachy keen." Each word hurt. There were little men with big knives carving on the inside of my temples, and demons with spiked shoes and flamethrowers walking up and down every tendon in my body. Never mind what was going on in my stomach. I don't like to think about what was going on in my stomach.

At least the settee was overstuffed and would have been comfortable if even softness didn't hurt. The luxury was not unexpected—we had taken a large suite of rooms at the Krellen Inn. When you're paying with real Pandathaway gold—even if you get back a lot of local coins as your change—you can usually get a spot of luxury.

I would have settled for a jot of comfort.

Ahira bit into a red, round apple; the crunching sound hurt my forehead.

My mouth tasted of sour vomit. Every time I turned to look at something I could feel my neck bones squawk, and the grit behind my eyes grated as I lay there.

There was a cure, but I couldn't use it. Wouldn't use it.

I forced myself up to one elbow and fumbled for the stone mug of too-hot Holtish herb tea that Andrea had brewed up for me; it was supposed to be good for both headaches and menstrual cramps. I had to remove the damp cloth from my eyes to find it. This is one time that I can swear that one out of two isn't good.

I eyed the flask of healing draughts. It would be wrong to take it just to cure the hangover. It's not just that healing draughts are expensive—although they are—it's worse: they're rare, hard to get hold of. We're supposed to save that stuff for serious hurts, for emergencies.

Granted, I once downed a half bottle when I was fleeing from a town—I've shown my heels to so many that I don't recall just which one now—but I had sprained my ankle, and while that's usually a minor injury, it would have gotten me killed then, and by my definition, an injury isn't minor if it gets you killed.

In all the times I've been banged up, and there are a lot of those, I've never used the stuff promiscuously—I've always preferred saving promiscuity for other contexts.

The wind was blowing hard from the west, in through the window; the fresh air helped just a little. Jason had been dispatched for food, and had returned with a basket of fruit, a dozen sticks of roasted pork, peppers, and onions from the market down the street, and a pail of ale from the eating room below.

The smell of food made me gag. The aroma of roast pork and a hangover don't mix.

Well, the tea was a loser. Maybe the ale would be better. I accepted Jason's offer of a battered pewter tankard, and sipped at the flat brew, hoping it would clear the painful fog behind my throbbing eyes.

It didn't. I've never had much luck with the hair of the dog as a hangover remedy.

Healing draughts are expensive, and hard to come by. Hangovers hurt. Balance the two in the scales, and the supply of healing draughts was still meager, and hangovers still hurt like hell.

Put it in proportion: I could lie here in pain for the rest of the day. In a day, tops, I'd be back to normal, and if we were going to leave Fenevar, we'd need at least a day to get horses and provisions, never mind about which direction.

The trouble, of course, was that Mikyn could have gone anywhere, in about three directions. On the other hand, while things in Ehvenor weren't likely to stay in one place, the city itself was considerate enough to stay in one place, and maybe that solved the problem for us.

How to travel was easy: we'd go by land. Fenevar isn't a major shipping center—the shoreline is too swampy and shallow.

"At least we don't have to travel by water," Ahira said, repressing a shudder.

Andy patted his knee. "Just as well, eh?"

Dwarves don't like water any deeper than what they wash in—and the traditional dwarvish washhouse is a small room, concave to a drain in the center, ringed with chest-high (to them) washbasins. Ahira was the only one I've ever known to use a bathtub.

It's obvious why, when you think of it—a human with a lungful of air is lighter than water. Swimming, for us, is just a matter of working with natural forces, sometimes bobbing up and down to rhythmically clear mouth and nose from the water in time with breathing. Dwarves, on the other hand, are denser than we are. Their bones aren't only thicker, with the correspondingly larger joints that confer a greater mechanical advantage, they're made of a slightly different, more compact calcium matrix than ours. Their muscle fibers are smaller and much more numerous, and they carry a smaller fat-to-muscle ratio—that's one of the reasons they're so fond of ale: starch and alcohol are good sources of quick calories.

Drop a dwarf in water, and he'll sink like a stone.

I trotted out Lou Riccetti's old joke: "How do you make a dwarf float?" I tried to grin, but the effort hurt.

Ahira smiled dutifully, while Andy answered. "Two scoops of ice cream, one dwarf, and fill with Coke."

Yup; because that's the only way. I guess you have to be an Other Sider to find it funny.

Jason wasn't having any of the humor. "I don't like any of it, but we've got to find him."

Tennetty sneered. "Wanting doesn't make it so. He left ten days ago. He could be anywhere."

Andy shook her head. "Not if he's maintaining a cover as a roving farrier."

"We need to find him."

Jason was right. It was one thing to kill slavers. Nobody shed tears for them. Fear them, sure; deal with them—well, what else was there to do with a conquered neighbor?

But express sympathy? Identify with them? Consider Home raiders a common threat?

Nah.

The trouble with creating a legend is that people will believe it. Ahira and I, and later Jason, had gone to some trouble to keep Karl's legend alive in the stories about the Warrior, and Karl was the archetype of a Home raider. By murdering the locals and leaving the note, Mikyn was fucking with the legend. I'm not sure whether I was more surprised or annoyed. Both, I guess—Mikyn had been raised in Home, and he should have *known* better.

I sipped some more of the hot tea and lay back. Just reach out, take the small brass bottle in my trembling hand, then break the wax seal with my thumb, and tilt it back . . .

No.

Ahira had been thinking. "Any chance you can put a location spell on him?" he asked Andrea.

She shrugged. "Perhaps." She shrugged. "Certainly. I've gotten very good at location spells."

I was going to ask how, but I caught myself. Back when she thought Karl was alive, she had labored long and hard to locate him. You do it a lot, you get good at it.

"I will need something of his," she said, "preferably some hair or nails, or something he's interacted with intimately."

"They say the note was written in blood."

"His?" Ahira was skeptical.

"Not likely, but it's a start." Andrea stood up. "There's a hedge wizard in town. As I understand it, he's a confidant of Lord Ulven. I think it's time for a bit of professional courtesy." She wasn't wearing wizard's robes, of course, but equally of course she could quickly demonstrate what she was, if necessary.

"Hold on, please." Ahira held up a hand. "You haven't done this for awhile."

"Magic?"

A frown twisted its way across his face. "No. The rest of it." He pursed his lips for a moment, then bit another chunk of meat off his skewer. "If you're going to brace a local, we'd best be able to get out of town quickly. That means horses."

Tennetty nodded. "Me. You part with gold too easy. Looks suspicious."

"Fine."

"Hmm . . ." she cocked her head. "One each, and two spares?"

"Three, if you can. We also should try to learn as much as we can about the local situation—there's a dwarf smith; I should go and see if he wants some word from the Old Country. Jason, it's you and me for that one."

Jason scowled. "Why me?"

"Because you speak dwarvish, and with a thick Heverel accent. Tall Ones who can speak the language, accent or no, are rare enough that you'll charm him. If he happens to be from Heverel, all the better." He turned to Andrea. "Which leaves you and Walter for the wizard. You need somebody to watch your back." He nodded at me. "You'd best leave now."

"Now?" I asked.

"Now," he said.

"Well," I said, each word a painful effort, "a bodyguard has to move around."

"True enough. Better drink that stuff," he said.

My hands trembled as I examined the wax seal perfunctorily, then broke it, tossing the cap aside. I brought the flask to my cracked lips, each movement hurting.

A spasm of nausea washed over me, but I fought it down successfully. The too-sweet liquid washed the vomit and sand from my mouth, replacing it with a warm glow, like good brandy. In between painful beats, my headache disappeared, various aches and pains sparking away, disappearing.

But I really hate magic. Honest. I just hate hangovers more.

"That feels better," I said, my voice deepening and strengthening as I tossed the damp cloth aside and swung off the couch and to my feet.

No pain, not even any morning aches. The air was just chilly enough to be bracing, and filled with the enticing smell of roasted pork, peppers, and onions. I was twenty again—strong, arrogant, and horny, ready to deal with anything the universe cared to offer up . . . starting with a stick of roast peppers, pork, and onions that Jason had left on the serving platter.

As I bit hungrily into the cold meat, Ahira caught my smile and returned it.

In divvying up the jobs, he was still looking after me, the way it had always been. He could easily have assigned himself as Andrea's bodyguard, even if that meant she would have to wait until he got back from the smith.

Tennetty scowled. "What are the two of you so proud of yourselves about?"

Ahira shrugged. "Private joke."

CHAPTER TWELVE

In Which I'm Too Smart for My Own Damn Good

A hasty judgment is the first step toward recantation.
—PUBLILIUS SYRUS

Figure it out fast—and so what if you're wrong? You might get lucky and implement the wrong one so that it works.
—WALTER SLOVOTSKY

THE SIGN READ—

REWNOR
Magician, Wizard, Mage, and Seer

—in typical convoluted Erendra lettering, although runes and symbols were scattered across its surface.

Andrea stopped five steps before the doorway, and reached into the bag at her waist.

I started to reach for her wrist, but stopped myself. "Hang on a second," I said.

She turned, her face creased in irritation. "What *is* it?"

"Look," I said, "I'm no expert on magic—"

"That's for sure."

"—but I do know that it's a risk for you. You've overdone in the past. Doria thinks you've been hooked on it."

She dismissed it with a frown and a wave. "You don't, or you wouldn't have let me come along."

I had been thinking about that, and I'd been thinking about how convenient it had been for me to think Doria wrong, and decide that Andy was safe to travel, because if I didn't, I don't know what we would have done for a wizard.

She tossed her head, sending her long black hair flying as she struck a pose, one hand on hip. That's who Aeia got that habit from, I guess. "I don't intend to spend the rest of my life living that down. I had a problem. I pushed myself too far, and made it worse by not taking care of myself. I've got it under control now."

I guess I didn't keep my skepticism off my face—not surprisingly, because I wasn't trying to.

Also unsurprisingly, that didn't calm her down. "Dammit, Walter, you know you need a wizard in on this, at least the Ehvenor and Faerie part."

I had to admit that was true. "Sure, but—"

"But nothing," she said. "Just navigating around the middle city takes magic. By some perspectives, it doesn't have a diameter."

"Eh?"

"I mean," she said, "looked at one way, there's a fleck of Faerie in the middle of the city, and the rules of Faerie are . . ." she grasped for a word ". . . indeterminate, by your standards. Not entirely determinate, by mine. When you get close natural laws break down.

"Well, no, they don't exactly *break* down; they kind of get neurotic. They don't apply in the same way, and there's a whole new set that you're not equipped to learn. You'll have to trust me there and then, and you have to trust me here and now."

An old friend of mine used to explain that what most women want from the men in their lives is loving leadership. I guess he hadn't met Andrea. Or Tennetty. Or Aeia. Or Kirah, for that matter. Or probably Janie.

Argh. Slovotsky's Law number whatever: a generalization that doesn't apply to anybody means you're missing something. Doria, maybe? Dorann, please?

"For now," Andrea went on, "you'll have to trust my judgment about when magic is necessary. Understood?"

She didn't wait for me to answer; she dipped two fingers into her bag, and pulled out a handful of dust and tossed it into the air, accompanying it by a pair of muttered syllables. Stubborn old habits die hard—I tried, once more, to make sense of what she was saying, to remember the words, but I couldn't.

Dust motes turned to a million points of light, and then dimmed to redness, and then further until all they left behind was a dazzle in my eyes.

She stopped. Her eyes closed, her lips moved slowly, silently for a full minute.

That's a long time to stand and wait.

Passersby stared at her out of the corner of their eyes, and then hurried on. Most normals—present company certainly included—tend to want to be away from a working wizard, preferably as far away as possible.

Finally, her eyes opened. "Okay; he's waiting for us. Let's go in."

"Hmmm . . . can I ask what that was for?"

"The first was just checking for . . . a certain class of trap. As to the second . . ." She smiled. "It's an old wizard's trick. You know how a spell is a collection of syllables, each in its right order? Well, if the spell is built right, there's often stopping points, short of the whole thing. You go almost to the end of the spell, and then leave the last few syllables— sometimes even one—unsaid. Sort of like building a car, then putting the key in the ignition—but not turning it. Then when you need it, out come the last few syllables." She gestured with her fingers. "And *vroom*. Lightning shoots from your fingertips, or whatever."

"I've never had lightning shoot from my whatever; it just felt like it once." I was trying to keep things light and friendly, but I didn't like her tone. There was a shadowy undercurrent in her voice, something dark and deadly. I took her arm. "Excuse me, old friend, but you've missed the point—we're not here to fight with the local wizard."

She raised her eyes to heaven and rolled them. "I know that. Silly. I didn't want to walk into Rewnor's shop with an almost-built spell hanging over his head, and mine. Not a friendly thing to do. I was busy," she said, and her lips split in a remarkably sexy smile, "eating my words, eh?" She patted my shoulder. "You handle the sneaking around; leave the magic to me."

She pushed through the curtains; I followed.

Some day, if I'm lucky, I'm going to walk into a magician's shop or workroom that's lit like a library, clean as McDonald's, and sterile-smelling as a hospital.

I wasn't lucky today.

Rewnor's workshop smelled like a gym locker, redolent of old dirt, unwashed sweat, and variously related funguses eating away at toes and crotches.

Ugh.

No, the standard history of me is right, but I'm not a witling; I decided in junior high that football was to be a way of paying for college without slashing a four-year hemorrhage in Stash and Emma's savings. What I did in the fall was a job, and that's all. The stink of unwashed sweat holds no whiff of nostalgia for me. I spent too many hours in gym lockers, back on the Other Side, and don't miss the stench at all.

What light there was came from a pair of sputtering candles set into reflective holders high on the wall. Not even a glowsteel. What light there was revealed a smallish room lined by workbenches, an open door at the far end leading to immediate darkness.

The day was heating up outside, but the air was dank and chilly in here.

Shaking her head, Andrea walked to a workbench, picked up a fist-sized copper bowl, and took a sniff. "Myrryhm, hemp, and cinnamon? *Really?* I am unimpressed." She turned to me. "I've always been unfond of love potions, but if you're going to do them, it's perhaps best to *do* them. A simple increase of libido is hardly the same thing, don't you agree?"

There was no answer.

"Oh, *please*," Andrea said to the empty air, with a sniff. "I know you're here just as well as you know that I am, and for the same reason. Trying to hide your fire is useless, you know; you're being *very* silly, and that's starting to irritate my

146

bodyguard. I wouldn't want to irritate him, and I suspect you don't, either."

A bronzed god of a man strode out through the doorway, into the room. He stood a head taller than me, and I'm not a short man, and his wide shoulders threatened to split the seams of his wizard's robe.

"I was doing nothing of the sort," he said. "I was busy with a preparation in my back room." His voice was a baritone rumble, almost smooth enough to be singing. He clasped his hands in front of him and bowed his head slightly. "I am known as Rewnor; you are welcome in my humble shop."

Andrea returned the salute. "Call me Lotana, although that is not now and never has been my name."

He raised a protesting hand and tried to smile ingratiatingly. "Please, please, dear lady. Name spells are beyond such as me, and I'd know better, in any case." He squinted, as though looking at something hovering over her right shoulder. "I can't tell quite what it is, but it's about one syllable away from eating me, eh?"

"Or something." Her smile seemed genuine. "I thought I'd hidden it well."

"I thought you said you'd swallowed all your spells," I whispered, not particularly afraid of Rewnor hearing.

She crooked a smile. "You'd have been telling the truth, if he'd put a truth spell on you, wouldn't you?"

"I don't see the need." Rewnor spread his hands broadly. "I've recognized you as my better, good Lotana, but that doesn't make me blind. You're here for some purpose, and I doubt it's for love philtres of guaranteed harmlessness and questionable efficacy. Can I be of help?"

"Possibly," she said, idly picking up a tool from the table, a fairly serious violation of wizard etiquette, as I understood it. It looked more like a dentist's probe than anything else, except for a dim glow at the point. She tested the point against the ball of her thumb. "There've been rumors of things coming out of Faerie. I'd wondered what you've heard."

Rewnor looked down at her, and over at me, his face studiously blank, as though he was forcing himself not to take offense at the cavalier way she was handling his tools. "Things have been happening, Mistress Lotana, and that's the truth. As to what, you'd have to ask the likes of better than I."

"There was a murder here, a few tendays ago. A note was left behind. We would like to arrange to see it."

"How did you know I had it here?" He frowned. "You *are* good."

Well, actually, we hadn't known it was here. We were going to ask his help getting access to it.

Andrea started to say something, but I stopped her. "You know that Lotana is better than you are. You perhaps don't want to know how much, or all that is involved."

I made a mystical sign. It didn't mean anything, not on This Side, although Sister Berthe of Toulouse—the nun we used to call "Sister Birtha de Blues"—would have been proud at how easily I did it.

Rewnor raised a hand. "Ah. I see."

Andrea glared at me, irritated at how I was interfering, but I spread my hands in apology. "I'm sorry, Lotana, but there was no avoiding it. Rewnor was always going to see that there are great forces involved. Friend Rewnor is safest just giving us the note and staying out of all this."

"Well . . ." A ghost of a smile kissed her lips, and I wouldn't have minded joining it. "If you think so. I would have preferred to enlist his help, despite the danger, but . . ."

We were out of there, the paper in hand, within two minutes.

The note was written in the blocky printing that Andrea used to teach at her school in Home, for both English and Erendra.

The Warrior Lives

—it said, in big brown Erendra letters, now flaking. And below, in English, just:

Don't try to find me. Please. I'm getting closer.

"No, dammit, there's nothing I can do with it. He just dashed it off, and while he used blood, it isn't *his* blood. I can't use

148

things he's only casually interacted with for a location spell, or I'd be able to track anybody, anywhere, just by sorting through a few quadrillion oxygen molecules to find one that the quarry breathed."

Andrea was not happy.

Neither was I, as I stood next to the window, trying to fan the fumes outside. Andrea's attempt to see if the note could be used to trace Mikyn had involved some odorous compounds, and I didn't need for any of the inn's servitors to smell the sulfur and hellfire of a magician's preparations.

Below, the horses were saddled, and the others waited. We didn't absolutely have to get out of town right now, but in whatever direction he was traveling, Mikyn was heading away from us as time went by, and we wouldn't be able to catch him by standing still.

Wait for word of another Warrior killing? That was possible, of course, but dangerous. Why would some travelers— ones with suspiciously too much money in their kip—be hanging around Fenevar? A good question—so best to be sure it wasn't asked. Much better to move along the coast in either direction, and see if a farrier named Alezyn had been through, and when.

We took the back stairs down to the alley, and to the horses.

Tennetty had brought a fairly broad selection, from a dull, listless gray gelding pony for Ahira—who never liked a horse to have a lot of spirit or speed; I think he would have preferred a lame one, really—to a prancing pinto mare for herself.

I checked the cinch strap, then swung to the broad back of my chestnut gelding, his torn right ear suggesting that he'd lost out to a stallion at some point before he'd lost out to the gelder's knives and irons. He wanted to move faster than I was interested in, but, thankfully, Tennetty had equipped him with a vicious twisted-wire bit, and we quickly agreed that we'd proceed at my pace, not his.

"So?" Jason asked, coming abreast of the dwarf as we started off in a slow walk, down the main street toward the coastal road through the swamp, maybe a mile ahead. "Where are we going?"

Ahira shrugged. "Tromodec is about two days that way, Brae three the other way. What we have to decide—what I have to decide—is if we let the search for Mikyn trump looking into the Ehvenor matter." Ahira was, by common consent, including mine, in charge strategically—and that's in part because he didn't make decisions arbitrarily. "Anybody got any advice?"

"Brae," Andrea said. "It's one step closer to Ehvenor." At that moment a cloud passed in front of the sun, so that a shadow quite literally fell across her face. There was something in her expression, something I couldn't quite name. Obsession, perhaps? Compulsion, maybe? I dunno.

"Tromodec," I said. "A couple days probably won't make much difference, we can catch up with Mikyn quickly. Tromodec is closer; it means knowing something sooner. By at least a day." And we'd be two days farther away from Ehvenor and Faerie. We could probably find out all that was known about the things coming out of Faerie anywhere along the coast, and I had little preference for examining the buzz-saw close up.

Besides, if Ehvenor was all that important, there were likely other folks than us, other wizards than Andy looking into it. Let them get in the way of the axe for once.

"Brae," she said. "The matter of Ehvenor is more important. Didn't you hear the rumors of a village that had been wiped out?"

"I never believe rumors. I've started too many myself. Tromodec."

"*Brae,*" she said, her petulance only partly an act. There was more than insistence in her manner; perhaps a touch of fear?

"Tromodec." I smiled my most charming smile, no doubt dazzling her from scalp to crotch. "Wanna wrestle over it?"

"Later, maybe." She returned the smile like she meant it, earning both of us a glare from Jason.

I wasn't any too pleased with him, either; it had occurred to me more than once that if it wasn't for his presence, I'd likely be bunking with Andy instead of Ahira. I could have stood consoling the widow a couple of times.

Ahira turned to Jason. "Baron?"

Jason's chuckle sounded forced. "Oh, you mean me?" He was irritated with me; no doubt he'd side with his mother. "I favor Tromodec," he said.

Well, you could have knocked me over with a quarter-staff—I wouldn't have thought to duck. I should have thought it through, though—Jason was more interested in the search for Mikyn than the investigation of Ehvenor, which put us on the same side.

"If it works right," he went on, "we're closer to Mikyn; if it's wrong, we've only lost four days instead of six, the way it would be if we wrongly go to Brae."

Tennetty snorted. "I've got a better way. Just figure out which way is more likely to get us into trouble, and pick that one. It's what always happens, anyways."

"By which you mean Brae," I said.

"Sure. One step closer to Ehvenor; one foot further in the grave. I say Brae."

Ahira tugged on his reins, hard; his pony wanted to canter, and he didn't want that. "We have two for Tromodec, two for Brae. Which means that if this was a vote, I'd cast the deciding one, and get to decide. Since this isn't a democracy, and it's my call anyway, I get to decide."

Jason started to open his mouth, then stopped himself.

Ahira sighed. "I remember him, too, Jason. I remember how mad Karl and I were when we saw how his father had beaten him." He lowered his head for a moment, perhaps to bid farewell to an abused little boy, but when he raised it, his game face was back on—cold and merciless.

There was a time when Ahira could have gone up against anything with a smile on his face and a joke on his lips, but that time had passed.

"On one hand, we have the fact that Mikyn's moving around," he said. "Tromodec is the right move if we want to chase him down. Ehvenor and Faerie will stay where they are. On the other hand, the matter of Ehvenor and Faerie is more important than the problem of a rogue Home warrior, no matter who he is." His axe was bound across his saddle with quick-release ties that would let it go from both the saddle and sheath with one quick tug. He rested his free hand on it, as though asking it for help.

"If we knew for sure that we could find him quickly," Ahira said, "I might think differently, but, as it is, I say Brae. Ehvenor's more important; we head for Ehvenor."

When I was a kid, I always thought of a swamp as of necessity something like the Florida Everglades or the Maevish bogs—brush lightly covering a few spots of damp land and water, but mainly immense patches of quicksand that would suck you down forever if you stepped in the wrong place.

It's just as well that there's no guaranteed penalty for being wrong; I'd have paid it too many times over, in my life. Which probably would have been shorter, a lot shorter. I'd rather be lucky than right—there was a time I got involved in a small political mess in Sciforth, and definitely picked the wrong side. The good guys would have, as it turned out, stuck my head on a pole, while the bad guys and I split a pot of gold.

The swamp road twisted across the cluttered ground, seeking the ridge line, probably built up where there was no ridge. To the right and left, the ground fell, through tangles of vines and creepers, to an impenetrable morass of cypress and willow, the mess punctuated by infrequent stretches of open water and a rare sodden meadow.

The odd jay—there is no other kind—would occasionally perch in an overhead tree, to crap on us, taunt us, or both, and every so often I would hear the sound of slithering on dead leaves, but while the swamp should have been teeming with life, most of the life had learned to avoid humans, and wasn't going to make an exception for a quartet of them just because they were accompanied by a dwarf.

There were a few exceptions. At one point, the road twisted in hairpin turns down the side of a coastal ridge, and the last of the turns revealed a small lake, half a mile across, rimmed by rushes and cattails. A small doe had been drinking at the edge of the water; at our approach, she lifted her head, eyes wide as saucers, and vanished off into the brush with swooping bounds, startling a covey of swans from concealment and into flight.

Tennetty, always alert for game—or at least a chance to kill something—brought her loaded crossbow up, but didn't take the shot. My guess is that she didn't have a clear shot, and a crossbow has little stopping power—if you don't nail a deer through the spine, heart, or (much more likely) lungs, you've got a long chase ahead of you.

"So much for a good dinner tonight," she said.

We camped that night by the side of a straight section of road, hanging hammocks between paired trees rather than trusting the ground. Snakes and all.

Even I couldn't have crept through the brush silently, and the road stretched out straight a quarter mile in either direction, so we lit a cookfire and relaxed, knowing that we'd see anybody coming up on us in plenty of time.

Jason took first watch, while Ahira sat up with him, the boy nervously stirring at the fire, the dwarf rewinding the leather and wire wrapping of his axe-hilt. Me, I couldn't sleep, not yet, so I improvised a pad of blankets in front of my saddle, and sat with them, stropping my dagger. It's hard to have too much of an edge on a knife.

Tennetty's eyes were sleepy as she joined the three of us, a brown blanket wrapped around her shoulders.

I looked up at her. "You look tired."

She nodded as she dropped a folded blanket to the ground next to me and seated herself tailor-fashion on it, huddling in her sleeping blanket.

"I feel tired," she said. "Just too wound up, I guess." She stared off into the dark like she was expecting something to leap out of it, then shook her head. "Happens, sometimes."

I scooted over a bit, to let her use my saddle as a back rest. She gave a quick Tennetty-smile—lips together, their ends barely curling up—and leaned against it, and against me. I could feel the warmth of her body through the blanket, which told me that it had been far too long since I'd been with a woman.

Still, I guess those are the times that I most like out on the trail—the end of the day, when there's nothing to do but sit and talk until sleep drives you to your bed, whatever it is.

Tennetty's arms were folded under her blanket. Knowing Tennetty, each hand would be resting on the butt of a loaded pistol. I don't mean to be condescending; it felt reassuring.

One thing I could always count on is that Tennetty would be ready for sudden violence. Too ready, maybe, but ready.

The dwarf was rewinding the leather in some sort of intricate weave that I couldn't quite follow, his thick fingers moving with their familiar delicacy, while his eyes and mind were elsewhere. On the ground in front of him was a fresh spool of bronze thread—combined with the leather, it would give a good, solid grip, be the handle or hands wet or dry. (Whenever it all hit the fan, my hands were always wet, as soon as I noticed them.)

Picking up the theme, Jason had his revolver and cleaning kit out, the cartridges, bottles, cleaning cloths, and other paraphernalia neatly lined up on the blanket in front of him, steel and brass flickering in the firelight.

He cleaned and oiled the pistol in just a few moments—doesn't take much if you haven't fired it—then wiped it down with an oily rag before reloading it and slipping it back into his holster, thonging it into place.

"Other one in your bag?" I asked.

"Eh?" He looked over at me. "Other—oh: the other revolver." His smile was a trifle too easy. "I doubt it. I left it with your daughter."

"Jane, I trust, and not Dorann?"

He decided to take that as a joke, which it was. "Just in case," he said.

Tennetty, her eyes still sleepy, nodded in approval.

I stropped my dagger some more. Nehera, the master smith, had made it from a single piece of iron, lightly sprinkled with just enough charcoal, then heated and folded over, hammered on hundreds of thousands of times, making it strong despite the thinness of the blade. It would bend rather than break, but it could still hold enough of an edge to cut through muscle and cartilage. The surface was covered with the marking of the process: dark striations, like a fingerprint. I could have recognized the pattern among a hundred similar knives.

I tested the edge of the blade against my thumbnail; even with a light touch, it bit hard into the nail, which was more than good enough, so I wiped it down with oil and slid it back into its sheath.

When I looked up, Jason was eyeing me, perhaps a bit skeptically. I tried to decide whether he was thinking that I was acting out some nervousness, or just unable to keep my hands still, but I've never been much good at mind reading, so I slipped one of my throwing knives out of its sheath and started to work on that. I don't *have* to keep my hands busy, mind; I just like to. Can quit any time I want.

Jason caught Tennetty's eye and smiled tolerantly.

Ahira had caught the byplay. "You make the common assumption, Jason Cullinane," he said. "You assume that the objects we live and work with are just that: objects, and no more."

The boy shrugged. "Useful objects," he said, "but sure." He patted at his holster. "I mean, this is more useful than six flintlock pistols, but it's a thing, and that's all."

"No. It's never just a thing. Not if you listen," Ahira said, with a sigh. "I spent a lot of time making this battle-axe," he said, taking another turn of bronze wire around the handle. "Only part of my smithing came with the territory— I had a lot to learn. It took me three tries to get just the *right* steel, and I had an expert steelmaker helping me. It took me more than a tenday to hammer that blob of metal into shape, working carbon and brightsand into the edge just deep enough. I had picked up ten pieces of ash and oak in my travels, and it took me even longer to whittle them down to thin laths, then glue them together so that they would hold, never splitting."

He rubbed the flat of his hand against the dark metal. "You work on or with something, some thing, long enough, and there's part of you in it. Not just for now, not just while you live, or even while you and it exist together, but for forever."

His eyes grew vague and dreamy. "There was a door, one night. It led to a room in which three children lay sleeping, two of them as dear to me as children could ever be. There had been assassins about that night, and while we thought them all dead, we could have been wrong. So your father and I sat in front of the door that night, perhaps just in case we were wrong, perhaps because we wouldn't have been able to sleep."

Tennetty leaned her head against my shoulder, her eye shut but her expression that of a little girl listening to a favorite bedtime story. I put my arm around her; she started, just a trifle, then relaxed. If I didn't know better, I'd swear she made a vague rumble, almost like a purr.

Ahira stroked the axe head yet again, then ran his rough fingers affectionately through Jason's hair. "And all night long, this axe whispered to me, *Don't worry. Nobody will ever get past us to hurt them.*"

I don't understand it, not really, but for the first night in longer than I care to think about, my sleep was deep, dark, warm, and dreamless.

Breakfast the next morning, as sunlight began to break through the brush, was bread, cold sausage, and cheese for the humans, accompanied by a clay bottle of resiny local wine; it was oats, carrots, and apples for the horses, washed down with stream water for all.

I bit into another hunk of sausage, and swallowed. Spitting it out would have been uncouth, and probably slightly less nutritious than swallowing. Look, I like garlic—I like it a lot; I swear to God—but I don't think of it as a breakfast spice.

A cookfire probably would have helped the taste, but we needed to be on our way.

I really wanted something hot, though. A mug of tea would have warmed my hands and middle quite nicely. I thought about having a nip from the flask of brandy in my pack—that would have done it too—but decided against it.

Ahira, Andy, and Jason broke camp; I helped Tennetty with the horses.

"I've ridden on worse," I said, just to make conversation.

She smiled. "Not too bad," she said. "I checked them over as carefully as possible—Ahira's pony is slightly spavined, but he's the worst of them. Not really bad. Mostly freshly shod, all saddle-broken. I'd like to see how they handle gunfire," she said, with a sigh, as though she knew how they would, which she did.

They would run like hell, that's what they would do.

For a horse to hold still when there's lightning cracking somewhere just above and behind his head isn't something that comes naturally, or in one afternoon. The way you shoot from any but the best-trained horse's back is to dismount, tie the horse to something that won't move, walk away, and then do it.

Either that, or be sure that

a) your first shot hits, and

b) you have a great need to be somewhere else quickly right after, and you don't much care where.

"The hostler must have had a large stock," I said. Supply and demand works even if you've never heard the term.

"Yeah. More than he needed." She nodded. "He bought a big string from an upcountry rancher, about eight, nine tendays ago; expecting a trader a few tendays back."

I know, I know, it's obvious—but nobody else had seen it, either. It's one thing to play armchair quarterback; it's another to be out there, calling the plays yourself.

"Andy?"

She swallowed a mouthful of bread before she answered. "Yes?"

"In order to locate Mikyn, you need either something of him, or something he's interacted with intimately, right?"

She didn't get it either, which is understandable. If you haven't ever made something from cold iron and fire, you won't understand how very much trouble it is, how every hammer stroke puts something of you in it, even if all you're making is something as humble as, say, the barbeque fork I'd made in ninth-grade metal shop, the pail hooks we used to churn out by the dozens during my summer at Sturbridge . . .

. . . or a horseshoe.

Jason was quicker—he had already approached his horse, and lifted its front hoof. "Nope—this one could stand a reshoeing, in fact."

"Try another one," I said, reaching for my own horse's left front leg. Tennetty, one hand flat against the side of its neck, kept it calm while I lifted the leg.

Nope. You can often tell a farrier by his style, and dwarf-trained smiths had a distinctive one, a lot cleaner than that of whoever had shoed this horse.

Two down, and no go.

Ahira checked his pony, and then Andy's nervous black mare.

"I think we're on to something. Eight nails," he said. "Nice dwarvish style." Ahira's broad face was smiling so hard I thought it might split. "Walter, you may take one 'nicely done' out of petty cash." He turned to Andy. "How long? And do you need me to get it off the horse?"

She shook her head. "Not if you two will hold it still. And ten minutes, if that."

It barely took five, although it left her face sweaty, and ashen. Like mine.

Her quivering finger pointed back the way we had come. Toward Fenevar. Toward Tromodec. Away from Ehvenor.

Ahira shook his head. "Damn it," he said, as he looked up at me. "We've got a rogue on our hands, but the reasoning still holds. Ehvenor is more important. We leave Mikyn for after Ehvenor; we head toward Brae."

Shit. Magic scares me.

CHAPTER THIRTEEN

In Which We Are Welcomed to Brae

Joint undertakings stand a better chance when they benefit both sides.

—EURIPIDES

Hey. The ruby was just sitting there. Okay?

—WALTER SLOVOTSKY

THROUGHOUT MOST OF my childhood, Stash's best friend was Mike Wocziewsky, a local cop. He had been either a detective or maybe just a plainclothes investigator, but he'd been caught in a wrong bed, and rather than taking a hearing on Conduct Unbecoming, he'd gone back to a blue uniform, and the streets.

I liked Big Mike. He was built like a big blue barrel, smoked cigars that looked and smelled like dog turds, and never stopped telling stories. He gave me my first jackknife, an official Scout knife. No, they weren't the best the money could buy, but there was something wonderful about having the real equipment. I loved that knife.

And the stories Big Mike used to tell.

"There are these five scuzzballs hanging around on the corner, and I know for sure that they are the same scumbuckets that had hit old man Kaplan's liquor store the week before and left him bashed up pretty bad.

"Now, you gotta understand: I *don't* like old man

Kaplan. The cheap bastard doesn't believe in a policeman's discount—well, didn't. These days I have trouble getting him to take my money. You should see the case I got for Christmas, Stash . . .

"—But never mind, even though I wouldn't give a shit if he'd fallen down the stairs at home, when he's on my street he's one of my people, and I don't like having one of the people on my block lying in a hospital bed with one tube running up his nose and another out of his shlong, understand?

"Back to the douchebags on the corner. I don't have anything to pull them in on, and besides, I'm a bluesuit now, not a shield, and so it's none of my business. Bluesuits don't investigate. Except, well, I don't let dogfuckers shit on my people, not on my block. So I go up to one of the cuntfaces, and pull him away.

" 'Pretend like you don't want to talk to me,' I say, kind of low, but just not quite low enough. He's not slow, and he gets the idea real quick, and shouts out something as he sort of swings at me. But I've got about a hundred pounds on him, and he knows better than to really slug me—I mean, if he does that, he knows I'll put in so much stick time that his *descendants* will hurt.

"But while he's swinging on me, I grab his arms, and shove him up against a wall, real gentle, just hard enough to distract him while I slip the hundred I'd palmed into his pants pocket.

"Now, the other dingleballs are watching all of this, and one of them sees it, which saves me some trouble. I just let him go.

"I didn't know how far it would go, and I didn't much care, but a couple of days later I visit the dickhead in the hospital, and he's in even worse shape than Kaplan, and very willing to talk. Lay a hand on him? Nah. I just offered to give him another payoff. For some reason, he didn't want that.

"Hundred bucks a lot of money? Sure is. To a cop. I got paid back. I bet old man Kaplan thought it was the best hundred he ever spent."

———

I'd been expecting to hit town in midafternoon, but we must have been making better time than I'd thought.

It was noon when Brae came on us suddenly, or vice versa, depending on how you look at it. The way I see it, the center of the universe is a couple of centimeters behind the middle of my eyebrows. The center of the universe just moves around a bit.

In any case, we rounded a bend, and there it was, a collection of one-, two-, and three-storied wattle-and-daub buildings and twisty little streets sprawled across the coastal hills, running from the crest of a ridge all the way down to the Cirric.

Not much of a city.

"Reminds me of an old joke," I said. "Waiter comes over to the table. Says, 'How did you find your steak?' 'I just looked under the parsley, and there it was.' "

Andy laughed dutifully, as did Ahira. Neither of the other two did. I guess you have to be raised speaking English in order to get the jokes—and Tennetty wasn't. And you've probably got to have a sense of humor, unlike Jason Cullinane.

At first, Brae stank of fish. Not surprisingly; the waters in that region are rich with fish, and dried alewife—ugly fish—is a major export. Despite the smell, my mouth watered at the thought of fresh spotted trout over an open fire, seasoned only with salt, peppers, oil, and maybe a squeeze from a small, sweet, Netanal lemon.

Ahead, straddling the road, stood a guard station at the entrance to town—antique construction, but freshly manned.

"Strange," Ahira said. He was handling the horse better than I'd expected, although I knew he would have preferred his pony. I had another use in mind for the pony.

I nodded. Along the Cirric, most danger to the locals comes from the sea, not the land. The domains tend to be on good terms with each other, generally saving their hostility for pirates and islanders.

"Okay, everybody," Ahira said. "Let's take things nice and easy; I don't see any need for a problem. Nice slow walk toward the guard station. Walter, you're on."

This is why we get along well—Ahira knows when to let

me be, and when not to. Actually, I'd been working up another cover story, but Ahira pointed out that we had met some of the travelers in Fenevar, and could easily be exposed as somebody with something to hide if we changed our story. Not that that would necessarily be horrible; a lot of folks who travel through the Eren regions aren't quite what they seem, and anybody who automatically believes what a traveler says is too trusting by more than half.

I turned in the saddle and gave everybody the once-over. The rifles were lashed in a bundle with the bows, and the pistols were safely stowed away. Andy was dressed in her wizard's robes, but had, as she put it, "dimmed her flame" to that of a minor wizard, much less powerful in appearance than in reality. I'd have to take her word for it.

She looked too good, dammit, and the smile on her face, while not too eager, was just a notch off.

Tennetty, a blue cotton shift over glossy leather riding breeches, was her maid, and if a maid carried a largish dagger, that wasn't particularly surprising.

Nor was a three-person bodyguard for a wizard, even one of them a dwarf.

We looked the part, I supposed. Except for Jason. There was a bulge under his tunic, which was okay; lots of people carried an extra knife or purse against their body, but the butt of his revolver peeked out. Which wasn't okay—while slaver rifles and pistols were becoming increasingly common-place as time went by, I didn't want to have to explain what we were doing with something that was so clearly the product of Home.

"Lace up your tunic a bit," I said. "And when you put the holster back on, shift it around so that the butt isn't visible, eh?" If everything hit the fan, I'd be more than happy for Jason's revolver, but I'd be less than happy if that's what made everything hit the fan.

We couldn't stand a search, but a search isn't a common custom when passing into an Eren town.

Last but not least . . . "Andy?"

She closed her eyes for a long moment. "Two local magi-cians. Not particularly bright flames; not terribly powerful or

accomplished. Or they're doing the same thing that I am."
She smiled. "Only better."

I would have shivered, but it was too warm out.

The guards at the station had been stamped out of the same
mold: medium-sized, stocky men, with walrus-style mustaches
and sharp chins, large hands that held on to the stocks of
their spears either for support or out of readiness. Me, if I had
to stand guard, I'd want a spear, too—gives you something to
lean on.

About three-quarters of a wagon wheel had been stuck
up on the side of the guardhouse, for reasons that escaped
me for the moment.

"Names and purpose in Brae?" one asked.

"Tybel, Gellin, Taren," I said, indicated me, Ahira, and
Jason. "Bodyguard to Lotana, wizard. Duanna," I said, indicating Tennetty, "wizard's maid."

Now, I won't swear that it's true, but I've always thought
of bodyguards as nontalkative types, and bet most people do.
A few clipped words might save us a lot of fast talking. "Passing through, or passing by—your choice; no trouble wanted.
May stay one night, two, three, or none. Planning on trading
further down the coast. We don't discuss what, where, or
who."

They would figure out that further down the coast meant
Ehvenor, but it wouldn't be in character for me to discuss it.

The two guards shrugged at each other. "By command
of Lord Daeran, be welcome in Brae," one said formally,
with a slight bow.

"The town is laid out like this," the other said, indicating
the broken wagon wheel. "Town square here." He tapped
the hub with the point of his spear. "Lord's residence here;
if you're looking to buy fish in quantity, you negotiate that
with the Valet." He did say "Valet," honest—it was the same
word as for the fellow who lays out your clothes and cleans
your room for you.

"You'll find inns along High Street," he went on, tapping
a spoke. "Fish markets along the docks." He tapped against
some of the broken spokes. "Ride through Main Street,"

another tap, "and through the center of town and by the Posts of Punishment on your way."

Andrea cocked her head to one side. "Wouldn't it be quicker to take the Street of the Eel up the hill to the Old Avenue?"

He looked at her suspiciously. "I hadn't realized you'd been in Brae before, Mistress Lotana."

She gave him a chilly smile. "I haven't."

She made a brushing gesture with her fingers, something halfway between a gesture of dismissal and the sort of finger movement a wizard often makes when throwing a spell. I didn't like it, but there wasn't much I could do about it, or even a good reason to argue about it. Andrea was, after all, good with location spells, and it couldn't hurt for one of our party to know her way around Brae.

It could, however, hurt for one of our party to shoot off her mouth, and I resolved to discuss that with her later.

The soldier decided to drop the matter. "By the Lord's direction, everyone is to pass the Posts of Punishment," he said. "Any other needs?"

I would have asked about the Posts of Punishment, but with Andy already having shot her mouth off, more curiosity didn't seem called for.

I jerked my thumb at the pony, trying to keep things casual. "Could use a good smith. Useless, there, threw a shoe this morning."

Shoeing a horse takes some tools and effort—removing a shoe takes a lot less.

A look passed between the guards, and one walked to the rear of our group, examining the gray pony's foot closely for a moment, then nodding.

The fact that I was ready for all of this didn't mean that I liked any of it, although as the guard let the hoof drop, the chill in the air warmed up. I wasn't born yesterday—I had pulled both front shoes the day before, to be sure that the hoof would be properly dirtied, and the sharp edges worn a bit.

"Smith? Not a farrier?"

I spread my hands. "That would be fine, too." I shrugged, calmly, casually, but not too casually. A bodyguard with no connections to Mikyn wouldn't be upset at the question, but would think it a bit strange. "I wouldn't have thought Brae large enough to need a full-time farrier."

That must have passed muster, because he nodded and said, "You'll find Deneral the smith on the Street of the Dry Creek," he said, returning to his tour-guide persona, "at the base of the hill. He does fair shoeing, so they say. Again, welcome to Brae."

We rode past the wattle-and-daub houses of merchants and town-bound tradesmen, toward the center of town.

"Posts of Punishment?" Jason asked.

I shrugged. "Common along the coast."

There's an Other Side variant of it called crucifixion—basically, you tie somebody up on a stick, don't let them have food or water, and let them die of thirst and exposure.

I frowned. Maybe I haven't seen enough death and suffering, but I really didn't need the local lord ordering me exposed to some more.

Ahead, the street narrowed; we shifted from riding two-two-one abreast to a single line, with me, as chief bodyguard, first, Ahira last.

Across the square were six posts, each about the size and shape of a telephone pole, each topped with a vaguely cigar-shaped iron cage barely large enough to contain a person. What amounted to a siege tower stood nearby, rolled just out of reach of the first cage.

That one, and three others, were occupied by motionless forms, all rags and bones, slumped up against the metal.

From that distance, I couldn't tell if any of the four were alive, but then I saw an arm move.

Tennetty grunted. I thought she had a stronger stomach than any of the rest.

Ahira hissed at her to shut up. So did I. I wasn't too worried; being nauseated by the sight of this wasn't particularly a break in character.

"Fine," she said, her voice low. "But I know one of them. I recognize her from Home. She's an engineer, name of Kenda. And the one in the far cage. That's Bast."

Ohmigod. I remembered Bast as a skinny little boy.

Jason's horse took a prancing step as he walked it up to my side. "What do we do?"

"Nothing quickly," I said. "Nothing at all, until Ahira and I say so. If we say so. Understood?"

His face was white, but he nodded.

CHAPTER FOURTEEN

In Which I Go for a Stroll

There are usually aleph-null ways to do something right, but aleph-one ways to do it wrong.

—LOU RICCETTI

Lou always makes things complicated. What he means is that if you choose how to do it at random, you will screw it up. What he's leaving out is that if you're careful about how you do it, you'll probably screw it up. Still, "probably" is better than "will."

—WALTER SLOVOTSKY

I'VE ALWAYS TRIED TO both keep and avoid a sense of proportion. Ever since the freshman philosophy class that James Michael and Karl and I were in together.

There's lots of ways to teach ethics. Professor Alperson tried a complicated one.

"Okay," he said. "Classical ethical problem, with a twist. You're in a specific city on a specific date and time, and you're walking along the railroad tracks. You hear the whistle of an oncoming train.

"Now, ahead of you, you see two people stuck to the tracks; each is wedged in by the foot. One is an old man, who you know to be a good and saintly type; the other is a young boy, who you know to be the worst brat in all of . . . well, never mind. You only have time to save one. What do you do, and does it matter what you do?"

We batted that one back and forth for awhile. I, of course, challenged the parameters he had laid down—never take a problem at face value—but he held firm. No, there was no way either was going to free himself, the train was not going to stop, and I knew that for sure, and we'd discuss epistemology some other time.

James Michael tried to take the long look, but rejected it. "In a hundred years, they'll both be dead, so it doesn't matter? Is that what you're getting at?"

Alperson shrugged. "Maybe. Maybe I'm not getting at anything."

Karl took it seriously. "You save one. Either one. You save the old man because he is good and virtuous and because virtue should be respected, or you save the boy because no matter how much of a brat he is, he still deserves to grow up, but you do save one of the two."

Alperson smiled. "What if I were to tell you that the date is August 6, 1945, and that the city is Hiroshima, and that in two minutes, the bomb the *Enola Gay* is about to drop will kill all three of you? Would that make any difference?"

Karl shook his head. "Of course not."

Alperson's smile grew larger. "Good. I don't know if I agree, but good. You've taken a position. Now support it."

It took us the rest of the day to put it all together, but the locals were still talking about it, and evincing curiosity didn't make us seem, well, curious.

There had been a murder just outside of the city of Brae, but well within the domain of Lord Daeran.

There had also been a contract team of engineers from Home here, laying out a glassmaking plant. Canning—well, jarring—of fish in glazed clay pots was one of the ways of putting down a larger-than-usable catch. While overcooked and oversalted lake alewife fillets in a sealed pot of brine was not my idea of a good time, there were folks inland for whom that was a great if expensive treat, and a very good supplement to a diet that consisted largely of bread and onion, with too little protein.

Real glass canning, though, would have been an improvement—safer, faster, cheaper. Good glassmaking was something that Lou Riccetti wanted, and the Cirric shore was the right place to put such a plant. So he had sent out an engineer team to negotiate and reconnoiter, led by Bast, one of his senior engineers. Bast was a good fellow, who I still, deep within my heart of hearts, thought of as a skinny boy who drew more than his share of guard duty.

A new idea of Lou's, contracting out labor.

Not a great one, as it turned out.

Farm slaves were increasingly rare these days, horses and oxen increasingly common. Of the circle of farms surrounding Brae, owing fealty to Lord Daeran, only a handful had even a single slave; most were worked by large families and their horses and oxen.

Except for one, a small plot worked by an old man named Heneren, his childless wife, and a superannuated slave, name of Wen'red. They had been visited by a traveling farrier, who was traveling through the arc of farms, reshoeing as he went.

He had swiftly murdered Heneren and his wife, announced to Wen'red that he was now free, and left the old slave alone as he headed off toward the city.

Wen'red had waited a day before he had started in toward the city, on foot. It took him several days—he hadn't been off the farm in thirty years, and got lost. But he knew his duty to his late owner, and reported the murders to a city armsman . . .

. . . the day after Bast had been seen helping the farrier book passage away from Brae.

The afternoon of the morning that Mikyn had sailed way.

Two days before an armsman returned to town, bringing word of the state of Mikyn's victims.

It was only natural that Bast and company would offer help and shelter to a Home raider, even one in a farrier's disguise that they would have pierced easily.

It was equally natural for Lord Daeran to try Bast and company for conspiracy in the murder of Brae subjects, and to stake them out in the hot sun and cool night, providing them only water, and only enough to keep them alive until they would die of starvation and exposure.

Nice folks, eh?

———————

"Just about midnight," Ahira said. "Guard will be changing any time."

My time. No matter how much intelligence you have, you can always use good intelligence, if you catch my drift.

We had taken conspicuously rich rooms that were even more conspicuously secure. They were on the third floor of the inn, with but a single door entrance, and two balconies, neither of which would be easily accessible from below, and only barely from above—the overhanging roof would prevent somebody from simply dropping down from roof to balcony.

There was nothing that would prevent me from rappelling down the side of the building into the edge of the square below, except the possibility of some passersby seeing what was going on.

But local light-discipline was lax, and two of the lamps on the street were out, the residents not yet braced by armsmen demanding they be lit.

More than enough shadow for the likes of me.

Walk out the front door? Sure, I could have done that— but it's always better to have the option of being officially somewhere else when there's skulduggery going on.

That's me, Walter Slovotsky: skuldugger.

I sat tailor-fashion on the floor, Andrea behind me, fingers kneading at my shoulders hard, just this side of bruising. I might turn down a massage from a pretty woman, but only rarely from somebody who is good at it, and never from a pretty woman who is good at it.

Jason scowled. I had a blindfold over my eyes, but I could hear him scowl.

"I should go too," he said.

Tennetty snorted. "Like you could get him out of trouble?"

His voice was too quiet. "Yes," he said. "Like I could get him out of trouble."

He was right—he had saved my life last time out—but it was irrelevant. We weren't configured for violence or flight, and I didn't see any way to change that, not tonight. If we had been more cold-blooded, we would have left the engineers in the hot sun for another day before I went reconnoitering—

giving the rest of the group time to get beyond town, ready to run if things went sour.

But no. They had been up there for days and days, slowly burning to death and starving in the hot sun, and while I didn't see any possible way I could get them out tonight, the sooner we knew what we were up against, the sooner we could get them out.

If we could get them out.

Look—truth is that the importance of something doesn't have a lot of effect on whether or not it's doable. I've had too many lessons on that already; I hoped this wasn't going to be another one.

Time for a quick sneak around, to find out whether rescue for the engineers consisted of a breakout, or a merciful death.

Or nothing at all. If you can't do it, you can't do it.

"Time," I said, rising to my feet. I opened my eyes, and could see through the blindfold that the lamps were still on in the room. "Lights out."

I heard several puffs of air, and then: "Lights are out."

The best way to see in darkness is to be born a dwarf— not only do they see better with less light, they can see three colors down into the infrared, and can find their way at a dead run through territory and conditions where you and I wouldn't have a prayer.

The best way wasn't open to me. The second best way to see well in darkness is, first, to have the heredity that gives you decent night vision; second, to eat your carrots, whether you like them or not—I don't; and third, to give your eyes enough time in darkness before you venture out into it.

Black is one of my favorite colors, particularly at night. The trouble is, it's the classic color of a thief. Similarly, it would have been nice to rub some black greasepaint over my face and hands, but that would have labeled me as someone skulking about.

Ahira gripped my shoulder for a moment. "Don't get too close, and don't get into trouble." He was always trying to keep me out of trouble, and it was only through the obvious necessity of it that he had agreed to my night walk.

"Trouble? Me?" I smiled. "How could anybody who looks this good get into trouble?"

He didn't chuckle, although his grim frown lightened a shade or two. "True enough. Don't try to get too close—you're much too high class to be concerned about the fine details of the Posts of Punishments. Just make a quick survey of the situation, then get back here."

"Sure."

What the well-dressed thief was wearing this year: black cotton breeches of a nice thick weave, neatly bloused in plain leather boots that were somewhat better made than they looked; a dark tan shirt, jauntily slashed to the waist, all that covered by a brown cloak whose collar would work as a hood, if need be. A particularly short shortsword, suspended from the swordbelt with cloth linkages, instead of metal—no clanking when I walk, thank you. A fine leather sap tucked into the belt—a footpad's weapon, but something a bodyguard might carry. Two braces of throwing knives hidden here and there, and a largish pouch slung pertly over the right shoulder, containing some money, a couple of flasks of healing draughts, and a few oddments. Gloves of the softest pigskin, which gripped the short woven leather rope quite nicely as I tied it into a rappelling rig, then passed one end of the long climbing rope through.

The street was quiet. With Ahira holding one end, I threw the other end over the edge, and stepped out into the night.

There's basically two ways around a city—you can stick to the main roads, or try to keep in alleys and back streets. I passed down several alleys before I found what I was looking for: a tavern across the street, its open door belching sailing songs into the night, and on this side of the street a raised walkway.

I pulled some dirt out, then stripped off my shoes, socks, gloves, cloak, belt, sword, and shirt, wrapped everything else tightly in the cloak, and stuffed the bundle under the walkway, patting dirt back into place over it.

Ahira was right. Somebody who looked the way I had wouldn't have any business skulking about the center of town, past the Posts of Punishment, alone or in company.

Shirtless, I straightened and slung the bag over my shoulder and strutted across the street toward the tavern.

First, a bit of beer. No, first, a *lot* of beer.

The street was cold under my feet as I walked across the street, and through the broad door, into noise and light and singing.

"Hey," I said. "Is there nobody who will drink with a sailor?"

CHAPTER FIFTEEN

In Which an Old Acquaintance Is Briefly Renewed

He is the best sailor who can steer within fewest points of the wind, and exact a motive power out of the greatest obstacles.
—HENRY DAVID THOREAU

It's always seemed to me that sailors spend most of their time making up funny names for things.
—WALTER SLOVOTSKY

THE FIRST TIME I WENT sailing, I don't think it went terribly well. Some people have no sense of humor . . .

I had a summer job at a Y camp in Michigan—just driving a truck, actually, although that was more fun than it sounded. What I got to do was haul campers out on expeditions—canoeing down a river in Canada, hiking through the forest in the Upper Peninsula, survival camping in a national reserve, like that—and hauling them back. All in the back of slightly modified trucks. Grossly illegal—all the laws specified school buses—but as long as there weren't any accidents, nobody was going to bother the Y.

There were two neat things about the job. One was the scenery; that part of the world is pretty. The other one appealed to my laziness: when there weren't campers to be driven around, I didn't have anything that I had to do.

So I hung around the camp. Ran five miles a day to keep my wind up; rebuilt a few forest paths and such, but mainly just goofed off around and read—Stash and Emma would send me a CARE package each week with five packs of M&Ms, ten new paperbacks, a couple pairs of socks, and a totally useless dozen condoms. (I didn't find any need for condoms in an all-boys' camp.)

One day, one of the campers—a sixth grader, I think— asked if I was willing to come out and skipper an E-scow for him and a few of his friends. It was a single-masted racing shell with twin daggerboards, fast and lovely as it skimmed across the lake, but if you didn't handle it just right, it could capsize in a breath of wind. Seems that while all five of them were very experienced sailors, the camp rules required an adult in charge, and I was considered one, being all of nineteen at the time.

It was strange. Mickey, the kid who was really in charge, would address me very formally—"Skipper, I think we should stand by to come about," and then I'd say, "Stand by to come about," and they'd framish the glimrod and farble the kezenpfaufer, or whatever needed to be done, and wait for me to respond to Mickey's nod with a "come about."

The only part they didn't like was when I told them stuff like, "All right, let's hoist up the landlubbers and batten down the hatches."

No sense of humor.

Particularly when I said, "Stand by to capsize."

"The thing is," my new friend said, his thick arm thrown across my shoulder, "is that the *Watersprite* may *look* like the slowest scow on the face of the Cirric . . ." actually, he said "Shirrick," but you get the idea ". . . and it may *smell* like the least-bailed excuse for a floating cesspool ever to dishonor the sewer-water in which it floats, and it may be *captained* by the stupidest man ever to risk falling overboard and poisoning the fish below, but, once you get used to her and her ways, she's even worse. Havanudda beer."

He was a broad, thick man, with a rippling sailor's beard that spilled down both cheeks, across his neck and down his chest. Beneath the beard, his face was sweaty and dirty in the light of the sputtering candles that dripped wax onto the filthy surface of the rough-hewn table. Absently, he crushed a beetle with his thumb, then drained some more beer, one hand on my knee.

I think he was about to launch into another long, drunken monologue—drunks do that, a lot—so I interposed another suggestion.

"So," I said, weaving in time with him, "you think I should not think about thinking about signing on." My slur was worse than his, but not much.

"Welen, my pet . . ." he waved a finger. He was trying to point, probably. "I think you'd be crazy to entertain the thought of considering contemplating the idea of thinking about signing on."

"Aw, it can't be as bad as all that, now can it?"

"Can't it now? I see right through you, Welen, and don't you think I don't. I know what you're up to."

I forced a warm smile. "Oh, you do, do you?" I didn't look toward the door, but with a bit of luck I could make it out into the night with a kick, a leap, and a dash.

"Don't you think I don't—been too long with dirt instead of a deck under your feet, eh? It shows, man, it shows. A man's got to eat—and drink, eh?—and a sailor's got to sail. I don't doubt that, Welen-pretty, but you can do better than the *Watersprite*, is all I say, except to add that you can't do worse."

He rose, wobbly as a newborn colt. "No time like the present—just let me finish this, and we're off. Hey, Tonen, Rufol—I'm off. Are you with me, or against me? Swear to the Fish, I do, you'll not find your way back alone. I think you are drunk, the two of you, the both of you are drunk."

"Drunk, us? No, just reefed a bit too tight," another sailor said, as he and yet another lurched to their feet, and we all lurched out into the night.

We staggered down the street, down the hill, toward the center of town, belting out a very pretty harmony on a sailing song usually used to time the pulling of a rope.

I took the baritone lead; I'd spent a fair amount of time impersonating—no, *being*—a sailor; it was one way to move along the coast and among the Shattered Islands without drawing any attention, and ships are always in need of crews.

The light-negligence that I'd seen higher up the hill

wasn't echoed in the center of town. The poles were ringed by a dozen lanterns, and a ten-man squad of soldiers stood guard from nearby. If I had to, I would have bet there was another troop in the dark of the lord's house, across the way, and certainly plenty more within call at the barracks. Coastal cities had always been subject to pirate raids, and local lords knew to keep troops handy.

"—so haul them hard, sailors,

"Pull them down and away,

"You'll work hard for your money,

"No drinking today.

"So haul them hard, sailors—"

One of the troop broke away and stalked across the darkened ground toward us.

"Be still, the lot of you," he said, smiling, "M'lord sleeps with his windows open, and if you wake him you'll not be finding him amused."

My new friend threw his arm companionably about the soldier's shoulders. "He doesn't like singing? What kind of lord is this?"

The poor soldier gagged at the smell of his breath. I didn't blame him. The sailor released him, then staggered toward the nearest of the posts, dragging me by the arm.

"Come look at what we have here. Eh, but what *do* we have here? Skinny little birds on their perches. Hello, skinny little bird? Would you like to come down from there and perch on my face?"

From the cage, Bast's skeletal face looked listlessly down, his eyes dull. There was no sign of recognition; I doubt he could even have focused properly. I wouldn't have wanted to bet he could take another day. Kenda looked even worse, and the two in the cages beyond were unmoving, perhaps already dead.

The cages were secured by locks, not apparently welded shut. No, not welded shut at all—as Kenda shifted position slightly, the door squeaked against its catch. Not good, but not as bad as it could have been—it was possible that they had been welded in there. There isn't a This Side lock I can't open, given the right tools and a few minutes. I had the right tools in my pack—the few minutes would be a problem.

Never mind that for now. Just get information.

One guard sat in the door at the base of the siege tower, a tall, thick column probably concealing a circular staircase—it was thicker than would have been needed for just a ladder, and it would be much easier to manhandle bound prisoners up a staircase than a ladder.

"Heyheyhey," the guard said. "No talking to the condemned, eh? Be off and on your way."

We staggered off into the night, belching out another chorus.

Dockside, my thick-fingered friend let the other two on first. "I want to have a little, oh, talk with our new friend, eh?" he said.

The other two laughed as they reeled off down the docks toward the narrow gangplank. They knew about his predilections.

I'd worked them out a while back, but I wasn't ready for it when he clumsily threw his arms around my neck and said, "Was that good enough, Walter Slovotsky?"

He didn't sound drunk at all.

His smile was crooked. "Did we find out enough, I asked you," he said quietly, then raised his voice. *"What's the matter with you? I jus' wanna be friends, don' you wanna be friends?*

"You should ask how I know you," he went on, lowering his voice. "You don't remember me, but we met once before. Years ago."

He fingered his neck, at the base of the black beard that ran down his chin and neck and into his chest. Perhaps it was the flickering lamplight, or maybe I did see, almost hidden beneath the mat of beard, white scars that an iron collar would have left behind.

Clumsy fingers groped where his collar would have been. Had been.

"Push me away now, Walter Slovotsky," he whispered. "A quick curse, too, if you please."

"I do it with women, damn you—keep your hands off my cock, or I'll geld you," I shouted, as I shoved him, hard. "I swear I'll cut your balls off and stuff them up your nose."

"Aw, let's be friends." And, again, *sotto voce:* "We sail in the morning. I'm not a brave man, or I'd stay and help you and your friends." He backhanded me across the face, hard enough to sting, no more. *"That* for your shyness." And, again, quietly: "If you're leaving by water, the two fastest ships in port are the *Butter* and the *Delenia*, but careful of both captains. They do much business here." He raised his hands in defeat.

"*I* know when I've been told no," he said, staggering away into the dark, gesturing a farewell with a casual wave.

I didn't even know his name.

CHAPTER SIXTEEN

In Which a Hearty Breakfast Is Eaten

In skating over thin ice, our safety is in our speed.
—RALPH WALDO EMERSON

Audacity is a virtue that should always be practiced with caution.

—WALTER SLOVOTSKY

THE OTHERS WERE ALL up waiting for me. Ahira hauled me up into the window so fast it felt like flying.

"How did it go?" he asked. "Did you find out what we need?"

"Maybe." I nodded. "I'll need to think about it."

"See," he said with a relaxed smile. I liked that smile. I hadn't seen it for awhile, not since Bieme. "You didn't have to get all that close, eh?"

I shrugged. "I guess I should have listened to you."

"Sometimes things are real simple," I explained to three others, as we gathered around breakfast in the central room the next morning. "I know the easy way to get them out."

Down in the town center, our friends were spending another day starving and frying in the hot sun. Tennetty was off running an errand.

Here, sunlight splashed in through the breeze-stirred curtains, onto the four-person dining table and the silver trays heavily laden with rashers of bacon, chicken pies, and little ceramic ramekins holding coddled eggs, among other things. Breakfast is traditionally the biggest meal of the day in Brae, which is fine by me.

Ahira cocked his head to one side. "Sure." Using a pair of silver tongs to protect himself from the heat, he took the lid off a baking pot, and sniffed. "Some sort of stew, I think." He slopped some onto his plate, and mopped at it with half of a golden fist-sized roll. "Hmmm . . . not bad. Kid, maybe."

I reached for a roll—it was still warm from the oven—then tore it in half and dipped one end into a crock of raspberry preserves. It was delightfully sweet, with maybe just a touch too much tartness, and the seeds crunched between my teeth.

Andrea wasn't having any of it—she and her son were only picking at their food.

Ahira crunched into a thick rasher of bacon, then washed it down with a swallow of deeply purple wine. "So tell me how we do it the easy way," he said, a suspicious twitch to his grin.

"You and Jason take over the siege tower, climb up, and run a cable through all four cages," I said. I dipped the other hunk of bread into a cup of golden butter, and bit into that. Hmm . . . it was hard to decide which way was better—I downed both halves of the roll in two bites. "We splice one end to the other, tying them together. Meanwhile, I wrap det cord around the base of each pole, and light the fuse.

"Just before it all blows, Ellegon swoops down out of the sky, and grabs the whole mess just as the explosives cut the poles free."

Jason frowned in disgust. Andy shook her head, tolerantly.

"I think I see some problems with that," Ahira said, dryly.

"Only a few," I said. "One, we don't have a cable. Two, last time we talked about it, Lou figured he's about five years away from being able to produce det cord or any other good plastique equivalent, so that part doesn't work—the closest thing we have is a handful of grenades, and they won't do it.

"Three, there's no rendezvous set up with Ellegon for another eighteen days, so we can't count on him for this.

"Four, there's too many soldiers out there, and they'd cut us down before we got anywhere."

There was a pyramid of three tiny roasted chickens on one of the serving plates; I took the top one and tore off the drumstick. It came off too easily—either the bird had been overcooked, or I was more pumped up than I was trying to affect. Not that it matters: the skin of the drumstick was crisp and garlicky; the meat was rich and firm.

Tennetty burst through the doors, shut them behind her, and gave a quick nod as she took her seat at the table and tore into a loaf of bread. "Passage for eight on the *Delenia*," she said, from around a huge mouthful. "We leave at noon, tomorrow."

"Boarding?"

"Any time in the morning, from first light on. One problem, though—she's riding too low for her dock space, and they're moving her out to a mooring today so they can finish loading her. Long Dock needs work—it's been silting up underneath, and Lord Daeran had a problem with his last set of silkie workers."

"Launches?"

She nodded. "Her own. Two. Each can carry eight, including crew. Both will be tied up at Long Dock from sundown on."

Andrea had caught on. "We've done this one before," she said. "One day after arriving on This Side."

Once we were safely on the ship, we would have a common interest with the captain in getting the hell out of here, just as we had done, long ago, with Avair Ganness and the *Ganness' Pride*.

"Almost makes me feel nostalgic." Her smile brightened the whole room as she reached for a chicken breast and tore into it with strong white teeth. "How about the other part?"

"All a replay." I shrugged. "Ahira and I did that one, too, the time we ended up having to put your husband on the throne." I shook my head. "This time, though, it's a solo."

It would have to be me, and me alone. I'm not a hero or anything, but Ahira wouldn't be able to get in. It was totally not Andy's sort of thing; Jason was just too young to pull it all off. Tennetty could do the threatening part of it—and well—but not the rest of it. I sat back, trying to think of a way I could make this work with a fortyish woman wizard, a reliable dwarf, a still-green kid, or a one-eyed psychopath in the lead role, but couldn't.

"Uh, excuse me? Last time you did this?" Tennetty cocked her head to one side. "As I recall, last time you went face-to-face with royalty was the time you got Baron Furnael killed, no?"

"Close enough." I nodded. "Hey, I'll have to do it better this time."

Jason looked from Ahira to me, and back to Ahira, and then back to me. "You love this, don't you?"

"Truth to tell, Jason-me-boy, I do. Consider it a personality defect." It also scared me shitless, but not out of an appetite. I reached for another piece of chicken.

One does have to keep a sense of proportion about such things.

While our friends baked in the hot sun, we spent the day preparing, and resting, and eating.

I had to get up too early for breakfast the next morning. It was important to be at the residence early.

CHAPTER SEVENTEEN

In Which I Have a Pleasant Chat with Lord Daeran

The same man cannot be skilled in everything; each has his special excellence.

—EURIPIDES

There's a balance you have to learn, between being able to do a little of everything, and therefore nothing at all real well, and becoming overspecialized and completely useless outside your specialization. Learning that balance is, I've always believed, part of becoming an adult. I figure I'm about twenty years overdue to learn it.

—WALTER SLOVOTSKY

OLD FAMILY STORY—AND it's one of the few that my mother used to tell, so it could be true. Nah. But . . .

It seems that when my parents were trying to have me, there was some trouble conceiving. The doctors didn't know much about infertility then, and were trying whole bunches of things, some of which made sense, others of which were just patent nostrums. Schedules, diets, temperature taking, boxer shorts—the whole bit.

Finally, according to Mom, the doctor said, "Look. Stop trying so hard. It may just be a matter of relaxation. So take it easy, don't worry about schedules, don't worry about time of the month. Just do it whenever you feel like, okay?"

"That's why," Emma would say, her mouth quirked into a smile that caused Stash to blush just a bit, "we can never, ever go back to Howard Johnson's."

The way to a man's heart is through his stomach—or his rib-cage, if you're playing for keeps; the way into a lord's residence is through the kitchen.

It only stands to reason—the formal front door is for formal visitors, and is well-guarded by people wanting to know the reason for somebody entering. There was a lot of traffic, mind; Lord Daeran wasn't just idle royalty, but like most of the rulers of the small domains along the Cirric, the equivalent of the village warden, as well—his time was spent in negotiating rates for dock space and bargaining over the cost of potted fish.

On the other hand, given the local refrigeration problems—there isn't any—there are constantly people arriving with food deliveries. Particularly in early morning, before the sun is fully up, before even those who are up and working are really awake.

Well, give them credit—this isn't the way an attacking army would work its way in.

The trick was to look like I knew where I was going, and to be sure that I didn't end up in a closet.

Fairly straightforward, actually—the kitchens occupied the alley side of the residence, and there was only one open door, through which I could hear the clanging of pots and shouting of cooks. (Why all cooks shout is a mystery to me.)

I was through the outer kitchens and into the cooking room itself before anybody braced me. It was a burly woman, who vaguely reminded me of U'len, although this one had an even meaner expression on her face, if that could be believed. She had been stirring a huge stockpot filled with bones and carrots and onions, but she stopped to look up and glare at me.

"Sweetmeats for Lord Daeran," I said, bowing deeply, holding out a small wooden box and a piece of parchment to her.

She didn't take either. "What am I supposed to do with these?"

"Lady, I've ridden all of a day and a night to bring this from Fenevar and Lord Ulven." I spread my hands. "The box is to be properly presented to Lord Daeran; the parchment is to be imprinted with the mark of Lord Daeran's Valet, attesting to my having delivered it in good order." I gestured at the parchment. "Good lady, I am sure that you can mark it for him, if you would be so—"

She eyed the broken wax seal that my carelessly spread fingers didn't quite obscure. "And what am I supposed to do about this?"

I smiled innocently. "Which?"

"This seal. It appears to be broken. Will I find some sweatmeats missing inside?"

"Please, please, good lady—do I look like the sort who would steal a sweetmeat from the likes of Lord Daeran?"

She nodded. "Yes, you do. Now, do I look like the kind of fool who would sign for something I knew to be short?" She shooed me away. "Now, now, Lord Daeran is normally a patient man, but be along with you," she said, brushing me toward the inward door. "Find somebody else to sign for it. Our lord has little patience."

"Oh, please." Please don't throw me in that briar patch.

"Be along with you."

One down.

I made my way up the service stairway, cold stone rough beneath my naked feet. Bare feet are quieter than shoes.

The next part was going to be easy. We knew where the lord's room would be—when you've got an appearance balcony outside, it's not hard to guess.

Security might be tightened up shortly, but it would be a while. Word of what he was doing to the engineers would get back to Home, but it would take tendays; Daeran would want to tighten things up soon, but he wouldn't want to put everybody on full war footing *too* early, for fear that his troops would lose their edge.

Alternately, he might assume that Lou Riccetti would think of contract engineers as labor to be hired out, but nobody to fight a war over.

In the last, he was right. Too much land and too many countries and too many domains lay between Home and Brae over which to fight a war.

In any case, Lord Daeran's quarters were going to be on

the second floor, and there weren't going to be any guards in front of his door, although he would probably sleep with the door locked.

I stopped at the beaded curtain across the entryway to the second floor, listening at the beaded curtain that hung over the doorway. Listening for the sound of feet padding down the hall, anything.

Nothing. Cautiously, slowly, gingerly, I pushed a strand of beads out of the way. There was no reason at all for there to be a guard standing in front of the door. So, there would be no guard standing in front of the door.

All I had to do was convince the guard standing in front of the door.

I eased the strand back and stood there too long, thinking. Not good, but harmless this time.

The obvious thing to do was to pull out the pistol and point it at him, because everybody knows that when somebody points a gun at you, you just do whatever they say, right?

Well, no.

A Grateful Dead fan once got backstage by buying a pizza and walking past all of the security stations loudly proclaiming, "Pizza for Jerry Garcia. Pizza for Jerry Garcia." It worked just fine, and, so I hear, the band was kind of nice about it, and let him hang out backstage for the rest of the show. And they ate the pizza, too.

On the other hand, some would-be presidential gatecrasher once tried just that with Jerry Ford—"Pizza for President Ford. Pizza for President Ford" and he didn't even get to the Secret Service. He was arrested at the first police checkpoint and spent the rest of the weekend in jail while the lab checked out the pizza to be sure the pepperoni wouldn't explode or something.

All of which goes to show that impertinence can work for you or against you.

The box held my finery—I had been intending to change in Lord Daeran's room before waking him, figuring that the plain muslin tunic and leggings of the lower classes might not intimidate him.

I dressed quickly.

The very best guards are the most literal-minded. If they have specific orders to cover a situation, they obey them; they show no initiative at all.

On the other hand, rulers, particularly harsh rulers, tend to want to have things both ways. They punish any violation of orders, but they also hand out punishments for violating unwritten, unvoiced orders—regardless of what the literal orders were, regardless of any conflict between the written and un-. Keeping quiet around a sleeping lord would be an unwritten, but enforced order.

I walked right through the beaded curtain, gesturing as imperiously as possible to the guard.

"Don't you have ears, man?" I asked, loudly. "Didn't you hear me call you?" I asked, slapping my hand hard against my thigh as I walked toward him. "Look at this mess," I said, gesturing back toward the hall. "Have you ever seen anything so—"

Either they don't hire terribly bright men as guards in Brae, or he wasn't a morning person. He hadn't decided what to do when I hit him hard in the throat with one hand—no windup; I'm good at that—and then slammed the box into the corner of his jaw—a blow to the chin gives a nice shock to the brain stem—before his panic circuits cut in. By then, it was too late. His eyes rolled up, his knees buckled, and he collapsed.

I didn't quite catch him before his head bounced on the floor—ouch!—but I quickly hauled him through the darkened doorway and into Lord Daeran's room. I've gotten pretty good at tying people up—the basic trick is to start by wiring the thumbs together, tight.

The room was large, light and airy, plaster walls newly whitewashed, the expanse broken by an occasional painting. A black-and-white striped Nevelenian rug covered the floor. Thick, too; I sank to my ankles. Lord Daeran lay snoring on the broad bed. Alone. Good.

The broad windows to the balcony were secured by a bar. I carefully lifted the bar and set it down on the floor, then pulled the windows open with one hand while drawing my dagger with the other.

Lord Daeran's bed was a huge canopied four-poster, silk ropes secured to each post. Hmmm . . . it was obviously for him, but which way? I smiled. Nah. I'd never get away with it.

It only took me a minute to set myself up.

Well, no point in wasting time—I turned him over, stuffed a wadded end of blanket in his mouth, and set the point of my dagger under his nose as he came very, very quickly awake.

"One loud word, Lord Daeran," I whispered, visibly trembling, "one shouted syllable, one raised voice, and I'll discuss this with your successor." I moved the point of the knife from his nose to his throat, and kept up a nice, vibrato quaver. I do a good tremble. "Understood?"

My voice cracked a bit around the edges, which I think scared him more than anything else. I wouldn't want a nervous man holding a knife to my neck, either.

Under other circumstances, I suspect Lord Daeran would have cut a better figure, but sleep had splayed his long goatee and bristly mustache, and fear had his eyes wide.

He didn't really want to nod—not with the knife ready to cut his nose off—but managed to move his head up and down a fraction of an inch.

I pulled the end of the blanket out of his mouth, and replaced it with the neck of a metal flask. I thumbed the flask open.

"Have a drink," I said, raising the flask to his lips and the point of the knife to his right eye.

It was pretty foul stuff, but he choked it down.

"Swallow good, now," I said, still obviously scared shitless.

I let out a sigh as I moved away from the bed. I set the flask down on the table, took a small glass vial out of my pouch. The cork came out with a loud *pop*.

"That's all over." I raised a hand as I relaxed into a chair, a man whose work was done. "Just keep your hands away from your mouth for a few moments, and we don't have to worry about you purging yourself. As an alternative, if you want to find out how much your successor loves you, just let out a yell. I'll dump the antidote out on the rug or shatter the vial against the wall. By nightfall you'll have died a particularly horrible death."

I tapped the point of my knife against the glass, and he winced. It was starting to get to him.

I smiled. "Careful. Don't get any on the bed." I didn't turn my head decently aside as he vomited onto the floor, a quick stream of green foulness. "Stage one. Even if you get to a bottle of healing draughts now, it won't do you any good. This mixture is special—the Matriarch of the Healing Hand could probably cure you, or perhaps the Spidersect Senior Tarantula, or whatever they call him. I don't think your locals can manage it."

Wiping his mouth on the back of his sleeve, he was able to summon up more composure than I would have had in his situation. "I take it there's an alternative." He tried to smooth his beard and hair into place.

"Yeah," I said. "You can get my friends out of your cages, down to Long Dock, and all of us away from here. You've changed your mind—they're going to be banished, not slowly executed."

I had been hoping for some quietly blustering threats, but he just nodded. "Who are you?"

I bowed. "Walter Slovotsky, at your service." His eyes widened marginally; he had recognized the name. "Or the other way around, eh?"

"So," he said. "I free your friends, and then I get the antidote? Enough to counteract the poison?"

"Sure." I nodded. "It doesn't take much—this is easily three times as much as is needed. To cure you, that is. You will still hurt some. Probably spend half your next tenday squatting over a thundermug—but it'll be loose stools; at least you won't be shitting out your whole insides."

He looked at me out of narrowed eyes. "I'm not sure I believe you."

I had been counting on selling him on the story.

It only stood to reason—I had taken a huge risk in sneaking myself in, and for what? Just to feed him a mixture of water, iodine, pepper oil, ipecac root, and some slightly raunchy mayonnaise we had pilfered from yesterday's breakfast and let sit out in the sun?

Of course not.

The bigger the bluff, the better chance it has of working, and this was about as big as I could arrange on short notice.

Hmm . . . we could always fall back on Plan B. The only trouble was, I had been counting on this one, and I didn't have a Plan B. I mean, I had the general outlines, but none of the nuances, and the nuances are always the best part. It ought to start with a thrown knife in his throat, to stifle his screams, and I could take it from there. The window? Not for me, but yes—strip the guard's tunic off, and throw him out the window. He would be the assassin, killed while trying to escape.

There was a desk next to the window; I could probably hide under it while everything went to hell, and maybe slip out during the confusion.

I'd gotten out of worse, but not often, and one of these days I wouldn't. When you're playing table stakes, you can't always push everything you have into the pot, and I had, and the son of a bitch was going to—

A universe was born in a cloud of gas, grew to a majestic spectrum of stars, and then aged and died to cold iron stars in the moment between when he said, "I'm not sure I believe you" and "You'll have to take the rest of the poison to persuade me that the antidote works."

Slowly, he picked up the flask and held it out to me. "I want to see some of it pour into your mouth."

I swallowed the horrible, thick stuff—God, we had done too good a job on it.

"See?" I said, as my gorge rose. I hate ipecac root. Waves of nausea dropped me to my knees as my stomach purged itself, but I held the flask out, threatening to throw it, as he retrieved a dagger from somewhere next to his bed.

I wiped my mouth on his sheets, then carefully, deliberately swallowed a third of the antidote, such as it was. It burned its way down. Just what I needed on a nauseous stomach: a shot of Riccetti's Best corn whiskey.

He hesitated for a long moment, then dropped the point

of the dagger. "I guess I'd best get dressed," he said. He was already planning to betray me, of course. I hoped I was one step ahead of him.

Two soldiers lowered Bast to the dirt of the town square, laying him next to where Kenda was already recovering—a dose of healing draughts was not going to do Mardik or Veren any good. There's nothing you can do for the dead.

It was a good time to think about that, and to think about Bast and Kenda, about Tennetty, Jason, Ahira, Andrea, and myself, for that matter. A horrible way to die.

I looked Daeran in the eye. It would be a mistake to move my free hand toward a knife. I had to remember that I had the antidote to the "poison" that still had his stomach a bit queasy, and that was weapon enough.

The fact that something isn't true has nothing at all to do with your not remembering it.

Daeran kept staring at my right hand, the hand that held the flask, measuring his chances of securing it in one leap, and deciding that he didn't like the odds. I kept my eye on the hefty soldier behind me who kept trying to circle around me so that he could move in and grab my arms. Eventually, he might try it. Or maybe not. I'd have to be ready to toss the antidote aside, and tell Lord Daeran that there was more on the boat already, but I wasn't at all sanguine about that working.

People would have gathered in the square, but squads had been detailed to close off the base of the streets.

Kenda was able to sit up by herself, and raised the bottle to Bast's cracked, bloody lips.

He swallowed once, convulsively, and the all-too-familiar miracle happened: pink washed most of the ashen color from his face, and the black hollows that were his eyes filled out. He was still half-starved—there was only so much that a healing draught can do. It would be days before he could walk by himself, and weeks before he could fight. If he could fight—self-defense was part of an engineer's training, but I don't remember Bast as being terribly good at it.

"No more than ten soldiers," I said to Lord Daeran.

"One each to carry my friends, eight more to make you feel secure."

The fullback behind me took a step forward, his foot scuffing the gravel. I was supposed to turn around and look at him, while the free safety to my left dived in and grabbed the flask. Granted, the flask didn't contain anything important. Just my life, and my friends' lives. That made it easy for me to forget that the liquid was only a gill of corn whiskey.

I raised the flask above my head, ready to dash it to the ground. "Tell them, Daeran."

He motioned them to desist. "Corporal Kino, pick out ten men. Two to carry Walter Slovotsky's friends." He included the two football players, of course.

Under a sky filled with puffy, peaceful clouds, a cool wind blew off the Cirric, blowing the smell of my own fear away.

Tennetty and Jason were waiting at the end of the dock. Jason's pistol was at his side, his finger near but off the trigger. Tennetty had her sword out in one hand, a flintlock in her other hand, and another brace of pistols in her belt.

Maybe three hundred feet off the end of the dock, the *Delenia* floated, secured at bow and stern by anchor and mooring. She was getting ready to leave. Her mainsail and mizzen were up, their booms swung out by the wind, sheets hanging loose as they flapped and cracked in the stiff breeze. The jib had been raised, but was bound to the foremast. Setting it would take only a few moments. Raise anchor, drop the mooring, haul in on the sheets, and the ketch would be off. It was rigged for several additional sails—they're called staysails on the Other Side; This Side the term is "leach sails"—but that would just add a little speed.

Andrea and Ahira stood on the high rear deck, talking with the captain. I don't know exactly what they were saying, but I hope they were being persuasive.

I don't think the sailors in the two launches were any too pleased. A Cirric sailor has to be able to fight as well as run, but the *Delenia* was a fast ketch, and they were undoubtedly much more practiced at running than fighting.

"The flask, if you please," Daeran said, holding out his

hand, "and then you may load yourself and your friends in the boats and go."

I laughed. "Really? Do I look that stupid?" I held the flask out over the water. "We'll all go out to the ship, and then send the flask back in one of the launches."

"How do I know you won't simply kill me once we're aboard?"

Jason spoke up. "You have the word of a Cullinane."

There are parts of the Eren regions where that would have settled it all.

Brae wasn't one of them, apparently. "No," Daeran finally said. "I don't trust any of you. You will go out in one launch, and six of my men and I will bring the prisoners along in the other. We will get on board, and then make our exchanges, and then each of us will go our separate ways."

I thought about it for a moment, and then shrugged. "Sure."

CHAPTER EIGHTEEN

In Which I Make a Trade and We Seek to Bid Farewell to the Friendly Natives of Brae

Crescit amor nummi quantum ipsa pecunia crescit. (The love of money grows as the money itself grows.)

—JUVENAL

So I said to myself, a two-way split can be profitable, but a one-way split might even be more than twice as good.

—WALTER SLOVOTSKY

LOGISTICS, FORMAL OR in-, has never been something that I've found terribly interesting. It's always been somebody else's department. Riccetti, now . . . hell, Lou would have worked out the problems just as a matter of practice. Logistics was why we put Little Pittsburgh in Holtun, rather than Home—Home is out of the way, and too near elven lands for the comfort of many, myself included.

That's Lou. Me, I had been vaguely wondering how they had managed to load the ship, but I hadn't really thought much about it until the launch pulled around the far side of it, revealing the floating dock.

Well, actually, it was more of a small, thin barge, stabilized at either end by floating barrels lashed to the water line, which presumably didn't let it dip or rock much. A wooden frame hung over the railing of the boat, basically locking the barge into place at the waterline. Clearly, the goods had been placed on it back on dockside, and then the whole thing poled out to the *Delenia*, the frame tied into place. That way, the barge could be emptied into the cargo net and the net lifted up by the winch with some reasonable amount of security for both crew and cargo.

Above, two crewmen were finishing securing the cargo crane, the cargo netting already having been neatly folded over the rail and lashed into place. They were late with that. You can't actually use the crane unless you've got the sail booms either stowed or, more commonly, lashed to the other side of the ship—they both swing through the same space, as the long-arm crane's boom has to be long enough to swing through a huge arc to provide the mechanical advantage that will allow one or two seamen to move a ton of cargo from dock to deck.

During my time at sea, working my way from port to port, I always used to like running the winch and crane. It's hard work, which I grant is atypical for me, but there's something special about being able to handle such massive forces, even by indirection.

Then again, maybe not.

I thought for a moment that it was all going to break loose as Tennetty leaped lightly from the launch to the floating dock, then helped me up, the flask still clasped carefully in my hand, as though everything depended on it.

Which it did.

Daeran and his soldiers followed us onto the floating barge, two of them carefully lowering Bast and Kenda to the ground. Above, the captain, his hands on the rail, leaned over.

I disliked him at first sight—from the neatly trimmed beard, framing the lips that were parted in an exhibition of straight, white teeth, down to the v-shaped torso of an acrobat or bodybuilder, all the way to treetrunk legs. All nicely bronzed, rather than browned.

Pretty men bother me.

"Greetings," he said, his voice deceptively calm. Or maybe not. Maybe maybe he was just an idiot who hadn't figured out how easily, how quickly everything could go to hell. "I am Erol Lyneian, captain of the *Delenia*."

I nodded. "Walter Slovotsky. Captain of my own soul."

"Oh, shit," Tennetty muttered. "I thought you were going to react like this."

"What?"

"You don't like competition, Slovotsky," she said. "Pay attention."

"I see," he went on, "that we have a problem. Why don't all of you come up and discuss it?"

It was just as well that Tennetty had cautioned me—it had been my intention to make the final exchange aboard ship, but something in his voice made me want to change my mind.

It was still the right move. "Very well," I said.

Ahira was waiting for me at the top of the ladder. "I think," he said, "that we may have a problem." His voice had taken on that level, overly calm tone he only used when things were just about to break. "*Delenia* and Erol Lyneian have been trading here for too long, and they're on good terms."

"How good?"

"Good enough that Erol Lyneian isn't even scared."

That was bad. Part of the plan involved the captain being sufficiently frightened of the local lord that he would want out of there, and quickly, not trusting Lord Daeran to believe that his involvement with us was innocent. It's sort of like Big Mike's routine with the stoolie, except Lord Daeran played more for keeps than any bunch of New Jersey street hoods.

Andy's eyes were glazed over, almost completely. If I'd had the genes for it, I suspect I'd have seen nascent spells hovering over her. But if everything went off, she would be like a flamethrower operator in combat—everybody's favorite target. She might have time to get a muttered, unrememberable syllable out, but she might not.

What we needed was something that would be worth more to Erol Lyneian than the ability to trade in Brae. A lot more. He only had a crew of five—it doesn't take many to run a well-designed ketch, and the more labor you have, the narrower the profits—and things didn't look like an even match, even with them on our side.

On the other hand, if everything hit the fan, he would know there was no guarantee he would make it out alive.

I smiled at him, as though to say, *You can count on being the first to go*, and he smiled back and made a gracious gesture, as though to say, *After you, my dear Alphonse.*

Okay. I know: there were twelve of them against five of us, and I've faced worse odds than twelve to five.

On the other hand, Daeran's soldiers looked like they knew what they were doing, both singly—which was bad enough—and worse, collectively. As though to underline that, three of Daeran's bruisers leaned their heads together and started divvying up targets.

Bad, bad, bad. We could probably take on the six, but it would be close, and if the seamen came in on the other side . . .

I did a quick sum of the party's possessions, including coin, gem, potions, and everything, and decided that wasn't going to do it, even if we threw in my charm. A sea trader has to be something of an adventurous type, but his ship comes first, unless—and maybe not even if—you've got enough to buy him another ship.

Lord Daeran had decided that wasn't going to do it, either. He held out his hand. "The antidote, please," he said, smiling, his men gathered around him in a semicircle. "Then we'll all leave," he said, lying, thinking that I would have to decide to believe him.

That's how a Mexican standoff ends. With somebody making a fatal error.

"What would you trade for passage on your ship, Erol Lyneian?" I asked.

"Oh," he said, idly, "you've already paid for passage." He didn't expect me to believe him, and I didn't.

Well, we'd been saving this for years. It was even a secret that anybody but the Engineer knew how to make it, although all of us Other Siders did.

"I will tell you how to make gunpowder," I said. "Not the magical slaver imitation. Real gunpowder, black powder.

It's very cheap to make. I'd tell you right now, except that they would know how, too."

Ahira's jaw dropped, and Jason's eyes grew wide. I wasn't looking at Andy and Tennetty, but I don't imagine I would have seen them beaming approval.

Look. It wasn't the best idea in the world. Maybe it wasn't even a good idea. The best I can say for it is that I'd just given Lord Daeran and Erol Lyneian a huge conflict of interest. One of them as the source of real gunpowder would mean an immense shower of wealth; two would mean just another competitive business. As the sole non-Home possessor of the secret, Erol Lyneian would be a happy ship owner sailing from port to port, selling cheaply made gunpowder at high prices; if it could be bought competitively, it was just another commodity.

If I'd had a day or more to think it over, I can't imagine anything else I could have said that would have made Erol Lyneian want to side with us, rather than with Lord Daeran. I've thought about it since, and I still can't come up with an alternative.

There was only one trouble in this admittedly brilliant piece of improvisation: I could see by the look in Erol Lyneian's eye that he didn't believe me.

I only realized that Lord Daeran did believe when he lunged for me, wrestling the flask from my hand as he shoved me up against the rail.

In retrospect, of course, it only stands to reason. I'd spent some time persuading Lord Daeran of my sincerity, and it had worked—he went for the flask of supposed antidote, after all. He was disposed to believe me; I could have sold him the Brooklyn Bridge, even though he wouldn't have had the slightest idea what a Brooklyn is. Erol Lyneian, on the other hand, had just met me, and had yet to discover what a charming and reliable fellow I am.

Things went to hell quickly.

One reason that wizards need good bodyguards is that in a fight, a wizard is everybody's first target; having Andy free and operating would have ended things in our favor quickly.

Two soldiers jumped at her; out of the corner of my eye

I saw Andy collapse from a blow to the head, and Tennetty hack down at the soldier who then tried to pin her against the deck, but I was busy with my own fight.

This would, in the old days, have been a great time for Karl to be there.

Once, when a trap we set for slavers went suddenly sour, he ended up inside a circle of four swordsmen—and good ones, too—armed with nothing more than an improvised quarterstaff. In about four seconds, it was all over—he had hit them hard, and fast, and they were down.

But Karl was dead and gone, and all we had was me.

I did the best I could—I flung a throwing knife into Lord Daeran's belly, and lashed out with my foot at the nearest of the soldiers, sending him crashing into one of his fellows.

That gave me enough time to get my sword free.

I batted a knife out of the way and slipped my blade in between a soldier's ribs. His bubbling scream cut off as he twisted spasmodically away, my blade jamming in his ribs, taking my sword with him. Ten years before, even five years before, I would have moved fast enough to extricate the blade, to twist it loose, before it was caught, but I was getting old and slow.

We would have had no chance at all if it hadn't been for Jason's revolver and for Ahira. The dwarf somehow got hold of a huge boarding pole, and flailed it around like a quarterstaff, hitting one of Lord Daeran's men so hard that he actually broke through the railing and slammed down hard on the floating dock below.

Jason's revolver spat flame and smoke at one of the soldiers, echoed by a gout of blood and gore from his thigh. Screaming, the soldier fell heavily, across Bast.

Bast's arms moved spasmodically, clumsy hands flailing away at the soldier's face. He was doing the best he could, but he wasn't going to be any help.

I ducked under a butt-stroke from a spear and lunged for the owner of it, drawing one of my Therranji garrottes as I did. I faked at him with my left hand, then neatly looped the garrotte over his head with my right, drawing it tight with a jerk that should have taken his head half off.

Face already purpling, he staggered away, fingers clawing

uselessly at his throat. It would take a bolt cutter to save him now, and I wasn't about to go digging in my kit for ours.

But there were so many of them; even without Erol Lyneian and his sailors taking part, there were just too many of them for us to take at such close range. I should have thought it out better. I should have insisted that Jason stand back, out of range, before everything hit the fan, but that sort of thing had always been Karl's department, and Karl was dead.

One soldier reached Jason, pulling his revolver down, his body shuddering at the shot that ripped through his belly and out his back, but before Jason could free the weapon two others were on him.

Tennetty had just fired one of her flintlocks, although I didn't see what, if anything, she hit. Moving even faster than I'd have thought she could, she was on the back of one of the soldiers wrestling with Jason, her shiny bowie rising then falling, then rising and falling again, now redly wet.

Jason managed to free himself and fire off two more quick shots, but his revolver clicked empty.

The revolver.

It fired cartridges, filled with the smokeless powder that Lou Riccetti and his top assistants had spent years perfecting; for now, it was one of two, one of only two repeating pistols, the most advanced weaponry in the world.

Jason was Karl Cullinane's son, and Karl Cullinane would have done his damndest to make sure that a weapon that advanced didn't fall into foreign hands. Jason Cullinane tossed the pistol over his shoulder, over the railing.

A priceless piece of blued steel tumbled end-over-end through the air, arcing outward.

I think that was when I heard Tennetty scream, as a sword pinned her by the shoulder to a mast, her knife falling from her useless fingers. I know that was when Jason went down under a rush of bodies. It was too late for him to get his sword free—

Something caught me upside the head, shaking the whole universe for a moment. I staggered, tried to recover as I drew my belt knife and stabbed backwards, rewarded by a scream.

"Walter, we—" I didn't get to hear what Ahira was trying

to say. The largest of the soldiers hit him with a flying tackle, neatly knocking the dwarf, his arms spread wide in helplessness, backwards through the hole in the railing, like a cue ball smacking into the eight, and the eight into the pocket.

Except that the pocket here was deep water.

Very deep water.

"No."

No, it was going to be okay. Ahira was tough. When he hit the floating dock, his superior musculature and thicker bones would protect him. But he had been hit hard, and at a sharp angle, and it arced him out past—

I can still hear his scream of terror, a high wailing cry. I can still see him falling backwards, out of control, his fingers reaching for the floating dock, missing it by inches. I can still see the splash he made, and see his wide eyes, and the panic written on his face as the water closed over it.

Dwarves don't float.

Dwarves can't swim.

Dwarves sink like a stone.

"No," I shouted. Asshole. You'd think that a man would learn, well before he's my age, that wanting something not to be so has never, ever changed it, that it doesn't matter what you want, what you desire, what you need, but what you do.

Reflexively, foolishly, idiotically, uselessly, I reached out a hand, but it was useless. The water was eight, ten feet below the rail, and Ahira had already vanished from sight.

Something hit me alongside my right ear, I think.

CHAPTER NINETEEN

In Which a Friend Has a Few Final Words with Lord Daeran

Pride, envy, avarice—these are the sparks have set on fire the hearts of all men.

—DANTE ALIGHIERI

I can think of two things I've been waiting my whole life to say. A friend of mine recently stole one of them.

—WALTER SLOVOTSKY

My KARATE TEACHER, Mr. Imaoka, gave me the best lesson on fighting that I've ever had.

"The most important lesson in karate is running," he said, as the lot of us reluctantly strapped our sneakers on. "The first thing you do in a fight," he said, "is to turn and run away.

"Run for at least a mile, preferably two or three. If he's still chasing you, he's probably out of breath by then. If it's still worth fighting about," he said with a smile, "you turn around and beat him up."

When next I could follow what was going on, Lord Daeran was looming over me, looking none the worse for wear, his hair and goatee now neatly combed, his face glowing with health and vigor.

He had gotten to our healing draughts, it appeared.

I would have rather had a hangover, thank you much.

There was a constant stabbing pain under my left shoulder blade, where I was sure that I had been stabbed. I had to breathe shallowly, broken ribs grating at even the slightest movement.

Not that I could have moved a lot. Lord Daeran had saved me that trouble by tying me to the rail near the stern, between Tennetty and Jason, my hands behind me. Andy, Kenda, and Bast lay tied on their sides on the hot deck, a soldier looming over each of them, although I don't know why.

Tennetty and Jason were cut in dozens of places, and while they hadn't bled out, neither of them was in any shape to fight: Jason was battered badly, and while the fingers of Tennetty's right hand were feeling around for the knots, her whole left arm hung limp—the sword she'd taken in the shoulder must have gotten to a nerve center.

Not good.

Over her gag, Andy's eyes were wild, even the heavily bruised right one, swollen almost closed.

Ahira was dead.

Our gear had been spread out across the deck, clothes scattered haphazardly, weapons and other stuff carefully laid out for Daeran's examination. Stooping over our gear, he fingered an unmarked gunmetal flask. I wouldn't mind if he drank that—it was a liniment for saddle sores, and the main ingredient was wood alcohol.

"First matters first, Walter Slovotsky," Daeran said. "The antidote. You have more of it, I'm sure."

Well, yes, we did—the more of it was in another flask, just out of his reach. I like an occasional nip to cut the dust of the trail.

I didn't answer, and I was very careful not to look either at the flask of Riccetti's Best or away from it. He didn't get angry. He just stalked over to me and carefully hit me across the face twice, first time with his palm, then with the back of his hand.

Not torture. Not yet. This was just to let me know that he was serious.

In my mind's eye, I could see Ahira taking the bastard in his broad hands, fingers crushing the life out of him.

But Ahira was overboard, in thirty feet of water.

Dead.

Only one chance, although not much of one. Things hung in a balance here, perhaps too delicate a balance. With the damage we had done to his party, Daeran and Erol Lyneian were at rough parity on the ship, and Daeran would know better than to endanger that by sending for more troops right now, threatening to cut Erol Lyneian out totally.

The two of them would come to terms before they could afford to torture the secret out of me; they would have to set up a cozy little arrangement that would have landed them with an antitrust suit on the Other Side.

I could think of only one card to play. We had managed to keep the secret of black powder for close to twenty years now, through the time that Pandathaway wizards had invented their expensive substitute, through Riccetti's re-creation of the smokeless powder for cartridge weapons, through all of it.

But it was now, or never. I voted for now. "Saltpeter—the crystals you find under old piles of manure."

"No," Bast shouted. "Don't tell him. In the name of the Engineer, shut your mouth. Don't—"

"Saltpeter," I said. I wasn't going to be stopped. "Fifteen parts by weight. Powdered charcoal—willow works best—three parts. Sulfur—two parts."

"That's the antidote?"

"No, no, no," I said. "That's *gunpowder*. Black powder. Manufacture is tricky, but those are the ingredients. Saltpeter, charcoal, sulfur. Fifteen, three, two."

A stray smile crossed Erol Lyneian's lips. "I think that Lord Daeran is more interested in the antidote to the poison right now. You managed to spill all but a drop."

I tried to shrug, regretting the effort instantly. "There wasn't any poison," I said, spitting out each word through a red cloud of pain. "All a bluff. The idiot went for it."

Think, dammit, think. I was just going through the motions. All I had done was my usual part of it: try to buy some time for Ahira to figure us a way out of this mess, to pry up some loose edge of the trap we found ourselves in for him to work on, but Ahira was gone.

Dead.

I'd have to do his job. Or somebody would.

No. There was another solution. We could all die.

Daeran took a step toward me, but stopped at Erol Lyneian's gesture. "You're lying."

"Then have some more out of that flask," I said, pointing with my chin. That hurt, too. "It's just corn whiskey, but enjoy. It'll taste the same. Enjoy. Compliments of the Engineer."

Below his angry eyes, Bast's lips were pulled back in a snarl. If he could have worked his way loose, he would have gone for me, not for them. The secret of gunpowder was the great treasure of the Engineer, and I had just given it away.

Well, my life and the lives of my friends were the great treasure of *me*, and I was hoping that I had just bought a better chance of survival for all of us. Neither of them would trust me, and Erol Lyneian now knew too much, as did all of his men.

But he wouldn't have to face that intellectually, not yet. Lord Daeran had three functioning soldiers aboard the *Delenia*, all of them with naked weapons, and Erol Lyneian had only his five crewmen, none of them visibly armed, all of them on deck. Erol Lyneian and his men could win a fight, probably, but only an extended one. He couldn't count on taking out all of Daeran's people before reinforcements arrived.

Daeran forced the mouth of the corn whiskey flask between my lips.

I took a large mouthful before he wrested it away. Last drink for the condemned man, and all that.

"Too eager, you are," he said. "I think you may be bluffing again. We'll wait and see what the effect is."

It wasn't going to work. I didn't have enough leverage to play Erol Lyneian off against Daeran. All I was doing was buying time. For what?

Maybe Tennetty could work her way free.

She clearly didn't understand the situation; she was smiling. Crazy, idiot bitch. Didn't she know how badly she had been cut, didn't she know that we were all dead, that I was just buying us some time for a miracle, and that it wouldn't come?

Jason started smiling, too. Imbecile.

Look, I don't mind people being heroic, but this was ridiculous.

Ahira was dead, we all were as good as dead, and the fucking idiot was grinning—

It was then that I felt the blunt fingers behind me, working on my knots.

Daeran saw something in my eyes, I guess. His brow furrowed, and he took a step forward.

I spat blood on the deck. Blood always makes a good distraction.

"Healing draughts," I said. "No more until I get them, for me and my friends."

"We'll see about it, after the details," Daeran said.

"Now," I said. "Or I bite my tongue off and you never know what the secret procedure is."

The secret procedure wasn't much—grind each ingredient separately, toss in a barrel, then wet it down with water (good), urine (better) or wine (best), then stir, stir, stir, until your arm feels like it's going to fall off. Then stir some more. Push the mixture, now vaguely dough-like, through a wire mesh to mix it more—it's called corning. Repeat, dry *very* carefully, and there you have it. It's dangerous—kids, don't try this at home—but it's not complicated.

"You're bluffing. Again," Daeran said.

"Try me," I said, bluffing.

He didn't quite sigh. "Not this time, I think. This time, I'll let you win." He took a step toward me.

Behind me, the fingers went away. Ahira, somehow clinging to the side of the ship, probably standing on top of the molding surrounding a porthole or something, had ducked down.

"No, them first." I nodded at the others. They needed it worse than I did, Tennetty and Jason in particular, and I needed my hands free.

Daeran had decided to control his temper. There would be enough time shortly to punish me for my insolence, and just because he'd fed them healing draughts, it didn't mean he couldn't kill them later.

"Very well." He moved over to where Tennetty was bound, and brought the bottle of healing draughts to her lips.

The fingers behind me returned, and finished their work,

then pressed a knife hilt into my hands, but the hilt was withdrawn. The fingers put leather thongs into my hands and closed my fingers around the thongs, giving my hand a final quick pat before the blunt fingers went away.

Thanks a fucking lot, Ahira.

It was him. There was no question of it. I knew the touch of that hand, and I don't look a gift horse in the mouth, not when it's the only ride out of town. My best friend was alive, and operating independently, and—

Of course. Sometimes I'm such an idiot—he wasn't teasing me. He had just given me the inventory of our weapons, and assigned me the one he thought suited our situation best, trusting me to read his mind.

We had leather thongs—the ones that had bound my wrists, no doubt—and we had a knife.

Okay; that was a start.

The knife would go to Tennetty, and Ahira would try to work his way around, clinging to the side of the ship, trying to stay out of sight. No. He wouldn't. If he fell again, he might not be able to make his way up out of the water. He would stay right where he was, perched on top of the rudder or whatever. He would free me, Tennetty and Jason, and then expect me to start things off.

How the hell had he gotten out of the water? I had seen him hit the water, and seen him sink like a stone.

Later, Walter, later.

And what had taken him so long?

Andrea, Jason, and Tennetty had been treated with the healing draughts; it was my turn.

Lord Daeran knelt in front of me. "Your healing draughts. Then you will talk. I promise you, you will talk." He brought the warm lip of the bottle to my mouth, banging it hard against my teeth.

I didn't care. The too-sweet taste of the healing draughts washed the blood from my mouth, my aches and pains becoming distant and vague.

No time to enjoy that now. I tied a loop in one end of the leather thong, and slipped the other end through it.

Lord Daeran's eyes went wide as I whipped the loop over his head and drew it tight around his neck.

"Now," I said, probably redundantly.

No time to finish him off—I kicked him aside then went low, toward our gear. Tennetty, the knife held in her outstretched hand, went high above me, bowling herself into a soldier who was reacting just a little too slow. I think she gutted him; his scream rang in my ears.

No time to think, either; I would have to do it all right, and by instinct.

I slid a sword hilt-first toward Jason, then tackled the soldier above Andy hard enough to have satisfied even Coach Fusco. Sonofabitch always thought I took it too easy on quarterbacks. Fuck him.

And to hell with the soldier, too—my rush carried him back to where the rail caught him across the kidneys. His arms flew apart as the tetanic shock hit him hard.

We were still overmatched, and even with Ahira back in action we wouldn't have had a chance unless . . . first, I'd have to get Andy free, and she would have to . . .

Of course. Trust your friends. I could see the boom out of the corner of my eye, and hear Ahira laughing about it in the corner of my mind.

"Tennetty, Jason—*down*," I shouted. The dark shadow swept toward me; I ducked under it and went for Andy as the boom, propelled by impossibly strong dwarf muscles, swept hard across the deck, bowling over soldiers, the sailors reflexively ducking.

I scooped up a knife and reached Andy's side. A slice and a twist and she was free, fingers already clawing at her gag; a leg-sweep knocked down the soldier who had been lunging at her.

Her arms spread wide, she rose to her feet, uttering just one syllable.

Daylight reddened and dimmed, and the sky went dark above us.

Time slowed. I'd been hearing my heart thumping hard and fast, but now with each beat was a slow double moan.

Gwa-thunnnnnk.

Long pause.

Gwa-thunnnnnk.

I could still think, I could still see, but I couldn't even fall fast. We were all stuck in the same clear molasses: Tennetty, her knife rising, unable to see the saber inches from her back, about to skewer her; Ahira, one hand clamped on a bloody mess that had been the face of a soldier, his other arm squeezing another's chest further than bones could give; Jason, in full lunge through the belly of the largest of the soldiers, his face grim as he saw another blade descending toward him.

We were all trapped in the red time. Except for Andy.

Leaning hard, like she was walking against a strong but steady wind, she walked smoothly across the deck, pushing up on the saber menacing Tennetty as she passed.

She reached her son's side, and brushed the attacking blade aside, then set one finger on either side of the soldier's head, muttering a word I could not have remembered even if I'd heard it.

Sparks leisurely leapt from finger to finger, strengthening as they did. Her mouth was moving, but I couldn't make out what she was saying. The sparks became a flow, and the flow became lightning, jagged forks piercing the soldier's head until a cloud of smoke gathered about his forehead and ears.

Slowly, gracefully, she turned toward me and smiled. It wasn't a friendly smile.

Over to you, she mouthed.

As the light blued again, and time returned to normal, Ahira had retrieved his axe from our pile.

There were only two soldiers left alive on deck. Tennetty had snaked her arm around the throat of one, and Jason, his sword shining in the light, had squared off against the other.

All that left was Lord Daeran, lying on the deck, loosening the garrotte that I clearly hadn't quite tightened enough.

Hey, I was in a hurry.

Ahira raised his axe.

"What . . . *are* you?" the lord asked.

If it had been me, I would have been tempted to make a speech, about how Mikyn was one of ours, and if he needed stopping, we would stop him, and no locals need apply, and about how putting friends and associates of ours to death for unwittingly helping Mikyn was just plain wrong, and wasn't going to be tolerated.

But Ahira didn't make premature speeches.

The axe fell, and then he spoke.

"Justice, you son of a bitch," he said.

I guess, back in the old days, James Michael and I saw the same movies.

Soldiers at the dock were loading themselves into boats, and two of the small boats were already on their way toward us.

"Captain," I said, "do you want to try to explain it all right now, or shall we get out of here?"

Erol Lyneian smiled as he gestured his crew into motion. "We still have an agreement, Walter Slovotsky. The *Delenia* is to take you safely to where you wish to go; you are to give me the secret of making engineer gunpowder."

He wouldn't apologize for his having made a virtue of necessity earlier, for siding with the late Lord Daeran. Business, after all, was business.

Bast pushed himself forward, staggering, probably both from the rolling of the ship. "No. Don't tell them anything, don't let the secret out, don't—"

Tennetty caught his arm, twisted it up and around behind his back with an economical motion. "Not now. Later, if at all." She pushed him away, then drew her sword again and took up an *en garde* position next to me.

I nodded to Erol Lyneian. "We have a deal. Let's just move this ship, asshole."

CHAPTER TWENTY

Immediately After Which I Strike My Forehead, Quite Briskly, with My Open Palm

It ain't what a man don't know that makes him a fool, but what he does know that ain't so.

—JOSH BILLINGS

Sometimes, it's good to be wrong.

—WALTER SLOVOTSKY

THERE IS A THING A friend of mine once labeled the "rhinoceros in the corner." Maybe she was just repeating it, but I always associate it with Peggy.

"The rhinoceros in the corner is the idea that hangs over a conversation," she said, "but that you don't talk about. You find them all over the place, in a lot of situations."

"Like, say, the first time you go to dinner with a girl?" I smiled. It was, of course, the first time we'd gone out to dinner.

"Woman."

"Woman." Fine.

"You talk about school," she said, "and about majors, and jobs, and movies, and politics—anything. But what you're both thinking about is whether or not you're going to bed together."

"Oh?"

"I mean, like, you're thinking about that, and she's thinking about that, but you don't talk about it."

"You mean like we're not?"

"Well . . ." She smiled and sipped at her beer. "Yeah."

Ahira didn't want to tell me how he had survived, not unless I asked; and I wasn't going to ask him. Just pure stubbornness on both of our parts, but it's a pattern we'd fallen into over all the years. Eventually, one of us would give in, but you wouldn't want to bet the farm on which.

Ahira and I stood in the spray on the foredeck, near the bow. He sat on the step next to the anchor, one arm hooked over a safety line as he honed the edge of his battle-axe; I leaned against the rail, doing nothing much.

Ahira whisked his stone smoothly against the edge of his axe. *Fsssssst. Fsssssst. Fsssssst. Fsssssst.*

"You're going to get that sharp enough to shave with, if you keep at it," I said.

He shrugged. "No such thing as too sharp an axe." Yes, a too-thin edge could chip in a fight, but that wouldn't make much practical difference, not with Ahira's strength behind it.

At least Ahira was talking to me, even if the stubborn bastard wouldn't volunteer the information I wanted him to. I was *persona non grata* with Bast and Kenda, and Jason wasn't sure, yet, whether I had brilliantly bought us more time—thereby cleverly saving the day—or if I had cravenly sold out everything that Home stood for, and for no purpose. I would have given him an argument, but I'm not sure which side I'd have taken, so I had given it a pass. Andy was asleep in her bunk, Tennetty watching over her, Bast, and Kenda.

"Feels faster now than it was before we tacked," he said.

"I know," I said. "But it just feels that way."

Running with the wind is fast, but despite the name it's stuffy and no fun. The faster the sailboat, the less pleasant it is—the more efficient the boat is at using the wind, the less breeze you have. You carry your effluvium with you. It feels like you're not moving, like the rest of the universe is moving around you. Slowly, and stuffily.

I much prefer sailing close-hauled, close to the wind, the rush of air in my face, occasional jets of spray refreshing me.

Magic and madness were loose somewhere out in the night, and we were sailing off into it all.

We talked, and kept watch on the night. Not the worst thing to do. The night was clear, the sky bright diamonds displayed proudly on the blackest velvet. To port, beyond where the starlight capered across the gentle swells, dark land loomed threateningly below the starry sky, the blackness broken only occasionally by the flickering of lanterns or fireplaces in some window ashore.

Off to starboard the roiling surface of the water, dark and glossy, shimmered and shattered the starlight.

A sailor only sees the surface of the sea, always is left to wonder what may wait below the surface. There's a lot you never know.

I guess I'd never know what the right thing to do about Kirah was. But maybe I didn't have to decide on the right thing, not in terms of effects. Maybe what I ought to do was accept the principle that if I wanted things to work out for me and Kirah, just maybe running around the Eren regions wasn't the way to cure it, that maybe the reason things had gone okay during the years in Endell is that I'd been there.

Or maybe not. Maybe what both Kirah and I needed was a long time away from each other.

I could still remember her, though, her hair floating in the breeze, her body soft and warm. Too long ago.

There comes a time when you just make a decision, when you stop fooling around pretending that what you're doing is weighing and balancing and considering and trying to decide, and you just decide. Fine.

I'd decide. Enough trying, enough whining and wondering and whereforeing. When I got home, I'd make things work between Kirah and me. Period. Never mind how, never mind why. I'd just do it.

"What are you thinking about?" Ahira asked. *Fsssssst. Fsssssst.*

"Just thinking that it's getting cold out here."

Straight ahead, perhaps only a few hundred yards, perhaps more than a few miles, a trio of faerie lights slowly circled each other as they pulsed gently through the progression of blues and greens. The tempo picked up, and the lights orbited faster around their invisible center, becoming all red and orange, the pace increasing still further as they circled each other faster and faster, tighter and tighter, until the circle could not hold. First one, then the other two shattered into a shower of fiery sparks that blued as they fell toward the dark waters below.

"Magic and madness are loose out in the night," I said.

"True enough."

"And we're sailing toward it."

"There is that." *Fsssssst. Fsssssst. Fsssssst.* He raised his head. "Where would you rather be?"

"Here's fine, I guess." Some of the best times are when you just sit and talk and think.

Erol Lyneian was very much a neat freak: the anchor cable, of that strange Therranji construction that left a brass-and-iron cable as flexible as rope, had been carefully flemished against the deck, not simply coiled in a heap.

Ahead of us, starlight danced on the water; the water rushed against the fast-moving boat. Above us in the dark, the jib strained to catch every whisper of wind, looming above us like a large vague ghost.

One of the crewmen worked his way forward. Vertum Barr, his name was: a short, bony man well into his fifties, naturally so thin that you could see his ribs despite the small potbelly, dark and wrinkled like a dried mushroom—the sort of sailor you find working all over the Cirric, from boat to boat. He would never own more than he could carry in his seabag, but as long as he could work he would always have a bunk under which he could stow his bag.

"Carrying a bit of weather helm as the wind picks up, eh?" I asked.

His face split in a gap-toothed grin. "How did you know that?"

"Please. I do have an eye for the obvious: she's heeling a bit. Whoever is back at the tiller keeps having to bear away. Costing us speed."

"Hmmm . . . and what would you be doing about it, were it yours to do?"

I shrugged. "Is this a test? Your center of effort's too far back. Me, I'd just crank the traveler leeward—flatten out the mainsail. Or maybe I'd heave to and reef the mainsail some. But I'm a lazy man. A captain who prides himself on every breath of speed is either going to fly one of those loose-footed sails you're rigged for, or more likely going to put on a bigger jib."

"He is, is he?"

"And somebody who has gone to the trouble of having the mainmast rigged with twin forestays isn't going to want to heave to and switch sails the easy way—it'll take at least four men to do the job, and I'll bet you'd like a couple of assistants to help with that huge mother of a jib."

"I wouldn't bet against you, truth to tell." He smiled. "I could use some help, at that."

"Sure; we'd be happy to."

Ahira nodded. "I can finish this later." He stowed his axe in its sheath and then bound it to a rack of belaying pins. "What are you getting us into now?"

"Just a bit of work." I still wanted to ask him how he had survived, and he wanted to tell me, but the two of us have always allowed ourselves to be stubborn over things that don't matter.

His smile was bright in the dark. "That I can handle."

We surprised them. Ahira and I managed to haul the huge bag with the balloon jib—we would have called it a genoa jib on the Other Side—all by ourselves, even though Ahira grunted with the effort as he hauled the sailbag up the hatch. It must have weighed four hundred pounds, but Ahira can carry weights like that.

Me, I just steadied the thing. I'm only human, after all.

The rigging was a bit different than I was used to, and they had folded and packed the sail according to their own idiosyncratic system; I wouldn't have wanted to try to rig the sail myself, but Vertum Barr and Tretan Verr knew their jobs, and it wasn't all that long before we had the balloon jib up on the leeward forestay, and the smaller jib down, folded, bagged, and stowed.

We returned to our spot on the deck, the huge jib ballooning in the wind above us, luffing just a bit as the crew worked to get the trim right.

"I don't know what you see in this," Ahira said. Not criticism. Just observation.

"Guess you have to be born with a taste for it." I smiled. "I had a bit of experience on the Other Side." Just a bit. "It's relaxing."

"Hmm."

"You've got something on your mind," I said.

He nodded. "That's a fact. I've been wondering if you're getting too slow, Walter," Ahira said, considering the edge of his axe, as he resumed his sharpening. "You all do seem to slow down, as the years go by."

"And not you?" I asked, maybe too harshly. "You missed a step today." If Ahira hadn't been bowled over the side, we might have won on the first round, instead of lucking into another shot at the game.

I shuddered. The locals have ways of getting people to talk, and I'm none too fond of even the *idea* of red-hot pokers being shoved up my ass. We all have our peccadilloes, and that's one of mine.

He shook his head. "No. Not me. I'm not aging like you are, not as fast." He stared at me out of sad eyes. "If I was losing it, bit by bit, I'd admit it. To myself."

I leaned back against the railing and closed my eyes. Possibly I was getting too old for this. I'd been saying that for ten years, and maybe it was coming true.

Damn silly time to be growing old. Magic was loose in the world and we were sailing toward Ehvenor, toward God-knew-what. The situation called for not only the wisdom that's supposed to come with age, but the reflexes of youth. We needed a cross between Alvin York, Natty Bumppo, George Patton, and Shadowjack, and all we had was me.

"Maybe," I said. "And maybe we just were unlucky this time. I don't think we did too badly. Getting out of Brae with all of us alive is about ten strokes under par, as far as I'm concerned. That was too close."

"No," he said, firmly. "Just par."

We sat silent for a long time.

"Don't be angry," he said. "It had to be said."

"Maybe it did, and maybe it didn't."

"Would ignoring it make things any better?" A broad hand gripped my shoulder. "I seem to remember somebody telling me, one rainy Friday night years and years ago, that I wasn't going to drive my wheelchair out of the dorm and into the rain, because I couldn't afford to risk getting a cold, not in my state. I remember him saying something about that it was fucking unfair, but the universe was fucking unfair, and we weren't going to pretend otherwise."

I shrugged. "Well, you couldn't."

It was hard to remember Ahira as crippled James Michael Finnegan, largely because I'd never really thought of James Michael as a cripple—his mind had always been sharp, sharper than mine. The body, sure, that was bent, but after you've known somebody for awhile, you learn to stop worrying yourself over it; it doesn't rub off.

"I also remember," he said, his voice low, "that you canceled a date to put together a poker game that night."

"Hey, I needed the money." I smiled. "Besides, I didn't really cancel it, we just pushed it back a week."

Bethany had been good about it; she had acted as James Michael's hands at the poker game, and had been amused at the way that the other players paid more attention to her cleavage than to their cards. Nice lady. Next weekend we had a nice steak dinner, complete with a bottle of Silver Oak cabernet, paid for with my winnings.

"Now it's my turn," he said. "You've got to start taking it easy." He chuckled to take the sting out of it, the laugh a deep rumble in his barrel of a chest. "You can't afford to get your neck broke, eh?"

"Hey, I wouldn't do that. Deprive all the women of my charm? But leave it for later. Not now. I'm still okay."

He had finished with his axe; carefully, gently, he wrapped it in an oilcloth.

"Maybe so," he said, "probably. But you will slow down too much, some day. We can push it back a bit, but there's going to come a time when you're not going to be able to go out and do things yourself." He bit at his thumb. "Next generation's coming along—Jason's getting sharper. We're going to have to be sure that he's got the right kind of people to back him."

"Until what?"

The dwarf shrugged. "Until things change. However they change. Until the revolution that Lou is building takes off on its own; until the gathering of Holtish and Biemish nobles becomes a true parliament, until Arta Myrdhyn takes a hand and screws up whatever the hell we think we're doing."

Starlight danced on the water, and a brief spray more chilled than refreshed me.

"In the meantime," he said, "you've got to do two things."

I knew what the first was going to be. "Practice, practice, practice."

"Yup. Starting in the morning. You and me . . . well, I can read your mind almost as well as you can read mine. Tennetty tends to bunt too much, and Jason can't coordinate with anybody."

I shrugged. "I keep thinking of him as his father. Karl would have ducked back and blown six of them away before getting into the fight, and then he could have taken out the rest."

Ahira looked me over, slowly, the way he always did when I said something stupid. "That's the second thing. Don't buy into the legend, or you might start to believe you're just as legendary." He looked out over the water. "You've got to remember you're tricky Walter Slovotsky, and stop trying to be Karl. Swaggering through the town square on a recon was a Karl sort of thing."

Well, I didn't say, *I actually didn't do it Karl's sort of way. I did it my way.*

But Ahira was off on his you're-getting-too-old-for-this kick, and I didn't want to complicate the issue.

Besides, he was right. I've always been best at sneaking and indirection, not taking on half a dozen swordsmen. I should have thought out a way around it, not confronted Lord Daeran in some sort of Mexican standoff.

"I'll try," I said.

"Good," he said, rising. "We start practicing in the

morning. In the meantime, get some sleep. I'll keep an eye on things tonight; I can catch up on sleep tomorrow."

Screw it. "*Okay*," I said. "O-fucking-kay. I give."

"Eh?"

"I give in. You win. If you won't tell me, I'll break down and ask."

He smiled as he ticked his thumbnail against the anchor. "Ask what?"

"How it happens that you're alive."

He smiled, again. "You mean because dwarves can't float, can't swim, right?"

"*Yes*. That's exactly what I mean. Are you going to tell me, or let me die of curiosity?"

He shrugged and he hefted the anchor chain. "I think I'll ask Erol Lyneian for a piece of this, as a good-luck charm. —Anybody ever tell you that dwarves can't *climb?*"

CHAPTER TWENTY-ONE

In Which I Face Off with a Fanatic, and Spend Time with an Old Friend

There are truths which are not for all men, nor for all time.
— VOLTAIRE

I changed my mind, okay?

— WALTER SLOVOTSKY

OLD FRIENDS ARE GOOD to have around. There's a story or two about that, but they'll have to wait, just a bit.

We stopped to trade at Artiven, bobbing safely at anchor offshore, while the launch took Erol Lyneian and some trade goods ashore—a few bundles of Sciforth ironwood, a couple of hogsheads of horrible-smelling Fenevarian glue, and, surprisingly, fifty-or-so pounds of Home wootz.

Maybe that shouldn't have been so surprising—Artiven was known for its knives and swords, and it would have been hard to think of a better start than the high-grade weapon steel that Home produced.

We could have gone right past, I guess, except for two things. For one, crew provisions were low. There hadn't been quite enough time to load them in Brae. Taking to your heels usually interferes with something important; this was above par. Two: Ahira wanted Bast and Kenda off the ship, and away from us.

Erol Lyneian had been pushing me for more of the details of powdermaking, and I'd been supplying them.

Bast wasn't happy. We hadn't had quite enough healing draughts to bring him and Kenda up to full health; the aftermath of his ordeal had left him frail, at least for the time being. Rest, food, and time would do everything else. Although he couldn't rest.

He caught up with me as I was getting a lesson in rigging and ketch sailing from Vertum Barr—I'm no dilettante, but I like learning new skills and polishing ones I already have—while Tennetty and Jason were working out on the rear deck.

It was good to play sailor again, wearing nothing but a pair of blousy pantaloons and a headband—well, and a knife strapped to my right calf, concealed by the pant leg—worrying about nothing more important than how to get a bit more speed out of the shape of a sail, whether the bilge hold needed pumping again, or how to fly a complex set of sails.

The *Delenia*'s gear was unusual, even by the idiosyncratic nonstandards of Cirric sailing: she used a lot of lacquered, layered wood rather than iron (okay) and brass (better); jibsheet fairleads anchored, instead of track-and-slider; reefing claws that looked like bear paws. Strange stuff, but not bad.

Tennetty had stripped down to a thin cotton shirt and shorts, and Jason down to just a pair of ragged Home jeans. They circled each other, hands reaching out for a grip on forearms or waist.

"Now," Vertum Barr said, chewing on a piece of jerky as he talked, "you hear a lot about how the mizzens don't add much to the speed of a ketch, and there's some truth to that. But when you're close-tacking, the faster you can come about, the better off you are, and that's why we pay particular attention to the trim of the mizzen." He frowned at the horizon, his forehead creased leather. "Probably fly the mizzen trysail, if things look shaky."

Far off, probably a storm was brewing. All kinds of storms.

Tennetty let Jason grab her by waist and arm, and as he

tried for a solid throw, she kicked her heel against his calf, knocking one leg out from beneath him, the two of them falling hard to the deck, Tennetty on top, her fingers stopping inches from his eyes.

She slapped the deck and rose. "Again."

"So why a ketch?" I asked.

He smiled. "*Delenia* used to be a fishing boat—and a fisherman has to be nimble more than fast. If it were up to me, I'd have her remasted and rerigged as a sloop, but Erol Lyneian likes the way she handles as is, and she's his ship, not mine, eh?"

This time, as Tennetty and Jason closed, their arms and feet moved so fast that I couldn't quite make out what they were doing, but when they parted, he was still on his feet, and Tennetty was lying at his feet, slammed hard onto the deck.

If it were up to me, the ship would lie at anchor here while the storm passed us by, but none of the crew seemed to think it looked threatening enough. You can pick up a lot of knowledge by working the coast, from boat to boat, but there's things that only years of experience teach you. "Now, if we have to run before the storm, we may be able to run quicker, without endangering ourselves, if we have a bit of cloth back here. Yes?"

I nodded. "That would seem to be so."

I'd heard Bast walk up behind me, but I hadn't done anything about it. Let him make the first move. Of course, if the first move was slipping a knife in between my third and fourth ribs, I'd probably regret it. I'm kind of funny that way.

Vertum Barr touched a bent finger to his brow and walked off.

"Walter Slovotsky," Bast said, as I turned. "We have to talk."

"We can talk. If you want to argue about taking passage to Sciforth, talk it over with the dwarf, not with me."

Ahira was ashore, finding a ship for Bast and Kenda, a) which I didn't want to argue about, and b) with which I agreed.

"Not about that," he said. "About something more important."

223

I remembered Bast as a gangling kid, with an Adam's apple that used to bob nervously up and down his skinny neck, never really concealed by the soft, downy beard that couldn't grow long enough to cover it, or to conceal his soft face. He could never look me in the eyes in the old days, always looking away.

Now, his black beard was trimmed back, like an overgrown hedge; his skin was pulled taut at the bridge of his nose and above his cheekbones; and his unblinking eyes never left mine. He was dressed only in a blousy pair of sailor's pantaloons with thick rolled hems at his ankles—they were much too large for him—and carrying only a waterskin over his shoulder.

I knew what he was going to say before he said it. It's a minority opinion, but Lou's disciples have always seemed to me to tend toward the fanatical.

"We have to silence everyone aboard this ship," he said, his voice stubbornly level and reasonable, his eyes obstinately refusing to glow with fanatical fire. He dropped the waterskin over the rail, letting the coiled leather thong pay out from his hand until it splashed in the water below. He hauled it up and tied the skin to the rail, letting it cool in the breeze.

Evaporative cooling, and all that. I bet he even knew the name of it.

"Just because they overheard the secret of powdermaking?" I finally asked.

"Yes."

As Hassan ibn-al-Sabbah would have said, *Death to all fanatics!*

I shook my head. "The secret would have to get out sometime. May as well be now. If the choice is the secret getting out now or me cold-bloodedly murdering the *Delenia*'s captain and crew, then it definitely gets out now." I reached down into my pouch and pulled out a stick of jerky, tore it in half, and politely offered him his choice of halves. I wouldn't have returned the courtesy, mind—if he had done it, both halves could have been poisoned.

He thought about it for a moment, debating the propriety of eating with the greatest traitor that he'd ever known, then decided that it wouldn't stay his hand, if necessary. He bit into the jerky.

"No," I went on, "our edge is always going to be progress, not secrets. If the process for making slaver powder was cheaper, the secret of black powder wouldn't be worth anything. It could have been cheaper to make; hell, maybe it could be made that way; I don't know enough magic." I chewed some more jerky. Too salty. "No, our edge is going to be in staying ahead of the game, not in controlling who plays what pieces. For now, staying ahead means smokeless powder weapons replacing black powder. More bang for the volume, less smoke, slower burning."

His look was too controlled to be a glare, but just barely. I wasn't supposed to know the advantage of slow-burning powders in long barrels.

Tennetty and Jason walked up, both sweaty from their workout. Well, Jason had that sweaty-but-satisfied look that the younger folks get; Tennetty's breathing was still fast, and a vein in her neck pulsed in a rapid beat. She looked more drained than anything else.

"We're thinking about going ashore for awhile," he said. "Stretch our legs a bit, maybe ask around some." His face was too much a mirror to his thoughts; I could tell he was too eager.

"Tennetty?" I cocked my head to one side. "He's leaving something out."

"He told you."

"I doubt that."

"Well, maybe he could have been more specific." A smile worked its way across her face. "One of the crew came back with some rumors about things streaming out of Ehvenor. We thought we'd see what the local gossip is."

I turned back to Jason, not asking why he hadn't come clean with me. He still had a lot to learn—I don't insist on doing all the fun things myself. Besides, looking into rumors wasn't all that much fun. "You asking permission?"

He thought about that. He thought about the fact that he didn't like me much, and then he thought about the fact that he was perfectly capable of making errors, too.

225

So he said, "Advice, at least," his face going studiously blank. He had worked out that he didn't have to take advice.

Tennetty kept her smile small. Good; the kid didn't need to see her beaming approval. Might swell his head fast enough to burst the skin.

"You ask the dwarf?"

He shook his head. "Him next, and Kenda." He looked over at Bast. "Would you like to come along?"

Bast shook his head. "No."

Delicately put. Bast reminded me of an Other Side friend I used to have. Brian would always turn down an invitation to go out to dinner with a guttural monosyllable, implicitly trusting to his friends not to take offense. Not a good bet, not altogether. Eventually we stopped calling, most of us.

Jason was waiting with simulated patience, and the day wasn't getting any shorter. Artiven was a relatively safe town, but there was no sense in pushing it, either way.

"Sure," I said. "Go on in, but don't try too hard to nose around. Spend a bit of money, eat some local food, keep your eyes and ears open, and your mouth chewing."

Jason and Tennetty walked away. Bast was still scowling at me.

Black powder wasn't as much of a secret as he thought. Andy had been around when Lou and I mixed up the very first batch, and helped stir, all the while chanting, "Bubble, bubble, toil and trouble." She knew the formula, and Ahira did, and I'm sure Doria knew what went into black powder, too, although I wouldn't have given odds that she knew the proportions.

Not that those mattered—you can get quite a distance from the classical mix and still get real gunpowder. The main secret is in knowing what to play around with, and going ahead and doing it.

So, the simple argument went like this: Bast, don't worry about the secret getting out, because there's a bunch of us who have known it for years.

With Bast eager to slice the throat of everybody who had heard the secret, it was probably not a good idea to give him more targets; better to reason with him. "Did you know?"

He shook his head. "I had . . . hints, but I deliberately didn't follow them up. I didn't need to know how to make powder, and I didn't want to know. Master Ranella does, and there are . . . arrangements if she and the Engineer were both to die. But no, I didn't know how." He unfastened the water-skin from the rail and took a polite swig before offering it to me.

I thought about the waterbag, and I thought about the drinking to show that I trusted him, but then I decided that it was too big a risk, even though I knew there was no point in Bast poisoning me. Maybe he didn't know that.

We'd had enough to do with poisons recently, albeit fake ones.

"I don't think so, Bast," I said, handing him the waterbag back.

"You ask me to trust you, but you won't trust me?" he asked.

I nodded. "Well, yeah."

It was, after all, a fair statement of the situation.

The door to Andy's cabin stood half open. Inside, the slatted blinds over the porthole cast bands of light and dark onto her bunk, striping its rumpled brown blankets. Dressed in a pair of shorts and a halter against the heat of the day, she was sitting tailor-fashion on her bunk amid scattered items: a silver knife, its handle the dull white of new bone; a spool of impossibly fine thread; a small lenticular crystal clutched in a clay claw; a foot-long feather that pulsed through a rainbow of colors as she idly stroked at it.

You know: the usual.

She didn't notice me at first; she was concentrating on the thick, leather-bound volume. I glanced at the pages, and found that not only couldn't I read them, but that the letters blurred and swam in front of my eyes.

More magic. I shivered. I don't like magic.

I stood in the doorway, silently. I'm good at that. I once crouched silently on a tree branch for more than a day, motionless while the sun rose and fell and rose again, although my thighs and lower back still ache at the thought of it, even now, years later.

"Close the door and pull up a seat," she said, not looking up. "I won't bite."

"Oh, darn."

She raised her head into the bands of light and shadow, and the light caught her eyes and mouth as she smiled for a moment. Just for that moment, all the years fell away, and we were kids again, back in our twenties. She looked too young for all the years, maybe, or maybe it was just that the years had finally settled well on her. I never believed the common Other Side nonsense about how a woman was necessarily the most beautiful at twenty or so, and over the hill by thirty.

But it was only a moment; she moved her head back, one band of shadow turning her smile into a dark and distant smirk, another masking her eyes. "What's everybody up to?"

I sat down on the bed, the spell book between us. "Jason and Tennetty have gone into town, just to look around. Ahira's over in the docks, buying passage for Bast and Kenda. We should have the two of them out of our hair by tonight. What are you up to?" Translation: How much have you been using magic, and how much is it affecting you?

Her mouth quirked in the shadows. "Trying spells that are beyond me, without success." I guess my alarm showed in my face.

She waved her hand, as though to wave my concern away. It didn't work. "No, not dangerous ones—this is subtle magic. Information magic, not power magic," she said. She touched a fingernail to a fuzzy line on the page. "This one, for example: I could, say, accent the second syllable of the instigator, reverse the suffixes for any of the hegemonics, lisp my way through the dominitives, and all that would happen to the power is that it would randomize, and that wouldn't do much. It might raise the temperature in the room a few degrees, but that's about all."

"What's it for? The spell, I mean."

"Mapmaking," she said. "Directional magic. We'll need it in Ehvenor. We're getting close to Ehvenor. Tomorrow night?"

I nodded. "Morning after, at worst."

Or at best. This time I didn't shiver. Reflexively, I

reached toward the knife—I'm comfortable with an edged weapon in my hands—but pulled my hand back. Messing with wizards' equipment isn't a good idea.

"Sometimes a knife is just a knife," she said. "Go ahead; you won't hurt anything."

I hefted it in my palm, the silver blade cool against my skin, the bone handle too warm, as though she had been holding it tightly, too long.

She looked up at me, her eyes probing from the slatted shadow. Bars of light and dark cut diagonally across her face, striping it.

"I worry about you sometimes," she said. There was an extra note in her voice, something high-pitched, perhaps. It bothered me.

"Me, too," I said. "I'm getting too old for this." I ran my thumb along the edge of the knife. I'd seen sharper.

The edge of her mouth touched the light as she smiled. "Too old for what?"

"This running around, getting ourselves in and out of trouble."

"You still seem good enough at it," she said, leaning back, considering.

I shrugged. "The trouble with this line of work is no matter how good you are at it, eventually you get unlucky. It's like . . ."

That was the trouble. It wasn't like anything else. "Okay, try it this way. Karl and I used to spar, back in the old days. Now, back at our peak, he had the edge on me in strength, and I had a bit more speed, but his reflexes were just a touch better than mine. He couldn't move as fast, but he could react faster, he could get started moving just a hair before I did."

She nodded, her face impassive.

"So, given that he was better at hand-to-hand than I am, he should have won all the time. But he didn't win all of the time—just *most* of the time. Big difference. We were operating close to the limits of human reflexes, and sometimes you have to, say, commit yourself to a block before your opponent strikes—if you wait for him to make his move first, there won't be time for nerve impulses to travel to the brain and make the return trip before he connects, yes?"

"So?" she said. "What's your point?"

"My point, such as it is, is that we live in a world of both skill and chance. If you put yourself into a situation where there's a random factor operating, no matter how carefully you've scoped it out, no matter how good you are, sometimes you're committed to a path, sometimes you've already entered into a course of action that'll smash you flat."

"Or blow you into hamburger," she said, her voice low but unnaturally even. She wasn't talking about me. "Turn his body into garbage," she said, her fingers digging into my arm, "and spread it across a filthy beach, gulls swooping down and pecking at threads of muscle and patches of skin, flecks and fragments of bone, and one eyeball, miraculously intact, lying on the sand, staring blindly at the sharp beaks, at—"

"Andy—"

"I can see him before," she said, the words coming faster and faster, "I can see him and I can feel it, except when the fire flares in my mind, except when the power plays through my fingers. I can see him smiling, not because he isn't scared, because he was never afraid to be scared, but because he knows that that will frighten them just a little more. I can see him lighting the fuse," she said, spitting out the words in a rapid-fire tattoo, "I can see him batting them away with his good hand while the fuse burns down, and laughing at them, smiling at them, maybe because they don't know enough to run, maybe because since he can't run he won't let them run, because he's decided that this is the end and they're all going with him." She looked up at me. "But sometimes he isn't wearing his face, because sometimes it's Jason's, and sometimes it's Ahira's, and it's been Piell's, and my God, Walter, sometimes he's wearing your face, sometimes he looks like you, sometimes it's you, Walter . . ."

"Shh . . ." I laid a finger against her lips. "Easy, Andy. Slow down."

With a visible effort, she stopped herself from talking.

Trembling fingers reached for my face, her touches tentative, light, like the brush of a cobweb.

"Sometimes it's yours," she said. "Sometimes he wears your face." Her breath was fast and ragged, and her voice was thick and liquid. "It's all getting so complicated," she said, "the closer we get to Ehvenor."

She touched my forehead with two widespread fingers and breathed out a spell, like she was blowing a bubble in the air.

Bright lights flared behind my eyes, in my mind, and I could see distant fires, to the horizon, and beyond. They burned too brightly; reds and oranges that intense, that vivid would have burned my eyes out of my head.

Off in the distance, beyond the horizon, the rolling waters of the Cirric roiled at the edge of Faerie, bubbling in places, freezing in others, while below the surface, immense dark shapes waited for release.

Somewhere far away but closer, a purple vein of magic had been cut open; strange things and strangeness bled out into the cold air, taking on a solidity that was nonetheless substantial for all its wrongness: a vision of a dagger-toothed, batwinged creature became real and flapped off into the night; a vague, insubstantial hulking shape took on precision and substance as it shambled across the ground, scratching at its hairy sides.

Off beyond, beyond distance, barely visible yet crystalline in its clarity, a landmass stood waiting, bright lights pulsing across the twisting shoreline in a gavotte somehow familiar in pattern but unpredictable.

"Faerie," she said. "Imagine yourself with all the problems and sorrows a human could have. You could lay it all before the Faerie, and they could send you home healed and well, or broken and misshapen, better than you ever were, or worse than you ever feared you could be."

Chances?

She laughed as she spread her hands in front of me, her fingers moving as though she was shuffling a deck of cards. "Imagine an infinite deck of cards, Walter. Each card has a number on it, from one to infinity. There is one one, two twos, three threes, four fours, and so on." She mimed fanning the deck. "Pick a card, at random, Walter, from one to infinity, and I will pick one, too, and what are the chances that my number is larger than yours?"

50-50, looked at one way; 100%, looked at another; zero, yet another.

"All are true," she said, dismissing the deck.

The inner vision turned away from the water, toward the land. We were used to thinking of powerful magical objects as few and far between, but I could see the flare of half a dozen charmed amulets or rings within the confines of Artiven itself. And not just the fire of an enchanted stone or piece of glass. Hiding, wrapped in long-rotted leather, an iron glove lay, its fingers thick worms of segmented steel, each finger tipped with a jagged blade like a shark's tooth, waiting while it lay beneath the sands at the shoreline, pushed down beneath the rotted piling of an old dock.

"Deathglove," she said. "It kills happily, it kills well, but it kills a bit of you every time you use it. Buried a long time ago, by somebody wise enough not to keep it. There would be those who would give everything they have for this."

Then how could it have lain there so long? I didn't voice the question, but she answered it anyway.

"Can't you see? It's hidden, it's hidden."

Not now it wasn't. But I don't need a deathglove, thank you very much.

"No, Walter, you idiot, not the deathglove, the rest of the picture, the summoning. It takes more power and control to find it, to see all of it. If I can just look deeper . . ."

The light started to clarify further, to brighten, but—

"No." I could feel the sharp clarity of the shapes cutting at my mind, sawing away at my sanity. I pushed her hand out of the way, and the light died behind my eyes. I wasn't meant to work magic, or to work with magic.

And neither was she, not at this level. Not like this.

"Stop it," I said. "Let it drop."

Her eyes had gone wide and unblinking, her jaw slack. A fat, red drop of blood hung at the swell of her lower lip as her lips moved rapidly, almost in silence, her breathing growing faster and more ragged.

"No."

I shook her once, gently, then again, hard, but she didn't stop. I tried to shake her even harder, but I couldn't. I don't mean that I wasn't willing to shake her hard. I tried, but it was like trying to push her first through water, then molasses, then through a wall—there was a limit to how hard I could shake her, how hard her magic would let me hold her.

"*Stop* it."

I tried to slap her, but my hand slowed as it approached her face, turning what had been intended to be a sharp hit into a gentle cupping of her cheek. Whatever was moving her was protecting her on the level of physical attack.

"*Andrea.*"

I couldn't hit her, and nothing I could say was going to do any good, so I pulled her close, my mouth over hers.

Her eyes were wide and her mouth was wet and warm, salty with the taste of blood, perhaps mine, perhaps hers. Her arms snaked around my chest, astonishingly strong fingers locking tightly behind my back as she pushed herself hard against me, her tongue warm and wet in my mouth.

Old reflexes died hard while long-time inhibitions died easily: I swept the spell book and her gear off the bed and onto the floor, not caring about the damage.

Her eyes, now more insistent than mad, locked on mine as we fell to the bunk, fingers struggling clumsily with clothing.

The part of me that's always analytical mused that I used to be a lot more expert at this, but I told it to shut up, and for once it listened.

She lay in my arms for a long time, her head resting on my left shoulder, her breathing so slow I thought she was asleep, which is why I didn't move my arm from underneath her, even though she was pressing against my biceps in just the right place to put the arm to sleep.

To tell the truth, the first time hadn't been all that good; we were both in too much of a hurry, or at least I was. The second time was better. Twenty years before, there had been a third time, but no matter how long it had been for me since I'd last been with a woman—and it had been *far* too long—I was years older, and was slowing down.

Well, I had seen this coming, and now it had happened, and the world hadn't ended.

What I hadn't considered enough was that Doria was

probably right, that Andy was overdoing the magic, and it not only was taking a toll on her, but was threatening to send her right over the edge, almost as though it was a personal force. I'd have to try to keep her away from magic, but I didn't have the vaguest idea as to how to do that. This worked once, but I didn't think that keeping it up twenty-four hours a day was a really live possibility.

I mean, assuming I was, er, up to it, how would I phrase the suggestion?

I smiled to myself, but it wasn't funny. Andy was pushing herself too hard, and I didn't see a prayer of stopping it. Maybe, just maybe, she could control it better. Maybe there was some other way.

I hate maybes.

I had thought she was asleep, but then she stretched and yawned, lifted her face to mine, and smiled as she stretched, one toe coming up and playing with the sheath still strapped to my right calf. I don't normally feel the need to be armed during sex, honest, but I hadn't spent a lot of time thinking this out.

Unsurprisingly, all the tension had gone out of her body. Even if you do it wrong, that still tends to happen, and while I hadn't been keeping score, I hadn't noticed a lot of mistakes on either of our parts, just the normal sort of first-time clumsiness. What did surprise me was that a lot of tension I hadn't known I'd had, had gone out of me. In my shoulders and right arm, particularly. (I suspect the tautness had gone out of my left arm, but it was numb, and I wasn't going to know about that for awhile.)

"What am I supposed to say?" she asked, her voice blurred with sleepiness. " 'Thanks, I needed that'?"

It would have been uncouth to observe that she obviously *had* needed that, even softened by an explanation to the effect that for an adult used to an active sex life, there were better things than having it cut off, as I could have explained from my own recent history.

Or I could have explained that I needed it too. No, not just the release; as much as I'd wanted that, I am more than skin and meat wrapped around a collection of gonads and hormones. What I had needed, what I had needed badly, was the touch of a woman who didn't shudder when I laid a hand on her.

But—

"Sure," I said. "That'll be fine."

Let me tell you two of the nice things about having old friends around:

You can do something that is at the very best morally ambiguous, and then, when questioned about it, you can try to shrug it off with a stupid one-liner, and all that will happen is that your old friend will stiffen for a moment, then relax in your arms and lay her head on your chest, and then she'll say with an affectionate laugh in her voice, "Walter, you are *such* an asshole." And then, quickly: "We'd better get dressed before my son gets back."

And, later, you can be standing next to a railing as a ship is blown through the night, watching the faerie lights dancing manically along the horizon, their reflections in the water shattered and dispersed long before they've ever reached you, and another old friend will walk up and rest a slim hand on your shoulder, lean her head against your arm, and say nothing, nothing at all.

CHAPTER TWENTY-TWO

In Which We Meet Three Slavers Snarling, Two Wizards Waiting, One Cleric Considering, but Skip the Partridge in the Pear Tree

Whoever loves, if he do not propose
The right true end of love, he's one that goes
To sea for nothing but to make him sick.

—JOHN DONNE

Peer pressure is a pain in the ass.

—WALTER SLOVOTSKY

THE SUN HAD JUST SET, casting fading bands and threads of gold and crimson on sky and water, as the lights of Ehvenor drew over the horizon and started to peek out between the islands.

The cold gray waters around Ehvenor were scattered with rocky, wave-spattered islands. Some thrust stony fingers through the surface and into the sky, and made me think of underwater spires threatening to gut the ship. Others, their backs covered in moss and brush, rose only a few feet out of the water. Their dark bulks loomed dangerously beneath the waves, threatened the *Delenia*'s bulk with grounding.

Mostly, they just got in the way.

Life's a lot like that.

Erol Lyneian pointed the *Delenia*'s bow high, toward what looked like a dangerously narrow passage between two islands, but he looked like he knew what he was doing, and I hoped he knew what he was doing.

"There's a landing on the other side of that. That's the closest I'm willing to go to Ehvenor these days."

There was a light behind Andrea's eyes—and no, that's not a figure of speech—as she laid a hand on Erol Lyneian's shoulder and said, "No. There is another. Further down, past the channel. Sail to that one." Her voice was a thick contralto, almost singing.

I looked to Ahira, and he looked back at me, but neither of us was going to say anything further.

Erol Lyneian started to protest, but she silenced him with a gesture. "Sail to that one."

The landing was a shelf cut into the side of the cliff, and three flights of steps carved up the side, zigzagging to the top above.

Delenia strained gently at her anchor as the onshore breeze tried to blow her up against the rocks, her sails flapping loosely in the wind. We unloaded our gear quickly, Jason and Tennetty descending first, Ahira and me throwing packs and parcels down to them and the four rowers in the launch.

I was the last one down. I turned to Erol Lyneian to thank him, but he hadn't gotten us out of Brae out of any goodness of his heart, but in return for a secret worth as much as a hull full of gold, perhaps. And worth nothing if I simply spread it around, telling everyone I encountered what gunpowder consisted of, how to make it.

Of course, it wouldn't be worth anything to me, either, but it never had been, not in the sense that Erol Lyneian thought of it. Which is why he hadn't thought of the possibility that I might spread the secret further—why would I give away something that I had so carefully husbanded all these years?

I smiled.

"Fare well, Erol Lyneian," I said, as I lowered myself over the side.

Only a few minutes later we and our gear were safely ensconced on the lower landing, watching the sailors row the launch all too quickly back to the *Delenia*.

Ahira looked at the lights brightening the sky overhead, obscured by the cliff, and then he looked at me.

"Walter," he said, "you're on."

Most of the time, the precautions you take are wasted, but you have to take them anyway.

A college friend of mine—she was a senior when I was a freshman—got married right after graduation. She wanted to get started on making babies, only to find after much effort and expense that she had a fertility problem, and that all the years and money she'd spent on contraception had been wasted. I don't want to count the number of times I've entered a room through a window, or perhaps an unexpected door, or poked my head in and out for a quick peek before going in. I can't begin to add up how often I've armed myself for the day or night without ever having to even touch a hand to a knifehilt or pistol butt. I won't try to remember the number of times I've loaded a pistol and hung it on the wall without having to fire it.

Still, you do it the right way, each and every time.

I crept up the steps slowly, carefully, hands feeling for any give as I slowly put my weight on each progressive step, eyes sweeping the steps ahead for a sign of anything out of the ordinary, happy that these were stone, and not wood. There's a thousand ways to gimmick a wooden staircase; a laid stone one is trickier, and carved stone is the toughest to rig, but it's not impossible.

The obvious place for a trap was at the top, where some idiot would poke his head and torso over the ledge, leaving himself an open target, so I paused at the last landing and gently straightened.

The plateau was overgrown by a thick vine that lay flat on the ground; it had long choked any grasses dead, so there was neither any obstruction nor concealment.

Still, in the dark, you wouldn't expect anyone to be looking for a forehead and a pair of eyes. You wouldn't expect there to be somebody right there, his eyes inches from mine.

Which is okay, because there wasn't.

What there *was* was a man, squatting easily, just out of reach, looking down at me, two men standing behind him. He was broad of shoulder and dark of hair and beard, and his thin lips barely split in a smile that held only a trace of cynicism, perhaps, or possibly just a hint of contempt.

The hilt of a saber hung near his left hip, canted forward, but his hands were clasped in front of him.

"Greetings," he said. Moving with exaggerated slowness, he unclenched his hands and gestured beyond, to the campfire, where three more shapes in dark robes huddled around a simmering pot. "They've been waiting for you, for all of you." He extended a muscular hand to help me up, but backed slowly away, palms up, when I didn't take it.

I looked beyond the three rough men toward the fire, toward the three hooded shapes there, watching us, not moving.

Six of them, five of us. I didn't particularly like the odds; the three robed ones sitting about the fire might as well have been wearing signs proclaiming themselves magic-user types.

The dark-bearded man spoke again. "Ta havath," he said with a smile. "We mean you no harm, not here and now." It was a genuine smile, but I didn't like it. "Even though I am called Wolkennen, and am a full brother of the Slavers Guild, as are my guild brothers here," he said.

Sometimes, everyone is lucky that I'm me, and not Karl—me included. Karl would have launched himself at Wolkennen, and damned be the consequences, figuring one down was a good start. Me, I just beckoned to the others to hurry the hell up the stairs, and straightened, slipping the hilt of a throwing knife to the palm of my hand.

I mean, I believed him, but I wasn't sure I believed that I believed him, if you understand what I mean.

Andy was at my side, one hand touching my arm to urge caution, a soft spell on her lips.

"Be easy, Walter," she said, walking up the steps and stalking across the mat of vines toward the campfire, and the three sitting around it. One of the slavers took half a step toward her, stopped by a glare from Wolkennen.

"No," he said. "Leave them be." The three slavers

backed off, away from us, away from the fire, toward the far end of the plateau where a pair of low tents stood pitched.

I walked the last few steps up the plateau. Down the slope, Ehvenor lay, waiting. Or maybe it didn't lie, and perhaps it didn't wait. Maybe it was doing more than lying.

Down the slope and below, Ehvenor flickered brightly in the night.

The last time I had been near Ehvenor, it looked pretty much like a normal city, except for the area around the Faerie . . . well, embassy, I always thought of it.

I'd say that part of it was unchanged, except that it had never *been* unchanged: that was the trouble with it.

It was a tall, dome-capped tower, rising perhaps four stories, seemingly woven of sunrise and haze, always best looked at out of the corner of the eye. When you'd look at it directly, it would seem to shift, to change, to melt from one shape to another, but always so subtly that you never could tell just what had happened, always knowing that something was different from what had been, but never able to tell whether the change had come on quickly or slowly.

It was still there in the center of the city, but now it was surrounded by three similar buildings, no, it was

a hundred buildings; silly, of course it had always been
—a thousand buildings, spread across
—no, tightly packed through
—miles upon miles of crooked
—no, curved
—no, straight streets.

I could have looked away, but it's a bad habit to look away from things that bother you; you have to get used to it. So I looked, my jaw clenched so tight I'm surprised I didn't break any teeth.

Okay; fine. The outer parts of the city were still streets of cobblestone and mud, still buildings of wood and stone, but the center of the city, a mass of great brightness and indeterminate size, was something that my mind couldn't quite grasp, no matter how hard I tried.

Big fucking deal. Nothing to be scared about. I'd never been able to do integral calculus, either; not understanding something didn't have to scare me.

So why was I shivering? I would have guessed that it was cold on the plateau, but I don't like the looks of that kind of intellectual dishonesty on anybody, present company included.

Okay; it scared me. Big, fat, hairy deal. I'd been scared before.

Off toward the edges of the light, dark shapes shifted into and out of solidity, some evaporating in the flickering whiteness, others shuffling off into the darkness.

I turned back to the others.

Trouble was brewing, at least from one quarter. Andy had quietly joined the three robed ones sitting by the fire, but Tennetty and Jason had dropped their gear and squared off opposite the slavers. No weapons had been drawn, but maybe it was only a matter of time. Jason had already thumbed away the thong holding one of his borrowed flint-locks in place.

Silly boy. I thumbed away the thongs of *all* of my flint-locks. I was willing to take Wolkennen's word for his harm-lessness—until it all started.

Ahira stepped in front of Jason. "Let's not start anything we can't stop, friends," he said, mainly to Jason and Tennetty, but maybe a bit to me, as well.

Something moved in the vines underfoot, and I started, stopping my hand at the butt of a flintlock.

"You know," I said, "this reminds me of a story I once heard about. Seems there were these two groups of combatants squared off against each other, trying to make peace. Only trouble was, one member of one party spotted a snake, and drew his sword to cut its head off. That's when it all broke loose. Not because anybody wanted it to, but because everybody thought it already was breaking loose."

Ahira nodded. "So we'll all stand very easy. Tennetty, you and I will just sit ourselves over there," he said, indicating a spot about halfway between the fire and the tents. "Jason and Walter, you join Andrea."

I didn't know whether to be flattered that he trusted me enough to back Andy on whatever was going on, or whether to be discouraged that he didn't trust me to either hold my fire or put it in the right place, so I decided to skip being flattered or discouraged and hurried over with Jason to where Andy was standing by the fire.

Well, I had long taken the position that if what was going on with Ehvenor was all that important, there would be magical types looking into it; I didn't know whether to be glad or disappointed to be proven right.

One of the three robed ones stood, throwing back the hood, and letting the dark robe fall to his feet. Beneath the robe he wore tunic and leggings, both of a light yellow. My prejudices are always to think of wizards as small, wizened men and women—the more powerful, the smaller and more shriveled—but that's really silly, when you think of it. Somebody who can take on a better appearance may well choose to appear young and strong; somebody with enough power to make that appearance real may well choose to be young and strong, and by no means are all wizards human.

He was tall and just barely slender rather than skinny, his black beard trimmed neatly, the movements of his hands graceful as he beckoned to Andy.

"Join us, good wizard," he said, clasping his hands in front of him and bowing. "We have been waiting."

Andy said nothing, and the silence hung in the air for a long time while the city flickered and the fire crackled. In the crackling flames, a burning log broke in two, sending a shower of sparks into the air and off into the night.

Andrea raised a hand and breathed a spell, and the wizard stretched further until he was impossibly thin for a human, the tops of his ears losing their roundness, as his hair and beard became finer, softer, like a baby's hair.

"Well done, oh, well, done," the elf said, his words almost a song. "You have unmasked me, I do depose."

She tossed her head. "I don't need false congratulations. I couldn't have overcome your seeming if you hadn't let me."

"True." His look wasn't quite condescending; neither was the way he clasped his hands at his waist and bowed. The look was penetrating, the kind of stare that made me think he could look through not only my clothes and flesh, but maybe even my self.

"I am Vair ip Melhrood, long resident in glorious Pandathaway, for these past two hundred years of the Wizards

242

Guild. I am known as Vair the Uncertain." His lips crooked into a smile. "At least, I think that's how I am known."

"You wear your age well," she said.

"Thank you."

The second rose, throwing robes aside in one rough motion. He came about waist-high on the first: a dwarf. My first thought was that he wasn't a wizard—dwarf wizards are rare—but when he seated himself tailor-fashion on the air, I decided otherwise. It takes a powerful wizard to use a levitation spell at all, and even more so to simply use it for the casual purpose of bringing his eyes to the same level as Andrea's—it could have been just showing off, but he was a dwarf, and dwarves don't tend to show off. No, he was a wizard, but he hadn't bothered with a seeming.

Dwarves don't mind how they look; there's no accounting for taste.

This one looked pretty ugly, even for a dwarf. He was only a little shorter than Ahira, but probably didn't weigh more than half as much. His skin hung off him in deep folds. The peeling skin didn't look particularly healthy, but I guess he didn't care about the heartbreak of psoriasis.

Where Ahira's big nose and massive jaw make Ahira look pleasantly homely, this dwarf's face was covered with deep wrinkles that made him look like shrunk leather.

"Nareen," he said, his voice a quiet rasp. "Nareen the Patient, Nareen the Glassmaker. I ask that you sit with us."

"I will hear you," Andrea said, "shortly." She turned to the third, who rose as the others had, pushing her hood back. Even though her hair was pulled back in a tight bun, she would have been lovely, except that her right eye stared unmovingly ahead, dead and unseeing.

She parted her brown robes to reveal pristinely white robes beneath. Despite the contradiction of the eye, I knew what that meant.

Shit.

"I have no name, nor am I called by one," she said, her voice a rich contralto. "But I am of the Healing Hand."

Double shit.

Shit: I don't like the Hand; it's personal. They took Doria away from us for years, and never really gave her back; she

243

had to break free, and was only barely able to. We had run into each other one time, her mind more melded than anything else into their collective conscious. I know that's part of how they relate to the Power they call the Healing Hand, and that's what enables them to act as a conduit for its blessings and providings, but I don't have to like it, and I don't like it.

Double shit: it seems that as Hand clerics develop more power, they give up more of their identities; the higher-ranking ones are known by their titles, having forsaken their own names. According to somebody who ought to know, the Matriarch herself no longer has any of her own personality, but is merely a reflection of the whole Hand consciousness, and that spooks me. I had a run-in with the Matriarch years before; she didn't find my rather charming self-centeredness, well, charming, and for some reason I'm uncomfortable being in the presence of someone of power who strongly disapproves of me. Always have been, ever since back in high school when I had a run-in with the principal about the awkward incident involving a hydrogen-filled basketball and a bunsen burner.

Call me picky.

Andrea gestured at where the slavers were camped out. "And these are?"

"They are with me," Vair said. "I required bodyguards. In Pandathaway, the slavers and my own guild have a . . . standing arrangement." He cocked his head to one side. "You seem surprised to see us; did you think you'd be the only ones interested in such an event?"

Nareen spoke up. "I have been waiting here for most of a year," he said, "living off roots and leaves, watching the changes below, waiting to learn more." He gestured toward the flickering city. "When I arrived, it was still only in the center. Fewer of the—"

"There," Vair said, pointing. "Another one."

I followed the pointing finger, but didn't see anything. Neither did Andy. "Another what?"

Vair shrugged. "Who knows? Something released from the shadows, to shamble off into the night. Dark and hulking it was, at the edge of visibility, now off in the darkness."

Nareen's eyes were following something I couldn't see for

a long while, but then he shrugged. "It could be anything. A fairy taking a shape, a shape taking identity, a myth taking reality." His eyes sought and caught Andrea's. "I've seen two dragons spurt forth and fly away, a dozen deodands stagger off into the night, and scores of large, hairy things, like humans but uglier even than humans." He watched the city flickering for the longest time. "There. A glimpse, a flicker, a taste of the Place Where The Trees Scream."

The Hand woman stroked the air in front of her. "Possibly. I know I saw a flash of meadow earlier, somewhere outside of Aershtyn."

I was going to ask how she was sure where the meadow was, but I didn't. Magic, after all.

She shook her head. "No, Walter Slovotsky, it was not that. The meadow was ringed by tiny firs, the sort that grow only high on the slopes of Aershtyn."

"What *is* going on down there?" Trust Jason to ask the obvious question.

Vair shrugged, again. "It could be any of a number of things. It's possible that this is but the first tentative feeler in a long time, an attempt to see if the powers of magic and the will of the gods still balance the faerie and the fey.

"Or it's possible that an immature one of them has been . . . Mmm. I don't think I have the words." He looked at me, then spoke a few low syllables, while distant fingers touched my mind. It was only then that I realized that he had been talking in English, not Erendra. "It is possible that an immature one of *them* is loose, creating magical creatures and spinning them off into the solid regions like a child blowing soap bubbles off into the breeze." He smiled, sadly. "Or it could be that I have been quite deliberately misled, and that this is just another part of the duel between the two long-mad ones."

Nareen smiled. "Don't ask an elf for answers; they always have too many."

"How about you?"

The dwarf shrugged. "I don't pretend to have any. Oh, anyone can see the obvious, that magic and the magical spurt out from Ehvenor like molten glass from a holed crucible, solidifying in the coolth of hard reality. But the cause? I'll not talk on causes, or you'll think me to be Vair the Uncertain."

Vair folded his arms in front of him, then brought up one hand and felt at his chin. "I don't know. It is unknown, and perhaps unknowable. Of a certainty, I can see no way of knowing without getting close enough, without getting to the Hall. Perhaps there is a breach between Faerie and reality; perhaps some of the Good Folk simply toy with Ehvenor; perhaps it is the end of the world."

The Hand cleric laid a hand on Vair's arm. "The unknown can be investigated. A breach can be healed, perhaps; the Good Folk may be persuaded to cease their play, if it is just play; the unknowable and the end of all that is can be met with serenity. It is the not knowing that is the problem, almost as much as the knowing too much."

Knowing too much can be a problem?

She gave me a look. Okay. It can fuck up your sense of proportion to all hell. I'd worked that one out years ago, even before Professor Alperson's class. Too much of a sense of proportion is a disability. See, the answer to the railroad problem is that it doesn't matter what you know or what you think you know—Karl was right. The answer is that you don't, for the lack of willingness to make a hard decision, let two people die when you can save one, even if it's only for a moment.

One side of Andy's lip curled up into a skeptical half-smile. "What are the chances of this being the end of the world?"

Nareen scowled. "There is no chance of that. Vair exaggerates. It may be important, but it is not of that importance. The feel is wrong. Lives hang in the balance, yes; but not the reality of reality, not the existence of existence."

Big fucking relief.

The Hand cleric chose her words slowly, with special care. "It is necessary that someone go down into the city, to the Hall. What you call the Faerie Embassy."

"And you think you've found your suckers, eh?" I asked.

Vair's thin lips twisted in derision. "Sucker, no. Someone who is . . . unusually expert at finding her way about, beyond her abilities in more traditional areas of expertise. Someone who was called, perhaps." He gave Andrea another one of his penetrating looks. "Though I cannot see who could call you against your will."

I turned to Andrea. "I don't like the sound of it."

"You don't have to." She dismissed me with a wave as she turned back to the Three. "Your problem isn't a lack of power, is it? It's a lack of knowledge. Vair alone has enough power to . . . cut a magical flow, given the right tools. You've made the tools, Nareen, but you can't heal over the cut, stitch space and time back together. The Hand has the power to cauterize the cut, if there should be need, but not if none of you can see through the indeterminacy."

Her lips were tight as she nodded once, tightly. "The three of you need someone who has been preoccupied with location and direction spells, someone who has skill in that area beyond what she should, someone who can plot her way through with some hope of getting out, and report to you what is happening in there, the shape of reality inside."

Nareen sighed. "That is almost the case," he said, sadly, his hand reaching down to a pouch at his waist and pulling a small leather bag from his purse. With exquisite delicacy, his large blunt fingers worked the knot open and slipped a glass eye onto the palm of his hand. "This is the second Eye I have made here."

"I have the first." The Hand cleric reached up and touched her dead, staring eye with a fingernail. *Tick. Tick.* "What one Eye sees, the other Eye sees. So. There are three of us: Me, to see. Nareen, to make the tools. Vair to use them. You are the fourth: one to place the Eye."

I held up a hand. "Now wait a fucking minute. Why can't you do this yourselves? Why Andy? Why us?" *Why me?*

"Why not us?" Vair nodded, conceding the validity of the question, if not the accusation. "Not me, because I would soon be lost within Ehvenor; my abilities are in a different area. Not she of the Hand or Nareen, because I need her sight with me, and I need the tools he will make ready." Vair the Uncertain looked uncertainly at me. "Andrea, because she can expand her powers to navigate through indeterminacy. Jason, because he will go in willy-nilly, as his father would have. Ahira, because there is danger in Ehvenor, and his strength may well be required; Tennetty, because where strength may not be enough, viciousness may serve; you, because where strength and viciousness may be insufficient, sneakiness, pragmatism, and pigheadedness may suffice."

I cocked my head to one side. "And all we have to do is get this Eye to the Faerie Embassy, or outpost, or whatever it is, and then get out?"

"All that is needed," Nareen said, slowly, sadly, "is that it be brought all the way *in*."

CHAPTER TWENTY-THREE

In Which We Foolishly Don't Take Our Time to Think This All Over

Though boys throw stones at frogs in sport, the frogs do not die in sport, but in earnest.

—PLUTARCH

Sense of proportion, pfui.

—WALTER SLOVOTSKY

A FRIEND OF MINE ONCE explained why she did her breast self-exam only once a month. You'd think, given the Other Side importance of spotting a lump early—there are only a few really solid cures for the wasting disease on the Other Side, and all of them work better if you catch it when it's young—she'd spend a few minutes every morning checking. And, hell, if she didn't want to do it for herself, I could think of a few dozen men, myself included, who would be happy to do it for her.

But she explained that those sorts of changes happen so slowly that if you feel for them all the time, you'll get used to the growth of the small lump, and it'll become part of the background—you'll miss the changes, until much later than you would if they surprise you.

Sometimes important changes happen right in front of your eyes and you can't see them.

I didn't like it. Any of it.

"What I don't see," I said, "is why her. Why us?"

"Because we're here?" Ahira shrugged unnecessarily hard as he settled the straps of his rucksack over his mail overshirt. He had put the strap buckles in their outermost holes; it now barely kept the rucksack on his back.

"Bullshit," I said.

"There have been things Andrea let drop. I think she's been pulled here, maybe. Think about it."

I remembered the time in her new workshop, and the momentary look of obsession, compulsion that had crossed her face. And then there was the time outside of Fenevar, when the idea of heading away from Ehvenor had scared her.

Ahira slipped a piece of rope under the straps of his rucksack, put a single knot in it, then tied a bow that held the two front straps together.

"By whom?"

He shrugged. "I don't know." He shook his head. "I could be wrong. It doesn't make sense—she's stubborn, and if somebody's trying to bend her will, she wouldn't go along without a fight. Who is there who might try to influence her that she wouldn't resist?" He threw up his hands. "So forget it. Not all my ideas are winners."

I couldn't think of anybody, either. "So why aren't we turning around and running away?"

His mouth twisted into a frown. "Because it doesn't much matter what anybody or anything else wants. The same principle still applies, only more so: strange things have been coming out of Faerie, and that's started to affect us and the people we care about." He looked at the three around the campfire for a moment. "And because Andrea is going in, no matter what you and I want her to do, and you'd no more let her go in alone than I would."

Well, one of us had to say it, and it was his turn.

"Turn around," I said. When he did, I gave a good, hard tug on the rucksack. Solid. Neither elegant nor comfortable, but wearing it this way meant that his rucksack would stay on his back, yet he'd be able to release it with one quick tug if need be. "It'll do."

"Good." He bit his thumbnail, and considered the ragged

edge. "How many individuals or things have you run into that you don't understand?"

"Well . . ." I couldn't help smiling. "Everybody except me and thee, and sometimes I'm not sure about thee."

His frown was sour. "Magical individuals or things."

I shrugged. "Including Deighton? A lot." I started to tick them off on my fingers. "The Wizards Guild, for starts. Does that count as one, or as one per wizard? The Matriarch. The Bright Riders. Boioardo. Those guys in the black robes we ran into outside of Endell a couple of years ago. Thelleren, although maybe I'm just being suspicious by reflex. I've never been sure about Henrad, and . . ." I shook my head. "No. She's stubborn, like the rest of us. I don't know of anybody who could make her do anything, not really."

"Nobody alive," he said.

I didn't envy Wolkennen his job; he was trying to make a case he wanted to lose.

"I still believe," he said, "that you should take the three of us with you. We're pretty good when it comes to blades."

Tennetty didn't quite sneer. "I'm sure you are." She pumped her bowie in its sheath a few times, hard. "Want to—"

"No," Jason said. "Not here and now," he said. "You'd kill him, but he might damage you in the doing of it, and we only have a few sips of healing draughts left."

"I don't understand why you're turning down help." Andrea shook her head in frustration. "We could run into trouble in there." This wasn't her part of the business, and she didn't like the way things were shaping up. But, bless her, she was willing to hear me out.

"It's a matter of practice and trust," I said. "I can trust Tennetty to watch my back when that's her job, and that'll leave me free to worry about what's in front." I looked down the slope. "I don't trust Wolkennen, and I don't know how good he is. I don't need to worry about my back."

Ahira slapped his hands together. "Enough. Case closed. Let's get ready. Tennetty, you've got the Eye?"

"True enough." She displayed Nareen's Eye on her palm. Turning away, Tennetty removed her eyepatch, and brought

251

her palm to her face. When she turned back, the Eye glared from the socket. A good place to keep it, although as she blinked, the blank back side of it rolled forward, and it stared out blackly into the night.

She worked her shoulders under her leather tunic. "Simple job: just bring this—" she tapped at the Eye "—to the Faerie Embassy, or outpost, or whateverthefuck it is." She dropped her hand and looked over at me, looking cross-eyed for the moment. She patted at her various and sundry weapons, then shouldered her pack. "I'm ready to go. Is there any reason why we're standing around?"

Yeah, there was. Maybe the horse would learn how to sing.

"No," Andy said. "Best done quickly."

"Okay, everyone," Ahira said. "Let's do it."

"Wait a moment." Jason turned to Wolkennen. "We know what you are," he said. "You trade in people's flesh. Here and now is not the time and place to settle with you for that, but there will be another time, another place—"

Wolkennen sneered. "Who are you to say what time and place there will be?"

Jason smiled. "Hey, Wolkennen, haven't you heard? The Warrior lives." He turned back to the rest of us. "*Now* it's time to go."

Tennetty and I took rear guard as we walked away. "I don't like it," she said. "They could cut across the top and swing down the east side, then ambush us ahead. Two in front of us, one in back. Nail us with arrows before we could get at them."

I shook my head. "Nah." Then who would they get to go into Ehvenor?

But I kept my eyes open anyway, and Tennetty and I both had our swords drawn.

Stone steps down the other side of the plateau dumped us down on a narrow road that twisted down the side of the hills toward the city, alternately revealing and hiding it as we walked on.

I couldn't figure it, not at first. The city was pulsating, and flickering, streets shifting position and constitution. At one moment, one would be a narrow lane, surrounded by low windowless buildings in the night, and without warning or apparent rearrangement, it was suddenly a broad avenue crisscrossed by walkways in the day, and I couldn't spot the moment where one had become the other.

But, then, as we got closer, the pace of change slowed. Streets stayed themselves longer, the changes coming farther apart, but nonetheless both sudden and unseen. I know: it's not possible for something to change instantly, right in front of your eyes, and for you to not see that it's happened.

Understand why I don't like magic?

The trouble is, of course, that my mind wanted to spot the changes, to catch the flicker or shuffling or shift or transformation, and it wasn't equipped to. Looking for it was like, say, trying to spot bands of color in the infrared: something else I wasn't equipped for.

I guess I was paying too much attention to the way the city was peeking out around the next curve when the pack jumped us. It's something you've always got to watch out for around Ehvenor; there's too much magic around there, and hanging around magic drives some humans crazy. I guess it must make them want to leave each other alone, because if it didn't, they would quickly kill each other off. I dunno; not my department.

What was my department, what I did see, and barely shouted a warning about, was the three dark shapes that dropped out of the trees, one claw-fingered hand gripping Tennetty's shoulder, dragging her down.

CHAPTER TWENTY-FOUR

In Which We Learn a Possible Origin of a Previously Familiar Term

Nonviolence is not a garment to be put on and off at will. Its seat is in the heart, and it must be an inseparable part of our very being.

—MOHANDAS K. GANDHI

Just once, I'd like to have an enemy against whom nonviolence would be a workable alternative—workable in the sense of me not ending up dancing on the end of a spear, or cut into tiny, bite-sized pieces.

—WALTER SLOVOTSKY

I SHOUTED A WARNING to the others as I cut down at its broad, hairy back, only hacking once before I had to bring up the sword to skewer the one charging me, its hands outstretched.

The standard drill on that is straightforward: you parry his weapons, thrust, then withdraw with a twist—turning a narrow wound that might not slow him down into a broad one that will definitely sting him a bit—as you pull out your sword and get it ready to parry or cut something else. What you *don't* want is for him to be able to pull either a distraction, where one opponent monopolizes your attention while another one gets to you, or a sacrifice, where he forces you to spend too much time killing him, setting you up for the next one.

Either way, it's parry, thrust, and out-with-a-twist-*fast*.

Trouble was, this thing wasn't only larger and stronger than a human, it was also faster—it rushed up my sword, burying the hilt in its hair-matted belly, and seized me in a bearhug as it lifted me up and off the ground. Or, not quite a bearhug—while it pinned my right arm to my side, I managed to get my left hand free, and smash a bottom-fist down on its leathery face once, then again, and again.

Wrong, wrong, wrong—that had less effect than the sword did. It was like slugging a leather-covered rock.

The two massive arms squeezed the breath out of me, and kept squeezing so hard that the hilt of my sword was pressed hard against my gut. Warm blood—its warm blood— was running down my belly and leg, but *I* was the one losing strength; it seemed unaffected by the sword that had run it through.

Darkness started to close in, but I was able to get my free arm over and around its hairy arm, and liberate one of my flintlocks from my holster on my left thigh. I cocked the hammer as I brought the pistol up to its head, and then closed my eyes as I set the barrel against its snout.

I pulled the trigger. Fire and wetness splashed my face; with a liquid gurgle, it slumped to the ground, releasing me as it did.

My next breath tasted of sulfur and fire blood and foul sweat and my own fear: it tasted wonderful. I drew another pistol and cocked it, but the others had already dealt with the other two creatures.

Tennetty's, the one I had wounded, lay dying on the ground, its chest heaving slowly up and down, bleeding from a dozen wounds, some light, some cuts to white bone; the third had been split almost from collarbone to waist, spilling dark blood and yellow viscera onto the cold dirt with callous indifference.

Ahira stood over the last one, panting heavily, his axe and mail slick with blood, glossy in the starlight. "Everybody okay?"

"Jason and I are fine." Andrea was behind him, Jason

beyond her, his sword in one hand, a flintlock in another. The two Cullinanes were unmarked, as far as I could see.

"I'll live," I said.

"Unh." Tennetty was on all fours on the dirt. She knelt back for a moment, then slowly, painfully got to her feet. "Been worse." Her hair was a bird's nest, and she had scraped her face badly just above the right cheekbone, but she looked not much the worse for wear.

The three things lay on the ground in front of us.

Take a human, blow it up to one and a half times its size, stretch its face and then cover it all with a thick mat of stinking fur, and that's what you have. Something big and too strong, if not overly bright—if the three of those things had been a bit faster, or a bit smarter, all of us would have been dead.

Ahira knelt over a severed arm and poked at the hand with the hilt of his axe. "Partially retractable claws, and the thumb's just barely opposable. It may be intelligent."

I felt at my side. It hurt like hell, but maybe that was all. I breathed deeply, and didn't feel the broken edges of ribs grate against each other, so maybe I was okay, too.

That's where age and experience had saved our asses. Most of the precautions you take are wasted ones; ninety-nine plus percent of the time that you post a guard, nobody's going to even bother him; the rear guard of the party is usually a waste. Young people learn that too quickly, and not only do their minds tend to wander—so does mine—they also tend not to be able to pay attention to what's going on.

You live through this sort of thing for a while, and your chances of surviving the next time go up.

Nothing to it, really. Nothing but effort and patience and concentration and luck. Nothing to worry about.

I wiped my trembling hands on my thighs.

"What the fuck *are* you?" Tennetty asked the dying creature.

The last of them rolled its head slowly toward her, its eyes wide with pain, certainly, or anger perhaps.

"Urrkk," it said, slowly, painfully reaching out claw-tipped fingers toward her.

And then it shuddered and died.

"Time's wasting," Ahira said. "Let's go."

CHAPTER TWENTY-FIVE

In Which We Enter Ehvenor and I Get Lost

Nothing endures but change.

—HERACLITUS

When you get to my age, you like a little stability. At least in the fucking ground under your feet.

—WALTER SLOVOTSKY

THE MOUNTAIN ROAD bled off onto flat land at the shoreline, as we walked on while the morning fog crept in and the city insisted on changing in front of us. The road narrowed, became little more than shoulder-width, surrounded on each side by dense brush; we had to walk single file.

We walked for what felt like hours and hours; Ehvenor drew slowly closer. Dawn threatened to break over the horizon, while a light fog blew in off the Cirric, chilling me thoroughly to the bone.

Tennetty and I had switched off with Ahira and Jason, taking the lead behind Andy while they watched our backtrail. So far, so good.

The only trouble was Andrea: she was too calm, her steps too light and easy as we stopped at a fork in the road. I shook my head. That fork hadn't been there before; the road had twisted at that spot, but it hadn't forked.

It did now.

She smiled, and muttered a few quick syllables under her breath. "Right fork," she said, then relaxed.

Her eyes met mine for a moment. "It's okay to talk now; there shouldn't be any decisions for the next half mile."

"It would be nice if it didn't change for awhile."

"Don't count on it."

I tried to smile confidently. "How are you holding up?"

She shrugged. "I'm okay. I can handle this."

"Fine," I said. "But we can turn around any time you want."

Her eyes had stopped blinking. I didn't know what that means, I still don't know what that means, but her eyes had stopped blinking.

"I don't think so," she said. Then she corrected herself. "No, we don't turn around here. We keep going."

"We just lost the fork behind us." Ahira's voice was too calm.

I turned to see the road twisting behind us, vanishing off in the fog well beyond where the fork was. Had been. Should have been. Whatever.

"Good," I said. "I never liked it anyway."

Ahead, the fog thickened.

"Hey, Ahira? What say you and Tennetty switch?" Infrared can pierce fog a bit deeper than visible light, and dwarves can see farther into the infrared than humans can.

They did, and as we walked on, the fog thickened further, until I could barely see six feet in front of me.

"Let's close up, people," Tennetty said, beckoning Jason in tighter. "One for all and all for one, eh?"

I would have been tempted to protest, but Ahira nodded. "Makes sense. Andrea?"

She shook her head. "I can't think. The fog is too thick, on the ground, in my eyes, in my mind." Her shoulders hunched, as though waiting to receive a blow, then slackened as she breathed a spell, her fingertips working in front of her, drawing invisible letters in the air.

The fog drew in further, until I could barely see my feet, and Ahira off in front of me.

My heart started thumping.

Look—I'm not normally claustrophobic. A dwarf friend

of mine (not Ahira; he doesn't like spelunking) and I once waited out a cave-in for three full days until rescue reached us. I didn't have any trouble; I taught him how to play Ghost in dwarvish. But there's something reassuring about the solidity of cave walls. Nobody can reach claw-tipped fingers out of a cave wall and pluck your heart out; the closeness of a dwarf passage doesn't hide pitfalls and tripwires, or strange creatures waiting to leap out of nowhere and . . .

Easy, Walter.

Andy was guiding us toward Ehvenor by magic; Ahira was looking into the fog, at least a little way farther than I could, protecting us from sudden attack. Tennetty, Jason, and I were useless, and a third of that really bothered the hell out of me.

"Just a little farther," Andrea said, off in the mist, just a shape, nothing more.

The fog rolled up to my knees, and then to my belly, and it was all I could do to see my hand in front of my face.

"Here," Andy said, "take a sharp right, and step forward. No, not the rest of you. Just Ahira. Okay, Walter, you're next."

I turned right and took a step forward, out of the fog, and found myself standing next to Ahira in the morning light and thick mud of a narrow Ehvenor street.

I wanted to run, I started to run, but the mud sucked at my boots. It would be like trying to run, well, through mud.

Besides, there was no reason to run. I had just been in dense fog, and now Ahira and I stood in clear light on a narrow street, surrounded by two-story wattle-and-daub buildings, up to our ankles in soft, brown mud. It could have been any street in any city, except for the way that faerie lights, bright even in the daylight, hovered motionless overhead, seemingly frozen in place.

Andy's voice was far away, but I couldn't tell in what direction. "Jason goes next," she said. "Right here. Yes, go right, right here."

And suddenly Jason, and then Tennetty, and finally Andrea herself were beside us.

I forced a smile. "Nicely done. I didn't know you could teleport."

Andy smiled; then reached over and gave me a peck on the cheek. "Thank you for the compliment, but true teleportation takes power and control that's only theoretically possible. For anything mortal," she added.

If that wasn't teleportation, I'd like to know what it is.

I guess the question showed on my face, because she shrugged and answered. "It's not teleportation. Teleportation is when you go from point A to noncontiguous point B, skipping the points between. This just happened to be right next to where we were, if you knew where to look."

The air was warmer than it should have been for this time of the morning; I'd expected it to warm up some, but not this much. Cold mornings are better. Give a hot sun a while to work on the typical city street, and it'll smell like it's been paved in well-aged horseshit. Which it has, come to think of it.

"Waddling Way," Andrea said, nodding to herself, beckoning us to follow her. A twisty street, lined by two-story wattle-and-daub buildings, it curved off sharply maybe a hundred feet behind us, and less in front. The buildings were too tall and we were too close to see much over them, except for the distant glow of the Faerie dome to the north.

It was all quiet, and empty, except for the mud, and the buildings, and the faerie lights.

"Is quiet," I said. "Too quiet, kemo sabe."

Ahira chuckled. "Shut up," he said, not meaning it, as we walked after Andy. "Take it while you can get it."

Tennetty turned about slowly, like a camera panning in a full three-sixty, which I guess she was, at least in a sense. I didn't blame her for wanting to take it all in—it was so ordinary, not at all what I'd expected Ehvenor to be. Where was the flickering? The street we were standing on was as ordinary and solid as any street I'd ever seen.

I was going to be the straight man, but Jason beat me to it.

"Where's all the flickers? Why is it all so stable?" he asked.

Andrea didn't turn around. "The flickering was from

indeterminacy. Ehvenor is never really sure what it is, and the uncertainty has been growing. But whatever it is, we're here, and that's determinate. We're in only one time and place."

I had my usual reaction to explanations about magic: "Oh."

There's three theories about how to make your way down a street in hostile territory. My favorite theory is to avoid it in the first place; you very rarely can get killed in places you aren't. Second best is to split the party in two, each group staying on one side, covering the other. It limits the field of fire of anybody hiding in buildings on either side.

Another theory is that you walk square down the middle of the street; the idea is that gives you time to react before anybody or anything can reach you.

I don't much like that one, so I moved away, toward the raised wooden sidewalk that skirted the alley.

"No," Andrea said, without turning around. "Don't. You might get lost. Can't afford that."

Lost? Look—I'm not the kind who gets lost. I don't have a perfect sense of direction, but nobody's going to lose me on the streets of a city, not without a whole lot of trying.

Right, Walter, so where's the fog bank that was up to your nose?

I stayed close.

Waddling Way twisted and turned for maybe a quarter of a mile until it forked around a vest-pocket park, the left road leading up a cobbled street, the right one down into more muck.

I bent my head toward Ahira's. "Want to bet which way we go here?"

"Right here," Andy said, clopping down into the deeper muck, sinking in almost to her calves.

"It rained hard here, and recently," Ahira said, his eyes never stopping moving.

"No shit, Sherlock."

We followed her down into the muck, our boots making horrible sucking sounds every time we lifted our feet and stepped—

_____

—up onto the hot, dry dirt of the street, under the heat of an oppressive noon sun and the whistle of music in the crowded marketplace.

"People," Ahira said. "It's good to see people."

That was the moment I expected them all to turn from their buying and selling, sprout long fangs, and leap at me, but sometimes I'm lucky enough not to get what I expect.

High overhead, a dozen wood flutes swirled and swooped and dived through the moist air, moving fast as they piped their tunes, the high-pitched whistling dopplering up and down in counterpoint to the manic melody. Not great music; they played an eight-bar theme, repeated without variation.

We had to step aside, quickly, to avoid two horses—huge things, about the size of Clydesdales, although dappled, not solid—pulling a heavily laden wagon.

We pressed tight around Andrea, like a bunch of school-kids staying with teacher. Which wasn't so bad an idea.

Okay, okay, I'm slow, but eventually I get it: Ehvenor wasn't just unsure what it was, it didn't know *when* it was. Normally, it's easy to get from mid-morning to noon, but you don't do it without skipping over late morning. Unless everything, time included, has broken loose. Hell, it was possible we'd stepped from today into yesterday.

It was a market day, and the trading was brisk under the whistling of the overhead flutes.

Over by a pyramid of reed bushel baskets, an apple-cheeked appleseller haggled endlessly with a tall, raw-boned man in a traveler's cloak and floppy hat. Beyond them, one of the hulking beasts—shit, I'll call them urks or orcs until you've got a better name for them, thank you very much—gestured clumsily that the butcher was asking too much for one of his hanging haunches of mutton. Well, I *hoped* it was mutton; it could have been shepherd.

Beyond the street, the dome of the Faerie Embassy waited, separated from us by maybe two or three cross-streets.

"This way, and try not to bump anything," Andy said, working her way through the crowd as a heavily laden wagon clomped by, pulled by two enormous horses. The trouble with a crowd is that you have to suppress combat reflexes. I don't like strangers pressing up against me—I'd rather do the pressing. That's how you work a crowd, and I'm a pretty good pickpocket, actually. Not that this was the time to see if my pickpocketry was up to snuff.

We made our way down the street, past the filled stalls where an overweight appleseller haggled endlessly with a tall man in hat and cloak, past the orc arguing with the butcher, past the shops where the candlemakers wielded their frames and dipped their wicks, where a fat old basketweaver took another turn on the base of the frame she was building.

Something about it bothered me, and I gave Ahira a quick touch on the shoulder, then slipped back to the rear of our group, and looked behind. Yes, yes, you can leave trouble behind you, but monkey curiosity is a survival factor, if you don't overdo it.

They were still at it. All of them. The orc was still haggling over the cost of meat, and the tall buyer was still arguing with the short appleseller, and the basketweaver still hadn't—

A heavily laden wagon clomped by, pulled by two enormous dappled horses, each about the size of a Clydesdale.

And the flutes were still swooping and swirling overhead through the same eight-bar theme.

I pushed my way up to Andrea's side. "Andy—"

She raised a peremptory finger as she muttered another spell. "We go this way." She elbowed her way through the crowd, between two stalls, and into the cool of the day and the—

—dark of the night near the middle of the square. Well, triangle—three streets dumped on it; the buildings at their ends wedge-shaped, triangular, like pieces of stone cake. No windows, no doors, nothing.

A pedestal holding a statue stood in the middle of the square, although I couldn't see what it was a statue of.

Ever do that experiment where you find your own blindspot? It's pretty simple. You put two dots on a piece of paper about six inches apart, close one eye, and stare at one of the dots as you move the paper closer, seeing the other one only out of your peripheral vision.

Eventually, you'll pass the dot through the blind spot of

your eye, the place where the optic nerve enters. And it'll disappear, although you'll still know it's there, and if you move the paper or your eye just a little, you'd see it, but don't: stare straight ahead.

That's what the statue looked like. Like I Can't See It.

Above and beyond it, straight up one of the feeder streets, the dome of the Faerie Embassy stood, flickering in the night.

Andrea hurried us along. "Quickly, quickly," she said, moving us toward another one of the feeder streets.

Ahira held up a hand. "No. Stop. What are we doing—"

She shook her head, her eyes growing wide. "No. We can't stop. It's all breaking loose." Her lips moved, her breath went ragged.

"It's not just the city anymore. It's falling apart." She gestured at the street that apparently led toward the embassy. "The Hand was right: it's connecting with the rest of the world." She gestured at the street. "Walk down that way, true, now it'll take you to Lost Lane, but Lost Lane won't dump you out on Double Circle—go north at the first corner and it will lead you down to the pits; the east road will bring you to a spot a hundred feet under the Cirric, just off the Pandathaway coast; west will drop you in a tree outside a village on Salket. It all," she wriggled her finger, "touches. But you won't walk down there, will you?"

Great. Andy had an n-dimensional map of the city so crowding the inside of her head that she couldn't remember that the rest of us barely knew what the hell we were doing.

"Let's get the hell out of here," I said.

"No, it's not all of Faerie. Not in the solid regions. Just a piece of it. We *go*, before he gets here." Dragging Jason by the arm, she ran off toward the street.

What did that mean? He? Who, he? I broke into a sprint after her, Ahira and Tennetty at my heels. There was something behind us, something huge, but I didn't take a look at it. We reached the juncture of square and street only a few paces behind her.

"Boioardo?" I asked, craning my neck to look as we lunged into the night and—

—skidded to a stop two feet from the edge of the hot, flat roof. I stuck out an arm and stopped Ahira from bumping into Jason. A bright noon sun beat down on us, but the blue sky was covered with black bands, arcing from horizon to horizon.

"Quickly, now," she said, "over this way."

We made our way down a ladder into an alley, and followed Andy down the alley and—

—into a vestpocket park, cool and green and minty against the heat of the late afternoon.

I would have said the trees were oaks, except that their bark was edged in silver, and the broad leaves chimed gently, like silver bells, as they rustled in the breeze.

Tennetty's breath was coming in ragged gasps, and I could have used a breather.

Ahira looked around. "Can we take a moment here?" he asked, over the ringing of the leaves. "Or do we have to run on?"

"Oh, yes," Andy said. "We rest here for a moment," she said. "I've muddied the trail enough for us to do that, at least."

One branch of the ancient oak hung long, within grabbing-and-hanging-on-while-you-grab-your-breath range, which I did. The bark was rough beneath my hand, its silver trimming cool.

Jason reached up and flicked his fingernail against a leaf. It rang like a tuning fork.

Ahira squatted on the ground. "Well, just in case we need to know, which way do we go next?"

She closed her eyes and thought about it too long, her lips moving almost silently.

I mean, I wasn't timing it or anything, but easily a minute passed before Tennetty started getting twitchy, only to subside at Jason's light touch on her arm. Jason was getting good at light touches; I would have wanted to punch her. (I wouldn't have *done* it, mind, but I would have wanted to. I get nervous around magic.)

Finally, Andy opened her eyes. "You can't see it from here, but there are steps down to the road about fifty yards that way, past the old oak. For the next while, at least, we'll be able to make it almost all the way down the steps—but do skip the top one; it connects off the roads."

I let go of the branch and sat slumped against a tree, letting myself go limp, which took no great effort.

The rough bark was somehow reassuring against the back of my tunic. Maybe I took some comfort in its solidity. My fingers played in the long grass. Long for a park, that is—about four inches in height, dense and fine and green, like a lawn.

Tennetty tapped a finger against the glass eye. "What is going on?"

Andrea opened her mouth, closed it, opened it again. "You don't have the background to understand it."

I've never liked that sort of explanation. The trouble is, it's true, sometimes. Try explaining Heisenberg's Uncertainty Principle to somebody who doesn't know that the smallest possible piece of matter isn't a dust speck, or the rudiments of atomic theory to somebody who thinks that if only you have a sharp enough knife you can divide a piece of clay endlessly in half—I've done both.

Andrea's fingers twisted clumsily. "We live under laws of nature. Magic is part of those laws. Gravity attracts matter to matter; magnetism attracts or repels; the weak magical force carries information; the strong force carries power." She waved her hand toward the dome of the Faerie Embassy. "But those are just a . . . a subset of the rules of Faerie. When we're in Faerie, or even just close to it, it's like we're a bunch of Newtonians trying to plot our way through Einsteinian space, and wondering why we can't break the speed of light no matter how much faster we run."

She gestured at the park around us, her movements jerky, like she was wired too tightly. "Ehvenor's always been part of the . . . outskirts of Faerie. The Good Folk don't like it much; it's too restricted there, too flavorless. But that's changing, and I'm starting to see too much of it." She stood, and as she stood, the tension in her body eased. "It's not just space that touches, but time. The here and the now." Her voice was low. "At the core of Faerie, at the singularity at the heart of it, all is chaos, all touches, there are all rules and none."

She shook her head, as though to clear it. "But that doesn't have to be here. The Three can anchor it all in reality, if only they know . . . where. Vair is the most powerful, but he's uncertain where to put his fire; Nareen's tools have the solidity and stolidity of his race, but little more." She reached out a finger and tapped at Tennetty's eye. "They need *her* sight."

I wouldn't have wanted to poke my finger at Tennetty's eye, even at a glass one, but Tennetty didn't react.

Andrea shrugged into her pack. "So we go."

"Why now?" There was a panicky tone in Ahira's voice.

"Because," she said, "I told you; I've seen the paths. In just a few seconds we hear his footsteps, and we . . ."

Heavy footsteps thudded on the ground; we ran down the steps—skipping the top one—and across the cobbled street, down the alley, and—

—into the dark of a cloudy night, lit only by the dim green glow of the stinking mosses lining the gutters.

Ahira pulled a glowsteel from his pouch, and the actinic blue chased the darkness away.

It was just an alleyway, a slim street between two rows of buildings that towered in the night, vanishing up in the distance. There was no sound behind us, but Andy shook her head. "He's too close here—we have to take a short cut by diving deeper into Faerie.

"This way," she hissed, vanishing in the darkness of a doorway. We followed her, through the darkness—

—and into the hard, cold wind of the Place Where Trees Bleed.

The icy air blew unrelentingly through the scarlet leaves, each one dripping crimson at the slightest movement. The giant limbs creaked in their pain. Pools of blood gathered beneath the trees, darkening, thickening in the air.

"*Nobody move*," Andrea said. "Let me move you. The rules are more . . . general here; there's no safety in solidity, not if you don't know where to step." She stepped quickly around, moving so fast it was as though her feet hydroplaned over the damp grass, gently touching Jason once on the cheek. He disappeared with a loud *pop!*

"You have to move just right." She pulled Ahira's arm forward. He staggered forward and then disappeared, too.

Only Tennetty and I were left with her, but I could hear the footsteps on the ground behind us. One chance only, and not much of one.

Andy's hand caressed my cheek. "Don't move, Walter," she whispered, her voice low. "He's behind you."

Tennetty spun, her sword raised high, but the grasses turned into snakes, winding themselves about her ankles, their long fangs sinking deep into her calves.

She screamed. I don't know why it surprised me that it was a high-pitched, horrible sound, like anybody else's. But she turned it into a grunt, as she hacked down at the snakes, her blade slashing them, turning the ground around her into a mass of bleeding, writhing pieces of reptilian flesh.

The voice was the same:

"Good day, all," Boioardo said. His face was too regular, too pretty, the cleft in his chin too sharp. He was all in black and crimson, from the cowl of a scarlet cape flung carelessly over one shoulder to the black boots with enough shine for an SS officer. His tunic was of red velour, cut tight at shoulders and belted at the waist to reveal the v-shaped torso of a bodybuilder.

He proceeded to sit down on the empty air, like somebody who had forgotten that there wasn't a chair behind him. But before he could fall, a swarm of tiny winged lizards flew down from the trees, the lot of them barely supporting a jeweled throne that they slipped behind him, just in time. Others pulled off his cape and folded it neatly over the back of the throne.

Tennetty grunted again, still slashing at the snakes.

Boioardo crossed one knee over the other and smoothed at the already-smooth black tights. "Oh, please. Don't make such a fuss." The snakes melted at his gesture, but the blood continued to run down her leg.

He blurred in front of my eyes, and when I could focus on him again, he was a slim man, about my age and height, still sitting easily on his throne. Maybe a touch older, less in shape, gray at the temples only. His jaw firm, his mustache evenly combed, an ever-so-slight hint of epicanthic folds at his eyes. He was dressed all in black, except for a brown cloak held fast by a blackened brass clasp.

Okay, okay, I'm slow: "I'm more handsome," I said.

Tennetty gave me a funny look. Funnier than usual, I mean. "Than me?" she said.

Andrea's fingers touched me at the temples, and for a moment, he flickered, becoming Tennetty, then Andy, and then back to me. He wasn't me, here, he was just mirroring me, in his own way.

Andy looked me in the eye for just a moment. She didn't need to say it: she had to get the Eye to the Faerie Embassy, and Boioardo had to be delayed enough for her to do that. She knew the path; Tennetty had the Eye. That made Andy essential, Tennetty next in importance, and me expendable.

But she couldn't. Expend me, that is. Not without my permission. That was the trouble with Andrea: she never was cold-blooded enough.

The dream was always the same. Except this time the Cullinane was asking me to do it by myself, and I didn't know if I could.

I froze, for just a half-second—

CHAPTER TWENTY-SIX

In Which I Find the Place Where Only That Which You Have Loved Can Help You

Involve yourself with the world. Reach out. Touch. Taste. Live. Trust me on this one, if on nothing else.

—WALTER SLOVOTSKY

I WASN'T THERE FOR A lot of the next of it, but it happened, at the same time that I was busy fighting for my life, I think.

Or maybe it didn't. I mean, it *happened*—reports for the rest of it are reliable—but there's that problem of time. We don't know much about Faerie, and probably aren't built to know much about Faerie. But we do know that time acts funny in and around Faerie, and there was no question that we *were* around Faerie. And there's no question that time was already acting strange in Ehvenor. That part is certain—when you turn a corner from afternoon and find yourself in dawn, I mean, you don't have to be Albert Einstein to figure out that time has been thoroughly fucked with.

What I can say for sure is that what happened with Jason and the dwarf happened during the next part of their lifespan, just as my fight with Boioardo happened during the next part of mine.

I guess that'll have to do.

And I can't tell you what finally made it all happen. I've been wondering ever since—was it me, or was it Andy and the Three? Both? Something else?

The trouble with this part of the story is that I don't know who the real hero is.

Well, that's not true, either. I do know.

She bought Andy and me a few seconds, and paid in full measure, without a whimper.

Damn it, Tennetty. I never got to say goodbye to you.

Ahira staggered out of the screaming grasses and into the dark, onto the soft carpet, Jason right in front of him.

They found themselves in a small room, suitable for a bedroom or a study, high above the dark streets below. Lit only by a single lantern mounted high on the wall, the room was empty save for the carpet, a desk of sorts up against one wall, and a pile of blankets and an empty chamberpot off in one corner next to several canvas sacks brimming with raw vegetables and dried meat.

The desk, such as it was, was interesting. The desktop was a smooth-sided door—the knob was still attached, but it was on the far side, near the wall—elevated by stone blocks at four corners that raised it to knee-height. Books and scraps of parchment lay scattered on its surface, held down by oddments of stone and scraps of ironwork. He made out some Erendra glyphs, and some of the rest was in scratchy runes that Ahira didn't recognize, but most of the writing blurred in front of his eyes. Wizard's work.

"Somebody has been living here," Jason said.

Ahira raised a finger to his lips. He wasn't irritated by the boy's keen attention to the obvious, but by his talking. Until they had a better grip on where they were, it was best to keep mouth closed, eyes and ears open.

A heavy wooden door stood half open, leading out into the dark hall. Ahira listened for a moment, but couldn't hear anything. So far, so good.

Gesturing at Jason to keep an eye on the door, he turned to the window.

Outside, just across the street, the Faerie Embassy stood gleaming in all its unfixed glory.

Was it three or four stories tall? And were there long, rectangular windows, like glass doors leading out to a balcony, or were the only openings in the solid expanse broad slits, too narrow even to be arrow loops?

He didn't like looking at it; he couldn't tell. Better to concentrate on the here and the now. Hanging around a wizard's workshop was a bad idea, it was time to—

Jason was beckoning silently to him; the boy had already flattened himself near the single door leading to the hall.

His lips moved. *I hear something*, he mouthed.

Good boy. This time, he wasn't scared. No, that wasn't true—Ahira could smell the fear on him. Jason was bright enough to be scared, he knew he could be hurt or killed at any moment, but that was just another fact of the universe, to be dealt with appropriately.

And he knew it. He couldn't keep a smile off his face. This time Jason Cullinane wasn't running away.

His axe held easily in his hands, the dwarf leaned his head close. Familiar footsteps echoed down the hall.

Ahira lowered his axe. "Hello, Andrea," he said.

Andrea walked through the door, but it was a changed Andrea. Her black leather vest and pants had been replaced by a gleaming white robe, woven of fog and light. Her black hair was shot with silver, and her eyes were red and rimmed from either crying or lack of sleep.

Jason took a step toward her, but Ahira seized his arm. "Wait."

She raised a slim hand. "Yes, it's me. Older, perhaps a year, perhaps more, or less? Time is so . . . different here, and I've been hiding and studying in nooks in time, trying to control the madness while I've learned more. I'm older, yes; somewhat wiser, I would hope; knowingly more ignorant, certainly. But I'm still me." A tear ran down one cheek. "May I hug you? It's been so *long*," she said.

—but Tennetty didn't spend any time thinking it out: she dug her finger into her eyesocket and flipped me the Eye while she launched herself at Boioardo.

The glass Eye tumbled through the air toward me.

No. "Tennetty, *don't.*"

But thinking or saying it didn't make any difference. Nareen's glass Eye, the one the Three needed in order to see through the veil of uncertainty into the heart of Ehvenor, floated through the air toward me. I snatched the Eye out of the air, slapped it into Andrea's hand, and started my turn, but it was too late.

Boioardo had already risen from his throne, moving so quickly that his sleeves and cape snapped through the air like the end of a whip. He batted her sword aside as though it was nothing, and had his hands on her.

She grunted once as his fingers tore through her flesh the way a backhoe claws through ground, and then he shook what was left of her once, twice, three times, like a dog shaking a rat, and tossed her aside, bloody, broken, dead.

His arms red with her blood, splashed to the elbows; it seemed to bother him in his fastidiousness. He looked down at them, at the red blood wetting his sleeves, and then he gestured once, idly, and the blood was gone. Tennetty lay on the ground, her dead eye and empty socket staring off into nothing.

You don't waste time grieving for friends, not during a fight, you don't.

"Now, Andy," I said. "Do it now. Take him. Like you did before."

She shook her head. "Not here, not on the edge of Faerie. I don't have enough power, not enough strength to do it."

Boioardo smiled. "She knows I can follow the two of you wherever in Ehvenor you try to hide."

I pulled Andrea close. God, why did you make women so warm? "Hide yourself for now," I whispered, "but get the Eye where it needs to be. Do what needs to be done."

She nodded, once, quickly, then touched soft fingers to my lips and pushed me away, hard; as she stepped away and vanished I staggered back—

Jason awkwardly hugged his mother, and Ahira let the blade of his axe drop to the carpet.

"How long?" Ahira asked.

She spread her hands as Jason released her. "I don't know. Possibly a year. Perhaps two. I used to keep count of

273

meals and sleeping periods, but I gave that up when I found that I didn't need to eat and sleep much here. Two years?" She walked to the window. "Long enough to learn what it will be necessary to do to walk across that street. Long enough to learn most of the paths through Ehvenor, long enough to learn some truths about myself, long enough to call myself here." She shook her head as she turned back to them. "I'm sorry to be so maudlin. I know it's been only seconds for you."

Ahira smiled at that. "That answers that question."

That part of it made sense, at last. He had known Andrea Andropolous Cullinane for twenty years now, and had known her to be every bit as stubborn as it was possible for a human to be. Her will wasn't subject to anybody else's command. She decided for herself, and nobody else did. Nobody else.

So: who could call Andrea to Ehvenor? Who could bring her here? Who had been calling her here ever since Castle Cullinane? Who was it who had made her stir-crazy enough to go out on the road into God-knows-what?

Andrea.

She returned his smile. "Me. Who else?" Her eyes went vague for a moment. "She'll be along shortly, with the Eye."

"And what happens then?"

She shrugged. "I only know a little. She didn't—I mean *I* didn't have time to talk much with her, with me. After we abandoned you two, she took the Eye, and then pushed me off into a strange part of Ehvenor, and I got lost. I had to learn how to find my way back to here. She said that she was going to, that *I* was going to try to walk across the street and bring the Eye there." She looked out the window. "No matter the cost. The rest is up to the Three." Her eyes widened. "Oh, *no*. It was so good to see the two of you that I forgot what she told me—" She turned to Jason. "Quickly, hand me your knife."

—I staggered back onto an empty street in a deserted part of town. Rows of tenements lined the dirty street beneath the dark sky, while cold white light shone up through the cracked ground.

I was alone, but I wasn't going to be alone long, not if

Boioardo was following me. I had to hope that Boioardo was going to chase me, that I could distract him long enough to give Andy time to do her thing, to get the Eye to the Faerie Embassy, and return to pull me out of trouble and away before Boioardo killed me.

Andy was good at locating people and things; it might work, if I could buy enough time. But I'd have to avoid him for as long as poss—

There was a tap on my shoulder, and there he was. It wasn't like looking in a mirror, not really; surely such a self-satisfied smirk would never be found under my mustache?

"A fine place," he said, reaching slowly for me. The light from beneath cast his eyes into shadow, but his too-white smile almost glowed in the dark. "Shall we end it here?"

I started out in high school as a running back; I ducked under his arm and ran, broken-field style. It didn't do any good. There he was, just a half step behind me. Not running, just gliding effortlessly over the ground, his feet never touching the dirt.

He frowned. "This is too easy," he said, giving me what looked like a gentle shove. It didn't feel that way—I slid six feet on the dirty ground, the grit and dirt scraping away the clothing over my left hip, then grinding a wide swath of skin and flesh from my hip and thigh. I slammed against a wall, hard, knocking the wind out of me.

I lay sprawled on the ground, trying to force some air into my lungs. Muscles just wouldn't work right. None of them.

He loomed over me. "Get up. You must be better sport than this."

I rolled to my hands and knees, then staggered to my feet.

"Wait," I managed to croak out. "Give me . . . time . . . recover."

I wasn't sure that my right knee would support my weight, and I could feel ribs grate against each other in the mass of red agony that I used to call my chest.

His smile broadened. "I don't see the need for that." He waved his hands once, and all my aches and pains were gone. It didn't happen with the wave of comfort and ease that healing draughts always provided; one moment I could barely grunt out words through the pain, and the next, all the aches were gone.

Even the scrape I'd taken on my left hip had healed, and the clothing over it.

Stall, Walter, stall. "Just wait a minute," I said. "This is too easy for you. Give yourself a handicap. Don't just look like me. Reduce your strength and speed to mine. Make it a fair contest." If Boioardo had a weakness, it was his arrogance—although who could call him on it? Incredibly powerful, invulnerable, able to assume any form he chose. I would rather have been in Philadelphia.

He cocked his head to one side. "Fair, no; I do not care to lose. Less unfair, certainly. That will make you better sport."

He eyed me carefully, then closed his eyes and concentrated. His form seemed to flow for a moment, then stop flowing, until he looked like me, again.

Boioardo took one step forward. "I'm only twice as strong as you, and but half again as fast." He blocked my punch and backhanded me back, lights flashing on the edge of my vision. "That ought to do."

If you practice something often enough, it becomes part of your muscle memory. Maybe the basic block-and-strike was like that.

He took a punch at me, and I had blocked it, moved in and brought my knee up quick as all hell.

The only trouble for me was that he was already blocking down, and hard.

The only trouble for him is that I'd finally slipped one of my throwing knives into my left—blocking—hand and slipped that in between his ribs. He staggered back, in pain. Not enough pain, but he'd taken on not just enough of my form, but enough of the reality of being human, to hurt.

I would have finished him off, but I'd been through that before with him when he was playing wolf. The best I could do—the best I hoped to do—was to fight him to a stalemate while the others did their thing.

And the best way to do that was to run.

I ran, down the street, and into—

—a forest of huge trees, the canopy of leaves arcing fifty feet above my head. Low brush clawed at my ankles and calves as I ran, my feet crashing through the dry leaves littering the floor. Above, tiny green lizards in the trees sang in easy counterpoint to the rhythm of my steps.

I was tripped, sent sprawling; I rolled to my feet, barely avoiding an immense projecting root, one of the huge trees at my back.

Boioardo moved his cloak aside as he faced off against me.

The only plan that occurred to me was to stall for a moment, just a moment, while I readied a knife. Maybe this one would hit something vital, knock him dead before he could regenerate himself.

"The Place Where One Speaks Only Truth," he said. "Just the outskirts of it. Shall we end it here?"

"No, I'd rather stall as long as I can," I said, truthfully, fingers clawing surreptitiously for a throwing knife. "And I'm going to try to stab you—"

Shit, shit, shit . . .

I ran up the root toward the trunk of the tree and leaped for another root, my next leap carrying me beyond the tree, toward a path. His footsteps crashed behind me as I scampered down the path through a bend, to where it intersected with another path, and leaped through—

Andrea turned to Jason. "Quickly, hand me your knife," she said.

Jason didn't move; Ahira shoved him aside, hard, snatching at his belt for the knife, flipping it easily, hilt-first, to Andrea.

She raised the knife and tossed it toward the open door, just as the other Andrea, dressed in black leather, flicked into being in the doorframe.

Ahira's breath caught in his throat.

—into darkness. I tripped, and fell backward, into water and slime, then forced myself to my feet, all wet and cold. I could barely stand without bumping my head on the roof of the tunnel; I steadied myself with my hands against the side. The walls of the tunnel were warm and soft to the touch, the fleshy feel of it broken every ten feet or so by hard rings of something white and bony beneath the surface.

There was light ahead, farther along in the tunnel. I staggered along, as quickly as I could. There was a juncture up ahead, barely visible.

Footsteps thundered behind me as I reached the junction and dashed through—

—into the next passage of the tunnel.

Sometimes, even in Ehvenor, a corner is just a corner.

I ran on, my feet making awful sucking noises in the muck, and into—

Ahira's breath caught in his throat.

"*No.*" It had to have been Andrea, but it couldn't have been Andrea. Andrea wouldn't try to kill her earlier self, but Ahira had just given whoever this was a knife.

The blade twisted through the air, barely passing over the new Andrea's shoulder, only to bury itself in an outstretched hairy arm.

Ahira smiled. By God, he *had* been right. White Andrea *was* his old friend.

White Andrea grabbed Black Andrea's arm and pulled her to one side as the thing staggered inside, all hair and muscle and stink.

It closed with Ahira, hairy hands fastening on his throat as it lifted the dwarf bodily from the floor, ignoring the knife still stuck in its arm. The new Andrea, the younger one, raised her hand, but the one in white batted it aside.

"No. We have to go. *Now.* This is where we abandon them. We don't have much time."

Over her protests, the white Andrea pulled the other one out through the door, and slammed it behind, quite neatly trapping Jason and Ahira inside.

—smoke, clawing at my lungs, tearing at my eyes. Strong fingers grabbed at me, but I kicked out once, twice, then dived away into blindness, his coughs and chokes behind me.

I was just starting to wonder if he'd locked himself into

a human form, stuck with human weaknesses, when the coughing shut off.

Fairy, you cheat. He had taken a moment to change a little, to allow himself to breathe smoke without pain, without coughing.

"Well, certainly."

I staggered forward, from the smoke—

The dwarves call themselves the Moderate People; and there is a saying among the Moderate People that condemns immoderate moderation. Balance is important, equilibrium is necessary, but only in its place. This was not the place for balance; here, moderation would have been recklessly immoderate.

The universe dwindled to Ahira's hands, each one on a wrist of the monster. That was all. There would never be more than that, and each hand would have to close, to pry the strong hands away from Ahira's throat.

His fingers clenched tighter, and tighter. But so did the choking hands. His lungs burned, needing air. Darkness crept into the edges of his mind.

There had been a time when sickness had bound him to a metal chair, but that time was gone, and it must not return. He could tolerate almost anything, but not being confined, not being held immobile.

His arms and legs thrashed, uselessly, helplessly.

I will not be held down against my will. I will never be held against my will.

There was nothing else but his fingers on the wrists, squeezing hard, harder against the creature's bone and muscle. Rage flared blue-white in Ahira's mind, giving strength to his hands, washing away thought and intelligence, as a berserker rage built, needing only one more spark to set it flaring.

Bones cracked beneath his palm, the hands eased, and Ahira dropped to the floor, while steel thunked into flesh—

—*again*, he realized.

He had been hearing the sound of a knife hacking into flesh for some time now. All the while that he had been trying to break free, Jason had been stabbing at the creature.

Ahira rose to his knees and sucked in a lungful of fetid

air. Despite the unwashed reek of the creature and the smell of his own sweat and fear, the air cooling his aching lungs was as exhilarating as a cold white wine. The cold and comfort flooded his body, pushing his rage back, leaving his mind intact.

He opened his eyes to see Jason hack again at the creature's neck, as blood flowed down its chest from a dozen wounds.

It staggered back, then forward again, and reached out for Jason, too stupid to know it was dead. Ahira dived at its knee, shoulder hitting hard against fur-covered muscle and bone, tripping the creature. He fastened his hands on its head, the fingers of his right hand tangling themselves in its stiff, wiry hair, while his left hand closed on the massive bony ridge over its eyes.

Ahira twisted once, giving it everything he had, rewarded by a single loud *snap*.

That was all it took. The creature shuddered once and went limp, its dead body voiding itself with an awful flatulence. It was all Ahira could do not to vomit.

Both of them gagging, Jason helped Ahira to the window.

"What's going on?" Jason asked.

"I don't know."

The cold outside air helped to clear his nose and his mind, but it didn't provide any answers.

Andrea had abandoned them, but she had done so knowing that they could handle the creature—orc, or goblin, or whatever it was. He leaned farther out the window and breathed in the sweet, fresh air.

Below, White Andrea stood on the sidewalk, facing the Faerie Embassy, the Eye held high in the palm of her right hand, an open, leather-bound book held in her left.

Ahira called out to her, but she either didn't hear him or was ignoring him. Andrea took one step onto the narrow street, but as she did, the air around her darkened, then solidified into three dark bands that looped about her body, and slowly, inexorably contracted, forcing her down and to her knees, trying to force her back.

Her gaze dropped to the book in her hand, and her lips moved.

Ahira's hands tightened on the windowsill. His mouth was painfully dry.

Andrea was a powerful wizard, certainly, and as White Andrea she had had plenty of time to prepare for this. But too much use of power could drive her insane, and she was fighting out of her league when she took on Faerie. And she'd known that, dammit. She hadn't impressed the spell she was using into her memory, but was reading it from the open book, not trusting her ability to carry it in her own mind and remain sane.

Curling the rest of her fingers around the Eye, she raised her right index finger and gently touched the outer corner of her right eye. A single teardrop swelled there, fattening, growing until it could hold no longer and ran down her cheek, bursting into fire as it fell from her jaw and onto one of the black bands.

Where the flaming tear touched, the band dissolved, leaving behind a ragged hole.

Andrea shed another fiery teardrop, and yet another, until she was crying a shower of burning rain, dissolving the bands of darkness until all that remained of either tears or darkness was a bit of dust, a little ash and soot that slipped from her white, misty robes as she took another step forward.

—and I staggered into the glowing fog, flagstones hard under my knees, a distant roar in my ears. I got to my feet, not sure which way to run. I could more feel than see a wall to my right, but the fog was thick around me, and there could have been miles of open space in any other direction, or a waiting open pit.

God, Andy, hurry up with whatever you're doing. It would be nice to be saved in the nick of time.

Maybe I could climb the wall. If Boioardo were to climb after me, I could drop down on him. Even with twice my strength, he wasn't invulnerable. Given enough of a start, if I could gain enough height, I might be able to land hard on him, smash him to the ground, and crush him either to death or unconsciousness before he could throw off the limitations of the flesh that he had assumed.

Yeah. Sure. And maybe I'd be elected fucking Queen of the May, too.

The fog thinned in front of me to reveal a series of niches, carved into the wall, each of a different size. There may have only been ten or so; there may have been hundreds, thousands, vanishing off into the fog.

In the first one, in the niche right in front of me, was a pair of sneakers.

"Holy *shit.*"

They weren't just sneakers; they were *my* old sneakers, my first pair of sneakers, or at least the first pair I remembered.

Stash had always believed in buying irregulars, and had picked up a pair of some famous brand—PF Flyers, maybe?— that the manufacturer had rejected because of a sloppy seam along the uppers. The sloppy seam was still there—just a little crooked; nothing important—and so was the spot on the sole, just below the heel, where somebody, probably Inspector 7, had neatly sliced off the little brand patch when the sneakers had been rejected.

Same blue stripe along the rubber sole, same flat cotton laces, clean and white like they had been the day they were new.

They reminded me of running fastfastfast on a hot summer day, of leaping over low picket fences and scrambling through backyards not just when that damn St. Bernard was chasing me, but because I was ten and it was summer, and that's what you did when you were ten and it was summer.

In the next niche was a fountain pen, a real chubby-barrelled Shaeffer fountain pen with the white dot on the clip, and I knew that if I took it down, and took off the cap, it would write with the blackest of blue-black ink, because that was the ink that was in it the day that Mom had given it to me, the day that I had brought home my first report card that was just Bs and As. How had she known that I was finally going to bring home a decent report? Had she had the pen waiting through most of my elementary school career?

Four As, and three Bs, the report card said; it was in the next niche, all clean and waiting.

It takes longer to tell it than it did to live it; I don't think

I'd stood in front of that wall for more than a second, taking it all in.

My teddy bear was in the next niche: an ugly stuffed panda in black and dirty white, one ear half torn off, glossy brown buttons from an old overcoat for his eyes. He waited, lying patiently, the way he always had at the head of my bed.

Bears are like that.

Boioardo had spoken of the Place Where Only That Which You Have Loved Can Help You.

Now I understood. It was a capital-P Place in Ehvenor, yes, on the edge of Faerie, surely, but it was also a small-p place in my mind.

I've lived some years now, and I've touched some things more than casually. You run through enough summer days in an irregular pair of PF Flyers, and they become part of you, not just for the few days and weeks and maybe months that the shoes last, but for as long as there are hot summer days just after school's let out, and as long as there are the tight, springy steps that you can only take in a new pair of sneakers and as long as there are fences and yards and dogs that surely can't be as big with teeth that can't be as sharp in reality as in memory.

It was mine, forever.

My bear was here. No nightmares here, not with my bear waiting at the head of my bed, ready to dispel a bad dream with its familiar warmth.

It was all mine. This was *my* place.

In the next niche was a jackknife. It didn't look like much, I guess, and it was smaller than I remembered it, but the Scout crest had the same scratch on it that it had always had. *My* knife.

It was my knife, the one that Big Mike had given me, so many years ago, and it was here, in my hand, the ripples cut into its plastic sides familiar under my thumb.

Look: I know I had a fighting dagger at my waist, and I know that it gave me more reach. But that was just metal, just a tool.

This was *my* knife.

It had meant something to me, and it was here to help me. What was it that Ahira had said? Something about how it's not just the people in our lives that matter, about how we had best be careful what we make, what we use, because we invest something of ourself with everything we touch.

And I know that a nonlocking jackknife is a silly weapon in a fight, so I thumbed open the awl on the back, and held the knife hidden in my hand, just a sliver of metal showing. One punch with it, and the awl could slice hard, deep, through flesh and into Boioardo's eyes.

My knife.

Okay; bring on the demons.

Off in the distance, something roared, a sound both familiar and strange. Not the growling of a beast, but the roar of an engine. I hadn't heard the sound of an engine in more years than I cared to think about.

Boioardo walked out of the fog, an immaculate imitation of me, his cape curling swirling about his ankles.

"Nice of you to wait for me, Walter Slovotsky," my face said, in my voice. "You ruined my fun; now I'll ruin yours." He smiled. "I always knew that it would end here, here in this Place."

He took a punch at me, but I blocked it with my left arm; it went numb and fell back at my side, but my right arm still worked, and I punched hard at him.

"Fuck you," I said.

His head moved to one side, but the slim steel edge cut his cheek open to the bone, and staggered him.

It wasn't enough. He backhanded me, lifting me up and off my feet. I fell hard to the flagstones, the knife skittering and bouncing away into the fog. I started to crawl off after it, but he blocked my way.

"You lose," Boioardo said.

The distant roar grew closer.

I knew that sound, by God, I knew that sound. Eight cylinders, generating more power than three hundred horses, hauling around tons of metal and glass, painted all black and yellow, like a bumblebee.

Ahira was right. We had best be careful of what we touch, what we make, what we use, because there is some of us in each bit of it, and we'd best be careful what we are. And in the Place Where Only That Which You Have Loved Can

Help You, you'd best have gone out in the world and touched a lot, because you never know what you will need there.

I forced a smile. "Wrong, Boioardo. You lose."

The rain of tears dissolved the black bands, and Andrea took another step across the street, toward the flickering of the Faerie outpost.

"She did it!" Jason sighed in relief.

"No." Ahira shook his head. "She's not there yet. Look."

The flickering below took on substance, shimmering shifting into a wall across the street, reaching down through the dirt and up to the sky.

Glassy hands reached out from the wall to push and pull at Andrea, several fixing on her robes of mist and light, others fastening tiny fingers in her hair. Small fingers twisted tightly as they became more substantial.

She turned to another page of the book, and hesitated for a moment, just a moment before she began reading.

Lips murmuring words that could never be remembered, she tucked the book under her arm, and touched her right index finger gently to her left wrist.

A trickle of blood ran down her arm, fat red drops turning all sparkling and golden as they fell to the ground.

She cupped her left hand in front of her. The trickle of blood ran down her wrist and pooled in the palm, swelling. When the pool began to drop golden sparks, she raised her hand, and shook it once, twice, three times. A cloud of golden sparks shattered the ghostly hands into fog, and then into nothingness.

The Eye held high, the book again open in her free hand, White Andrea took another step forward.

"Wrong, Boioardo," I said. "You lose."

It doesn't cost anything extra to die with brave words on your lips, but I wasn't going to die, not here and not now. It was his own fault; he had chosen the Place. Perhaps, in his alien cruelty, he had thought that it would be amusing to finish me off here in this place, in my Place, but his arrogance had betrayed him.

This was *my* Place.

At first, he didn't believe me. Then his smile vanished, and his eyes widened. He looked from side to side for an avenue of escape, but there wasn't any. The wall was to one side of him, and it was coming out of the fog from the other.

Boioardo tried to cheat, he tried to change, but he was too late, and too slow. He had been faster in his changes; now it was as though he was trying to do too much at once.

Too bad for him. You don't face off against the Big Car when you've got other things on your mind.

It was among the last and absolutely the best of the standard American bigmobiles. A huge car, pulled around by a three-hundred horsepower V8, easily enough for the job—a monster of an eight-cylindered engine, it roared like a lion. Two-toned, black and yellow like a bumblebee, wraparound windshield, curved fenders, and a rear deck large enough to camp out on.

Tires squealing as it swerved to miss me, tons of black and yellow steel roared out of the fog and smashed into Boioardo, knocking him back up against the wall.

He tried to rise, but the Big Car shifted into reverse, tires smoking as it lunged back, then shifted into drive and lunged forward to smash him against the wall, steel squealing as the impact crumpled the grill, starred the windshield.

Boioardo had been caught in transition; he rose once more, battered and bloody, too broken to concentrate and change. His fingers bent at impossible places as he threw up his broken hands to protect himself.

"No, *please.*"

Pity wouldn't have stayed my hand, and I had no pity. You don't go around playing with people like they were toys, not if you expect any sympathy from me. You don't rend somebody I love to shreds of bloody flesh and then ask me for compassion.

"Do it," I said.

The air in front of Andrea solidified, warped itself into a black wall that separated Andrea from the flickering of the Faerie Embassy.

She put out her right hand, the hand that held the Eye, and pushed hard on it, lips never quite stopping their motion.

Light flared around her fingertips, cold, silent balls of red and whiteness that vanished as they hit the black wall.

She murmured another spell, and waves of thunder crashed, making Ahira's ears ring. But the thunder beat uselessly, harmlessly against the blackness.

She took a step backward, looking from side to side, as though deciding not whether to run, but where to run. Andrea shook her head, black hair shot with silver settling about her shoulders, eyes closed tightly.

Ahira couldn't hear her over the crash of thunder, but he didn't need to hear the words.

Ahira found that the windowsill was splintering under his grip; he forced his hands to open. Crushing the windowsill would do no good. He had been wrong again, dammit. He had thought that a wizard didn't know how far to push magic, what moment would cost sanity, when that sacrifice would be made.

It was clear that Andrea knew that her next spell would cost her more than tears and blood.

She straightened, her shoulders back, and opened the book to a new page, reading slowly, carefully, as she raised the hand that held the Eye, her index finger straightening as she touched it to her temple, as though to say, *I'll feed you with this.*

Her right hand glowed, and as she pushed it forward the black wall melted in front of her. She pitched the Eye toward the flickering of the Faerie Embassy, and then fell to her knees, her face buried in her hands. Her shoulders shook.

Far off, a distant voice spoke slowly, thoughtfully, the way elves tend to. "I see it, I think."

"Don't be so tentative," another answered. "Use this, and seal it all off."

The world exploded into brilliance, and then faded.

"Do it," I said.

The Big Car gunned its engine once more. Tires squealed on the stones, and the stink of burning rubber filled my nostrils.

It smashed into him one last time, steam from its shattered radiator vying with the fog as it ground what was left of him against the wall. It backed away, leaving Boioardo broken, bloody, dead. If I hadn't known, I wouldn't have been able to tell what he had been.

Slowly, brokenly, the car circled around to me, one crumpled fender nudging gently up against me, as though to ask if I was okay.

The Place faded out around me.

I barely had time to lay my hand on its cold metal flank. I didn't know the Polish, and it didn't matter anyway. It would understand, no matter what the language.

"Thank you, thou good and faithful servant."

And then the mists swirled up, and around, and washed all traces of consciousness away.

CHAPTER TWENTY-SEVEN

In Which We Part Company, and Two of Us Head Homeward, Well, Holtun-Bieme-ward

Every parting gives a foretaste of death . . .
                                        —ARTHUR SCHOPENHAUER

When you say goodbye to a friend, assume that one of you is going to die before you ever get to see each other again. If you want to leave something unsaid, fine . . . but be prepared to leave it unsaid forever.

                                        —WALTER SLOVOTSKY

I DON'T REMEMBER HOW we got there, but the next thing I remember was being back on the plateau above Ehvenor. It was like I had been going on automatic pilot. It could have been a shock reaction, I suppose; my extensive collection of bumps and bruises showed that I had taken more than a few blows to the head.

No, that wasn't the next thing I remember. Ahira and I had been talking about what happened, while I looked off into the distance. Andrea, wrapped in a woolen blanket, had been leaning up against Jason, sobbing.

There were seven of us, some sitting, some standing, the fire to our backs, looking out at the ruined hulk of a city below.

The three slavers had fled, or just plain decided to leave.

Ehvenor had stopped flickering, and the mass of creatures flickering through its changes had been unceremoniously dumped in the here and now. Bands of hairy beasts fought with each other through the narrow streets, the wise ones fleeing outward, while creatures of the night ran for the darkness of the hill, escaping the oncoming day.

Dark shapes moved outward, fleeing the solidity of the city, some shuffling along the ground, others taking to the air or diving into the Cirric. I could almost have sworn I saw a dragon take wing and flap off toward the south, but I could have been wrong.

What I wanted was a drink. No, what I wanted was a drink with Tennetty. Maybe a nod and cold smile that said I'd done okay, although why I ever gave a fuck about that cold-blooded psychopath's opinion escaped me.

Damn it, Tennetty.

I'd have to settle for the drink; I fumbled through my pack and brought forth the flask of Riccetti's Best. It was heavy enough, there was still some left, enough for maybe half a dozen good-sized drinks. I pulled the cork and drank deeply, letting the fiery corn whiskey burn in my throat and warm my middle before I passed the bottle to Ahira.

"Well," he said, considering, "I think we earned that." He took a swig and then offered the bottle to the Hand woman, surprising me.

She declined the offer with an upraised palm, her eyes, both real and glass, never leaving the pageant below. "Magical beasts loosed into the wild, into the earth and air and water," she said. She cocked her head to one side. "Things haven't been like this since I was a little girl."

It only occurred to me later that most magical creatures had been gone from the Eren regions for centuries.

Shouldering a small canvas bag, she turned and walked away into the darkness.

It took me almost a full minute to realize that she had just left, and wasn't coming back. Ahira passed the bottle to Jason, who passed it along to Nareen.

Vair polished a coin-sized ruby, then fit it into an open wire frame. He threw a handful of powder on the fire, and considered the smoke through the lens.

"It could be worse, perhaps," he said. "All of Faerie could have poured through, possibly. If the breach had not been sealed, if the one who cut the breach had not been stopped." He looked at me through the fire of ruby, then tucked it in his belt pouch and crossed his long arms over his chest. "It all would have failed if we had not seen the breach, with the Eye. You have done well, the lot of you." He rose. "Or so it would seem to me." Without another word, he turned and walked off into the darkness. I was sure—I *am* sure—that he disappeared while he should still have been visible in the firelight.

Andrea, leaning up against her son, still sobbed. Quietly. Jason glared furiously at all of us, as though we could do something.

Nareen chuckled gently, for that is the way the Moderate People chuckle. "There is nothing to be done, young Cullinane. There is only much to be endured." Nareen walked to the two of them and gently, slowly, pried Andrea away from her son, and took her small, delicate hands in his huge ones.

"You see," he said, as though he was talking to Jason, although he really was talking to Andrea, "those of us with the gift know a truth, that there is no pleasure quite like using it, like refining it." His broad hands stroked hers. "Most of us know that we must be careful in its use; that if we use too much of the gift, push it too far, we will have to choose between it and sanity, and who would choose sanity compared to the glory of the power rippling up and down your spine, eh?"

His words were gentle, but each struck Andy like a blow; she sobbed even louder, trying to turn away. But the dwarf wouldn't let her.

"No," he said. "You made your decision. To feed your power not with your sanity, but with your ability." His index finger moved in the air, his rough fingernail tracing a fuzzy red glow that swiftly faded. "Your ability to see this as sharp lines instead of a red blur, and all that that implies."

I thought about how, a long time ago, another friend of mine had sacrificed his ability to do magic, and how that had worked out well for him, and I hoped. Maybe it would be so for Andrea, too. Or perhaps not.

Nareen nodded his head, perhaps admiringly, perhaps

291

with just a trace of condescension. "My compliments," he said. He lowered her to the ground; she squatted gracelessly, her face in her hands.

Nareen turned away.

"Don't leave yet." Jason held up a hand. "Wait. I—we, that is. We helped you. I'd like some help, from you." He swallowed. "There's a friend of mine, running around, doing some horrible things. I need to find him. Help me."

There was that Cullinane grimness about his face again. No matter that he loved his mother, and no matter that she sat on the ground at his feet, weeping—there was something out there that he had to do, and he was about to do it.

Nareen nodded. "Perhaps just a little."

"Okay."

Shit. That's the trouble with trying to be Hercules. You clean out the Augean stables, and then you have to go chase down Pegasus.

Ahira looked over at me, and he was smiling. "What am I going to say?" he said.

I smiled back. "Ask Jason. It'll be good practice."

Jason thought about it for a moment. "That somebody has to take Mother home, but that I'm still too young and stupid—"

"Inexperienced," the dwarf put in.

"But close enough," I added.

"—to be running around on my own." He swallowed, hard. He wasn't going to say anything about Tennetty. I don't know why that was important to him, but it was. "So," he went on, a catch in his voice, "one of you had better come with me. The one that's better at keeping out of trouble, not the one that's better at getting into it."

Ahira smiled at me. "I wonder—who could that be?"

Jason turned to me, and gave me another shot of that grim Cullinane look. I never much cared for it.

"You'll watch out for Mother?" he asked, although it really wasn't a question, but a command.

That was okay. "Sure," I said. "Andrea needs some rest. The two of us, at least, had better camp here for tonight, head up into the hills tomorrow."

It would take a week at least to get to Buttertop, the hill north of Ollerwell that was the nearest of the regular rendezvous places. We could wait there for Ellegon's next circuit through. Might be a few days, a tenday at worst. I could live off the land for longer than that.

I wouldn't get any rest worth talking about, not tonight. I'd have to leave somebody on guard, and a nonspeaking, incessantly weeping woman wasn't my idea of a great guard.

Nareen smiled reassuringly. "That can be taken care of, at least for tonight."

I guess I should have been irritated that the dwarf wizard was reading my mind, but his grin was infectious. He reached into his pouch and brought forth a small glass ball, about the size of a big marble, which he placed in the air, and set spinning with a flick of his thumb and a few muttered syllables. "Sleep easily tonight; this will scream at any danger. For us, the sooner we leave, the sooner we can book passage at Artiven."

I wondered how they were going to make their way through the dark of night, but Ahira tapped at his brow.

Darksight, remember?

Oops.

Ahira nodded. " 'Twere best done quickly, eh?"

"There is that."

I clasped hands briefly with Nareen, and gave Jason a hug—which he tolerated with admirable patience—before turning back to Ahira.

"Watch your six, short one," I said. "And if you need me . . ."

He nodded, once, and gave a half-smile. *We'll be fine,* he was saying. *But if we need you, we'll send word.* His grip on my shoulder was firm.

I fed some more wood to the fire while they walked off into the night.

Below, Ehvenor stood in the dawn light, empty, no sign of life save for the gleaming building in its center.

Just as well Nareen left the marble-or-whatever-the-hell-it-was on guard. While I do recall spreading my bedroll and lying

293

down on it, I don't remember actually settling myself in for sleep. Before I was completely flat, I was out.

And I slept like a dead man, only awakened at dawn by the *tink!* of the marble-or-whatever-the-hell-it-was bouncing off a stone.

PART THREE

NEW WORK

CHAPTER TWENTY-EIGHT

In Which the Living Dead Not Only Speaks, but Eats Both Trout and Chicken

Travel, it seems to me, has always done more for flattening the arches, callusing the feet, and irritating the hemorrhoids than broadening the mind.

—WALTER SLOVOTSKY

I EYED THE SKY OVER Ehvenor as I broke camp.

Blue sky, puffy clouds, no dragon. Damn.

Hmm, I guess that should be "as we broke camp" except that "we" weren't doing it. I had made breakfast—jerky and oatmeal; sticks to the ribs. I had packed the rucksacks—fairly, honest; I was putting out the remnants of the fire—okay, I was biologically better equipped for that job.

Andy was waiting for me down the path. She had taken a battered leather book out of her rucksack, and opened it. The letters swam in front of my eyes; I'm not built to read magic.

They probably swam in front of hers, even forgetting, for the moment, that she had burned out her magical ability. Tears do that.

She wiped her eyes on the back of her hand and put the book away, tying the rucksack tightly shut before she slung it over her shoulder.

"Well," I said, "day's a-wasting." I love it when I talk colorful. "Let's get going."

She set off in a slow walk. At least she wasn't crying now. Her eyes were red, and there were dark baggy circles under them. Her hair looked like a bird's nest, and her mouth was set in a permanent frown.

But at least she wasn't crying.

Big fat, hairy deal.

I scanned the skies, hoping for a pair of leathery wings. This would be a handy time for Ellegon to show up and save some wear and tear on both my bootleather and my tender tootsies. But the sky was just full of blue and clouds and birds, and you can never find a dragon when you need one.

We headed off down the path.

There's any number of things one can do with somebody who is busy withdrawing from the world. You can just be patient and let them retreat into their navel, coming out whenever they please. *If* they please.

Now, I'm not saying that's a bad plan. It's probably a good way to handle it; maybe even the best way to handle things. But it's not a Walter Slovotsky way to handle things. Sorry.

"Now," I said, babbling over the babbling of the stream, "anybody can get lost in the sense of not knowing where you are. No big deal, as long as you know how to get where you're going. Not knowing how to get where you're going is the dangerous kind of lost."

It was a nice-sized stream, maybe three yards across where we were, its broad banks providing a wide path. During rainy season, the stream probably overflowed the banks, but it wasn't rainy season.

"This is one of the easier orienteering tricks," I said. "Avoid heading across unfamiliar territory for a point-destination: a town, an oasis, whatever. Points—okay, okay: areas— are easy to miss.

"Roads and streams, on the other hand, are long skinny things. You tend to trip over them.

"So you aim for a road that you know leads to your destination, even if that means breaking right or left of whatever you're heading for. Now, I know the road from Heliven to Ollerwell—it's a long, wide one, crosses a lot of streams up in the hills, certainly including this one. So, unless there's a good reason not to, we follow this stream until we hit the road. Q.E.D."

She didn't answer.

"I know what you're saying," I said. "You're saying, 'Walter, that's all well and good,' you're saying, 'but you've walked out of Ehvenor before, and so this isn't unfamiliar territory to you.'

"You've got a good point, and that's a fact. But there's a difference between having been through this area before and knowing it well. Now, I do know the route that we took the last time I walked out of Ehvenor, but that was more than ten years ago, and I think they may even remember me in one of the towns we passed through, so perhaps we'd be just as well skipping it."

She looked at me, trying not to glare. That was an improvement. At least she was trying something.

I was tempted to try something; I've been in worse-looking company.

If you ignored the reddened eyes and the slumped shoulders, Andy was still an awfully good-looking woman, in or out of her boots and leathers.

But she still wouldn't talk.

There are things I like less than traveling with somebody who won't start a conversation, who won't answer in other than monosyllables, and who cries herself to sleep each night, honest. But most of those involve things similar to sitting up on the Posts of Punishment.

The stream bent up ahead, and I suspected there'd be some fish feeding under the fallen tree that didn't quite bridge the stream. The morning was getting old, and the food in our pack wasn't getting any more plentiful, so I shrugged out of my rucksack and beckoned to Andy to wait.

She dropped her own rucksack and squatted on the ground, silently obedient.

I would have rather she spoke up and spooked the fish.

I crept out on the log. Sure enough, just under the surface of the rippling water, in a quiet space sheltered by the tree, a trio of largish trout hovered in the shadow, either having a quiet chat about fishy life or eating something.

Not for long.

One of the gifts I got in transition to This Side is my reflexes, and while they've been more important, they've never been a lot more fun than when I lunged, scooping up one of the fish and flinging it high into the air, just like a bear with a salmon, except that I'm much prettier than any bear.

The trout thunked down on the riverbank, flopping madly. *Flibitaflibitaflibita.*

Nice-sized, the way local speckled trout often get. Maybe three, three and a half pounds.

I'd sort of hoped Andy would take over, but she just watched it, so I pulled the utility knife from my rucksack—I don't use my dagger or my throwing knives for this sort of thing—then quickly gutted the fish, rinsing off both the fish and my hands in the stream. Ick.

"Now, the *right* way to cook trout involves poaching it with vinegar and spices," I said. "Blue trout is one of the greatest meals that ever there was.

"A good second choice is to tie the trout to a green stick and then shove it head deep in nice, hot coals. On the other hand, we don't have nice, hot coals, and I'm not going to spend an hour building up that kind of cookfire."

Keeping up a steady monologue, I gathered some dry wood and built a quick cooking fire on the riverbank—if you've got some birch bark handy, which we did, and if you're willing to waste a little gunpowder, which I was, you can start a fire real quick.

I cut the fish down the back and seared the halves on the ends of a pair of green sticks, using a rough stone to grate just a taste of wild onion onto it. It only took a few minutes; all you really have to do with freshwater fish is cook them enough to kill any parasites.

A bit of salt from the saltwell in my pack, and, *voila:* fish on a stick. Lunch for two.

"What are you going to have?" I asked.

She didn't rise to the bait, and I wasn't irritated enough

to let her go hungry, so I handed her one of the sticks and then quickly wolfed down my own.

Not bad. Not bad at all. Fresh trout, no more than fifteen minutes from the stream, is a dish fit for a king.

Or even for Walter Slovotsky.

I washed my hands in the stream and then scooped some water onto the fire. "Let's go."

The first days were like that. Andy slept when told to, ate what I put in front of her.

To my surprise, she stood her turn at watch and stayed awake and alert while she did, but that was about all.

The nights were cold, and I wouldn't have minded not sleeping alone. But it didn't seem like the right time to bring up the subject, not even of sleeping. I'm a sensitive guy, eh?

So, instead, I kept up the constant monologue as we walked. I swear, I began to run out of subjects; by the third day, I'd covered damn everything I knew (well, almost everything. Some things Woman Isn't Meant to Know). About how to set up a staff in a castle. About how to keep in practice with a bow. About why you keep flintlocks loaded, and how poor old Tennetty always scared the shit out of me.

We hit the Heliven-Ollerwell road late on the second day, and left the stream and trout dinners behind.

Just as we were breaking camp the next morning and I was launching into today's monologue—a reconsideration of the Nickel Defense and its suitability for college football—Andy looked up at me and frowned.

"Walter, shut up," she said.

"Well, well, well. It lives." I hefted my rucksack to my back and we started to work our way back toward the road through the forest.

She should have snorted, but she just looked at me dead-pan. "Your sympathy is underwhelming. You don't know what I had to give up."

"Better than sex, so I'm told."

The corner of her mouth may have turned up a millimeter. "Depends on with whom."

"Was that an offer?"

"No."

Sometimes no doesn't mean no, but when it's accompanied by a weak shake of the head, lips pursed just *so*, that's exactly what it means. Which is okay. I can take no.

On the other hand, I was heading home to my wife, to make things work. It would have been nice to have one last dalliance. On the other hand . . . I've run out of hands.

Just as well.

We walked along, not talking. I can take silence, although you'll never get that in the forest. There's almost always the far-off cry of a bird, the chittering of insects, and if nothing else, a whisper of wind through the trees. Not silent at all. Not even quiet, not really; it's only the tallest trees that are quiet.

"What now?" she asked. Or maybe said.

I hadn't taken this route before, but I had passed through Ollerwell once or twice. "Ollerwell's just a few miles ahead, just across the river, and down aways. We can buy some fresh food. I don't think we'll be able to get more trout—they tend to fish it out around Ollerwell—but maybe some eel, or some of that bass you find in the lakes up this way. Not beef—I mean, they might have some, but the locals don't eat a lot of beef, and we'd smell of it for days. We *could* splurge on a chicken, if—"

"Shh." She waved it away, tiredly. "I mean, what do I do now? After we get back."

I shrugged. "Whatever you want, Andy. Except magic, so I'm told."

For the thousandth time, she took the battered leather volume out of her pack and opened it.

The letters blurred in front of my eyes, and apparently in front of hers, too.

They would have, even if she hadn't been crying.

Sometimes I call it right: a farmer at the edge of town had a fire going, and a fat capon turning over a spit, sending delicious flavors wafting off into the breeze. We could probably have made a better deal in town, but the crackling of crisp skin over the coals made me part with a Holtun-Bieme copper half-mark with Karl's face on it, which bought me a huge chunk of breast (no comments, please), and Andy an over-sized thigh, each served on a fist-sized loaf of fresh brown bread hot from the oven.

I didn't wait for it to cool, and ended up burning my tongue. It was worth it.

I'd like to report that Andy wolfed hers down with hunger and gusto, but she just ate as we walked through the village, past a couple dingy rows of wattle-and-daub houses and onto the northern road.

Another couple of days and we'd be at Buttertop.

"How about you?" she asked.

At first I didn't answer. It took me a moment to realize that she'd picked up our conversation of hours ago where we had left it off. I hate it when she does that.

"Me?" I shrugged. "I think I'd better take it easy for awhile. Spend some time with the kids, and with Kirah. You?"

She sighed. "I might go back into teaching. English, basic math, the usual. Even if some of the Home youngsters do it better than I could. I don't know."

Maybe, just maybe, if I gave Kirah enough patience and attention, maybe that would do it. Life's like a fight, some-times; there's times when you have to commit yourself, to lunge full, all stops out, not worrying about what happens if it doesn't work. See, you don't just put something of yourself in what you touch, but you put it in who you touch. After close to twenty years together, Kirah was part of me, and I wasn't going to cut that out, any more than I'd throw away my left arm.

Ellegon found us that night.

I was a bit nervous about camping on the ground close to a road broad enough to be navigable by stars and faerie lights, so we had moved well off the road, onto a wooded rise, and slung our hammocks high in a giant old oak tree while it was still light enough to see.

Actually, I'd done the slinging, and it had only been one hammock. Climbing was hard enough on Andy, but I picked her branches to make getting in easy for her. It had been some trouble, but we'd gotten her settled in and pretending to be asleep, while I climbed farther up the tree and seated myself in a crotch between two old limbs, too lazy, or maybe too tired to mess with it all. I just whipped one end of a piece of rope around the tree, and knotted it in front of my chest, so that if I leaned forward instead of back I wouldn't fall out and break my neck.

I let the day slip away. What was that old dwarven evenchant? Something about—

That was, of course, the moment that flame would have to flare loud and bright over the treetops, accompanied by the rustle of leathery wings.

Wake up, folks. Your ride's here. If you hurry, we can be in Holtun-Bieme in the morning.

CHAPTER TWENTY-NINE

In Which We Decide What Those Who Can Do, and Why

It is better to travel hopefully than to arrive.
—ROBERT LOUIS STEVENSON

Never come home unexpectedly. It's a break-even proposition, at best.

—WALTER SLOVOTSKY

E LLEGON SET DOWN QUI-etly outside the walls in the gray light just before dawn. I slid down his scaly side and landed hard on the hard ground, twisting my ankle.

"You're getting old, Walter," Andy said, as she lowered herself more gently down from the dragon's back.

Happens to the best of them, the dragon said, turning its broad head to face the two of us. *So I understand. What are you going to do now?*

"Me, I'm for bed," I said. "I don't sleep well in the air."
So I noticed.

Andy patted at her belly. "I'm going to go eat something, then probably some sleep. You?"

The dragon walked away, toward the main road, his wings curling and uncurling. *There's a sheep in the south pasture with my name on it. I'm hungry.*

It was nice of Ellegon to walk away far enough that we wouldn't be battered by dust and grit when he took off. Although, at this point, that would have been wetting a river.

In that case . . . the dragon leaped into the air, leathery wings sending dust and grit into the air to batter at my eyes and face.

"Me and my big mouth," I said.

Andy didn't answer.

The watchman at the main gate let us in through the small-door; we waved aside his offer to wake a welcoming committee. I just wanted to look in on my kids and wife, and then find an empty bed. Or, better, grab a few blankets and curl up in a corner of Kirah's and my room, and let her find me when she woke. I wouldn't slip into bed with her unexpectedly; that would set her off.

Andy touched my shoulder for a quick moment. "Look me up when you get up. I've got an idea I want to talk over with you."

I nodded, too tired to bother asking what it was.

Dawn had been threatening to break outside, but a castle is always dark until the sun is well up, and well before it's down. Not that the staff believed that. Some wisely frugal servitor or penurious asshole had put out most of the lanterns; I had to get one from the rack outside the kitchens.

I don't believe in madly tittering darkness, but the mirk kind of giggled at me as I made my way up the stairs toward the bedrooms.

Dorann's room was next to Kirah's and mine. I crept in for a quick moment.

Barely illuminated by the flickering lantern, my baby daughter lay under her blankets, all curled up and tiny. It was all I could do not to sigh out loud, although I couldn't prevent a tear or two from running down my face. Dammit, but she looked like she had grown an inch since I'd been gone. You miss so much when you're on the road, whether your business is sales or steel.

I rested my hand against her warm cheek for a moment, and she stirred just a little, then reached up a pair of chubby hands and pulled my hand closer to her face, never coming close to waking. After a few minutes, I gently detached my hand.

God, little one, I never realized how much I missed you.

I shut her door gently behind me, then went to Kirah's and my room. The knob refused to turn; it was locked. Good; Kirah was still practicing ordinary security. I was willing to bet that the secret passage to the room next door was still properly blocked.

I dug in my pouch for my key. I turned the key in the lock with exquisite slowness, and gently pushed the heavy door open, hoping that the hinges wouldn't squeak and wake her.

The bed had been moved in my absence, and a full-length mirror had been set up next to the window, angled to reflect the first traces of dawn light down onto the pillows, to wake the occupants.

Very clever.

But a hint of predawn light was enough to let me make out the faces of both occupants: my wife, and that asshole Bren Adahan.

I don't know how long I stood there, not thinking. It seems long in retrospect, but it probably wasn't.

I do remember, vaguely, what I thought about, in between the moments of anger, and hate, and jealousy, and shame, and guilt.

I thought something about how I didn't believe in a double standard, really, truly I didn't, no matter how hard and fast my heart was beating, no matter how much anger flared red behind my eyes, in my mind.

I do remember realizing how it wasn't being touched that disgusted Kirah, it was being touched by *me*, that it was the feel of my hand, my body against her that she associated with her old life, with rape and slavery.

What had I ever done to deserve that? Nothing, maybe. Fine. Who the fuck says you get what you deserve?

I do remember thinking, just in passing, that I could probably pick the lock to Bren Adahan's room next door, and be waiting for him when he made his way back through the secret passage.

And I do remember thinking that standing in an open doorway, tears running down my face, wasn't going to do any damn good, so I swung the door slowly closed and wiped my face on the back of my hand. I had the key almost completely turned when I heard soft footsteps behind me.

I hadn't been listening. Bad policy.

I finished turning the key, carefully pocketed it, and slowly turned, my weight on the balls of my feet.

Janie and Aeia stood side-by-side in the gray light. Janie in a heavy black sleeping-robe, belted at the waist with a thick velvet rope. The robe was far too large for her; its hem touched the floor, and her hands barely peeked out of the sleeves. It all made her look younger, far too young to be around for this.

Aeia had thrown on a thigh-length white silk robe. Slim fingers nervously toyed at the belt at her waist. Her eyes were puffy from sleep, but just a bit wide.

I was trying to figure out who had wakened whom, and decided that Aeia had probably wakened Janie. Aeia knew—hell, everybody knew—that Janie could always handle me.

"Hi, Daddy," Janie whispered.

"Hi, sweetness," I whispered back. "What's new?"

With a sad little smile—damn, I'd never seen Janie smile sadly before; I didn't much like it—she took my arm and brought me down the hall to the top of the stairs.

"Some things have happened while you were gone," she said, "some things we all pretend we don't know about. Aeia's been worried you'd do something stupid, but I've been telling her that my Daddy will handle things in a nice, civilized manner, that nobody's going to get hurt." Her face grew somber. "Tell her I'm right, Daddy."

Look: I am more than a collection of hormones and reactions. I could be livid with rage—and I was—but *I* decide what Walter Slovotsky does, not my anger. *I* decide, and I decided that I wasn't going to blow up. Not here and now; not ever. You don't solve this kind of problem with a knife and gun, you really don't.

So I forced my fists to unclench.

"Sure, sweetness. No problem. Truth to tell, I'd decided that your mother and I were through." Well, that was probably true. Since just a few minutes ago, no matter what I had decided on the *Delenia*. Hell, we might go through the motions for awhile. But every time I saw her, I'd replay the scene of her and Bren in bed, and each time I'd try to touch her, she'd see whatever private hell she saw.

Fuck it.

Aeia smiled. "It's going to be awkward," she said. Her golden brown hair was mussed from sleep; I wanted to run my fingers through it. She slipped her hand into mine, and gripped tightly. "But everything will be fine," she said. "Trust me."

"We'll manage," I said, weary past imagining.

She nodded, once.

"In the meantime," I said, "how about somebody finding me a bed?"

Janie led me down a flight to an unoccupied room on the floor below, and gave me a peck on the cheek. "See you this afternoon. Sleep well." She turned back down the hall, almost stumbling over the hem of her too-large robe.

Aeia came into my arms for a brief moment, her arms pulling, not pushing, her body warm and alive against mine. She rested her head against my chest, then raised her face and kissed me quickly, gently on the lips.

"Later," she said, then turned and walked away down the hall.

The room was dark, and smelled vaguely musty. The bed was lumpy, and smelled more than vaguely musty. But there's one great thing about being dog-tired: you can cry yourself to sleep in about two seconds.

The nightmare is always the same:

We're trying to make our escape from Hell, millions of us streaming down the streets of Ehvenor, running from the wolf-things that think of us only as toys and prey. Everybody I've ever loved is there, along with faces familiar and strange.

There's a street corner up ahead, a place where I somehow know that a right angle turn will bring us to safety, and I shout out directions.

It seems to be working. They flicker out as they turn, and I somehow know, as you can only know in a dream, that they've escaped, not found themselves in the Place Where Trees Scream.

But the wolf-things approach, accompanied by the shambling orcs, their fangs dripping blood.

And then I see him: Karl Cullinane, Jason's father, standing tall, face beaming, his hands, chest, and beard streaked with blood and gore.

"We're going to have to stall them," Karl says. "Who's with me?"

He smiles, as though he's been waiting his whole life for this, the fucking idiot.

"I'm with you," somebody says.

Figures push out of the crowd, some bloodied, some bent. Tennetty's the first. Not the aging, wasted one, more used up than aged, but a younger, vigorous Tennetty, her sneer intact. "Count me in."

Andy's next to her, looking foxy in her leathers, a small leather shield strapped to her left arm, a smoking pistol in her right. She smiles at me. "You don't think I need magic to count, do you?"

Big Mike hefts his baton, tapping it lightly against his thigh. "Never need anything, eh?"

My brother Steve fixes the bayonet to the end of his empty M16. His smile is reassuring. "Sharp edges don't jam, eh, Cricket?"

Karl looks at me—they all look at me—his bloody face puzzled. "Walter? What are you waiting for?"

I was about to say something, to tell them something important, but—

I woke in a cold sweat, in the dark.

Just a dream. No big deal, I tried to persuade myself as I wiped the sweat off my forehead.

It was dark; I'd slept—or nightmared, if you want to be accurate—all through the day and well into the night.

Somebody had snuck in while I was sleeping and had not only laid out some fresh clothes, but had filled the copper washbasin, then set the lantern underneath it to keep the chill off, if not keep it warm.

I stripped down to skin and scabbards, then splashed a

little on my face and chest before pulling on the trousers and slipping the shirt over my head. A full bath could wait until I had some food, but not much longer. A nice hot soak was just what the cleric ordered.

I swallowed. Okay. Now, what?

There was a knock at the door.

"Come," I said, slipping the handle of a knife into my hand. I mean, I didn't need to fight with Bren, but maybe he wouldn't know that. It does *not* take two to have a fight.

Andy walked in, a lantern in one hand, a tray of food balanced on the other. "I had one of the guards listening for any sign of movement in here," she said. "I wanted to get to you before things get . . . hectic."

I forced a smile. That was a good word for it. Hectic. I liked that. "And you wanted to talk to me," I said. I bit into a cold drumstick. "You wanted to talk to me about something else, about, say, about how now that you're no longer a wizard, you want to go into what Karl used to call the family business, and about how you need a teacher, and about how I'm not going to be completely comfortable around here for the next while, and about how maybe I ought to be the teacher, eh?"

She nodded. No smile. Just a nod. I wondered if the only place she ever was going to smile again was in my nightmares. "Good," she said, matter-of-factly.

"And what did you think I was going to say?"

"Yes. I thought you'd say yes."

"Okay: yes." I nodded. "I've got to straighten out some things, some family matters, but then we go into training, and we hit the road as soon as we can."

She looked like she had a question.

"Lesson the first: ask it. When you've got time, always ask."

She thought it over for a moment. "Why are you so eager to get back on the road?"

"You want the truth?"

"Sure." She smiled. "Why not."

I shrugged, and looked back to the sweat-soaked rumpled blankets heaped on the bed and floor. "So I can get a good night's sleep."

Author's Note

The heroes in Walter's dream sequences are intended to be Walter's, not mine; there'd be some overlap, but my list wouldn't include many of his selections, and vice versa.

Each of us, after all, does get to—and has to!—pick our own.

—J.R.